SYNDICATE RULES

BOOKS 4 & 5

by Lucy Monroe

1st Printing 2025

Syndicate Rules

Ruthless Enforcer

Brutal Capo

Lucy Monroe

LUCY MONROE LLC

Copyright © [Year of First Publication] by [Author or Pen Name]

All rights reserved.

Contents

Ruthless Enforcer

Lucy Monroe

LUCY MONROE LLC

Dedication

We are all broken. That is how the light gets in. – Ernest Hemingway

Writing about broken and imperfect people finding love and acceptance is one of my favorite things. A perfect vessel doesn't allow anything in. Not light. Not moisture. Not sustenance. It is completely self-contained, but that is not how human beings survive. We are in this thing called life together.

This book is for all of the imperfect people who enrich my life and accept me for the less than perfect person that I am. Especially my husband, Tom and my oldest and dearest friends, Mona, Myra & Carolyn.

*Greek Mafia Hierarchy**

Ádis Adelfótita **| Hades Brotherhood**
Territory: West Coast & Parts of Western Canada
Nonós tis Nýchtas **| Godfather of the Night**
Constantin Petros
Kai **| Second-in-Command**
Tobias Nikolaides
Eidikós **| Specialist: Lawyer**
Vasileos Rokos
Anax **| Head of the Local Territory**
Zeus Rokos
Kai **| Second-in-Command**
Orion Rokos (Lawyer)
Eidikós **| Specialist**
Enforcer & Assassin
Atlas Rokos
Eidikós **| Specialist**
BookkeeperHelios Nikolaides
Eidikós **| Specialist**
Smuggling & Weapons
Zephyr Nikolaides

* While the criminal syndicates found in this book are loosely based on known hierarchies within Greek mafia and Russian bratva organizations, they are fictional. They do not represent any actual mafia or bratva family. Nor are their hierarchies meant to be an exact replica, but rather inspired by research.

Prologue

LUCIA

5 Years Ago

*P*orca miseria!

The left side of my head throbs. There is a faint tang of copper in my nose and on my tongue.

Opening my eyes, I groan. The sunlight coming in through the open curtains is too bright. I am on the floor of my father-in-law's office.

I sit up, shifting so I can lean against the side of the desk. Trying to remember how I got here, I reach up to my forehead. It hurts. I touch something wet and sticky and look at my fingers. I blink. They are smeared with red. Blood.

Memory comes back in disjointed flashes.

Leo screaming at me. Trying to shove me at the safe. Shaking me so my head snaps back and forth on my neck. Me falling.

Terror makes my heart pound erratically in my chest. I jerk up onto my knees so I can see the gun safe. It's still closed.

Grazie a Dio. Thank God.

Relief washes over me. I didn't open it for him.

Leo needs professional help. However, my husband, Tino, and his father insist I figure out how to care for Leo on my own. We don't go outside the family for help.

Only, there is no one in the Detroit Cosa Nostra trained to deal with a man who suffered traumatic brain injury at the age of twelve. Leo is now 20, only three years younger than me, but he still responds like the twelve-year-old he was when he took a shot to the head while out learning the business with his father.

Only now he's the same six feet tall as his brother and equally as strong. However, while Tino would never hurt me, Leo has. Not on purpose, but that doesn't change the outcome. This is only the second time he's gotten this bad.

My mind shies away from memories of the first episode like this and what it cost me.

I don't know how long I've been knocked out, or where Leo has gone. I can't expect help from Tino or my father-in-law. They are doing their weekly inspection of the nightclubs they run for the Cosa Nostra and will not be home much before dawn.

Leo didn't get into the gun safe though, and for that I have to be grateful. He is obsessed with the idea of becoming a made man like his father and brother.

The prospect of the unpredictable man with a mind of a child carrying a gun and thinking it is okay to kill people sends chills down my spine.

My phone rings and I pull it from the back pocket of my jeans.

My father-in-law prefers me in dresses, but during the day while he and Tino are gone, I wear casual clothes and tennis shoes. Keeping up with Leo requires flexibility of movement and the ability to run, even on the marble floors that cover so much of the first floor of the mansion.

The phone keeps ringing and I see that it is Tino. I tap to answer. "Hi, Tino."

"Listen, *amore mio*, there's paperwork in the safe that has the information you need to access my accounts in the Caymans. Get it and then you and Leo have to get out of there."

"Tino—"

He cuts me off. "Go to the cabin and wait for me to call you there."

I don't waste time trying again to ask why, or what's going on. Tino's voice is tight with tension and an emotion I don't think I've ever heard in it before. Fear.

"Okay. I'll get Leo and we'll go."

"*Ti amo.*" In the three years we've been married, Tino has only told me he loves me three times.

When I told him I was pregnant. The day I lost the baby and now.

Dio mio, this is serious.

"Be careful," I say.

I don't know if he hears me before he cuts the call. Something bad is happening and I've got to find my brother-in-law and get us both out of Detroit.

I get Leo to the cabin and we settle in. My texts to Tino go unanswered, but I don't contact anyone else. That is the protocol.

Protocol doesn't stop me from checking the online news outlets for information. I am horrified by what I find.

Two, possibly three, gangs are waging war in Detroit. The initial violence erupted in one of our clubs.

Reading between the lines from who is quoted as saying what, I realize the Irish mob and Russian bratva have teamed up to take over Cosa Nostra territory in Detroit. And everything is being played off as a war between rival gangs.

It's warfare all right, but the main players aren't street gangs. They are organized crime syndicates vying for territory.

Rumors of bystanders shot dead abound, but by the next day, twenty deaths are confirmed. The vise around my heart tells me that one of those people is Tino.

He still hasn't answered my texts. The one call I made to him in the middle of the night, breaking protocol, went straight to voicemail.

Hoping against hope, I read the news obsessively over the next two days, sleeping very little and only eating when Leo gets hungry. I gasp as I read the headline to a breaking story. My home has been fire bombed. Leonardo and Lucia Revello are presumed dead, burned to ash with our home in the chemically enhanced fire.

My stomach cramps.

Reading about the tragedy of our *entire* family being killed on the same night sends me running to the bathroom before I vomit bile all over the cabin floor.

Tino is dead. Agustino Sr. is dead. Leo and I are presumed dead.

Tino and Agustino are considered collateral damage to the gang warfare. The death toll has risen to nearly forty people. Authorities are baffled as to why our home was bombed. Right now, the two incidents are being treated as unrelated.

They aren't. I am Tino's legal heir. The Irish and the Russians don't want me around to be able to fight their possession of the nightclubs on a legal front.

Not that I would be the one doing the fighting, but my standing as owner to the properties would give my don legal leverage in this war.

The same don who allowed the mounting tension between the bratva and our mafia to continue. Don Russo took the path of least resistance too many times and now my husband, father-in-law and more than two dozen other Cosa Nostra men are dead.

From the names listed of the victims, it seems only nine are Russian or Irish. No names are given for the supposed gang members engaged in the conflict.

Returning to the city would be signing my own death warrant. Leo's too.

Just as important is the promise I made to Tino when we got back from our honeymoon. He and Agustino Sr. told me that I would be responsible for Leo's care. Tino made me promise him that if anything ever happened to him and his dad, I would take care of Leo as if he was my own brother.

I look over to where Leo is playing a video game on the cabin's big screen television.

Tino would expect me to take Leo back to Detroit, to his grandfather, the Revello patriarch. But my promise was to take care of Leo as if he were Rocco. If

Leo were Rocco, I would make sure he got the medical treatment denied to him since his accident.

Family takes care of family.

Well, me taking care of Leo means doing what is best for him, not what is best for *la famiglia*.

When I discover that the papers Tino wanted me to get show me how to gain access to several accounts in both our names in the Cayman Islands, I know I can do that. It means letting my family continue to believe I am dead.

My heart hurts at the thought of never seeing my parents or brother again, but if I go back to Detroit, chances are both Leo and I end up dead for real. And maybe my family with us. Our enemies bombed one house. What's to stop them from bombing another?

It is better for everyone if me and Leo stay dead as far as the Detroit Cosa Nostra and their enemies are concerned.

Chapter 1

ATLAS

Present Day

The pounding bass of the club's music thrums through my body. Swirling lights play above the gyrating bodies on the dance floor.

A woman on the edge smiles and crooks her finger at me. I pretend not to notice.

Instead of wearing my usual dark suit, I'm dressed to blend in. My black dress shirt is a snug fit and open at the neck. No tie. My slacks are clubwear not the bottom half of my usual designer suit. Nothing about me screams enforcer for a Greek mafia family.

Ádis Adelfótita, the Hades Brotherhood, is my family and my life. Tonight my job is to gather intel on potential business tithes for our protection racket before anyone realizes we're claiming territory here.

It's nine o'clock and Nuovi Inizi is already half full. People are dancing and drinking.

I take note of the bar to my left, staffed with three bartenders. I count four waitstaff serving customers on the floor. I bet that number increases once the club gets busier. Very promising.

This place is doing well even though it's in a suburb of Portland and not downtown. Whoever did the décor, knows how to draw in people who want to party in a trendy setting. I bet the drinks are expensive and the booze to make them is cheap.

I make my way to the bar and order a Scotch, neat. I'm right that the price is at the high end. Exactly one shot is served in a rock glass by a smiling bartender.

I toss it back and am surprised. The Scotch is a higher quality than I expect. It's not top shelf, but it's not bought for profit margins alone.

That could be good, or bad. Higher quality liquor might bring in more customers to the club, but overall the profit margins are going to be lower.

The percentage we require for tithe once we take over protecting an area can go up or down depending on the profit margin for the business. We can't expect 10% of net out of a restaurant when their profit margin is only 7%. Doesn't leave enough money to put back into the business. A bankrupt business doesn't make us any money.

A nightclub like this should be able to support ten though. The owner might need some advice on how to increase their liquor margins, but that's an easy fix.

A feminine voice interrupts my calculations. "*Ciao, bella*. Give me a cranberry juice and soda would you?"

The husky tone of the woman's voice sends an arrow of desire zinging straight to my cock. I have to control my body's instinct to spin and face her and force only my head to turn. And I stare.

She is beautiful. No more than five-foot-four, her red heels give her an extra three inches. She still only comes up to my shoulder. I want to reach out and touch the silky waves of her chestnut brown hair. My hand starts to lift and I have to press it into my side.

Pretty dark eyes observe me from her heart shaped face. One sculpted brow raised in silent question.

I'm too busy looking my fill to answer.

Encased in a red dress that barely brushes the top of her knees, her body is all curves. The sleeves are long; the neckline does not plunge and it's still the sexiest damn thing I have ever seen. Her generous tits are lovingly accentuated by the red silk clinging to them. The skirt fits her luscious hips like a second skin. If I could see her ass, it would be a perfect, juicy peach.

I *need* to get my hands on it. *Gamó*. What is happening?

I'm never like this when I'm on the job. I would like to blame this reaction on how long it has been since I got laid, but I got my rocks off last night.

My cock is hard as steel, wanting *this* woman. Women are interchangeable to me. A pussy is a pussy. But not this one. This one I crave.

I will have her.

This job just got a whole lot more interesting.

A practiced smile curves lips I want to crush under mine. "Are you enjoying yourself?"

I am now.

Even if I can tell she is not hitting on me. She's asking like someone who works here, even though she's not dressed like one of the servers. A manager maybe?

Not only a woman to fuck, but someone who will have good information for me if I ask the right questions.

"It's a bangin' club," I say.

Pride shines in her chocolate brown eyes. "Thank you."

"Do you work here?"

Her laughter is a sexy trill that hardens my cock further. This time her smile is genuine. "It's worse than that, I own the place."

I am not often surprised, but I am now. She seems young to own the club. I'd assumed the L. Esposito behind the LLC was older and probably a man. She's neither and my dick is thrilled.

"That means you're not on the clock." I shift my body closer to hers.

She doesn't move away, but takes a sip of her cranberry juice and looks up at me through her lashes. "Or I'm always on the clock. It depends on how you look at it."

"Dance with me."

She's opening her mouth to turn me down.

I can tell, but I'm already taking her drink from her hand and putting it on the bar. "Watch it for her," I instruct the bartender.

The woman nods, her eyes wide, like she's never seen anyone pick up her gorgeous boss before. Good. That means I don't have anyone I have to incapacitate to claim all of this woman's attention. And that is what I plan to do for the foreseeable future.

Sliding my arm around her, I settle my hand onto the curve of her hip and guide us to the dance floor. She gasps, but she doesn't try to pull away.

When we reach the dance floor, I turn her body into mine. I lift her left hand and put it on my neck and place her right hand over my heart. Then, pressing her against me, we grind. Her red painted lips are parted, her eyes filled with the same sexual need crashing through me.

LUCIA

What am I doing? I don't dance with customers. I haven't danced with anyone in more than five years.

I don't even know this man's name, but his hard thigh is between mine and our bodies are moving together like we've been doing this for years, not seconds. One of his hands is pressed against the top of my ass, holding my body close to him. The other is on my nape.

It's a possessive, dominant hold and my ovaries are exploding.

It's wild. Unbelievable. And irresistible.

Since Tino, I don't date. I don't let men get close.

Suddenly, my body is telling me how starved it is for touch. My inner sex kitten that has been hiding my whole darn life comes out to play. *Dio mio.* She wants to rub against his thigh and push my breasts against the hard plains of his torso.

He reads my mind and his leg shifts so he's making my dress ride up my thighs. If I don't get a hold of myself soon, I'm going to be dancing with my thong exposed and the round globes of my butt along with it.

I can't get that inner sex kitten to care. She wants this. She craves it.

He leans down and nips at my earlobe. "Tell me you have a storage room we can go to."

"I..." I try to shake my head to clear it, but he's kissing a spot under my ear that has my vagina clamoring for more.

Somehow, I find myself leading him through the club and to the right of the bar, down the hall and to a nondescript door. I press the unlock code into the keypad and the heavy steel door clicks open. He reaches around me and yanks it so he can push me through.

The lights go on, revealing the stairs. He picks me up and throws me over his shoulder, taking the stairs two at a time.

I laugh breathlessly and push myself up so my soft stomach isn't bouncing on his hard muscles with every step. "Take a right at the top."

These rooms were used for storage, but I renovated the area into a small, one-bedroom apartment when I started Nuovi Inizi.

Living here makes sense financially, but right now all I care about is that my bed is only two doorways away.

He stops in front of the entrance to my place and lets my body slide to the floor in front of him. "Get us in, *ílios mou.*"

"My name is Lucia."

"You burn hot like the sun. You are my *ílios.*"

His sun? Isn't it enough he has a body to die for and his voice sounds like sex? Does he have to be charming as well?

"What language is that?"

"Greek, like my family," he growls in a deep, sexy tone that goes straight to my core.

My fingers slip and it takes two tries to get the code into the keypad and my apartment door unlocked. I don't remember ever being this hot. Desire runs through my veins like lava.

Is it because it's been so long since I had sex? I'm not like this though. My vagina keeps clenching and it feels empty.

Sex is fun, but it's not necessary.

At least that's what I've told myself for the past five years. It's how I thought of it before my husband was killed in the war over territory in Detroit. I don't want to think about Tino right now, or my life before I came to Oregon.

I am a new woman and apparently my body got the memo. Because I want this man who uses Greek endearments and makes my heart race in my chest. Enough to leave the club in the hands of my employees and bring him into my personal sanctuary.

I don't bring strange men home. I don't bring men home at all. I don't even invite my friends over, but this man? I want him here. In my bed.

Is it because I'm finally realizing my dreams? Have my body and mind slipped the tight leash of relentless work and effort of the last five years?

He shoves the door open and pushes me inside. His roughness doesn't make me nervous. It turns me on. But then I was once married to a mafia soldier. Normal men don't scare me.

This one though. He is something else. He wouldn't even be intimidated by the don.

Kicking the door shut behind him, he starts unbuttoning his shirt. "Do you like that dress?"

"Yes."

"Then take it off before I rip it from your body." There is no teasing in his blue gaze, merely intent.

I'm so freakin' aroused right now. My panties are soaked, and I can feel slick wetness where my thighs rub together.

Reaching behind me, I undo the zip and then pull the dress off, leaving me in the red lace panties and matching bra I never expected anyone else to ever see. Lingerie has been a private indulgence since I ran from Michigan with my brother-in-law. The single reminder that I am still a woman, not just a nightclub owner earning money to support the last living member of my family.

Those blue eyes heat, burning over my body like a physical touch. "You are fucking beautiful."

I feel beautiful with his gaze on me. Sexy.

"Your turn."

His shirt is unbuttoned, giving me a glimpse of his sculpted chest, but that's as far as he's gotten. Shrugging out of his shirt, he reveals the rest of the chiseled perfection of his arms and chest. He has tattoos. Lots and lots of tattoos.

His right arm has a full sleeve of monochromatic images inked into his skin. A snarling three headed dog guards his heart. Under it is something written in Greek letters.

I had no idea I found body art such a turn on. Does he have ink on his back? Wanting to know, I ask, "Can I see your back?"

He gives me a smoldering glance and then turns around. His entire back is covered with a tattoo so detailed, it looks real. A Spartan warrior stands victorious over a dead bear with a sword sticking out of it and rivulets of blood running from the wound.

The blood looks wet; the warrior's muscles almost ripple.

Unable to stop myself, I step forward, my hand outstretched to touch.

Something about the Spartan feels familiar.

The only facial features showing behind the Corinthian helmet are the warrior's eyes, mouth and chin. The eyes are the same blue as the man on whose back I'm ogling. The lips and jaw are the same shape too.

"It's you," I say.

"Yes."

My fingertips trace the tattoo, and I discover small ridges under the colorful ink. Scars?

What caused them? Are they why he got such a huge piece of artwork on his back? What does the bear symbolize? I'm pretty sure these questions are too intimate to ask a one-night stand. So, I don't.

But I wonder.

The man I am practically drooling over bends to take off his boots, giving me a delicious view of his perfect backside. Okay, there's nothing *practically* about it. I swipe moisture from my lips with the back of my hand, greedy to see it all.

I wait with bated breath while he undoes his trousers and shoves them, right along with the black knit boxers clinging to his muscular buttocks, down his legs. He turns back around, and I finally suck in air that almost chokes me.

Fully aroused, his penis juts out and upward with impressive length and girth. He's huge.

If I'm going to jump off the bridge of celibacy, there could be no better specimen of masculinity to do it with.

He crosses the space between us so fast, I barely realize he's moved. Wrapping his hand around my hair, he holds it like a ponytail, keeping my head in place. He dips down so our lips touch. Just that. A simple touch.

I make a needy sound and I push up toward him, wanting a deeper kiss.

He gives it to me, suddenly devouring my mouth and I respond with an alien, wild passion. His big hands are on my back, touching and pressing me closer. Then he undoes the clasp of my bra and pulls it from me.

My soaked panties are next, but when I go to step out of my heels, he says, "Don't. Leave them on."

With an arm under my bottom, he picks me up and carries me across the room until I feel the wall at my back. Then he lifts my body like it's nothing and drapes me over his shoulders. My sex is right in front of his face. He breathes against my most intimate flesh and I shudder in response.

Inhaling like he's savoring my scent, he nuzzles forward. My own head thunks back against the wall, my hands digging into his hair of their own accord.

How is he holding me up like this? I'm not tall, but I'm by no means tiny. I don't wear a size two, in fact I shop in the plus size department when I have time to look for new clothes. My boobs and butt are what is referred to as curvy. I have thighs that will never be referred to as pencils; my tummy is not flat, much less concave.

Yet, he shows no strain from this position. That is so freaking hot.

His tongue flicks out to taste me, laving my folds and then pressing against my clitoris. Already so hot, I am gasping on the verge of orgasm. How did he get me here so fast?

Uncaring, my body responds to his teeth and tongue with unabashed delight. He eats me out like he's enjoying himself, not like he's chasing my climax so he can get his rocks off. His tongue is all over my vulva, but then he thrusts it inside my vagina and I cry out.

I haven't had anything but my own finger in there in five years. I touch myself to get off to relieve stress. It never feels like this.

Rubbing his nose up my labia and over my clit, he sends jolts of pleasure sparking along my nerve endings. When his mouth settles against my swollen nub, he nips it with his teeth.

"Oh!" I gasp out.

Then he sucks on my clitoris and ecstasy radiates out from my core.

I scream when I come, squeezing his head with my thighs, shoving myself forward to press against his willing mouth. He's not done though, and he keeps eating me until a second climax hits with even more ferocity than the first.

Then I'm begging. "*Basta!* Stop. It's too much. *Per favore*...please..."

I'm American, but in the Detroit Cosa Nostra, Italian is the first language we teach our children and it falls from my mouth too easily when I experience deep emotion. Or incredible sexual pleasure.

I don't even know this man's name and I don't care. Not right now. I'm begging him to stop, but my thighs aren't relaxing so he can move his head back, are they?

How am I twenty-eight years old and only now realizing I can feel like *this*?

When my leg muscles finally give and they nearly slip off his shoulders, he does a little jog with his shoulders and I slide back. He doesn't let me fall. He doesn't even let my feet hit the floor. He puts his arms around me and unerringly carries me to the bedroom.

I would say it's instinct for a sexual master like this man, but really, there is only one door. The bathroom is through the bedroom.

He lays me on the bed before turning to go.

No way did he just give me multiple orgasms with his mouth only to leave without getting off himself. Right? Before I can fret too much about it, he's back, a small foil packet in his hand. He rips it open and rolls the condom down his length.

Then he joins me on the bed, positioned between my legs.

Before he can put that monster inside me, I say, "Wait."

He does and something inside me cracks. This man.

"What is your name?"

His smile is sexy as hell. "Atlas."

"I'm Lucia. When I say it's a pleasure to meet you, I mean it."

He's still smiling when he lifts my legs and pushes my thighs wide so he can press the head of his big dick against the entrance to my body.

"The pleasure is mine." He thrusts forward, hard.

A string of Italian curses explode out of my mouth.

Sliding into my wet heat, he stretches my vaginal walls until I'm sure I can't take another millimeter. But do I want him to stop?

No. And he does not.

He keeps thrusting in and out, going deeper with each thrust until he's hitting my cervix. A different kind of pleasure explodes in my core. Tinged with erotic pain, it's so intense it radiates outward, devastating every nerve ending in its path.

He pistons in my body, dragging his thick penis along the hypersensitive tissue of my inner walls.

And all I want is more.

Then he discovers my breasts. Or at least that's what it feels like. Because he stops moving to play with his new toys and as frustrated as I am, I'm also experiencing an overload of sensation. Every tweak of my nipples results in a burst of pleasure in the flesh clinging so tightly to his hardon.

It's a feedback loop that I never want to stop.

I cant my pelvis, taking him deeper and suddenly he's moving his hips again, but his hands are still on my fleshy mounds. His fingers playing a catch and release game with my nipples.

He grows impossibly big inside me and then he shouts his release so loud my ears ring. It takes me over the edge again and I scream too. His name.

"Atlas!"

When he comes back from taking care of the condom, he doesn't get dressed, but joins me again on the bed. His hands explore my body, running over already sensitive skin and dipping between my legs with intent.

"Again?" I ask.

"I am nowhere near done with this gorgeous body." Delivered in that deep, masculine tone, it is both a sensual promise and a threat.

At some point, I slip into exhausted slumber only to wake sometime later with his rock-hard erection rubbing up and down my labia. My overworked clit is swollen and super sensitive, and I can't help wanting him all over again.

"More?" I ask with sleepy disbelief.

Does this man ever go soft?

"As often as you'll let me."

My body thrills to his words and I say, "As often as you like."

He likes hearing that and shifts so his bulbous head is pressing against my entrance. "You might regret that offer," he warns.

"Never." I'll drown in the pleasure I find in his body tonight and do so willingly.

His growl is the only warning I get before he surges inside me and takes me on another wild ride that leads to yet another screaming orgasm.

It doesn't surprise me when he makes good on his promise and wakes me twice more in the night. The man is a machine.

However, when I wake up in the early morning hours and his big body is still curled around mine? That shocks me.

I expected him to sneak off during the night. I have no personal experience with morning-afters and only know what I hear around the club. The one man I had sex with before this was my husband. Our first morning-after was after our wedding.

Will Atlas expect me to make him breakfast? The idea doesn't bother me. In fact, I like the thought of feeding him and fall back to sleep planning the perfect morning-after menu in my head.

Chapter 2

ATLAS

I wake with Lucia pressed close to my body and my cock already throbbing with the need for another round inside her tight pussy.

I've never had sex with a virgin, but I swear her pussy is tight enough to be one. There was no blood though. Even though she must be at least in her mid-twenties, I checked when I took care of the condom the first time. She is that tight.

Maybe it's been a while for her. She responds like a dream, but I would swear there were times when the pleasure she felt was a surprise to her.

She's too beautiful not to have men in her life though. My muscles bunch with the need to hurt any other man who dares to touch her. The urge to kill those faceless bastards who already have rides me hard.

I let my hand slide along her generous curves. I will fuck all memory of other lovers from her mind and her body. I will ruin her for anyone else.

This possessiveness is new.

Sharing women with my brothers has never been an issue. In the past.

If one of my brothers or cousins makes a move on Lucia, I'll beat him into next week. It's a new thought, but I don't question the rightness of it.

This woman is mine.

She makes a soft sound when my fingertip circles her nipple, but she doesn't wake. I wore her out last night.

Let's see what I can do with her this morning.

Reveling in the feel of her satin smooth skin under my hands, I touch her slowly and gently. The idea of keeping her asleep a little while longer as I rev up her body turns me on. I've never done anything like this before.

Never been interested in exciting a woman who wasn't offering anything back to me.

When I brush two fingers over her mons, sliding over her lips without dipping between them, Lucia moans and rolls onto her back, unconsciously giving me better access.

I'm hungry for her pussy, but I want to taste all of her. I start with the join of her neck and shoulder, kissing her there. Goosebumps form on her skin, revealing this is an erogenous spot for her. I slide my tongue up her neck and tug her earlobe gently with my teeth.

She shifts restlessly but doesn't open her eyes.

Is she pretending to be asleep?

Her breathing is still that shallow, even inhalation and exhalation of sleep though. Her heartrate remains steady, even though I can smell her arousal on her skin.

Gamó. My heart is pounding wildly in my chest.

My hands shake with need and excitement as I touch her body. Her body's instinctive response calls to something primal in me. That her subconscious trusts me enough to allow her such deep sleep when I am in the bed with her? It makes me want to beat my chest and stake my claim.

I don't sleep with women. When the sex is over, I leave. Or they do. The only people who I can sleep in the same room with are my brothers and cousins. Even with them, I sleep lightly, atavistically alert for any danger.

No one shares my bed.

Last night I shared hers though and I slept deeply and well.

I sip at her lips and even in sleep, her mouth clings to mine as I pull my head away. But I'm on a mission. And when I am on a mission, I am hyper focused. Right now, I'm determined to kiss and taste every inch of her skin.

I learn the spot below her ribs makes her shiver. She kicks her legs restlessly when I kiss the bottoms of her feet, but her thighs part invitingly when I sample the skin behind her knees.

Seeing the glistening folds of her pussy, my mouth waters and my focus shifts to waking her with pleasure.

LUCIA

I wake from the most amazing sex dream of my life, only to discover that it's real. Atlas has his head buried between my thighs, his tongue thrusting inside me.

Tino didn't do this. He always said real men got their wives off with their dicks. Which was probably why my climaxes were few and far between with him.

I've had more orgasms in one night with Atlas than I had during my first year of marriage. Maybe *all* the years of my marriage.

All thoughts of Tino and his limited view of sex fly out of my head as Atlas shifts his tongue up to my clitoris and thrusts a finger inside my swollen core. I grab his head, holding him in place and thrust my hips upward toward his talented mouth.

He hums in approval and the sound vibrates through my sensitive, intimate flesh adding to the blissful sensations.

My body is buzzing with ecstasy, like we've been at this for hours, not minutes. My muscles contract and I go rigid as it coalesces inside me before exploding, sending ricochets of pleasure outward.

I scream his name and I'm still chanting, *"Bene...bene...bene..."* when he surges up my body and slams inside me, hitting my cervix and causing another climax to overlap the first one.

He pistons through my orgasm, never letting me come down completely and I grab his ears, tugging his head down so our mouths meet in a passionate kiss. I taste myself on him, the proof of how he pleasured me increasing my excitement.

I meet his thrusts, my body aching in the best way possible from a surfeit of sex. My vaginal walls cling to his demanding penis each time he pulls back, but give way again with every thrust forward. He grinds his pelvis into my overworked nub of pleasure, twisting his hips and forcing my body to surge toward cataclysmic release again.

This time when I come, he comes too, his erection buried as deeply inside me as it will go. He wraps his arms around me, pressing our bodies together as we ride out the waves of ecstasy together.

He kisses me over and over again until my panting breaths settle into a normal rhythm and my body goes lax under his.

Then he lifts his head. "You sleep really deeply, *ílios mou.*"

"I don't," I deny. Though I slept better last night than I have since the early months of my marriage.

"I'm a light sleeper." Have been ever since I lost my baby. My body and subconscious mind are always on alert for danger. Even though the danger is gone, happily living in a beautiful facility in another state. "I guess you exhausted me last night."

Or I felt safe with him in my bed like I haven't in a very long time.

He tugs at my earlobe with his teeth and huffs a breath of warm air, sending pleasurable shivers down my neck. "You are so responsive. I could stay inside you all day."

My stomach snarls. His rumbles right after and I laugh. He joins me and I have another revelation. Laughing while a man is still inside my body is wonderful.

"I think I need to feed us before anymore bedroom gymnastics."

"You want to feed me?" he asks, smiling.

"Yes. I already planned out the perfect breakfast, but you're going to have to let me up to make it."

"You planned it?"

My face heats, but I nod. "I woke up earlier, around dawn, and you were still here. I thought—"

"That you would feed me. I like that *ilios mou*, almost as much as I like being inside you."

"Glad to see you have your priorities straight," I tease. But when his stomach growls again, I shove at his chest. "Up. Time to eat."

"I've already eaten." His blue gaze traps mine. "And it was delicious."

"Your libido may be satisfied, but your stomach isn't. Neither is mine. We need sustenance if we're going to keep this up." I blush again, realizing I may have put my foot in it.

Why should I expect that he'll want to stick around for more? We'd barely shared first names before having sex. I don't have experience with one-night stands, but I'm pretty sure that's an indication of one.

"If you are promising me both food and further access to your body, who am I to deny you?" he asks, like he didn't get the memo on the one-night stand thing either.

Was this wild, amazing, unexpected and terrifically intense sex the start of something more?

Chapter 3

ATLAS

I disengage from Lucia's body, wanting nothing more than to go for another round, but she's hungry too. So, she must be fed.

As I stand, I look down at my still semi-erect cock and the sight of my seed mixed with her juices gives me a primal sense of satisfaction. I've claimed my woman.

And she enjoyed it, chanting how good it was in Italian. Like me, her American English has no accent, but Italian slips in when she's excited. I like it.

It's sexy.

In a flash, what I'm seeing on my cock registers on a whole different level. *My seed mixed with her juices*. Oh, Fuck.

"I forgot the condom." Shock nearly strangles me. I don't fuck women without gloving up. Ever.

Not one time since I started having sex have I forgotten that layer of protection. Not even when I was a teenager discovering the joys of dick in pussy.

She's up on her knees, staring at me, horror etched in her beautiful features. "You didn't use a condom? *Dio mio*, tell me your clean."

"I am clean."

"Can I believe you? I met you last night."

"You can believe." I cross the room and dig my phone out of my slacks. With a few taps I have my most recent test results on the screen. I show her. "Clean."

She grabs the phone and reads carefully, but then she grabs her throat. "This was taken three months ago. How many women have you had sex with since then?"

"None without a rubber."

"But..."

"I have never had sex without one." I'm glad her primary concern seems to be about STDs.

She must be on birth control. A beautiful, sensual woman like her would need to be. I'm sure I'm not the first man she's brought up here from the club.

My mind throws up images of other men standing where I am. The beast inside me roars. I'll need a list of names.

Any man who has known her sweet pussy needs to die and who better to kill them than me? Called Dímios, the executioner, because I am *Ádis Adelfótita's* most brutal assassin.

Her chocolate brown eyes search mine, like she's looking for the truth in their depths. I will never lie to her about something important like this, so I let her look her fill.

"I'm clean too," she says, "But we should probably both get tested."

"If you want our second date to be a trip to the clinic, I'll indulge you," I tease.

I never tease women. Sometimes I give my brothers or cousins shit, but this lighthearted man? He isn't me.

Only he is with Lucia apparently.

"I'd call it our third date. Breakfast will be our second," she sasses back with a grin.

A grin that goes straight to my cock, which fills with blood until I'm once again fully erect. I have a strong sex drive. It is a Rokos family trait, but this is next level. I am insatiable for this woman.

Her gaze slides down my naked body, only increasing my desire to rejoin her on the bed.

When she sees how ready I am, her eyes widen. "It's only been a few minutes. How..."

"Last night didn't clue you in to how fast I recover around you?"

"Around me?" she asks.

I decide to answer her with my body rather than words. Breakfast is put off for another hour, but this time she reminds me about the condom. And for the first time in my life, I resent gloving up.

I don't want barriers between us.

LUCIA

While Atlas showers, I put together the breakfast I planned in the early hours.

I can't wait to have a full-size kitchen again. Not that the kitchen in the modest house I'm buying is big, but it will be a huge improvement over this kitchenette.

Even if I had something bigger than a toaster oven, there's no space in here to do any real baking. I'm only able to cook frittatas because I have a special pan for making them on top of the stove. It makes single serving sized frittatas, which is all I've needed up until now. Because I'm only cooking two eggs at a time, it has the added benefit of cooking them faster as well, so I wait to pour the egg mixture in until I hear the shower shut off.

Imagining him drying off his naked body in my tiny bathroom has my mouth going dry. I've been fighting the temptation to join him since I told him if he didn't shower alone, we'd be eating breakfast for dinner. Because I didn't like our chances of being naked together under water and not having sex again.

I've never been this *horny* in all my life.

I was married to a husband I loved for three years and even our honeymoon sex wasn't this good. Is it my age? I'm not thirty yet, but my ovaries want to explode every time I look at Atlas.

The shock of the forgotten condom didn't diminish my desire for the sexy, tattooed man one iota. Right now, I want to go into the bathroom and explore every single one of those tattoos with my tongue.

Instead, I put the croissants in the toaster oven to heat up and pour the egg mixture into the frittata pan. I set my kitchen timer for two and half minutes before putting the jam in the center of my bistro style table. Small and round, it's the only table that would fit in the efficiency maximized space of my apartment.

The timer goes off and I flip my frittata pan, setting it again for a minute. I've prepared two cappuccinos and I'm starting the second pesto frittata when Atlas walks into the room. He's wearing black knit boxer shorts that form to his muscular body. No shirt, no slacks. His gorgeous body is on display for my enjoyment.

And I do enjoy it. I fan myself. "Do you usually eat breakfast in your underwear?"

"I wouldn't want you to feel underdressed, considering you aren't wearing any." He pulls me in for a kiss, his big hands sliding under the silk of my robe to grope my naked flesh.

The timer goes off for the second frittata and I force myself to pull away from his mouth and his touch.

I put the food on the table, and he smiles when he sees it. "You went to a lot of trouble. Thank you."

I shrug. "I like to cook, and frittatas are easy."

"If you say so." He hums appreciatively when he takes his first bite.

It's so surreal to have a nearly naked man sitting at my table, I almost forget to eat, but then my stomach growls and reminds me the last food I had was sometime around lunch yesterday. I reach for a croissant and slather some raspberry jam on it.

I have a sweet tooth. So, sue me.

We eat in comfortable silence until he's polished off his eggs and I've managed to drink most of my cappuccino.

"Were you having a nice dream this morning?" he asks me, his blue eyes filled with sensual heat.

I choke on my last sip of coffee and start coughing. He gets up and hands me my glass of water, encouraging me to drink.

"You know I was," I tell him.

He winks. "You must have been. You took a long time to wake up."

Mortified, I gulp down more water rather than answer.

He squats down beside me, his hamstrings bulging. "It was sexy as hell."

"You liked doing that while I was sleeping?"

"Tasting you gives me pleasure, but bringing you to the point of climax while your body slept? That was fucking hot."

"You want to do it again?" I ask.

"Absolutely. The question is: do *you* want me to do it again?"

Atlas is a complicated man, one who has shown he'll take what he wants. However, I sense that he won't take more than I want to give. Hence his question.

"Yes. I do." I'm not going to play coy.

I want all the pleasure this man wants to lavish on me because it's beyond anything I've ever experienced. And we've only had one night and morning together.

"Good." He leans forward, putting his face into my neck. "You smell like me. Like sex. It's fucking addictive."

"I like being addictive, but I'm still going to shower after breakfast."

He inhales deeply, kisses my neck and then stands and returns to his chair. "I'd prefer you didn't."

"I have things I have to do today, and I can't do them reeking of sex."

"You don't reek. You smell good." He takes a croissant and starts to eat it without any jam.

Warmed by his blatant sexual approval, I take a bite of my frittata. I make my own pesto and the eggs are yummy if I do say so myself.

"What do you have to do today? Besides go to the clinic with me?" he asks.

To get tested. Right.

I am not a slut for sleeping with a man I met last night. I am free. Sexy. Things I haven't been in a long time. "We can go there first thing so you can get back to your day."

"I plan on spending my day with you. What are we doing?"

He doesn't ask if I mind. And that turns me on instead of irritating me. Which is all kinds of wrong, I'm sure, but no one else is inside my head to judge me.

Not anymore.

No longer a mafia princess, I am Lucia Esposito, nightclub owner and newly discovered sex kitten.

I stand up and start clearing the table. "I need to pick up packing boxes."

"You're moving?"

"I'm buying a house." My voice holds all the delight and pride I feel at that reality.

I've worked hard to get to a place where I can take care of Lenny and have a home of my own. The one thing I've missed since leaving my family behind that I can actually do something about.

Atlas grabs the rest of the things off the table. "I'll do the dishes while you shower."

Surprised, I put the plate I'm holding down and stare. "You're going to wash my dishes?"

"You cooked. It's only fair."

"But I don't have a dishwasher." No room in the kitchenette.

He gives me an odd look. "I can wash a few dishes and pans by hand. I'm not helpless."

"Okay."

Why does the thought of him doing dishes in my kitchen make me wet?

Ignoring my body's response, I hightail it to the bedroom and grab a short floral dress I usually pair with dark leggings. Fall has been warmer than usual this year, but it's nearly the end of October and there's a nip in the air despite the bright blue sky.

The dress hits me a few inches above the knee but I don't put on my usual leggings. Instead, I toss a pair of thigh-highs on the bed beside the dress. They have elastic at the top to hold them in place and I won't have to wear a garter belt.

The scooped bodice of the dress shows off my cleavage while the stretchy fabric clings to my curves. The a-line skirt drapes flatteringly over my ample bottom and hips.

I would normally wear yoga pants and a sweater to run errands. After leaving Detroit, I stopped dressing up to leave the house. I'm no longer a capo's daughter-in-law, constantly under scrutiny.

Here, I am simply me. A woman who doesn't have to impress anybody when I'm out and about. That doesn't mean I'm wearing my yoga pants to hang out with Atlas though. I guess I still have some vanity.

I put my long hair up so it won't get wet, before stepping into the shower. Washing quickly, but thoroughly, I'm finished and drying off less than fifteen minutes later.

While I'd love to luxuriate in my own body right now, I'd rather be with the man who made me feel so decadent to begin with.

Besides there really is no luxuriating in my small shower cubicle.

That doesn't mean I rush through getting ready.

Apparently, my inner sex kitten wants to look her best for the man who gives such copious and amazing orgasms.

Chapter 4

LUCIA

Atlas offers to drive and I let him. I'd planned to run my errands using the MAX and taking a rideshare home once I picked up the boxes.

He presses the button on his key fob to unlock the doors on a shiny black metallic BMW X7.

Opening the door for me, he gives me a hand up so I can slide into the leather passenger seat of an SUV nicer than the don's. I'm surprised Atlas felt comfortable leaving this vehicle parked in the unsecure lot overnight.

Put the luxury SUV together with Atlas's designer clothes and shoes, and that spells serious money. His own? Or his family's?

It doesn't matter to me. I'm not looking for a sugar-daddy. Or even a boyfriend. Heck, until last night, I didn't think I was looking for a sex partner either. I might change my mind about the boyfriend thing. We'll see how this goes. For the first time in years, I have breathing room and can consider the possibility.

The fact that I want to? I blame on my ovaries.

Maybe a little on his amazing sex skills too.

Pulling into traffic, he says, "Tell me about your house."

"It's a ranch style house built in 1957, but the kitchen is fully updated."

"What about the wiring and plumbing?"

"Oh, that too, but it still has its original charm. The carpet someone used to cover the floors in the 1970s has been pulled up and it has hardwood throughout. There's an extra half bath and a laundry room."

I have a stackable washer and dryer in my place, but it's in a closet with no space to hang things up when I pull them out of the dryer. It's funny the things you learn to miss that you've taken for granted your whole life.

I don't miss having a maid, or bodyguards, but a place to bake? That I can't wait to have again.

"The garage has been converted into a family room too."

"Where will you park your car?" he asks, like he doesn't see that as a bonus.

"Well, if I had one, I could park it in the driveway."

"You don't have a car?"

"No."

"How will you get to and from the club?"

"Both the house and Nuovi Inizi are within walking distance to a MAX stop." It's one of the reasons I was so happy when my offer on the house got accepted. "Would you like to see it?"

Hearing the words come out of my mouth startles me. I haven't invited anyone to see the house. I'm still trying to decide if I want to have a housewarming and have my employees over after I move in.

He doesn't hesitate. "Yes."

"I'll text the realtor." The house doesn't have anyone living in it, so it should be no problem.

While I'm texting back and forth with my realtor, Atlas drives to a private clinic near Portland's downtown.

Once we get there, he guides me into the discreetly elegant building with a hand against my lower back.

It feels nice. Not like the actions of a one-night-stand. Though can it be called a one-nighter if he stayed for more in the morning and breakfast after?

I have very little experience with this kind of thing, but it feels like the beginning of something and not a casual hookup.

Which scares me a little, but I'm in a better place to start a relationship than I have been since Tino's death.

Atlas and I go separately to get our blood drawn for the tests.

The nurse asks me the usual screening questions.

"Is the day after sex too early to take a pregnancy test?" I ask her when she's done.

"Ten to fourteen days is preferred," she replies without judgment. "Do you need the morning after pill?"

That gives me pause. It should be a no-brainer. Getting pregnant with a man I met so recently would be foolhardy, to say the least.

But the prospect of pregnancy tastes sweet to my soul in a way it hasn't since I lost my baby. Not that there's much chance of it happening. I never went on birth control after my miscarriage. Once Tino and I started having sex again, I never got pregnant.

Still, if there is a chance, I want to take it. I *can* take it. A year ago, I wouldn't have been able to, but the club is making enough profit now to cover Lenny's care and my own living expenses. Including paying the mortgage on a house that could easily accommodate another person.

I shake my head. "No, thank you."

"Are you sure?" the nurse asks, this time with a tiny bit of judgment.

Or is that me judging myself and blaming her?

Whichever it is, I say, "Yes, I'm sure."

After I am done giving my urine and blood samples, I find Atlas waiting for me in the reception area.

He looks big and forbidding until he sees me and then he smiles. "Ready?"

I nod.

He guides me out to the car. "Some of the tests will be ready later today, but a couple require time to culture and won't be available for a few days."

"You asked?" I shouldn't be surprised.

Atlas hasn't shown any reticence asking for what he wants so far.

"You didn't?"

I laugh. "I didn't have to. The nurse offered the information."

"My nurse wasn't nearly as helpful." There's something in his voice.

"Why not?"

"She was too busy trying to give me her phone number."

Unreasonable anger surges through me.

It's not as if Atlas and I are a *thing*. But I am hoping we might become one.

"That's very unprofessional." But then, so is a nightclub owner having sex all night with one of the patrons.

"I told her I am seeing someone."

"You did? You are?" I stop before getting into his SUV. "You'd better mean me."

If he's in a committed relationship with someone else and I spent all night and morning naked with him, I'm going to feel like crap. I didn't even think to ask.

The look he gives me could sear concrete. "Who else but you, *ílios mou?*"

"Okay, good. Just so we are clear, I'm not seeing anyone either."

"If you were, you wouldn't be any longer."

"Sure, caveman." I roll my eyes and climb up into the truck.

Atlas pulls the seatbelt across me and hooks it and while he's still leaning over me, presses his lips firmly to mine.

"No one else touches you." He closes my door.

I wait for him to come around and get into the driver's seat before I say, "I don't share either."

He smirks and starts the engine.

The smile I give him is filled with the delight coursing through me. We *are* starting something and neither of us wants to see anyone else while we see where this thing goes.

I give him the address for the house I'm buying and he puts it into the GPS.

It takes twenty-five minutes to get there and we talk the whole way. Atlas tells me he's only moved to the Portland Metro area recently.

"What brought you here?" I ask.

"Business and family."

The same reasons I settled in Oregon. To start a business that could support me and Lenny's care and to get away from what was left of our families. I doubt Atlas is trying to get away from his family though.

"Where did you move from?"

"San Francisco. Our parents still live there, but my brothers and I wanted to build our own business."

"That's admirable." So different from the mafia culture I was raised in.

Sons in the Russo Famiglia followed in their fathers' footsteps to become made men, never straying from the same zip code. Unless it was for an alliance.

Atlas reaches for my hand and puts it on his thigh while he drives. "Does your family live here?"

It takes me a second to answer. The gesture feels so intimate, like we are a couple already. "I don't have any family."

It's why I use Esposito as my surname now. It's common in Italy to give it to children without family. For all intents and purposes, mine is gone.

"I am sorry."

"Don't be. Life happens to us all." And it is my choice to live without any connection to mine.

It is the price I pay to keep both me and Lenny safe.

"How long have you lived here?"

"So sure I wasn't born in Oregon?"

"Besides your slips into Italian? I hear some Michigan in your voice. Maybe Detroit."

Ice washes through my vein, momentarily freezing my vocal cords. "How?"

"I notice things."

I wish he hadn't noticed that. It makes me feel exposed, and I'm not about to confirm or deny it. "I moved here five years ago to open Nuovi Inizi."

"Why a nightclub?"

Memories of another life in another place assail me. "I started the nightclub because that's what I knew."

After I lost the baby, Tino thought keeping me busy would help me get past the grief. It worked to an extent, but losing a baby isn't something you get over quickly.

Tino and his dad ran the Cosa Nostra clubs in Detroit. He asked me to take over doing the books for the clubs. I discovered an aptitude for bookkeeping, both balancing the real income and expenses and for ways to launder money.

I liked my new job. It was a respite from babysitting my adult brother-in-law and it gave me a chance to spend more time with my husband. Every aspect of running a club goes through the books in one way, or another. Hungry for knowledge of any kind, I ate it up.

What I didn't learn about running a club from doing the books, I learned from listening to Tino. Once I started working for the clubs, he never hesitated to talk business in front of me. Not that he was ever interested in my opinion about running them.

However, back then? I thought he was a modern thinking man because he let me listen in. Other mafia wives I knew weren't allowed to work and their husbands never talked shop in front of them.

I never got used to the noise and the crush of people at the clubs though. Mostly Tino made sure I spent time in them during the day.

I could have suggested he bring the paperwork to me and I do the books at home, but I never did. Because I didn't trust my husband not to expect me to watch over Lenny and do my work at the same time. So, I put up with the sounds and smells of the clubs. Something I still struggle with at Nuovi Inizi.

My favorite part of owning the nightclub is the administrative stuff that happens during the day, when the club is closed.

"I'm good at it," I add, realizing I've been silent too long while lost in my memories.

"You are. Nightclubs fail at a rate of 75%," Atlas says. "That you made Nuovi Inizi a success shows you're savvier than most."

I'm surprised he knows that. "Are you a trivia geek as well as an accent savant?"

Why did I say that? It implies he's right about where I'm originally from. Not that he'd find my family looking for Lucia Esposito.

"It's not trivia to me," he dismisses. "My family owns a few clubs in San Francisco and LA."

Woah. Okay. Seriously rich family.

"What would you do, if you didn't own the nightclub?" Atlas asks me.

"That's not an option." Lenny's care will always require a level of income I can't make anywhere else. "I'm not a dreamer I'm a doer."

Although the profit margins for Nuovi Inizi are good, they will just cover Lenny's care, my new mortgage and putting aside the money monthly that will be necessary for expansion.

Once I have enough saved, we will open up the second floor to private parties and install a VIP area for patrons willing to pay what will be hefty membership fees.

"Why here? Why the suburbs and not downtown?"

I answer his second question because answering the first would reveal too much. Unless I lie. And for some reason, even though I've spent the last five years lying about myself to pretty much everyone, I don't want to outright lie to him if I don't have to.

"A combination of factors. Rents and property are less expensive in the suburbs and there are more options available. Onsite parking is a huge bonus, but not something I could have offered in a downtown nightclub." Not with what I had for starter money.

Maybe, not even if I'd had twice as much to work with. Getting space in a building with a parking garage in downtown Portland can take a year, or longer, on a waiting list.

Properties that have their own parking lots are real estate unicorns and I've never believed in magic.

"It was busy last night." He brushes the top of my hand with his thumb.

Pleasure travels up my arm and zings along no well-traveled nerve endings to my nipples and core.

This man.

"Yes. The customers that would have gone downtown for the latest boutique bar are happy to find something closer to home that offers the same sense of urban sophistication." I work hard to make sure the ambiance and music feel of the moment.

It requires subtle updates to décor, which I assess monthly. Sometimes, it's a simple matter of removing some tables and rearranging others. Other times, it requires paying a graffiti artist to repaint the wall outside or a muralist to do one inside.

I bring in new DJs weekly. When they hit, I have them back. Bringing in popular guest DJs from bigger cities is also important.

"I'm exploring the possibility of doing live music once a week," I tell Atlas. "Portland's music scene is vibrant and popular local bands can bring in their own clientele with them."

"You're a savvy businesswoman, Lucia."

My cheeks warm, I smile. He has no idea how much the compliment means to me. To be recognized for my brain and not only my body. Born a mafia princess, I was considered good for two things by my family:

1. The potential to make a good marriage alliance, which I did.

2. Having babies. Which I didn't.

But that last one wasn't my fault. I got pregnant like I was supposed to. What happened after, well that wasn't on me.

Chapter 5

LUCIA

Atlas pulls his SUV into the driveway of the house that is going to be mine in less than three weeks. The pale-yellow ranch style home with its partial brick façade gleams brightly in the autumn sunshine.

Crimson mums fill the brick flowerbox that runs under the picture window in the front of the house.

It's not a big lot, but there's a fenced-in back yard and well-maintained flower beds in the front. Most importantly, it will be mine. My sanctuary. My home.

Elaine, my realtor, is waiting by the front door.

She eyes Atlas with interest before turning to me. "Lock the door from the inside on your way out. I'll leave you to it."

"You don't have to stay to see us out?" Atlas asks, his eyes narrowed.

"No." Elaine smiles at him. "Practically speaking, Lucia is the homeowner."

"If that is the case, then you should install a deadbolt. A lock on the door handle won't keep an intruder out."

"Oh, is he your security consultant?" Elaine asks me.

"No." But apparently, he's very security conscious.

I don't tell Elaine who Atlas *is* because I don't have a label for him.

Hookup? Embarrassing.

Boyfriend? Not quite ready to use that label, despite our discussion about exclusivity.

"Right, well. Once you take possession, you can install all new locks. I always suggest doing that to all my clients."

"I intended to," I tell her.

"If you don't need anything? I've got a showing in half an hour. I need to hop to it."

"Thanks for letting me in," I say, waving her off.

I turn to find Atlas glaring dourly at the door. "How does she know no one else is inside?" he asks.

"Why would they be?"

"I can think of at least five reasons and none of them good."

Laughing, I grab his arm and pull him inside. "No one is waiting inside to rob us, I promise."

Atlas comes in, but an air of watchfulness surrounds him now. His muscles seem bunched, ready to spring into action while his gaze darts around the living-slash-dining area as if someone is going to jump out at us.

"You really do have a thing for security," I say wryly.

He looks down at me. "Whereas I would say, you do not show enough concern for your own wellbeing."

"What do you mean?"

"You are standing in an empty house with a man you met only last night. I could do anything I wanted to you and the only person who even knows I was here with you is that dippy realtor. You didn't even tell her my name."

"You did what you wanted with me last night. And this morning," I remind him with a teasing smile, trying to keep things light.

"You are safe with me," he says, no humor lightening *his* features. "But if you had allowed another man up to your apartment last night, or gone with him in his car this morning, you might not be."

"If another man had wanted to go up to my apartment, I wouldn't have let him. Do you think you're the only guy to hit on me in the last five years?" I ask, irritation starting to take over my delight in being in my soon-to-be new home.

"Did you at least get the names of the others before you took them up?" he asks, almost snarling.

What the heck does he have to be mad about?

"There were no others. I've been too busy building up the club to date anyone." And why did I admit that?

My dating life, or lack thereof, is none of Atlas's business.

He goes to grab me, stops himself, makes an honest to goodness growling sound and stalks off. He does a quick but thorough walkthrough of the house before coming back to where I'm still standing, fuming in the living room.

"The house is clear."

"What are you, a cop, or something?" I demand.

"I am not a cop," he says with such disgust, there's no doubt Atlas is no fan of law enforcement.

I cross my arms over my chest and cock my hip. "So, why are you acting like one?"

"I am acting like a man who cares about your safety."

"Oh, I thought you were just a guy who got off on insulting the woman he had sex with. It goes both ways you know? I could have been a serial killer and you followed me up to my apartment like a lamb."

The look he gives me questions my sanity. "I can take care of myself."

"So can I."

"Your code for the downstairs door and your apartment are the same. Anyone could get inside."

I can't believe he noticed that. Or that I let him. He might have a teensy-tiny point about my lack of caution with him.

"No one else knows them," I say defensively.

"I know them."

"You watched me type them in?" He must have to know they are the same.

I'm appalled at myself. I never let anyone close enough to see me enter the code. Not even the employees that have been with me since the beginning. But he didn't merely see me enter it and notice the two doors have the same code. He remembers that code.

I'll have to change it when I get back. On both doors.

"Yes."

"That's rude."

"Most criminals are not polite," he grits out.

All belligerence, I ask. "Are you a criminal?"

"That is not the point." He glares down at me.

"I didn't think so," I say with narrowed eyes. "The point seems to be you trying to make me feel like I'm not very smart."

"What the hell are you talking about?" His glacial blue eyes spear me with ire.

"This was a mistake. *Uscire*." Realizing he's not going to understand me telling him to get out in Italian, I say, "You need to go."

Why did I think I could build something with a one-night stand?

He's right. I treated him like I could trust him without any reason to do so. I blame it on lust. That's better than thinking of myself as desperately lonely.

I hate that word. *Desperate*. I am not desperate and I'm not lonely. I'm not.

I have my friends...well, my employees.

My brain stops there. Because there is no one else. Not a single person would miss me if I were gone. Not really. When I ran from the Detroit Cosa Nostra, I left behind family and friends.

And I haven't replaced any of them in five years.

I didn't want to. Letting people in puts me at risk of being found out. Which is a paranoid way to look at relationships, but I was raised in the mafia. Paranoia keeps you alive.

Only it didn't keep Tino breathing. Or his dad, or the dozens of other made men that died that day when the Irish mob and the bratva joined forces to take over Cosa Nostra territory.

"I'm not going anywhere." Atlas runs his hand along my arms, the back of his fingers brushing my breasts.

I should jerk away from his touch, but I stand there, staring up at him. What is wrong with me?

A second ago, I was furious with him. Now, I want to know where else those fingers of his are going to go.

He pulls me closer to him until my chest presses against his warm body. "You are safe with me."

"I believe you, but I shouldn't." I really, really shouldn't.

I am an intelligent and usually cautious woman. But with this man, I throw caution to the wind and run almost entirely on instinct.

"You should because it is true. I will protect you, *ílios mou*. I need you to protect yourself when you are not with me."

"I do. I'm only like this with you." And I hate admitting it. Even to myself. "None of my employees know the code to get upstairs at the club."

His expression is skeptical.

"I don't let people close enough to see over my shoulder and I always, always block it with my body."

"Except with me." He sounds confused by that, but his expression? It's 100% male satisfaction.

I step back, away from his touch. "We should leave."

Chapter 6

ATLAS

At least she is saying *we* should leave now, not trying to get rid of me.

Telling me to get out in Italian. Should I tell her that I'm fluent in the language? The *Ádis Adelfótita* has a close relationship to the Camorra in California and men of rank in the *Ádis Adelfótita* are required to learn a language of either our allies, or our enemies.

I learned two. Italian and Russian.

Being able to understand my little sun when she is angry, not to mention passionate, will give me an edge. I decide not to reveal that edge yet.

She is so irritated I pointed out her deficiency in security that her generous tits are heaving. She frowns when she notices me looking at the mouthwatering cleavage on display.

I shrug. What does she expect? My cock might feel like it's been chiseled out of granite when I'm around my beauty, but I'm not made of stone.

"You were going to show me around," I remind her.

She rolls her eyes at me. "You already took your own tour."

"No. That was me confirming no one else was here." Lucia coming here alone when someone could break in so easily gives me an unfamiliar sick feeling in my gut.

Ilios mou needs to be more cautious.

I will kill anyone who hurts her, but that won't undo the harm already done.

She frowns and shakes her head. "And I thought I was paranoid."

I shrug. It's not paranoia, but knowledge. The world is a dangerous place. My family contributes to that danger, so I should know.

But I will keep any risk away from my woman.

"You seriously want me to show you the house?" she asks, her voice dripping with disbelief.

"Being able to see it how you do is why I came with you." I don't care about the house, only what it means to her. "Tell me what it will be like when you live here."

She sucks in a breath. "How can you have me so angry one minute and say the most perfect thing the next?"

I don't answer because I don't know. I don't know why me wanting her to stay safe made her mad or why telling her the truth about why I'm here made her happy.

Giving me a tentative smile, she waves her hand around her. "This is the living area. It's not huge, but the way the living and dining room flow together in the L shape makes it feel bigger. I'm going to put a sofa facing the fireplace. I don't have a lot of other furniture for in here, but it will come."

She takes my hand and walks me through the rest of the house, telling me her plans for now and for later when she can buy more furniture and make more updates.

Her whole house would fit in my suite in our family mansion, but I like how happy this space makes her.

She shines like the sun I call her. Her parents named her Lucia. Light. I call her *ílios mou*. My sun. For a Greek man it is the same. I could call her *astéri mou*. My star. Both fit her. She is beauty and brightness. But she is not *a* star. She is *my* sun.

Warmth, illumination and beauty for my world.

Her voice goes dreamy talking about her plans, turning me on.

When we reach the master bedroom, I have some ideas for how to christen it. There is no furniture, but that's not a problem. Images of taking her against the wall play an arousing montage in my head.

I've been sporting a semi this whole tour, but now my cock grows hard as a pike.

I like sex. It's a good way to blow off steam. Not a necessity though. I never think about the woman after I leave her. I don't go back for seconds.

With Lucia, having repeated and prolonged access to her sexy body is fucking necessary. It's a good thing I need to spend so much time with her over the next couple of weeks.

I am so insatiable for her pussy, my hands cramp with the need to grab her tits.

She pulls her hand from mine and shakes it out. "Is something wrong, Atlas?"

"No." I grab her hand again and rub her palm until she relaxes. "Better?"

She nods and turns to leave the room. "Come on. There are only two rooms left to see."

I'm not interested in those rooms. I want to stay here and put the master bedroom to its intended use.

Reaching out, I clasp her shoulders and I pull her to a stop. "Come here."

Lucia's eyes widen, her beautiful face filled with confusion. When I yank her body flush with mine, she gets it.

Her soft lips part and her breath stutters, but she shakes her head. "We can't. The house isn't mine yet."

I don't bother arguing. She's a firecracker in bed, but innocent in ways I'm not sure I ever was.

I slam my mouth down on hers, staking a claim on her berry red lips. She tastes so damn sweet, but she has plump and juicy lips between her legs that are even sweeter. Getting her to let me eat her out here, in a room with no curtains on the windows, is going to take some doing though.

Lucky for me, backing down from a challenge is not in my skillset. I kiss Lucia until she stops fighting my hold, spearing her mouth with my tongue like I want to spear her silky, warm pussy.

She moans and wraps her arms around my neck, making her own effort to close any distance between our bodies. Taking two handfuls of the delectable ass under the skirt of her flirty dress, I lift her, moving until her back is against the wall. She lifts her legs and locks her ankles behind my back.

She's wearing thigh-highs, not tights.

Fuck. Me.

Lucia writhes against me, trying to increase the friction, her thin panties and my slacks no barrier between her soft pussy lips and my hard cock.

That's right. Let it go, *ilios mou*. Let me have what is mine.

Her movements grow erratic, telling me she's nearly there. Not ready for her to come, I move back. Breaking the hold of her thighs on my torso, I lower her to the floor and let go of her ass.

"No," she mewls. "I was so close."

My smile is diabolical as I slide my thumbs under both sides of her dress's neckline and slip them under her bra straps.

She's too lost in her passion for self-preservation or to worry about who might see us. Exactly how I want her.

I yank the stretchy fabric of her bodice down her arms along with her bra straps until her large tits bounce free.

Puckered and rosy with blood, her nipples call to my mouth. Leaning down, I take one between my lips and suck. Hard. Lashing it with my tongue, I cup her other breast in my hand and start to play. When I pinch the tender peak between my thumb and forefinger, she moans, her body straining toward me.

Her nipples are so fucking sensitive. Can I make her come from stimulating her beautiful tits alone?

I bite softly on her tender flesh, eliciting another long, high-pitched moan.

"Basta!" she cries.

No way is it enough. And with her arms trapped in her dress there's nothing she can do but take the pleasure I give her.

"Oh, Atlas, *bene,*" she breathes.

It is better than good. She is perfect and so is her response to my touch.

"Don't stop. *Per favore,* don't stop."

Her pleading words act like kerosene on the fire of my libido.

Kneading her fleshy mounds, I suck and bite on her nipples until she's breathing so harshly it sounds like she's sobbing. She's close to coming, but my patience is gone.

I reach under her dress and tear her panties right off her. The sound of silk rending draws another long moan out of Lucia.

I lay her on the floor, glad the carpet that was removed in the rest of the house was replaced in here instead. Shoving her skirt up her thighs, I push her legs apart and upward so she is open to my gaze.

Her thigh-highs frame her pretty pussy. The dark pink flesh is swollen and glistening. My mouth waters and then I dive in.

Her sweet honey bursts onto my taste buds. She's so wet, her juices slide across my tongue. A litany of pleas and demands in a mixture of Italian and English falling from her lips, Lucia bucks up against my mouth, trying to get what she needs to climax.

Not yet, beauty.

Her little pearl is hard and protruding from her hood. I suck on it and she screams, but I pull back.

She starts swearing.

I grin and then lick around her tight little asshole. I haven't taken her here yet, but I will. For at least the next couple of weeks, this woman is mine. Every sexy inch of her.

Sucking one plump nether lip into my mouth, I sweep my tongue side to side along the engorged flesh.

She's still fighting to get her arms out of the dress. *"Porca miseria,* Atlas, help me."

But I like her the way she is. As good as trussed up for my pleasure.

I give her other lip the same treatment until she's moaning, begging me to put a finger inside her. I'm a generous man. I give her two.

Her pussy walls suck at my fingers as her hips buck. She's trying to ride herself to completion, but that's not happening. Not until I'm ready.

And I'm not ready. I'm having too much fun.

LUCIA

I don't know how many times Atlas brings me to brink of orgasm before backing off, but I'm sobbing and cursing. And yes, *begging*. When I realize I'm doing it in Italian, I switch to English. Not that it makes any difference to the sadist torturing me with pleasure.

My arms are trapped in my dress. As much as I fight it, a secret part of me thrills to the knowledge I can't get free.

He has me exactly where he wants me, my over stimulated breasts on display and my thighs spread wide in lewd invitation.

He lifts his handsome head. His eyes should glow demonic red with the look in them, but they are still blue.

"Please, Atlas," I beg again. "Let me come."

He stands and I whimper. He can't leave me like this. He strips out of his clothes, leaving them in a heap on the carpet. He's not going anywhere.

Dark with blood and aggressive with need, his heavy erection bobs upward.

Kneeling beside me, he helps me out of my dress and bra with surprisingly gentle hands. I don't wait. I'm too far gone. I shove him on his back and mount that oversized steel pipe between his legs like a trick pony.

But the only trick is how swollen my inner flesh is. Despite my gushing wetness, I have to keep rocking to get his big dick inside me.

He grips my hips with his inhumanly strong fingers and guides me up and down on his shaft. A galaxy of stars exploding inside me, ecstasy pounds through my blood with every beat of my heart as my muscles seize with the ultimate pleasure.

I scream so loud the neighbors probably hear me.

I don't care. I have never come so hard. My soul is tethered to my body by the hard flesh filling me and stretching my inner walls.

Flipping us, Atlas starts to pound into me, bringing another earth shattering climax piggybacking onto my last one. This is no aftershock. My womb clenches with extravagant need. My muscles contract and I cry out, incoherent words, demands...but one word resounds around us.

His name. *Atlas*. I scream it, over and over again.

He keeps thrusting into me, grinding down with his pelvis and keeping me on the edge of bliss, before toppling me over again and again. It's too much. Too good. Too intense.

I start to hyperventilate.

He cups my breasts and caresses them in what is probably meant to be a soothing manner, but I'm so over sensitized, it only adds to the overload of sensation. My vision goes black around the edges.

I am going to pass out and I can't get the breath to tell him so. My body bucks and writhes, but he meets me thrust for thrust, forcing layer after layer of pleasure into my system.

It's too much.

I gasp out his name, but it's barely more than a whisper. "Atlas." Then everything goes black.

I don't know how long it is before I wake up, but I'm straddling his lap while he leans against the wall. My head rests over the Cerberus tattoo. The sound of his steady heartbeat against my ear comforts me.

My vaginal walls contract around him. His still hard erection is deep inside me. Although the copious amount of fluid leaking out of my vagina tells me he came too.

He's petting my back and whispering things to me in Greek that make goosebumps break out on my flesh even though I don't know what they mean.

I nuzzle into his neck. "We did it again."

"What?"

I yawn. "No condom."

I could nap right here. Even with him inside me. Maybe especially because he's inside me. I am safe. Protected. Connected to another human being in a way I've never experienced.

"The tests are for your peace of mind, *ílios mou*. I am clean. You are clean."

"I could get pregnant." Yes, I decided to take the risk and not use the morning after pill, but he deserves to know it *is* a risk.

If he has reasons for not wanting to father a child, I will take the pill. I'm still well within the window of effectiveness. Regardless, it only decreases the chance of pregnancy by 75%. Odds improved by my lack of ability to get pregnant the last two years of my marriage.

Atlas goes still, his hand halting midway down my back. "You're not on birth control?"

"No."

"Why not?"

Here it is. The moment of truth.

"I haven't had sex with a partner in five years." I've masturbated, but there's no risk to pregnancy with that.

His penis grows impossibly bigger inside of me, stretching well used flesh in a silent claim to my most intimate flesh.

Cupping my shoulders, he pushes me back far enough so he can see my face.

His is an emotionless, impenetrable mask.

A chill goes down my spine and I shudder. It's like the man sitting under me, still buried deep inside me, is not the same man I've been with since last night.

This man is a dangerous stranger.

And then he smiles and the fear sending icicles along my nerve endings evaporates like the mist.

"You could be pregnant with my baby." He doesn't sound angry, or even worried.

If I didn't know it to be impossible, I would say he sounds pleased by the prospect.

"You're not upset about that?"

"I am not."

"Most men would be." I think. Not like I have a ton of experience dating.

He shrugs. "I am not most men."

"I guess I'm not most women either."

"What does that mean?"

"I'm not upset by the idea of having a baby, even though I'm not in a committed relationship and I've only recently managed to get my life to a place where I have breathing room." I've always wanted to be a mom.

But I thought that dream died with my husband. Now, I realize I can fight for it, like I fight daily for my independence and the ability to take care of Lenny.

"I'm not looking for you to play daddy, or anything. If you hate the idea of your progeny out in the world, I'll take Plan B." Now that I know what I want, I can save up for a trip to the sperm bank.

Why not?

"No," he says forcefully. "No morning after pill. If you carry my child, we will work it out together. Family means everything to me, my brothers and cousins."

"Not your parents?" I ask.

"No." His tone doesn't invite further discussion.

I can't help wondering why his parents are excluded. This thing between us is too new to press for answers though.

Regardless of how much of his family he included in the sentiment, it is not a foreign concept to me. It is a familiar refrain in the mafia. I guess it's not so surprising that normal people feel that way too.

So, I nod. "Okay. We'll work it out together."

It's not a promise of a future together, but an understanding that we are both responsible for the life that could be growing inside me. We're both culpable for forgoing the condom and we have both agreed that I won't take the morning after pill.

Against all odds, and knowing what a long shot it truly is, I can't help hoping I'm pregnant.

Chapter 7

ATLAS

After dropping Lucia off at Nuovi Inizi, I drive home.

I need fresh clothes and Zeus wants an update. After showering and dressing in my usual suit, I find him in his office.

"What did the computer do to you?" I ask.

Zeus shifts his glare from the laptop screen to me. "Nice of you to finally show up."

"I wasn't aware I was expected, *anax*." I emphasize his title.

The head of *Ádis Adelfótita* here in Portland, Zeus is my oldest brother. I respect him, but I'm nobody's lapdog. The ability to bend knee was tortured out of me when I was ten years old, and the Golubev Bratva kidnapped me.

Zeus leans back in his chair. "You never spend the night with women."

I shrug. It is true, but Lucia is different. "I slept."

Zeus's eyes widen. "You slept, as in went somnolent beside another human being? A *woman*?"

My brothers and I don't trust people in general, but we are particularly wary of women. Our mother lied to my brothers when I was taken and told them I had been sent away to school. Our nanny colluded with the Golubevs.

Both women betrayed us for their own comfort and security.

The bratva wanted part of my grandfather's territory in Los Angeles. They believed I was the leverage to get it. I believed my grandfather, who was the *Nonós tis Nýchtas* (the Godfather of the Night for the *Ádis Adelfótita*) would rescue me.

We were both wrong.

The Golubevs tortured me, sending videos of my abuse to my grandfather as incentive. He was unmoved and by the time I returned to my family, I no longer allowed emotion to move me either.

"There was a hell of a lot of sex too." The memory has my cock wanting to surge in my slacks.

"Didn't need that bit of information."

"Maybe she wore me out." It would explain why I was able to sleep next to Lucia.

I don't feel worn out though. After burying myself in her body and eating her pussy so many times, I am ready to take on a whole nest of enemies.

Too bad we're lying low right now.

"Maybe." Zeus doesn't look any more convinced than I am. "Should I be worried?"

"About me getting a lot of phenomenal sex?"

"About you being compromised." The *dipshit* goes unsaid, but I hear it anyway.

"My loyalty to you will never be compromised."

My grandfather didn't rescue me nineteen years ago. His men, including my father, did not rescue me.

Constantin, who is my uncle and the current *Nonós tis Nýchtas*, defied his father and came into Golubev territory to get me. He brought my older brothers along, who were twelve and thirteen at the time. Constantin was only seventeen himself.

Nearly a whole generation younger than my mom, he rules over the *Ádis Adelfótita* very differently than my grandfather did. He'll order the death of an entire family without blinking an eye, but his loyalty to his men and his family is absolute.

That started nineteen years ago when he, Zeus and Orion breached enemy territory to save me. We all became made men that night, killing all my captors staying at the compound. Three, and the most brutal, of those kills were mine.

After a year of torture, I had a lot of rage. The beast the Golubev bastards woke inside me had his first taste of retribution that night. It has had many tastes since. I have killed so many Golubev bratva soldiers, they have a permanent bounty on my head.

I'm not worried. Their bratva is a shadow of what it once was because of me. One day, I will make sure the Golubevs cease to exist altogether.

"You've got that look in your eye," Zeus says.

"What look?" But I know.

"You're thinking about them."

The Golubevs. He doesn't have to say their name. We both know.

My destiny as an enforcer and assassin is carved into every scar they put on my back.

Constantin gave me the nickname *Dímios* when I killed my captors so brutally the night my uncle and brothers rescued me. In an ironic twist of fate, the bratva call me *palach* and whisper about me like the bogeyman. Like the Greek word *dímios*, it is Russian for executioner.

"Other than getting lucky, how did it go last night?" Zeus asks sourly.

We all have our damage from that night.

To survive the torture, I built a wall between me and any of my soft emotions. Ruthlessly killing my captors only put a layer of cement over that wall.

Zeus drowned the nightmares in sex. He was a manwhore until the girl he was promised to was murdered by the bratva. Now he's so celibate, we call him The Monk.

Orion seems the most normal of all of us, but that's only because he hides his damage behind humor and charm. It's there. Every bit as ugly and remorseless as mine and Zeus's.

"Luck didn't come into it." Lucia is as hot for me as I am for her. "Like I thought, the Nuovi Inizi is solid. With the other businesses in the area, our yearly take on protection will be eight figures easy."

Laundering money through some of those businesses will only sweeten the deal.

"How many businesses did you recon last night?"

"One."

"One?" Zeus does not look impressed.

It's a good thing, I don't worry about impressing my brother, or anyone else.

"One," I repeat. "I met the proprietor. She researched the area before building her club and keeps tabs on it to keep Nuovi Inizi running successfully."

"You're cultivating her as an asset." It's not a question.

So, I don't answer. "Has Zephyr locked down our dock access?" I ask.

"He's working on it."

Establishing a new territory is never easy. We'll succeed, whatever palms we have to grease and blood we have to spill.

We plan a controlled start though. Recruitment, the port and marking the boundaries of our protection territory are top priority.

Later, we buy our own clubs. The plan is to own at least two strip joints and one nightclub within a year. Lucia's knowledge will help with the latter. Maybe the former too.

Zeus closes his laptop and studies me. "Tell me about the owner of Nuovi Inizi."

"Her name is Lucia Esposito." I found her last name on one of the escrow documents for her new house when I searched her apartment while she showered.

There is nothing in her purse with her full name on it. No driver's license. No library card. Her credit cards are for Nuovi Inizi.

"She's in her mid-twenties. Young to own a club, especially as a sole proprietor," I add.

"You're sure she's alone? No backers?" Zeus sounds skeptical.

"I'll do more digging, but it doesn't look like it." She talked about building her life by herself and didn't mention anyone else when talking about choosing the club's location. "No close family by the look of it either."

My sexy little nightclub owner puts up a friendly front, but she's a loner. The LLC is a dummy corporation for one L. Esposito. Now that I know her last name, I know that is her. No other names are included in the articles of incorporation.

If she has silent business partners, she's done a damn good job of hiding it.

"Married?"

"No." Fury at the thought of another man touching her erupts inside me.

I put a lid on the volcano, like I always do. Unless I need to use my rage to serve me in my role as *Dímios*.

The look on my brother's face says he noticed my reaction. And he's surprised by it.

Not sure why. I'm not incapable of feeling emotions. It's my choice not to let them rule me. Most of my emotions are locked down so tight, they are atrophied.

Anger is a useful emotion though. As long as it is controlled. Anger feeds the beast that kills for our family without remorse.

Lust is also a useful emotion, but I will never let a woman lead me around by the dick. Last night, I chose to give into the carnal hunger Lucia arouses so easily in me. And I plan on feeding that sexual fire until it burns out.

"You think I would fuck a married woman?"

"No. Make her a widow so you could fuck her without remorse? Yes."

If she had a husband, would I off him? Memories of how many times and how many ways I fucked Lucia flip through my brain. Would I get rid of anyone in the way of me having her? Yes, and I would enjoy doing it.

"The fuck is that look on your face?" my cousin, Helios, demands as he plops down into the other chair facing my brother's desk. He looks to Zeus. "Is he smiling?"

Zeus and Helios both stare at me.

"What's going on?" Zephyr asks from the doorway.

We live together in the compound. My family lives in the main house, described as a mansion by the realtor who sold the property to us. The soldiers we brought up from California live in a separate building.

Security is tighter with us all in one compound, but it has its drawbacks. The chief one being my brothers and cousins all under the same roof with me, getting in my business.

The only one missing right now is Orion, my middle brother. A lawyer, with a practice in the city, he takes on clients that can build our network of contacts.

"Atlas was smiling," Helios tells his brother.

"What the hell?" Zephyr demands. "I don't believe you."

Zeus gives me a look. "He's banging the target."

"She's not a target," I deny. "She's a resource."

Zeus shrugs. "Who you plan to collect protection money from."

"You went to the club for the first time last night and you're already bumping uglies?" Zephyr asks. "What's this chick's name and where do I find her? If she put a smile on Atlas's face, she's got a magic pussy and I want me some."

I'm on my feet and Zephyr is flying across the office before I'm even conscious of standing. My cousin shatters the glass on the watercolor Mom painted for Zeus before we left LA and lands with a loud thump on the floor below it.

"What the hell?" Zephyr jumps to his feet.

My lungs bellowing like an enraged bull, my hands fist tightly at my sides so I don't reach out for him again. "Lucia is off limits."

Zephyr's hands go up, palms out. "Whatever you say, cousin. There's plenty of pussy if you don't want to share this one."

"Brother?" Zeus asks.

My gaze locks with his. "What?" I snarl.

"Something you want to tell us?"

"She's different," I grind out.

"How?"

"I want her." She's mine.

"You've screwed plenty of women. You've never been possessive of any of them."

I don't have an answer for that, so I speak my truth. "If anyone touches her, they die."

"Shit," Helios breathes.

"Do the rest of the men going to her club know that?" Zephyr asks, sounding too damn amused.

"She doesn't fuck the customers."

My brother and my cousins all look at me like I'm not making sense.

Finally, Zeus points out, "She had sex with you."

"Enough sex to keep you with her all night and part of today," Helios says.

"You keeping tabs on me, cousin?" I ask, wondering if I need to remind him to keep his trap shut like his brother.

Maybe use my knife. I won't kill him. Just cut him a little. Shooting him would be overkill.

"I want to live to see another day," he says.

I take that as a *no*.

"It's not a secret you didn't come home last night," Zeus says.

I acknowledge his words with a slight dip of my chin, my body still in battle ready mode.

"You going to keep seeing her?" my brother asks.

"As long as it takes."

He doesn't ask, *As long as it takes to what?* He thinks he knows what I mean. That I will fuck Lucia until I get her out of my system.

But that's not what I'm talking about. I mean until I get her pregnant, which is fucking news to me. Since when do I want to have a kid with somebody?

She might be pregnant already though and the thought of using a condom with her again makes my skin itch. So, a pregnancy is more likely than not.

If it happens, there will be no letting her go. Ever.

Something inside me, in the dark depths of the soul I'm pretty sure atrophied along with my more tender emotions, is deeply satisfied at that possibility.

Lucia will be mine forever, not a few weeks.

We could raise a child separately, but why would we?

She and our child will be safer with me there to protect them. Besides, Lucia runs a nightclub. She doesn't need the stress of raising a child on her own. I'll be good for her.

It's a strange concept. Me being good for someone as something other than a stone-cold killer. I like it though.

I'm thirty years old and I've never known another *magic pussy* as my cousin calls it. Lucia's is the only one I want to lock down and keep for myself.

It's not merely her banging body though. It's her quick mind and the way she makes me laugh. And smile.

"That's creepy as hell," Zephyr says.

"Right?" his brother agrees.

"You're smiling again, brother." Zeus's eyes narrow. "Are you thinking about her?"

"It would be hard not to since we are talking about her."

My brother nods, but there's something in his eyes. Like worry. It must be a trick of light. No way is Zeus worried about me. I'm the last person Zeus needs to worry about. I left the weak little boy behind the night I made my first kills. And he knows it.

I am *Dímios*, the executioner. I can take care of myself.

And I will take care of Lucia too.

Chapter 8

ATLAS

I change into street clothes and pack a duffle before returning to Nuovi Inizi. I don't plan to return to the house tonight. Maybe not tomorrow either.

The service door is open when I arrive, and I can hear Lucia's soft tones talking with someone.

Someone who sounds like a man.

The presence of a delivery van near the back door does nothing to dampen the instant rage flooding my system.

Shoving the door all the way open, I step inside the club, but she's not in the hallway.

Her laughter sounds from an open doorway about ten feet along the corridor. My long legs eat up the distance in a couple of seconds.

This door smacks against the wall when I push it open.

Huh. Might have hit it a little hard.

Lucia jumps and spins to face me. "Atlas! I didn't know you were coming."

"I told you I would be back." I'm talking to her, but my eyes are fixed on the man who is standing way too close to my woman.

He takes a hasty step away from her and toward me, thinks better of that and shuffles to her other side. "I didn't know you were seeing someone."

"Is there a reason you thought she would tell you?" I ask in a tone I usually reserve for interrogating our enemies.

"What? No. We're friends, that's all." The guy swallows nervously.

Wonder what is stressing him out? Is it his imminent death he sees in my eyes?

"Are you friends? Or are you an inventory supplier for her club?"

He flinches at my tone. Huh. He's a pretty perceptive guy. He knows when he is in trouble. Too bad he's not as good at staying out of it to begin with.

Lucia lays a hand on my arm. "I thought you'd text before coming."

That small touch brings all my focus onto her. Big brown eyes blink up at me in confusion.

"Didn't think I needed to."

Her brows furrow and her pretty lips tilt down. "It's polite behavior to warn a friend before dropping in on them."

"You are not my friend," I bark.

She snatches her hand away and steps back, hurt darkening her eyes. "Fine. We aren't friends. You still could have texted to say you were on your way. I might have been gone."

I don't like the distance she's put between us, so I close it and pull her close. "You are not my friend. I don't fuck friends."

She gasps. "Atlas!"

She doesn't want Mr. Invading Her Personal Space to know we're lovers? Too bad.

"You are *mine*." I flick a glance to the other man to see if he gets the message.

He is looking at Lucia, not me. I revise my estimation of his smarts.

"Possessive much?" she teases, letting her body relax against mine.

What is her first clue? "Yes."

"There's no need to be jealous. I'm taking a delivery. That's all." She licks her lips and that seals it.

I pull her body up at the same time I crash my mouth down on hers.

She tries to shove at my chest, but I'm not budging. She might not see the supplier as anything but a business connection, but he looks at *ílios mou* like a starving man in front of an all-you-can-eat buffet.

The only man allowed to feast on her voluptuous curves is me.

Sliding my forearm under her ass, I lift her higher, so I don't have to bend to kiss her. Her feet leave the floor, and she makes a startled sound, wrapping her arms tightly around my neck.

Determined to remind her who she belongs to, I eat her lips and press my tongue against the seam of her mouth, demanding access to the sweet heat within.

She keeps her lips tightly sealed for a heartbeat and then she sighs, melting into me. Her lips part and I don't hesitate to slide my tongue inside. She tastes like no other woman ever has.

Like mine.

Hell, I don't kiss. I fuck. But with Lucia, I want it all.

The sound of a throat clearing and rubber soles squeaking on the floor reminds me we are not alone. Unfortunately, it reminds *ílios mou* too because she tears her mouth from mine.

"*Basta!* Stop! Let me down, Atlas." She pounds on my shoulder with one of her small fists. "I have work to do."

Letting her body slide down mine, I glare at the man interrupting my hello kiss with Lucia. I guess he has a death wish.

"If you'll sign for the delivery, I'll get out of your hair," he says to Lucia, doing his best to ignore me.

It won't work. He and I need to set some ground rules. Like if he touches Lucia, I will break every bone in his hand.

When *ílios mou* pushes away from me, I let her this time.

"Thanks for personally making the delivery, Shawn. Customers wouldn't have been happy if we tried to get through the weekend without your ale." She uses her finger to sign the digital receipt on his tablet.

He smiles at her, showing his sense of self-preservation is much worse than I thought. "You should think about increasing your order."

"Maybe. It's not fair to you to keep asking you to make these emergency drop-offs between our scheduled deliveries." The look on her face tells me she doesn't want to though.

Why not? I'll ask her after I have a little talk with the beer supplier.

"Leave the crates there. I'll help you with them after I walk your *friend* out," I tell Lucia.

Settling her fists on her hips, she gives me the stink eye. It might have the effect she intends if her posture did not make her generous tits stick out in a way that has my mouth salivating for a taste and my hands itching to touch.

The beer supplier notices too, and any possibility our little talk would only be a verbal one explodes on the impact of his gaze on my woman's breasts.

I grab Shawn's arm and hustle him out of the temperature-controlled storage room. Lucia is a hell of a businesswoman. Nothing in this club is below par, not even the storage facility for her alcohol.

"No need to see me out. I know the way." Shawn tries to pull away from my hold.

Good luck with that.

I don't say anything until we are outside. Then, I let my fist make the first conversational salvo and punch him in the stomach.

He gasps and doubles over, his arms windmilling to keep him upright.

"She is mine. Get within two feet of her again and I'll break both your arms."

"Who are you?" he wheezes, trying to stand up straight.

"Her man."

He sucks in air and then manages to pull himself together enough to stand. Neither of my brothers or my cousins would have taken that hit without retaliation.

"You think she's going to thank you for losing her account with us?" he sneers.

I crack my knuckles. "I think you're smart enough not to inconvenience her like that."

"I'm going to the cops. I'll press charges," he says, all bravado.

Some guys need an extra lesson to really learn. I give it to him. This time kicking him in the side of the knee. Not hard enough to break bone, but he goes down.

"Go to the cops," I dare him. "Five men will say I never left the house."

He's crying and holding onto his knee, showing enough smarts not to get up. "But Lucia saw you. She's not going to lie to the cops for you."

"She won't have to. You make a nuisance of yourself and I'll take care of it. It's my specialty."

"Are you threatening me?"

"If you need to ask, you're not paying attention."

"You can't do that."

I roll my eyes. "You'll keep supplying Lucia's club with as much of your product as she wants. You will not call the cops, or tell your Uncle Harry—"

"I don't have an Uncle Harry."

"Are you really this dense?"

"No." He shakes his head and wipes snot and tears from his face with the back of his hand. "I understand what you are saying."

"How close are you going to stand to Lucia?"

"Two feet." His answer is immediate.

He's finally getting it.

"Are you going to tell anyone about our discussion?"

"No."

"Good. Lucia's customers like your beer. It would be a shame if you weren't around to make it for them anymore."

To show what a reasonable guy I am, I help him to his delivery van. If I drag him so he has to hustle on his sore leg, well, what can he expect?

I don't have time to mollycoddle the man. Lucia is waiting for me.

Chapter 9

LUCIA

There's something wrong with me. When Atlas comes in acting like Cro-Magnon man, I soak my panties. I should feel badly for Shawn. Atlas clearly intimidates him.

Only, the ale distiller has always been flirty, and lately he's gotten a little aggressive with it. I've turned him down no less than four times for dates, but he never gives up.

Maybe now he will.

Atlas comes back into the storage room as I'm setting one of the crates of ale on the shelf.

"I told you to leave that for me," he growls.

His voice goes through me like an electric current. My heart races. My thighs clench in an involuntary spasm.

But I finish what I'm doing before turning to face him. "Who do you think does it when you're not around?"

There's something wild in his eyes. Intent, like a predator.

An atavistic shiver goes through me.

He grabs the last two crates and brings them over, stacking them neatly in the spaces left empty by my dwindling supply.

"I am here now." Sliding his hand under my hair, he grips my nape. "Do you need anything else before?"

"Before what?"

His eyes smolder at me. "Going upstairs and using your bed instead of bending you over these boxes."

He waves toward my whiskey inventory, which happens to be stacked three boxes wide and waist high. My waist.

The wetness between my legs becomes a veritable flood.

There's still lots to do before opening the club tonight, but my body isn't listening to my brain. My core clenches and releases over and over again, wanting to be filled. My nipples tighten, aching for his mouth. I lick my lips, not because they are dry, but because they crave stimulation.

"If I bend over here, how fast can you get me off?" I challenge.

Unable to believe the words that came out of my mouth, I barely breathe as I wait for his reply.

He yanks me toward him and mashes his lips to mine, kissing me until I'm rubbing against him like a cat in heat.

His mouth breaks away from mine to find that spot on my neck that sends me into the stratosphere. "Here it is then."

Wanting bare skin, I tug his black t-shirt up his rock solid abs. He helps by grabbing the back of the neck and yanking it off over his head.

I rub up his torso with both hands, mapping his bulging muscles and then tunneling my fingers in his silky chest hair.

"I love that you don't shave this," I tell him.

"Why would I?" he asks.

"I don't know, but some men do."

"Who?" he asks in that gravelly voice that makes my ovaries want to explode. "Who have you seen without his shirt?"

I should roll my eyes, but my body is going haywire again. His possessiveness should not turn me on, but it does. So, so much.

"Men take off their shirts to dance." I don't mention my dead husband.

I never understood why Tino waxed his chest. I guess he thought it was sexy. He never asked me what I thought. He was too macho to need my opinion. About anything.

I loved him, but if he'd lived, I'm not sure I still would. I am a different woman at twenty-eight than I was at twenty-three. Even without losing him and going into self-imposed exile, the years would have changed me. Matured me.

The truth is, that those last two years of my marriage, the cord tethering my love to him had grown pretty taught.

"Not anymore, they don't."

"It's cute that you think you can stop them." I sound sarcastic, but my vagina is yelling, *gimme, gimme, gimme.*

He doesn't reply, but shoves up my shirt and unhooks my bra, tugging it up too so my breasts spill out.

He steps back and looks down. "I could look at your naked body all day."

"I'd rather you touched it."

His expression is filled with male confidence. "That's right. We're on a timer."

He spins me around to face the boxes, bending me only far enough that I can stay upright with my hands on the top of the boxes for stability. Then he shoves my leggings and underwear down together, exposing my wet folds to his gaze.

"Perfect," he breaths as he reaches around to massage my already sensitive clitoris.

He shifts behind me. There is the sound of a zipper. His blunt head presses into my dripping opening and I arch back, wanting more.

He gives it to me, thrusting forward powerfully to fill me with his engorged penis. For a second, it feels like he's splitting me in two and then my inner walls give way and he surges forward even more.

I can feel the bite of his open zipper against my bottom and the rough denim of his jeans against my thighs. I don't know how he's maintaining the squat he needs to keep himself inside me, but his show of strength makes my lady bits swoon.

All thought flees my brain as he sets a pounding rhythm, driving me toward climax.

"You're so fucking tight." Both of his hands grip my hips as he pounds in and out of me.

Releasing my arms, I bend over the boxes, my breasts hanging over the edge, my belly pressing into the cardboard. He shifts his body further over me, reaching around with one hand to pinch my nipple.

Pleasure shoots straight from my nipple to my core and I moan.

"Touch yourself," he grits into my ear.

The angle is tricky, but I get my arm in front of my thigh and manage to press my middle finger against my clit. That's all I need before my body detonates in wild ecstasy.

Atlas isn't finished and he keeps pounding into me. I let my hand drop away and float on the feeling of being taken by this powerful man.

"I didn't say to stop touching yourself." He grabs my hand and puts it back where he wants it, so I'm once again massaging my clitoris with every thrust of his hips.

My body jolts with sensation after sensation. "It's too much."

"No, it isn't." He nips my earlobe. "We're not done."

Porca miseria! No way is he going to get another orgasm out of me right now. I shift my fingers off the over sensitized bundle of nerves, but don't move my hand away.

He knows immediately about my disobedience and makes an animalistic sound. Pulling out of me, he steps away.

Despite having got off already, my whole body rebels at the loss of him inside me.

Oh, crap. We forgot the condom again. He's going to come on my naked backside. An unexpected frisson of desire pulses through my core at the thought. I want his cum on me.

But he's not jacking off behind me. He's ripping my leggings and panties down my legs, taking my ballet flats with them. Then he finishes taking off my bra and shirt, so I'm completely naked.

"Atlas?"

He shakes his head. Then he picks me up and lays me across the boxes with my butt right at the edge.

Grabbing me under my feet, he pushes until my knees are at my torso. "Hold them."

He is so damn sexy and his bossiness is catnip to my inner sex kitten.

I wrap my arms around each thigh, gripping with my hands to hold myself open like he wants me.

"Good," he praises in a guttural voice.

A frisson of bliss arcs straight to my core.

I am wrong. I'm not done. Pleasure tightens like a spring inside me and he hasn't done anything but put me where he wants me.

His arms wrap around my legs, his hands gripping the front of my thighs with inescapable strength. He slams his thick column of steel inside my slick channel, bottoming out on the first thrust. And his hold keeps me from sliding backward even an inch.

My nerve endings explode with sensation and my vaginal walls grip him impossibly tight.

"Such a good little pussy." He pats my mons in approval.

I am drowning in lust and an unfamiliar sense of happiness. Do I have a praise kink?

"Keep your legs where they are."

"Uh huh." It's all I can say, intelligible words beyond me.

"Good girl."

Oh, lord. Those two words in *that* tone.

One hand still keeping my body from sliding up the boxes, he reaches between us and rubs his thumb in circles over my clit as he pulls back until his swollen crown is all that is still inside me.

I mewl.

He smiles diabolically before ramming back into me, setting a punishing pace. The orgasm I deny I'm capable of is growing closer and closer.

Atlas speeds up his hips and unbelievably increases the power of his thrusts until my body shakes with every drive forward.

"Come for me," he demands, his handsome face set in a rictus of pleasure.

He's close.

I want to obey him. My body is craving the release now and my heart is set on getting another *good girl* out of him, but I can't crest this wave of pleasure.

Then he pinches my clit. I scream as I explode with the power of a nuclear blast.

He roars as his seed washes my insides with heat.

My chest heaves, my heart pounding so hard, I can feel my pulse in the tender flesh wrapped around his still hard member.

Awareness of where we are and what we are doing comes back to me slowly, but when it does, I jerk under him and start shoving at his chest. My bar manager is going to show up any minute and I do not want to be caught naked in my cool storeroom, with Atlas still inside me, when she does.

He shakes his head. "Give it some more time."

Give what? His penis? He'll be ready to go again if he stays inside me much longer. I'm not convinced he isn't ready to go now.

"We don't have time. Willow is going to be here soon."

"Who is Willow?" he asks without moving.

"She's my bar manager and more importantly, she can let herself into the building."

He grunts but doesn't move.

"I'm serious, Atlas. I don't want her finding me like this."

"She won't."

"You can't be sure."

"I will not allow you to be embarrassed." His words are a promise.

But I don't know how he'll keep it if Willow gets here before I'm dressed. Feeling compelled to trust him, I stop trying to move.

"Good girl."

Heat surges into my cheeks. I like that way too much. For several long seconds, we stay there, him deep inside me, his eyes locked on mine.

The sound of the outer door opening reaches us and I panic, but Atlas cups my face. "It will be alright. You are not doing anything wrong."

"Not sure health and safety would agree," I mutter, but my body responds to the command in his voice and settles.

Dio mio. This man.

Atlas pulls out slowly, careful of my overused lady bits. "Do not move."

He yanks his t-shirt on and tucks his still hard shaft into his jeans, but he doesn't zip them. The t-shirt won't hide the fact he's aroused, but it covers his naked flesh.

He steps out into the hallway and shouts, "Hey, Willow. I'm Atlas. Lucia wants you to start in the main area."

"You're the dude she took upstairs last night."

"And I'm the man who will be staying up there tonight too."

"I need to see my boss. You're hot and all, but how do I know you aren't a serial killer who stuffed her body in the deep freeze?"

Someone kill me now. "I'm fine," I yell, loathe to move when Atlas told me not to.

I have no idea why. I hated when Tino and his dad tried to boss me around, but this feels different. It feels right and I'm going with it.

"Do you have a deep freeze?" Atlas asks Willow, sounding weirdly interested.

"Well, no. It's a figure of speech."

A beat of silence and then, "I'm serious, Lucia, tell me something that lets me know you're okay."

"You're the one that's always telling me I need to blow off some steam." I put my hands over my face, unable to believe I said that.

No way does Willow not know what we are doing in here. But she hasn't seen me and for whatever reason, that makes it okay.

Her laughter echoes from down the hall. "Good for you!"

Atlas doesn't say anything else, but comes back into the room and closes the door behind him. I shudder to think how much extra power we used keeping it cold with the door open this long.

I didn't build a successful nightclub ignoring the little things like that.

He crosses the room to stand between my legs. "Put your feet on my chest."

Is he going to keep going? Part of me wants to. Very much. The responsible business owner knows we can't though.

He taps his chest and sex kitten wins over responsible businesswoman. I let my feet rest against his hard pecs and feel immediate relief in my strained thigh and arm muscles.

Atlas slides two fingers deep inside me. My core clenches around his hard fingers and my clitoris pulses in renewed interest. But he doesn't move them. He stands there, pressing inside me, his rugged features intent.

I can't help squirming a little. "What are you doing?"

"Making sure." He presses down on my lower belly so I can't move.

"Making sure of what?" This is getting bizarre.

"That my sperm stays inside you."

What? It's a shout inside my head, but nothing comes out of my mouth as I gape like a fish.

"No...what..." I try to get more words out, but they are locked in my tight throat.

Choosing together for me not to take the morning after pill is miles away from him actively trying to get me pregnant. Isn't it?

"What the hell are you talking about?" I am finally able to demand.

"You want my baby. I want you to have my baby."

I try to scoot back from his invading fingers. "Let me up."

"Not yet."

"We have to talk and I'm not doing it with your hand in my vagina."

"It is only two fingers. I've never been interested in fisting, but if that is something you want."

"No," I practically shout.

His dick is oversized enough. His whole hand? Not in this lifetime.

"Good. I would worry about hurting you."

How are we having this conversation? In this situation?

"Please, Atlas, you have to let me up."

He looks down at me. "I like touching you."

"I figured that out." But right now I need my brain online and it goes haywire when he's touching me. "I mean it, Atlas."

He pulls his fingers out and my body mourns the loss. *Mamma mia.* I am addicted. What am I going to do when he moves on?

A man from wealth like his doesn't have to settle. But why the heck is he *trying* to get me pregnant?

I sit up and wetness gushes from me. That's one box that is going to be unpacked, broken down and buried with the other recycling before anyone else gets a chance to see the proof of my poor decisions.

Ignoring his dictate, I clamber off the boxes in a less than graceful fashion. When my feet hit the chilly floor, a big shiver wracks my body. Standing naked in the cold storage is probably not one of my best moves.

Quickly yanking on my leggings and top, I say, "I need a shower."

And there was me thinking we could get off fast and I could go on with my preparations for tonight. I didn't factor in the lack of a condom and the mess that would make. Or how sweaty I would get either.

Sex with Atlas is messy. And overwhelming. And wonderful. But really, really messy.

Slipping my feet into my ballet flats, I grab my underwear and bra. No point in putting them on only to take them off again. Hopefully, I won't see Willow on the way to my apartment.

"Here." I shove my lingerie toward Atlas. "Make yourself useful and put these in your pocket, or something."

He takes the undergarments from me and tucks them away.

Turning back to the box, I see the wet spot testifying to what we did and cringe. I rip open the top and start putting bottles on the shelves.

"What are you doing?"

"Getting rid of the evidence." Inhaling, the scent of sex assaults me. *Caspita!* "Can you open the door, and I don't know, wave some air in here?"

The most amazing sound erupts behind me. I spin in time to see the pure amusement covering Atlas's face. His laughter is deep and masculine. Also delicious.

"You want me to get rid of the smell of our sex?"

"Yes."

He opens the door and walks out. A second later I hear the back door opening too. He comes back carrying a flattened cardboard box and using it like a fan, he waves fresh air from the hallway into the room.

Finishing with the bottles in the box my bottom was on, I break it down, flatten it and join him in his efforts.

Atlas stops, inhales deeply and nods. "Better."

I have to agree, but a trace of the scent remains. Shaking my head, I hand my flattened box to Atlas. "Will you put those in the recyclables?"

He must have figured out where we store them near the garbage dumpster to have found the one he's using.

Taking the cardboard from me, he nods. "I'll meet you upstairs."

Because he can. Because he knows my security codes.

I frown. "I need to change the codes on my doors."

"Not on my account."

Why did I know he was going to say that?

Shaking my head, I pull the door to the cool storage shut behind me. "I'll leave them for now so you can get upstairs."

"Save me some hot water," he shoots over his shoulder before jauntily walking toward the backdoor, whistling a tune I can't quite place.

And then it hits me. He's whistling "Moves Like Jagger."

Chapter 10

ATLAS

The shower is still running when I let myself into Lucia's apartment. The urge to join her is so damn strong, but my woman has a club to run.

After dropping my duffle in her bedroom, I clean up at the kitchen sink. Zipping up my jeans, I feel the bulge in my pocket from her panties and bra. I pull out the bra and go back into her bedroom to drop it in the clothes hamper she has there.

The panties still damp from her juices, I keep.

"Oh! Atlas. You're here." Steam follows her out of the small bathroom.

Another reason I don't join her. That room is barely big enough for me. With both of us in the shower, I doubt either of us could turn around, much less bend down. Could be fun to try though.

Lucia's hair is wrapped up in a towel and another one covers her luscious curves. I make no effort to hide my interest as she pulls lingerie from her tall dresser.

Turning, she wags her finger at me. "You stay over there, mister."

"Sure, *ilios mou.*" I lean back against the wall to show her she's safe from my sexual advances.

For now.

My willpower is tested when she steps into a red silk thong and tugs it up her lush hips. When she settles her gorgeous tits into a matching bra, I growl.

Her head is down, but I see those lips of hers curve into a small smile.

"I'm being good, but if you keep teasing me, you're going to end up under me instead of in your club."

She lifts her head, her dark eyes filled with fire. "Don't even think about it."

"Seems to me you're doing your best to make sure that's all I'm thinking about."

Biting her lip, she nods. "Maybe. You deserve it though, after that incident in the cold storage."

"Incident?" I ask carefully.

"What would you call it?"

"Amazing sex."

Color surges into her cheeks and she turns away to get something out of the tiny closet. "It was more than that."

"Yeah?"

"You know it was. You *tried* to get me pregnant."

"You want a baby."

"Theoretically." She pulls another sexy red dress down her body. "Choosing not to take Plan B is very different than actively trying to get pregnant."

"Not really."

She spins to face me. "Yes, really. You can't seriously want me to have your baby."

"My mother has been on me and my brothers to give her grandchildren."

"Are you kidding me? Your mother wants to be a grandmother, so you decide to knock up a practical stranger."

I give fuck all that my mother wants to be a grandmother. Her and my dad accepted my grandfather's decision to leave me at the mercy of the bratva, telling my brothers I'd been sent away to school.

Of course, she cried and acted horrified by what had been done to me in captivity. My grandfather hadn't told either her or my dad about the videos. According to my uncle, my mom begged her father to get me back right after I was kidnapped.

He told her he would in his own time and his own way. She believed him. Trusted him. So did my dad.

Which means I will never trust either of them again.

No, my mom is not the reason. The woman I'm fucking wants a baby and she's not getting pregnant with any other man's child. "You'll be a good mother."

"How can you know that? We met last night!"

"When you know, you know." Ever since I didn't listen to that voice inside me that told me danger lurked around the corner and I got kidnapped at the age of ten, I do not ignore my instincts.

And they are telling me this woman would make an amazing mother. Not only that, but I want her to be the mother to *my* children.

It's fast. I don't care. I know what I know.

I am not letting this woman go and nothing will hold her to me with stronger glue than my baby inside her.

Convincing my family to accept her will take some doing. She's an outsider. From the look of horror on her beautiful face, convincing her is going to be even harder.

"You're serious about this," she says, her voice high with disbelief.

Keeping my cum insider her didn't clue her in? If she needs to hear me say it, I will. "Yes. I'm going to get you pregnant."

I don't tell her my plans to keep her. That might make her nervous.

"Do you always wear red to work?" Yes, it's a blatant attempt to change the subject.

There's no point in arguing about something that will not change.

"You can't say something like that and then calmly ask me about my work attire."

"Pretty sure I can."

"Atlas! Be reasonable."

"Was it reasonable not to take the morning after pill?" She has good instincts, but it's clear she's not used to following them. "You knew it was the right choice."

"I can't get pregnant."

"If that were true, I'm pretty sure you would have led with it when we talked about you not being on birth control earlier."

"Are you calling me a liar?"

"No, but you're not telling the whole story either."

"How can you know that?" She shakes her head. "Do not say it. You *do not* know me, no matter what you think."

She'll learn differently, but for now, I won't push that particular point. "Tell me why you think it will be hard for you to get pregnant."

Her face freezes in a grimace of grief, an old agony deep in her gaze. "I'm not ready to talk about that."

"Okay."

"Okay," she echoes.

"Should you take the towel out of your hair before we go back downstairs."

"We?"

"You're not spending the night around a bunch of horny, drunk men without me."

"Has anyone ever told you that you are pathologically possessive?"

"No."

Her expression is pure skepticism. "Right."

"I've never cared before if the women I was fucking wanted to fuck other men."

"Never?" she asks, her voice breathy.

"Never. My cousin asked me to introduce you because he wanted to get with you and I threw him across my brother's office."

"You told your brother and cousin about me?"

"Yes."

"And you *threw* your cousin?"

"I didn't kill him." That's restraint right there.

"Good to know."

"Don't be afraid of me. I will never hurt you."

"That's easy to say, not so easy to follow through on."

I want to know what she means by that, but Lucia refuses to talk anymore while she's getting ready. She tells me if I can't be quiet, I need to go in the other room. She needs to center herself before going down to the club.

"It's Friday night and that means all hands on deck. I'm running behind. I won't have time to come back up here and go through my usual routine to get my head in the right space to deal with a noisy, crowded club."

She doesn't like the noise and the crowds? Why the hell does she own a night-club then?

I don't ask because I can see that she means it. Lucia needs some time to find her Zen. She's stressed and it's not all because of a busy night at the club.

My decision to get her pregnant has her discombobulated. But she's not trying to kick me out of her apartment. Hell, she's not even kicking me out of the bedroom as long as I keep my mouth zipped.

That's pretty damn telling, even if she doesn't want to see it.

Her instincts tell her she belongs to me, but her brain is fighting it.

Chapter 11

LUCIA

Atlas helps me with my preparation and I'm grateful for two reasons. One, I'm running behind and two, his presence stops Willow from grilling me.

She doesn't even try to pretend she isn't watching us though. Every time Atlas touches me, her perfectly shaped eyebrows waggle at me and she makes a ridiculous expression of exaggerated approval.

And he touches me a lot. A hand on my shoulder. A caress over my hip as he walks by. Brushing my fingers with his when he's taking a box of inventory from me on my way to the bar. He's really got a thing about me not carting heavy boxes around.

It could be annoying, but it's not. It's sweet.

It's too much to expect Willow to keep speculation about Atlas to herself. But I don't expect my servers and bartenders to show up armed with curiosity born of knowledge.

She texted them.

My stomach knots. They all know that I took him upstairs last night. That he's still here is proof positive that my ovaries are in charge and not my brain.

The DJ arrives and my worries get tabled out of necessity. Although Chaos is a favorite with the patrons, he is not on the regular rotation. A bit of a prima donna, the DJ expects my undivided attention while he sets up. Tonight is no exception.

"Get your shit together," Atlas growls at the DJ. "Lucia has more important things to do than hold your hand."

Chaos looks Atlas up and down with a sneer. "Who are you?"

"I am Atlas Rokos. I'm in business with Constantin Petros. Change your fucking tone or this is the last gig you play on the West Coast."

Dio mio. I'm going to lose my DJ. On a Friday night.

But Chaos doesn't pick up his toys and go. He stares at Atlas like he's seeing a ghost. "*The* Constantin Petros, the nightclub owner?"

Atlas jerks his head in a nod, his jaw like granite.

Chaos puts his hands up. "Sorry, man. I didn't mean to monopolize Lucia's time. You sticking around tonight?"

"Yes." It sounds like a threat to me.

But the DJ grins. "Great! Maybe you can put a word in for me with Leon."

Who is Leon?

"Impress me and I will." His hand at the small of my back, Atlas turns me and leads me away.

"Who is Leon?" I ask out loud this time.

"He books the DJs for my family's clubs."

"Family!" Chaos exclaims behind us. "You're part of the Petros empire?"

Atlas ignores the DJ and guides me away from the sound booth.

"They must be pretty successful for Chaos to turn darn near obsequious," I say wryly.

"Successful enough." Atlas stops in a secluded corner and pulls me around so I'm facing him. "Is he always so demanding?"

"Talent usually is. One way or another." I shrug. "It's the price I pay for getting the best. Chaos brings in clubbers from all over. People will drive eight hours to be here on a night he is running the music."

The lines will be down the block tonight. I have two extra bouncers coming in.

"How did you get him to come here?"

I don't take offence at the question. My club is successful, but it's not big and I only have the one location. In the suburbs.

"One of my bartenders is his cousin." I've spent five years leveraging every person I have contact with to make Nuovi Inizi profitable.

"He'll leave for LA if Leon offers him a gig," Atlas says warningly.

"Can't be helped. Chaos refuses to sign a contract with any of the area clubs because he wants to break into either the Los Angeles or New York club scenes." Even without a good word from Atlas, Chaos is on the right trajectory to do that soon too.

Which is why I put up with his need to be the center of my attention when he plays my club.

Atlas grunts.

"Is there a reason you haven't mentioned the name of your family's clubs?" I ask.

"Zesti." He waits for my reaction.

I open my mouth. Nothing comes out. I close it. Then I try again. "Your family owns the Zesti clubs?"

There are three in Los Angeles that I know of, and he mentioned that they have clubs in San Francisco too. I'm pretty sure they have locations in San Diego as well.

Tino and his father tried to emulate their success in Detroit. They managed well enough to draw the attention of the local Irish mob and Russian bratva. My husband died trying to keep control of lucrative nightclubs that laundered money by the millions.

Cold suspicion runs up my spine. "Are you here scoping locations for another Zesti?"

Does he want to take over Nuovi Inizi?

Atlas pulls me in for a kiss. "No, Lucia. I told you, me, my brothers and my cousins moved here to build our own thing, not extend what others have already done."

I believe him, but I still say, "Promise me you're not using me to get information so you can start your own club and destroy mine in the process?"

"On my honor, I do not want to destroy your club." He presses his forehead against my own. "I promise."

Again, I believe him. Either that makes me hopelessly naïve, or a really good judge of character.

"Break it up you two." Willow looks down at her tablet. "The bachelorette party cancelled. The groom eloped with the bride's pregnant cousin. I didn't think you'd mind us refunding the reservation deposit for the tables. I wanted to check with you first though."

We usually require a minimum of twenty-four-hour notice to cancel a table reservation without charging a fee.

"We won't have any trouble filling them tonight with Chaos in the sound booth. Have Cheryl contact the waitlist before we open them up to walk-ins though."

"Will do. Barry wants to talk to you about security tonight."

I don't roll my eyes because this is typical of Barry. He has a plan, approved by me, but insists every night on going over it one last time before we open the doors.

Probably comes from being in the military.

I don't complain though. We've never had a major security incident and the minor ones get handled quickly and efficiently.

Without giving it any real thought, I take Atlas's hand and lead him toward my office where Barry will be waiting with his team.

And so it begins. Friday night at Nuovi Inizi.

I won't be able to take a full breath again until the doors shut behind the last patron.

~ ~ ~

The night is every bit as busy as I anticipated. Chaos is on fire. Probably trying to impress Atlas into putting a good word in for him with the booking agent for Zesti.

No servers call in sick. The bouncers are focused. The bartenders and barbacks sling drinks with all the flair they're supposed to.

The music is loud. We are packed to capacity.

It should annoy me having Atlas hovering like he is, but it doesn't. He knows how to stay out of the way, but he also knows how to step in and help when I need it. I've never had that.

My staff are good at their jobs, but as they say, *the buck stops here*. There are too many fires only I can put out. No doubt because of experience with his family's clubs, Atlas knows how to help me douse the flames.

I warn myself not to get used to it.

Atlas isn't a permanent fixture in my life. This thing between us is about a minute old and new relationships fail as often as new nightclubs.

~ ~ ~

But he's still there. Later that night. And the next. And the next after that. The sex is incendiary.

Even though his inexplicable desire to get me pregnant does not abate. In fact, his insistence on holding his cum inside me is a huge turn on. Not that I'll ever admit that to him.

At times I wish my body could cooperate and at others I'm grateful for whatever made me incapable of conceiving again after the miscarriage.

Because the idea of having a baby is both tantalizing and terrifying.

Especially with Atlas as the father.

Nuovi Inizi is closed Sunday and Monday, but I still have work to do.

On Sunday, Atlas leaves while I'm in my office. He says he's going home to get fresh clothes and check in with his brothers, but I fully expect a call or a text saying he won't be back today.

Not because he doesn't intend to come back, but because no matter how intense this thing between us is, Atlas can't give all his time to me.

He has a life and he's in Portland to build a business with his family.

Chapter 12

ATLAS

Everyone is on the back deck when I get home. Zeus is grilling steaks and the scent of charred meat makes my mouth water.

It's not exactly barbecue weather, but it's not raining either. I don't take off my hoodie though.

"About time you showed your face." Zephyr punches me in the shoulder. "I thought you disappeared in that magic pussy."

I punch him back and he staggers. "Don't mention Lucia's pussy if you want to keep your tongue."

"It's true then, you're falling for her?" Orion hands me a bottle of my favorite beer from Santorini.

Lucia's customers aren't the only ones who like craft beer. "I'm keeping her."

"You think that's wise?" Wearing jeans and a polo, my middle brother still manages to look like a high-class lawyer.

"Don't care." This is about following my gut, and my gut says that Lucia Esposito belongs to me.

Orion's eyes narrow. "You have a job to do with her."

"And I will do it." I'll enjoy doing it. Spending time with her is no hardship.

"You think she's going to let you keep her once you start charging her club protection money?" Orion asks.

"She'll have no choice." I'm not letting her go.

Besides, Lucia will be better off under my protection in the long run. A highly intelligent woman, she will realize that once I explain things to her.

Orion takes a sip of his own beer. "Tell me about the club."

"She built it up from nothing, turning a furniture store into a bangin' night-club. Lucia has her finger on the pulse of her clientele and the area. She keeps everything fresh."

"Fuck me," my brother breathes.

But I'm not done. "She doesn't like crowds or noise, but you'd never know it by how she is with the patrons and her staff."

"He's doing that creepy shit again." Helios glares at me.

Orion asks Zeus, "Are you seeing this?"

"I told you. He was smiling the other day and he threw Zephyr across my office when our cousin suggested getting with the woman too."

Remembering my cousin's colossally fucked up proposal, I shoulder check him and he crashes back into the table.

"What the hell? I didn't say anything," Zephyr complains.

I shrug. Zephyr is the youngest of us, and sometimes it feels like he's a lot more than two years younger than me. Maybe because he didn't make his first kill until after he was legal to drink.

"Do you smile when you are with her?" Orion asks.

I give him a look. That's a ridiculous question. Of course, I do. "What's not to smile about when I'm with the sexiest, most beautiful and intelligent woman I've ever met."

My cousins gape at each other, but Zeus and Orion are fixed on me.

"She's an outsider," Orion says the same way he'd warn me Lucia had a communicable, deadly disease.

"The fuck do I care about following the traditions of the *Ádis Adelfótita*?" Those traditions left a ten-year-old child in the hands of monsters for a year.

"It's not just about tradition. Outsiders don't understand our way of life."

"She might already be pregnant with my baby."

"*Gamo*!" That's Helios.

"Did the condom break?" Zephyr asks. "Why isn't she on birth control?"

"Remember that redhead in Athens?" Helios reminisces. "She said she couldn't use anything because she was a magnet for side effects."

"Yeah, she gave a hell of a blow job though." Zephyr shakes his head.

Zeus pulls the steaks from the grill and brings the platter over. We all troop inside and gather around the table in the breakfast nook. No one says anything about eating in the dining room.

Zeus puts the platter of steaks in the center of the table beside a cucumber salad and a basket of rolls. He's frowning, but he doesn't add to the peanut gallery.

"You didn't wear a condom," Orion guesses as he sits down.

"No."

"How do you know she's clean?" Helios asks and immediately puts his hands up. "I'm not saying anything against her."

"This lack of caution isn't like you," Orion adds, eyes the same blue as mine trying to see into my soul.

Good luck with that, brother. My soul withered nearly twenty years ago under torture and the knowledge my grandfather would rather hold on to his territory than his grandson.

"We got tested." I grab a steak with my fork and plop it on the plate in front of me before adding some cucumber salad.

I hope Gina made it. Zeus can grill, but none of us are good cooks otherwise. Not like Lucia. What that woman can whip up in her tiny kitchen is amazing.

"Your idea, or hers?" Orion asks.

I finish my bite of salad. Our housekeeper definitely made it. It has the perfect amount of feta, olives and dressing.

"What's with the twenty questions?" I ask, instead of answering my brother.

"I'm worried about you."

"Yeah, it's almost like you're human, or something," Zephyr teases.

I shrug. I don't allow emotions to be used as weapons against me, but that doesn't make me a robot. It makes me smart.

This weird lightness inside? It's okay. "I think I'm happy."

"You're volatile is what you are." Helios cuts into his own steak. "Like an elephant in musth."

"What are you? A zoologist now? The fuck are you talking about elephants?" Zephyr demands.

Helios ignores his brother. "They go into this thing when they want to impregnate a female. It's called musth and it makes them violent and unpredictable. Dangerous."

"Are you saying I'm dangerous?"

"You're the most dangerous man on the west coast, hell maybe the continent," Zeus says drily.

"That's not what Helios means." My cousin is talking about me being dangerous *to my family*.

Maybe to Lucia.

My cousin looks worried. "You're right. It's not. Your special skills as an assassin makes controlling your emotions even more important."

"I'm not going to shoot one of you." Or break their necks, or shove a stiletto through their hearts, or...okay the list could get pretty long.

I know more ways to kill than there are letters in the Greek alphabet.

"Just throw your cousin across a room." Orion's tone is hard. "Listen, brother, seeing you smile after all this time. It's pretty damn terrific, but if you lose control of your emotions after keeping them locked down so long..." He shakes his head.

"You could burn this city down and the whole state with it," Zeus says.

I frown at my oldest brother. "A few smiles and some laughter doesn't mean I'm out of control."

"You laughed?" Helios asks, dumbfounded.

My brothers and cousins all stare at me with varying degrees of disbelief.

Done with this, I surge to my feet. "You gave me a job to do, Zeus. I'm doing it."

"Sit down, Atlas." Zeus doesn't make it an order. There is almost a plea in his eyes. "Eat with us. Tell us what else you've learned."

"You want to grill the steaks? Fine. You keep trying to grill me and I'm out of here," I warn before returning to my chair.

It would be a shame to waste Gina's salad.

"I don't like the potential I see for the situation with this woman to blow up in your face and that's the last I'll say about it." Orion takes a sip of his beer. "For now."

Doesn't matter what my brothers or cousins say. I'm keeping Lucia. Hell, I'm not sure it matters what she says.

I tell them the observations I've made and the name of the distiller who sells Lucia his handcrafted ale. Too bad for Shawn, his craft distillery is in our territory. I won't mind extracting protection money from him at all.

"What did he do to piss you off?" Helios asks.

I shrug. Telling them he stands too close to Lucia might make me sound unhinged. I'm not. I'm protective. And a little possessive. Maybe a lot. Okay, yeah, definitely a lot.

I would be as happy to kill Shawn as let him live to pay us.

"There's an issue with the port," Zephyr says when I'm done giving my report.

"I thought you had it locked down," Zeus says. "We already put the offer in on the abandoned shipping yard."

"Someone else came in and made a backdoor offer. They're trying to outbid us."

"Who?"

"I don't have a name, but I saw a group of tatted up men down there today. They were with someone who never got out of the car, but they each reported to him after checking out different parts of the yard."

"What kind of tats?"

Zephyr looks at me and then back to Zeus. "I can't be positive, but they looked like bratva tats."

What the actual fuck? We spent a year investigating the Portland metro before we made our move and there was no sign of a bratva presence.

Street gangs and militia groups, but no bratva, no Irish mob and no Italian mafia. We chose our new home carefully because establishing a new territory for the *Ádis Adelfótita* isn't going to be easy.

Zeus doesn't look as shocked as the rest of us.

"You know about this?" I ask him.

"I got a tipoff that bratva activity is increasing in Portland."

"Tipoff from who?" Orion asks.

Zeus grimaces. "That anonymous guy who has been sending me texts."

We don't know who the unknown informant is. But the intel Zeus has received so far has been accurate.

"Did your CI give any details?" Helios asks.

"He's not a CI," Zeus snaps. "I'm not a fucking cop."

Unfazed, Helios says, "He's keeping his identity confidential and he's an informant, so CI."

"You're not as funny as you think you are." Zeus looks at me. "My *anonymous* informant gave me the name of a bar the bratva are hanging around. Atlas, I want you there. You have the best chance of recognizing bratva soldiers by face alone and knowing what family they are from."

I am a little obsessed with any bratva even remotely connected to Golubev. No one in my family will ever go through what I did because the bratva want something from us.

I send a message when I need to and even when I don't. Loud and clear, with dead and dismembered bodies.

"I'll do the recon, but otherwise I'll be with Lucia." I let my brother see my commitment to this family in my eyes. "If you need me, I'll be here."

Zeus nods. "I know. Zephyr, take some soldiers and set up cameras at the shipping yard. Orion, see if you can find out who made the backdoor offer. We aren't losing this port."

No piece of shit bratva are getting a foothold in our territory either.

Chapter 13

LUCIA

I get a text from Atlas, but it's not what I expect.

Atlas: *Want to check out a bar on the east side with me?*
Lucia: *Sure. When?*
Atlas: *Tonight. I'm on my way back to your place.*
Lucia: *I'll make dinner.*

I love cooking for Atlas. He's so appreciative, regardless of what I make, and I like keeping him to myself. I miss cooking for other people.

Letting others into my personal space is hard for me though. Maybe I'll invite Willow and Barry for dinner after I move into the new place.

I don't have to open myself up to close friendship to have work colleagues over. If you asked her, I bet Willow would say we are friends already anyway.

We're not. We can't be. She knows nothing about the real me.

My heart stutters at the thought. Because if that is true of Willow, it is equally true of Atlas. He doesn't know where I come from and that cannot change, but there's so much more I'm keeping from him.

Is it worth changing that to keep him in my life?

The weight of my secrets has never felt so heavy. Can I make myself tell him about losing the baby at least? I don't have to reveal that my dead husband was mafia.

Most regular people would never even consider that possibility anyway.

~ ~ ~

I'm finishing the last touches on my electric skillet lasagna when the door to my apartment opens.

"Gamó."

A smile plays around my lips. I've figured out that means *fuck* in Greek.

Him saying it like that tells me that my current attire is having the effect I planned. I'm wearing a pair of black panties, no bra, and a frilly bib apron.

It is from a Halloween costume I wore the year before last. Sheer white organza, it is not a practical apron, but serves its purpose. Cooking naked isn't safe.

Pretending nonchalance my body is far from feeling, I sprinkle the fresh basil leaves over the top of the lasagna. Atlas starts whistling and after a couple of bars, I recognize the song. "Centerfold."

I'm already wet. Cooking naked waiting for my lover to show up will do that to me, but that whistling? It has me gushing slick onto my inner thighs. It takes everything inside me not to turn around. Swaying my bottom side to side, I put the lid back on the electric skillet and turn off the heat so the lasagna can rest.

Strong hands land on my hips sending jolts of electric energy through me, before sliding up to cup my breasts.

"I like this." Making circles with his palms, he rubs my sensitive flesh through the slippery organza.

My nipples perk under his ministrations. "I like that," I say throatily.

What this man does to me with a simple touch.

"Do you need to turn anything off?"

I shake my head. "Everything is off. The lasagna is resting. We can eat it whenever."

"Good," he growls. "Put your hands on the edge of the counter and don't move them."

Anticipation shudders through me as I obey his instructions, planting my palms flat on the countertop.

"Good girl," he rumbles in my ear, his hot breath sending sensual shivers down my neck and into my shoulders.

Kneading my breasts, he tugs at my earlobe with his teeth. I want to lean back into his hard body, but I can't with my hands where they are. I whimper.

"Problem, *ílios mou?*"

"I want to touch you too."

"More than you want to feel this?" He pinches one nipple and then the other, alternating back and forth between them repeatedly.

Something about him doing it through the stiff, but slick organza adds to the sensations and arousal arrows down my body, making my vaginal walls contract in need.

"Atlas." That is all I say, but my voice drips with need.

Making an animalistic sound, he spins me around and covers my lips with his in a bone-melting kiss.

My body softening against his immediately, I open my mouth for his questing tongue. He tastes like beer and the addictive flavor that I have only tasted on his lips. It is pure Atlas.

Skimming his hands down my body, he sends more shivers of arousal cascading along every inch of naked skin his fingers touch.

My body reacts to him so quickly and completely. One caress and I am going up in flames.

Reaching behind me, he unties the apron. Our pressed together bodies are all that is keeping it in place. I shift back a little so it can fall before pressing my now naked breasts and diamond hard nipples against his chest.

When he cups my bottom, and lifts me, my legs automatically go around his hips. He jostles me so my core presses against the erection in his jeans. Pleasure zings through me and I moan into his mouth.

Not breaking the kiss, he effortlessly carries me into the bedroom. But he stops at the bed. "You're not too sore?"

I shake my head. Am I sore? The truth is, I've been pleasantly sore since that first morning after and I love the way it feels. Every twinge in my nether regions reminds me that right now, for as long as this thing lasts, I am not alone.

I'm not only sore though. I'm also extra sensitive too. Even wearing underwear stimulates me and keeps me in a constant state of arousal.

He kisses along my jaw. "We went at it pretty hard this morning."

"I remember," I purr. "Maybe we can do that again."

My vagina pulses in agreement.

"You're so perfect for me." He lays me down on the bed and steps back to strip out of his clothes. "Don't touch your thong."

That commanding tone sends shivers of need cascading through me. I slide my hand inside the front of my panties until my middle finger dips between my wet folds.

"I said—" he starts to growl.

But I interrupt him. "To leave them on. I have. You didn't tell me not to touch myself."

Drawing the silky wetness my body has made upward, I get my clitoris wet and make light circles around the bundle of nerve endings. My hips jerk upward and I moan.

The feral sound that comes out of Atlas goes straight to my core.

He grabs my wrist and pulls my hand away from my sex and puts it in his mouth. He sucks my fingers, sliding his tongue between them.

I revel in his attention, moving my body decadently on the bed.

He releases my fingers. "You taste so good, *ilios mou*."

"Do I?"

"Taste." Bringing my hand to my mouth, he waits for me to obey.

I open my mouth and suck my own fingers in. Flavors burst over my tongue. My arousal. Him.

Tugging my fingers out of my mouth, he places my hand above my head and then slides his fingertips down my arm and over to my breast. He cups my breast and brushes his thumb over my aching nipple.

I cup my other breast with the hand not above my head, pinching my own nipple and sending sharp shards of pleasure slicing through me.

Moaning, I cant my hips upward, my core achingly empty. "Please, Atlas."

"Not yet." His jaw is taut with need, his control so close to breaking.

But he doesn't break. His erection, dark and engorged with blood, leaks pre-ejaculate and bobs in front of him like a baseball bat about to take a swing.

He tugs my hand away from my body. "Not yet," he says again. "You're not ready yet.

"I'm past ready," I argue.

Atlas smiles. And it's not one of his nice smiles. This one is all sorts of devious and it sends anticipation running along every one of my nerve pathways.

He places my hand above my head beside the other one.

Lying like this, I am vulnerable, but powerful too. I am the absolute center of his attention.

In this moment, nothing exists outside this room for either of us.

"Clasp your left wrist with your right hand."

Relishing the release of control, I do exactly as he says.

"Good girl." He says something in Greek and even though I don't understand the words, the tone makes arousal gush between my legs. "Now, close your eyes."

Letting my eyelids lower, and unable to see him now, I can only focus on what I am feeling. Both of his big hands cup my breasts, squeezing and releasing in rhythmic movements. Then he pinches my nipples and jolts of pleasure zing between them to my clit.

Gasping, I turn my head from side to side, but I don't open my eyes.

I don't want this game to end.

His hands slide away from me, and I mourn their loss, but I don't protest. I want to know what comes next.

Strong fingers grip my ankles and he pushes my legs up so my knees bend until my heels are practically touching my butt. "Spread your thighs, Lucia. Let me see my silk covered pussy."

I part my thighs and he guides my feet until I am fully open to him.

"Your panties are soaked." The air shifts and that is the only warning I get before his mouth is on me there.

He inhales my scent and groans and then he's biting against my tender flesh, but the fabric of my thong acts as a barrier, dulling the sharp sting of his teeth.

There is a snick, like a switchblade opening. Cold steel slides up my calf and a shiver of atavistic fear goes through me.

I don't move a muscle. I barely breathe as the flat of the knife glides along my skin until it presses against my center.

"Atlas," I moan.

"You are such a good girl. So damn trusting."

"Only you." I don't know why I trust him so deeply, but my certainty that he will not harm me is absolute.

"Only me," he growls. Then the knife goes under the side of my thong and cuts through the silk with barely a whisper.

How sharp is it? Sharp enough that if Atlas were to slip even a hairs breath, it would slice right through my skin to muscle.

He doesn't slip though. He drags the flat of the knife over the apex of my thighs, sending my intimate flesh quivering. And then he slices through the other side of my panties.

The silk tugs against my skin and then it is gone, my entire vulva now on display for him.

Two thick fingers press inside of me, and my vaginal walls clamp down on them, trying to suck him in deeper. When he pulls back, I whimper, but then he's thrusting forward again, pistoning in and out of my tender channel with quick, powerful thrusts.

His thumb glides over my clitoris when his fingers are embedded as deep as they can go inside me. Pleasure so deep, it is almost pain, radiates through me. I can hear myself moaning, pleading, but it is as if I am removed from it. So in tune with my pleasure receptors that I'm drunk on it, but also feeling like I'm floating beyond my body.

My eyes fly open. I need to connect to the here and now or I will be lost forever.

His eyes are waiting for mine, his gaze locking us together as intimately as his fingers inside my channel.

"Close your eyes, *ilios mou.*"

I shake my head, almost frantic. "I need to see, or I'll float away."

I never knew passion like this before him, so intense it consumes me completely.

"I'll keep you here," he promises and reaches to brush his hand down over my eyes, forcing my lids to shutter.

"Atlas, I need you inside me." I want to reach for him, but I don't.

"I am inside you."

"Your sex. I need that big dick stretching me wide."

"You'll come this way first." There is no give in his voice. "You will gift me your pleasure."

The thrusts of his hand picks up pace and his thumb circles my sensitive nub with every deep penetration. Ecstasy builds inside me and I give myself over to it, once again trusting Atlas to keep me safe, even from himself.

A cataclysm of pleasure detonates inside me and I scream as my body bows upward, my muscles tensing in a pleasure pain rictus. With talented and determined fingers, Atlas drags me through the aftershocks and right into another orgasm before I've caught my breath from the first one.

Not giving me a chance to come down, he's there, between my legs, his blunt head pushing against my swollen flesh. His crown breaks through my opening and my inner walls contract.

He presses inexorably forward, forcing my oversensitive, inflamed flesh to accept the intrusion of his iron hard penis. Pleasure thrills through me as he claims my body the way I've been craving.

Every time is like the first one, and I wonder if this will be the time when I cannot accommodate his length and girth. But he bottoms out inside me, pressing against my cervix and stretching my sensitive tissues beyond what I think he can.

"You're like a damn virgin every time."

Or he's monster sized. "Had sex with many virgins?"

"None."

"Then how—"

He doesn't let me finish. "You are tighter than any other pussy I have fucked."

"Not so much with the other vajayjays you've conquered," I instruct him.

"You make me forget every single one."

I don't want to know how many there are for him to forget.

"I never wanted to keep a woman, Lucia, but I'm keeping you."

Typical arrogant man. He's not asking.

Why my inner sex kitten thrills at this, I can dissect later.

"You're going to come again," he tells me with confidence. "And you are going to soak my cock before I bathe your womb with my seed."

"You're so primitive."

"Is that a complaint?"

With my arms willingly planted above my head and my eyes voluntarily shut because that's what he wants?

"No."

"I didn't think so." He pulls back until only his head is still inside me.

I whimper at the sense of emptiness.

"Is this what you want?" He slams forward, filling me completely. "What you need?"

I can't answer because there's no air left in my lungs as he slams in and out of me with addictive force. My breasts shake and my hips jerk with every powerful thrust, each one taking me toward the precipice again.

"Please," I beg.

"What? What do you want?"

I'm so wet, that despite how tight I am around him, he slides in and out of me with ease. The sound of our intimate flesh smacking together, the squelch of my juices bathing us both is satisfying on a primal level.

"I need to see you," I gasp out. "Please."

"You can open your eyes when you come." He leans down, sliding his arms under me and gripping my shoulders to hold me in place as he rams into my body.

He surrounds me completely.

I didn't know sex could be like this. If I had, I would have been sure I would hate it. But I don't. I adore the feeling of being claimed so forcefully. I crave it.

Electric currents run along my pleasure pathways, coalescing in the center of me over and over until it explodes with sparks I can see behind my closed eyelids.

"Yes!" he shouts. "Oh, fuck. Milk my cock, take everything out of me."

Needing to see his pleasure, my eyes snap open and lock on his. Intense pleasure stares back at me and that look hits me deep in my core, lighting off another shower of sparks inside me.

His body stills, his arms locked around me like bands of steel, and he grows impossibly large inside me before a cascade of heat bathes my cervix.

If my ovaries weren't so temperamental, this would be the moment I got pregnant. The thought sends a powerful aftershock through me.

Atlas groans. "You squeeze me so tight, *ílios mou*. Even if I wanted to pull out of you, I don't think your pussy would let me."

"You know it's not exactly rational to want to get a woman you've known only a few days pregnant."

"The dark ember left of my soul knows yours."

Emotion threatens to overwhelm me. "Why only an ember?"

"It's a long story."

"And if you follow past patterns, you're not going anywhere anytime soon."

He acknowledges that truth with an inclination of his handsome head. "It's not a pretty story."

"Does it have anything to do with this?" Breaking his stricture not to move my hands, I trace the Cerberus tattoo and the Greek writing under it.

Placed over his heart, it has to be important to him.

"Yes."

"What do the words mean?" Or is that too personal? Will he refuse to answer?

"Give them nothing, but take from them everything."

"That's grim."

"I told you. Not pretty."

I wave between our bodies. "This isn't pretty either."

The way our bodies connect is too brutal for *pretty*, but it is also soul stirringly beautiful.

"If you are going to connect with my soul, I want to know why yours is only a *dark* ember." I *need* to know.

"I was kidnapped when I was ten years old."

My hands move of their own volition to curve around his neck and my legs come up around his hips as I hug him with my whole body. "I am sorry."

Wealthy families are always at risk for kidnappings. Because in the mafia, that risk is increased, especially if there's a war going on, I had training from early childhood how to react if I was taken.

It never happened to me, but I remember the nightmares after sessions for me and my brother with our instructor.

"What happened?" I ask.

"They demanded a ransom from my grandfather."

"Not your father?"

"Grandfather had what they wanted."

That's not surprising. As the patriarch of the family, his grandfather would hold the bulk of their wealth until his death.

"Your grandfather couldn't pay what they were asking?" I find that hard to believe.

His family owns Zesti, but maybe they weren't as affluent when he was a child.

"He *refused* to pay." There is a wealth of feeling in those four words. Resentment. Disillusionment. Anger.

His grandfather's refusal is still affecting Atlas today. Memory of something he said tickles the back of my mind. Family is everything to him and his brothers. Not their parents.

Clearly not their grandfather.

Atlas swallows and then speaks again, his tone low. "They kept me for a year, sending my grandfather video proof of the torture they were putting me through."

That's where the scars under the giant tattoo on his back come from. The Spartan makes sense now too. A symbol of strength and stoicism.

"A year? Were they holding you in another country?" I'm not surprised the authorities couldn't find him.

Children go missing every day and many are never heard from again.

"I got away. That's all that matters now."

"How?"

But Atlas shakes his head. "If I talk about this anymore, I'll go soft and then I won't be able to hold my cum inside you."

"I know you say you're trying to knock me up, but somehow we always end up going for Round Two when you do this."

His smile devastates my heart. "Added benefit."

My giggle gets cut off as he starts to move again. My last rational thought before pleasure takes my brain offline is that being betrayed by his family would definitely have killed part of his soul.

Chapter 14

ATLAS

The bar is not in the seediest part of Portland, but the businesses around it wouldn't generate as much protection money as Lucia's club all together.

"This is where you wanted to bring me?" Lucia asks as I help her out of the X7.

"My brother asked me to check it out."

"Unless you're willing to invest a lot in not only the building, but the neighborhood, anything but a pop-up club here doesn't have much of a chance."

"What about a strip club?"

Her hand tightens in mine. "You're opening a strip club?"

"We're planning a couple, yeah."

"I thought you'd do a night club."

"That's in the plan too."

"Wow, that's a lot of businesses to run. How many brothers do you have?"

"Two brothers and two cousins."

"Older or younger?"

"Does it matter for running a club? We're all well over the age to serve alcohol."

"I wasn't thinking about your suitability to run the clubs. I'm doing that thing people who date do, getting to know you."

"Are we dating?"

"You keep saying you're going to keep me, so I'm going with yes." She looks around us as we step inside the bar. "Though this is not my idea of great date night material, in case you are wondering."

It's a typical neighborhood bar. Low lighting. A little run down, but clean. A single waitress works the floor serving drinks and a bartender serves behind a bar that covers nearly the length of the back wall.

Round tables are scattered throughout the space. No booths. The hallway to the bathroom is the only brightly lit area. The bright lights send a clear message.

No dealing and no sex inside the club. In case the patrons don't get the hint from the brightly lit corridor, there is an obvious camera pointed toward the bathroom. That is unexpected.

The two tables with men speaking Russian is not, but I don't recognize any of them. I step in front of Lucia anyway, blocking her view of the bratva soldiers and their sightline to her.

I'm not supposed to engage, just check the place out and try to figure out which bratva is trying to find a foothold in the Portland metro. Having Lucia with me gives me better cover than coming alone and sticking to the shadows.

It's a solid move. So, why am I second guessing making it?

Leading her to a table as far away from the Russians as I can get, I pull out Lucia's chair for her.

She smiles her thanks, slides out of her coat and hangs it on the back of the chair before sitting down. Her back is to the Russian men, the way I want it. The location is not ideal for gathering intel, but Lucia's safety takes priority.

Even over getting the information my brother wants.

Hell. "I shouldn't have brought you here."

"It's not that bad." She smiles at the waitress approaching our table.

I don't tell her it's not about the ambiance, but her safety. I will keep Lucia from harm. Whatever it takes.

Leaving my leather jacket on because that makes accessing the knives in the hidden interior sheaths easier to get to if I need them, I sit down.

Wearing skintight jeans and a t-shirt that molds her curves and shows a slice of skin between the hem and the waistband of her pants, the waitress stops beside our table. She's easily in her late thirties, if not early forties, but she's taken pains to look younger. Mostly successful, it's the lines around her eyes that give her away.

She gives Lucia a once over, dismisses her and turns a big smile on me. "I'm Wanda Sue, but you can call me Wanda." She winks and her red tinted lips tilt in a smirk. "What can I getcha, sugar?"

"What would you like, *ilios mou*?"

Lucia looks around the bar again and then up at the server. "Do you have any craft beers?"

"This is Portland. What bar doesn't?" the waitress asks, like she thinks Lucia isn't very bright.

My sweet sunshine remains polite though. "I'll have whatever craft IPA you have on hand. With a glass."

That's my woman. All class.

The waitress nods. "And you, sugar?" she asks me.

Lucias's lips draw into a tight, flat line. Oh, she does not like this woman calling me *sugar*. Despite all the action it got earlier, my cock jerks to attention.

Jealous Lucia is our new favorite flavor.

"I'll have the same as my wife. Wait to open the bottles until you bring them to the table," I instruct her.

Lucia jerks and then she kicks my ankle under the table. "I am not your wife," she hisses at me as the waitress flounces away.

"Would you rather she kept hitting on me?" I taunt.

"A wedding ring is no deterrent for some women." She frowns. "You aren't wearing one anyway," she mutters.

"I am aware."

Lucia crosses her arms, thrusting her tits up in a temptation I have to ignore. I can't even look as long as I want to because I have to keep my peripheral vision on the Russians. And when I look at her luscious curves, it takes all of my attention.

She's wearing her signature red again. This time in a tight thin sweater with sleeves that reach an inch past her elbows. No jeans for my sun. She's got a short black skirt on that swishes around her gorgeous thighs when she walks, teasing me.

I could slide my hand up her thigh and be touching her pussy through the red lacy panties she's wearing under it. Her demibra isn't doing anything to camouflage her hard nipples either.

"You're a fucking temptation, you know that?"

"We're on a date. Isn't that what I'm supposed to be doing? Tempting you." She looks me up and down. "You're certainly tempting me."

"What are you newlyweds, or something?" Wanda Sue asks sourly as she plops two bottles of beer on the table.

Opened bottles.

"Take those away." My tone suggests she not argue.

Rolling her eyes, she says, "Jed opened them before I brought them over."

"I told you I wanted them opened at the table."

Her look asks if I'm kidding.

My glare back tells her I'm not.

One of the Russians gets up and goes down the hall toward the bathroom, only he walks right past it.

What is back there?

"I'm going to use the little girl's room while our server is getting us our *unopened* beer." Lucia stands up.

No way is she going down that hallway alone. Cameras be damned.

I stand.

"Are you going to escort me to the bathroom?" she asks with a laugh.

"Might as well drain the elephant."

"Elephant is right," she says sotto voce, but loud enough for the snarky server to hear her.

Putting my hand on the middle of her back, I walk with Lucia right past the table of bratva.

"The *pakhan's vtoroy* expects it to be handled by the time he gets back from San Francisco," one man says in Russian.

That one word confirms who they are. *Pakhan* is the head of a bratva. The fact their *pakhan's* second is in San Francisco is also a wealth of information. There are only two bratva families active in that territory.

The Golubevs in Oakland and the Semenovs, a neutral bratva that controls most of San Francisco proper. I don't recognize these soldiers as being from either bratva brotherhood.

The man closest to the wall says, "There's some company trying to buy the shipping yard. They already put their bid in."

They're talking about the abandoned shipping yard at the port on the Columbia River, and our company, Cerberus Inc. No chance they'll find us. The principals listed on the paperwork don't exist anywhere but in falsified records.

Like a lot of so-called legitimate businesses, we handle buying and selling property through a shell company based in the Cayman Islands. For us, it's not only a tax shelter, but an additional layer of security between us and the enemies that we don't want to know what businesses we own, the FEDs included.

"After tonight, we will have the leverage we need to make the broker accept our terms of sale. The port is ours," the first man replies.

That's something we need to deal with immediately. The Russians like to use threats to family as leverage. We don't, but that doesn't mean we are ignorant of who is important to the commercial real estate broker.

I shoot a text off to Zeus telling him what I heard as I follow Lucia down the hallway.

She stops at the door of the women's restroom. "I'll meet you back at the table."

I'm not leaving the hallway, but I nod anyway. No point arguing and *ilios mou* would tell me she doesn't need a babysitter. Like she tried to do repeatedly in the club on both Friday and Saturday night.

Didn't stop me from sticking close then and it won't now.

Keeping the door she went through in my line of sight, I walk casually toward the men's room and then beyond it. There are three more doors at the end of the hallway. The one on the left has a scratched and grimy plexiglass insert, allowing me to see a kitchen beyond.

A woman is loading trays of glassware for the industrial dishwasher. I suck in a shocked breath and then force my lungs to release it, shaking my head.

It's not her.

I can't see the dishwasher's face, just her profile. But it doesn't matter. The woman she reminds me of is dead, killed by bratva scum allied with the Golubevs.

My mind is playing tricks on me. I turn away and examine the other two doors, the women's bathroom never out of my peripheral vision.

Clearly leading to the outside, the center door is big and made of steel. Lifting my phone, I pretend to text and move so I lean back against the third door. Dropping one hand behind me, I try the handle and it turns. With the camera app open on my phone and set on selfie mode, I push the door open a crack.

It's another hallway. This one not lit nearly as brightly as the one I'm standing in. I catch movement on my phone screen and slide sideways so I'm leaning on the wall when the bratva soldier I saw earlier comes out of the doorway.

He jerks to a halt when he sees me. "What are you doing here?" he demands in heavily accented English.

"Checking my messages while waiting for my wife to finish in the bathroom. What's it to you?"

"Leave."

My eyes never leaving the man stupid enough to think he can order me around, I tuck my phone into my back pocket. "I'll leave when she comes out."

"Get lost." His voice is louder, like he thinks I didn't hear him the first time. "Fuck off."

"Hurry up, Boris." The man who said they were going to get leverage on the broker tonight is standing at the other end of the hallway.

He looks at me, but what should be a cursory glance takes everything in. I know because I'm doing the same thing. Boris is only a couple of inches shorter than my six and a half feet. He's twice as broad though and should be a lumbering ox of a man.

But he holds himself with a readiness that I recognize. He won't go down easily. His compatriot is coming closer, the movement overtly casual but he's a predator.

Like recognizes like.

These bratva soldiers have an edge the Golubevs I've been hunting since my teens don't.

I flick my wrist with a minute movement and my stiletto slides into my palm.

"I told this asshole to get lost, but he says he's waiting for his woman to come out of the toilets."

Boris's friend narrows his eyes at me while I pretend not to understand what they are saying.

Lucia steps out of the bathroom as the bratva soldier comes abreast of the door. She gasps and stops short. "Oh."

"Hey, sweetheart." I move quickly to get between Lucia and the dangerous man standing too damn close.

Her smile belies the worry I can see in her eyes. "Ready to get that beer?"

No fool, she can sense the tension in the hallway, but she's acting like she doesn't.

"Are you the asshole that told Wanda Sue you would not drink the beer she opened?" This man's accent is even thicker than his pal's.

"What's it to you? She your girlfriend, or something?" More likely his interest is in the bar's nightly take.

This place is either paying protection to the Russians or owned by them. They're too at home here for it not to be under their control one way or the other.

"You order beer. She serve you beer. You pay."

"Fine." If Lucia wasn't standing two inches behind me, I would argue. "Let's go, sweetheart." Shifting sideways, so both men stay in my line of sight, I take Lucia by the arm.

She's stiff and glares at the Russian man. My feisty Italian lover does not like my easy capitulation. As a club owner who makes sure her staff offers stellar customer service, she takes it personally when others do not.

Anger is coming off her in palpable waves. If I don't get her out of here, she's going to start something I'll have to finish.

Not that I mind killing these two, but Lucia doesn't need to see me do it. She doesn't know I'm Greek mafia yet and she will *never* see Dímios in action.

My phone vibrates with a text, but I ignore it. The situation is too volatile to let my focus splinter even a single shard.

The two Russians follow us until we're out of the hallway and then they veer toward two more bratva standing near the tables they'd been sitting at before. They talk together in tones too low for me to catch.

Not that I'm lingering by their tables. I'm hurrying Lucia toward ours. When we reach it, I don't pull her chair out, but grab her coat and help her into it.

Then with my left hand on her arm, I pull out my wallet with my right and extract a twenty to toss on the table.

She glares at me. "Oh, hell, no. You are not leaving that bad excuse for a server a ten-dollar tip." Pulling her arm from my grasp, she digs through her purse.

Holding up two fives and two ones, she says, "This covers it."

It's not an extravagant tip, but it's still twenty percent.

She grabs the twenty and hands it back to me.

"Keep it," I tell her, refusing to take the money. "You're not paying for the beer we didn't drink."

"Don't be a chauvinist."

"I brought you to the bar. I pay."

"So, if I invite you someplace, I get to pay?" she asks suspiciously.

I shrug. It's not something that has ever come up for me before. I don't date and the few times I have had drinks or dinner with a woman before fucking her, she never balked at me paying.

"Why do I get the feeling that shrug means *no*?"

"Because you're intuitive like that."

"Don't try to charm me into keeping your money. It's not going to work."

I smile. She's the only woman, hell the only person, who has ever accused me of being charming.

"And keep those bedroom eyes to yourself. I'm angry."

"That is a challenge I am willing to take on." Once I have her out of this bar and away from the bratva soldiers.

She rolls her eyes at me, but pink tinges her cheeks and her breathing speeds up. Guiding her toward the door, I keep a watch on the men who are still talking.

Some of them are looking this way. Two guesses who they're talking about right now and the first one doesn't count.

Chapter 15

ATLAS

As soon as we get outside, I rush Lucia toward my X7. It automatically unlocks when my RKE is within a few feet so I can yank her door open as soon as we reach the truck. I grab her by the waist and lift her into her seat, then slam the door and jog around the SUV to the driver's side.

Pressing the button to start the car, I bark. "Seatbelt, *ilios mou.*"

"I told you that's not on right now," she huffs, mistaking my urgency for a desire to get back to her apartment for sex.

Not that she's wrong. I always want sex with her. Right now, I want to get her away from men, who would kill her without a second thought, more.

"Now." I start backing out of the parking spot as the men come outside.

Boris is watching my truck like he's memorizing the plates. He probably is. It won't do him any good.

We don't register our vehicles under our own names. No one in our business with a healthy sense of self-preservation does.

Lucia does up her seatbelt. "*Caspita.* You could have waited until I was buckled."

Keeping an eye on my rearview mirror for a tail, I voice activate a call to my brother.

It connects and before he can speak, I say in Greek, "You are on speaker and Lucia is in the car with me."

At the sound of her name, she gives me a questioning glance.

Traffic isn't heavy, but there are a few cars on the road with me. Unless they pulled out of the bar parking lot with their lights off, the Russians aren't one of them.

They don't know who I am and have no reason to follow us. However, they recognize I am a dangerous man and if they are as well trained as I believe they are, they'll pay attention to that.

Neither of the soldiers liked that I was hanging around in the hallway by the bathrooms, which tells me that the rooms behind the other door are worth looking into.

"What is going on?" Zeus asks me in Greek. "Did you overhear anything else useful? Do you know who they are going after tonight?"

"No. My guess is either the broker's wife or mistress." The information Zephyr compiled did not list any children and the man's parents are living their retirement dreams out in Arizona.

"Helios took his team to the broker's home. Zephyr and his team are on the way to the mistress's apartment. "

"He thinks the mistress is the target?" If he didn't, my youngest cousin would have insisted his team be the one to go to the broker's house.

The port deal is his baby.

Lucia's arms cross and she looks out her window. Away from me.

"Stay with Lucia. We'll handle the bratva bastards."

I wasn't planning on leaving my woman, but don't bother telling Zeus that. No reason to get my *anax* pissed at me if I don't have to.

"Be careful," he warns me. "We don't know how many soldiers they have in the city."

We have five teams of 3 to 5 men. We're working on recruitment, but if the bratva have a large contingent of soldiers, we'll be stretched thin.

My brother hangs up and I tell my phone to send a group text to my team.

Atlas: *Get a hotel room near Nuovi Inizi. Bring your kits. 3 days.*

I am telling them to bring their weapons and at least three days' worth of clothes.

Theo: *Something going down boss?*

A year younger than me, Theo is third generation Greek mafia, but his father left the Drakos outfit in Chicago to join the *Ádis Adelfótita* when he married the daughter of the *anax* in Sacramento.

In the wrong place, at the wrong time, Theo had been taken by the white supremacist under my kill order. He and his mouth-breathing cronies were beating the hell out of Theo for looking too much like his biracial mother.

His Cerberus tattoo is on his neck, so I knew right away he was a member of the *Ádis Adelfótita*.

After killing my target and his shithead friends who thought they could lay hands on one of my brothers, I took Theo to a mafia doctor. It took him six weeks to recover from the beating.

He asked to join my team while he was still in the hospital.

Atlas: *Just left a bar infested with bratva.*

Bobby: *What family?*

Bobby is a straight up product of the American foster care system. I recruited him to the *Ádis Adelfótita* when he was sixteen. That was eight years ago, and he's been loyal to me ever since.

Atlas: *Don't know.*

And I hate not knowing. When I get back to the club, I'll instruct my team to cover Nuovi Inizi in shifts while rotating in groups of two to stake out the bar Lucia and I left. We need intel.

Yesterday.

Michael: *This got anything to do with why Zephyr and Helios's team took off loaded for bear?*

Michael's mother is Greek mafia. His father is a professor at USC. After six years in the Army, Michael decided he'd rather beat up and kill people for the mafia than the government. According to him, we're more honest about our motivations.

I don't follow politics, so I wouldn't know, but he's been an asset to my team for the last two years.

Atlas: *Yes.*

Bobby is the only one who had to learn to speak Greek and now he's fluent. We do all of our texting in Greek as a matter of course.

With every text my phone reads out to me over my car's speakers, Lucia grows more visibly irritated. Her whole body is turned away from me by this point and her posture is rigid.

She huffs out a sigh after the last text. "If you miss having someone to talk to in Greek so much, maybe you should go home and hang out with your family in person."

"I'm not going anywhere but back to the club with you."

"Maybe I want some time to myself."

No chance in hell.

Seeing an empty parking lot for an industrial building, I yank the steering wheel to the right and pull the SUV into it.

"What are you doing?" Lucia demands.

Not bothering to answer, I pull my truck around to the back, so it's not visible from the road. Once I maneuver it so I'm facing the way we came, I put it in park, but leave the engine running.

"What are we doing here? Why did we stop?" Lucia is looking at me finally, her dark eyes snapping with annoyance.

"You are angry."

"You think?" she snarks back.

I don't take the bait. "Yes. What I want to know is: why?"

"Oh, I don't know. You take me to a dive bar where the service sucked and you paid for beer we didn't drink. If it was busy, I could understand the server forgetting and opening our bottles, but the only people there were those two tables of thugs."

Thugs is right. Lucia has good instincts, even if she's too innocent to know what they are telling her.

"You're mad because I paid for the beer?" If I had known it was going to cause me grief with my woman, I would have taken the bratva bastards out back and eliminated them. "It was ten bucks. Twelve with tip."

"You gave me twenty, so essentially that's what you paid because we both know you'll get sneaky about not taking the extra eight dollars back once we get to the club and I can break the twenty."

She knows me pretty damn well for such a short time being together.

"What is this really about?"

"You talked to your family in Greek to exclude me."

And then I see it behind the ire. Hurt.

"I wasn't trying to exclude you." Just maintain her innocence about the reality of my business.

Yes, I'm keeping her, but even I realize it is too early to start inducting her into the mafia life. Some wives never know about the *Ádis Adelfótita* and their husband's true vocations. I don't fool myself that Lucia can be kept in the dark indefinitely.

She's too smart.

"That's not what it felt like." She sighs. "I learned to speak Italian before English. My mother preferred it, but she taught me and my brother not to speak it in front of our friends and exclude them."

"You have a brother?"

"Not anymore."

Shit. He's dead. "I'm sorry."

"Me too."

"Were you close?"

"When we were kids." She wraps her arms around herself. "But not for a long time."

"You still miss him."

Moisture pools in her beautiful brown eyes. "Yes."

Shit. Fuck. Damn. "Don't cry."

She blinks furiously and turns her head away. "I'm not."

That is worse. Dealing with her tears has me tied in knots, but having her turn away so I won't see them? That is fucking excruciating. Any other woman and I'd be glad for it, but not Lucia.

I cup her cheek and turn her face back toward me, brushing at the wetness trickling from the corner of her eye with my thumb. "Cry if you want, but don't turn away from me."

"Why not?" She sounds genuinely confused.

"I don't like it."

"Most men would be relieved."

"I am not them."

Lucia gives me an assessing look. "When I turned my face to hide my emotions, did that make you feel excluded?"

A pit yawns before me. I'm not a fool. I know the parallel she's drawing for me.

"I will try not to speak in Greek around you."

"It's not speaking in Greek that bothers me, it's you having whole discussions that exclude me."

"My family and I are used to talking about business in Greek, *ílios mou*."

"I like when you call me your sun. Sweetheart is more generic. Why did you start using it at the bar?"

She noticed? Of course, she did. Lucia is as observant as I am.

"It seemed appropriate." For reasons of expediency and hiding my identity as a Greek man from the bratva.

I am not ready for them to know who I am. They will soon enough. They'll be aware exactly who they set themselves against. Right before Dímios wipes them out.

"Well, I like *ílios mou* better." She pronounces *my sun* with a perfect accent.

I smile. "I will remember that, *eromenis mou*."

"What does that mean?" she asks breathily. "Only you said it with that tone you usually use when we're making love."

"It means *my lover*."

Her eyes soften and small puff of air gusts out between her lips. "Oh. I like that too."

"Sometimes I will talk business in Greek. It is not meant to hurt you."

She sighs and turns to kiss the palm of my hand.

My muscles clench from that small act of affection, my cock swelling to aching readiness in seconds.

"I miss my family more than I realized. Having you talk in Greek to yours brought home that I don't have that anymore. I am alone."

"No. You are with me now." She will never be alone again.

Tilting her head up, her parted mouth invites my kiss. I give it to her, plundering her sweet heat with my tongue. She grabs at my shoulders and tries to press forward but the seatbelt stops her.

She scrabbles at the release and breaks the kiss with a curse when she can't get it to disengage.

Breathing heavily, I put my hand over hers. "Stop. I'll get us home and you can ravish my body then."

"Ravish? Who says that?"

That would be me. "I read a lot."

"Romance novels? Because I'm pretty sure they're the only ones that are going to mention ravishing."

I shrug. Some of them are seriously hot and when I'm in the mood to get myself off instead of searching for pussy, they work better than porn.

All that emotion that I don't let myself feel is a huge turn on.

"Really? You read romance?"

"Sometimes."

"That is unexpected."

"The erotic kind," I explain.

"That makes more sense."

"What do you read?"

"I used to read romance, all kinds. For the past five years the only reading I've done is invoices and tax statements though."

That is going to change. The woman needs time to relax and I'm going to make sure she gets it.

"Who is your favorite author?"

She names an author I've read before, and I like that we have similar taste.

"Do you read thrillers. *Did* you?" I correct myself.

"Yes."

I name an author this time and she smiles. "I love his books."

As I put the X7 into gear, I say, "He's one of my favorites too."

For the rest of the drive, we list favorite authors and books. There are only a few we don't have in common.

"I need to download a couple of those." Reading is a good way to decompress when I'm off the job.

She pulls out her phone. "What's your email address?"

I tell her.

She goes silent, tapping away at her screen. I hear a notification from my phone.

"I sent you some books."

"You bought me books?" I ask. Has anyone ever bought me a book?

"By those two authors I was telling you about."

One thriller and one spicy romance. "With you around I don't need the romance."

"Maybe it will give you ideas."

Fuck me. She wants to play. "Do you think I need them?"

"No, but I wouldn't want you to run out of inspiration."

"You are the only inspiration I need." I grab her hand and put it over my hard cock.

She squeezes. "Good to know."

I whistle "Don't Worry, Be Happy" and Lucia gives me what would be a heart melting smile.

If I still had a heart.

Chapter 16

ATLAS

Lucia is passed out from pleasure and exhaustion beside me when the text comes in from my brother.

Zeus: *Bears neutralized. Need you at the warehouse.*

We bought the rundown warehouse before we even started looking for a place to live. Priorities.

And having a place to interrogate and intimidate is high on the list for men like us.

Atlas: *One hour.*

I send a text to Theo, who is on guard duty for the club tonight.

Atlas: *Inside. Guard the door to upstairs.*

Theo: *You going to the warehouse?*

One of the other soldiers must have let him know about the successful operation. Theo hadn't been happy to learn that he and the rest of my team were on guard and recon duty when shit was going down.

He'll get over it. They do what I need them to do.

Atlas: *Yes.*

Theo: *I'll watch over your woman.*

I don't bother to reply. Theo will be waiting for me outside the backdoor when I get downstairs.

After a military shower, I dress in a black t-shirt and jeans, strap on my weapons and pull on my leather jacket over the holstered gun and the knives strapped to my forearms. There's another knife in the sheath in my right combat boot and a gun strapped to my ankle.

The inside of my leather jacket is lined with throwing knives on both sides.

From now and until the bratva threat is neutralized, we will all be heavily armed wherever we go.

My body is a deadly weapon. Up close and personal, I can take out an enemy quietly and effectively without hardware. A shot to the head is more efficient in distance situations though. My throwing knives are best for incapacitation, or slowing down my prey.

Every tool has its purpose.

Lucia is still sleeping when I finish dressing and come out of the bathroom. The light is off before I open the door, so I don't wake her. It works, but I risk rousing her anyway when I lean down and kiss her lips softly.

Her mouth molds to mine, even in her sleep. When I pull it away, those pretty lips go lax again and I smile.

This woman.

There is no way I am ever letting her go.

~ ~ ~

When I reach the warehouse, there is no sign of anyone else. As it should be. I drive around the back and open the bay door with my remote. It looks rusted into place and decrepit. But it is made of reinforced steel and swings up on silent hinges.

I pull my X7 in next to Zephyr's bright yellow Lambo. My truck is more useful for transporting bodies, something important in my line of work. It's also a hell of a lot less of an attention seeker.

From the other vehicles parked in the warehouse, it looks like Zeus and Helios are here as well.

I go down to the basement, the top selling feature for this property. It is not on the blueprints filed with the planning office and the access is now hidden behind a bank of broken down filing cabinets that look like they haven't moved in the past two decades.

Following the sound of murmuring voices, I find my brother and both of my cousins in the interrogation room. Two men are stripped naked and hanging by their wrists from a chain in the ceiling.

Satisfaction unfurls in my gut when I see that one of them is that fucker that got me in trouble with Lucia for insisting I pay for the beer. Lucia's safety and my family's interests made the timing bad for taking him down earlier, but now?

I'm going to have some fun.

"I don't think I'm ever going to get used to seeing you smile," Zephyr grouses as I walk closer. "Although this one looks damn evil."

"I'm looking forward to *talking* with the prisoners."

"Oh, shit, what did they do to you?" Helios asks.

I shrug.

"You! I knew you were trouble," the Russian on the right says malevolently.

"Good instincts," I acknowledge. Then look him up and down and shake my head. "Bad choices."

The man on the left spits toward me. "When my bratva is done with you, you'll all wish you'd shot yourselves in the head."

"Strong words for a man about to cry for his mommy," I say with disinterest.

My toolchest is designed for garage tools, but the things I keep inside the grey metal drawers are a lot more interesting. Or their use is.

"Hell," Zeus says. "You're pissed."

I shrug. "Do I look angry?"

"No, you look like an emotionless psychopath, but we both know that's not you."

I'm feeling emotion right now. Most of it, rage. These fuckers came into our city and they want to disrupt our plans. Plans my brothers and cousins and me have spent years developing.

"What are you doing in Portland?" I ask them.

"Fuck you." The man on the left spits at me again. His saliva falls short and splats on the cement, but the disrespect is there regardless.

"I would teach you some manners, but there's no point when you're never leaving here alive."

"If you're going to kill us anyway, why should we tell you anything?" the man on the right asks.

A more intelligent response, if shortsighted.

"Because there's a world of pain in difference between a clean death and a dirty one. I can keep you alive for days and you *will* talk." I have only run across one man who didn't respond to any of my interrogation methods.

Serbian, he was a tough mofo that earned my respect if not my mercy.

These two? They're professional, but they aren't immune to pain. I'll prove that to them soon enough.

I open the top drawer on my tool chest and pull out the blackjack that belonged to my grandfather. My dad's father, not the asshole who left me with the Golubevs for a fucking year.

Pappous gave it to me when I turned thirteen and spent the next two years training me how to use it with lethal efficiency.

"First lesson. Don't spit at the *palach*." When I mention the title the Russians have given me, the bratva scum both jerk in their chains. "So, you know who I am."

"*Palach* is a bogeyman. There is no assassin acting as executioner to the bratva."

"Tell that to the dozens of your brothers I sent to hell when you meet up with them later." I smack the man who spit at me with my blackjack at the right angle to knock two of his teeth out.

He grunts but doesn't cry out. Anticipation sends my blood rushing through my veins. I like a good challenge.

Two hours later, my muscles burn from a good workout, and I have a sheen of sweat on my arms and chest. Bloody and missing some teeth and fingernails, both men are covered in red blotches that will bruise if they live long enough.

My methods of interrogation ultimately cause them to shout their throats hoarse, but the information they reveal is minimal. Not useless though.

Knowing they are from Russia and do not plan to stay in Portland tells me they are acting as temporary muscle to help take over territory for a US based bratva. They stubbornly refuse to tell me which one, but I already have a good idea. And there is a long road of pain driven revelations between here and death for them.

Helios is doing a deep dive based on their vehicle registration. It's not a rental and it isn't owned by a shell company. Not good planning.

The man who owns it lists an apartment address in SE Portland as his home. Zephyr is hitting it now with his team.

I will be surprised if they find anything but an empty unit, used solely for the purpose of filing paperwork. But I recognize the name on the registration. The man is dead. I killed him two years ago.

Using his credentials is a forward-thinking security move. Too bad I know his bratva and all their connections as well as I do. The dead man was a shot caller for the Golubev Bratva.

Sure, it could be someone else with the same name, but I don't believe in coincidences.

So, the Golubevs, not the Semenovs. The *Ádis Adelfótita* will be able to maintain our truce with the Semenovs.

Maybe I should have expected this. The Golubevs are moving their territory north, where they believe they won't have syndicate competition. Portland would be a good location to rebuild their decimated ranks, especially with help from their bratva brethren from the homeland.

If we did not live here.

But what they do not realize is that they are trying to relocate to territory now claimed by their enemies, the *Ádis Adelfótita*. Worse for them, their *palach* now calls Portland home.

Coincidence? No.

It is Nemesis at work. They would have been safer staying in California. Because I am Dímios, the instrument of Nemesis.

Chapter 17

LUCIA

After a night of intense lovemaking, we sleep in. Or I do. Atlas isn't there when I wake up, but there's a text on my phone.

Atlas: *I'll be back to take you to lunch at 1:30.*

The door to my office opens at precisely 1:30. Atlas stands in the opening, his gaze locked on me. "Ready?"

"Let me just finish this beer order."

"You need more of Shawn's ale?" Atlas asks, his tone sneering when he says my supplier's name.

"No. This is my monthly order for the national brands. My clientele likes craftsman ale, but the margin on it isn't as good as what's mass-produced."

"I notice your liquor is higher end than I expect in a nightclub."

"We don't serve rotgut and because of that we are busy on nights the local bars are practically empty."

"But aren't you losing margin on the other nights? And you're closed on the quietest nights already."

She shrugs. "I'm not serving top shelf, but what is the point of offering my customers swill, I wouldn't serve a guest on a bad day?"

"You see your customers as guests?"

She closes her laptop and stands up. "Yes. My staff are trained to see them that way too. We're more than a dance club to spend a couple of hours getting wasted with your friends. Nuovi Inizi is an experience."

His expression is blank, but I see the minor tells around his eyes and the edges of his lips. He thinks I'm wrong, but he keeps his mouth shut.

"Thank you for not trying to educate the little woman." Tino and his father would never have held back.

They assumed they knew better.

"Your success speaks for itself. I wouldn't presume to question the method that got you here."

"But you don't agree with it."

"We don't see the club business the same way, but there's more than one way to build a business. If your goal was to have multiple locations, your methods would have to reflect that."

"One club is plenty for me to handle." It pays for Lenny's care and provides me a decent livelihood.

That is enough.

"Even with only one club, I think you need a general manager to take some of the load off of you."

"That's in the long-term plan." But can't happen right now. Not if I want to buy my house.

Having a home that isn't an efficiency above my nightclub is more important to me than having more time in my day to revel in my aloneness.

Though I'm not alone right now.

I grab my purse. "You ready to go?"

"Not yet." He pulls me into a kiss.

My brain is fuzzy from pleasure when he pulls his head back. "I like this look on you."

"What look is that?" I tease in a sultry tone that only came into my repertoire after meeting him.

"The just kissed and thinking about fucking look."

"Accurate."

Growling, he lays another lip-lock on me that sets fire to my core.

This time I'm swaying on my feet when our mouths break apart. "Maybe we should go upstairs and see if you can't keep me looking like this for the rest of today."

I'm caught up on paperwork. There are always things I could be doing, like updating our social media accounts and looking into new suppliers. But I deserve time off too.

Atlas looks tempted but shakes his head. "You need to eat."

"I had breakfast." My stomach chooses that moment to snarl loudly.

I guess my body doesn't count a single croissant eaten a few hours before as adequate sustenance.

He takes my hand and tugs me out of my office. "And now you're going to have lunch."

Once we're in his SUV, he asks me where I want to eat. "You know the area better than I do."

"There's a family-owned Italian restaurant a few minutes away. Let me call and see if they have a table." Listening to him talk and text in Greek with his family last night triggered a hunger for the familiar.

He thinks my brother is dead, but Rocco survived the war with the Irish and the bratva. When I'm overwhelmed, or sometimes really tired, I consider calling him. I let myself imagine that his love for his sister will be bigger than his loyalty to the don.

But that's a pipe dream.

If I want to keep Lenny safe and happy where he is, if I want to avoid another mafia marriage, Rocco and my parents have to continue to believe that I'm dead.

Does that hurt? Yes.

But the alternative would hurt even more. Or that's what I tell myself. Honestly, if Lenny's welfare wasn't part of the equation, there are times I would pack it in and return to Detroit. To my family.

The lunch rush is pretty much over, and the small Italian restaurant has an open table. I give them my name and ask them to hold it for us.

Over lunch, Atlas asks my opinion of the different businesses in the area. And he listens with rapt attention when I give it.

For a woman raised to accept the very traditional role of first mafia daughter and then wife, his interest in my thoughts and opinions is heady stuff.

"Are you and your brothers really considering opening a strip club near that bar we went to last night?" I ask Atlas, making no effort to hide my disapproval of the idea.

He gets a strange look in his eyes I can't quite decipher. "It might be a strategic move."

"I'm not so sure about that." Those thugs last night sounded Russian.

Which in and of itself is not concerning. There are over 40,000 Russian, Ukranian and other immigrants from the Baltic states in the Portland Metro. Many came to Portland to escape religious and other types of persecution.

I considered starting Nuovi Inizi in the Dobro Pozhalovat, a predominately Baltic neighborhood in East Portland, before ultimately deciding on my current location in Portland's west suburbs.

Before making the decision, I did my research on Portland's large Baltic community. There was no bratva presence when I did it.

What is concerning is that the men from last night had familiar tattoos. Ones like those the bratva that killed my husband and father-in-law wear proudly.

"There are places in and around the city that would be more profitable." Not to mention safer. "Besides, if you're working all the way over there, when will I see you?"

He keeps saying this thing between us isn't temporary. Well, if it's not, then him working across the city and with more than a couple of suburbs between us isn't going to be conducive to seeing each other.

"Running the club won't be my job."

"I thought you were doing this with your brothers."

"And cousins," he corrects while topping off my wine glass. "We each have our roles to play. Mine isn't management."

"What do you do?"

"Facilitate."

I'm not sure what that means, but no doubt he and his family have a system.

"You've been spending so much time with me, I'm not sure how you are facilitating anything."

"I worked this morning."

"That's where you went? Were you looking at properties?" Hopefully not near that seedy bar.

If those are bratva soldiers, no one working, or living in the vicinity of that bar, is safe. Especially not the Baltic immigrants building a life for themselves here.

Like all organized crime, the bratva prey on their own first, exploiting and drawing from the population for new recruits.

Worse is the potential for human trafficking. The bratva in Detroit traffic humans for both the sex and employment slave trade.

The very thought of it nauseates me.

Not all bratva generate income from human trafficking, but chances are any bratva looking to establish territory in Portland does. It's a matter of the path of least resistance. The city ranks in the top twenty for human trafficking in the US.

"What's wrong?" Atlas leans forward, his hand outstretched. He lays it against my forehead. "No fever, but you look sick."

"I'm fine." Just nauseated at the idea of my city being infiltrated by a syndicate willing to buy and sell human beings.

A sparkle comes into his glacial blue eyes, warming them. "We'll stop at the pharmacy on the way to my house."

His meaning sinks in and everything inside me seizes. With longing that won't be fulfilled.

It makes me grumpy. "Forget it. Even if I were pregnant and we both know I'm not, no way would I be morning sick yet."

The nausea didn't kick in until I was six weeks along, which my mom thought was early. It didn't go away when I hit the three-month mark either. I was miserable right up until the sixth month. I only had one month to enjoy being pregnant. I'd be nauseated every day of my pregnancy not to have lost my baby at seven months.

"We *don't* both know you aren't pregnant."

"Well, I do."

"You're not on birth control."

"I told you I probably can't get pregnant." And when he accepts that, will he dump me?

Chance of rain 90%.

"Probably is not *can't*."

Leaving his ridiculously optimistic viewpoint aside for the moment, my brain screeches as the rest of what he said penetrates. "What do you mean *your* house? We're going back to my place."

"Zeus wants to meet you."

"You want me to meet your family? Already?" Wow.

"Yes."

"I'm not sure I'm ready for that."

"What's there to be ready for? I'm not asking to fuck you in the ass. I'm taking you to meet my brother."

That he considers backdoor sex a sign of deeper intimacy than meeting his family is something for me to unpack later. Also, that he considers it a natural progression of our sexual relationship.

Chapter 18

ATLAS

The look on Lucia's face says the last thing she wants is to meet my brother. Should I mention it won't only be Zeus?

Helios and Zephyr are dealing with the fallout from last night, but Orion should be at the mansion.

Deflection seems like a good strategy right now. "You ready to explain that *probably* to me yet?"

She's silent so long, I think she's going to refuse, but then she huffs out a long breath of air. "I was married."

Dark fury that another man called her wife rises up in me. I don't care if it is reasonable. Lucia is mine.

The only thing keeping me sane in that single word, *was*.

My jaw so tight, my back teeth are grinding, I ask, "Where is he?"

"That is not the question I expected you to ask."

Too bad. I repeat it. It is the question I want answered.

"In the cemetery."

The man is dead. Good. Lucia's soul is not dark like mine. She would not like it if I had to kill the man she married.

I pull the SUV onto the freeway. "Did you try to get pregnant with him?"

The idea is doing nothing to abate the rage inside me.

"I got pregnant the first year we were married, but I..." She pauses, her voice thready. "I tumbled down the stairs and lost the baby."

"I am sorry." Not words I usually say, but in this case, they are the only ones that matter.

How the hell did her husband fail to protect her from something like that happening? Or did he cause it?

My grip on the steering wheel is so tight, I'm surprised it doesn't crack under the pressure. "Did he push you?"

"No." Something in her voice tells me that's not the whole answer.

"Did the fall do damage to your reproductive system?"

"I don't know. Maybe. After I healed from the miscarriage, we didn't use birth control, but I never got pregnant again, not in two years."

"How often did you have sex?"

"I don't think that's any of your business."

"Tell me."

"Hardly ever," she huffs, crossing her arms under those generous breasts.

I reach over and run my hand along the tops. "Why?"

"He got busy with...with work and I..." Her voice peters out like she ran out of battery.

"You what?" Am I being intrusive? Hell, yes.

She'll get used to it. I'm not going anywhere. And I want to know everything about her.

"It was hard for me. Having sex with him. I think he suspected it. Losing the baby so late in my pregnancy was hard on both of us."

"But he's the reason you lost it." It's a shot in the dark, but I'm a damn good night sniper and I expect it to hit my target.

Her gasp and the way her body goes stiff tells me it does. "I never said that."

"He didn't push you down the stairs." She said that. "Were you running from him when you fell?"

Maybe I can find a necromancer to bring the bastard back from the dead and kill him all over again. This time with my own special nuance.

"I didn't fall."

Gamó. "Tell me."

"Lenny is my brother-in-law. I can't believe I'm telling you this. He was in an accident when he was a child and suffered a traumatic brain injury. I was supposed to watch him when my husband and father-in-law were out of the house."

Traumatic brain injury can mean a lot of things. "What was the impact of the injury on Lenny?"

"He lacks impulse control. He'll get fixated on an idea and lash out at anyone who prevents him from following through."

She doesn't have to spell it out. With her being her brother-in-law's primary caregiver, that person would have been Lucia, more often than not.

"He's an adult now?" I ask.

"Yes."

"And when you lost the baby?"

"Yes."

"A large man?" Even an average size man would be bigger than Lucia, but a large one would be damn near impossible for her to control physically.

"Yes." Her voice is soft, laden with old grief.

"Your bastard of a husband expected you to care for and protect his brother who was an adult sized male?"

"Yes."

"What happened?"

"Lenny wanted something I wouldn't give him. We fought. I tried to get away. He shoved me. The stairs were too close, and I went flying. When I woke up, my baby was gone."

And those bastards probably blamed Lucia for not being able to handle Lenny. She said her husband is dead. Is her father-in-law?

"How did your husband die?"

"A workplace incident. Something went wrong at the club and both he and his father died."

I am not a good man. I hope those bastards suffered before death. "That's why you came to Portland. You left your old life behind."

"Yes."

I can't stand the pain that single word holds, and I pull off at the next exit. We're close to the mansion, but I'm not ready to take her there. I discovered a park with a sunken rose garden when I was doing recon for the area. Finding a parking spot on the street near it, I pull in, maneuvering the X7 to fit between two cars.

I turn it off and get out. Lucia is still sitting in her seat with her seatbelt fastened when I come around the passenger side of the truck and open her door.

I reach over her and press the button to release it, and then carefully pull the belt away from her as it retracts. "Come on."

She looks past me. "Where are we?"

"Someplace I can hold you while you talk."

"A park?" she asks, like that's the strangest place I could have brought her.

I wrap my arm around her waist and pull her close. "Yes, a park."

The roses have bloomed and died already, their bushes in hibernation for the winter, but it is still a peaceful place. A few walkers and joggers power along the path that runs the perimeter of the park, but only a couple of people are in the sunken garden itself.

Exactly what I wanted.

"I didn't know this was here. I've visited the Rose Garden in Washington Park, but no one ever mentions this place. I bet it's beautiful in full bloom."

"We'll come back in July and you can see."

"That's nine months away. You keep talking like we have a future."

"Because we do."

"Isn't it too early to be sure about that?"

"How long did you know your husband before you knew?"

She makes a strange sound before she shakes her head. "We knew each other our whole lives. Our parents were matchmaking before I learned how to walk."

"Is that why you married him?" Had she loved the man who put her and their baby in such a dangerous situation?

"Family expectation was a big part of it, but I fell in love with Tino. He was handsome and sophisticated."

"He was older than you?"

"Only a couple of years, but he had way more life experience than I did at twenty."

"Were you happy?" Can she be happy with me?

She'll have to learn to be.

"For a while."

"Until the baby?"

"Things were hard before that. We argued over getting Lenny professional help. Tino and his dad were adamantly against it."

"Why?" Was it money? But somehow Lucia had ended up with enough money to start a nightclub.

"They were old fashioned Italians. Everything was supposed to be taken care of by the family."

Sounds like the mafia. Only family takes a backseat to the wellbeing of the syndicate. Not for my uncle though. For him, family comes first.

What happened to me shaped all of us, Constantin, Zeus, Orion, and even Zephyr and Helios. They weren't part of the rescue, but they learned how little our grandfather valued us and how easily he controlled our parents.

"You deserved better."

"So did Lenny. He was devastated by the loss of the baby. It set him back for a long time." She sounds sad.

"You have a lot of empathy, don't you?"

"Not so much anymore, but back then, I cared too much about the people in my life."

She's saying she cared about that piece of shit she was married to. "Are you saying you don't care now?"

"I don't have people in my life now."

Bullshit. "You have me."

And when she is pregnant with my kid, I'll be her shadow. A man who knows so many ways to kill also knows how to keep someone safe.

She takes care of her employees too, not just her club. They care about her. Does she not see that?

Lucia's laughter is hollow, but there's a thread of amusement there. "Do you make these pronouncements expecting everyone to fall in with your plans, or is it just me?"

Zeus is *anax*, but my crew looks to me first for orders. As it should be. When I tell them what to do, of course, I expect them to obey. When I told them we were moving to Portland, I assumed they would make the move without resistance.

Theo told me I should have asked them. I told him to fuck off and get his place packed up.

Lucia's face is tilted up toward me. "That look on your face. It's definitely more than me."

"Only the people closest to me." I don't care enough to tell other people how it's going to be. Not even my parents.

"How did we get so close so fast?" she asks, not like she's denying it, but finds the closeness hard to believe. "It's only been a matter of days."

I shrug and start us down the wide cement steps leading into the sunken garden. "Sex."

She smacks me in the stomach with the back of her hand and then yelps. "That hurt."

"I'm sorry?" She hit me. Not the other way around. That will *never* fucking happen.

"You should be, having such a hard stomach."

"You like my muscles." She spends enough time touching them.

"You got me there."

We walk in silence until we reach the fountain in the center of the rose garden. Lucia stops and watches the water shoot into the air until the pattern starts repeating. Then she sighs and pulls my other arm around her, holding both of my forearms.

It's not a good position to protect her from, but it's not an impossible one either. She seems to want to be surrounded by me. So, I give that to her. Maybe she's cold. Her coat more fashionable than warm.

I stay alert to our surroundings. My instincts tell me we are alone and not being watched.

"I want to be a mom. I don't know if my body will let me."

"You have to have sex to get pregnant."

"We had sex, but not very often."

"Repeated occurrences increase the chances for most things."

"But..." She stops talking and grips my forearms harder. "You really think I can?"

"I think if you are worried, we go back to the private clinic and have them run some tests."

"I'm not sure I want to know. If something inside me was damaged, it will bring it all back."

"And if nothing is wrong with you except an inept dead husband."

"Tino wasn't inept."

"So, the way you respond to pleasure with surprise so often has nothing to do with his ineptitude. Right."

"It's been five years."

"Which might explain your sexual hunger, not how shocked you are by the things I do to make your body sing."

She turns in my arms and looks up at me, doing her best to frown. "You are so darn arrogant."

"Confidence is not arrogance when it is justified." I have absolute confidence in my ability to kill and make this woman come until she passes out.

Both of which I have proven over and over.

"I'm nervous about meeting your brother."

"Brothers," I admit.

"Both of them will be there? I thought Orion was a lawyer. It's Monday. Isn't he at his office?"

"He'll be there for dinner."

"Oh. So, now I'm nervous about meeting both of them. Do you all live together?"

"Yes. My cousins live there too." She doesn't need to know about our men who live on the grounds too.

They won't be at the house. Theo, Michael and Bobby want to meet her, but their recon job at the bar is the reason I have Lucia with me.

I need all three to infiltrate the bar. Unlike some of the specialists that came up under my grandfather, me and my brothers never send our guys in without enough backup. Neither do my cousins.

Which is why we've never lost a soldier from our teams. Doesn't mean we won't. Death is a part of this life. I should know, I'm usually the one dealing it out.

But it will not be because of us.

"That's a lot of men in one house. Do any of your brothers or cousins have significant others?"

"It's a big house. And no, they're all single."

Chapter 19

LUCIA

He says *they're all single* like he's not. With anyone else, I would worry he'd slipped and was revealing a committed relationship to me.

But that's not it.

Atlas considers us a couple. I'm his and he's mine.

It's surreal. So, why does it feel so right?

I'm still asking myself that question after we finish our walk in the rose garden and he drives us to his home.

He uses his phone to open the gate, but there are guards on either side. And I can see others patrolling the grounds.

How rich are these men?

Wealthy enough to worry about their security. Then what is Atlas doing running around without a protection detail? I ask him.

He laughs. "I don't need anyone else to protect me."

"You can say that after what happened to you as a kid?"

"Anyone coming after me is signing their own death warrant."

"I guess you took a lot of self-defense courses after you got back home."

"Something like that."

"It worries me that you see yourself as invincible. You aren't. No one is."

"If you say so."

"I mean it, Atlas. It's obvious you and your family are worried about security. You shouldn't be going to clubs alone, much less picking up strange women."

"You are not a strange woman."

"It's not so nice from the other side is it?"

"What?" he asks with barely restrained patience.

Yep. Not so nice when he's the one getting chastised for not being cautious. "Being told you aren't careful enough about your own personal security."

"Lucia, it is my job to protect you, not the other way around."

I laugh. I can't help it. "This isn't the stone age and you aren't a caveman, no matter how much you might act like one in the bedroom. Watching out for each other goes both ways."

With an arrested expression, he puts the SUV into park and turns it off in front of the ginormous mansion he apparently lives in.

"How do you stand being in my tiny apartment when you have all this?" The house is easily twice the size of the home I left in Detroit and that place was ten thousand square feet of opulence.

"You're there."

"There you go, saying the perfect thing again."

"Come on, I'll show you around."

"That sounds good." At least it will get me out of meeting his family immediately.

Or that's what I think until we walk into the marble tiled foyer. Another man with the same dark hair and blue eyes as Atlas is standing there and his expression isn't friendly.

He's sizing me up.

I slide my hand into Atlas's bigger one. He squeezes and whistles "Don't Worry, Be Happy" under his breath.

It makes me smile and I'm able to greet his brother. "Hello, you must be either Zeus, or Orion," I extend my hand.

"That's Zeus," Atlas says, shifting his body between me and his brother, forcing me to abort my attempt at shaking hands. "He's the oldest."

"I remember."

"Were you whistling?" Zeus asks Atlas.

Atlas shrugs.

I roll my eyes. "He likes to whistle, as I'm sure you know." And he uses the songs as messages.

Or is that just with me? Maybe he doesn't pick his music to communicate with his brothers. Maybe he just whistles tunelessly around them? The thought makes me go warm and squishy inside.

This man is so dangerous to my heart.

"My brother hasn't whistled since he was ten years old," Zeus says accusingly.

But what is he accusing me of? Bringing out the musical side to Atlas?

I stand up straighter and give Zeus my best mafia princess look. "You wouldn't know that by me."

The older man's eyes widen fractionally. *Is he not used to women standing up to him? Then we are in for a long and probably unpleasant evening. Because I am no pushover.*

Not anymore. Not that I ever was one, but I let Tino and Antonio Sr. convince me to take on responsibilities I did not want. Not only that, but I strove to do them well so I wouldn't disappoint the two men.

I worried more about what Agustino Sr. thought of me than my own father.

Now, my father believes I'm dead and I refuse to twist myself into a pretzel to impress any other man. Even Atlas's older brother.

His tune changes from "Don't Worry, Be Happy" to...is that "We are the Champions"?

"Knock it off," I admonish Atlas. "I'm not fighting with your brother."

"If you were, my money would be on you."

"What the hell, Atlas?" His brother sounds annoyed. And a little disbelieving.

Removing his hand from mine, Atlas slides it up, under my hair, to clasp my nape. "Lucia is a strong woman," he says, like he's explaining. "And she has the advantage of having me on her side."

There's a warning in his tone that I can't miss. Which means, neither can his brother.

"Are you threatening the *anax*?" someone asks from my right.

I turn my head and yet another ridiculously gorgeous man with black hair and blue eyes is walking toward us.

"Did your parents use PGT before doing IVF, or something?" *The level of masculine beauty in this foyer is absurd.*

"What is PGT?" Zeus asks with narrowed eyes.

"Preimplantation Genetic Testing," the other brother says before I get a chance to answer. "Why would you ask that? A lot of siblings look alike."

Is he seriously trying to pretend he doesn't realize how good looking he and his brothers are? I mean, sure Atlas takes the hotness up to nuclear levels, but no way are his brothers having any trouble getting dates.

"You are Orion, the lawyer if I'm remembering right." I don't bother to offer my hand to shake this time. Zeus wasn't particularly keen, I could tell and then there's the Mr. Possessive-Pants with his hand on my neck

Orion jerks his head in assent and glares at Atlas. "What else have you told her?"

"The only thing that matters."

Oh, crap, he's going to say it in front of his brothers.

"What's that?" Zeus asks this time.

"That she's mine."

He said it. Heat flashes up my neck and into my face. Neither brother seems any happier about Atlas's claim than I am. Though their reaction leans toward anger, not embarrassment.

"Are you sure you're not triplets? I mean, you've all got that swoony black hair and blue eyes thing going on. Chiseled jaws and handsome features that could have been carved by Michalangelo himself. Don't even get me started on all that height and muscles." I fan myself and not only because I'm hot with mortification from Atlas's words. "You even scowl the same."

Zeus and Orion turn those matching frowns on me.

Atlas pulls me around to face him and yep, he's got the hot Greek daddy glare going on too. "You do not think my brothers are swoony."

"You're the swooniest." I pat his chest and then let my hand rest against his heart under his leather jacket, because, well...I want to.

"Is that even a word?" Orion snarks.

I ignore him, staring up into my boyfriend's eyes and trying not to drown in the intensity I find there. "I don't think your brothers are happy you are dating. Do we have to stay for dinner?"

I thought mafia men gave off dangerous, primal vibes. *Caspita!* The men in the life I knew back in Detroit had nothing on these uber wealthy Greek brothers.

Zeus grunts. "We are not unhappy Atlas is dating."

"Shocked more like." That's Orion. No surprise the lawyer is the snarky one.

I don't answer, but look up at Atlas appealingly.

"You will not find my brothers attractive."

"You're still stuck on that?" I don't roll my eyes, but it's close. "You're acting like a caveman again, just in case you wondered."

"I am the only man you will find sexually desirable."

"I didn't say I found them sexually desirable," I practically shout. I can't believe he said that. "You're the only one that makes my panties wet."

Did I say that? Out loud? In front of his brothers? Oh, well.

In for a penny, in for a pound. "I said they are good looking. Which they are. Until Orion opens his mouth and then the appeal wanes quickly. The jury is still out on Zeus."

A crack of laughter sounds behind me.

"Hey!" Orion says, sounding offended. "Women like my mouth fine."

"Well, of course they say that when you pay them enough," I say without turning around.

Atlas bursts into laughter, which is what I was going for. He was looking way too unhappy about the similarity in looks between him and his brothers. I can't help they are hot, but I don't want to bang them.

I tug his head down so I can whisper in his ear. "Five years, Atlas. *Five years*. I wouldn't have broken up with B.O.B. for your brothers."

"Remember that," he says in that growly voice that soaks my panties.

Porca miseria. I have no hope of getting through this evening with a modicum of dignity intact.

"Whose Bob? Do we have to get rid of someone?" Orion asks.

I jump and shove myself away from Atlas. Orion moved closer while I wasn't looking and I practically run into him.

"What are you, part bat?" I demand. "And also, have you heard of the concept of personal space? As in, you are standing in my bubble."

Orion takes an unexpected step back. I didn't expect him to listen to me and react so easily. He doesn't give off cooperative vibes.

It's not far enough for Atlas. He tugs me another two feet away from his brother, taking the opportunity to divest me of my coat and slide off his own jacket. He opens a hidden door in the wall and hangs them both up in a freaking walk in coat closet.

"Who is Bob?" Zeus asks when his brother comes out of the closet and shuts the door, leaving the wall looking as seamless as before.

An earthquake opening up a fissure in the floor I could sink into would be welcome right now. You could fry an egg on my cheeks at this point.

"I assume she named her vibrator," Atlas says when I remain silent.

"That did not earn you any good boyfriend points," I mutter.

"B.O.B.?" Orion asks, like he's amused. "I get it now. Battery operated boyfriend."

"You would have earned a gold star for your ability to state the obvious, but the need to spell it out is your fault because you were listening to a private conversation. So, no gold star for you."

"You're standing in a foyer with two other people. That's hardly private."

"Have you heard of the concept of whispering? Clearly my words were not meant for your bat ears."

"Your woman is mouthy," Zeus says.

"Not usually. Apparently, you all bring it out in me." I haven't been this willing to pop off with what's in my head since me and my brother were kids. When we were still close.

Training to become a mafia princess included learning to stifle any and all sarcasm. It wasn't considered ladylike. I'm kind of glad it's back.

Too bad my brother isn't here to use it on, but Atlas's brothers will do as stand ins.

Sudden emotion wells up inside me at the thought.

I turn to look up at Atlas and poke him in the chest. "You'd better mean it, when you say you're keeping me," I say fiercely.

He can't offer me a family and take it away. I won't survive that.

"My brother never says anything he doesn't mean." Zeus doesn't add that's what has him worried, but it's in his tone.

I'm worried about this thing between Atlas and me too. It's fast and incredibly intense. There's the whole what-happens-when-I-don't-get-pregnant thing too.

If he dumps me, I will hunt him down and shoot him in the knee. Too bad for him, my father taught me to shoot when I was ten, right alongside my brother, who was only eight at the time.

I take Atlas's hand and tug. "You said you'd show me around this place."

"It will have to wait," Zeus says. "Gina made dinner and it's ready now."

"Who is Gina?" I ask Atlas as he starts walking down a hallway off the left of the foyer.

"Our housekeeper."

"She has to clean this place *and* cook for you all? When does she sleep?" I ask, "I'm pretty sure there are labor laws against hours like those."

Atlas smiles and shakes his head. "She has two people working for her."

I look down the long hallways with several doors off of it. "Not sure that's enough. Especially if they're picking up after you all and not just doing the deep cleaning."

"You're inordinately interested in our domestic staff arrangements," Orion says. "Did you do work as a maid?"

"I was married. Same difference." I had a service that came in weekly to do the deep cleaning, but I did all the cooking for the Revello family. "It was a traditional household."

"Where is your ex-husband?" Zeus asks, his tone dark.

"That's the first question Atlas asked too."

"And your answer was?"

"In a cemetery."

Zeus nods, like that's good.

I roll my eyes this time. "You do know that the customary response to learning someone is a widow is to say you are sorry for her loss, not look like you're pleased by the death of another human being."

"Was it a loss?" Orion asks way too perceptively.

"I loved my husband." It's the truth, if not all of it.

"Do you love Atlas?"

Chapter 20

LUCIA

I ignore Orion's question as we walk into the dining room.

Not merely because it is ridiculously intrusive, but also because I don't know the answer. I mean, I think I *do* know the answer, but my brain rebels against me feeling something so deep for Atlas after a matter of days. It's not possible. Love builds over time.

At least that's how it was between me and Tino. We always knew we were going to get married, and I knew him as well as I knew my own family. It was natural to love him. Tino was a charismatic, smooth guy.

Atlas is not smooth. The more time we spend together, the more I realize he is more caveman than charisma. I guess I like cavemen, because I'm falling into the deep end of my emotions.

The sound of chairs scraping across the dark hardwood floor brings my attention back to where I am. The dining room is huge, with a table that would easily seat twenty.

"Planning to do a lot of entertaining?" I would have thought they would be too busy starting their clubs.

I know from experience that doesn't leave a lot of time for anything else, much less dinner parties for twenty guests.

"Why do you ask?" Atlas pulls my chair out and waits for me to sit down before practically lifting it up with me on it to scoot me closer to the table.

This little show starts a slow burn of desire in my core.

"The size of your table."

Atlas looks at the long table that wouldn't look out of place in a palace. "Sometimes, we meet with our men in here."

They must have a pretty friendly relationship with their security team if they have their meetings in the family dining room.

Yanking the chair to my right several inches closer, Atlas sits down and puts his arm over my shoulders.

Orion shakes his head. "Are you going to piss a circle around her next?"

"Nice," I snark.

Orion narrows his eyes at me. "Do you have brothers?"

"I did. One. Rocco was two years younger." And right this minute, I miss him like a lost limb.

"I am sorry for your loss." Orion's voice rings with sincerity, his expression serious.

"He was lucky to have you for the time he did," Zeus says.

And my eyes tear up. What is it with these Rokos men? Assholes one minute and then worming their way into my heart with the right words the next.

I turn my head away, hiding my emotions from them, and stand up. "Excuse me. Where is the restroom?"

Atlas isn't having any of it. He grabs me and pulls me onto his lap. "You're not going to the bathroom to cry alone."

I don't ask how he knew what I planned. This man notices everything about me.

"Men aren't comfortable around a woman in tears." I learned that lesson quickly after the loss of my baby.

Neither Tino, nor his father wanted to see me cry. My own father and brother weren't any better.

Atlas puts his fisted hand under my chin and tilts my head back so I can't hide my emotion from him. "We talked about this."

"Your brothers don't need a crying woman ruining their dinner."

"Who told you that?" he asks, his voice hard.

"Whoever it was is an asshole." That's Zeus.

Atlas grabs the cloth napkin from his place setting and gently dabs at the moisture on my cheeks. "Let me guess, your first husband."

"He was my only husband," I say with some asperity.

I don't have a string of dead husbands in my past. I'm no black widow.

"Until now."

"Don't say things like that."

"Why not? If they are true?"

I shake my head and squirm, trying to get up. Hardness that is not his muscular thigh presses against my hip and I stop moving fast. How long has he been this way? Do his brothers know?

"Losing a sibling is devastating. If you need to cry, cry," Orion says.

And he knows, doesn't he? He lost Atlas for a whole year when they were children.

"We're not weak men. We can handle a woman's tears." Zeus's tone brooks no argument.

Was Tino weak? I would have staunchly denied it five years ago, but looking back, I know he wasn't the husband I needed. Meeting Atlas has forced me to look at the past through different eyes.

There's no ignoring the stark difference between the two men.

"I am not Tino," Atlas says, reading my mind.

"No, you aren't. In so many ways," I whisper under my breath.

"He sure as hell isn't," Orion says, like he's judging my dead husband and not favorably.

Zeus grunts in agreement. It must be his go to sound. Another thing he has in common with Atlas. I wonder if Orion does it too.

"The more I learn about Tino, the more satisfying I find it that you don't think I'm like him, but I want to know exactly what you mean by that," Atlas says.

Bat ears is another common genetic trait, it seems.

I sigh. "I'm not spending dinner talking about my dead husband. He is in the past. I am also not eating sitting on your lap."

"Why not?" His arm settles over my lap like a steel band.

The silent message is clear. I'm not going anywhere.

"It's not polite, Atlas."

"I don't care."

"Maybe your brothers do."

"It's weird, I'll give you that," Orion says.

I frown at Atlas. "I told you."

"It's not that you're sitting on his lap," Orion clarifies. "It's that my baby brother wants a woman in his personal space at all."

Is Orion trying to imply that Atlas, Mr. Handsy himself, has an issue with people in his personal space? Because I don't believe it. He's always invading mine.

Not that I mind.

Somehow, I find myself sharing a plate of food with Atlas. But I draw the line when he tries to feed me.

"I have my own fork," I say with asperity, grabbing said fork. "I'll stab you with it if you try to feed me like a child in front of your brothers."

"Does that mean you don't mind him doing it when we aren't around?" Orion again.

I give him the stink eye. "None of your business."

There are so many lies of omission in my life that I will not lie about anything else. And the image of sitting in Atlas's lap with a blindfold over my eyes, and my hands tied together, while he feeds me has my ovaries sending messages to all my other lady bits.

I'm so wet, it's a miracle I don't slide right off Atlas's thighs.

"You will tell me whatever is putting that look on your face later."

I shove a bite of delicious chicken cooked with artichokes and tomatoes into my mouth and chew with gusto. Not answering him. N. O. T.

Under the cover of the table, Atlas shifts his arm. His hand settles on my knee, but it doesn't stay there. He starts sliding those thick fingers up the inside of my leg.

I squeak.

"Did you meep?" Orion asks.

"Will it offend you if I deck your brother?" I ask Atlas.

"No. I'll hold his arms for you."

"Not necessary." I level an ire filled glance on Orion. "I've taken down bigger men than him."

All three men growl. In unison. Excuse me while I expire from arousal. "You know, I'm not attracted to your brothers, but that growl in stereo? Seriously hot."

"You should never have been put in a situation you had to take a man of any size down." Atlas makes the pronouncement more appropriate for a different era, but his brothers nod in agreement.

All three men look ready to take on my past.

My inner feminist takes a nap and I revel in all this testosterone directed toward my protection.

Atlas doesn't even grumble about my comment regarding the hotness of his brothers. He's too busy looking furious about my past. He knows about Lenny and he hates I was put in the position I was.

I hate it too, especially on the anniversary of my baby's death. But I despise it as much for Lenny. He deserves to be happy and his life in Detroit was a lot of things. Dangerous. Chaotic. Uncertain. Happy was not among them.

"Newsflash, it is the twenty-first century, gentlemen. A woman can take care of herself," I am compelled to say. Even if knowing I don't have to is sweet like honey to my soul.

"Not my woman."

"Your caveman is showing again."

"You mean it ever goes into hiding?" Orion snarks.

Zeus shakes his head, like his brothers are too annoying for words. My father used to do that when Rocco and I were acting up and feeding off each other.

These men are all adults, but the dynamic is so precious, it hurts.

I don't get time to dwell on that heart pain though, not with Atlas's hand moving inexorably higher on my thigh. Another inch and he's going to feel my soaked panties.

I'm regretting my decision to wear the short sweater dress with thigh-highs and no tights. I'm way too accessible to that wandering hand.

"Why a nightclub?" Zeus asks.

Ah, we've reached that part of the evening. The grill-the-new-girlfriend over dinner phase.

"It is what I knew."

"You worked in a nightclub before coming to Portland?" Zeus probes.

I'm adept at avoiding answering questions I don't want to, but there's not harm in answering this one.

"I did the books for the nightclubs my husband and his father ran." Both the ledgers the government saw and the real ones. "I couldn't help learning a lot about the business side of things in the process. When I left, I knew my best chance at making the life I wanted would be running a nightclub."

It wasn't what I wanted, but it was what I knew. The only thing I knew that could make the kind of income I needed to take care of both me and Lenny. Unless I wanted to start my own criminal enterprise and without the support of a syndicate, that option was way too risky.

"Considering how many fail in the first year, you must be good at it." Zeus doesn't sound like he's giving me a compliment. "Do you have silent backers?"

"Not that it's any of your business, but no, I don't. Nuovi Inizi is 100% my responsibility." After paying ahead five years for Lenny's care, I invested the rest of the money I drained from Tino's accounts in the Cayman Islands in Nuovi Inizi.

"And fully your triumph." It's not Atlas who says this, surprisingly, but Orion.

Maybe we'll get through the evening without me doing him bodily harm.

"It is. Lucia is a damn fine businesswoman." Atlas's fingertip brushes over the gusset of my panties and ecstasy fizzes over my labia and up into my core.

It is all I can do not to squirm.

I grab Atlas's wrist. Too little. Too late. Why didn't I stop him before he reached fingertip to vulva contact?

"You must have done your research before opening the club where you did."

I nod, not about to open my mouth when embarrassing noises might come out instead of words.

"Atlas said you have some recommendations for us in regard to buying our own clubs," Zeus says leadingly.

Shoving another bite of food into my mouth, I nod again.

Atlas's finger slides under the fabric between my legs to touch my naked lips. *Dio mio.* I am not going to make it through this dinner.

"What are they?" Zeus asks.

He wants me to answer him? Now? I accidentally, on purpose stab Atlas in the hand with my fork while ostensibly going for another bite. He grunts.

He grunts!

Is it murder when it is provoked? Asking for a friend.

"You okay there, Atlas?" Orion asks, his voice laced with laughter.

Oh, he knows something is going on.

Torture just got added to the table along with the murder possibility. I may have left behind the mafia, but I haven't forgotten everything I learned.

"I think I need to sit in my own chair," I say from between gritted teeth.

Atlas's hand slides back down my leg and he lifts his fingers right up to his mouth. I watch in mortified fascination as he sucks my juices off of them.

O-M-G. My mouth parts and I gasp as desire rips through me with the power of a tsunami.

Kissing my forehead, Atlas says, "Answer my brother, Lucia."

I look toward Zeus, cringing inwardly at the judgement I'm going to see in his face. What kind of woman lets her boyfriend touch her like that at the dining table? Not one raised to be a perfect mafia princess, that's for sure.

Zeus isn't looking at me with disgust though, he's looking at his brother with concern.

What is that about?

"Answer me first why you and Orion seem so worried about Atlas dating." I wait in silence for one of them to answer me.

"When Atlas was ten..." Zeus looks to my boyfriend, like he's asking permission to continue.

Atlas shrugs. "I told her already."

"You told her?" Orion asks, sounding dumbfounded.

I get that it's early to be talking about such heavy stuff, but we both laid our past bare for the other. Well, my past is almost bare. I haven't mentioned the whole mafia connection. How do you tell someone your family is part of a century old criminal syndicate?

"Yes." Atlas takes a bite and chews unconcernedly.

My whole body is still buzzing with the electric current caused by his shenanigans.

Zeus gives his brother a strange look before saying, "When Atlas came home, he was different."

"Inevitable after spending a year going through what he did." I shift my hips, trying to alleviate the ache between my legs without being obvious about it.

"For fuck's sake, let the woman sit in her own chair, brother," Orion says with exasperation.

Atlas's arm contracts around me like he's stopping me from leaping form his lap. "I like her where she's at."

"This." Zeus waves between me and Atlas. "This is what I'm worried about."

"I told you your brothers would be uncomfortable with me sitting in your lap for dinner." Let's not mention the inappropriate touching that I very much want to go back to.

In private.

"They'll survive." Atlas has zero concern about the awkwardness of the situation.

"You're really stubborn."

Atlas shrugs.

"Before he met you, Atlas hadn't smiled in years," Zeus says.

Orion nods in agreement. "I hadn't heard him laugh since before the kidnapping."

"He's happy." And being with me makes him that way.

Warmth unfurls inside me and I want to hug Atlas so hard. When have I ever been the source of someone's happiness?

Never.

"I didn't know he *could* be happy." Zeus doesn't sound all that joyful about it himself. "What happens when you two break up?"

Hearing the question from someone else's lips throws my own worries into perspective. It doesn't matter how long Atlas and I have known each other. He's the puzzle piece that has been missing from my life, and I'm the one that completes the picture in his.

"We're not going to break up."

"Glad you finally realize that." Atlas rewards me with a bite of crisp asparagus from our plate.

I take it off the tines of his fork and savor the perfectly prepared vegetable. So much for feeding myself.

"Well, at least you are living in the delusion together," Zeus says acerbically.

"There are things you don't know," Orion says, clearly not content to let things lie.

Zeus lays down his own fork and pushes his plate away. "That's for a later time." His tone is one of command, not suggestion.

I don't mind. Atlas will tell me what he needs to in his own time. How can I expect anything else when I'm hiding so much about the woman I used to be from him?

Chapter 21

ATLAS

After dinner, which my brothers managed to make ridiculously awkward by implying I'm emotionally stunted to Lucia, I give her the tour of the house I promised.

She loves the media room and sighs over the indoor pool, but when we get upstairs, she says, "I want to see your room now."

Grabbing her hand, I drag her down the corridor to my suite and press my palm to the reader beside the door before swinging it open.

We've both been on a razor's edge of desire since dinner. It's time to take care of it.

"You have biometric security on your bedroom?" she asks with disbelief.

"It's more like an apartment within the house."

Her perfectly shaped brows draw together in a frown. "You don't trust your brothers?"

"They're two of only a handful of people I do trust. The lock is there for everyone else."

"Like your housekeeper?"

"And everyone else who comes inside the mansion."

"I guess after what happened to you that level of paranoia makes sense, but it must be exhausting."

"Security is second nature to me now."

"Were you like this before you were taken?"

"I don't remember." I was a kid. I came home a made man at the age of eleven, no longer a child, but not an adult either.

"Your brothers are really worried about you. I'm assuming you don't date a lot."

"I don't date ever."

"That's hard to believe considering how quickly you went from one-night-stand to committed couple who don't see other people."

"I knew you were mine the first time our eyes met."

"I want to scoff at that, but it felt like that for me too." She sounds worried about that.

And she doesn't even know the half of why she should be. The fact that we got together so quickly is nothing compared to the identity of the man she's dating.

Dímios. The executioner.

It is inevitable that she will eventually find out about my connection to the Greek mafia, but she never needs to know how many men I have killed. Or how much more blood I will spill in the future.

She looks around my space and her eyes widen as she takes everything in. "You weren't kidding when you said apartment. This living room is three times as big as mine. You even have a freaking kitchen."

"More like a snack area." There's a stove that I never use, a small fridge and a wall of cabinets and drawers.

"It's bigger than my kitchen and I bet you never cook for yourself."

"That's a bet you would win." I'm not interested in talking about how my meals are prepared right now. "Tell me what put that look on your face at dinner."

"What look? There were so many ranging from embarrassment to confusion, not to mention trying my hardest to hide how turned on I was by what you were doing."

"It was definitely a turned on look. And it was before I started touching you under the table."

"Oh." Lucia looks away. "That."

Definitely that if this is the effect remembering what caused it is having on her. "What were you thinking?"

"You were trying to feed me."

"I did feed you." She kept forgetting to eat because my damn brothers were talking to her, so I had to feed her a few times to remind her about the food on our plate.

She swallows. "Yes. You did."

"So?"

"So, I liked it," she says in a small voice.

"So did I."

She ducks her head, her dark hair falling like a curtain over her cheeks so I can't see her face at all. I don't like it.

Pulling her around to face me, I lift her chin so her eyes have to meet mine. Their chocolate depths are swirling with emotion. And desire.

Fuck me.

"It turned you on when I fed you?" I'm surprised. She'd made a big deal about wanting to eat with her own fork.

"Yes, but thinking about you doing it...a different way, turned me on even more."

"What way?"

"I had this picture in my head."

I pull her close with one arm while cupping her nape with the other, keeping her face tilted up. "What did that picture look like?"

"I was sitting on your lap."

"Were you dressed?"

She shakes her head.

My cock, which is in a perpetual state of readiness around her, goes painfully hard. "What were you wearing?"

"My panties and bra."

"The ones you have on now?" Sheer crimson stretchy fabric, the bra barely contains her generous tits. Her matching thong reveals her shaved pussy lips and showcases her ass.

"Yes."

"And?" I don't ask what I'm wearing because it doesn't matter. My clothes aren't going to stay on for much longer.

"And I'm wearing a blindfold."

My knees about buckle. "What else?" I ask hoarsely.

"Handcuffs, or a tie, or something, but my hands are bound behind my back."

"*Gamó.*"

"What do you think?" Fear and lust fight for supremacy on her beautiful face.

"What are you afraid of?"

"You thinking I'm a freak."

"I think we didn't eat dessert."

She frowns, opens her mouth and then snaps it shut again. Swallows. And then, "Oh."

It takes me only a few seconds to tear off my clothes and Lucia watches me the whole time with blown pupils.

"Take off everything except your bra and panties."

She grabs the hem of her tight dark red sweater dress and tugs it up slowly, revealing her body inch by inch. Her thong is so wet it sticks between her pussy lips. My mouth waters to taste her, but that's not what is happening right now.

Stopping as the hem of her dress reaches the underside of her breasts, Lucia lets out a small puff of air.

"Finish it," I say in a guttural tone usually reserved for interrogations.

She shivers like she can feel the barely leashed violence behind it. Not that I will do her harm, but I am going to fuck her so hard, she'll need to sit on a pillow tomorrow.

She tugs the soft red knit up a sliver at a time until her pebbled nipples poke at me through the sheer fabric of her bra. Stopping when her body is revealed but her face is hidden by the dress, she puts herself on display, making herself vulnerable to me.

My plan to have her undress herself going up in the fiery inferno of my need for her, I step forward. We pull her dress the rest of the way off together.

I toss it away from us before cupping her generous mounds. "Your tits are beautiful."

"I'm glad you think so."

"You never told me why the red." Not sure why my brain offers that as a distraction. "Is it because you're so passionate, *eromenis mou*?"

I need to get a handle on the lust surging through me, or I'm going to rip off her soaked panties and destroy the matching bra. Finding out why she always wears red is as good of a brain interrupt as anything else. Or should that be little-brain interrupt?

She shakes her head. "The shade of red that represents passion is brighter. Besides, I didn't even know this kind of desire lived inside me before we met."

My little brain likes hearing that. Too much. "So what does that dark red mean?"

"A lot of things, but the one that matters to me is courage. Making the choices I did that led me here took a lot of it. Wearing something crimson every day is my way of reminding myself I have the courage I need to get through whatever comes."

Gamó. "When I think you can't get any more perfect, you do." And as distractions from my lust go, this discussion is a total bust. "Take off your boots."

"Aren't you going to help me?" she teases.

"I'm busy." I could play with her rack for hours. I pinch both nipples at the same time. "Be my good girl and do what I say."

She shudders.

She loves being called a good girl. It fucking fascinates me. She is my good girl though, even when she's being bad.

"I need to bend down to get my boots."

Nodding, I release her tits and step back. "Turn around, I want to watch your ass."

Blushing, she turns. That blush makes me want to throw her over the couch and drill her without mercy, but we've got plans.

She squats to take off her boots, popping her ass cheeks out and putting the crotch of her panties stained dark from her arousal on display.

"Never wear tights again," I order.

She shakes her ass a little. "Like my thigh highs, do you?"

"Yes." The way they stop midway up her juicy curved thighs and frame her ass and pussy gets me every damn time.

She tugs off first one boot and then the other, before straightening her legs. She does not lift her torso, effectively leaving her bent over and touching her feet.

She stays that way until I am breathing heavily from the view of her ass. "You're a fucking tease, Lucia."

Standing, she turns and sweeps her long hair back over her shoulders so every inch of her luscious tits is on display for me. "I'm not teasing, I'm tempting."

"Stay there."

"You're so growly."

Jogging down the hall to my bedroom, I don't answer. I grab two of my silk neckties that will not survive the night. There are a box of zip ties in my equipment room I use for jobs, but I am not binding her tender wrists with a zip tie.

There's a sex toy store near her club. I'll have to drop by and get some leather cuffs, maybe some other bondage equipment. Being restrained for me excites *ílios mou* and that means I need bindings that won't hurt her.

When I get back in my suite's living room, Lucia is standing exactly where I left her. Her eyes are hazy with desire, her nipples diamond hard peaks and the perfume of her arousal permeates the space.

Staying there because I told her to is turning my woman on.

I approach her in silence, my eyes eating up her delicious body. I don't ask if she's ready. I can tell that she is. Stopping behind her so my aching cock presses against her back, I cup both of her naked shoulders. I'm holding a tie in each hand and the ends dangle, brushing along her silky skin.

She moans. I slide my hands, still holding the ties, down her arms, leaving gooseflesh in my wake. She moves restlessly when the ends brush against her legs.

So beautiful. So fucking responsive.

Trailing my hands up her torso, I cup her tits again and play with her nipples until she's leaning against me for support. She's making those little sex noises that act like tinder to the fire inside me. I want to bend her over and shove my cock deep inside her tight, wet pussy.

My dick is drooling, leaving a streak of precum on her back. Rocking forward, my boner slips against her slickened skin. If I don't stop, I'm going to come all over her back and that is not the plan.

I force myself to step back.

She sways and I catch her hip with one hand. "Can you stand?"

"I don't know."

"Try."

She shivers.

Gamó.

I let her go, but give it a beat to see if she's steady. She doesn't sink to the floor.

"Good girl." I squeeze her ass.

"Atlas," she says in a breathy, barely there voice.

Wrapping one of my ties around her head twice, I blindfold her, and tie the ends together behind her head.

"It's dark."

"Good." It should be. I'm an expert at blindfolding targets.

Next, I create a double loop with my other tie, before pulling one of her hands back and sliding it in the right loop. She offers the other one before I can grab it.

Smiling at her eagerness, I slide the loop over her hand and secure the tie so that it will not tighten if she yanks against it but will not loosen either.

"Stay there."

"What are you going to do?"

"Get our dessert."

She swallows and nods.

I know exactly what I want to feed her. My brothers prefer *kaimaki*, traditional Greek ice cream with swirls of cherry preserves and infused with rose water. It's too sweet for me. I like lime sorbet and Gina makes sure I always have a pint in my freezer.

No surprise, the pint of gourmet sorbet is there, when I open the freezer. I grab it and a spoon and put them both on the coffee table. Then I return to my sweetly patient lover.

Too sweet for a man with a dark soul like mine, but I am not letting her go. I sweep her up into my arms.

Gasping, Lucia contorts her body, trying to hold on, but her hands are secured behind her back.

Holding her tightly against my chest, I say, "Relax. I will not drop you."

She instantly stops squirming and rests against me. "I know."

I sit down and settle her on my lap facing me, maneuvering her thighs on either side of mine. The scent of her pussy juices are even stronger with her legs spread.

My cock bobs and my mouth waters. My favorite sorbet isn't what I want for dessert. "You make me so fucking hard."

Chapter 22

LUCIA

Blindfolded, with my hands tied behind my back, I should feel vulnerable. Maybe even scared.

I'm not. Not even a little. I feel empowered.

I'm so excited, my heart is going to beat out of my chest. The strength in the hard thighs under mine only makes me feel safe.

"You are so beautiful like this." Atlas's voice is even deeper than usual.

My inner muscles involuntarily contract and pleasure pulses in my core. Shifting side to side, I try to get some relief.

Atlas grips my hips, stopping the movement. "Ready for your dessert?"

Dessert? All I want is him. "Dessert later."

"No chance." His laughter is a little diabolical. "You want this *eromenis mou* and I will give it to you."

"Why does that sound like a threat?" I ask, panting.

His big hand presses against my bottom and he jerks me forward until the soaked gusset of my panties is flush with the base of his sex. Vibrating with sensation, my clit rubs against his iron hard tool.

"Not a threat. A promise." He kisses me, licking my lips before pulling his head away.

I extend my neck, trying to chase that sexy mouth.

He wraps my hair around his fist and uses it as a handle to pull my head back. "Open your mouth."

My lips part of their own volition.

A cold spoon touches my bottom lip. "Taste."

Shivers of arousal cascade through me as I obey. Flavor explodes across my tongue. Lime. Sweet. It's sorbet. The frozen treat melts almost immediately in the heat of my mouth.

The next thing to touch my lips is not a spoon, but the blunt tip of Atlas's finger. Covered in the sorbet.

I suck the dessert off his appendage without having to be told and somehow the saltiness of his skin mixes perfectly with the sorbet to create my new favorite flavor. He feeds me bite after bite with me taking longer and longer to suck his finger clean.

Desperate to touch him, I yank against the tie around my wrists. It doesn't give.

I let his finger go with a pop and ask, "Aren't you going to eat any?"

"Yes."

"Do you want me to feed you?" Please untie me.

"Yes," he says gutturally.

He reaches behind me and does what I'm craving, removing the tie binding my hands. But I have no chance to enjoy my new freedom before I find myself on my back on the couch.

Atlas shoves my thighs wide apart and arranges my hands in the crooks of my bent knees. "Hold them."

"I want to touch you." I'm not whining.

I'm stating, in a sort of pleading tone. Is pleading better than whining? Does it matter when I feel this good?

"You want me to control your body," he says, his tone deep and commanding. *Dio mio.* He is right.

Unable to see him because I am still blindfolded, I clasp my legs tightly and pull my thighs even further apart for him.

He hums his approval and then my panties yank tight against my hips before the fabric gives way completely to the strength in Atlas's grip. Pulling the ruined underwear upward, he tows the thin strip of fabric that sat between my butt cheeks up between my nether lips. It drags against my clitoris before he rips the torn panties completely off my body.

Wetness gushes from my core. Not being able to see makes everything I experience so much bigger. We are definitely doing this again.

"I'm going to leave a wet spot on your couch," I pant.

"Good. Every time I see the stain, I will think of you like this," he growls.

Nothing he could say could turn me on as much as knowing he thinks about me when we aren't together. It is not out of sight, out of mind, like it had been in my marriage.

Freezing cold against my clit shocks a scream out of me. My legs automatically try to snap together to protect my tender bundle of nerves. Atlas's head and shoulders are there though. His hot mouth covers my clitoris and he sucks, nipping gently. Then, swirling his tongue around my clit, he warms my chilled flesh.

He pulls back. "Pussy and lime sorbet. My new favorite flavor."

I laugh.

"What?"

"That's what I thought when I sucked it off your finger."

He grunts.

Oh, caveman. Why are you so damn sexy?

Another dollop of frozen confection lands against my clitoris and I cry out. He doesn't put his mouth on me right away this time but holds my thighs open while the chill permeates my sensitized bud.

I squirm as the sorbet slowly melts against my heated flesh, sending a message to my nerve endings that I cannot decide is pleasure or pain.

"Please, Atlas."

"What do you want, *eromenis mou*? Do you want me to finish my dessert?"

"Yes," I practically yell.

"Soon." He runs his finger through my slick folds. "So pretty."

"Atlas," I wail.

There is no warning before he shifts and his mouth is back on me. He licks all over my vulva, before gently sucking one of my labia into his mouth. Holding it carefully between his teeth, he runs his tongue along the plump and sensitive flesh.

Porca miseria! I am not going to survive this.

I realize I said the words aloud when he stops eating me and lifts his head.

"Yes." His voice so fierce it sends a shudder through me. "You will survive and thrive."

His visceral reaction beats against me, but I do not know what he wants from me. I want his mouth back on my intimate flesh. I thrust my hips upward in silent supplication.

"Say it," he demands.

My brain addled by unfulfilled pleasure, I can only cant my hips again, seeking more of his mouth.

"Say you will not die. I will not let you."

His sheer arrogance gets through my arousal fogged brain. "Pretty sure that's not your decision. You are not God."

"I am your lover," he says, like that's something more powerful. "I will never let you go."

If anyone can hold onto me by sheer will alone, it is this man.

"Don't let me go." It's a plea for so much more than sex, but I do my best not to acknowledge that. Even to myself.

"Say it."

"Not dying right now. I need." Him. His mouth. A climax.

The original Atlas held the weight of the world on his shoulders. This Atlas could give the ancient son of Titan a run for his money in stubbornness though.

He proves it by taking me to the edge over and over again, no matter how much I beg for and demand my release. Only when my body is covered in a sheen of sweat and tears of frustration leak from my eyes does he finally allow me to come.

Two big fingers drill into my intimate tunnel while he suckles my clit with the strength of a vacuum. My orgasm blasts through me like a case of C-4 going off. I scream so loud and so long, my throat hurts.

Feeling light-headed, I sink, boneless, into the couch. My body is so replete, even the aftershocks of my seismic climax can't make my muscles tense again.

Fingers work behind my head and then the tie is being removed. Light assaults my eyes and I wince, closing them.

"Look at me," Atlas orders. "I want your eyes on me."

It takes a few seconds for my eyes to adjust to the light and then I'm able to focus on him. His handsome face is set in rigid lines, his gaze feral. I release one of my legs so I can wrap my fingers around his turgid erection.

Rearing up, he puts his hand over mine and jacks himself off with our combined grip. Our eyes are locked the whole time, his showing an intensity of feeling that cannot be mere lust.

"Yes, like that," he says, as if I have anything to do with the strength of our grip, or the speed of our hands moving over the hard column of flesh.

Then his face sets in a rictus of pleasure and he shouts my name, ejaculating all over my vulva. Globs of his warm semen hit my sensitive flesh and send residual waves of pleasure through my core. He keeps my hand wrapped tightly around his sex as he prolongs his own pleasure.

"Keep your hand there," he demands as he removes his own to rub his essence into my nether lips, scooping some on his fingers, pushing it inside me.

Tingles of pleasure, that can't quite turn into arousal in my exhausted body, follow his fingers' path.

I am connected to him on an intimate level I never experienced in my three-year long marriage.

Why this man? How is the bond between us so strong already?

~ ~ ~

I wake up surrounded by familiar heat in an unfamiliar bed. The mattress is harder than mine and bigger.

Atlas's bed is huge, like the man it belongs to. The man whose arm holds me so tightly, my body is flush with his. The need to pee forces me to try to squirm out from under the heavy appendage.

His hold tightens and pulls me back into his heat.

I groan. "Atlas, I have to pee," I hiss.

Mumbling, he nuzzles my hair, keeping me close in his sleep.

It should feel claustrophobic. I used to hate when Tino smothered my body with his in sleep. But I like this. Too much. Atlas's hold makes me feel safe. Warm. Secure.

My bladder isn't going to let me revel in the pleasant feelings though. If I don't get out of bed soon, it won't be my arousal or Atlas's cum leaving a wet spot soaking through the sheet to the mattress.

I pinch his forearm. Hard. "Atlas." My voice is loud in the dark and silent room. "Let me up."

"No."

"I have to pee."

Grunting, he sits up, pulling me with him and proceeds to guide me out of bed and to the bathroom without turning on any lights.

Plopping down on the toilet just in time, pee gushes out, splashing into the water below my butt.

"Sounds like Multnomah Falls down there," Atlas says in a sleepy grumble.

"You could have let me come to the bathroom alone."

"I like being with you."

"In the bathroom?" I roll my eyes in the dark. "How pleasant for you."

"All the time I spend with you is pleasure." He yawns. Loudly.

I can't believe how good his words make me feel, but I snark, "Obsessed much?"

The subtle shifting of his body and the air around us lets me know he's shrugging.

"Seriously, Atlas, your brothers are going to get sick of you being with me so much."

"They'll get over it." His tone implies he doesn't care if they don't.

I'm sure that's not true though. He, Zeus and Orion are really close. That was made abundantly clear to me from the moment I met the oldest brother and all through dinner.

It's only a guess, because they weren't there, but I suspect they are as close with their cousins. After all, the five men moved up from California together for a joint business venture.

"You're lucky." My voice reveals my grief at the estrangement from mine, and I wince.

For five years, I have done my best not to think about my family, but being around Atlas with his brothers makes my heart ache missing my own.

His big hand lands unerringly against my neck and curves around it possessively. "Why are you sad?"

I wipe and stand, lowering the lid before flushing. "You and your brothers remind me of what I lost."

"Now you have two brothers to annoy you, not one." He reaches out and suddenly a dim light above the sink goes on. "And two cousins who will be up in your business, whether you want them to, or not."

"Don't say things like that," I say sharply as I wash my hands with jerky movements. "They're not my family."

"They will be. Once we marry."

"We're not engaged." No matter how right things feel with Atlas, I'm not jumping blindly into the deep end of this thing between us.

That's a good way to drown.

Chapter 23

ATLAS

Lucia is quiet when we wake up. I fuck the thoughtful right out of her in the shower, but she's back to staring off into space by the time she gets dressed in her clothes from the night before.

Knowing she's going commando is doing nothing for my ability to control the urge to touch her.

I'm cupping her ample ass when we reach the kitchen, where my family is eating breakfast. Seeing everyone there, Lucia squeaks. She jumps away from me, smacking my hand away from her ass.

Worse, she insists on sitting in her own chair. When I go to grab her and put her in my lap, she threatens to turn me into a eunuch with her fork. My cousins and brothers find this hilarious, laughing like hyenas.

Zephyr shakes his head. "Woah, you'd better watch out for this one, Atlas. She's a firecracker."

"Talking about me like I'm not here is a good way to learn how big I can explode like one," Lucia says sweetly to my cousin.

Laughter erupts from the peanut gallery while Lucia pretends to ignore my annoyance. Zeus, being Zeus, formally introduces her to our housekeeper, Gina, and my two knucklehead cousins.

"Too bad Atlas saw you first," Zephyr says, because he clearly wants an early grave. "If you ever decide to upgrade models, keep in mind that I'm younger and have more stamina."

The asshole won't have any stamina when he is dead, will he?

"Yeah, not buying that, even if you gave me the nickel to do it." Lucia smiles at Gina and takes a laden plate of breakfast from her. "Thank you."

"Getting a peek at my *stamina* is worth more than a nickel," Zephyr claims then shouts as his chair tilts backward from my foot lifting it under the table.

He crashes to the floor.

"What happened? Are you alright?" Lucia asks while Gina rushes over to help Zephyr up.

Grinning like a fool, he winks at *ilios mou*. "I'm fine. The chair had a mind of its own there for a second."

"More like a nudge from Atlas." Gina glares at me.

I shrug.

"Did you knock his chair over?" Lucia's brows are drawn together in confusion, like she's trying to figure out how I did it.

Long legs and strength can accomplish a lot.

I grab a fresh roll from the basket on the table. "He had it coming."

"Atlas!" Lucia looks at me with shock while the hyenas around the table laugh again.

I roll my eyes at her. "He's fine."

"That was uncalled for." Lucia glares at me.

Irresistibly drawn to those pursed lips, I kiss her until she forgets she's mad and kisses me back.

"Save it for the bedroom," Orion snarks.

Lucia goes stiff and yanks her head away from mine. She forgot where we are. I like that so much, I decide I won't kill my cousin today.

"I can't believe you knocked your cousin's chair over. What are you, twelve?"

"He offered to show you his cock. He's lucky he didn't end up with a knife in his junk."

"You can't say stuff like that, even as a joke," Lucia admonishes me, standing up like she's going to check on Zephyr's nonexistent injuries herself.

I give my cousin a look to let him know how much I do mean my words and he waves her off. "I'm fine. It's nothing."

Smart man.

Tugging Lucia back into her seat, I ask, "What time do you have to be at the club today?"

She looks up at me, worry darkening her gaze. "Have you considered therapy? I think you might have anger management issues."

Orion turns his laugh into a cough, but Helios nearly falls off his own chair in hilarity.

Ignoring them, I take Lucia's hand in mine. "Been there. Done that. My mother made me go after my rescue."

The psychologist was connected to the life and even she couldn't know it all. I read once that for therapy to work, you have to be honest. Since there was more that I couldn't tell her than I could, the sessions were doomed to fail.

"This is as good as it gets."

I don't know what Lucia sees in my face, but hers goes all gooey and she caresses my cheek. "It's pretty darn wonderful from where I'm sitting."

"You'd better keep her, Atlas. She's the only woman with rose colored glasses tinted enough to see you as boyfriend material through them," Orion offers his two-cents.

Lucia turns a censorious glare on my brother. "I have twenty-twenty vision and you should be more affirming of your brother."

While she and Orion trade barbs, Zephyr joining in to back them both up, Zeus gives me a disapproving glare which I ignore.

My cousin knows better than to say shit about Lucia seeing his stamina. He had his warning in Zeus's office last week.

"What time do you need to get to the club?" I ask Lucia again, when I'm on my second cup of coffee.

She sighs. "I should be there already. I'll need to leave right after breakfast. I can get a rideshare though, if you have things to do."

"I will drive you." Like hell is she getting into a car with a stranger. "You work too much."

"Whereas you are not working enough," Zeus says.

When Lucia bites her lip and starts looking guilty, my hand itches to toss a throwing knife at him. I would hit him in the fleshy part of his arm. He is my *anax* and brother, after all.

"I'm doing everything I'm supposed to," I remind him.

He tips his coffee cup to swallow the last sip and then sets the empty mug down. "Are you though?"

Enough of this shit. I stand up. "Let's go, *ilios mou*."

"It sounds like Zeus needs you. Let me get a cab back. It's not a big deal."

The look I give my brother should set his head on fire.

He doesn't see it because he's frowning at Lucia. "You aren't taking a damn cab back to your club."

Finally, he says something that makes sense.

"Don't worry about Zeus," Orion says to Lucia. "If he's not busting somebody's balls, he's not happy."

"For that, you can drive Lucia home. I need to meet with Atlas."

I'm about to tell him to shove his meeting right up his ass when I notice the expression on Lucia's beautiful face. She looks stressed. I don't like it.

"You okay, *ilios mou*?" I ask her.

"I don't want to cause trouble between you and your brothers."

"You're not causing any trouble," Zeus and I say at the same time.

Lucia smiles. "Have you thought about taking that act on the road?"

"I'm happy to drive you home," Orion says. "I want to see Nuovi Inizi. Atlas has talked it up and I want to see if it lives up to the hype of a man whose dick is addicted to the owner."

"It does," I say.

Lucia gives my brother a look. "Do you talk to your mother with that mouth?"

"As infrequently as possible."

Aw, hell, now Lucia is giving my brother her compassionate look.

"If you touch her, I will cut off your fingers," I warn him in Greek.

"I'm not about to touch your girlfriend," he answers me in English.

Lucia beams at him. "Thank you for speaking in English."

"Keep making her smile at you like that and we'll need a new lawyer because you'll be six feet under." I stick to Greek.

Lucia doesn't need to hear my threats. Only Orion does. He knows they're more like promises.

~ ~ ~

"She's got you tied up in knots," my brother says.

"Stop trying to be an agony aunt and tell me why I had to let Orion drive Lucia to the club."

"I want to check in with you."

"Not this shit again. I am fine. Yes, I want to keep her. No, that doesn't change who I am or what I do for the *Ádis Adelfótita*."

"Maybe it should."

"What the hell do you mean?"

"Do you think Lucia will be able to accept you as Dímios?"

"She never has to know about my job as executioner. She'll know I'm an enforcer soon enough."

"Not as soon as we planned. I want to take care of the bratva problem before we start collecting protection money. Securing the shipping yard has to be our top priority right now."

A flood of relief I don't understand washes over me. It shouldn't matter *when* Lucia finds out I'm an enforcer for the Greek mafia. She's going to accept it because there is no other choice.

But I'm still glad I have more time to get her as addicted to my cock as I am her pussy.

Or get her pregnant.

Chapter 24

ATLAS

It's early on a Wednesday night. The club isn't packed yet, which is why they stand out like nudists at a convent.

Three of the bratva soldiers we saw at the bar the other night are looking over Nuovi Inizi with greedy eyes.

What are they doing here?

When their gazes land on Lucia in her signature red wrap dress that shows off every banging curve and two inches of mouth-watering cleavage, that greed gets tinged with lust.

A crimson wash of anger darkens my vision until all I can see are their bloody, lifeless bodies in my mind's eye. Moving so that I am between Lucia and them, I text Bobby, my guy watching from the outside tonight.

Atlas: *How the hell did three bratva get past you?*

Bobby: *Didn't get past me, boss. Just texted you to tell you they are on the way in. Do you want backup?*

Alone, I wouldn't need backup against three men. No matter how well trained. But Lucia is here. So is her favorite bartender. Hell, she'll be upset if *any* of her employees get hurt. Only way to guarantee that doesn't happen is to lure the assholes outside.

Atlas: *Call in Theo and Michael and meet me by the back door.*

The bratva bastards make it easy, coming toward me on their way to Lucia. I bump into one, lifting his gun on contact. The clueless bastard doesn't even realize it, but he does shove me and start yelling at me in Russian.

"Watch out, bitch."

I smile at him, a Dímios smile and he frowns. One of his friends backs up a step. The other looks at me warily.

"Your brothers cried like the little bitches they were when I killed them," I say in Russian.

Fury turns all three men's faces even uglier than they already are. The one I bumped jumps toward me, but I spin away, grab his arm, whip him around and shove his own gun into his side. His body now acts as a shield between me and his buddies.

"What's going on?" Lucia asks from behind me.

An unfamiliar feeling makes my heart pound.

Fear. This woman has a nose for trouble, or a magnet drawing it to her. She attracted me, didn't she?

Turning slightly so I can see her, I keep my body between her and the bratva soldiers and tighten my hold on the man acting as my shield. "Nothing for you to worry about, *ílios mou.*"

Her eyes narrow. "He was yelling at you. In Russian."

She heard that? She doesn't understand Russian, or she would have asked questions at the bar that night. Lucia is too curious and intelligent to have done anything else.

"No big deal. I was surprised to see them in the club and bumped into Ivan here." I've got no clue what the man's real name is, but Ivan will do.

Other than the name, I'm careful to tell Lucia the truth. Something inside me roars like a beast at the idea of lying to her. There's a hell of a lot I'm not telling her, but that isn't the same as telling her something that is not true.

That feels like a betrayal and I won't do it.

"Right?" I dig the gun harder into the Russian's side.

"*Da.*"

"English, asshole," I bark.

"Yes."

"Friends of yours?" Lucia asks, her dark eyes glowing with curiosity.

"They want a word. I'm taking them outside," I answer ignoring the actual question. "Right?"

"*Da.* Yes," my hostage corrects himself when I squeeze my fingers together on his shoulder, pinching the nerve there. "We talk outside."

His voice is hoarse with pain, but he also doesn't sound terrified. His two compatriots get self-satisfied looks on their faces when they hear we are going outside.

Which tells me three things. One, they all speak English. Two, they think they can take me. And three, the Golubev Bratva's kill order on me is about as effective as a paring knife against a machine gun.

Not a single bratva soldier I've run into has recognized my face. If these three recognized me, they would not be so eager to go outside with me.

Maybe I killed the soldiers who were tasked with researching me. Chances are good, considering how many I have taken out.

Regardless of the reason, the bratva know nothing about who their *palach* is and the bounty they have on my head is worthless. Not one of them knows what their bogeyman looks like and that has already cost three of them their lives.

Tonight, it will cost three more.

After I find out what the hell they think they are doing in Lucia's club.

"You can use my office if you want," Lucia offers.

My innocent, too-generous-for-her-own-safety sun.

"Thank you, *ílios mou*." I don't care if these men know her importance to me. They won't live to utilize the information. "We'll be fine outside."

"If you're sure."

I nod. "I might be gone a while. We have a lot to catch up on."

"Take your time." The guilt is there in her voice. Again.

It pisses me off, but I can't deal with it right now.

My woman needs to get over this idea that spending time with her is a hardship. Not only am I doing my job for my mafia, but even if I wasn't, watching over her would be my priority.

Especially with the infestation of bratva in the area.

I guide the men outside. My grip on their friend making me the Pied Piper for the other two.

As soon as we step out the door, I shove my hostage to the side and follow, keeping a firm hold on him. When his friends come out the door Bobby and Theo grab them, pressing guns to the back of their skulls to keep them docile.

We force them away from the back entrance to the club. When we are on the other side of the dumpster, I signal to my men to stop. No one using the back parking lot will see us here and garbage isn't taken out until after closing.

The employees that smoke are the only potential problem and I don't plan to be here long enough for it to become an issue.

I don't have to tell Michael what to do with our captives. This isn't our first rodeo and my team works together like a well-oiled killing machine. He slaps duct tape over their mouths and then zip-ties their hands behind their backs and their feet together at their ankles.

"I want you inside the club, keeping an eye on Lucia," I tell Michael in Greek when he is done.

He nods and disappears through the door we came out of with his usual silence.

I toss my keys to Theo. "Get the SUV."

The three trussed up men are now watching me with wariness. Is it the Greek? Or how quickly we incapacitated them?

"You thought you were the baddest motherfuckers in the area, didn't you? But now you know you're three little bitches about to spill the secrets of your brethren."

The one I called Ivan glares daggers at me, but one of his friends looks worried. He'll be the one to break, but not until after I prove with his friends how far I'm willing to go to get information. He's the kind who is impacted as much, or more, by seeing torture happen than being hurt himself.

We toss the three on top of each other in the back of the SUV and secure the specialty cargo net over them before shutting the tailgate. They aren't going anywhere.

Theo drives while Bobby keeps his eye on the prisoners. I call Zeus.

"What's up, little brother?"

"I'm on my way to the warehouse with three bratva soldiers."

"The fuck? Where?" He means where did I come across them?

"At the club."

"I'll be there in twenty. Don't start without me."

There's a lot we can do without *getting started*, so I don't argue with my *anax's* order.

When Zeus arrives, we have the three men hanging by their zip tied wrists from the rafters. Their feet are bare, making access to toenails and the fragile bones in their feet easy. Right now, their toes can touch the floor enough to take pressure off their shoulder joints. One turn of the winch and they lose even that level of comfort.

I'm ready to turn it.

I despise the Golubev Bratva and their allies. For what they did to me as a kid, but also because they make most of their money from human trafficking.

"Hey, brother. We've already done introductions. They know my name but aren't ready to return the favor." Though I have not told them I am the bratva killer their brethren in California refer to as *palach*. "I'm calling them Larry, Curly and Mo."

"You and your old movie references. Do they even know who the Three Stooges are?"

"Does it matter?" Sure, the psychological advantage of them knowing I am insulting them every time I use the names would be welcome.

But there's a psychological benefit to me calling them by names other than their own in and of itself. It implies they aren't real people to me. That they don't matter.

Zeus shakes his head at me. He approaches the dangling men.

"You are hellishly unlucky, aren't you?" he asks in Russian. "To walk into the club where your *palach* is hanging out with his girlfriend."

"He is not our executioner," the one I dubbed Mo says with misplaced bravado, completely missing my brother's inference to their *palach*.

"You are allies to the Golubev Brava." I throw my knife up high, letting it flip three times before catching it again. "I am death to you."

"What do you have against our Golubev brothers? They have no enemies in this state." This is Curly and he accompanies his words with a globule of spit landing on the floor a few inches from my boot.

Pig.

"Wrong." I punch him in the nuts with my knuckle duster while stabbing into the flesh of his thigh with my knife. "They are trying to establish territory in the same city as their greatest enemies."

Curly screams and jerks in his bonds, his toes losing their hold on the floor. He screams again when the weight of his body pulls against his strained shoulder joints.

Huh. Might have pulled one or both out of their sockets with that move.

"I was going to let you watch me play with your friends." I wipe the blood off my knife on his shirt. "But then you had to spit."

Curly moans.

"What no warmup?" Zeus asks.

"I have places to be." Almost as lethal as I am, I trust Michael to watch over Lucia.

That doesn't soothe the itch to get back to the club, so I can protect her myself.

Mo and Larry look at Zeus and me with dawning understanding. "You are Hades Brotherhood," Larry says.

He's been silent until now. He didn't react when we hoisted him up. No empty threats like his fellow soldiers when we ripped the duct tape from their mouths. No curses or insults.

"Curly's not the boss of your crew," I say. "It's you."

The man stares back at me with dead eyes. Eyes that before I met Lucia would be a mirror of my own. I don't know what Larry sees there now. His death? Yes. But a dead soul? Not so much.

She's fanned the dark ember of my soul into a flame. Though I'm pretty sure the fire is from hell, and it only burns for her.

"You are *palach*." He eyes me up and down. "You have killed many of our Golubev brethren."

"They started the war." And I will finish it.

"When they kidnapped a child from the Hades Brotherhood."

"You know your history."

He inclines his head, showing no discomfort in his situation, but his shoulders have to be burning. With normal interrogation techniques, he might crack in a week, or two. If we can keep him alive long enough to torture him effectively. My eyes scan the other two men.

Mo is the one I'm betting on, but does he have the information we need?

"The Godfather of the Night did not care enough to ransom the child back. How is the offense worth making mortal enemies of the bratva?" Larry asks.

My grandfather didn't value my life, but my uncle did and still does.

Content to let me do my thing, he ignores the San Francisco Golubev *pakhan's* demands to turn over the executioner. He also ignores the *pakhan's* offers of money and territory in exchange for a promise of safety for his men from the *palach*.

Never going to happen and Constantin will never ask for it.

"The only mortality being faced in this war is by the Golubev scum." There are no innocents among the Golubev Bratva soldiers and their allies.

Every one of them stinks with the shit clinging to them from the skin trade. They kidnap, torture, buy and sell human beings. Adults and children alike.

Larry's eyes narrow fractionally at my words, reflecting raging fury before it disappears and his gaze is once again soulless.

Interesting. The reaction was there, even if it is gone now. For a man like him to react implies a more personal connection than allies.

I do not lose my cool when allies of the *Ádis Adelfótita* are threatened. But for my brothers? And now, Lucia? I will burn down cities.

Chapter 25

LUCIA

When Atlas doesn't come back inside after thirty minutes, I go outside to look for him. There's no one there. Not the men he said he wanted to talk to.

Not Atlas.

His swanky SUV is gone from the parking lot too.

I text him.

Lucia: *Where are you?*

Biting my bottom lip, I wait for him to answer. Five minutes later, I go back inside. Where is he? There's no reason to be worried. Atlas is a grown man and can take care of himself.

But what if those men are bratva? I should have told him my suspicions so he would be more cautious.

Only how do I explain my ability to spot Russian criminals without revealing my own past, or making up some ridiculous story that would feel like acid on my tongue to tell?

I do one of my usual walks around the club to take the temperature of the room. It's more crowded than it was earlier, and people are having fun.

The dancefloor is more than half full. Two men have stripped off their t-shirts to dance with their oiled pecs on display. Atlas will be mad when he sees them and if he follows the pattern he's set, he'll demand they put their shirts back on, or leave.

But he's not here to go caveman on my customers.

My phone buzzes in the hidden pocket of my dress. I pull it out.

Atlas: *Had to do some work for my brother. I may not be back tonight.*

Disappointment fills me, but my text reply is all happy, happy.

Lucia: *Okay. Talk soon. [smiley face emoji, kiss emoji]*

Atlas: *I will be there tomorrow morning, if not before. Be good.*

I take a picture of the shirtless men dancing and send it.

Lucia: *Maybe I'll do a little dancing myself. [dancing woman emoji, devil emoji]*

Atlas: *[dancing man emoji, knife emoji, knife emoji, knife emoji]*

Laughter bubbles up in me.

Lucia: *You should have said goodbye.*

I'm the one that told him he shouldn't neglect his work to spend time with me. I can hardly complain about him listening to me. But it was rude to leave without even texting me that he was going.

What kind of work is he doing this late at night though? Maybe Zeus wants Atlas to check out a club he's thinking of buying.

I wish Atlas had asked me to go with him. I would have left Willow in charge and gone.

ATLAS

Fuck.

I should have texted her I was leaving. Now, she's dancing with shirtless men. I send a quick text to Michael.

Atlas: *Keep the naked men away from Lucia.*

Michael: *She's talking to patrons at the reserved tables. Nowhere near the dance-floor.*

The little tease. But nothing says she'll stay away from the dancers. I need to hurry this damn interrogation along.

Feeling stabby after my text conversation with Lucia, I turn to my brother and say in Greek, "I don't think these bratva are *allies* of the Golubevs. They're family."

"How big is the Golubev Bratva in Russia?" Zeus asks, knowing I've done my homework.

"Big enough to be a problem." This is about more than relocating their rapidly dwindling California counterparts. It has to be. "They want something here."

My brother nods. "We know they want the port, what we need to know is why."

There's a lot we need to know, and I'd bet my bank account in the Caymans that Mo has all the answers. Getting him to talk is the tricky part.

Pulling open the second drawer down on my tool chest, I examine the vials lined in neat rows before grabbing the one in the center. It is a cocktail I helped our chemist perfect before we left California.

It decreases inhibitions while increasing a sense of fear and visualization. Twenty minutes after I administer a strong enough dose, the blood dripping from a single cut will be warped by Larry's mind into a gushing river.

Knowing how to use it, requires knowing how it works, so I administered it to myself and had my brothers put me through various scenarios.

The drug magnifies everything. Pleasure and pain. Fear and euphoria.

I give a starter dose to Mo and Curly, but twice as much to Larry. He'll be hallucinating within thirty minutes on the outside and won't be of any use answering questions until he starts coming down. It's then, he'll be at his most vulnerable.

"You think we haven't trained for this?" he asks when I stick the needle in the vein running down the inside of his elbow.

I don't bother to answer. Him believing I'm using something like sodium pentobarbital will only make the real reaction to the drug harder for him to handle.

Extracting information is 10% torture and 90% mind fucking.

Larry starts screaming warnings about monsters and the devil to his bratva brothers thirty minutes later as I slice another shallow line down Curly's chest.

Curly barely reacts to my cut, but his face drains of color as he watches his leader lose his mind.

"Don't worry. I didn't give you as much as I did him. Tell me what I want to know and I won't."

Curly spits at me. Again. I dodge. It's a defiant act by a desperate man. And gross.

Blood doesn't bother me, but spit? Is so fucking unhygienic.

Giving Curly time to let his panic grow, enhanced by the drug in his system, I focus on Mo.

"Ten bucks says Mo pisses himself," I say to my brother.

Mo shakes his head and moans. "No. Leave me alone."

Zeus shakes his head. "Not taking that bet."

"I'll bet dinner with Lucia you can't make it happen in under five minutes." Orion saunters into the warehouse.

I signal to Theo and Bobby. "Get back to the club and watch over *ilios mou*."

Now that my brothers are both here, my team can focus on what I prize most. Keeping my woman safe.

"You have got it bad, brother," Zeus says.

"She could be pregnant with my baby," I remind them. "Not taking any chances."

"But are you taking my bet?" Orion pushes. "Or has fucking one so often made you a pussy?"

"I want your car if I win." Lucia needs a car.

Sure, I could buy her one, but taking my brother's is more fun. Besides, it can take up to a year to get the make and model of his Mercedes E Class fitted with armored body and bulletproof glass.

My woman needs her own wheels *now*.

Orion's eyes narrow. "You think eating dinner with Lucia is worth my car?"

"Yes."

"Fuck. You're on." He taps his phone. "Timer is running."

It only takes a minute and a half. I cut Mo's clothes from his body and then make two shallow slices near his testicles. When I offer to castrate him and save the world from his progeny, Mo pisses down his leg.

"Shit. I thought he was going to hold out longer than that," Orion complains. "He seemed calmer than the other two."

"While showing me the whites of his eyes. You can taste his fear in the air."

Orion sniffs and grimaces. "The only thing I smell is his piss."

"There's a reason you're the lawyer and I'm the head enforcer." I pull out the scraping tool and pliers I use to remove fingernails.

"I thought it was because you're so good at killing people."

"That too." Not that Orion is a slouch in that arena.

He doesn't have as many kills as me, but he's no choir boy.

Mo is crying when I place the tip of my blade under his chin. "What were you doing in Nuovi Inizi?"

"We wanted to meet the owner. Heard it was a woman."

That was more than I heard before that first night. "Where did you get your intel?"

"Shut the fuck up," Curly yells.

"You shut up. It's not your balls he's threatening, is it? I'm not telling them anything important anyway. He knows the bitch owns the club already."

All information is important, but more important is the fact that once someone starts giving answers, it gets harder to stop when faced with escalating pain.

"Do not call my woman a bitch." I punch him in the jaw, satisfied when blood and teeth spray out of his mouth.

"Don't break his jaw so he can't talk." Zeus frowns at me.

Curly does some very creative cursing in Russian.

He's realized they aren't getting out of here, but Mo keeps looking toward the door as if he's expecting to be rescued. Not going to happen. Even if they've got trackers embedded in them somewhere, we've got the signal jammers on.

Zeus's guy has a program running that has their phones pinging off cell towers all over the city while he downloads their data too.

"Why did you want to talk to Lucia?" I ask with a friendly punch to the kidneys.

Mo groans. "Protection money. Clubs are good targets."

I am aware.

"The club is nowhere near your bar."

Curly jolts, like he's surprised we know about the bar. Which goes to show how unobservant he is. Because I saw him at the bar. He sure as hell doesn't remember seeing me.

What did they think happened to the men that went after the real estate broker's mistress? They went on a journey to find themselves?

So, I ask.

"We thought it was a street gang. We've had a few run ins with them."

They're trespassing on gang territories? Or businesses? Or both?

I learn it's both. After some not so gentle persuasion.

"The gangs aren't running protection rackets," Mo offers when Curly clams up.

He doesn't want his ball sac peeled off. I explain how it works in detail that makes him heave and then start vomiting words.

"You can't protect businesses all over the city." Not unless they have a damn army over from Russia.

"They pay to stay safe from us." Mo looks at me like I'm not very bright.

But that's not how the *Ádis Adelfótita* operate. When we charge a business tithe for protection, we protect them. And not just from the disasters that might befall them if they refuse. Which is why I've been doing so much research on the businesses we are taking on.

Geographical location is important, but so are the threats they face. We're not stepping into gang neighborhoods until we've got the numbers to take what we want and protect it when we do.

Chapter 26

ATLAS

"We need to make recruitment a priority," I say to my brothers.

Orion narrows his eyes. "Agreed. We should offer a bonus for bringing in foot soldiers."

"Already on it," Zeus says. "Constantin is sending us a contingent of soldiers. Some may choose to stay in Portland, but as long as they are here, it is our responsibility to bankroll them."

Good. It's one thing to fly under the radar while we establish our control in a city with no syndicate presence. It's another to be ready to go war.

"Our brothers will hunt you down like pigs in the street," Curly spits.

I know their real names now, but I'm sticking with Larry, Curly and Mo.

"Like you hunted us down after we dispatched the team you sent to that woman's condo?" Orion asks with derision.

"They were soldiers."

"You implying you're something more?" I ask, sounding bored.

Better to get the information I want.

"Not us," Mo says.

"Shut up," Curly shouts.

"You said it first." Mo looks over at Larry. "They'll send an army from Russia to avenge him."

That's worth knowing.

"Who is he?"

"The *pakhan's* son."

Not the *pakhan* in California. New to his position after losing his father, because of me, *his* son is only a child. Curly is talking about the Golubev *pakhan* in Russia.

What is his son doing here in Oregon? Proving himself? But by doing what exactly?

"What is he here to do?" I ask Mo.

He doesn't answer. I turn the crank on the winch, lifting them until the three men dangle above the floor. Finally breaking for real, Curly screams and begs me to lower him back down. "My shoulders, my shoulders," he whimpers.

"Answer my question."

"The *pakhan* wants the port to bring our cargo in."

"What cargo?"

Neither Curly nor Mo are willing to tell me. Not even after I crank the winch twice more and threaten Mo's testicles again. It takes a surprising amount of bloody and painful persuasion to get the answer.

When it comes, it's not a surprise, but rage boils through my blood at the confirmation of what I suspect.

They're moving people. The *pakhan's* son is here to establish one end of a new east-west pipeline for human trafficking. Worse, they have plans to use Nuovi Inizi as a source of inventory. Lucia's DJ program brings patrons from the surrounding counties and even states.

"Better to take women from out of town than locals," Curly wheezes.

I grab my weighted baton, bring it up over my shoulder and swing down against his tibia. The bone cracks and he howls. I didn't think he had that much vocal juice left in him. One broken end of the bone makes a lump under the skin on his calf.

What these men would have done to my beautiful lover when she refused to let them use her club as part of their flesh trade, has me swinging my baton again. Curly's scream this time sounds like it's coming from the bowels of hell. Where I plan to send him.

"What is your problem?" Larry demands with more lucidity than he should be capable of.

His pupils are still blown. That last scream must have given him a shot of adrenalin.

"No fucking syndicate is moving into our territory to buy and sell humans." Zeus throws a one-two punch to Larry's kidneys.

The *pakhan's* son screams unintelligible things about fire, proving he's still well under the influence of my drug cocktail. A well aimed kidney punch can feel like you're being skewered with a hot fireplace poker, I guess.

Leaving him to writhe in his agony, Zeus takes a turn at questioning the other two.

Curly is barely conscious, but reveals that the current contingent of bratva soldiers isn't as large as we thought. Only a handful of Golubevs from California are here. I've decimated their numbers so much they can't afford to send more than that to Oregon until they make the move out of California entirely.

According to Curly, that move is supposed to happen once the shipping yard is secured. Which is never going to happen. There are only two dozen soldiers here from Russia. I like my odds.

As expected, Larry gives up more intel as he comes down from the drug cocktail I injected him with. He knows the names of all the major players, what they are supposed to be doing and where they live.

Helpful.

It would be more helpful if his location directions referred to neighborhoods in Portland, not St. Petersburg. There are drawbacks to using the drug.

He also knows who the contacts for the rest of the pipeline are and those he gives to me in a more coherent revelation.

"You've got to help him. He's dying." Mo tries to shout, but his voice is more of a whisper at this point.

I look dispassionately at Curly. He's pale and barely breathing. I must have damaged a large vein, or an artery when I broke the bone. His lower legs are purple and swollen. Internal bleeding.

"You're both dead. You just haven't stopped breathing yet."

"But we told you what you wanted to know." Mo cries, snot and tears mix with the blood on his face.

If he wants mercy, he'll have to ask for it in the afterlife, because he's not getting it here. "What were you going to do with Lucia?"

"Who is that?" Mo tries to wipe his face against his dislocated shoulder and only ends up spreading his blood and snot around.

"The club owner."

"Oh, her." His eyes go shifty.

I make a shallow cut under his right testicle and wait for him to stop screeching before saying, "Yes, her. What are the plans for her?"

"Ivan wants her."

"Who is Ivan?" No surprise one of the bratva pigs is really named Ivan.

I picked that name to give to Lucia earlier for Mo because it's so common. "The *pakhan's vtoroy*."

Larry didn't mention Ivan, which shows how well he trained to withstand interrogation. Knowing that makes me suspicious of the rest of the intel we got from him. We will have to verify it. Discreetly.

"What does Ivan want with Lucia?"

"He likes curvy women with dark hair."

They've been watching Lucia? I would have noticed. "How does he know what she looks like?"

"The recon team we sent in three months ago. They took pictures of the club and its owner."

Before we set our sights on Nuovi Inizi. Timing. Sometimes it is off like a bitch. If we'd moved earlier, I would have known about the bratva presence before they got more entrenched in the city.

"Ivan usually likes them younger, but she's a beauty though. Thought about trying her out myself." Mo's admission earns him another punch to his balls.

He moans, but is in too much pain to react like he did the first time.

"What does he do with these beautiful curvy brunettes?" Every word out of my mouth is a bullet that makes Curly flinch.

"He fucks them."

Ivan is now at the top of my kill list.

"If he really likes them," Curly mumbles. "They last longer."

"And if he doesn't?"

"He kills them while he's fucking them. His movies make the *pakhan* a lot of money, but it's the *vtoroy's* viciousness that got him so high in the ranks." Mo is rambling now, his words barely intelligible and all in Russian.

But I have *very* good hearing and I catch it all. "Where is Ivan?" I ask in a deadly tone.

"California."

So, he's still in San Francisco. "When will he be back in Portland?"

"Don't know." Mo drools blood and spit out of the side of his mangled mouth.

I ask again with more persuasion, but get nothing. Mo is not high enough in the food chain for that kind of information.

We ask Larry about Ivan's return. He tries to hold back the information, but now that I know he hasn't been as forthcoming as I thought, I change my interrogation tactics. Eventually, he tells us Ivan is supposed to return to Portland in two days, via private jet arriving at one of the smaller airports west of the city.

Not only will his men not secure the shipping yard like he wants, but when he gets back, a good number of them will be dead. I can accomplish a lot in two days.

Not that it will matter to him. He is going to die. The only question is how much information he will part with before he does.

When I am done questioning Larry, I clean up my tools and then myself.

"We should take a page out the Golubev playbook and find out if the *pakhan* values his son more than Grandfather valued me." I clean the blood from my hands and forearms with the essential oils wipes I keep in my toolbox.

The smell of blood doesn't bother me, but most people prefer the scent of mint and tea tree oils. I'm sure Lucia will.

"You want us to keep him a hostage until they cede Portland to us?" Zeus asks.

"Oregon, but yeah, that's the idea. We can see how the *pakhan* reacts to getting videos of his son being tortured."

"It's not a bad idea," Orion muses. "The containment cells are operational."

Every part of the warehouse is ready for business. The interrogation rooms, containment cells and the incinerator in the basement that burns at 1600°. Hot enough to cremate human remains in under two hours.

We also have three levels of climate-controlled storage in subterranean rooms accessible via tunnels from the basement.

The only thing we need now, are more soldiers.

"We kill and incinerate Mo and Curly."

"Curly is already dead," Orion says.

I look over and see my brother is right. "Saves me a bullet. Larry goes in a cell."

"His name is Dimitri."

"I give a fuck." I throw away the wipes in a paper trash bag that will be tossed in the incinerator along with Mo and Curly's bodies.

Zeus grabs one of the wipes and rubs it on my face. "For now, we let the *pakhan* wonder where his son is and who has him. It sounds like they've already made enemies with more than one street gang. The bratva will start their searching there."

I knock his hand away. "I haven't been a kid in a long time."

"Didn't think you'd want to go back to Lucia with blood spatter on your face."

He's right, but I'm not about to say thank you.

"So far, none of the bratva even know we are here," Orion says. "We should capitalize on that."

"Yes," Zeus agrees.

I do what I'm best at. I kill bratva soldiers.

"We need them neutralized," Zeus says to me, thinking the same thing. "It's time for you to go hunting."

"I'll start tonight." At the bar.

"Take your team," Zeus orders.

"I need men watching Lucia and the club."

"They aren't going to send another team there before they even realize this one is missing. And once they do, they'll be busy looking for their *pakhan's* son."

"That search could lead them right back to the club." It's what I would do. Trace the last known steps of one of my missing men.

"I'll drop in on the club tonight," Orion says. "But I'll post a man in and outside the building."

"Text your men," Zeus orders me.

I frown. "They aren't leaving until Orion shows up."

"Then I'd better get going." My brother takes off.

"My guys will handle this." Zeus waves his hand toward Larry, Curly and Mo. "Start with the soldiers. Bring in the shot callers in a couple of days so we can interrogate them for updated information."

"That was my plan." But I shoot Mo in the head before I leave.

I promised him death and I always keep my promises.

Chapter 27

LUCIA

I spy a familiar dark head near the entrance and my heart skips a beat. He's back. I skirt the dancefloor and the quickest path to intercept him.

When I get close enough to see his face, disappointment mixes with surprise inside me. It's not Atlas, but his brother, Orion.

His lips tilt in a mocking smile. "Don't look so happy to see me."

"Are you here to check out the competition?" I ask, when what I really want to know is where his brother is.

"Competition?" He lifts a single dark brow in question.

I roll my eyes. "Nuovi Inizi may be a stand alone club and not part of the Zesti empire, but we do alright."

"More than alright by the look of it." His blue gaze so like his brother's takes in the now crowded club and the busy waitstaff serving drinks. "You should charge a higher cover to get in. This place is worth it."

"Thank you. The cover goes up by 25% on Friday and Saturday night and I charge for table reservations besides the minimum drink order required."

He nods, clearly approving. "So, not just beautiful, but smart too. Atlas is a lucky man."

"Come on, I'll get you a drink." I turn to lead him back toward the bar, ignoring his blatant flattery.

Willow is working the bar and turns to us after handing a customer their drink.

She eyes Orion up and down. "There are two of them? Why didn't you say so, boss?"

Her implication she finds Atlas hot irritates me. "Flirt on your own time," I tell her.

Willow's eyes widen and she puts her hands up. "Didn't mean to step on any toes."

Crap. That's not the impression I want to give. "No toes to step on. I'm dating Atlas, not Orion."

"Maybe you should give me a try, make sure you're getting the best brother?" he teases.

Unless my instincts about them are way off base, and they never are, Orion would sooner walk in front of a car than try to poach his brother's girlfriend.

That doesn't mean the annoying man won't flirt to get a rise out of Atlas.

"Put a sock in it, Romeo," I tell Orion. "Atlas isn't here to get a rise out of."

And by the way, where exactly is he? Not asking. Not. I am not that needy, clingy girlfriend.

"I'll have my usual," I tell Willow. "What can I get you?" I ask Orion.

"Do you have plomari?" He asks about a traditional and high rated brand of ouzo.

"Drinking ouzo is a little cliché of you isn't it?"

"I am Greek." He shrugs. "Why should I settle for anything less?"

"We have Metaxa. Will that do?" We carry Ouzo 12 too, but I suspect he wants the less common brand.

His eyes light up with surprised approval. "Very nicely."

I signal to Willow to pour him a shot.

"Ice, or no ice?" she asks him.

"No ice."

"A purist, huh?" She pours a finger of the clear liquid that smells faintly of black licorice into a rock glass.

"No one has ever accused me of being pure," he purrs.

Willow hands him his drink. "I bet."

Ignoring their banter, I take a sip of my cranberry juice and soda water. The fizzy bright tang slides over my tastebuds.

"Where's your table?" Orion asks me.

It's my turn to shrug. "I don't sit down long enough to keep one free for me."

"No VIP area?" He swivels his head from side to side, like he'll find one if he looks hard enough.

There's a space upstairs, but buying my house takes precedence. "Not yet."

The renovations needed to make it something more than a few extra tables with a view of the dance floor will take a significant monetary outlay. Not to mention the additional staff necessary. The VIP area is something that will have to wait for the next phase of my business plan.

"I was hoping to get to know you better," Orion says. "But this shouting every word isn't working for me."

"Come on." I lead him to my office, unlocking the door when we reach it.

Orion follows me inside and puts his drink down on my desk before throwing his arm over my shoulder. "Smile."

"Watch it. You're going to make me spill my drink."

He snaps a selfie before I realize what he's doing and then steps away quickly, a devious expression on his face.

"What was that for?" I demand. As if I don't know.

"Letting Atlas know what he's missing."

"He's doing his thing for your brother," I chastise as I lean back against my desk. "Do you think it's fair to tease him?"

Orion shrugs and grabs his drink. "Where would the fun be if I couldn't give my baby brother a hard time?"

He saunters over to the chair near my desk that Atlas likes to use and sits down.

Looking down at his phone while his fingers are busily sliding across and tapping on the screen, he says, "It's a lot quieter in here, but I still think you need a VIP area."

"We don't all have a ridiculously rich family backing us with a gazillion dollars for a startup business. Expansion upstairs, including the VIP area will come when I have enough saved up to do it without taking out a loan."

Extra debt means that if something unforeseen happens, Lenny's place in his facility is in jeopardy.

I'll never let that happen.

And I have my employees to consider now too. Expanding too quickly puts everyone's livelihoods at risk.

"Atlas would lend you the money. I doubt he'd even charge you interest." There's something in Orion's tone.

I shake my head. "No chance. I don't need my rich boyfriend offering me money and I would appreciate you not suggesting it to him."

"Why not?"

"I've built this place on my own. I'm proud of that." Owning a nightclub isn't my dream, but it is what I need to do to keep me and Lenny safe and Nuovi Inizi is a success. "I'm not giving anyone else a stake in my club."

"Taking a loan isn't handing over the reins to your business."

"I don't want to owe anyone, least of all my boyfriend."

Orion's phone buzzes and he looks at the screen, his eyes flaring before he schools his expression.

"Was that Atlas?"

Orion nods, giving me a long look. "He's a little intense where you're concerned."

"You think?"

"And what about you?"

"What about me?" I ask with my brows raised and arms crossed.

"You never answered my question."

"Which one would that be?"

"Do you love my brother?"

I knew this would come up again. Nothing about any of the Rokos men makes me believe they give up easily. "Not something I am going to discuss with you."

"Just tell me you're serious about him."

"Is this you asking me what my intentions are?"

"Yes."

"I don't know what is happening between me and Atlas," I say honestly.

A thunderstorm of negative emotion blows over Orion's features.

"I mean at first, I thought it was a one-night stand. But it wasn't. I'm not sure what it is, but Atlas isn't the only one feeling things intensely."

ATLAS

If my brother doesn't watch himself, I won't only be killing bratva soldiers tonight.

That fucking picture, with his arm around Lucia. I texted him a warning. Keep his hands to himself or I will break every bone in them. Unlike Orion, I don't have a sense of humor. He knows I mean it.

His response was a picture of my sun leaning on her desk. The angle of the shot indicates he's at least four feet away from her.

His hands might survive the night.

Not like the bratva I'm here to kill.

Itching to get back to Nuovi Inizi and Lucia, I pull into a parking lot of a closed paint store across the street from the bar. I park my X7 in the shadows and put a single earbud in before turning on the app on my phone for monitoring the bugs my guys planted.

The devices have been acting up since the guys placed them. Like there's interference. The Russians could have jammers in the bar, but then the feed would only produce static. Not this interrupted shit. Maybe they've got equipment close by that causes interference.

Doesn't matter. I'm able to tell there are four guys at one of the tables talking. A deep, impatient voice demands the others tell him where Larry, Curly and Mo are. None of the others know.

The surly man, who is probably one of the shot callers, thinks they had a run in with a street gang. He expects them to prevail. Unfortunately for him, two of his men are already dead and in our incinerator.

Larry-slash-Dimitri is cooling his heels in one of our basement cells.

Orion was right about them believing the gangs are responsible for their brethren's disappearance. My brother is a smart guy. Hopefully smart enough not to take any more selfies with my lover.

Knowing he is there watching over her, even if he's being an ass, helps. But this fucking anxiety. This need to be with her and watch over her. It's like nothing I've ever experienced.

It's a damn good thing we're putting her club under our protection. How hard is it going to be to convince her I'm moving in?

Knowing my sun, she won't make it easy for me.

She'll let me do anything to her body, but she holds onto her independence fiercely. Better to stay the nights and start leaving my clothes there. No conversation that will make her think she has to assert her autonomy necessary.

There are only a few cars in the bar's parking lot. I run the plates on all of them while I am waiting for Theo, Bobby and Michael. Two of the vehicles are registered under the identity the bratva are using as a front.

Grabbing what I need from the kit in the back of my SUV, I look around to make sure no one is watching. My truck is hidden from the street by one side of the building. I lope across the nearly empty four lane street, stopping when I'm on the side of one of the bratva vehicles away from the bar.

I listen for anyone coming outside who might see me. There is nothing. No door opening. No crunch of shoes on asphalt.

In my earpiece, I can hear the bratva inside the bar still debating about going to look for Larry, Curly and Mo.

My vote is yes. It will make it easier to covertly eliminate them.

With another look around to make sure I'm not being observed, I place trackers and remote devices that will blow the tires on both vehicles.

Then I go back to my SUV and wait.

Theo's truck pulls in next to mine before the bratva come to an agreement on what to do. We all get out to confab quietly.

"I've got trackers on the two vehicles I could identify. When they leave, Theo, you and Bobby follow the silver sedan. It's tracker VD048 on the app. Michael, you're with me."

Fifteen minutes later, the four men exit the bar. Three got into the blue pickup truck I'd put a tracker on. An older man they referred to as boss, got into the silver sedan.

If we are lucky tonight, Theo and Bobby will track the shot caller back to their real domicile.

I am going hunting and plan to have three more bodies for the incinerator before dawn.

Chapter 28

LUCIA

Atlas climbs into my bed in the early hours of the morning, his body warm and hair damp from a recent shower. His arms go around me, pulling me close to him. Under the clean scent of the shower gel he prefers is a faint whiff of mint and...is that tea tree?

Weird, but I'm too tired to worry about making sense of it.

A few minutes later, I'm too turned on. Atlas touches me everywhere, his big fingers gentle but insistent between my legs.

When he slides into me from behind, I moan. Setting a leisurely pace, he acts like he has all the time in the world. He doesn't pull back very far, using short, deep and slow thrusts to keep me on the cusp of orgasm, but never quite taking me over.

My body is on fire and I undulate against him. It's not enough though.

I reach between my legs and press my middle finger against my clit. Ecstasy shoots outward from the bundle of nerves, making my womb contract. Shivers of pleasure travel up and down my thighs.

His hand grabs mine, pulling it away and I cry out in protest.

"You want something?" he asks, his voice husky in my ear.

"I want to come."

He wraps our fingers together. "Do I ever leave you hanging?"

"Now. I want to come now."

"You're not ready."

I'm so ready, I'm vibrating with it. But instead of arguing, I touch myself with my other hand. It's more awkward because that arm is under me, but I'm able to reach my pleasure button and I push it.

Circling the bundle of nerves and then scissoring my fingers around it, my orgasm builds.

"Uh...uh...uh..." Atlas tuts, grabbing that hand too.

He guides it up to his neck, shifting my body as he needs so he can. He pulls my other hand up. "Clasp them behind my neck," he growls in that bossy voice that sends arousal arcing along every nerve ending.

All the while, he keeps up that maddeningly slow rhythm with his hips. His thrusts take him deep inside my body, his oversized sex stretching me perfectly, on the pleasure side of pain.

I interlock my fingers behind his neck.

"Good, *eromenis mou*. So good for me. So good to me." His hand travels up and down my body.

Squeezing my breast, pinching my nipples, caressing my neck, trailing his fingers down my inner thigh, he touches me everywhere but where I need him most.

"Touch me!" I plead.

"I am touching you."

"There, I need you to touch me *there*."

"Here?" His fingertip barely skims over my clitoris.

"Yes," I moan.

He does it over and over again and I'm sure it's not enough. I plead and shift against him, but I don't move my hands. He doesn't change the slight pressure of his touch.

I am mindless with pleasure when my climax hits me out of nowhere. Screaming, my body arches and somehow he moves his hand enough to keep the same light touch. There is no respite from the pleasure, it builds to a second crescendo almost immediately and I scream until I am hoarse as shudder after shudder of ecstasy works through my body.

Then he shoves forward, buried so deep in my body his scrotum presses into my bottom. His hand clamps down on my tender flesh and pleasure wars with pain as my overstimulated clit reacts to the firmly possessive touch.

He comes shouting my name and holding my body so tight, it feels like he'll never let me go.

Like so many times before, he refuses to pull out after, his still hard erection holding his essence inside of me.

Exhausted from my prolonged pleasure, I fall asleep with him still inside me.

~ ~ ~

He's still wrapped around me when I wake up late the next morning. We shower together, have breakfast and he accompanies me to my office. I settle down to work, but he gets a phone call and takes it out in the hallway. He comes back later, to take me for a late lunch at a local restaurant.

That sets the blissfully happy pattern of the next few days. We spend the day mostly together. During breakfast and lunch, Atlas works on getting to know me. He is keenly interested in my opinion on the local economy, my plans for my club and anything else I want to talk about.

He never acts bored with me and although he's a little more taciturn, I love listening to him talk.

Especially about his brothers and cousins. I swear he acts like he's not telling funny stories, but their dynamic cracks me up. He's gone in the evenings and late into the night working with his brothers, but Atlas always wakes me up to make love in the early hours of the morning.

ATLAS

Ivan does not come back to Portland when expected. He flies to Moscow instead. It's not a surprise, considering how many of his soldiers I kill before he is supposed to arrive.

Apparently, he doesn't think Portland is safe for him. He's right. But him running back to Russia won't stop me hunting him down and killing him.

He is a threat to Lucia, so he cannot live.

At first, the bratva soldiers remain, beating the bushes to find their boss, Larry. Dimitri if you want to be accurate. Their search makes my hunting easier because we haven't found their base yet.

They don't return to the bar either, but they are out on the streets at night, roughing up gang members and making more enemies. I am the predator, keeping to the shadows, tracking them, and killing them one-by-one.

When the gangs start hunting them too, things get more fun for me. I have to find the soldiers first.

"Do not start killing gang members," Zeus says, glaring at me, like he knows I'm going to argue. "We're still deciding which gangs we want to negotiate alliances with and you're not going to make that decision unilaterally with your gun."

"Or your knife," Orion drawls.

I roll my eyes. "It's like you two don't trust me, or something. When have I ever been caught doing my job?"

And the only way I have to kill a gang member is if I get caught.

Before the *pakhan* can send major reinforcements, it is time for implementing the Hostage Plan.

A week after my interrogation of Larry, Curly and Mo, we send a video to the *pakhan* in Russia. It shows him the *enthusiastic* hospitality of *Ádis Adelfótita* toward his human-selling piece-of-garbage son.

Three days and three more videos later, the *pakhan* agrees to parlay with Zeus. It takes another recorded session between Larry, me and my tools, but ultimately, the *pakhan* proves to care more about his son's wellbeing than my grandfather cared about mine.

The *pakhan* over all the Golubev bratva agrees to our terms. Leave Oregon and stay the hell away from *Ádis Adelfótita* territory here. Constantin has given Zeus permission to negotiate the withdrawal of the American Golubev bratva from California.

That discussion is more heated, but finally, the *pakhan* agrees that his bratva will cease all organized criminal activity in California. They have six months to sell their legitimate businesses and get out of the state.

He agrees to put a leash on the *palach*, me. I will not kill any more Golubevs during the transition as long as they keep to the terms.

"One breach of this agreement and the entirety of it becomes null and void," Zeus says.

The *pakhan* nods. "Yes, yes. Just release my son."

"He will accompany your men when they leave," Zeus says.

"At least get Dimitri medical treatment."

"We have a doctor on standby to treat him."

Relief washes over the *pakhan's* features, something Zeus would never allow to show. He doesn't let his enemies see his emotions. The *pakhan* shouldn't either. If Zeus was without honor, he would have the leverage now to demand more concessions.

"There is one final detail," the *pakhan* says.

Zeus doesn't show his anger at the Russian man trying to renegotiate the terms of the deal. If he is angry. The *pakhan* opening up negotiations again, leaves Zeus free to ask for more too.

"As a token of good faith, turn the *palach* over to us. He has murdered many bratva from our family. Making an example of him will ensure the commitment of my people to our agreement."

"As a *token of good faith*, I will not send the executioner to Russia to kill your men off one-by-one. It is your job as their *pakhan* to make sure your men abide by the terms of the agreement, not mine."

"Do not threaten us," the *pakhan* snarls in Russian.

"It is not a threat. It is an outcome you can avoid. Whether you will, or not, remains to be seen."

"Your *palach* is a danger to my bratva. He cannot be allowed to live."

"Your men have nothing to fear from their executioner if they abide by the terms of our agreement and stay out of our territory in the future. If they don't, it won't be the *palach* that they have to worry about."

That is true for everyone but Ivan. But when I go to kill that bastard, I won't leave anything for them to trace the hit back to the United States, much less our mafia.

"If you expect us to act as allies, you must make this concession."

"At no time have I implied an ally relationship. We don't do business with human traffickers. This agreement is for a truce and it only extends so long as all of the conditions are met."

"You do not have the position of strength you think you do. I could send over an army and destroy your Hades Brotherhood in a single day."

"You could try, but the only syndicate that will be destroyed is your bratva."

Someone says something to the *pakhan* but the words are too low to understand.

The man slams his fist down on his desk. "A truce. For the return of my son."

Zeus nods, in complete control of his emotions. "Since you have reopened concessions, you have two weeks instead of a month to vacate Oregon and three months for your American brethren to get out of California."

That cuts both departure times in half.

Zeus cuts the connection while the *pakhan* is still sputtering.

"You don't trust him to keep his word, do you?" I ask before my brother can say anything.

"No, but this buys us time to build our numbers, so when they come for us, we're ready to destroy them."

I nod.

"You heard me give my word."

"That I won't kill any more of their men as long as they get the hell out of our territory and stop doing any business in it? Yes."

"They may not be men of their word, but we are. You don't kill another bratva in Oregon or California unless they break the truce."

"I won't be the one that breaks terms." But neither of us is convinced the Golubev Bratva is as determined to keep their word as we are.

Men who make human beings a commodity have no honor and cannot be trusted.

~ ~ ~

Over the next two weeks, I take my turn watching the bratva still in Portland while they put their properties up for sale and vacate the apartments they rent. Cars are sold or returned to leasing agencies and business is cancelled.

The listening devices we planted in the bar were found a few days after we took Dimitri, but that doesn't stop us watching them. We always have someone inside the bar they congregate in.

The *pakhan* is probably scrambling to figure out another port to use for the human smuggling operation. Too bad for him his partners won't be available to do business. Zeus agreed to let the bratva live, but not their partners responsible for establishing the other segments of the new route.

Chapter 29

ATLAS

Carrying the two items I bought today while taking my turn watching Dimitri's second in command.

The man seems to be obeying the terms of the agreement, but I take nothing for granted. When he goes into a sex toy shop, I follow.

He informs the owner that she will have to work with suppliers from another state to get what she wants to order from them. The bratva are smuggling sex toys from China so they aren't subject to tariffs or commodity restrictions.

It's a lucrative market. We should be in it too and I text as much to my brother before purchasing a pair of pink satin lined leather cuffs and matching sleep mask, clearly intended to be used as a blindfold.

Lucia is in her office when I get to the club. It's Sunday and she doesn't work tonight. The perfect time to play with our new equipment.

Her beautiful gaze lights up when she sees me standing in the open door of her office. "Atlas." The way she says my name sends blood surging to my cock. "You're back."

I hold up the handcuffs and sleep mask, dangling from my forefinger. "Time for a break."

Her eyes dilate and her lips part as she starts to breathe shallowly, but she doesn't get up.

"Come, *eromenis mou*. You have been working all day." It's not a shot in the dark.

"I need to finish this..."

Shaking my head from side to side, I stalk toward her. "You can finish tomorrow. You didn't even take a break for lunch."

The tracker I put on her phone shows she has not left her office since I drove away this morning.

"How do you know that? Did Willow rat me out?"

"Willow didn't have to. I know you, Lucia." I don't mention the tracker. It only confirmed what I already suspected.

And she doesn't need to know about all the measures I take to keep her safe.

Her smile is blinding. "Yes, you do."

I put my hand out toward her

Getting up from her chair, she takes it. Her eyes are focused on the leather pieces in my other hand though. "Are those new?"

"Yes." I am surprised she feels the need to ask. "I will never use something on you that has touched another woman."

A small puff of air escapes her mouth as she shivers. "Good."

"Is anyone else here?" Bobby says there isn't, but I want confirmation from Lucia.

She shakes her head, her silky dark hair swaying over her shoulders. "Willow left an hour ago."

"Any deliveries scheduled?"

"We have two cases of spirits that should arrive in a couple of hours," she says.

"I will take care of it."

"There's no need. I know you think I can't lift a case of liquor, but I promise I can. I'll accept the order."

"You'll be tied up." I watch for when the meaning of my words penetrates.

She gulps and darts a look down at the handcuffs. "Tied up...by those?"

"Yes."

"In two hours?"

Longer than that if I have my way, but I simply nod.

"Okay."

Predatory satisfaction settles deep inside me. "Take off your clothes."

She doesn't ask any questions, or demur with a false sense of modesty. Not my beautiful, adventurous lover.

Lucia unbuttons the front of her jumpsuit and then slides down a hidden zipper before pushing it off her shoulders and down her body to pool around her feet. She's wearing a black lace bra and panties under the crimson red jumpsuit.

Reaching out, I unclip the front closure of the bra with a flick of my wrist. The stretchy lace separates and her gorgeous tits spill out in all their glory. Looking like perfect little raspberries, her nipples are already hard and flushed with blood.

"You are beautiful, *eromenis mou*." My mouth waters to taste her sweet raspberry peaks.

She slides the boy short panties that leave half of her ass bare down her thighs and then steps out of them and the jumpsuit. She's so graceful, she manages to keep her sexy black heels on and stands before me naked except for them.

She knows seeing her in only her heels turns me on. Not that I need anything more than her presence, but the way they make her legs look a mile long makes my cock surge painfully against the zipper of my jeans.

"Lift your arms and put your hands out." My voice is low and guttural.

Her small, elegant hands rise putting her wrists exactly where I want them. I run my fingertips down her arms and she shudders.

"So damn responsive."

"To you."

I like the implication she wasn't like this for the man she married. Shoving thoughts that make me murderous away, I buckle a cuff on one of her wrists and then do the other.

The lightweight chain between them is about six inches long, preventing immediate strain on her shoulders from the cuffs.

Lifting the sleep mask, I ask, "Are you ready?"

"Yes." Her voice is barely above a whisper, but it does not waver.

I put the blindfold on her, running my fingers through the silky strands of her hair after tightening the sleep mask so it will not slide off.

Wrapping the long tresses around my fist, I gently tug Lucia toward me. "We're going upstairs."

"Okay."

Bending down, I grab her clothes and hand them to her. "Hold these."

She curls her bound hands upward, tucking the clothing between her forearms and her torso.

I adjust the position of her arms so her breasts are completely unfettered and then guide my sun out of her office by my hold on her hair.

LUCIA

The darkness behind the blindfold is not absolute, but it doesn't have to be. I can't see anything. No shapes. No obstacles in our path. Not where we are going. Not the expression on Atlas's face.

I'm so wet, my thighs are slippery. Just from having my wrists restrained and the blindfold put on me. Atlas's hold on my hair only adds to my arousal.

The hand not guiding me cups my breast, tweaking my nipple and I gasp.

"Is your pussy wet for me?" he asks, his mouth near my ear.

Moaning, I nod.

"Use your words, *eromenis mou*."

My lover. I am that. His. In every way. Yes, it's fast, but it's right too. I have never felt this way. Not with Tino. Never.

I trust Atlas implicitly and I have no fear as he guides me through the club and up the stairs.

"Yes, my pussy is wet." I never use that word, but saying it sends a jolt of pleasure straight to my core.

Is it the naughtiness of it? Or simply that I'm telling Atlas about how turned on he makes me?

He growls and slides that errant hand down between my legs, his long fingers slipping between my slick folds easily.

We keep walking, even though his fingers delve into my hungry cooch. *Dio mio.* The things this man does to me.

He plays with me as we cross the club and stops only to put the code in to unlock the door. Then his fingers are back, rubbing over my swollen clit as we mount the stairs. The shift in our bodies as we go up each stair jostles his fingers, giving and then taking away the friction I'm craving.

His big bulge rubs up against my bare bottom every couple of steps too and I can't help pushing back into him. Wanting more, knowing I can't have it.

Yet.

He opens the door to my apartment, guides me inside and then both of his hands fall away from me.

"No," I protest.

"Be a good girl and stay there."

Porca miseria! Can he say anything in that voice that won't turn me on?

I hear him moving around the kitchen and then his steps take him to the bedroom. I remain where I am, my body vibrating with need as images of what is to come play through my head.

The cuffs on my wrists tug and I realize Atlas is back, right in front of me and he's pulling on the chain between the cuffs.

"Everything is ready. Come with me."

Everything? What is everything?

"*Che cosa?*" I ask in Italian.

Before I can get my befuddled brain to translate to English, Atlas stops and his lips press almost reverently against mine before the kiss turns carnal and I find my leg up around his hip as I seek the stimulation I need against his denim clad leg.

He breaks the kiss and gently shifts my leg so my foot is once again on the floor.

"No," I moan.

His hand cups my nape. "Trust me."

He waits and I realize he wants my agreement.

"I do," I tell him. With my body and my heart.

He gets us over to the bed and pulls me into his lap, so I am straddling him. A sweet, fresh scent makes my mouth water as something cold presses against my lips.

"Open." He's being bossy again.

And it's making my core go molten. If I were a nuclear reactor, I would be in danger of exploding from the heat.

My lips part without a thought from my brain and a cold morsel settles on my tongue. A grape. I chew and swallow before he kisses me again. But as soon as it gets interesting, he pulls his mouth away and puts another piece of fruit against my lips.

It's a chunk of pineapple this time. He keeps kissing and feeding me until I'm humping mindlessly against his jean covered erection. I eat each bite without thought waiting for the kiss that follows.

Until he doesn't stop kissing me and his hands play with every erogenous zone.

I tear my lips from his. "*Per favore*, Atlas. *Ho bisogno di te.*"

"What part of me do you need, *brava regazza*?" he asks, calling me good girl in Italian.

So, I answer him in kind, telling him I need his cock. "*Ho bisogno del tuo cazzo.*"

"Not yet. I'm still hungry." He flips me on my back on the bed and yanks the chain between my cuffs upward.

I hear a small click and try to pull my hands down, but I can't. He's attached the cuffs to the bed somehow. A thrill zings through me and I tug harder, my heartbeat speeding up when there is no give.

So turned on I cannot form words, I moan and twist my head side to side, unable to see what Atlas is doing because of the blindfold. Every nerve ending tingles with anticipation for his next touch.

Strong, warm hands push my legs apart and guide my knees upward. "Hold yourself open for me."

Fluid gushes from my core as I do what he says.

And then he feasts. On me. Two thick fingers press inside me while he licks up my labia. He draws them out and shoves back in as he swirls his tongue around my clitoris. He eats me out like he's starving.

Something not as hard as his finger presses into my opening. It's strange but he pulls it out before I can figure out what it is. He shifts between my legs and then he traces my lips. The scent of my own arousal mixed with the sweeter scent of pineapple calls to something primal inside me as he wets my lips with my juices.

The he presses the pineapple piece into my mouth. "Taste yourself. You're sweeter than the pineapple."

He moves again and his mouth is back at my core, his teeth tugging gently on my swollen nether lips. He presses something inside me again, but follows it with his tongue and then he eats the piece of fruit saturated with my arousal.

He nuzzles my monz, inhaling deeply. "Your honey is delicious."

Nothing but garbled sounds make it past my lips.

"I know, *pethi mou*." He sucks and licks and nibbles on my most tender flesh until I am writhing and straining against my restraints.

I need more, but I will only get what he gives me. And that revs my engine, making my body purr like a million dollar sportscar.

His mouth pulls away from me, but he has three fingers inside me slowly pistoning in and out of my tight, wet channel.

"Do you know what *pethi mou* means?"

I shake my head side to side gasping as he keeps me on the precipice of coming with his fingers. If he would just touch my clitoris. A single caress with his thumb is all it would take.

"It means my death. You are the death of me being alone. Your light fills my darkness, *ilios mou*."

"You...are...not...dark..." I gasp out.

His laughter is drowned out by my scream as his thumb finally finds my clitoris and I climax. He forces me into another climax almost immediately, never letting up with his hand.

And then he's on top of me, shoving his hard shaft into me, stretching the tender walls of my vagina in a delicious pleasure tinged with stinging pain. It morphs into unfathomable bliss as he thrusts deeper than he should be able to go.

His balls slap against my bottom and I mewl. It's too much, but he won't let up.

"You can take it. Give me one more climax, *eromenis mou*. I know you can." He pounds into me, grinding his pelvis against my over sensitized clit.

Ecstasy washes over me, wringing a hoarse cry from my already strained throat, my entire body convulsing.

"That's right, *brava regazza*. Milk my cock, draw my seed into your body. Take it all." His filthy words of praise fall on me like warm rain.

My inner muscles grip his hardon as his hot seed shoots inside me.

Sometime later, he undoes the cuffs, rubbing my shoulders and arms before taking off the sleep mask. He shadows my face with his body so the light does not hurt my eyes as I blink, trying to adjust.

"You are so perfect for me, Lucia." My name on his mouth sounds like the sweetest endearment ever.

I wrap my arms around his neck and inhale his earthy post-coital scent. "I could never have done all that with Tino."

It's probably against all sorts of dating rules to bring up the dead husband while naked with the current lover, but I need Atlas to know that what we have is special. Profound.

"Why?" He slides to the side of me, his gaze searching my face for something.

I'm not sure what he wants to see, but I give him the truth. "I didn't trust him like I trust you."

Even before we lost the baby.

My gaze skims down his body and a laugh is startled out of me. His jeans are shoved down around his hips, his still partially engorged penis laying against his hairy thigh.

"What?"

"You never got your clothes off."

"I was busy." He strips now, but climbs back onto the bed with me.

Neither of us makes a move to shower.

"You are mine, *ílios mou*. I will never let you go."

His fervency should make me nervous, but it doesn't. It tells me that this thing between us is mutual. We're both all in.

Chapter 30

ATLAS

"Our offer has been accepted on the shipping yard." Zeus looks at me like he's trying to see something in my face.

I take a draw from my beer. "That's good."

Zeus called an in-person meeting with me and Orion. I don't like leaving Lucia, but we've got eyes on the remaining bratva in Portland and Theo is watching over her from outside the bar.

I need to introduce her to my crew soon. They will be part of her life, like they are part of mine. Besides my brothers, they are the only men I trust Lucia's safety to.

"It's a step toward getting us back on track," Zeus says.

Finally. The bratva issue took a lot of time and resources we weren't planning for.

"You want me to finish setting up our protection racket." It is as important for potential money laundering outlets as the income it will provide.

"Constantin wants us to build numbers and make a move to establish our physical territory." Zeus's expression is even more constipated than usual. "That means getting the protection racket up and running."

"Okay, I've got it locked down. I know exactly which businesses to start with and how wide to go with our territory." My discussions with Lucia have paid off. My beautiful lover is a font of information.

"If Lucia balks, we get her to sell the club to us. Constantin agrees."

A pit yawns inside me. None of us trusts the Golubev *pakhan*. The recent conflict with his bratva makes establishing our territory now imperative.

But Zeus is talking about *forcing* Lucia into cooperating with the *Ádis Adelfótita* laundering money through her club, or selling Nuovi Inizi to us.

That is not going to happen. "We are not taking her club from her."

"Then get her to cooperate."

"I'm not threatening Lucia." I stand up and lean over my brother's desk to let him see my rage close up and feel how much I mean my words.

"Fuck her into compliance, for all I care, but we need Nuovi Inizi working with us," Zeus says harshly.

"Piss off!" I slam my knuckles down onto his desk. "I am not touching *ílios mou* for any other reason than that I want her bangin' body."

Not to threaten her and sure as shit not to fuck her into submission. No matter how fun that might be in fantasy scenario.

Instead of lurching to his feet and taking a swing at me like I half expect, Zeus rubs his eyes the weight of his position in the lines of fatigue on his face. "Then use fucking logic and *convince* her. We can't get our own clubs up and running soon enough for what we need."

We have twenty soldiers coming up from California to fill our ranks. Even after we recruit the numbers we need, some may decide to stay. All members of the Hades Brotherhood need jobs to do and a source of income. Nuovi Inizi is pivotal to all of it.

Because I made it that way.

But how is Lucia going to react to having her club become such an integral part of the Greek mafia? We're beyond setting her up to pay a protection tithe now. Too many of our plans hinge on access to the club. Access to her and her knowledge of the city.

"We have to expand our numbers now for all our safety. Including hers," Orion adds when I scowl in silence at my oldest brother.

Zephyr and Helios haven't said a word during the discussion, but both are looking at me like they're wondering if they can trust me. Like my loyalty is in question.

Fuck that. Fuck them. And fuck this situation.

Maybe I have been hoping we could figure a way around charging Lucia a protection tithe, much less using Nuovi Inizi in any other way. So, the fuck, what?

Lucia's club is about to become our contact spot like that seedy bar on the other side of Portland has been for the bratva. A move like that makes Nuovi Inizi ours even if her name stays on the deed to the building.

Gamó.

"Your girlfriend is a savvy businesswoman," Orion reminds me. "She'll understand what has to happen once you tell her what the bratva planned to do with her club."

Like hell I'm going to tell her that. Unless I have no other choice. She doesn't need to worry about something that never happened and I will not allow to happen in the future.

"No one is going to hurt her," I warn my brothers.

"Of course not," Orion says but the look on Zeus's face puts our middle brother's assurance into question.

Orion ignores Zeus's glower and appeals to me. "Her business must be brought under *Ádis Adelfótita* oversight for Nuovi Inizi to have all of our protection."

"If she refuses to pay a protection tithe and does not want to sell, we will buy in as partners," Zeus offers his version of a compromise with cold finality.

My *anax* is only willing to go so far to appease my woman. The *Ádis Adelfótita* comes first.

What I don't say is that Lucia will be forced into cooperation, taking a partner she doesn't want or selling the business she worked so hard to build over my dead body and maybe theirs.

LUCIA

I'm so happy, I'm fizzing with it. It's the final walkthrough of the house before closing.

"You need to sign off on the repairs the seller made and then the final paperwork will be drawn up by the bank," Elaine says. "The inspector has already approved them."

He is leaving as I arrive and tells me that everything looked good. But as the homeowner, I'm expected to give my authorization as well. I like that, so I don't mind taking time from my day to essentially rubber stamp what the inspector said.

I only wish that Atlas could be here with me. It's an important milestone for me, and I want to share it with him. He's way more important to me than he should be after only a matter of weeks, but there's no help for it.

The heart wants what the heart wants. And the dreams I thought dead are coming to life again inside mine. But he's working with his brothers today and I could hardly ask him to tell them no when he spends so much time with me already.

Walking into the master bedroom where one of the windows had to be repaired, my gaze automatically goes to where we made love on the floor.

There's a tell-tale spot on the carpet. Elaine doesn't notice it. I doubt the inspector did either. It's very faint, but I know where to look. Atlas's fluids mixed with mine, right under where the bed will sit.

Does it make me sick that I want to leave it there? Something private and secret just for me. A memory no one can take away.

Reveling in joy stronger and deeper than any I have felt before, I have to stifle the happy laughter the sight of our cum stain on the carpet elicits in me. Me and Atlas together.

A sign of things to come, of a future not filled with the loneliness of the last five years.

Lenny has a home he loves and feels safe in, and now I will have mine.

"You look really happy, Lucia. Clients like you are the reason I am in real estate."

"Honestly?" I ask with a smile. "I'm bubbling over with it like a bottle of champagne somebody shook before popping the cork."

I wasn't sure this could ever happen for me. No matter how much I want this, Lenny's care and safety must come first. He doesn't have anyone else to look out for him.

But I am finally able to buy a house that's mine. It's a place where I can be myself. Not the mafia princess I once was. Not the nightclub owner I don't really want to be. But simply the woman I am deep down inside in my own space.

"Everything came together like you needed it to," Elaine says.

It's such a typical realtor saying, but she means it. She's not only here for the commission. Especially on such a small property.

"When I started Nuovi Inizi I was pretty sure I could make a go of it, but not certain I could bring in enough to pay for my brother-in-law's care."

Elaine knows about the facility because my contract to pay for Lenny's care came up when the underwriters started digging into my finances to determine if they would approve a mortgage for me.

"So many new businesses fail," Elaine says with her usual enthusiasm. "But you have the club making enough profit to cover his care and the mortgage for this place. You should be really proud of yourself."

I grin. "I am."

I might wish I could do something else, something quieter, but I've made Nuovi Inizi work for me and I'm proud of that. Maybe even more proud than I would be if it was my dream. I did the hard thing and succeeded.

As another successful businesswoman, Elaine's approval feels good. When I explain everything about Lenny to Atlas, he'll respond in the same way.

We walk back through the dining-slash-living area bathed in light from the autumn sunshine coming in through the large picture window.

It feels like a bright, happy omen.

My house. My home. A place for me.

I sign the papers for it tomorrow, and I can't wait.

~ ~ ~

Wearing my favorite red wrap dress, I'm still buzzing with excitement hours later.

The club is hopping and soon we will be at capacity. My staff are all where they are supposed to be. The DJ is here and spinning tunes.

Atlas said he will be here before close tonight. I can't wait to tell him about signing the papers and taking possession of my new home tomorrow.

He lives in a mansion. Is it a pipe dream to think he'll want to share my little house with me?

He spends every night in my even smaller apartment, I remind myself. The house will be an improvement.

Am I really going to ask him to move in so soon? I should wait. I should wait, but if he does what he is doing now, he'll be my de facto roommate without me ever asking. I want it to be my choice.

I need him to know that I want him there.

My gaze flicks to the entrance for the millionth time tonight, but this time I am rewarded with the sight of Atlas. There are three men with him. I recognize two of them. They've been in Nuovi Inizi before, when Atlas wasn't here.

I'm pretty sure I've met all of his family in Portland. Only, the way they all walk close together, it's clear they don't mind being in each other's personal space. Which means they know each other pretty well, even if they aren't family.

It's strange they never introduced themselves to me when they were here before. Had Atlas not told them about me?

They break through the crush of bodies and I notice how they are dressed. Unlike his usual attire of tight-fitting dress shirt and slacks or dark jeans, Atlas is wearing a charcoal grey, tailored suit. Open at the neck and with no tie, his black button up shirt reveals the strong column of his neck.

My brows furrow as my eyes take in how his companions are dressed the same way. Their suits are a rung down on the designer ladder, but nowhere near off the rack.

I go cold inside, a fist squeezing my heart so tight if it was a piece of coal, it would become a diamond.

Atlas looks like Tino used to when my husband went out to work. The suit is probably Hugo Boss and not Armani like Tino's, but that attitude Atlas wears it with is all too familiar. Confidence oozes off him in overwhelming waves.

The look he gives to the people stepping out of his way is both expectant and arrogant. He's used to intimidating others. How am I only just now noticing that?

Because my ovaries have been overriding my common sense since the first moment our eyes met.

That emotionless expression on Atlas's face is eerily familiar too. Every made man I knew back in Detroit had perfected that cold and detached air.

Suddenly everything clicks into place in my brain.

Atlas coming to Portland with his brothers and cousins. They're here to build a business all right, but they aren't simple nightclub owners like me.

They're mafia. Freaking *Greek* mafia and they are claiming territory in the city I have made my home.

Why didn't I know? When Tino and his father talked about Zesti, they never mentioned the clubs are owned by a syndicate. I should have realized though. My husband and father-in-law would never have admired a completely legitimate business the way they did Zesti. Much less want to emulate them.

Atlas's blue eyes warm slightly when they catch mine, but he doesn't smile. Why should he? He's not here for me. He's working.

Nausea rises in the back of my throat, and I force myself to swallow. The only way I get through this encounter is if I can pretend to be as disconnected from my emotions as Atlas.

If I have a single doubt about what Atlas is, the three large men flanking him pound the final nail into the coffin of any hope he's a regular guy. I've known men like them before. I grew up around them. They are like the men my father has working for him, some of whom I even called uncle.

The way these men's watchful gazes take in my club's patrons, the tense set of their shoulders, like they are ready to spring into action...it all spells one thing.

They are the muscle. Not that Atlas needs any, but like my dad used to say, it's all about perception.

Atlas stops in front of me, and I want so badly for him to say something, *anything* that tells me my instincts are wrong. To do something to show me everything hasn't changed. But he doesn't go to kiss me like he usually does.

"Lucia." He reaches for me. Finally.

But I jerk back so his fingers do not connect with my skin.

Surprised, he stares at me in silence and the longer it drags on, the more certain I am of why he's here tonight. It's not to see me.

Inside, my brain is screaming, *this cannot be happening*, but I smooth my face into a blank mask and turn to head toward my office. This discussion isn't taking place in front of my employees and patrons.

Not for Atlas's sake, but for mine.

The prickles on the back of my neck let me know that he is following me. I'm careful to maintain enough distance that he cannot touch me though.

Not that he would want to. His need to play besotted boyfriend is over.

Chapter 31

LUCIA

When we reach my office, I hurry to unlock it before Atlas catches up. However, his hand lands against the small of my back, burning me through my dress.

Getting the door open, I leap forward, away from him and rush to get behind my desk, though I don't sit in my chair.

One of his men follow him into my office. The other two remain outside in the hall.

"Shut the door." I'm impressed with how even my voice is when every word coming out of my mouth feels like glass shards shredding my vocal cords.

Giving me a look like he's trying to figure something out, Atlas waves toward his man. A moment later, the door shuts with a soft bang. I don't see it. My eyes are fixed on Atlas, and I watch him like he's a cobra and I'm a mongoose.

I am not helpless, but neither am I foolish enough to dismiss the danger my deceitful *ex*-lover represents.

Not anymore. I should have listened to my instincts about the danger I sensed lurking around him. How did I trust him enough to tie me up and blindfold me?

We didn't just do it once either. Atlas showed up one night with a pair of leather cuffs and I let him use them on me. More than once. I have to swallow back bile again at the memories.

He's mafia. A criminal.

He probably has more blood on his hands than Tino ever did. Because Atlas doesn't run nightclubs. Unless I'm badly mistaken...again...he runs the protection racket. Like my dad.

These men are his collections team. They're here to set up *protection* for my club, for a price. Like my dad and his men did to so many businesses in Detroit, probably still do.

"Are you okay, *ilios mou?*"

"Don't call me that." My fingernails dig painfully into my palms with my hands fisted at my sides to stop them shaking. "I am not your sun."

Though I sure illuminated plenty for him. I see everything so clearly now and the need to vomit increases.

He's been using me to get information on the area, the businesses, and my club. And all the time I took his interest as proof of his affection and respect, when in fact, it is the opposite.

"Introduce me to your friend," I say.

With a frown Atlas, steps toward me, like he's going to come around the desk.

Panic screeches through me and I lift one hand in a stopping gesture. "Don't come near me."

Atlas has the effrontery to look wounded. If I had a knife right now, I'd really wound him. I'd cut out his black heart and let it die right next to mine.

The other man rubs his hand over his closely cropped black hair, a gold pinkie ring glinting under the light. "Maybe I should go out in the hall with Bobby and Michael."

But I shake my head vehemently. "No. You stay."

The man looks toward Atlas who gives a miniscule jerk of his head. Watching me like I'm a dangerous animal set to attack, the man takes a seat in the chair furthest from my desk.

"Introduce me." I jerk my head toward the other man in case Atlas is in any doubt who I'm referring to.

"This is Theo, Lucia, a fr—"

"I know what he is," I interrupt. "I just didn't know *who* he is."

The fizzy bubbles of happiness have all popped, leaving my insides hollow and my heart aching.

He does not smile, and I wonder if any of his smiles were ever real. His gaze is unemotional, and I know the warmth I thought I saw there was fake.

There's no point in dragging this out. "How much?" I ask.

His glacial blue eyes flare with surprise, like he's shocked I realize why he's here. He doesn't have to give me the spiel. I've heard it all before from the other side.

"What's the name of your outfit?" I ask, pain and fury a dangerous cocktail inside of me.

I want to hit him.

But you don't strike out at made men unless you're prepared for them to strike back, twice as hard.

When he looks at me with confusion, I say, "Syndicate. Mafia. Whatever the fuck you want to call it. I've never heard of the Rokos Mafia."

I would have remembered if I had, and it would have saved me a lot of pain. And even more disappointment. If only he had told me what he wanted from the start. Why did he have to use me like he did?

My body aches like I have the flu.

"You said fuck."

So? "You say it all the time."

"You don't." His eyes narrow.

"How does that matter?" I demand. "Just tell me what outfit you are with."

I hate being in the dark about anything now that I know what a big secret he has been keeping.

"We are part of the *Ádis Adelfótita*." Atlas still looks like he can't believe I know what he is.

I look at him blankly.

"The Hades Brotherhood."

"A Greek syndicate?" It sure sounds Greek. He and his family are Greek.

"You're not the..." I trail off. "Does the Greek mafia have dons? Or godfathers?"

"My uncle is the Godfather of the Night. He rules the entire West Coast territory."

"Even territory you haven't claimed yet. There were no syndicates here when I moved to Portland."

"How do you know?" That is from his cohort, Theo.

I ignore the question. "Your uncle told you to set up protection territory here?"

"No. Zeus is my *anax*."

So, like a don, while the Godfather of the Night is like the Godfather in the Cosa Nostra. However, the Italian Godfather is the head of the entire Cosa Nostra in the United States and his uncle's territory is the West Coast.

Does it go up into Canada?

My brain is focusing on the minutia so I don't have to deal with the hurricane of pain from Atlas's betrayal.

"How much?" I ask.

"How much what?" he asks back.

His tone is neutral, but the words taunt me. He knows exactly what I'm talking about.

"Don't. Just don't." I inhale as deeply as I can, letting the air out of my lungs slowly in an attempt to keep my roiling emotions under control. "You know I'm talking about protection money. You've got two soldiers standing outside my office to make sure I don't leave before agreeing to your terms."

"Bobby and Michael are out there to make sure we aren't interrupted."

Is that supposed to imply a difference? If it is, I don't see it.

"How do you know why I'm here?" he asks and then glares. "Did the bratva approach you while I was gone?"

Theo makes a scoffing noise. "Nobody got past us, boss."

I refuse to answer. I will *not* explain how I know what is going on. Atlas deserves no explanations from me.

When neither Atlas nor I break the silence between us, Theo says, "10% of net profits."

Theo must be Atlas's second. He wouldn't speak for his boss otherwise. He's got the made man stoic mask down pat, his brown features showing not a single emotion.

The protection tithe could be worse. It could be 10% of my gross takings. Regardless, the money they want is too much for me. Not that they'll see it that way, or care if they do.

"We'll be checking your books to make sure you aren't shorting us. You don't want to steal from us." Theo's voice is laced with threat.

Atlas turns a glare on him before looking back at me. Something roils in the blue depths of his eyes, but he says nothing to deny the other man's words.

Something inside me shatters. My ability to trust. My hope for the future. My soul. I don't let it show though. I am stronger than that.

I am stronger than either of these men will ever know.

"When is the money due?" My tone is cool and my voice doesn't break. I'm proud of that.

Theo sighs dramatically when Atlas remains silent. "One of us will come by every Sunday to collect."

I nod my understanding. It's Wednesday. That means my first official payment is in four days. I'll have to make sure I have enough cash on hand to cover it.

"We'll take our first payment now," Theo says and I wonder why Atlas came at all if his soldier is doing all the talking. For intimidation factor? "Whatever cash is in your till."

I want to refuse, but I can't. I want to say I'll have to pay again in four days, can't they wait? But they don't care if it is fair, or even reasonable. Only that I pay what they consider I owe them for doing business in the territory they now claim.

I know this game. My dad tried to keep work away from his family, but I was a curious child. I overheard plenty when no one realized I was around.

This is how it works. If I were a restaurant, they would be asking less because profit margins are lower. If I owned a casino, it would be more.

They don't care that I was going to buy a house. They don't care that I have to pay for Lenny's care. Nothing matters but me paying them what they require for their protection now that they have moved into the city.

If the payment meant closing the club, they'd adjust it, or force me to take them on as partners and change the way I do business to bring the profit margins up.

Sure, they'll keep the other gangs and syndicates at bay, as long as they're the strongest. Not that anyone else was demanding money or making problems for me.

"Were those Russian guys the other night bratva?" Is Atlas moving in on Nuovi Inizi before they get a chance to?

Atlas knew them. Said the one guy's name was Ivan. He took them outside and I haven't seen the three men back in my club since.

Theo gives Atlas another long-suffering look and then answers my question. "Yes."

"Were they here to claim my club for their syndicate?" I direct my question to Atlas and dare him with my eyes to let Theo answer for him again.

"Yes," Atlas says with a frown.

He doesn't want to talk about this. Too bad. It's my life going into the crapper because organized crime finally decided Portland has potential.

"You'll be better off under our protection, believe me," Theo says, his dark brown gaze earnest.

"You think? Considering the fact that you are here demanding payment for that protection, you'll understand me not taking your word for it."

"They would have taken more than money from you," Atlas says through gritted teeth.

"So, you say."

"It is the truth."

I let him see how much I believe his so-called truth. "Why should I believe you about anything?"

"I have no reason to lie to you." Atlas's handsome lying face demands I believe him.

Not going to happen. "Your credibility is suspect."

"You need our protection," Atlas grounds out. "Larry, Curly and Mo coming here shows how much."

The bratva soldiers are named after the Three Stooges? No way. It must be some kind of code Atlas uses. "You told me that one guy's name was Ivan."

Something terrifying flashes in Atlas's gaze when I say the name Ivan.

"They won't be a problem for you anymore," he promises. "Neither will Ivan."

I guess I'm supposed to take his word for that too. So not happening.

"You lied to me and used me for my own good? Is that it?" I ask, sarcasm dripping from every word. "Newsflash, it's never for my own good."

The surprise on his face is almost amusing. Only nothing is funny right now. My lover is my extortionist. Nothing funny about that.

"Okay, lets go rob my till." I wave toward the door.

I'm not moving until they do. I don't want to be within two feet of either Atlas, or his man, Theo.

"We aren't robbing you," Atlas says forcefully.

"To-may-to, to-mah-to." He can call it protection money, but he's stealing from me. And we both know it. "Let's get this over with."

Chapter 32

LUCIA

Atlas and I stare at each other, both waiting for the other to move. Too bad for him, I'm stubborn as hell. I'll wait here until the club closes if I have to, but I'm not walking past him.

"Come on, boss. Let's get the money and go. It sounds like Miz Esposito has things to do."

Like scream into my pillow until my throat's raw.

Atlas puts his hand out to me and a laugh that has zero humor in it barks out of my throat. I shake my head and lift the hand he wants to hold with my middle finger extended.

Theo makes a sound between choking and laughing.

I stare daggers at him. "I'm glad someone finds this situation amusing."

His face slides into a stoic mask and he turns to open the door.

Atlas doesn't move. "Why are you acting like this? You'll get more out of this relationship than you'll lose by it."

"Says you."

"I did my calculations."

"Based on?" I know what he had to have done.

Get on my computer and look over my books. Will he admit it?

"Your password for your computer is the name of the club." He sounds put out by that.

Like he supposedly was when he realized I used the same number combination on the lock downstairs as my apartment? That's going to change tonight. Both of them.

I will set two *different* unlock codes he has no way of guessing.

"Are you trying to imply it's my fault you betrayed my trust and got onto my computer and looked at the club's ledgers?" I'm glad there's nothing about Lenny's care home on the computer.

Would it change anything if Atlas knew about Lenny? I shake my head. It wouldn't. So, I'm glad I never told him all my secrets. I gave enough of myself to this man.

"I didn't say that."

"You implied it."

"Your protection tithe won't take too much out of Nuovi Inizi," he says, clearly unwilling to argue. "We'll launder money through the club and within a year, you'll make it back in the fees we pay you. With our contacts, you'll save money on stock too. If you make a few changes, your profit margin will increase too."

"You've got it all worked out, don't you?" I mock angrily.

He calmly nods. "Yes."

"Only you didn't take into account that I don't want to launder money for criminals, much less use your contacts to get a better price on alcohol."

"Boss, we've got two more stops to make tonight," one of the men from the hall says.

Frustration bleeds through Atlas's blank mask. "We'll talk later."

Later never.

Finally, he leaves my office and I follow, locking the door behind me. I skirt around the wall of men in my hallway and head to the bar. Walking to the end, I signal to Willow to release the lock on the access.

Betrayal eats at my gut like acid. I go behind the bar and straight to the till. Feeling so brittle, one wrong word or touch will shatter me into tiny glass fragments of my former self, I avoid the bartenders and barbacks.

If there wasn't Lenny to look after, I could tell them all to go to hell. Especially Atlas. The lying, conniving snake.

But it's not just me. If I want to keep Lenny where he is, I can't afford what Atlas and his crew will do to bring me in line. A fire in the bathroom. Armed burglary. Things that will not destroy the club but will cost me enough and cause enough fear to make me amenable.

For my own sake, they could burn my club to the ground. I wouldn't pay a single cent to a man who used his body and my weakness for it to manipulate me into giving him access to my knowledge and my business.

Because it isn't just for my sake, I open the till and pull out most of the large bills. Leaving a few along with the smaller ones so my bartenders can continue to make change, I shut the drawer. I stack the money together and exit from behind the bar.

Ignoring his lackeys, I walk over to stand directly in front of Atlas, getting closer than I have since he walked into my club.

Glaring up at him, I offer the stack of money. I make no effort to hide what is happening. If the Hades Brotherhood wanted to keep this little extortion agreement a secret, Atlas and his crew should have waited to approach me until the club was closed.

For a breathless second, he makes no move to take the money. A curl of hope unfurls inside me. Maybe he's going to say this was all a mistake. He'll tell Theo and the others my club is off limits.

Atlas's hand comes up and those ridiculous pipe dreams turn to ash.

"You told me there was a dark ember left of your soul, but there is no smoldering fire there, just darkness," I hiss.

He flinches, but the hurt I see in his expression must a trick of the club lights. A heart as dark as his can't feel pain.

I smack the cash onto his palm and immediately yank my hand away. Or try to.

His fingers curl around mine too fast for me to pull back and his other hand comes down over the top of mine. "It's going to be okay, *ílios mou*. You'll see. I will protect you."

I flinch when he calls me his sun. Of course, he didn't listen to me when I told him not to. I can't stand having my hand trapped between his. Because even knowing what I know, the electric connection between us is not gone.

My fury only seems to heighten it.

"Those words might mean something if you weren't stealing my money to pay for that protection." I jerk at my hand.

He lets me go.

I look at Theo. "Nuovi Inizi is closed on Sunday. Come by at three and knock on the back door if you want your payment."

Theo looks at Atlas, but his boss is looking at me and I am *not* looking at him.

"I'll be here at three," Theo says finally and Atlas doesn't correct him.

The last tendril of hope dead inside me, I turn and walk away from them without another word.

But I don't get more than two steps before a hand lands on my shoulder. I know who it is. I jerk away from his touch and spin to face him, letting him see my fury, but not my pain.

His blue gaze traps mine. "This is business. The money..." He shakes his head. "It's not personal."

Is that supposed to make it better somehow? "Don't worry, I am under no delusion that we have anything personal between us. I'll have the money for your men on Sunday."

If Atlas comes instead, I'm not sure I'll be able to refrain from stabbing him in the eye.

His mouth works like he wants to say something but there is nothing he can say that I want to hear.

"Your guy said you have other businesses to shake down tonight." It's a not-so-thinly veiled hint for him to leave.

"Theo can take lead on the last two stops."

Oh, heck, no. Atlas is not sticking around here. "Then I guess you had better head home to check in with Zeus."

What did he call him? The *anax*? Men in his position are usually older. Men my dad's age, or older. Like almost always. There *is* a thirty-five-year-old don for one of the Five Families in New York, but that's unusual.

Zeus is around that same age, but I'm not asking Atlas how old his brother is.

I'm never asking him anything personal again.

"Are we done here?" I ask, finished with subtle hints.

He hands the money over to Theo, who tucks it away inside his jacket.

"Our business is done." He reaches for me.

I jump back, nearly tripping in my need to get away from him, to stop him from touching me. "No."

"I am not your enemy."

Is he really that clueless? "You are the very definition of my enemy."

"No, I am not. I will always protect you. Your club will thrive. I promise."

"You mean like you protected me tonight?"

His mouth snaps shut, something like guilt flashing in his gaze. It's too late for guilt. He already gutted me. Remorse won't change how he used me. How he played me.

This situation is bringing back memories I buried five years ago.

Tino's face superimposes over Atlas's and I see my husband the first time he wanted to have sex after I lost our baby. Tino's touch made my skin crawl and I nearly vomited. He'd slept in the guest room that night and for a month after.

Eventually, we'd reconnected. I'm not sure I ever forgave him.

I may never forgive Atlas for using me the way he did. If only I reacted to his touch like I had Tino's at first. Instead, even now, my body yearns to lean toward Atlas, to put my hand back in his.

Not happening. My ovaries are done calling the shots.

"I suppose it's too much to hope that you'll never come back, but if you do, it won't be for me. Because I never want you to talk to me again, much less touch me." Without drawing him a map to the exit, I can't be any clearer.

His jaw like granite, Atlas glowers. "We are not over."

We so are, but I'm done arguing.

"Leave." I will not plead with this man. I will not let him see me cry, but the tears are burning the back of my eyes and making my throat tight. "Now."

He clenches his jaw and nods. "I'll be back later."

No words left, not even *no*, I shake my head.

Finally, he turns to leave.

My shoulders drop from around my ears as I take the first full breath since I realized what he was doing here. I will him not to turn around again and for once, I get my wish. Atlas and his crew make their way across the club, other patrons unconsciously stepping aside to clear a path for the predators among them.

How had I not seen the hunter lurking in Atlas's eyes? I cringe at my own willful ignorance, because it was willful. Atlas is apex predator through and through. I made myself see something else when I looked at him. Something human and trustworthy when he's neither.

"You alright, Lucia?" Willow is standing right next to me.

How long has she been there?

"I saw you give your boyfriend the money from the till. Not trying to tell you how to live your life, but lending money to him like that could come back to bite you in the ass."

I spin to face my bar manager, unable to believe she thinks I would do something so foolish.

Opening my mouth to tell her just why I gave Atlas the money, I snap it shut again. Atlas and his mafia aren't the only ones who would be in trouble if the cops get involved. And I don't know if I can trust Willow not to call them.

She doesn't understand that if they're collecting protection tithes, the Hades Brotherhood have local law enforcement and probably at least one prosecutor and judge in their pockets. The only one that will be damaged in the long term is me.

I've been very careful to keep my name and image out of databases. Everyone back in Detroit thinks I'm dead and I'm going to keep it that way.

Doing my best not to let my inner devastation show, I shrug at Willow. "Sometimes, you just have to do what you have to do."

"Love makes fools of us all." Willow squeezes my shoulder in commiseration.

Love, or our ovaries.

Chapter 33

ATLAS

I throw Theo up against the side of the SUV. "Why the fuck did you tell her we'd be checking her books?"

"It's what we always say. So, they don't try to cheat us." Theo cocks his head, like he's trying to figure me out.

I'm not the one doing stupid shit.

"Yeah, boss. You always say it's better to threaten them before they get greedy than to have to punish them after," Bobby adds. "Better for business relations."

"Lucia isn't just a business owner. She's my woman." And they know it.

Michael looks at me levelly. "I'm pretty sure she doesn't see it that way."

"If she's yours, why are we shaking down her club?" Theo challenges me.

I shove him away. "Because our *anax* ordered it. I shouldn't have to explain that to you."

This whole damn night is a shitshow of epic proportions. I wanted to do Nuovi Inizi last, take my time explaining the protection tithe and how it will benefit Lucia and her nightclub in the long run.

I knew she'd be upset to learn how much I've been hiding from her. I planned to explain all of it. Well, almost all.

She doesn't need to know about Dimios.

She didn't give me the chance to explain anything. Somehow, she knew why we were there before I said a word.

How? Has she paid protection money before? To one of the gangs? She never said anything about it.

Like you never said anything about being part of a syndicate?

I ignore the voice in my brain to scowl at my crew.

"She's pissed, but she knows she's mine." I dare any of them to argue.

None of them do.

"Let's get the last two businesses set up." Neither owner had been around when we showed up earlier.

We're hitting both at closing.

"Theo, you and Bobby take the Vietnamese restaurant. Michael, You're with me."

Staying at the club would have meant waiting until tomorrow to hit the second location. We never go in alone.

Lucia needs time to cool off.

And I need time to figure out what to say to make her understand. Nothing I have said so far did the trick. She doesn't want to do business with criminals.

Gamó.

I'll change her mind. Once I figure out how.

I'd ask my brothers for advice, but Zeus is the one who insisted I collect the fucking protection tithe to begin with and Orion is better at poking the bear than soothing it.

I don't even consider asking my cousins. Both are man whores like Zeus used to be before he turned into The Monk. And the way they looked at me in my brother's office, neither understands how important Lucia is to me.

I'll figure it out. Lucia is mine and she's staying that way even if I have to cuff her to my bed.

My cock twitches at the image in my head. She would look beautiful spread eagle on my bed, her hands and ankles tied down.

LUCIA

Refusing to give in to the emotional pain that wants to take me to my knees, I force myself to work the floor like I do every night. I talk to patrons, check in with the DJ, help my bartenders keep the inventory stocked behind the bar and answer questions Willow can't.

All-in-all a typical Wednesday night. Only tonight, when it's time to clear the club, I am militant about getting everyone out. I instruct the DJ to make the announcement and then switch to soft jazz. We turn the lights up and I tell the staff and bouncers to hurry people on their way.

I want time to lick my wounds in solitude, if not peace. There is no peace trying to wrap my head around Atlas's betrayal.

Whether they can sense the mood under my calm exterior, or they're ready to go home themselves, everyone does their closing tasks quickly and without the usual joking around. When they are all gone, I lock the door, arm the alarm and then think better of it.

I turn it back off and reset the code to one Atlas doesn't know. I use the date of Tino's death. Another day when my world exploded around me.

Once the alarm is set, I head upstairs. On the way, I change the code on the door to the stairs to the date I married Tino. A reminder of the past and how naïve it is to trust a man with my heart. When I reach my apartment, I reset the unlock code to Lenny's birthday. This time it's a reminder of what is at stake and what my priorities have to be.

Walking inside the small space, I immediately regret coming upstairs. I should have slept in my office, even if I had to do it on the floor. Atlas's leather jacket is lying over the arm of the small sofa. His duffel is against the wall. The scent of his cologne lingers in the air but it's the memories that hurt the most.

The two hand-cast ceramic mugs he bought from the Farmer's Market because I like them sit on the counter waiting for our morning coffee. The table where we share breakfast and other things. My disloyal brain throws up an image of me riding him while he sits on one of the chairs at that small table.

It plays like a high-definition video in my head and it's not a fantasy, but a memory.

Another memory assaults me. Us making lo—having sex against the wall. Over the back of the couch. Him eating me out on that same couch.

I try to shake the memories loose, but the images won't stop and my heart shreds in my chest knowing I will never experience that level of sexual pleasure again. Worse, I will never know that kind of emotional intimacy.

It was fake for him, but it wasn't for me.

It wasn't for me.

My legs fold under me. There's no one here to see me give into weakness. I let myself fall to my knees, the tears I've been holding back for the last three hours coursing down my cheek.

I worked my butt off so I could buy that little house, that tiny part of the world that was just for me. But giving the Hades Brotherhood 10% of my net profit doesn't leave enough money to cover Lenny's care and the mortgage on the house. Not without strapping me so tight there will be no money left for emergencies.

And there are always emergencies.

For five years, I have worked long hours with no days off in order to get to a place where not only can the club profits support Lenny's care going forward, but I can take on a home mortgage and live a life away from the club.

Where I can take a day off here and there. But the only way the club stays solvent is to reinvest, to expand, to follow the plan. That plan only works with enough money.

I can't do that. It's not fair to the people who work for me not to be prepared for the unexpected. They're all relying on me to keep Nuovi Inizi going.

There is no point in putting it off. My realtor won't be in her office this late and I'm hoping she won't answer her work phone either. I want to leave a message. Maybe it will hurt less to say what needs saying that way.

I call and relief flows through me when the call goes to voicemail.

"I am sorry, Elaine." So, so sorry. As much for myself as the work she's wasted on this listing. "I have to cancel the purchase on the house. I know that means I give up my earnest money, but I have no choice."

I will lose thousands between the earnest money and everything I have paid for the appraisal, inspections and repairs for the underwriters to approve the loan.

It does not matter.

Nothing matters now.

ATLAS

It takes me longer to get back to Nuovi Inizi than it should. Zeus calls and wants a report on tonight's activities. In person.

There's no putting it off until tomorrow. My brother is in a piss poor mood and pulls the *anax* card. Our meeting takes twice as long as it should because Zeus refuses to take anything at face value.

By the time I'm back in my X7 and headed toward Lucia's place, my mood is as black as my brother's.

After the second attempt to turn off the building alarm, I realize Lucia changed it on me. *Gamó.*

Bringing up the disarming app on my phone, I get it started in time. I hope. When the beeping stops and the little light on the panel turns green, I let out my breath.

After the fiasco with the alarm, I am not surprised to find out she changed the unlock code on the door to the stairway. There's no app for this. It requires my analog skills at lock-picking. Same with the door to her apartment.

I would be happy my woman finally listened to me about changing the codes on her doors, except she did it to keep me out. Opening the door, a strange sound reaches me.

Like there's a wounded animal in Lucia's apartment.

The wounded animal is her. *Ilios mou.*

Halfway between the door and her bedroom, Lucia kneels on the floor, curled into herself. Her shoulders shake with her sobs.

What do I do? I am the executioner. Comfort is not in my skillset. But I cannot leave her like this.

First, I have to get her off the floor.

Squatting, I get one arm under her legs and wrap the other around her back. Lucia goes rigid before I can stand and throws herself away from me, landing on her side on the floor.

The skirt of her wrap dress rides up, showing every inch of her gorgeous legs. But the horror in her beautiful brown eyes throws a bucket of ice water on my libido.

"What are you doing here?" she demands, her voice hoarse.

How long has she been crying?

"I came to see you."

"I changed the locks." She scoots back and uses the wall behind her to help her stand, but she keeps her wary gaze on me.

What does she think I'm going to do?

"Criminal." I point to myself. "Remember?"

Her eyes darken with accusation. "How could I forget? You need to leave."

"We need to talk."

"There's nothing left to say. You used sex to get access to me and my club. You used me." Her voice breaks on the last word and more tears track down her face. She swipes at her cheeks angrily. "Just go."

"I'm not leaving you like this." Does she think I'm a monster? Sure I don't want the answer to that question, I don't ask it.

"Why not? You got what you wanted."

"I want you."

"Stop," she shouts hoarsely. "Just stop. No more lies."

"I never lied to you." I left a lot of shit out, but I never flat out lied to her.

"Like hell you didn't."

That voice of hers is killing me. I go into her kitchen, fill the electric kettle and turn it on.

"What are you doing?"

"Making you tea with honey and lemon." It's what my mother gave us when our throats were sore when me and my brothers were kids.

She yanks on my arm, trying to pull me from her kitchen. "I don't need tea. I need you to leave. Now."

I'm a big guy and even though she's furious, she's not shifting my body unless I let her. And I am not leaving her like this. I'm not leaving her at all.

"You are mine to take care of," I explain.

"I am not yours. Not one bit of me." She throws my arm from her and goes to the door. Opening it, she glares at me. "Get out."

"No." I turn back and open the cupboard she keeps her tea in.

I don't want to give her caffeine this late at night, so I grab the ginger tea. After I put a teabag in the mug she keeps out for her morning coffee, I turn back to face her.

Her eyes are puffy and red from crying, but her glare is sharper than my favorite knife.

Shrugging out of my suit jacket, I watch her eyes narrow. I hang it on the back of the chair I sit in when we eat together at her little bistro table. My shoes go next.

"What are you doing? Stop undressing. You aren't staying."

"We already had this discussion," I remind her.

"You refusing to leave is not a discussion."

"You insisting I leave when you are upset isn't one either."

She barks out a laugh. "Are you trying to convince me that you care you hurt me? You knew!"

"I knew what?"

"That you were using me. You knew you planned to steal from me. You knew it would hurt me."

"The protection tithe isn't stealing. We aren't the bratva. There are benefits to being under the protection of the *Ádis Adelfótita*."

"Like being poorer?" she snarks.

I hold onto my temper. She's not herself and she doesn't understand, but she will.

"Like being protected from the bratva."

"What difference does it make if it's you extorting money from my club, or them?"

"They didn't just want money." I hate having to tell her this. It will upset her, but she has to see the truth. She needs me.

"Oh, really? What else did they want? A better place to hang out than that dive bar with the terrible service?"

"They wanted to use your club as a hunting ground for women." I spell it out for her. "They wanted to give you to Ivan to use and abuse before he killed you making a snuff film."

"Ivan, the man in the club that night?"

"No. That man's name is actually Dimitri and his is the son of the *pakhan*. Ivan is his father's second in command. The *vtoroy* has a type and you're it."

Remembering what Mo and Curly said, fury boils through me. Lucia is my woman. I will protect her, and I will kill anyone who is a danger to her. Including Ivan.

"I'm supposed to take your word for that?"

"Why would I lie?"

"Oh, I don't know...because it's what you're good at."

"Damn it, Lucia, I didn't lie to you."

"You said you and your brothers were in Portland to start a business."

"We are."

"You're here to claim territory for the Hades Brotherhood."

"That too."

"You told me you're a facilitator for your family."

"I am." And an assassin. Sometimes the killing is part of the facilitating.

"You told me you weren't using me to get information," she says like she won the argument.

She didn't. "I promised you I was not trying to use your knowledge to compete with or destroy your club. I didn't."

"I guess our definition of destruction isn't the same."

The kettle boils and clicks off. I pour the water in her mug and let it steep while I find the honey and a lemon. "Destruction is destruction, Lucia. Yes, the tithe will lower your profit margin at first, but we'll get you making more money than you ever were before."

"Don't talk like we're a team. We aren't."

Pain pierces my chest. I've been having these aches all night. I need to up my cardio, or something.

I slice a wedge out of the lemon and put the remainder in the little lemon keeper she has in her fruit drawer. Lucia has weird but cool shit in her kitchen. Probably because she likes to cook. She's going to love having a full kitchen again when she moves into the house she's buying.

I need to find out when she takes ownership so I can get an alarm system installed and other security measures implemented on the property. I've already looked into the houses on either side. Neither are for sale, but I don't anticipate a problem convincing the owners to change that.

If I'm going to be living there, I want my men living in the other properties.

Chapter 34

LUCIA

My hand gripping the edge of the door so hard, it hurts, I watch Atlas make me tea.

Once he has the honey and lemon juice stirred in, he adds a single piece of ice to cool it down enough for me to drink without burning the roof of my mouth.

Too bad he isn't as worried about causing me emotional pain as physical.

What is wrong with him? He's acting like we're still together when we both know he was using me and my weakness for him to get information for his damn Hades Brotherhood.

Atlas lifts the mug. "Do you want to drink this in here, or in the bedroom?"

I want him to leave, but that doesn't look like it's happening until I drink the damn tea.

Leaving the door open, I approach the table. "In here."

I'm not inviting him into my bedroom. My body is still reacting to his like he's safety, affection, sex and everything good in between, but my mind? My mind knows the truth.

Atlas is my enemy, not my boyfriend. No matter what my ovaries try to tell me. Those little buggers are in a timeout for leading me into this situation in the first place.

He puts the mug down on the table and then takes a step back, like he knows I won't sit down until he does.

He's right.

As I shuffle over to the dinette chair, I'm in a nightmare, every move at the treacle slowness of a dream. Only, unlike in my dreams, I feel every ache in my body and heart.

Atlas watches me, his gaze never once wavering as I sit down.

Taking a sip of the tea, I realize how thirsty I am. All that crying. It's not like me. I didn't lose it like that even after I learned of Tino's death. How can I be more devastated by Atlas's betrayal than the death of my husband?

The tea helps the soreness in my throat with the side benefit of settling my stomach that has been roiling since Atlas and his crew showed up in the club earlier. No way am I going to admit that to my ex-lover though.

Atlas leans against the counter, his arms crossed over his chest, and watches me drink.

I pretend not to notice.

"When do you take possession of the house?" His deep baritone shatters the silence.

Glaring at him, I consider which is better: not to answer at all, or to tell him it's none of his business.

I go with, "None of your business."

There won't be any signing of the papers.

"I know you are angry right now."

"Do you? How astute of you."

He frowns. "We can work this out."

Yeah, not happening. "There is nothing to work out."

"I am not giving up on us."

"There is no us!" The shout strains my already abused vocal cords. "There is no us," I repeat in a near whisper before gulping down hot tea.

It soothes my throat and I concentrate on that sensation, not the ache in my heart.

"There is an us. You are mine. I am yours."

"No." I shake my head.

There is so much more I want to say, but not enough to croak it out through a strained throat. He and the Hades Brotherhood cost me my home.

Laundering money for the Greek mafia is a losing proposition for me. The risks outweigh the rewards big time. If the authorities come knocking, it won't be Atlas and his brothers that end up under indictment. It will be me, their associate with no actual affiliation to their syndicate.

I know how these things work and I am expendable to them. To Atlas. Especially to Atlas. How can I be anything else when he was willing to use me like he did?

Regardless of how I feel about it, the Hades Brotherhood isn't going to let me refuse to launder their money through Nuovi Inizi. That's not how it works. They targeted my club and I'm still in their crosshairs.

Looking around my small studio apartment, at the life I thought I was changing, an idea begins to form. A solution to my dilemma that has the side benefit of being something that will infuriate Atlas.

I'm pretty sure his brothers aren't going to be any happier. That only makes my plan more attractive to me.

I am a woman with agency and tomorrow they will all learn how powerful that agency is. Under the layers of pain and betrayal, an ember of joyful vindication burns deep in my chest.

Finishing my tea, I stand and leave the mug on the table. "I'm going to bed. Let yourself out like you let yourself in."

Not waiting for Atlas to answer, I head to my bedroom and shut the door once I am inside. There is no lock, but I'm too tired to care.

I want to sleep, but I force myself to take a shower. I need to wash the work and stress sweat off my body. Not wanting to go to bed with wet hair, I pile my long tresses into a messy bun on top of my head before I step into the shower.

After drying off, for the first time in weeks, I pull on my comfy pajama pants and a sleep tank top.

Climbing into my bed, I'm so tired, I ache with it. But my mind still spins with everything that happened today and what it means for my life.

The sound of movement filters in from the outer room and I realize Atlas hasn't left. It's then I notice that the pillow he usually sleeps with is missing from the bed and so is the throw that I keep at the end of it.

The stubborn, arrogant man plans to spend the night. On the couch. That is at least a foot too short for him.

A grim smile tilts my lips.

Neither of us is going to get much sleep tonight.

~ ~ ~

I wake feeling safe, warm and surprisingly rested. The source of the heat against my back does not register at first, but then the weight circling my waist does.

Swearing, I throw myself out of the bed.

Atlas came into my room last night. After tossing and turning between stress dreams, I didn't even wake up. My body has not gotten the memo that he cannot be trusted.

He sits up instantly, looking around for a threat. "What?"

"What are you doing in my bed?"

"Your sofa is too short." He finger combs his tousled hair away from his face. "For you."

"I was the one trying to sleep on it." He looks and sounds disgruntled. "I finally came in here a couple of hours ago."

It's the first time I've seen him wake up grumpy like this. Poor baby really didn't sleep well on the too short sofa. Sucks to be him.

"You have a bed the right size for you at your house. You should have gone there, not come into my bedroom uninvited."

"I didn't touch you."

"You sound proud of that fact."

"I am."

I roll my eyes. "Your arm was over my waist when I woke up and your hard dick was pressing against my back."

He doesn't look even a little bit sorry, just disappointed he wasn't awake to experience our unintentional cuddling. Unintentional on my part anyway. The jury is still out on his intentions.

Yawning, he stretches his arms above his head. The covers slide down his muscled body and I swallow the moisture that pools in my mouth from the desire to taste his salty skin. Wetness pools somewhere else too, but we aren't talking about that.

Tilting his head first to one side, and then the other, he rolls his shoulders. "If you really want me to pay penance, make me sleep on that damn sofa a few more nights."

The idea is intriguing. I cannot lie. But I'm not giving him a chance to make up for his betrayal. If things go the way I want today, I won't care if he sleeps on my sofa a hundred nights. I won't be here to see it.

I rub between my heavy breasts, trying to assuage the instant pain that thought causes in my chest.

It's a good plan, damn it.

"I'm going to take a shower. Want to join me?" Atlas climbs out of the bed completely nude.

I spin away, but not before I get a full monty view of his morning erection. A condition I have happily taken full advantage of in the past weeks.

Not today. *Not ever again*, I remind myself.

Self harrumphs, not in the least impressed.

Pulling open the drawer with my leggings, I pull a pair of fleece lined black ones out. "I showered last night."

"Don't make breakfast. We'll go out," he says as he disappears into the bathroom.

Can he really be that oblivious, or is he pretending everything is fine because he's hoping eventually it will be? And why does he care? He got what he wanted.

Or at least he thinks he did.

The Greek mafia is about to find out that messing with a Cosa Nostra princess is dangerous.

Dressing quickly, I quietly sneak out of my bedroom when the shower goes on. The keys to Atlas's SUV are in the dish he's taken to using for them. Predictability can be a good thing.

I grab the keys, careful not to clink them together in my hand and head downstairs.

In my office, I take the sheaf of papers sitting in the printer tray and tuck them into my tote style purse. I created the sales contract on my phone last night during one of my restless bouts and then sent it to the printer.

Before Atlas joined me and I slept like a baby. Not something I want to analyze right now.

Opening the safe, certainty settles over me as I spy the manila envelope with legal documents I had drawn up, signed, witnessed and notarized as soon as I took possession of Nuovi Inizi's building. I stuff the large envelope in my purse too.

I grab one last item from the safe. My gun and the belt holster that will be hidden by my oversized sweater. After checking and loading it, I put the belt on and slide the twenty-two into the holster.

Thirty seconds later, I'm climbing into the driver's seat of Atlas's luxury SUV.

Chapter 35

LUCIA

When I arrive at the Rokos mansion, I roll down the window to talk to the guard. I recognize him as one of the men that was here guarding the gate when I came with Atlas the first time.

I dismissed all that mafia security as typical for billionaires, which it probably is. But I willfully blinded myself to the other similarities between the Greek mafia and the Cosa Nostra because I didn't *want* to see syndicate when I looked at the Rokos lifestyle.

It wasn't just willful ignorance though. It has been decades since the Russo mafia moved into new territory. The idea that a mafia family would expand like Atlas and his brothers are doing for the Hades Brotherhood never occurred to me.

"I'm here to see Zeus," I tell the guard.

His eyes widen fractionally and then almost comically when he realizes whose vehicle I'm driving. He's surprised I'm here with Atlas's SUV and no Atlas. But the days of that fake relationship are over.

"Does Zeus know you are coming?"

"No. Why don't you tell him I'm here?"

The guard talks into the comm unit on his shoulder, listens to the response and then the gate opens. Driving through, I hear the gate close behind me and apprehension slithers down my spine.

I am not trapped. I am here of my own volition. This is the plan.

Parking in the same spot Atlas used, I turn off the SUV and hop out of the truck. Gina opens the door before I have a chance to ring the bell.

She smiles like she doesn't work for a bunch of extortionists. "Good morning, Ms. Esposito. Atlas isn't here, but if he said he would meet you, I'm sure he'll arrive shortly."

"I'm here to see Zeus." I don't return her smile and my tone isn't friendly.

I can't help feeling like Gina is part of the conspiracy to keep me in the dark until Atlas extracted all the useful information from me that he could.

And didn't I make it easy?

"Zeus is in his office," Gina says, her smile slipping in the face of my lack of friendliness.

"Would you mind showing me where that is? It wasn't part of the tour Atlas gave me."

"Of course, but let's hang up your coat before we go."

I shake my head. "I'd rather keep it with me."

When I'm ready to leave, I don't want to have to wait for my coat to be fetched before I can do so.

Gina cocks her head. "If you're sure?"

"I am."

Without any further questions, the housekeeper turns and leads me down a hall to the right of the foyer. Zeus's office is at the end.

Gina knocks lightly on the door.

"Come in," Zeus calls from inside the room.

Opening the door, Gina steps back so I can get past her into the room. "Ms. Esposito is here to see you."

"Thank you, Gina."

The other woman leaves without another word.

I don't look at Zeus right away, but give myself a moment to gather my thoughts while I take in the room. It's more traditional than I expected considering how modern the décor is in Atlas's suite.

Large windows look out into the well-manicured backyard. The wall behind me is lined with heavy wood bookcases filled with books, and the large executive desk Zeus is sitting behind looks like a well-preserved piece of the past. Two leather wingback chairs face the desk and there are two more chair pairings against the walls on either side of the desk.

Plenty of space for him to have meetings with his brothers and cousins.

Nothing about the office screams crime boss of a syndicate, but the weight of the atmosphere makes it easy to believe Zeus does both legitimate and back alley business here.

"Atlas isn't here." Zeus lets the words drop between us like a challenge.

I raise my brows in response as I pull off my coat. "I am aware. I left him showering in my apartment."

"He will be worried when he realizes you aren't there."

"You want me to believe you haven't texted him already?" I tsk and shake my head. "All evidence to the contrary, I'm not that gullible."

"Atlas didn't—"

"Stop, right there," I interrupt, my hand up. "I am not here to talk about Atlas."

Zeus's eyes narrow. "Then why are you here?"

"I have a business proposition for you."

If he is surprised, he does not show it.

He waves to one of the wingback chairs facing him, inviting me to take a seat.

I do so, crossing one legging clad leg over the other, placing my coat over my lap. Sliding my hand under the hem of my red tunic style sweater, I unlatch the holster and draw the gun out under the guise of adjusting the coat.

Unwilling to allow him to see my grief or even a glimmer of my nervousness, I refuse to fidget. My hold on the twenty-two secure but loose, I force my breathing to remain steady.

Taking out my phone, I show him that I'm turning it off. "I'm going to assume you have a jammer going so nothing we say here can be listened to or recorded regardless."

He inclines his head but does not answer.

"Good, I'm not interested in wading through euphemisms."

His lips tilt the tiniest bit at the corners, like he finds that amusing.

Then he's back to the serious, stoic eldest brother, crime boss persona. "If you are here to try to talk me out of the protection money—"

"That's not why I'm here."

"Whatever your reason for being here, this conversation should include Atlas."

"Why? He's not my boss. Is he yours?" I taunt.

Zeus frowns, but he doesn't take the bait. "He is your boyfriend and that makes private conversations between us problematic."

"One, he is most emphatically *not* my boyfriend." I tick off on my finger. "Two, I'm here to offer you a business proposition, not the other kind."

Heartbreaking sex with one brother in the Rokos family is my limit.

"Glad to hear it."

Lifting my purse, I pull out the sheaf of papers I grabbed from the printer in my office before I left the club.

I lay them on his desk. "I'm here to offer you a very good deal to buy my club."

Glacial blue eyes flare with surprise that is gone quickly. I have shocked him. Good. Last night I got a shock too. We will both survive.

"Here are the terms." I push the sales contract toward him.

I am not a lawyer, but with my experience doing the paperwork for the mafia clubs as well as a template I bought off the internet for the sale of a viable business, I am confident I have my bases covered.

It offers him the club and the building it is in at a steep discount from fair market value, with one stipulation. He agrees to take over payment for Lenny's care.

Zeus reads through the document, taking his time. When he is finished, he looks up at me and there is a question in his eyes. "Who is Lenny Smith?"

He says the name Smith in a way that makes me know he is aware it's an alias. I don't care. There's nothing linking Lenny Smith to Leonardo Revello.

"Someone I am responsible for. Once I sell the club, I will not be able to continue to pay for his care long term."

"Why should I take on this burden?"

"Think of it as protection money." I make no effort to hide the irony in my tone.

"Explain," he says, no amusement in his voice.

Oh, it's not so fun having the shoe on the other foot, is it, Mr. *Anax*?

"First, if Atlas told me the truth, then the Hades Brotherhood plans to start at least two nightclubs in the Portland Metro. Nuovi Inizi is already established and owning it gives your organization a material foothold in the territory you are claiming."

"That may be true, but I don't need to take on this unending debt, to get it."

"Yes, you do." I let the implication of my words settle between us. This is a nonnegotiable clause to the purchase agreement.

"You called it *protection*?"

I'm not ready to go there yet. "I am aware that clubs are perfect for money laundering, and Atlas has implied that is part of your plans for Nuovi Inizi. However, as long as I own the club, it won't be."

His brows draw together in an expression so like his brother's it hurts to see it. "Why not? Your cut would more than cover the expense of Lenny Smith's care."

He's not wrong there. Although I don't know what mafia business they have already established, I do know how organized crime works. If they don't already need it, the Hades Brotherhood will soon require a place to clean millions of dollars in dirty money each year.

"At first, maybe. But eventually I end up dead or in prison as a fall guy for your syndicate. And then who looks out for Lenny's interests?"

"That's a dark prediction for the future."

"But not an unrealistic one."

"You think Atlas would allow you to be made a fall guy?"

"I have absolutely no doubt." After last night, there is no place for trust between me and Atlas Rokos, or his brothers.

They were all part of the conspiracy to use my knowledge and set me up to pay protection.

Zeus doesn't like my answer. Tough. Sometimes the truth hurts.

"If I turn down this offer?" he asks.

"Then you can negotiate with the new owner for both protection money and the money laundering scheme." Although it's unlikely the Brotherhood would willingly let me sell the club to someone else.

Zeus's expression changes subtly and an atmosphere of menace fills the room. "You seem to be under the misapprehension that you can sell the club without our approval."

I was expecting this, but that doesn't stop the frisson of fear that goes down my spine. The Rokos men can be intimidating when they want to be. But I was raised around scary men and trained from childhood to hide my fear.

"I know there are things you can do to stop me selling, to cut me out entirely," I acknowledge.

"Then why are you here?" The *wasting my time* goes unsaid, but I hear it anyway.

I don't let his anger faze me. "Because, unlike the owners of the other businesses around me, I have a failsafe."

The sense of menace goes up a notch.

I'm not worried. Zeus is the *anax*. Like a don, he will not make any rash decisions. He will hear me out, if only to make sure he has all the information he needs before he deals with me. And my backup plan *is* full proof. Once he hears it, he isn't going to kill me.

The tense silence stretches between us.

"What kind of failsafe?" he finally asks.

I start with an explanation. "In another lifetime, I was a Cosa Nostra princess. I had a don."

A husband. And a family. I had people and many of those people are still alive.

Once Lenny is protected and his future is secure, can I go back to my family? Do I want to?

"That explains how you knew what was going on last night without having it explained to you." Zeus measures me with his gaze. "Does Atlas know?"

"Do I really need to answer that? If he knew, so would you."

An odd expression goes over his face, like maybe he's not sure of that.

Wishful thinking. I won't indulge in it. Atlas lied to me. He used me, I remind myself.

He's 100% on his brother's side in all this.

"What is your supposed failsafe?" Zeus asks again.

There's no *supposed* about it. If his mafia was better established in their territory, they might risk it, but not when they're getting up and running.

"In the event of my death or disappearance, the original of these documents will be delivered to the don." I put the manila envelope onto his desk.

The originals are with a firm of lawyers with whom I have weekly check in protocols. If I don't contact them via our agreed upon method, they send those documents to Don De Luca in New York, a man powerful enough to guarantee Lenny's safety.

"What are these documents?" There is no mistaking the anger in his tone now.

"You can read them for yourself." I indicate the envelope he will have to reach across his giant desk to get.

I won't be moving it closer to him. I'm not in an accommodating mood.

"You tell me."

I roll my eyes at his domineering order, but in the interest of expediency, I comply. "First, there is a letter explaining Lenny's whereabouts and copies of his diagnosis and treatment plan from an eminent neurologist."

Zeus makes a continue motion with his hand.

"Second, there is a witnessed and notarized will that leaves the club and any of my assets in a trust for Lenny, administered by the don."

His eyes narrow at this, but Zeus doesn't say anything.

"Last, there is an enduring power of attorney for all business matters related to the club and Lenny. Whether I disappear or die, the don will have legal claim to Nuovi Inizi."

"You believe we would disappear you?" Zeus asks, clearly offended.

Too bad. So sad. Send your brother in to seduce a woman into spilling information and making herself vulnerable to racketeering, and that woman doesn't trust your intentions toward her. *Shocking*.

Zeus shakes his head when I don't bother to answer what should be a rhetorical question. "My brother may want to chain you to his bed, but he won't do it."

Memories of the times Atlas handcuffed me to my own bed assail me. He made good use of the handcuffs he bought after he tied my hands to feed me up in his suite.

It takes all my mafia princess training to stifle my reaction to the x-rated movies playing in my head.

"If the don receives these documents, it will give him and the Cosa Nostra a foothold in your territory. Something your Hades Brotherhood cannot want right now."

Zeus doesn't look worried. Even a little.

I narrow my eyes and study him. No, not even a tiny tell to show my failsafe concerns him. Why?

"You want me to believe you put all of this in place since last night?" he asks derisively answering my *why*.

"You think I'm bluffing." I nod toward the envelope. "Look inside. You'll see I'm not."

"I don't need to. You're a smart woman. I'm sure you did your best to make the documents appear legally binding, but there was no time between last night and this morning to get them witnessed and notarized, much less set up to be delivered to a Cosa Nostra don."

My hand tightens on the gun and I have to force myself to relax my hold. No matter how pleasurable I might find shooting Zeus, I'm not going to.

Unless I have no other choice. "You're making a dangerous assumption, especially if you believe I'm as smart as you say."

"What's that?"

"That I wouldn't have set this up already."

He shakes his head. "It's a good bluff, but I don't believe you. This little drama isn't necessary regardless."

Little drama, my ass.

Shooting him is becoming more *necessary* by the second. Not for my safety, but to assuage my anger.

How angry would Atlas be if I shot his brother? I don't have to kill Zeus. Maybe maim him a little. And why the hell do I care what Atlas will think?

Zeus stands up and comes around the desk. He leans against it right in front of me. "Your club is in my territory and you will do what I say. If that means laundering money, you will do it. If that means running whores out of your back room, you will do that too."

The kid gloves are off and instead of being afraid, a sense of power courses through me. It's the familiarity of it all. He has no idea who he is dealing with. I might have been a naïve fool with his brother, but I'm no pushover. I was raised in the mafia, not the suburbs.

"No. I won't." I stand up and glare at him, moving until I'm out of striking range before revealing the gun in my hand.

Chapter 36

LUCIA

"What the fuck, Lucia? Put that away." Atlas's voice comes from the door.

I swiftly move back so I can cover both brothers. "I won't ask how you got here so fast. I don't care. Go stand by your brother."

"You're not going to shoot me." Instead of doing as I said, Atlas stands *between* me and Zeus.

Taking a two-handed grip to steady the gun, I aim at his torso. "I won't shoot to kill, but I will incapacitate you." I drop the aim a few inches. "Or maybe I will castrate you, stop you from seducing other women into being your dupe."

"I think she means it brother," Zeus says. "Right now, she's less likely to shoot me."

I nod. "Your *anax* is right, but that doesn't mean I won't shoot him. Now move further away from me, Atlas. If you rush me, I will pull the trigger and I won't be aiming to wound."

"You are hot with a gun in your hand, *eromenis mou*."

"I am not your lover. Not anymore."

"We'll have to agree to disagree." He sounds so darn complacent. I'm tempted to shoot him just because.

Atlas must see something in my face because he moves closer to Zeus. He still keeps his body between me and his brother though.

Protecting the boss. It's what a good soldier does.

"Do not make the mistake of thinking that because I fell for your brother's lies, that I am weak," I say to Zeus, ignoring Atlas acting like a wall between us. "I put the failsafe in place the week after I opened the club so that Lenny would always be taken care of."

"What do you think, brother? Is she bluffing?" Zeus asks Atlas.

I expect Atlas to ask what about, but he doesn't. He looks at me, trying to read my sincerity. My honesty about this is not something I need to hide. I let him see my sincerity as well as my hurt anger at his betrayal.

Atlas winces. "It seems like she's telling the truth, but she could be lying. She hid her affiliation with the Cosa Nostra from me."

My brows furrow. "How..."

Atlas points to an earbud in his left ear. "Zeus had me listening to the conversation from the time you came into his office."

"You told me you had a jammer," I accuse Zeus.

It never occurred to me he wouldn't use it. His business is the one that cannot come under scrutiny, not mine.

"I do have one. It isn't turned on." Zeus returns to his chair. "Please lower your gun, Lucia. You do not need it."

"I'm supposed to believe you?"

"Atlas would kill me if I so much as threatened you, much less touched you."

I make a production of showing my patent disbelief at that statement.

Atlas growls. "Damn it, Lucia, you know you're safe with me."

That's the trouble. I *do* feel safe with him. I have since the first moment. But that safety is an illusion.

"Sit down over there." I indicate one of the chairs across the office from me. "Then I will lower my gun."

Atlas doesn't hesitate to do what I say. He sits back and even puts his right ankle up on his left knee, the picture of relaxation. His stance is a stark contrast to his brother's looming presence only minutes ago.

The reason I felt the need to draw my gun in the first place.

"We have a lot to talk about." Atlas looks at me as if he expects me to agree.

I roll my eyes. Heart-to-hearts with the conniving jerk are so not happening.

"You're part of a mafia family?" Atlas asks, his tone casual.

Oh, so, not a heart-to-heart, but more intel gathering. There's no point in trying to hide what I've already admitted to.

I lower the gun to my side, but I don't put it back in its holster. "I was."

"Why didn't you tell me?"

"Are you being real right now?" Are we even on the same planet? "Why would I have?"

"We are lovers. Lovers tell each other stuff like that."

"You mean like you told me that you're part of a Greek mafia and came to my club to scope it out for your protection racket?" I scoff.

"That was different."

"Yes, it was," I breathe, furious all over again. "Me not telling you about my ties to the Cosa Nostra had no malice behind it. My past cannot hurt you, but you can't say the same about your present. Can you?"

"I didn't mean to hurt you."

Undeserving of an answer, I ignore that supremely ridiculous statement.

Shifting my gaze to Zeus, I say, "If you kill me or even kidnap me, that document packet will be delivered to the don."

"You set up a check-in protocol?" Zeus's tone sounds admiring.

I don't answer the question. The less they know about that, the less able they are to dismantle my precautions.

"Like your syndicate, the Cosa Nostra is always hungry for new territory and the don won't hesitate to claim it." It's a bald-faced lie.

The Cosa Nostra hasn't had a major expansion of territory for over a decade, and it has been even longer in Detroit.

"If you wanted the mafia taking care of Lenny Smith, you wouldn't be working so hard to do it yourself," Zeus says, clearly thinking he's got a point.

But I'm not letting him believe that. "The don might not keep him in his facility because of the entrenched belief that *it stays in the family*, whether that's good for family or not. But Lenny won't be homeless, and they won't hurt him on purpose."

That doesn't mean my brother-in-law won't be hurt, or that he might not hurt someone else if he is put back into a family household. Yes, that makes me feel guilty, but not enough to stay here and run Nuovi Inizi for the Hades Brotherhood. Whether they buy it, or not, my club won't be mine anymore.

I am emphatically not running sex workers out of my club. Atlas tried to tell me he saved Nuovi Inizi from being taken over by the bratva and used as a hunting ground for women. As if.

"Who is your don?" Zeus asks me.

"Does it matter? Do you want any of the Cosa Nostra to have a foothold in your territory?"

"Why give up a club you've worked so hard to build? You would make so much more money stay—"

"As a glorified manager? No, thanks," I interrupt him to say. "I'm not running your money laundering or a brothel out of the unused space upstairs. Like I said, I have no intention of ending up dead or in prison."

"No one is going to kill you," Atlas barks out, sitting up, all pretense of insouciance gone. "And you will never be a fall guy for the Hades Brotherhood. As my wife, you will be protected."

"Did we get married and I don't know about it?" I ask with sarcasm. "Only, I think I would remember."

"We aren't married yet."

"Or ever," I tell him flatly and turn back to his brother. "Do we have a deal?"

"Would you stay and run the club if you have my word you would be protected, married to Atlas, or not?" Zeus asks.

I don't know why he would offer that, or if I could trust him if he did. But it does not matter because it's not going to happen.

I am done.

"You can either agree to buy the club. Now." I'm not giving him time to come up with a plan to counteract my failsafe. "Or not. If the only way out is for me to give it to the don, then that's what I'll do."

The mafia will take care of Lenny. I did my best to protect my brother-in-law, but I can't do that from behind the bars of a prison cell. One way, or another, Lenny's safety will end up reliant on someone else.

Better I control who that someone is and what they do for him, than leave it to chance. Lenny deserves better. I deserve better.

"I'm not afraid of Russo," Zeus says mildly, like he's letting me down gently and letting me know he's aware I'm from Detroit. "He couldn't hold onto his territory; he's not taking mine."

Zeus knows I learned about running a nightclub from my husband and that my husband is dead. If he knows about the clubs in Detroit being taken over by the Irish and the Russians, he can easily work out that my husband is one of the men that died trying to protect them.

Which means he also knows who my husband was and probably who Lenny is too.

"Who said anything about Don Russo? Five years ago my husband and his father were murdered during the mob-bratva takeover," I say like I'm telling him something new. "Russo couldn't protect my husband. Why would I trust him to protect my brother-in-law?"

"You named a different don as his guardian and owner of the club," Atlas says, drawing my attention back to him.

Though, if I'm honest with myself, and I try to be, he's been the center of my focus since arriving. No matter who I'm looking at.

"Only the most powerful don in the Five Families. Everyone knows that when Don Caruso dies, Severu De Luca will be named Godfather of the Cosa Nostra."

Finally, Zeus looks like he's listening and not just humoring my *little drama*.

"If I buy the club, I want three months for you to train the new manager," Zeus says in a complete about face.

"No. I'm not staying."

"You want me to keep Leonardo Revello in that fancy facility? You will train your replacement." There's no give in Zeus's tone.

Worse is the look of utter implacability in his eyes.

Nausea roils in my stomach and I have to breathe shallowly so I don't throw up. Stress. It's a thing.

But the last thing I want is to stay in Portland where Atlas is. I shake my head.

"You are a very intelligent woman, Lucia Cattaneo."

Making a sound like a wolf facing its enemy, Atlas surges to his feet and takes a step toward me when Zeus uses my married name. "Do not call her that. She is not a Revello."

"Calm down, Atlas. The man is dead."

But Atlas doesn't look calm. He's one misspoken word from tearing Zeus's office apart.

What is wrong with him? He knows I am a widow. And I am not *his*, no matter what he says.

"As I was saying, Lucia, with a brain like yours, you know that negotiation requires compromise. I'm not taking over your club without you offering a smooth transition."

"You talk like you have room to negotiate in this."

"Do not make the mistake of believing I don't."

His words send unpleasant shivers along my nerve endings. I listen to my instincts telling me to take the win, even if it comes with a transition period. I'll just have to avoid Atlas.

Like I did last night. Right. That's going to work *really well*.

"Thirty days," I counter.

Zeus's eyes narrow. "Two months."

"Thirty days," I reiterate firmly.

"What happens if I don't pay for your brother-in-law's care? The facility isn't going to hire a lawyer and sue me for it," he points out.

So arrogant, like his brother. But he's right.

"So much for your word," I say sarcastically.

Probably not smart to taunt the criminal boss, but I'm so done with this conversation, and I have run out of fucks to give.

"You can't hold Lenny's care over my head. The facility knows to contact the don if his fees aren't paid." They'll contact me first, but Zeus doesn't need to know that. If I can't pay the fee, then they will contact Don De Luca.

"So?" Zeus asks, clearly unperturbed by the possible outcome.

I shake my head. "Funny. Despite how he used me, I would have said that Atlas had a sense of honor and you by association."

Zeus doesn't look so uncaring now. He's scowling at me. So is Atlas.

I ignore the wounded pride of both men. "If the facility has to contact the don, you will be in default on the terms of our contract. Don De Luca will have legal recourse to take the club from you."

Whether he exercises that recourse is anyone's guess, but one thing I know for sure. Severu De Luca puts *la famiglia* first and he won't allow Lenny to end up on the street.

"You're determined to make sure this guy is taken care of." Zeus's gaze fills with speculation.

Atlas is vibrating with emotion, though I'm not sure if it is anger, or something else. "Why is he so important to you?"

"He's my family."

"But he cost you your baby."

I wince, wishing I hadn't told Atlas about what happened. The dirty betrayer doesn't deserve my confidences, but I didn't know that at the time.

"It wasn't Lenny's fault."

My heart came to terms with his role in my baby's death a long time ago too. I tried to forgive Tino and Agustino Sr. too. But I couldn't forget the price my baby and I paid for my husband and father-in-law's choices.

"It sure as hell wasn't yours."

"Of course not." Though a small part of me has always shouldered some of the blame.

Watching over Leo, as he was known at the time, was my job. I was supposed to anticipate his needs and protect him from himself. I failed and failed my baby too.

Atlas moves like he's going to touch me and I jerk away. The gun knocks against my thigh and I almost drop it. I tighten my grip now slick with sweat. If I'm not careful I'm going to shoot someone accidentally.

The Rokos brothers might deserve it, but I could shoot my own foot if my grip slips again. Sighing, I unchamber the round and put the gun back in its holster.

"I made a promise to Tino, and I care about my brother-in-law," I say, my emotions even more raw than they were earlier. "I've done my best to take care of Lenny, but I'm not giving up my own freedom for his."

If that makes me a bad person, so be it.

Nausea rises again and I force myself to hide it. Okay, I'm not as insouciant about this as I want to appear.

I need to be out of this office. Away from Atlas and anyone named Rokos.

Chapter 37

ATLAS

Lucia pales, sweat beading on her upper lip.

I want to kill the demons putting that look on her face, but they are me and my brother.

"Thirty days," I say. She's not going anywhere, and a month is plenty of time to convince her of that fact. "And we will adhere to the terms of the contract."

Zeus looks at me and I let him see that I'm willing to go to war over this. He jerks his head in agreement. "Thirty days and we will pay for Lenny's care."

Lucia lets out a soft breath, but then she glares at my brother. "You won't be using Nuovi Inizi for any money laundering until I'm gone."

He opens his mouth to say something. Probably to argue. He is my *anax* and my brother, but Zeus is a few seconds away from my fist in his face.

Showing more courage when confronted by my brother than most made men, *ilios mou* puts up her hand and shakes her head. "No. I am not giving you the leverage to force me to stay and manage the club for the Hades Brotherhood."

She has a very Machiavellian mind. I like it, but I don't like her lack of trust. Even if I earned it.

"We aren't trying to trap you into staying to manage the nightclub." I don't care if she manages the club, unless that's what she wants and then I'll make sure she gets Nuovi Inizi back.

It's not her business that will work as leverage to keep her here. Though her move to force my brother to buy Nuovi Inizi and take on the financial responsibility for Leonardo's care is hella unexpected.

Lucia will stay because my plan to hold onto her has a lot more heft than my brother's. If I'm right, her pale face and obvious nausea have more to do with pregnancy than the stress of confronting my brother.

Ilios mou is not afraid of anyone.

"I told you," I remind her. "I will protect you."

"Like last night?" she scoffs.

"Yes. Getting Nuovi Inizi under the protection of *Ádis Adelfótita* is necessary to keep you and your employees safe." I'll protect her with my life, but that's not enough.

She doesn't want Nuovi Inizi used in human trafficking, even if she doesn't own it anymore. She cares too much about her employees and even the patrons. I can't protect the club and her alone.

I need my brotherhood behind me.

"Right." Her voice drips sarcasm. "Until they get arrested during a raid by the vice squad."

I remember what Zeus said to her about running sex workers out of the club. He was pissed, but he still shouldn't have said it.

"We'll use the strip clubs to run the a la carte sex trade," I inform Lucia with a glare for my brother. "We only use our nightclubs for the escorts to meet their client dates, for *their* safety. Transactions are never done on site."

"That's not what Zeus said."

"He was angry and pushing your buttons." My brother doesn't like his authority questioned.

He barely tolerates it from me and Orion.

If I know my brother, Zeus is angry that Lucia rejected me last night too. Even if he told me it served me right for letting my softer emotions rule me.

I told him to fuck off. There's nothing soft about what I feel for Lucia. It's hard, raw and primal.

Zeus does not need to protect me from Lucia or myself. Because I am not letting her go. She is *ilios mou* and I am not going back to the darkness.

"This time he threatened me. What happens the next time your *anax* gets angry? Maybe he drops me in it. I'm not going to let that happen." She sounds tired.

She was restless last night until I joined her on the bed. She thinks I came in there for my own sake, because of the short sofa, but I heard every toss and turn of her body.

Worried she would not get enough rest, I laid down beside her and took her into my arms. She settled immediately after that. No matter what she thinks she knows about me, her body trusts mine.

Her mind needs to get on board though. Or things are going to get awkward with the whole pregnant with my baby thing.

"That will never happen," I tell her. "You need to trust me to take care of you."

She stares at me with rampant disbelief. "You cannot be serious. I *do not* trust you and that isn't going to change now. Because now I know what you are and if there's one thing I've learned about made men, it's that I can't trust you to put my safety first."

"Who taught you that?" Zeus asks, mining for information.

That's my *anax*. Always looking for an angle to use. What he hasn't figured out yet is that I'm not going to let him use any angles against my woman.

"Besides your brother?" Lucia asks drily.

"Yes, besides Atlas."

I'm glad my brother doesn't try to argue that Lucia can trust me. She's stubborn and him getting in her face about it will only solidify her position.

She shrugs, her hand pressing against her stomach. "Who didn't?"

The nausea is getting worse. I need to look up remedies. Or take her to the doctor today. Yes, that's a better idea. They'll make time for her at the clinic.

The head of the clinic started his practice in L.A. with a loan from *Ádis Adelfótita*. He knows the importance of not crossing my family.

"That's not an answer," my brother pushes.

I stand up. "Leave it." I cross the room to Lucia. I can't watch her struggle with discomfort from a distance.

"I don't owe you an answer," she says to Zeus, pretending not to notice my approach.

That's better than her running away.

"Tell me anyway."

"That's something else you Rokos men have in common. You're all pushy." She looks at me now, censure glinting in her brown gaze.

"Then you know you might as well answer my question."

Lucia sighs. "My father, my brother, my husband, my father-in-law, and the list goes on. Every single mafia man who had a chance to put me first didn't." Her eyes catch mine and don't let go. "Including you."

She's wrong. Like last night, she's dismissing the truth of how precarious Nuovi Inizi's position is with at least two syndicates vying for territory.

The Russians are gone. For now. We can't trust the *pakhan* not to try again with bigger numbers though.

"Do we have a deal?" Lucia asks Zeus, her voice strained.

"Yes." My brother reads through the papers in front of him and then sends a text. "I will pay for Leonardo Revello's care in the facility, but his don deserves to know where he is."

"What?" Lucia jumps up and shoves past me to glower down at my brother across his desk. "You can't tell him. Even if Don Russo is willing to leave my brother-in-law where he is, Lenny's grandfather won't be. Agustino Sr. was a stickler for keeping it in the family, but his father is militant about it. He's totally old school."

"Lenny has a living grandfather and you've had sole responsibility for his care since his father's death?" I put my hand on the small of Lucia's back.

For a single breath, she leans back into me. But then she pulls away and shrugs. "I told you, his grandfather is old school. I wouldn't put it past him to kill Lenny to protect the Cosa Nostra."

"His own grandson?" Zeus asks.

"Considering your grandfather's protection of the Hades Brotherhood is the reason your brother's back is riddled with scars, I'm surprised you have to ask that question." Lucia casts a concerned glance at me.

Like she's worried I'll be hurt by her bringing up the scars. I'm not surprised she figured out the real circumstances behind my captivity, now that she knows the truth of my background.

I didn't lie to her about it. I left some stuff out. Like she did. My mafia princess.

She'll be the perfect wife for me.

After a perfunctory knock, Orion and Zephyr come into the office. Helios is right behind them.

"Let me look at the contract." Orion puts his hand out. "If everything is in order, Atlas and Zephyr will sign as witnesses and I will notarize it."

Zeus jerks his head in the affirmative.

"I need some air." Lucia spins around and pushes my cousins out of her way to get to the door.

I follow.

When we get in the hall, she looks to the right and to the left, her face creased with worry. "Which way?"

The bathroom. She's turned around and doesn't remember where it is.

I grab her hand and lead her to the guest bathroom closest to Zeus's office.

Lucia barely makes it to the toilet before throwing up bile. There is no food in her stomach because she skipped breakfast. I assumed she would have grabbed something before sneaking out of the apartment.

"You can't miss meals right now," I tell her.

She rinses her mouth with water from the sink. "Breakfast was not a priority for me this morning."

"No, stealing my SUV and meeting with my brother was."

"I *borrowed* it."

"Without my consent." She needs her own car though.

And as soon as I'm not sure she'll use it to run, I'll have Orion sign the title to his G-Wagon over to her.

"Do you see a chop shop anywhere around here? I didn't steal it, but I can drop it in one of the gang neighborhoods for you if you want."

My gut clenches. "You aren't going anywhere like that alone."

"You're not the boss of me." Wilted and leaning against the sink now, her words lack oomph.

"You keep thinking that."

"I know that. Even if I was still your girlfriend, you wouldn't be my boss."

"You're not my girlfriend," I agree.

She winces, hurt flashing in her dark eyes, but she ducks her head, hiding her reaction.

"You are *ilios mou*. You bring light into the darkness of my soul. You are the flame that burns there." I sound fucking poetic.

Her head snaps up, her eyes wide and disbelieving in her pale face. Then she shakes her head. "We are not talking about this right now."

Fine by me. No matter what Zeus thinks, I am not suddenly wrapped up in soft emotions. Acknowledging them once is enough.

"You didn't tell me you are mafia," she accuses.

I shrug. "Neither did you."

"I'm not mafia. Not anymore."

"You used the threat of Cosa Nostra involvement to get what you wanted from my brother. You're still mafia."

"You have an answer for everything." She doesn't sound impressed by that. "But what is your answer to my broken heart? That it shouldn't be broken."

I snap my mouth closed on my instinctual response, because that is exactly what I think. Her heart shouldn't be broken. If she trusted me, it wouldn't be, but according to her, it is.

That damn pain twinges in my chest again.

"I want to go home." She looks at me like she's waiting for something.

For me to move? That's not happening. She's fragile. She needs my support. "Don't you think we should go to the doctor first?"

"I don't need a doctor for stress nausea," she dismisses.

"Are you sure that's all it is? You've been tired the last few days and getting up later." I looked up symptoms of early pregnancy so I could watch for them.

She rolls her eyes. "I own a nightclub. Running it can be exhausting."

"Are your breasts tender? I noticed your areolas are darker. Your reaction last night and today could indicate hormonal based emotions."

She looks at me with confusion and then dawning understanding.

"You think I'm pregnant? And that's why I'm so angry with you?" Her voice rises steadily until she's almost shouting. "I'm angry with you because you betrayed me, not because I'm hormonal."

"Okay, but you have other symptoms of pregnancy. You haven't had a period since we met." That was eight weeks ago.

It only took a few seconds to realize I wanted her and one night to know I am never letting her go. And if I'm right, less than two months to get her pregnant.

The primal part of me is very satisfied by that fact.

"I...you...you got me pregnant on purpose!" She's definitely shouting now.

"Yes." I have made no attempt to hide my desire to do so.

"But I thought..." She shakes her head then the confusion disappears completely as her temper ignites. "You knew. You knew everything I didn't know and you got me pregnant anyway. You bastard!"

Every curvy inch of her vibrates with outrage.

Pain explodes in my cheek and my head snaps back. I don't expect the punch, or the shove that comes after so she can scoot around me to get out of the bathroom.

My feisty woman has a helluva right hook. I'll wear her bruise tomorrow.

I follow her down the hall whistling.

Chapter 38

LUCIA

The infuriating man is whistling again. I know this song. "Love is a Battle-field." Aargh!

I spin around and point at him. "Knock that off."

His brows raised, his handsome face the picture of innocence, or as innocent as a made man can look, he stops whistling. Shaking my head, I turn back around and stomp toward the front door.

The whistling starts again. It takes me until I reach the door to recognize it. "My Girl" by the Temptations.

Are you kidding me?

Refusing to give him the satisfaction of a reaction, I storm outside, only to stop at the SUV when I realize my purse and coat are still in Zeus's office. Along with the contract. That I still have to sign.

Porca miseria.

I don't know how long I stand there staring at the truck, telling myself I need to suck it up and go back inside to get my stuff.

Then the sound of whistling reaches me. He's still on "My Girl" like a smart speaker set on repeat.

"Why didn't you get in the truck? It's too cold to be standing around outside without your coat." Atlas sounds so dang reasonable.

Not at all angry I punched him in the face.

My hand still hurts. I shake it and wince. I'm not so lucky.

He notices. Of course, he does.

"You need to ice that. Here, put on your coat and then get into the truck. I'll be back with an icepack." He hands me my coat.

Avoiding looking at him, I take it and slide into the sleeves, grateful for the near instant warmth. It's a bright autumn day, but the air is chilly enough to cause gooseflesh to erupt on my arms.

I put my hand out for my purse. "My bag."

"Here." He holds it out toward me, dangling it from his big hand by the straps.

I reach for it, but he doesn't let go.

My gaze snaps to his face. There is a red mark on his cheek that will bruise, but no swelling that I can see.

His blue eyes are waiting to snag mine with that invisible tractor beam I swear he has. "There you are."

I roll my eyes. "Here I am. Now, will you let me have my purse?"

He releases it and because I'm tugging on it, I stumble back a step.

Reaching out, he grabs my arm. "Steady."

"Don't touch me." I jerk away.

His big body swells with affront, but he lets me go. "Orion said you can sign the contract tomorrow."

Of course, Atlas asked when he grabbed my coat and purse. He thinks of everything, except telling me who he really is before I find out on the other side of a demand for protection money.

"I'd rather get it over with." Though the idea of returning to Zeus's office makes my stomach roll again.

Atlas shakes his head. "He'll bring the contract by the club tomorrow. We have somewhere else to be."

What is he talking about? Then it hits me. The doctor. He wants to take me in for a pregnancy test. "I can just pee on a stick."

He hums, but I can't tell if he's agreeing or humoring me. "I'll get that icepack."

"Get one for your face too." I don't tell him it's not necessary. My hand is throbbing.

Besides, there's a chance I can get out of here the same way I arrived. Alone and driving his truck.

He heads back into the house without responding, probably thinking he's too tough to ice his cheek.

Men!

Disappointment makes my tender stomach clench, but there's no surprise as I dig through my bag only to determine that his keys are missing.

I could call a rideshare, but Atlas will be back by the time it gets here and will just follow me. If he doesn't scare the poor driver off all together.

He's intimidating on his best days. The Greek mafia enforcer pretty much only smiles around me. It took me a while to realize that, but the more I see him interacting with others, the more obvious it is.

Today is not one of his calmest. The driver might not recognize the leashed violence in Atlas's strong body, but her atavistic instincts will.

Why are so many rideshare drivers women? It feels like it wouldn't be the safest job to have.

And why is my mind taking me on a tangent?

Because I don't want to think about what Atlas pointed out in the guest bathroom.

I might be pregnant.

Even thinking the words fills me with stress, making the nausea rise again. Swallowing back the urge to retch, I force my mind away from an image of my stomach swollen with child.

Like I was before. Only this time, giving birth.

Dio mio. I have to stop thinking about this.

In desperation, I move toward the SUV. Feeling more than a little contrary, I consider climbing into the driver's seat. But I am also feeling lightheaded after my bout with nausea in the bathroom. Another symptom of pregnancy?

Don't go there. But my brain refuses to go anywhere else.

My hands come up of their own volition to press against my breasts. Tiny jolts of pain twinge through my generous mounds. Sighing, I pull my hands away.

They *are* tender and my bras are fitting more snugly lately.

What if I am pregnant?

Everything has changed since my epiphany that I still want to be a mother. I no longer own Nuovi Inizi, or won't once I sign the papers tomorrow, but neither am I responsible for the cost of Lenny's care.

With the sale of the club, I'll have enough to start over somewhere else. If I live frugally, I can even stay at home with the baby until he, or she, starts school. I will have to get a job at some point though.

None of this takes into account that I *didn't* visit a sperm bank to get pregnant. If I am pregnant, I have no doubt about who the baby's father is.

Atlas.

Moving away and starting over again would mean taking the baby away from him. Can I do that in good conscience?

No matter how angry I am at him, there is no world in which I allow my baby to pay for my mistakes.

What kind of father would he be? Protective. That's for sure. Bossy. That's a given. Will he expect our child to become part of the Hades Brotherhood, or marry to be advantageous to it?

One thing is certain. I may no longer be part of the Cosa Nostra, but I was raised in it. And I'm not afraid to raise my child adjacent to Atlas's life as part of the Hades Brotherhood.

I am terrified of what that means for me though. Will Atlas insist on marriage, if only for name's sake? He's Greek mafia. In the Cosa Nostra, certain old fashioned ideas are still rife.

If my father knew about my pregnancy, he would give Atlas two choices. Death, or marriage.

A shiver skates up my spine at the thought of my father and Atlas meeting. How would that even work? Do I call my parents and say, "Ta da, I'm alive?"

Questions whirl through my brain, one after the other until I start feeling sick again.

"Why aren't you inside the SUV?" Atlas demands.

I look at him. "What if I'm pregnant?"

"Then we will be parents."

"You make it sound so easy." For him, it probably is. "You don't have to carry new life inside your body." And worry if that life will survive to be born.

"I will worry about both you and the baby until you give birth safely. But I will protect you both with my life."

That's like a pathological thing with him. He sees protection money as an investment, not merely a payment for doing business in a syndicate's territory. My dad has the same attitude.

Papà says the mafia provides a service for what they charge their *clients*. Does Atlas see Nuovi Inizi as a client, or a cash cow?

It doesn't matter now, I remind myself. Because as of tomorrow, I will no longer own it. And in thirty days my obligation to the club and its employees will be finished.

Grief should be weighing me down, a sense of loss. I worked hard to build Nuovi Inizi into what it is, pouring my time and energy into it to the extent I have no life outside of the club. Not before Atlas anyway.

But I never wanted to own a nightclub. If I could have made enough money to support both Lenny and me with an office job and no crowds, I would have.

Opening Nuovi Inizi was the only legitimate way I knew to make enough money to pay for Lenny's care. Now, Zeus is responsible for the financial part of it.

Unexpected relief washes over me.

I'm not alone taking care of Lenny anymore, even if my partners in it are unwilling.

I will continue to personally oversee my brother-in-law's wellbeing. He's my family even if he doesn't want to see me. For whatever reason, being around me riles Lenny up. The doctors think it is wrapped up in the loss of my baby.

At first, that hurt. I gave up the life I knew and the rest of my family to protect Lenny. To keep my promise to my dead husband, if in a way he would not have expected or necessarily condoned.

But starting Nuovi Inizi took all my time and energy and being discouraged from visiting Lenny took away the guilt of not being able to.

I get weekly emails with pictures and a daily diary of his care and commentary about his mood, health and interactions. I make unscheduled visits to the facility every few months to check on my brother-in-law in person. Though he does not see me.

"Zeus won't tell Don Russo about Lenny, will he?" I ask Atlas as he opens the passenger door for me.

"No."

"You're sure?" My hand hurts and I don't want to use it. So, I sit back and allow Atlas to buckle my seatbelt like he usually does, doing my best not to breathe in his masculine scent. "He sounded like he might."

"He won't."

"Why are you so certain?" I expect Atlas to say because he knows his brother, or something.

What he actually says is, "I told Zeus I would kill him if he upset you by doing that."

The serious and determined note in Atlas's voice tells me he's not joking.

"You threatened to kill your brother?" My voice rings with disbelief I cannot hide.

"Yes." Atlas settles a cloth wrapped icepack on the back of my hand. "Hold this in place."

I do as he instructs because it's what is best for my hand, not because he tells me to. "But you wouldn't, and he has to know that."

As their *anax*, Zeus is the one person none of the Hades Brotherhood would consider killing. Especially his own flesh and blood.

"I would and *he* knows me well enough not to doubt that like you do."

"But the mafia comes first."

"No." He closes my door before I can respond to that ridiculous denial.

Once we are off the property, Atlas asks, "Why are you so determined to keep Leonardo in that facility? You implied him staying there keeps him free, but isn't it the opposite? Are you enacting your revenge against him for hurting you?"

"What?" I gasp. "No! I can't believe you think that of me."

"It's what I would do."

"Well, I'm not you."

"No. You aren't. You're filled with kindness and grace. I deal in cruelty and death."

"Is that how you *facilitate* for your family?" I ask with bite.

"Explain about Leonardo," he says without answering, but his silence is answer enough.

If he's in charge of racketeering for the Greek mafia in Portland, then he hurts people. Even kills them when necessary.

"He goes by Lenny."

Atlas shrugs, like Lenny's preference for what people call him doesn't matter. And I suppose it doesn't under the circumstances. Atlas will never meet my brother-in-law.

"When Tino and Agustino Sr. died, I became responsible for Lenny's wellbeing, not just his care. I had promised Tino to keep Lenny safe as if he were my own brother."

Atlas makes a sound of displeasure. He really doesn't like me mentioning my dead husband.

Possessive much?

Ignoring the little flare in my belly that thought gives me, I continue my story. "After Tino and his dad were killed and our house was blown up, Lenny and I were presumed dead. Incinerated in the blast."

"That explains how you got away from the Cosa Nostra, but not why you wanted to leave."

I'd already told him all the reasons, but not in connection to the action, so I spell it out for him. "First, the only way I could get Lenny the specialized medical help he deserved was to take him away. Second, I knew if I stayed in the Cosa Nostra, eventually, I would be expected to marry again. To make more Cosa Nostra babies."

"The Detroit Cosa Nostra are backward," Atlas says with judgment.

"The Detroit mafia, my family and the Revellos especially, have very traditional views of the roles for men and women. I was allowed to work, but only to get me over my grief after losing my baby." Tino would have expected me to quit my job as bookkeeper if I had gotten pregnant again.

"So, you ran?"

"Yes. Tino left me money in offshore accounts no one else knew about. It was his failsafe for me."

Atlas growls again.

"I was married once. He left me money to start a new life." Even if that was not how Tino expected me to use the money. "Get over it."

"What about Leonardo? How did he end up at the facility if you weren't trying to get rid of him?"

"Don't judge. Living with family isn't always best for someone with challenges like Lenny's. Living with me only agitated him. Hoping to figure out why, I took Lenny to a renowned clinic that specialized in traumatic brain injury."

"What did they say?"

"Lenny's diagnosis wasn't great, but it wasn't awful either. The damage to his brain meant that he would never mature emotionally past his current state, and he would always be prone to outbursts."

"That sounds all not great."

I like that he doesn't say bad because Lenny's condition isn't *bad*. It *is* challenging though.

"Untreated, his outbursts would grow worse and more frequent." I go silent, remembering how I felt when the doctor told me that. My fear for Lenny, my renewed grief for the loss of my baby, the result of one of those outbursts.

"I knew I wouldn't be able to keep Lenny safe, or the people around him on my own."

"You should never have been put in the position of needing to."

"That's easy for you to say, with your brothers and cousins to back you up." Even if I agree in principle, I don't tell Atlas that. "Regardless, there *was* treatment available. Inpatient treatment. The doctors were adamant. There could be no question that Lenny needed supervised living both for his safety and to ensure he got the most out of treatment."

"Did it work?"

"If you mean by work, did his moods and behavior stabilize? Yes. Lenny loves living there. He thrives under the supervised conditions. Lenny gets to spend more time doing things away from the facility than he was ever allowed to leave while living in the Revello home." In Detroit, he was a virtual prisoner.

In his current situation, he goes to the movies with friends. He shops at the game store and goes out to buy his own clothes.

"My brother-in-law is allowed every bit of autonomy he can manage without compromising management of his condition."

"Don't call him that."

"He's my family. I'm not going to pretend otherwise."

"Then call him brother."

"You're offended by me calling him my in-law?"

"It doesn't offend me. It fills me with rage."

The violence of his feelings should scare me. It doesn't. I know to my very core that Atlas will never physically harm me. Break my heart? He's already done that. So, yeah.

But break my person? Never. "Why does it make you angry?"

"It reminds me that you belonged to another man."

"Your caveman is showing again. I belong to myself."

"Yes," he agrees easily, surprising me. "But you are also mine."

And that last claim doesn't surprise me at all. Though it does exasperate me. "I told you, I'm not your girlfriend anymore. If I ever was. Not after last night."

"And I told you: you're something more important."

"Your sun. Your light." I sigh, frustrated with myself more than him because the claim touches me when it shouldn't.

Not after the way he used me.

"Yes." His tone leaves no room for argument.

But I'm good at wedging in places I shouldn't. "Can you use your light like a naïve fool?"

"I did use you to gain information and insight into the area," he admits without a tinge of remorse.

Glaring at him, I say, "I know."

"Stop frowning at me. I don't like it."

"Should have thought of that before you made me your dupe."

"You aren't my dupe or a fool," he says with all the exasperation I felt moments ago. "You are intelligent and knowledgeable enough to be a resource and an asset."

"Maybe you should be a spin doctor instead of a facilitator." He sure makes my gullibility sound like something better. "But believe it, or not, no woman aspires to be an information asset to the man she has allowed into her body."

"I didn't have sex with you for information."

"Yeah, right," I sneer.

"We made love because neither of us can keep our hands off the other. Your pussy is made for my cock. Your womb meant to carry my babies. My strength exists to protect and cherish you."

These damn maybe-pregnancy hormones. I swipe at my cheeks, but fresh tears wet them again. His use of the term *made love* robs me of my ability to think, much less retort coherently.

And the rest? The rest shatters something inside me, something I refuse to examine.

Chapter 39

ATLAS

"This is the wrong exit." They are Lucia's first words in ten minutes.

"No, it isn't."

She sighs. "It is unless you want to add twenty minutes of slow traffic on surface streets before we get to my club."

"Our club now," I remind her, pushing for a reaction.

I don't get one. "Whatever, you know what I mean. There's a pharmacy right off the exit nearest the club if you're wanting to stop and get a pregnancy test."

"Do you want to keep Nuovi Inizi?"

"That's no longer an option, and don't change the subject. Why did you take this exit?"

I am not trying to change the subject, but I want to know how she feels about selling her nightclub to us. "What if it was an option?"

"To keep the club?" she asks derisively. "We've been over this. I'm not laundering money for your mafia. I'm not running sex workers out of my club, even if it's their job of choice. I am not, under any circumstances, setting myself up to take the legal fall for you and your brothers."

"I will never let that happen."

"Two days ago, I might have believed you. Now, where are we going?"

Willing to leave the discussion for now, but not forever, I say, "I had Zeus call and make an appointment with an OB at the clinic we had our tests done."

"You told your brother you think I'm pregnant?" she practically shrieks.

"Fuck, Lucia. I could have lost control of the car with you shouting like that."

She snorts. "Not likely. I can't believe you told Zeus I might be pregnant."

"If you are, it won't stay a secret for long." Eventually, she'll start showing.

I wonder when. I didn't look that up. I have more research to do on pregnancy. A lot more if I want to keep her safe like I promised. That includes keeping her and our baby healthy.

I have a lot of questions for the doctor.

"It's not a secret," she huffs. "It's just *my* business."

"Our business." Lucia will not cut me out of our child's life, or her own.

Though I don't expect it to be easy to convince her of that. She took learning I am the head enforcer for our mafia badly. She never needs to know about my job as top assassin for the *Ádis Adelfótita*.

"Fine. *Our* business. But *not* your jerk of a brother's."

Her easy acceptance that I have an interest in her pregnancy loosens something in my chest that has been tight since the night before. "I thought you liked my brother."

"I did. He's a grump, but I liked Zeus." Sadness permeates her tone. "Before. Now, I know he never saw me as anything but a source of income and information. Like you."

I promised myself I would be patient with her, but this shit has got to stop. "I never said that."

"You didn't have to. Your actions said it for you. So did theirs. Zeus showed his true colors today."

"My brother is a short-tempered asshole on his best days." He used to be the charming one. Before the bratva killed his fiancée. "Today was not one of them. You blackmailed him into taking over the cost of Leonardo's care and it pissed him off. How did you expect him to act?"

Me promising to kill him if he told Don Russo about Leonardo's whereabouts, and by default Lucia's, only turned a bad mood into a vile one. But Zeus grudgingly admitted his threat was empty. He has no plans to tell the don.

"Oh, poor Zeus, having to do something he didn't want to. I wouldn't begin to know how that feels." She crosses her arms and stares out the window away from me.

"We all do things we don't want to, *ílios mou*."

"I'm not your sun."

"You bring warmth and light into my world even when you're mad at me."

"Stop saying stuff like that."

"No."

We drive in silence for a few minutes before she sighs. "I thought your brothers liked me too; it hurts to know it was all an act. Orion reminded me of Rocco and for a little bit I didn't feel so alone."

"My brothers do like you."

"You all put on a good show, I'll give you that."

Is her stubborn insistence on attributing the darkest motives possible to our actions from pregnancy hormones, or is it Lucia? My woman does have a temper and there's no signs of it cooling since last night.

Only time is going show her how wrong she is. "You said Rocco is dead."

Did she lie to me?

We know about the Revellos because they owned clubs that got taken over by the bratva. Information is power and we keep tabs on key players. That Tino Revello's wife and brother died in an explosion after his clubs got taken is also in our files. Who his wife was is not.

Now, I know it is Lucia. But I don't know what family in the Detroit Cosa Nostra she comes from. She's too smart to have gone back to her maiden name. That would make her too easy to track down.

"I didn't lie, but no, Rocco isn't dead. I said my brother is lost to me, like my parents. Which they are. I couldn't keep in contact with them and get Lenny away from the backward thinking mafia. My father would have insisted on Grandfather Revello making the decisions for Lenny's care."

"It's the way families like ours work. And you gave yours up to make sure Leonardo gets the treatment you think he needs. Why?" The promise she made to a dead man doesn't cut it.

"The day I lost the baby was as traumatic for Lenny as it was for me. He wanted me to have that baby so bad. Even more than Tino. He talked to my stomach all of the time. It destroyed him when his actions led to me losing the baby."

"How did he know they did?"

"He has the mind of a twelve-year-old, not a two-year-old. He lacks maturity and impulse control, but he can put two and two together. If he hadn't, his father made sure he knew. Agustino Sr. thought it would help Lenny control his rages to know what they cost the family. All it did was ensure that Lenny was as hurt by the outcome of that day as I was."

"Asshole."

"I didn't grieve his death like I did Tino's, that's for sure. And Agustino's father is even worse."

I don't need to hear how she grieved her asshole husband's death. He was as responsible for her pain and loss as her father-in-law.

"What will happen to you if your don finds out you've been hiding and keeping Leonardo hidden?"

"If you weren't lying, then he isn't going to find out."

Taking a second to control the anger her words elicit, I pull into the clinic parking lot.

"I was not lying," I bite out. "My brothers risked their lives as fucking children to rescue me when I was kidnapped, and I am prepared to kill Zeus if he rats you out to Don Russo."

Or at least make my brother wish he were dead. Not that Zeus will do that, threat, or no threat. But I had to have his vow and I used the threat of death to get it. Because it is important to Lucia.

"You wouldn't kill your brother." Her derisive tone scrapes my last nerve.

Getting out of the car, I don't bother to answer. She's determined to piss me off with her lack of trust. Showing some measure of self-preservation, Lucia waits for me to come around to open her door. My anger ratchets back a notch.

When she refuses to take my hand to get out of the SUV, it climbs right back up again. I grab her around the waist and lift her out of the truck.

She gasps. "That wasn't necessary."

"I disagree."

"You can be so infuriating."

"I do not have a corner on that market."

"Are you saying I annoy you?" She tries to avoid my hand.

But I catch hers and hold onto it. "Your determination to mistrust everything I say and do is pissing me off, yes."

"Poor you."

LUCIA

I realize the second the words leave my mouth that I've pushed Atlas a step too far.

His big body swells with the fury he's clearly been doing his best to bank and he yanks me around to face him. As angry as he is, he is still careful with me.

"No, Lucia, I am not poor, because I have no intention of going without."

I don't know how he gets that interpretation of poor, but we are so not going there. "If you thin—"

His mouth cuts off my words. The kiss is brutal, but my traitorous libido responds. I kiss him back, giving angry passion for angry passion until someone behind us clears their throats.

"Uh, if I could get inside." It's a woman's voice.

I try to jump back from Atlas, but he holds onto me, shifting us both out of the way of the heavily pregnant woman. One arm around my waist to stop me from moving, Atlas opens the door for her with his other hand.

She smiles her thanks and then winks at me. "Lucky you."

I don't feel lucky right now. My heart is one slice away from bleeding out. Knowing I am in love with a man who is only using me is devastating my usually resilient spirit. If I'm pregnant, Atlas is going to pretend to want me. I just know it.

"You don't have to pretend," I tell him. "I'm not going to try to keep you out of the baby's life if I'm pregnant."

"What exactly am I supposed to be pretending, *agape mou*?" he asks, his voice dangerously soft.

What does *agape mou* mean? Normally, I would ask, but not right now. Because I'm not sure I want to know.

"To want me," I answer his question.

He jerks my hand to the front of his jeans and presses it against the massive bulge there. "That is not a pretense."

"Atlas!" We're right in front of the clinic. "Anyone could see."

"Let them."

I try to jerk my hand away, but only succeed in sliding it down his erection. Heat burns in my cheeks. "Let go."

"No. Admit it."

"Admit what?" But I know.

"This is not fake. I am hard for *you*, and I don't care who knows it."

"Fine, you're hard for me. After the last two months, I'm convinced you can get hard in a stiff wind."

"Only if that wind carries your scent."

"You have to stop saying stuff like that."

"No, I don't."

"You're so stubborn."

"And you aren't?"

I shake my head. "Come on. Let's find out if our lives are permanently entwined."

"They're already that, *agape mou*. Believe it."

Taking a page out of his book, I don't bother to answer that provocative statement.

Thirty minutes later, I sit in stunned silence as the doctor tells us that I *am* pregnant.

"I didn't think I could get pregnant," I tell him.

"Why is that?"

When I explain, the doctor frowns. "We'll do an ultrasound and run some extra tests to see if there is anything to worry about. I would also like to see your medical files from your first pregnancy."

I curl my fingers into my palms in stress. The mafia doesn't recognize HIPPA guidelines and my previous obstetrician is a Cosa Nostra doctor. The private hospital where I lost the baby has ties to the mafia as well.

"You will need to sign a release, but we should be able to get them immediately," the doctor blithely continues, unaware of my growing agitation. "Unless your previous obstetrician does not have digitized files."

Atlas, who has been grinning at me since getting the news, goes rigid and shifts his now glacial gaze to the doctor. "You think her reproductive system could be compromised?"

"Honestly? From what Ms. Esposito has described, no. However, it is always better to err on the side of caution."

I agree. Of course, I do. I don't want to risk this baby's health in any way, but I don't want to reveal my whereabouts to the Detroit Cosa Nostra either. Much less the fact that I am alive.

But can I withhold my baby from my parents and brother? It's one thing to let them go on thinking I'm dead, but another entirely not to tell them about a grandchild.

My mother wanted to be a grandmother so badly the first time around. From social media, I know that my brother has not married yet and there are no grandchildren for my parents to dote on.

The weight of everything presses down on me.

"Do you have the equipment?" Atlas stands up, looming over the doctor's desk. "Or do I need to take her to the hospital?"

The silver-haired man makes an obvious effort not to lean away from Atlas. "We have the best ultrasound machines available here in the clinic, but your wife—"

"We aren't married," I rush to correct.

"Your...um...partner, needs to hydrate. If you could drink four cups of water over the next hour, Ms. Esposito, the ultrasound images will be clearer."

I remember how that full bladder feels with the ultrasound wand pressing down on my stomach and grimace.

Atlas frowns at me and demands, "Is that necessary?"

"If we want the best diagnostic results, yes."

"It's fine, Atlas. I've done this before."

"Water with no bubbles is preferred, but you probably remember that from your last pregnancy. You'll want to avoid carbonated beverages going forward to decrease the chance of painful heartburn."

"Where do you want to spend the next hour?" Atlas asks me. "Here or at a restaurant?"

"Here is fine."

"Get her some water," Atlas demands. "I have some questions for you while we wait."

The doctor stiffens at being ordered around, but he texts someone on his phone and a couple of minutes later, a woman comes in with a sixteen-ounce glass water bottle. It has the logo for the clinic on it and a pretty lavender lid.

Atlas has already started asking his questions.

Flipping the lid back, I drink from the water bottle, happy to discover the liquid is chilled, if not ice cold. Room temperature water is supposed to be better for hydration, but I don't like it.

Atlas is still asking questions when I indicate the empty water bottle to the doctor. He nods and puts his hand up to pause his discussion with Atlas.

Sending another text, he gives Atlas a bemused look. "You weren't joking when you said you had some questions."

"Why would I joke about something like that?" Atlas asks, his voice flat.

He really doesn't show much animation with other people. Unless you count intimidation.

"I don't remember ever answering as many detailed concerns with another spouse...uh, partner," the doctor hastily corrects at my glare.

The nurse comes in and takes my water bottle away.

"Do *you* have any concerns?" the doctor asks me.

I blink at him, still processing everything Atlas has asked and the doctor has answered. "I don't think so."

"Are you sure?" Atlas turns to me, his gaze probing. "Just because you have been through this before doesn't mean you won't have questions."

"Did you read that in a book?" I ask wryly as the nurse returns with my second sixteen ounces of water.

I take the bottle from her and immediately start sipping.

"It's in one of the brochures I read while we were waiting for the results." If Atlas is embarrassed to admit he read the brochures, it doesn't show.

Tino wouldn't have read them on a dare. And if he had read them, he never would have admitted it. Not macho enough.

Apparently, Atlas has no such issues.

"You have enough questions for both of us," I tease and then suck in my lips.

I don't want to be teasing him. Finding out I am pregnant does not undo his betrayal. What it does do is raise the question: why did Atlas want to get me pregnant in the first place?

And that is not a query I am going to make in front of the doctor.

Chapter 40

LUCIA

After I finish my water, we are led to a room housing a high-tech ultrasound machine. It has two screens and enough buttons and dials to double as a plane cockpit.

Atlas refuses to leave the room when the nurse instructs me to change into an exam gown.

"You're being unreasonable," I assure him.

He leans against the wall, a silent testament that he is not budging from the room. "I will turn away if you want, but I'm not going anywhere."

"What do you think is going to happen to me here?"

He raises his brow at me.

"Fine. Stay, but avert your gaze."

"Why? I have seen every inch of your body and tasted it too."

Not about to touch that statement with a ten-foot pole, I remind him, "You said you would."

His gaze burns into me for long seconds but then he turns his head. I quickly strip out of my clothes and put on the exam gown. It is open in the front but has enough fabric to wrap over itself and protect my modesty.

Which seems really important right now.

Ten minutes later, I realize that my modesty has nothing on Atlas's on my behalf.

"Transvaginal as in vagina?" he asks the doctor in clipped tones.

"Yes. And transabdominal refers to the ultrasound we will do via Ms. Esposita's abdomen."

"The fuck you are touching her vagina." Atlas moves his body between me and the doctor. "Get a female doctor in here."

"Mr. Rokos, vaginal exams will be a regular part of your wife's...uh..." He gives me an apologetic look. "Uh...partner's prenatal care. Nevertheless, the ultrasound will be performed by an ultrasound technician."

The doctor speaks patiently, like he expects Atlas to calm down once he is shown reason.

I have no such expectation. Now that I know Atlas is a mafia made man, so many of his idiosyncrasies make sense. The one thing the doctor should not expect is a rational response from my caveman when it comes to another man seeing, much less touching my most intimate flesh.

My caveman? No, *not* mine. But still very much a caveman.

"If you would be more comfortable stepping out of the room," the doctor has the lack of foresight to suggest.

Atlas grabs him by the shoulder and shoves toward the door. "The only man leaving this room is you. Get a woman doctor in here. Now. And if she can't perform the ultrasound either, you'd better get a woman technician too."

"While I appreciate your concerns..." The doctor is still talking when Atlas pushes him out of the room and closes the door behind them.

I can't hear what is being said through the door, but Atlas comes back into the room a few minutes later. "Their top female OB-GYN will be in shortly. She will be performing the ultrasounds and taking over your care."

"I never doubted it for a minute."

"If he touched your pussy I would have to kill him."

I roll my eyes. "Of course you would. How did I not realize you are a made man?"

"Knowing that you were raised in the mafia, it *is* strange that you didn't suspect anything."

His words flay my conscience and I sigh. There is nothing like willful ignorance. "I didn't put the pieces together, that's for sure. I didn't want to."

He cocks his head, like he's wondering about that but he asks, "Are you happy about the baby?"

"Yes."

"Even though I am the father?"

That is a question I'm not ready to answer. Atlas being my baby's father means I cannot walk away from him completely. That should not cause a flutter of relief in my heart.

Avoiding that emotional quagmire, I say, "You aren't the only one who decided not to use birth control."

"That's not an answer."

"Yes, it is. I am an adult and I take responsibility for my choices."

"And you chose to get pregnant with me."

"Yes." I trusted him too easily, but that is on me. "What I don't understand is why you chose to get me pregnant."

The door opens, interrupting whatever answer Atlas would have given. Part of me is thankful. I'm not sure I want to know if I'm a convenient womb to carry the next generation for the Rokos mafia.

A tall woman with long blond hair and wearing glasses comes into the room. "Hello, I am Dr. Lida MacGowen."

"MacGowen is an Irish name," I say suspiciously. Don't tell me that the Irish mob is moving in on Portland too.

"Yes, it is. And Esposito is of Spanish origin."

"Italian," I correct, still looking at her with suspicion.

Atlas cups my neck. "Relax, *ílios mou*, she's not part of an Irish syndicate," he tells me in perfect Italian.

"That day when I told you to get out of my house, you understood me fine," I accuse.

That triggers another memory. Him calling me good girl in Italian. I was so lost to passion, it didn't register then, but now I realize he's understood every word I've spoken in Italian since we met.

"Why didn't you tell me you speak Italian?"

"Calling you *brava regazza* didn't clue you in?"

"I was too far gone at the time to register it," I admit. But I remember now and I also remember how good it made me feel.

Why this man? Why does he have the key to my every lock?

"That is good to know," he replies in English, reminding me it is rude to carry on a conversation the doctor cannot understand.

"I apologize," I say to her.

"It's fine. It must be nice to be able to share a private conversation in front of others. But I didn't realize Rokos is an Italian name too?"

"It's not," I say.

"It's Greek," Atlas adds, pride infusing his tone.

"But you speak Italian?" she asks as she sets up the equipment.

"Yes." Atlas makes no attempt to explain.

The doctor doesn't seem offended. "We are going to start with the transvaginal ultrasound. It will give us a more detailed picture of certain parts of your repro-ductive system. It also offers the most likely chance of seeing Baby at this stage."

While it's small, the wand up my vagina is every bit as uncomfortable as I expect it to be. However, the 3-D image that comes up on the monitor is fascinating.

The doctor explains everything we can see, including a bunch of medical terminology that basically says I'm healthy and so are my reproductive organs. A whoosh-whoosh repeats in a rapid pattern.

The doctor smiles. "That's the baby's heartbeat."

Tears wash into my eyes as I grin up at Atlas. "Our baby."

I'm such a sap, but he looks utterly flabbergasted. "That is our baby?" he asks, like he didn't believe it the first time, or the second time, it was said.

"Yes." The doctor moves the wand inside me, clicks a couple of things on the space age instrument panel. "According to the measurements you are eight weeks along, Ms. Esposito."

"Eight weeks?" I ask faintly. That means I got pregnant the first time we had sex without a condom.

Like it was meant to be.

"I told you," Atlas says to me.

"You've told me a lot," I remind him.

"Your body was made to carry my baby. You got pregnant on the first try."

"We weren't trying that first time."

He shrugs.

"Your partner has a bit of the Neanderthal in him, doesn't he?" Dr. MacGowen asks.

"You have no idea."

~ ~ ~

Atlas calls his brothers to tell them about the baby as soon as we are back in his SUV.

"So, my brother knocked you up, huh?" Orion asks, humor lacing his tone over the vehicle's speaker system. "I guess you were doing more than playing Parcheesi on all those sleepovers."

"No, we played Monopoly."

"Pretty sure that's not how you got yourself a Greek bun in the oven."

"Half Italian," I reply with a snap.

"Don't Worry, Be Happy" is a low-level background noise as Orion and I trade barbs.

"Is my brother whistling?" Orion asks, his tone astonished.

I roll my eyes. "Yes."

"You sound happy brother," Zeus speaks for the first time.

"Can you doubt it?"

"Does this mean Lucia isn't planning to leave Portland after she trains a manager for Nuovi Inizi?"

"I will not withhold the baby from Atlas." My temper burns bright, but I'm not vindictive. "I am not that woman."

"That's good to know."

"Uncle Orion has a certain ring to it."

"Like a doorbell," I snark back.

"When are you going to introduce Lucia to your crew?" Zeus asks.

"They're waiting for us at the club."

That's news to me and butterflies start step-dancing in combat boots in my tummy. "I met three of them last night."

It's not a memory I want to hold onto.

"That was different."

"How many men are on your crew?" I ask.

"Three full-fledged members of *Ádis Adelfótita* and we are testing four more for potential initiation. They won't be at the club."

"You're recruiting for your crew? Why? Is the bratva fighting over territory?"

"Not now," Atlas replies.

Which is not reassuring because it implies they could be in the future.

"We have a truce with the *pakhan* in Russia. He has ordered his men out of Portland."

"Back to Russia? Or somewhere else nearby?" I ask.

"Good question," Orion says with grudging approval.

"Two of the men flew to Seattle, but the *pakhan* thinks we believe they all went back to Russia, or California." Atlas maneuvers around a slow car in the center lane on the freeway.

"California?"

"The Golubev Bratva have just over two months to sell or close their business and other assets before leaving the state," Orion adds. "They agreed to stay out of *Ádis Adelfótita* territory."

"And the Hades Brotherhood doesn't claim Washington as part of their territory."

"No, but British Columbia and Oregon are. There's only so much the bratva can do hemmed in from the north and south." Zeus's words imply the problem is taken care of, but his pensive tone indicates something else.

"We won't let them get to you," Atlas promises.

"Should I be worried?"

"No."

But I remember what Atlas said about the bratva coming to my club to shake me down. A frisson of fear makes the hairs on the back of my neck stand up.

As angry as I am at him and his brothers for doing the same thing, I don't fear them.

The bratva is something else all together. They showed no conscience, much less pity, when taking over Cosa Nostra territory in Detroit. They blew up my house, believing I was in it.

It was a different bratva family, but if the Golubevs approach bratva business the same way, I really do owe Atlas my gratitude for keeping them out of Nuovi Inizi.

I have no plans to tell him that though.

Chapter 41

LUCIA

"I 'm surprised you took the time to assess my club too," I tell his crew when Atlas formally introduces me to them, letting them know I remember seeing them in the club before last night. "Atlas had access to everything."

Including the profit and loss ledgers for the Nuovi Inizi. What could his men add to his already minutia level knowledge?

Bobby puts his hand on the back of his neck and looks over to Atlas, who is giving his stoic face. "Uh, yeah. We weren't here for that."

Did they come to check out the woman their boss is...*was* banging?

"Why were you here then?" I dare them to tell me but they all stand there like silent robots.

Deadly robots if the aura they give off is to be believed. And I'm done ignoring my instincts.

I turn to Atlas. "Why were they here? Did they want to know what the woman you duped looked like?"

Atlas's jaw ticks and I am ridiculously pleased with myself for getting to him so easily.

"No, ma'am." Michael's hair is cut short, a high and tight like a Marine's and he talks like one too.

Ma'am. For crying out loud.

"Then why?" I demand.

"We were here to protect you when the boss was out hunting those bratva bastards," Bobby blurts out.

He's the youngest and most impulsive of their little group.

I shoot a glance toward Atlas, but he's letting his men speak for themselves. He's made it clear that as long as they don't get too close, he wants me to get to know them.

"We weren't the only ones watching over you," Theo adds when I don't respond to Bobby's revelation.

Why is he telling me this? Atlas's crew should be more circumspect, shouldn't they? They're doing their version of talking their boss up.

A tendril of warmth unfurls inside me. His crew wouldn't want to talk him up if they didn't think he wanted me. Which means they never thought he was banging me for information.

Putting that away to take out and examine later, I turn to Atlas. "Hunting?"

He shrugs.

"Atlas is the Golubev Bratva's *palach*." Bobby's youth shows in his enthusiastic hero worship of his boss. "No one has ki—"

"The guys will be with you when I am not," Atlas says, cutting Bobby off.

Theo smacks Bobby on the back of the head and the younger man turns on him instantly, his entire demeanor changing. Gone is the affable young man proud of his boss's accomplishments, whatever they are, and in his place is a stone cold killer.

"The fuck?" Bobby demands.

Theo barks something at Bobby in Greek and the other man's eyes widen. He looks from me to Atlas and then back at me again.

He asks Atlas something in Greek.

Michael simply stands in stoic silence during this interaction, his attitude one of watchful readiness. I'm not sure what he's watching for in a closed nightclub, but his behavior is familiar.

Maybe if the Detroit Cosa Nostra had men like that on their payroll, that final night in Detroit would have gone differently. But Augustino Sr.'s men were like his son. Fourth or fifth generation mafia with an attitude of entitlement and certainty no one would be brazen enough to storm their kingdom.

They'd been wrong and unprepared for warfare when it came to them. Atlas will never be caught unaware like that. The fact he went hunting for the bratva, rather than waiting for them to try to attack him and his brothers shows how different he is from the Revello men and my former don.

Atlas shakes his head. "English from now on, when Lucia is around."

"Unless we need to keep things private," Theo says.

It's not a question, but Atlas nods.

Maybe it's time I learn Greek. I give Atlas a sugary sweet smile that makes him flinch.

"It's a good thing we aren't a thing," I say conversationally. "I don't want to be part of a world again where I don't have a voice because I have ovaries."

Even if those ovaries go gaga over Atlas. His eyes narrow, tension emanating from his big body.

"That's our cue to leave. It was good to meet you under less stressful circumstances, Lucia. When you can't get ahold of Atlas, call one of us. We'll be watching out for you." Despite the evidence of last night, Theo is clearly the charmer of this crew.

"I don't have your numbers."

"I put them in your phone," Atlas says without the slightest qualm.

Putting my hand out, I say, "Give me your phone."

He doesn't hesitate, opening it before he hands it to me.

Shock at his easy capitulation surging through me, I grab the phone and open his contacts. It only takes a minute to add Willow, Barry and my head server to them.

"What are you doing?" Bobby asks when Atlas doesn't.

"Putting the staff manager, bar manager and head of security for Nuovi Inizi in Atlas's contacts." I smack Atlas's phone back into his hand. "Tit-for-tat."

"Are you going to go through my computer too?" he asks, understanding immediately what I mean.

"Yes. When I'm done, I will have invaded your life as thoroughly as you have invaded mine." It's not an empty threat and I hope he knows it.

"Good."

He doesn't mean that. He can't. But the challenging expression in his blue eyes defies me not to believe him.

"I am not going to shut up and have babies," I warn him. "And I'm not going to marry you because I'm pregnant."

One marriage for duty's sake is enough in any lifetime. I might have loved Tino by the time we married, but I realized after losing the baby that he never loved me.

He married me to continue the Revello line. Out of both duty and necessity. Agustino Sr.'s uncle had lost his position as capo because he and his wife hadn't been able to have children.

That's how Agustino became a capo and took over running the clubs. Tino made it clear he wasn't going to let that happen to him.

If I get married again, it will be because the man I'm marrying loves me.

We aren't in the Cosa Nostra and I'm not a good little mafia princess anymore. Even if the father of my baby is the nephew of the freaking Godfather of the Night for the Greek mafia on the west coast.

"Good to meet you, Lucia." Bobby is backing up fast, Theo and Michael moving right along with him. "See you later, boss."

They leave via the hallway to the backdoor.

Atlas's focus is 100% on me though. "Make no mistake, *eromenis mou*, you will marry me. If I have to kidnap you, fly you to Vegas, roofie you and get married with the fucking video package as proof of the deed. You're my woman and the child inside you is my child."

That absolutely should not turn me on and make my heart pitter-pat. Should not. So, why does it?

"Not if it means going back to being a mafia princess who is seen and not heard," I snap right back.

"The Cosa Nostra in Detroit might be stupid enough not to value your smarts. But I appreciate your brain as much as I incessantly crave your body."

"Your mafia might be Greek, but you can't tell me they're so different from the Italians, not with your crew slipping into Greek to protect the *little woman* from knowing too much."

"Protection is right. The less you know, the less of a target you are."

"That's not why you cut Bobby off when he was talking. What kind of hunting do you do? What does *palach* mean?"

"You don't want to know."

"Oh, but I do," I assure him.

"Leave it alone, Lucia."

"Not going to happen. You've been picking my brain for weeks. Now it's my turn."

"I never pushed you to tell me something you didn't want to."

"Are you saying you never will because I don't believe you. Either this thing goes both ways or it doesn't go at all." Darn it. I didn't mean to imply there is a *thing* between us, but I'm not taking the words back either.

"Dimios." He heads toward the door to the upstairs.

"What is dimios?"

"Who I am."

Dimios is a name? "Why do you have so many names?" Dimios. Palach.

They have to mean something. That's how it works in the mafia.

Without answering me, he stops at the door and waits for me to key in the code to unlock it. Atlas, or is it Dimios? Whichever, he makes no effort to hide that he's watching the movements of my finger over the keypad with keen interest.

Since he can pick the lock as easily as use the code, I don't bother trying hide which buttons I press.

Standing in my apartment, for the first time, the space feels too small with him in it. He won't be here long, I soothe myself. But we do have things to discuss. Like the baby and what having a child together will look like for us.

"Sit down. Do you want tea?"

Slipping out of my coat, I lay it over the back of the sofa. "I would rather have coffee."

"Caffeine isn't good for the baby."

I sigh. "I know. Herbal tea is fine."

I don't know why I'm letting him act like a host in my apartment, but I'm suddenly tired. The last two days catch up to me and I flop down onto the sofa.

He fills the electric kettle with water. "Dimios means executioner in Greek."

Ah, so not a name so much as a title? "What does *palach* mean?"

"I dispense justice."

By dispense justice does he mean punish, or kill? Dimios-slash-executioner implies the latter. But what does *palach* mean exactly?

A cold chill works its way down my spine. "That sounds like you're more than an enforcer."

He shrugs.

"Are you? More than an enforcer?" I press.

He's silent so long, I don't think he's going to answer, but then he says, "Yes."

"What more?"

"I am the executioner."

"For who? Enemies of the Hades Brotherhood?" I guess.

"Sometimes. The Golubev Bratva is the syndicate that kidnapped me when I was ten."

Air whooshes out of me as I process this. He's saying that he dispenses justice on his own behalf too, killing his enemies. The tattoo on his back makes so much sense now. A Greek Spartan warrior conquering the symbol of Russia, a bear.

Wait. Another truth hits me. "The same bratva that you just made a truce with?"

"Yes. They wanted to make turning over the *palach* part of the terms."

"*Palach* is Russian for executioner, isn't it?" A picture is starting to form and despite his betrayal, my heart hurts for the little boy he was and the killer he became.

"I started when my uncle and brothers came to save me. I made my first kills that night."

"You were only eleven!"

"Yes."

"When did you start executing them again?"

"I never stopped. I hunted the Golubev Bratva soldiers who participated in my torture over that year first. I learned my skills on the backs of their corpses."

Atlas began slaying his enemies at the age of eleven and never stopped.

"Are there any left?"

"Of the men who kidnapped and hurt me? No. Golubevs? Obviously, yes. I only killed bratva connected to my capture, or ones who tried to do business in our territory."

"Killed. That's what Michael was going to say."

"Yes. No one has killed more bratva than me."

I shiver. "Who named you Dimios?"

"Constantin."

"Your uncle."

"Yes. For the first few years, only he and my brothers knew what I was doing. Later, when Constantin took over as *Nonós tis Nýchtas*, he made me an official assassin for *Ádis Adelfótita*."

Legitimizing what his nephew was doing anyway. "He was protecting you."

"Yes."

"If your grandfather knew you were doing unsanctioned killings, you would have been punished."

"I would be dead."

A man who left his ten-year-old grandson in the hands of monsters for a year would not have hesitated to kill that same grandson for disobedience. For some in the mafia disobedience equals betrayal.

"I don't want to live in the mafia world again." That brutal world where a child is sacrificed for power and the broken man he becomes could be killed by his own people for seeking the vengeance due him.

"I am sorry."

Because he knows I have no choice. I can remain "dead" to my family in Detroit, but because the baby inside me is Atlas's, I will always be connected to his Greek mafia.

"Why did you *want* to get me pregnant?" I don't get it. The consequences are lifelong for both of us. "You were fucking me for information. Why connect our lives inexorably like this? What was the point?"

"The point was keeping you. Pregnancy is an unbreakable bond between us."

I shake my head in useless denial. This man sees only one way forward. To take what he wants and keep it by whatever means necessary. He's utterly ruthless.

He wanted me locked down. So, he went for the jugular in terms of cementing our relationship.

Knocking me up. "You said you were sorry."

He nods, clearly unwilling to repeat the words.

"If you were really sorry, you would have given me a choice. You would have told me about what you are before getting me pregnant."

"You got pregnant before either of us made a conscious decision. I am not sorry I got you pregnant. I am sorry you don't want to live in my world."

"But I can't leave it."

He hands me the mug of tea. "No."

"What if I ran? I disappeared from one crime family. I can do it again." Especially without having to worry about Lenny's long term care.

"If you run, I will follow."

"To drag me back." I curl my legs up under me. "I don't know how many men you have killed, but you've done a great job of assassinating my future."

"I won't drag you back."

I don't believe him. "What then?"

"My role as Dimios is not locked into a geographical location."

Is he saying what it sounds like? "You're saying you would chase me, to what...visit your child?"

"I am keeping you."

It's not the first time he's said it, but maybe it is the first time what he means is truly sinking in. "But what about your brothers?"

"I wouldn't be able to continue as their head enforcer."

"You would leave your family for me?" I shake my head decisively. Not possible. "I don't believe you."

"We'll work on that."

Chapter 42

LUCIA

Orion brings the contract for me to sign the next day as well as his cousin Helios to begin training as my replacement. The club isn't open on Monday, so I start Helios on learning inventory and suppliers.

Atlas isn't happy when I sign the papers, but I ignore his brooding presence.

Over the next week, teaching Helios the ropes of running Nuovi Inizi goes surprisingly smoothly. He picks things up quickly and gets along with the staff. By the end of the week, I'm convinced it won't take a full month to train him.

Atlas is always here and when he's not, one of his crew is. He doesn't bring up marriage again though.

Which does not disappoint me.

I'm not great at lying to myself and can't help wincing at that whopper. No matter how angry I am at him, how used I feel, the thought of building a life without him, or having him only on the periphery is way too depressing.

"Doesn't Atlas trust you?" I ask his cousin.

Helios shrugs. "Sure, but he knows my focus isn't your safety."

So, Atlas makes sure someone is always here that sees my safety as a priority. Because of the baby?

What else am I supposed to think?

Other than his threat to kidnap and marry me, we haven't discussed what being coparents will look like. As determined as he is to invade every aspect of my life, when I start asking questions about the future, there is always someone, or something else, that needs his attention.

Every night I go to bed alone, but every morning I wake up wrapped in his arms.

The first morning, I cut up rough about it, but Atlas pointed out that like the night before, I didn't fall into a deep sleep until he joined me. I still don't invite him to sleep with me. I don't even invite him to stay on my sofa, but Atlas does what he wants.

He doesn't initiate sex. Neither do I. No matter how out of control my ovaries are from my pregnancy hormones. I know why I don't, but I don't know what is holding him back.

He's already proven that I'm easily seduced by him. I might think he doesn't want me anymore, but when I wake up in his arms it is always with his raging hard erection pressing into my back too.

"Shit, cousin, you need to get laid," Helios says after Atlas bites his head off about asking me to order the craft beer for the weekend.

Atlas glares at me.

"What did I do?" I demand.

It's not my fault that Shawn is interested in me. I don't do anything to encourage him. Not that he is as pushy lately. In fact, if I am there when he makes a delivery, he keeps a wary eye on Atlas and respectful distance from me.

"I think it's what you won't do," Helios says. "Have you cut my cousin off since we took over your club?"

"One, my sex life or lack thereof, is none of your business. Two, you didn't take over my club. I sold it to Zeus."

The look Helios gives me says he doesn't see the difference. But there is one. I took my fate into my own hands and forced Zeus to buy the club with the stipulation that Lenny would always be taken care of.

I am not powerless.

"You ready for lunch?" Atlas asks me, his tone clipped.

"Wow, how can I turn down such a charming offer?" I roll my eyes. "Yes, I'm ready."

The best way to control my nausea after waking is to snack throughout the day. If I don't each lunch soon, I'll need a granola bar, or something if I want to maintain my new normal.

"Let's go upstairs." Atlas lifts a to-go bag from my favorite Italian restaurant up.

"When did you get that?" I follow him up to my apartment.

"I had Bobby pick it up."

"Thank you."

He grunts.

I shake my head, having to stifle a weird urge to smile. He's kind of cute cranky. Knowing he's in a bad mood because of me is just a bonus.

Again, not powerless.

We plate the food together and Atlas puts it on the table while I get us both a drink. "Cranberry-cherry juice okay?"

He shudders. "Water is fine."

I hide my smirk. He doesn't like any form of cranberry juice, but it's my favorite drink.

After placing both beverages on the table, I sit down.

"When are you moving into your house?" he asks.

The impulse to smirk, much less smile, leaves like a puff. "I'm not."

"What do you mean you aren't? Did something go wrong with one of the repairs?"

Looking away from him, I swallow back emotion at the loss of my dream. "I canceled the purchase."

"Why?" he growls.

"Why the heck do you think?" Now I meet his eyes, my own filled with the temper coursing through me. "I couldn't afford it once you decided to take a cut of Nuovi Inizi's profits."

"But you sold the club to us. You have enough to buy the house outright now."

"I had already texted my realtor to cancel the sale when I realized the only true option was to sell the club to your brother."

"It wasn't your only option."

I give him a look that says, *right*. "My only safe option."

"I will never let you be the fall guy for our business," he practically shouts. "That was never the plan. You can run Nuovi Inizi and I will always keep you safe."

Jumping up from the table, he starts pacing in the tiny confines of my kitchen.

"That's not the only reason."

He stops and glowers at me. "What else?"

"I didn't think I was pregnant and had no intention of staying in Portland after I trained Helios."

"Where were you going to go?"

"Does it matter? Away from here."

"Because of me."

No reason to sugarcoat it. "Yes."

"And now?"

"Now what?" I don't know what he's asking.

"Are you going to run?"

"What would be the point? You already said you'd come after me." And no way am I escaping the Hades Brotherhood's assassin.

He's a hunter. His men said as much.

I have no intention of becoming prey.

"You hate me."

Do I? "A week ago I would have agreed," I admit.

"But now?"

"Now, I've spent the last week only sleeping well when you sneak into my bed. You take care of me and it's not all about what's best for the baby. You rub my feet and tell your cousin to figure stuff out himself when it is my job to teach him."

"But none of that changes that I used you to get information."

"No." I sigh. "None of that changes why we met."

"Does *why* we met matter so much?"

That's the million dollar question I've been asking myself. "You hurt me."

"I didn't mean to."

"Maybe not, but I don't think it would have mattered to you if you realized what the outcome would be."

"The hell it wouldn't have. If I knew asking for a protection tithe would cost me you, I never would have done it. I would have protected you and your club no matter what. You have to know that."

Part of me does, but part of me is still struggling with it. "I want to believe you because it hurts thinking it was all about using me."

"It wasn't." He drops on his knees in front of me. "Damn it, Lucia, the second I saw you, I knew you were mine. Maybe that's where I messed up. I thought you had to feel something that strong too."

"I did," I admit, my voice hoarse with emotion.

"Then why the hell do you doubt me when I say I will leave my brothers to be with you? That I will protect you with my life? I will never let you be hurt."

"Because no one has ever put me first like that. They're your family."

"*Agape mou*, you are my sun." He grabs both sides of my face and presses our foreheads together. "You are my future."

I want to believe him so badly, it scares me.

~ ~ ~

Two days later, Atlas takes me out to the parking lot. "I have something for you."

When we get outside, there is a metallic silver Mercedes parked near the back door. A soft chirp sounds and the quiet snick of door locks disengaging follows.

Atlas holds a black key fob with the silver Mercedes logo in the center out to me. "It's yours."

"You bought me a car?" Shock and excitement course through me. The luxury sedan is beautiful.

"I won it from Orion in a bet, but I had it detailed so his cologne won't assault you every time you drive."

He talks like his brother wears some cheap aerosol spray crap. When in fact, like everything else in Orion's life, his cologne is expensive and classy. However, Atlas knows my nausea can be triggered by smells.

So far, that doesn't include sophisticated men's colognes, but he's not taking any chances.

"What kind of bet gets you a car?" Unable to help myself, I open the driver's side door and peek inside.

The custom grey leather interior is pristine. I inhale. Atlas is right. I don't smell his brother's cologne. Or anything. Nothing to trigger the pregnancy nausea.

Nice.

"It was about how efficiently I can do my job."

Considering what Atlas's job is, I don't ask for more details. "Were you going to give him your BMW if he won?"

"No. He wanted dinner with you."

"Atlas!" I glare over my shoulder at him. "You cannot bet my time."

"You like to cook."

"That's not the point."

"I knew I would win, so it wasn't really a bet," Atlas dismisses.

"I'm surprised your caveman nature didn't balk at promising your brother dinner alone with me, even if you were confident you'd win."

"I never said it would be alone."

That sounds more like the Atlas I know.

"Whatever." I slide into the driver's seat and adjust it to fit my frame. "No more bets about anything to do with me."

He shrugs. Which is not a promise. "It got you an armored car nine months before a new one could be delivered."

His tone says it all worked out so what is my problem?

"Is Orion driving a regular car?" I ask, worried. "Is that safe?"

He's the family lawyer, which makes him a target on two fronts.

"Don't worry about my brother," Atlas grumps, his possessive nature reasserting itself. "He's fine. He can drive one of the security vehicles until his new car arrives."

Chapter 43

LUCIA

A few days later, I am working in my office on payroll.

It's not something I need to teach Helios. He'll be using a bookkeeper going forward. So far, they haven't recruited anyone local with the skill set. For now, the payroll and monthly bookkeeping will be done by someone in California.

The Hades Brotherhood can't hire a regular accountant any more than the Cosa Nostra can. With the mafia, there are always two sets of books. Those for the tax man, and those for the syndicate with record of all money laundered through the club and where it came from.

I haven't suggested myself for the job because I'm still wary. Bookkeeping is a lot safer than running one of their front businesses, but there is still risk. Lessened significantly if the Rokos brothers protect me, like Atlas promises.

I want to trust him, but I'm scared that if I do, he'll hurt me again.

Both our secrets are out in the open, but I wait for the other shoe to drop. Are there still things I don't know about him? Will Atlas start treating me like Tino now that I'm pregnant?

Chance of rain, less than 20%.

My ruthless enforcer still asks my opinion about things, even though the Hades Brotherhood have made their move to secure territory and taken over my club to do it.

So does Zeus. Which is weird. He can be a jerk when challenged, but apparently one that respects my intelligence. He even told me he would never threaten to run sex workers out of Nuovi Inizi again and that he shouldn't have done it the first time.

It's not an apology, but it's an admission of wrongdoing by a man with the same authority and power as a don.

Orion is the same snarky man with the typical god complex of an influential lawyer. He doesn't tell me he's sorry. He tells me to stop dicking his brother around and to get over myself.

The attitude is so much like Rocco that I start to cry. Orion gives me an awkward hug to comfort me and tells me not to be such a crybaby. It's like these Rokos men are intent on proving that I'm part of their family, whether I like it, or not.

"Hey, boss, you look pensive." Willow stands in the doorway of my office, or rather Helios's office.

"Come in sit for a minute." Other than announcing the change in ownership to the employees, I haven't talked to Willow about what's happening.

She relaxes in the chair closest to my desk, no stress or anger evident in her posture. "I guess you weren't loaning your boyfriend money that night, huh?"

I shake my head. "Not exactly, no."

"At first, I worried you were being coerced into selling. You worked so damn hard to make this place a success." Willow eyes me thoughtfully. "But every day that Helios takes on a little more responsibility, you get more relaxed."

"I do?" It surprises me she can tell. I put a lot of effort into hiding my real emotions behind an even-tempered façade.

"Not sure anyone else has noticed, but I've worked for you since you opened this place."

I nod, encouraging her to go on.

"In the beginning, I saw how hard it was for you to deal with the crowds and the noise. You tried to hide it, but it was there in a tightness around your eyes. The way you never wanted to socialize outside of work because you needed time to regroup away from people."

That isn't the only reason I hold myself distant from Willow and the others, but it is part of it.

"You don't think I'm being forced to sell?" I ask, to make sure.

Atlas and his brothers don't need that kind of gossip spreading about them.

"Nah. The more I think about it, the more this move makes sense for you. Besides, that overgrown boyfriend of yours is way too protective to let anybody push you into doing anything you don't want to."

"I'm not exactly a shrinking violet," I argue. "I can stand up for myself."

"Absolutely. Still, it doesn't hurt to have someone like him gaga over you."

"How is everyone doing with the transition?" I ask.

Willow shrugs. "Helios is a cool guy. A little scary sometimes, but I feel like that's a common family gene."

I can't help laughing. "Agreed."

"As long as you're happy, Lucia, we're all doing great. Helios said they want to open more Nuovi Inizis around Portland. They'll be looking for management and I'm keen."

The Hades Brotherhood are going to open other clubs under the Nuovi Inizi name? Not Zesti? I remember Atlas said they wanted to make their own way, but building on what I started is still a very cool thing for them to do.

Warmth expands inside my chest.

Why didn't Atlas tell me? Not that we talk about a whole lot lately. He's busy training new mafia guys. There are a lot more members of the Hades Brotherhood hanging around the club than I even realized were living in Portland.

"I'm glad you're happy about the transition. It's the right thing for me," I tell Willow. "But I didn't want to leave you all in the lurch."

"You so haven't. Helios made it clear that no employee you hired gets fired unless they screw up. Even though they've got their own people, they're finding places for all of us here, or in the new clubs."

"That's good to know." And something I wish Atlas had told me.

He's drawn back into the shell I didn't even know he had until our fight. He's so careful with me, but there's a barrier between us and I'm not sure how to take it down. I've only realized in the last couple of days that I want to.

Very much.

After my chat with Willow, Atlas finds me and tells me it's time for lunch. Today, he has grilled chicken salad and breadsticks ready for me when we get upstairs.

After we finish eating, he herds me toward the bedroom like he has every day for the past two weeks. Atlas expects me to nap, which is ridiculous. I'm not a child, but somehow, I always fall asleep and wake up feeling better. I don't get as tired at night while the club is open either.

I have a feeling that as soon as Helios is fully trained on closing, Atlas will suggest I go to bed earlier. By suggest I mean, carry me up the stairs if I don't go of my own volition.

Like the caveman he is.

I walk into the bedroom and stop short, my breath seizing in my chest.

Crimson leather cuffs sit in the center of my bed with a sleep mask in the same color beside them. My heartbeat stutters.

There is a message here, not just in the presence of the cuffs and blindfold, but in the color of them. Atlas had to have bought them special and he knows what crimson symbolizes to me. Courage.

Atlas is asking me to be brave. To take a risk. On him. On us. He stands so close behind me that I can feel the heat of his body. My thighs clench. My nipples ache. My lips part for kisses that haven't been offered, or welcome, in two long weeks.

Big hands cup my shoulders, their warmth seeping into me. "It is time for you to remember that you trust me, *agape mou*."

"What does that mean? *Agape mou*?" I ask him, finally ready to know.

"My love." He pulls me back against him and wraps his arms around my front. "Some people use it like darling, but I have never called another woman *agape mou*."

Does that mean he loves me?

"You want to have sex."

He thrust his hips forward a little so his hard erection presses into my back. "What gave me away?"

Wrapping my arms with his, I sigh softly. "I'm afraid."

"Of the handcuffs?" he asks, his tone heavy with emotion.

"Of being hurt again."

"I cannot promise not to hurt you, *ilios mou*. My soul died a long time ago. You resurrected it, but that doesn't make me perfect. Or even a different man."

Something in his voice tells me he wishes that were not the case. But I don't want a different man. I want the heart of the one holding me right now.

"I bet you called my OB and confirmed which sex positions are okay for me right now."

"I did, but then I called another doctor too."

"Why?"

"Doctor MacGowen isn't a fan of anal."

My whole body flushes. "You want to..." I let my voice trail off, unable to give voice to the tantalizing picture in my head.

It's not something I ever wanted with Tino, but my panties are soaked from thinking about Atlas touching me in that forbidden place.

"Take your ass? Yes. I want to own every part of your body, Lucia."

"And the other OB said it is okay?"

"I talked to six of them and all of them said yes as long as we go slow, use lots of lube and stretch you so there is no chance of tearing. Like I wouldn't do that anyway. What kind of monster hurts his woman when he's claiming her body?"

Uh...the kind that she asks to? I don't know, but I do know some women love pain with pleasure and others hate it and I'm somewhere in between. Though I doubt I would ever be okay doing anal without lube.

And right now? Pregnant?

I'm totally on the side of caution and care. "Okay."

Chapter 44

ATLAS

"Okay."

Lucia's voice hits me in the solar plexus with the power of a punch. She is saying yes.

"To the blindfold?" I need to confirm.

"Yes."

"To the handcuffs?"

Her body shudders. "Yes."

"To me claiming your ass?" Every muscle in my body goes taut waiting for her answer.

"*Yes.*"

I don't wait for her to change her mind. Pulling her top up and over her head, I start undressing her.

Her hands come behind her to pull at my belt, her fingers brushing over my rigid cock.

I groan. That feels good.

The clasp on her bra releases with a flick of my fingers and I peel the sheer, stretchy fabric away from her generous curves. "You know how much this bra turns me on."

"Mmm hmm." She's still trying to get my belt unbuckled.

I'm enjoying the feel of her hands sliding over my engorged penis too much to help her.

"Are you wearing the matching panties?" I ask with a puff of warm breath in her ear as I cup her tits, brushing my thumbs over her swollen nipples.

She moans out an affirmative.

Picturing the sheer thong revealing the bare lips of her pussy is enough to make my cock start drooling. Good thing I have clean boxers to change into later.

I pick her up and put her on the bed, so I can take her boots and socks off. Running my fingers down the center of her arches I revel in how she gives a whole body shiver at the stimulation.

"I want your tits in my mouth."

"Then hurry up and get us naked," she demands.

A predatory smile curves my lips. "There will be no rushing this."

"It's been two weeks, Atlas!"

"I am aware." If I didn't rub one off every morning in the shower, I would explode from sexual frustration.

It's a near thing regardless.

Yanking my clothes off, I watch her squirm on the bed, her fingertips sliding over the handcuffs and then away again. She wants to be bound. She loves it, but it makes her shy sometimes.

Lucia is it for me, whatever iteration she gives me of herself. The sexually confident siren or the demure angel. Both are her. And both are mine.

Once I am naked, my cock sticking out like a flag pole from my body, I tug Lucia's leggings down her legs one slow inch at a time.

"Come on, Atlas. I know the other has to take time, but not getting undressed."

For all her complaining, she doesn't take matters into her own hands. She trusts me to take care of her, even if she isn't saying so out loud.

Or maybe she is. She did say *yes*.

I leave her panties on so I can look my fill at how they cling to her puffy pussy lips because of how wet she is. "You are so beautiful, *eremenos mou*."

"So are you." Licking her lips, she stares at me with eyes glazed with lust.

This woman.

Kneeling on the bed, I grab the handcuffs. "Give me your wrists."

She offers them without a murmur, the scent of her arousal permeating the air around us.

I buckle one around her wrist and then the other, before attaching them with an eight inch leather cord. Positioning her in the center of the bed, I put a pillow under her head.

The crimson chain I attached to the headboard earlier this morning rattles when I pull it out from where I have it tucked behind the pillows.

Lucia's head jerks up at the sound and her eyes widen when she sees the chain. "You really want me to be brave."

"Maybe I need the reminder to show courage in our relationship." I've been giving her space, but that wasn't working.

I realized I wasn't initiating sex because I was afraid of Lucia's rejection. Fuck that. I don't give into fear. That's not the man I am.

So, I bought the handcuffs from a specialty shop that only sells by appointment. The leathersmith was willing to dye the natural cuffs crimson to match the silk blindfold I brought him. I painted the chain myself.

"What are you afraid of?" she asks, cutting straight to the heart of it.

"Your rejection."

"But I'm so easy for you."

"The past two weeks haven't felt easy," I let her know.

"No, they haven't." She smiles softly. "This is what we both want."

Pulling her cuffed hands above her head and attaching them to the chain, I say, "You know what this means."

"Deeper intimacy than meeting your brothers."

She remembers.

"Yes."

"I've never had anything in my butt. Not even a finger," she informs me.

I almost come right there. "You're a virgin."

"In that way, yes."

Fuck me.

She laughs. "I think it's going to be the other way around."

I said that out loud. I'm losing it. "Let me get the blindfold on you."

"Okay."

Her sweet acquiescence goes straight to my cock and I have to kiss her. She lets me sweep her mouth with my tongue, relearning the taste I've been missing for too long.

When I break the kiss, we're both panting and she's writhing on the bed, her legs splayed wide in invitation. My beautiful lover is so needy right now. Just the way I want her.

I trace her lips with my fingertip after I get the blindfold on her. "Can you see anything?"

"Muted light."

It's not a blackout blindfold, so that's to be expected. "Good."

I cup her breasts again, squeezing gently. "You're all mine to play with."

She arches up toward my hands. And I pinch her nipples in reward. I use everything I have learned about her body to bring her to the brink of orgasm before I rip her panties off, shove her thighs wide and feast on the pussy denied me for fourteen days.

Her scream of release is music to my ears, but I don't stop. Only this time, I cover my finger in lube and circle her asshole over and over. She undulates, clearly enjoying the stimulation of the nerve rich tissue. Some women don't like this.

I knew *eromenus mou* would. And she does. I suckle her clit as I press a fingertip inside her. She moans, canting her hips between my mouth and hand. Not trying to get away from either, but get more of both.

I finger fuck her with one digit until her passage is completely relaxed around my finger. Then I add another, pushing her closer to her second orgasm with my mouth. But she likes having her ass played with and it's not me compensating with the pleasure to her pussy to make up for discomfort in her ass.

She's enjoying both, her ass muscles milking my fingers like her pussy does when she comes. She's so tight. I scissor my thick digits, stretching her for what comes later. We have a ways to go before she'll be able to take my cock.

It takes another climax and a third finger before she's ready for me.

But it's only when she pleads, "Please, Atlas, I want you inside me. There. I need you," that I move up her body and kiss her again.

Forcing my tongue into her mouth so she can taste her own honey, I gorge on her sweetness. She moans and kisses me back, sucking on my tongue. Her earthy delight in our combined flavors turns my crank until I'm revving in the red zone.

I've got to take this slow, no matter how aroused she is, or how turned on I am.

Turning her over, I position a firm pillow under her hips. My mouth waters at the sight of her full, round ass on display, the lube glistening at her crack. I pull her ass cheeks apart and groan at the sight of her pretty stretched hole.

After slathering more lube on the steel monster between my legs, I press my weeping head against her sweet little pucker.

She goes still under me, but doesn't ask me to stop.

So, I don't. "Press out, *brava regazza*. It will make it easier for me to go in."

I'm so hard, there isn't going to be any trouble with me penetrating her backdoor, but I don't want to hurt her. She's going to feel nothing but pleasure giving this virgin hole to me.

She does what I say and my head pops inside. Her muscles clamp around me in a near painful grip. I press forward about a half an inch.

She groans.

"Too much?"

"Not enough. Give it to me, Atlas," she pants. "Make me yours."

"You're already mine," I growl, but surge forward because I can't not.

She gasps as I enter heaven. Are those angels singing? No, it's my woman's sweet little moans.

I pull back and she cries out.

Stilling, I force my raging body to wait until she's ready.

But she slams her ass toward me. "Do that again. It feels so good."

I get halfway inside her before I pull back this time.

A decadent moan of pleasure snakes out of her as I withdraw until only my head is inside her.

We do this over and over until I'm finally seated fully inside her tight virgin channel. No one else has ever felt her velvety heat around them like this and no one else ever will.

The thought unleashes the last of my restraint and I fuck *ilios mou* until she burns me as hot as the sun I call her. Reaching around to play with her clit, I rub circles and brush my finger side to side.

Her ass muscles grasp at my cock, revealing how much she enjoys this.

"Harder, Atlas, more!"

I give it to her, sliding in and out of her lubed tunnel, fucking her with all the power of my bigger body until she screams out her climax. Her ass milks me and drives me right over the edge until I'm coming deep inside her bowels, claiming her in the most primal way possible.

I wait for my breathing to regulate before pulling out slowly, relieved to see nothing but lubricant on my cock. No blood. I did not tear her. With the way she shouted for more, I didn't think it was likely I was hurting her, but I'm still satisfied to see the confirmation.

After I remove the blindfold and handcuffs, I pull her body into mine, surrounding her with my heat. Her hair is sticking to her forehead and temples with sweat, her breathing coming in shallow pants.

I rub her back in soothing circles until she nuzzles into me and says, "I need a shower."

"We both do." We shower together in her tiny stall.

We're going to have to move into the mansion until our house is built because we need a bathtub. Right now my sweet girl needs to soak and she can't.

Doing the next best thing, I bathe her with soapy hands. No wash cloth or loofah to abrade her delicate skin.

When I go to wash her backdoor, she balks. "What are you doing?"

"Washing you. What does it feel like?"

"Uh, that, but I can wash myself."

"You are mine to care for, *ilios mou*."

She relaxes her tightly clamped thighs. "Okay."

"That's becoming my new favorite word," I tease her.

Smiling, she washes what she can reach of my body with soapy hands. We cherish each other in the shower until the water cools.

I pull her out and gently dry her body before rubbing a towel vigorously over my own.

She wraps her arms around me and lays her forehead against my chest. "Thank you."

This woman. "The pleasure is mine."
"It was both our pleasure, but it was more than that."
"Yes, it was." And I'm glad she acknowledges that.

Chapter 45

LUCIA

Atlas's phone rings in the bedroom and he ignores it as our souls connect in the silence between us, the steamy bathroom our refuge from the world.

The ringing stops, only to start all over again a few seconds later. Then my phone starts up.

I lift my head. "We should probably answer. I don't think they're going to stop calling otherwise."

His jaw taut, like he wants to say something, he nods and steps away.

I follow him into the bedroom. Atlas grabs his phone. "What?" he barks.

He listens, his body going rigid, an emotionless mask dropping on his face as he carries on a conversation in rapid fire Greek.

He hangs up and starts yanking on clothes. "Get dressed, we have to go."

Urgency laces his voice and I don't hesitate to tug on fresh underwear and then my legging. I don't bother with a bra but grab a t-shirt to pull over my bare breasts. Even with the sense of urgency surrounding us, my sensitized buds zing with pleasure at contact with the soft cotton.

I yank one of Atlas's hoodies on and zip it up halfway. It smells like him and helps the tension in my body ease. While I put on my socks and boots, Atlas slides his arm through his shoulder holster and adjusts the gun.

After grabbing a brush and a scrunchie, I swipe my phone from the table and grab my purse. "Ready."

"Is your pistol still in there?" Atlas takes my hand and pulls me after him.

"Yes."

"Good." Tugging me into the kitchen area, he grabs a gun and extra ammunition from the top of one of my cupboards.

When had he put that there? I don't ask.

Now is not the time to discuss his tendency to make himself at home in my apartment. The fact that he feels the need to grab the extra gun when he's already wearing one in a shoulder holster, says whatever is happening is serious.

He slips the extra ammo into his pocket and holds the gun up and ready. "Hold onto the back of my shirt. I need to know you're there."

With no thought to argue, I slide my hand under his jacket and grab his shirt.

He jogs out of the apartment and down the stairs. I stay with him the whole way. Helios, Theo, Bobby and Michael are all downstairs in the club when we get there.

"I'll get her to the mansion." Helios reaches out like he's going to take my arm. "You need to go hunting."

"I'll hunt down the walking dead men *after* I get her safe," Atlas snarls. "You, Bobby and Michael stay on our six. Theo, you're driving my SUV."

He hustles me outside and into the SUV's middle seat while the other men get into another SUV parked behind the club.

Atlas gets in beside me. "If I say down, you bend over and keep your head below the line of the window. If I say floor, you unbuckle and get on the floor, curled into as tight of a ball as you can."

"Okay." Childhood training comes back and I sit slanted sideways so my head is not a target.

"*Brava regazza.*"

It's a totally inappropriate time to be getting wet, but my body reacts predictably when he calls me good girl again in Italian.

"What's going on?" I can finally ask since him giving me an answer will no longer slow us down.

"Zeus's informant contacted him. Two teams arrived yesterday, maybe earlier, from Russia. Their orders are to take me and Zeus out and to nab you."

"What do you mean nab me?" I brush my hair into a smooth, wet ponytail and hold it in place with the scrunchie. "Why?"

"Ivan."

Dropping the brush into my purse, I go hot and then cold, remembering what this Ivan wants to do with me.

Atlas calls his brother and puts him on speaker. "I'm heading to the mansion with Lucia."

"Do you think that's wise? One of the teams is targeting me and I'm here."

"They don't know we are aware of them. If it were me, I'd wait until you leave the estate. Easier to get to you. Our biggest point of vulnerability is when we arrive."

"There's no vantage point for a sniper. You made sure of that," Zeus says. "If they attack it will be at close range."

"It doesn't look like they had anyone on the club yet. We aren't being followed."

"Good. They got in yesterday. They may still be sourcing their weapons. Plenty of time for you to hunt."

Why does Atlas have to track these guys down? He's one of the targets, for goodness' sake.

Only I know. This is the way it is in the mafia. It's his job.

"I'm not going hunting until I know Lucia is in the saferoom where no one can get to her." It's the second time he's put that out there.

Warmth unfurls inside me. He's determined to keep me and the baby safe. After what he said in my apartment, I don't believe this is only because I'm pregnant either. I am his sun, the star around which his world turns.

His future.

"Of course not, brother. Your woman's safety comes first." There's a strange tone in Zeus's voice and I wonder what it means.

The SUV lurches to the right, goes up on a curb and back onto the street with a bone jolting thump. A rock hits the back window causing small cracks, but the window doesn't shatter.

Another rock hits and I realize they're not rocks. They are bullets.

"Down, Lucia," Atlas barks.

I tuck under the chest strap of the seatbelt and bend in half, my arms wrapped around my knees, my head resting sideways on them.

The car swerves right to left and then back again.

"We're taking fire," Atlas says to his brother, his voice filled with quiet rage.

"Orion and his team are heading your way."

Atlas climbs into the far backseat and I hear a soft whir, then the road noise gets louder. He's opened the back window somehow.

"Atlas, get away from the window," I yell, but I don't lift my head.

"Don't worry, Lucia, my X7 is designed for this."

For firefights? How dangerous is his life? Armored cars are not uncommon in our world, but SUVs tricked out to make shooting at pursuers possible? Not so much.

He shoots at whoever is pursuing us and then grunts. "One down, nine to go."

He starts whistling *Another One Bites the Dust* and despite the situation I smile.

"Are you whistling, boss?" Theo demands from the front.

Two more shots sound and then the cacophony of a crashing vehicle. The window whirs as it rises back into place and Atlas comes back over the seat.

He rubs my back. "You can sit up now, *ilios mou*."

I jerk upright and examine Atlas for any injuries. But there's nothing. "You're okay?" I ask.

"I am. Were you worried about me?" He sounds almost bemused. "No reason to be. I'm very good at what I do."

"Like gold medal good," Theo pipes up.

Great. The man I love is a gold medal killer. Better that than dead though.

And yes, I do love him. I knew before the whole protection money debacle, but have been trying to convince myself it was anything but love for the last week.

"I'm so glad for you. Everyone should have something they are good at," I say acerbically. "But don't scare me like that again. What if they had shot you through the open window?"

"Nah. The opening was too small and both of our vehicles were moving. Only a handful of shooters in the world could have made that shot."

"It's a good thing they weren't using armor piercing rounds," Theo adds. "The window would have shattered then."

I gasp.

Atlas barks something at Theo in Greek.

"Sorry," the other man says contritely. "I didn't mean to upset you, Lucia."

"Um, you didn't. I mean, if they had used armor piercing rounds, I would be more than upset. But Atlas is okay."

"You care," Atlas teases me.

I'm not reacting to that statement. At all. Of course I care. If I didn't, I wouldn't have been so devastated to learn he was using me.

In a blatant attempt to change the subject, I point out, "Your entire whistling repertoire is from a different century, or haven't you noticed that?"

"So? I like the songs. And they fit." He starts whistling "My Girl" again, but sings a single line, "I've got sunshine on a cloudy day," before he slips back into whistling.

I swipe at wet eyes. "Darn pregnancy hormones."

"If you say so."

I glare at Atlas. "I do."

"If you two are finished," Zeus says from the car speakers.

Oh, sheesh. We have been on speaker phone all this time.

"We need to check my SUV for trackers. Unless the bratva bastards are that good at tailing a car undetected, they found me with technology."

"I assume you didn't take time to check for a tracker before you left the club."

"No," Atlas bites out between gritted teeth. Oh, he's angry with himself for not doing it.

"They shouldn't have been able to act that quickly," Zeus says, like he's giving his brother an out.

"They might be sourcing a specialty weapon, but they obviously brought guns with them. No reason to assume they didn't bring everything else they needed for their op."

"I'll reach out to my informant."

"I thought he only contacted you, that you didn't have a way to contact him," Atlas says.

"Sh...they called me with this intel instead of texting me," Zeus says. "They didn't block their number like usual."

"Helios needs to scrub the traffic cams," Atlas says.

Zeus grunts an assent. "I'll put him on it as soon as you all get here."

"Helios is your hacker?" I guess these Greek mafia men wear multiple hats in their organization. "He's really good at managing a club."

Atlas scans the empty streets around us. "Helios has tech geniuses on his crew. They run the online gambling operation and money laundering from that angle."

"And cover your asses with traffic cams in their off hours?" I tease.

"Pretty much."

Zeus grunts and Atlas frowns. "I'm not hiding shit from her."

"You got brotherly disapproval of oversharing with me from that grunt?" I ask, impressed.

"More like *anax* disapproval," Zeus says.

"Are you worried I'm going to take my newfound knowledge to the FEDs? Really?" Zeus misses my epic eyeroll because...phone and not video call.

But Atlas sees it and winks at me.

I grin back at him.

"The thought crossed my mind."

"Well uncross it. Or whatever. I'm no rat."

"Good to know."

"Will you be very upset with me if I shoot your brother?" I smile sweetly up at Atlas.

"I knew that look meant nothing good."

"You're so astute."

"You cannot threaten to shoot me." Zeus sounds ticked.

"I just did, so it looks like I can."

"Lucia," he barks.

Ooh, the *anax* is angry. Atlas doesn't look worried, but Theo is gripping the steering wheel tighter than he was when trying to avoid the Russians chasing us.

I sigh. "Fine. I won't threaten to shoot you anymore."

"Thank you."

Theo jerks and gives me a wide-eyed look in the rearview mirror.

"You're welcome. Don't call me a rat and we're good."

Zeus sighs. "You should not threaten your *anax* regardless."

I shrug. The obedient mafia princess has been squeezed right out of my DNA.

"Lucky for you all, this happened on this street." Portland is a population dense metropolitan and not many areas are like this one with no foot or car traffic.

Even luckier, Portland decided against using the gunshot recognition system that was hotly debated for several months. Unless a security guard for one of the warehouses calls in suspicious sounds, the cops won't be the wiser.

No doubt by the time another car drives down the deserted street, Atlas's people will have removed all evidence of the gun battle and car accident.

"Not luck. Planning," Zeus says. "We located our compound where we did for a reason."

"Because it is surrounded by mostly industrial buildings, or no buildings at all." East of the city, it is closer to the seedy bar we first saw the bratva soldiers in than to my club.

"You have a very mafia centric mindset." Atlas puts one hand on my thigh, but the other holds his gun ready and his eyes are fixed on the world outside the SUV.

"I guess. It was fun living like a normal person for a few years though." When I wasn't stressing over making a success of the club and keeping Lenny where he's happy.

Or worrying about if someone from my past would walk into the club once it became so popular with out-of-towners.

Okay, normal might be overstating the case.

Chapter 46

LUCIA

We reach the mansion without further incident. Rolling right through the gates open to let us in, Theo brings the SUV to a lurching halt in front of the house.

Neither he, nor Atlas, open their doors though.

Theo is watching something behind us. Atlas is casing the area with laser focus. I wait in silence.

"It's shut." Theo must mean the gate.

Atlas nods. Takes another look around the house and then opens his door. "Let's go."

He steps out and then puts his hand out to me.

I slide across the seat to take it. By the time I get out of the SUV, Theo and the rest of the crew are there, creating a protective barrier around me.

"I thought Zeus said there are no sniper vantage points," I say as I'm ushered inside.

"There aren't," Zeus himself affirms.

Bobby shuts the door behind us. "But the boss won't take any chances with you."

This over-the-top protectiveness is for me. I shudder to imagine what he'll be like once our baby is born. I'm thinking helicopter dad with an automatic rifle.

"I'll take Lucia to the saferoom," Zeus says. "Timio has some intel for you, Dimios."

Executioner. That's what that means. I do a quick internal check, but the reminder that Atlas is an assassin doesn't impact my feelings for him at all.

"He can tell me on the way to the saferoom." Atlas is serious about seeing me there with his own eyes before he's willing to go hunting.

"You don't trust me to see to her safety?" Zeus asks.

"If I had no other choice, you are one of a few I would trust. But I do have a choice and I will not leave *ilios mou's* safety to anyone else."

Zeus nods. "Protect your sun well, brother. Our souls are darker than Hades' Lair."

Tears prick my eyes. These pregnancy hormones really are a bitch. But Zeus sounds resigned to an immutable truth. Like Atlas did when we first met.

Atlas takes me by the hand and leads me down the hall toward Zeus's office, but we stop halfway there and he slides a picture upward and puts his hand on a scanner pad. The once seamless wall slides outward and the next scanner is for his eye.

He then tugs me forward. "Try not to blink so it can scan your eye for access, *agape mou.*"

Once the heavy door swings outward, he pulls it wide enough for me to step through the opening. Inside, is a smaller version of his suite upstairs without the kitchenette, though there is a microwave and a minifridge.

Gina is sitting on the small couch watching something on her phone. She looks up with a smile. "You hanging out with me while they get whatever sorted?"

I nod.

"Theo will be staying too," Atlas says from the open doorway.

"No." The word comes out louder than I intend. "You need him with you. We'll be fine here on our own."

Atlas shakes his head. "I am gold level good at what I do, remember? I don't need Theo with me, but I do need to know you are safe so I can concentrate on doing my job."

I can't help noticing he's a lot more circumspect about what that job is in front of the housekeeper. It surprises me, but I don't comment on it. If the brothers and cousins don't tell her all the details of their business, I'm not going to point that out.

Zeus would prefer *I* didn't know the nitty gritty details either. Too bad for him.

If Atlas and I have any chance at a future, it will not be with him treating me like a mushroom. Keeping me in the dark and smothering me with shit to cover what's really happening.

Atlas turns to go.

"Atlas!"

He stops and faces me. "I will be fine, *agape mou.*"

"I know." He has to be. There is no other option. "When Tino left that night to go into work, he didn't kiss me goodbye."

Atlas's eyes flare with emotion. "You want me to kiss you?"

"Yes."

"I thought she hated his guts." Orion says from the hallway.

The snarky brother has joined them. Good. I want as many people watching Atlas's back as possible.

Atlas ignores his brother and cups my face with both hands. "Remember to eat something."

I nod.

He kisses me, his lips soft at first, but the kiss quickly turns possessive. I mold my lips to his, parting them in invitation. His tongue delves into my mouth, claiming and arousing. Proof of his constant desire for me, even when the world is burning around us.

No one rushes the kiss. Not even Orion.

When Atlas finally lifts his head, his blue gaze is dark with desire. "Do not leave this room until I come for you."

"Okay."

His face shifts into an emotionless mask and he turns away. A predator's energy emanates from him and it turns me on way more than it should. No matter what I tell myself, I have always sensed the danger in him. The darkness.

And I am in love with it as much as everything else about him.

The way he treats me like I'm the only person in the building even when the club is filled with gorgeous women on the make. The way he listens to me and values my opinion. The way he makes love to me like I am the only woman he will ever want.

The way he takes charge in the bedroom to take care of me, not keep me under his thumb.

An apex predator, Atlas doesn't need to treat me like I am less than to make himself more.

"Be careful," I call as he leaves.

He nods without looking back. I know why. It's as hard for him to leave me as it is for me to let him go.

But Atlas has a job to do.

He has to go hunting to protect his family, me and the baby included.

ATLAS

"We are staying at the house..." He names a surprisingly populated area, but it is in the Dobro Pozhalovat community.

Hiding in plain sight, this property is not on the list the *pakhan* gave us. Does that mean he hid it from us deliberately, or doesn't know about it? Both are equally likely scenarios.

Its location explains Dimitri naming the neighborhood in Moscow during interrogation. While there are many Baltic immigrants living in the area, the name for the community is Russian. *Welcome.*

No way do the inhabitants want to welcome the Golubev Bratva.

Pricking slightly deeper into my *guests* ballsac, I ask, "House number?"

He shakes his head and I drag my knife slowly down, making a clean cut right between his testicles. His scream tells me he's close to giving me what I want.

It's a myth that soldiers can be trained to withstand torture indefinitely. If the man has a certain personality type, he will die an excruciating death before giving up information he isn't supposed to. If he doesn't, he will break. And I am not just a gold medal assassin; my torture techniques do not fail.

I wipe my bloody knife on his cheek. "House number."

The words are a whisper, but I hear them. Helios is there and he sends the address to one of his tech geniuses for confirmation.

It takes fifteen minutes, during which the prisoner sobs and begs for death.

"Satellite images and traffic cams close to the address confirm the arrival of sixteen men the day before yesterday. There is no sign of Ivan. My guy is tracking two four man teams through traffic cams now for approximate locations."

"What about the other four men?" I took out three of the four men trying to kill me earlier.

My current 411 connection to the bratva is the one still living picked up by the clean up crew.

"What was your directive?" I ask the now weeping man.

"To kill the Rokos brothers."

All three of us? "Why?"

I can guess, but I prefer to know.

"In...our...way..." he gasps out.

"The *pakhan* agreed to a truce." Not that any of us trusted him.

"We take our orders from Ivan."

Now, that is interesting. Bratva and mafia have one thing in common. The second-in-command does not issue orders counter to the boss's. That is treason, a capital offense, regardless of what syndicate you are in.

"Does the *pakhan* know that Ivan sent you here?"

"Ivan said...was gift."

Ah, so the *pakhan* doesn't know. He is still responsible because it's his job to control his men.

"You came here to kill me and my brothers?" I toss my knife and catch it right in front of the Russian man's face.

Will he confirm Zeus's source's intel?

"After you are all dead, we take the woman."

"What woman?" I press harder.

"Owns a club."

My woman. The mother of my child.

"I will bathe in the blood of you and your comrades." Making no effort to move, I slit his throat.

Arterial spray splatters my face and clothes, the warm droplets anchor me to the present and *my* directive. To kill every one of these motherfuckers.

Helios's guy tracks one team to an unpopulated spot outside the city where they have been for the last hour. Getting the specialty weapon that they ordered?

The other team is on a major street near the mansion and I smile. Lucia and Gina are safe in the panic room and the compound is equipped to handle any attack short of one from a rocket launcher.

The bastards are making this too easy for me.

Currently in the onsite interrogation room in the basement of our mansion, I am ready for them.

We prefer to keep things to the warehouse, but that's not always possible. When we set up the compound, we designed this room for easy disposal and mop-up.

Barking orders to my crew, I jog to the armory and get my sniper rifle with a suppressor. It won't block the sound of the shot entirely, but it will be enough to make it unlikely anyone outside our compound will hear it.

There are no vantage points outside of the compound property where a sniper can create a nest and wait to take one of us out. We purchased and demolished the only two buildings that might have worked, with the added advantage of preventing any nearby neighbors moving in.

However, the top level of the mansion has several sniper nests in place that cover all approaches to the compound. Once we confirm the team's approach, I will get in place to take them out.

I prefer up close and personal kills, but with twelve more men to dispose of before *ílios mou* is safe, I need to keep things fast and efficient.

~ ~ ~

The head of the last man on the kill team explodes inside their vehicle when Helios's guy tells us that the last team and the one in the industrial district are both on the move. Because I do not know the nature of the weapon, or weapons, they have procured, I need to take them out before they come to the compound.

A rocket launcher is unlikely but not out of the realm of possibility.

They are heading toward the same area of the city. It could be the compound, or some other rendezvous point.

If I play this right, I can intercept the team from the industrial area first. Since I was eleven years old and made my first kill, I have always played it right.

This time is no exception.

I take out the tires of the SUV they are driving in from my sniper position. Then I wait for it to crash into a nearby building and pick off the two men who get out. The driver is still at the wheel, either knocked out or dead from the collision. The man in the front passenger seat shows more self-preservation, diving to the back.

Bobby moves in on the SUV and takes him out with a head shot through the back window while Michael secures the driver. Alive then.

The cleanup crew arrives with a tow truck. They're trained as well as any Formula One pit crew and have the SUV up on the tow truck bed in less than three minutes. They take the prisoner. He'll be waiting for me at the warehouse when I'm ready to interrogate him later.

I want confirmation that Ivan instigated this attempt to take me and my brothers out and to kidnap Lucia, more intel on the Golubev bratva in Russian and information on Ivan's routines and whereabouts.

My crew and I move on to intercept the last kill team. They are driving through more populated areas and we have to wait to make our move. It soon becomes obvious the rendezvous point is supposed to be the compound.

It's almost anticlimactic how easy these assholes are making this for me.

Not that I mind this time. Not when Lucia's safety is at risk as long as the bratva soldiers are at large in the city.

I challenge myself to take them alive, and succeed with all but one. He jumps from the sedan, brandishing an automatic rifle and starts spraying automatic fire immediately. I take him out with a shot to the head before joining my team to surround the car.

One of the other bratva tries to be a hero, but I take him down with a shot to the shoulder and knee. He won't die before I get the information I want, but he'll wish he did.

Once the threat is neutralized, I want to get Lucia out of the panic room, but I don't. I need confirmation the four teams are the only Golubev bratva in the city before she comes out.

If I wait to get the other intel I want, there's a good chance the injured man will die before he can give up what he knows.

~ ~ ~

It's the early hours of the morning when I finish. Blood covers my face, arms and clothes.

"Good work, brother," Zeus says. "Go. Take a shower. Get your woman. She refused to leave the saferoom when I let Gina out because she'd promised you she would stay until you came back."

That's Lucia. She makes a promise and she keeps it.

"She's too good for me."

"You think? You're one of the best men I know. Loyal. Strong. Honest."

"I'm an assassin. I have killed more men than any serial killer on death row."

"War has casualties."

"She lost her first husband to a syndicate war." I hate acknowledging Lucia once belonged to another man.

"She won't lose you."

"I hid who I am from her. What we are. It hurt her."

"You didn't mean to."

"Does it matter?"

Zeus sighs. "I don't know. Intention doesn't prevent outcome."

"No." I wipe the blood from my hands, but don't attempt to clean it off anywhere else. "I didn't want her to know about Dimios. When I told her about being an assassin, I didn't plan on giving her details."

"Did something about today change that?"

"Not today. Just thinking about what she said. I'm not hiding anything else about who I am."

"Are you prepared for her rejection if she can't accept what it means for you to be Dimios?"

"No." She's mine. Now and always. "But she deserves to know what she is allowing into her life."

"You are not a thing, but a man."

"Sometimes, I don't feel human."

"We all lost part of our humanity when Grandfather refused to negotiate your return."

"Not when we made our first kills?"

"No. For you, the first time they tortured you, they took away a little bit of what makes you human. For me and Orion, the day Constantin snuck us into his father's office to show us the videos of you being beaten peeled away part of ours."

"Lucia deserves a man with his humanity intact." But I am the man she gets.

"Your sun deserves the man she wants. If that is you, you will only hurt her if you try to protect her from yourself."

"When did you get so wise about women?"

Zeus shakes his head. "Go. Talk to her, but take a shower and change your clothes. You look like an extra from a horror movie."

Maybe that's exactly what Lucia needs to see. Me as I am, not how I wish I could be for her.

Chapter 47

LUCIA

At the sound of the saferoom's door opening, I leap from the bed and rush into the outer room. The low-level light reveals Theo standing near the small sofa.

He nods toward the front door. "Boss. She's sleeping in the bedroom."

"I'm right here." And I haven't been sleeping.

Gina left the panic room hours ago when Zeus came and told her she could, but I promised Atlas I wouldn't until he came for me. So, I stayed.

"Uh, boss, do you want to go take a shower? I'll bring Lucia up to your suite."

Something dark is speckled over Atlas's face and arms. The scent of old copper permeates the air.

"Are you hurt?" I rush over to him and start patting his body, looking for wounds.

"The only men hurt are the ones who wanted to kill me and my brothers and kidnap you." The way he says *kidnap you*, that's the part he holds against them the most.

Because I matter to him.

Atlas cups my shoulders. "You don't look like you were sleeping."

"I wasn't."

"Why not?"

"I didn't know where you were."

"Didn't Theo tell you my mission was a success?"

I nod. "But no one would tell me where you were. I didn't know if you were hurt. Theo said you weren't but..." I shrug.

"You didn't know if you could believe him."

Theo puts his hand up like he's going to touch me. Atlas growls and Theo's hand drops. "I wouldn't lie to you, Lucia."

"You would if Atlas told you to, or one of his brothers."

Theo has the grace to look chagrined. He knows I'm right.

"I didn't tell him to lie."

"You didn't tell him to answer my questions either."

"I was torturing the men I did not kill for information." Atlas holds his body tight, his expression stoic.

He didn't take time to wash up before coming to get me. Because he couldn't wait to see me? Or because he wanted me to see him fully for who he is? He's not hiding anything from me anymore.

This is him as much as the sexy man in a black leather jacket and jeans, or the ruthless enforcer in his custom-tailored designer suit. And he wants me to see, wants me to accept him for who he truly is.

No more secrets. No more hiding behind half-truths.

"Yes, I see the blood of our enemies on you. It doesn't scare me." I lay my hand over his heart. "The only thing that scares me is that you don't love me."

"Uh, that's my cue to leave. Good luck there, boss." Theo grabs something off the back of the sofa and leaves the panic room.

Atlas is staring at me like he's trying to see into my head. "Not love you?" he demands. "What the fuck do you think I have been saying?"

"You say I'm yours. That you will never let me go, which is pretty arrogant, you know?" My hand fists in his shirt.

It's damp. More blood.

"I don't feel arrogant." His arm comes around me, pressing me flush with his big, muscular body.

"You said that our baby makes us a family. Would you have let me go if I wasn't pregnant?" I need to know.

"I told you I wasn't going anywhere before we found out you are pregnant."

True. "You know what you haven't said a single word about?" I frown up at him. "Loving me."

I am deeply, irrevocably in love with my Greek mafia assassin but don't know if he feels the same. Yes, he's over-the-top protective, but is it about ownership or love?

"What do you think I'm saying when I call you *agape mou*?"

"You said it can mean darling as well as my love."

"And I told you I'd never called any other woman *agape mou*. Like I've never called another woman my sun or my lover. You're it for me, my one chance at happiness."

Dio mio. The things he says.

"Are you saying you love me?" I need it spelled out. My heart needs the words, not endearments.

"With everything left of my fractured soul." The emotion in his eyes defies me to disbelieve him.

"There's this quote," I say softly. "We are all broken and that is how the light gets in. I think it's Hemingway. Anyway, if I'm your light then the only way I get into your soul is if it is a little broken."

Pain fills Atlas's expression. "It's more than a little broken. It's shattered."

"Is it? Knowing you love me has brought the pieces of my broken heart back together. What does knowing I love you do for your soul?"

"You love me?"

"What do you think I have been saying?" I use his words back on him.

"Say it."

"I love you, Atlas. Dimios. Enforcer. All of you."

He shakes his head. "No. You cannot love me. Not after what I did to you."

"Did you have sex with me to get information out of me?" That's the idea that hurt the most.

"No. When I saw you, I wanted you like I have never wanted anyone or anything. Making love to you that night wasn't smart, but I couldn't help myself."

His words soothe the rough edges of the raw wound inside me.

"I should have left your club alone. It's my job to protect you and I cost you your dream."

"Nuovi Inizi is not my dream." It never was.

"But your little house." He shakes his head like he can't stand to think of it.

"I hope whoever buys it has the carpet in the primary bedroom cleaned. We left a stain from our lovemaking," I tease.

"That person should be you."

"No. You can't live in that house with me. I can't live there pregnant with your baby. It's not safe."

"I've turned your life upside down."

"Yes, you have, but love has a way of doing that. Didn't you know?"

"No. I have never been in love before."

"But you are now." I need to hear it again. It seems so impossible that Atlas loves me as deeply and irrevocably as I do him.

"I love you my beautiful sun. More than life. More than my family. More than the *Ádis Adelfótita*."

"Blasphemy." I'm teasing. A little. Part of me is deadly serious. "Nothing can come before your syndicate."

"Nothing can come before you."

Tears wash into my eyes. "You mean that."

"Yes."

"You said you would leave Portland and your brothers to be with me."

"Yes."

"But they are your family."

"You are my everything."

"You say stuff like that and it feels like there's a vice in my chest squeezing my heart."

"Good. If I have hold of your heart, I have hold of you."

"You know me so well."

"And you know me."

Done arguing truths my heart and my mind agree on, I nod. His kiss reforms my broken heart to an organ that beats only for him.

When he lifts his head, he frowns, swiping at my cheek with his thumb. "You're crying. And I got blood on you."

"Emotions can be messy. And I don't care."

"I should have showered before coming to you."

"No," I disagree vehemently. "You wanted me to see you as you are, to hide nothing from me. And I do."

"Yes."

"I'm glad. I love *you* Atlas. All of you." I'll say it as often as he needs me to.

"You deserve someone better, but I will never let you go." He squeezes me tight.

"If you try, I'll hunt you down and make you sorry."

"Would you?"

"Oh yes."

"If anyone could find me, it would be you."

I smile. He sees my stubbornness and my intelligence. Neither intimidates him. Because his strength of will easily matches mine. So does his smart brain.

I like it.

"How do you feel about sex in the shower?" My body is craving the kind of orgasms only he can give me.

But even more, I crave the closeness physical intimacy brings.

He doesn't answer, but he swings me up into his arms and jogs out of the room. My body on fire for his touch, I kiss along his neck and the underside of his jaw. I don't care about the blood.

I want him any way I can get him.

Reaching the bathroom in his suite, he sets me on my feet and turns on the water in the large shower enclosure. Watching each other, we both strip out of our clothes.

We don't even wait to wash before he's kissing me again, his tongue deep in my mouth, his hands roving over my naked body with purpose.

Atlas knows how to touch me to have me writhing against him. I rip my mouth from his. "I need you, Atlas, now."

He lifts me under my arms and slams me back against the wall of the shower. Spreading my legs, I wrap them around his hips, inviting him inside. Still tender from before, my pucker twinges.

But the small pain adds to the pleasure.

Lifting me so the head of his erection is pressing against the opening of my body, he surges upward, filling me with one powerful thrust.

My vaginal walls stretch and sting a little, but it feels good and I want this too much to stop and prepare my body more.

It's like he knows though, and he slows down, pulling out one slow centimeter at a time before sliding back in just as slowly. I try to shove downward, but his hold on my bottom is like steel and I'm not moving anywhere he doesn't want me to.

His kiss turns languid as well and the inferno inside me burns brighter and hotter than ever before.

"I need more." My words are both a demand and a plea. "Be gentle another time. Not now. Now, I need you to remind my body of our connection."

"I can do that without plowing you into the wall."

"Plow me. Please."

His laugh is evil. He knows how turned on I am. His huge, rock hard penis tells me he is as aroused as me. But he doesn't increase his pace.

Hot water falls around us, steam filling the large glass enclosure as Atlas takes me on a hellishly slow ride to heaven.

"Touch yourself," he demands, his voice dark and commanding.

Without thought, my hand slides between our bodies and my middle finger slips across my engorged nub. I keen, my head going side to side.

"It's too much."

"No." That's all he says. No.

And I believe him. Because he's right. It's not too much. It isn't enough. I circle my clit with my fingertip and then press against it, sliding my finger side to side and my climax storms over me.

I'm not moving my hand anymore, but Atlas is causing it to jostle against my bundle of nerves with his now hard and deep thrusts. Aftershocks roll through me and I cry out, over and over, the pleasure never fully abating.

Throwing his head back, he shouts while the heat of his semen pulses inside me causing another onslaught of ecstasy to wash over me.

I'm crying when we finish and he licks my tears away. Then he washes my body meticulous inch by meticulous inch. After washing my hair, he puts conditioner in it and then starts washing his own body.

I help him, making sure every droplet of blood is wiped away.

"Turn around," I tell him. "Let me get your back."

After kissing me, he does and I wash his back and buttocks before sliding my tongue and lips over every scar that has made him into the man he is today.

"Ilios mou," he grinds out. *"S'agapo."*

Pretty sure that means I love you in Greek. So I say the words back to him. Over and over against his marked skin.

He bends forward, his hands on the opposite wall, holding him up. I lean against him, pressing my breasts against his back, wrapping my arms around his torso.

We stay like that in tender silence for long seconds before he tugs me around so he can rinse the conditioner from my hair. Afterward, he turns off the water and we step out of the steamy cubicle to dry each other off.

We're careful with each other, like it's our first time.

In a way it is. It is the first time we make love that we both know we *are* making love.

He knows all my secrets and I know his. I will hold them in my heart for the rest of our lives.

Chapter 48

LUCIA

I finish training Helios to take over Nuovi Inizi, but there's a subtle shift in things now. Atlas always stays close, but now he touches me constantly.

While Helios, and every other man in the Hades Brotherhood, keeps their distance. And woe betide anyone clumsy enough to bump into me.

Bobby grabs my arm. "Where do you want these crates?"

Before I can answer, Atlas is in front of me and the thunk of flesh hitting muscle sounds.

Expelling a harsh breath, Bobby doubles over.

"Atlas, you psycho. He was just asking me a question." I rush to help Bobby stand but he backs away from me with his hands up. "I'm fine."

His face is red and he's still breathing shallowly, trying to control the pain.

"You're not fine," I contradict and turn to glare at my boyfriend. "What is your problem?"

"He knows not to touch you. They all do."

"What if I was going to walk in front of a bus? Would you prefer he let me do it instead of grabbing me to save me?"

"You will never do something so stupid." Atlas's glower is sulfuric.

I roll my eyes. "Okay, fine. Bad example, but you know what I mean."

"If it is a matter of your safety, exceptions can be made."

"How are they supposed to know that?" I indicate the men milling around the bar where the staff is preparing for the night ahead.

There are always at least two other members of the Hades Brotherhood hanging around, sometimes more. It's for my security because they are there even when the club is closed.

I know it's about me because they follow me when I leave too. I might as well be royalty or something with my own security detail.

Tino was never this possessive, or protective. But then Tino was nothing like Atlas on so many levels.

"I don't like you punishing Bobby for trying to get my attention."

If anything, Atlas's frown gets more ferocious and it's directed toward the member of his crew.

"It's all good, Lucia. I won't forget again, boss."

I spin to face Bobby. "Don't let him off the hook like that. He should apologize."

Bobby's face contorts like he swallowed a lemon and he backs away quickly. "Yeah, no. The apology wasn't my idea, boss."

"Ask Helios where he wants the crates. He's in charge now, not me," I call as Bobby disappears down the hall toward the office and the back door to the club.

Atlas's hands land on my shoulders. "Is that what you really want?"

This again. "I don't want to talk about the club. Atlas, you can't threaten your men for trying to get my attention. It's not Bobby's fault my mind was elsewhere."

"Where was it?" Atlas turns me to face him, but doesn't let me go.

My hands automatically settle against his chest and I revel in the strength of his muscles and warmth of his body.

"Helios doesn't need any further training."

A tick develops in Atlas's jaw. "So? You promised Zeus thirty days."

"I'm not going anywhere, Atlas. I already told you that."

"You gave up your house and even though you have enough money to buy it outright now, you haven't talked to Elaine about renewing your offer."

"How do you know that?"

"I asked her."

Sighing, I rub my hands over his pectoral muscles. "That's a little invasive, don't you think?"

"No. You are mine."

"You say that a lot." Every time we make love and sometimes when we don't. Like now.

"Because it is true."

"I don't deny it."

"Orion thinks you want to keep a nest egg to fall back on. Is that it? I can buy the club for you, but you'll never be without resources. I'll make sure of that."

"That's a very generous offer, but I don't *want* the club. Opening Nuovi Inizi was the best way I could think of to make enough money to care for Lenny long term, but I never wanted to own a nightclub."

"You spent five years building the business. You want me to believe none of that matters?"

"No, of course not." I lean against him, inhaling his scent. Leather, bergamot and spice, but underneath it all, Atlas. My man. "I'm proud of what I did here, but that doesn't mean I want to keep doing it."

"Why not?"

"Why do you think?" I challenge back. He says he loves me. Does he know me?

Atlas pulls me closer to his body and rubs my back. "You don't like crowds. You won't miss working the floor."

"True." But that's not all.

"Managing the talent takes a lot of patience."

"It does."

"You put up with shit I wouldn't."

"Which is why Helios is running the club and not you."

A laugh rumbles deep in Atlas's chest, vibrating under my hands. He's not offended.

"I'm better at killing than cajoling." The words are filled with humor, but they are laced with a question.

One I am happy to answer. Again.

Tilting my head back, I smile up at him so he can see the acceptance in my gaze. "Yes, you are. Lucky for all of us, or that situation with the bratva kill teams would have gone very differently."

His kiss comes as no surprise and I let myself fall into it for long minutes, but then my stomach growls.

He moves his mouth from mine. "You need to eat."

"For a top assassin, you have a real mother hen complex."

"Eat some lunch and I'll show you my cock tendencies."

"That was bad, Atlas." But I laugh. I love his humor, especially since he doesn't reveal it very often.

Lunch is leftover pasta from last night. Atlas makes a salad while it's heating and I set the table.

"So, you don't want me to buy back Nuovi Inizi?"

I make a sound like a kettle letting off steam. "Seriously? How many times do I have to say it? I'm glad not to have the responsibility anymore. If I could have supported Lenny with a job as a bookkeeper, I would have."

We finish getting the food on the table in a companionable silence. Atlas isn't mad and if he finally hears me about the club, I'm not either.

"Are you interested in doing the books for us?" Atlas sounds intrigued by the possibility.

"That's something I've been meaning to talk to you about." Only, I don't want to get caught up in business with California's Hades Brotherhood. "By us, do you mean the Greek mafia here in Portland?"

"My wife doesn't work for the *Ádis Adelfótita*. You are family with as much of a stake in our success here in Portland as me, my brothers and my cousins."

"I am not your wife," I remind him with some bite. "We haven't discussed marriage."

"We did."

I roll my eyes. "That was a threat, not a proposal."

"I'm working on it."

"What's to work on?"

"I'll explain tonight."

He's going to propose tonight? And he's telling me about it? But then I did ask. Sort of.

"Yes, I would be interested in taking over the accounts for you and your brothers. I know a lot about laundering money."

"I thought you didn't want to work for criminals."

"Not as your patsy, but as a part of the family? That's different. I am not morally opposed to cooking the books, but I am categorically opposed to taking the fall for the organization."

"I will never let that happen." He looks dangerously angry at the idea.

"I believe you." Which is why I'm so intrigued by the idea of becoming their bookkeeper. "Talk to your brothers about me taking over the books."

"Don't you want to wait until after the baby is born?"

"No. I'd rather get stuck in now and get things running smoothly so that after the baby comes, I can cut my hours if I need to."

"You've thought about this."

"I have."

"And you want to be part of both sides of our business?"

"I do." I have no intention of existing on the periphery of Atlas's life. "You promised me I would always have a voice in your world. I'll hold you to that."

"There is no voice I would rather listen to."

"Not even your Godfather of the Night?" I tease.

"Not even my brothers."

And he puts his brothers over the head of the Hades Brotherhood. Atlas's priority is family over organization. That settles into my heart and fortifies my foundation for trust in this man.

Easier to believe I come first when he's already shown that, but also because his brothers come before the Hades Brotherhood.

I could argue they are one and the same, but Atlas and I both know that isn't exactly true.

Chapter 49

LUCIA

Atlas hands me my coat. "Put this on."

"Where are we going?" I'm used to his abrupt ways.

Sometimes I push back to prove I can. Right now, I'm curious. Is this when he takes me somewhere romantic to propose?

"To the compound." He never calls it home anymore. He's even referred to the mansion as his brothers' house.

So, not someplace romantic, or I guess it could be. It depends on what is waiting for me in his suite. Crimson handcuffs? "Okay. I wouldn't mind eating Gina's food again for dinner. She's a great cook."

"Not as good as you," Atlas replies loyally.

Only, I'm pretty sure he means it, even though Gina prepares his favorite Greek dishes. She's offered to teach me and I'm looking forward to taking her up on it.

"You like my food because you know I make it with love." That is something my mom used to say.

She probably still does.

Atlas stops on the way to the backdoor, turns and pulls me in for a hard kiss.

When we get to the mansion, after taking off our coats, we head straight for the dining room. However, it isn't food spread out on the table. It's design plans for a house.

"What's this?"

"Our house."

What is he talking about? We don't have a house. "Did you ask me to move in together and I don't remember it?"

"No. We *are* moving in together, but you get final say on the details of the house."

"You know it doesn't work like that. You can't just tell me I'm moving in with you. It's not like showing up with extra clothes in a duffle and never leaving."

"I am aware."

"So?"

"What do you think of the plans for our house?"

"Seriously? That's how you're going to play this?" Though why I'm surprised, I don't know.

Irresistibly drawn to the design plans, I study them. The house is a lot like the one I planned to buy, only bigger. A lot bigger. It's one floor with four bedrooms, a giant kitchen with a sunroom breakfast nook, and formal living and dining rooms. Unlike the house I planned to buy, this one has a large family room too.

"It has the big windows you like, but these ones will be insulated with automatic blinds installed between the panes of glass."

"Where is it going to be built?"

"We'll expand our security wall to cover one of the properties we own to the east of the compound. It will give us enough distance for privacy without compromising security." He frowns. "We can't have a tree in the front yard because it poses too much of a security risk."

Flabbergasted at all the plans, I nod. "Is that a Wolf and Miele range in the kitchen?"

"Yes. Elaine said it was on your wish list."

"But totally out of my budget. Or at least it was." Sometimes, I have to remind myself that I have the money from the sale of the club and it's all mine.

It's not as much as I had to start the club, but it's plenty to do the things I want. Atlas is right. I could buy a small house and pay cash and still have enough left over to live on for quite a while.

He cups my nape. "Not out of *our* budget though."

I adore the way he can't keep his hands off me.

"You talked to Elaine," I say as his words click in my brain. "About what kind of house I wanted."

"She worked with me and the architect to design something that fulfilled all your dream elements and your absolute musts."

"The sunroom breakfast nook," I say.

He nods.

"Is there an herb garden in the back yard?"

"There will be. We'll have landscapers come in and create the front and back yard you want to raise our family."

"Raise our family. You're talking marriage again, but I can't help noticing, there has been no proposal." I step back and glare up at him, my arms crossed over my chest. "You are not dictating we get married, Atlas Rokos. You are going to ask like a normal person."

"But we are not normal," he points out.

"I don't care. In this, we are as normal as they get. I'm not getting marched down the aisle under duress and speaking vows I don't mean like with so many mafia marriages."

"Is that how you ended up married to Tino?"

"No. But it happened to my cousin. I wanted to marry Tino, but that was before."

"Before what?"

"Before I knew you existed in the world."

His face reflects his shock. "That is not what I expected you to say."

"The love I feel for you is intense and consuming, so much bigger than the crush I had on my first husband."

Love is not the sweet, gentle emotion I thought it was when I married Tino. It is powerful and sometimes dark, sometimes overwhelming. And always protective. At least that's how mine and Atlas's love is and that's the only love that matters to me.

He pulls a dark blue ring box with gold lettering in Greek from his pocket. I suck in suddenly desperately needed air. Opening the box, he holds it out to me.

The diamond is blindingly large.

Blinking away emotion filled tears, I say, "They'll be able to see that rock from space."

"As long as the men on planet Earth can see it and pay attention to what it means, no one has to die."

Of course, he goes there. "Maybe dial that back a notch. I'm pretty sure you don't need to kill someone for hitting on me."

"Agree to disagree."

I shake my head, my gaze locked on that ring. "You're so possessive."

"You are just realizing that?"

"No, but that ring." I shake my head. "It's huge. We could buy a house for what it cost you."

I'm a mafia princess. I know what a diamond of that quality costs.

He shrugs, not denying my claim and I groan. "How wealthy is your family?"

No wonder he is able to offer to buy the club back for me.

"Rich enough, but I'll use my own money to provide our home."

Oh, I hit a nerve with that. I didn't mean to though.

I hug Atlas. Hard. "The house is beautiful, and I love that you talked to Elaine about what I wanted. How long will it take to build?"

"It will be finished in four months."

"That soon?"

"Money talks, among other things."

"Tell me you didn't threaten to kill anyone."

"I didn't threaten to kill anyone." His face gives nothing away.

"Really?"

"The contractor has family that works for the Hades Brotherhood in California." Atlas takes the ring from the box and holds it between his thumb and forefinger, the diamond glittering under the light from the dining room chandelier. "So, you'll marry me."

I step back and look up into his face. "That wasn't a question."

His blue eyes narrow. "The nonvoluntary trip to Vegas is still an option."

"No. It isn't. Ask me, Atlas. You already know I love you."

Heat flares in his gaze and then he kisses me breathless. He never ignores when I say I love him. He treats the words as a gift every single time.

When I'm boneless against him, he says, "Marry me, Lucia. Be the light in my darkness for the rest of our lives."

"Yes," I sigh against his lips. "And you didn't have to kiss me into submission to get a yes out of me. Of course, I want to spend the rest of my life with you."

"Even though it means being part of a mafia again?"

"A mafia that is as much family as business. A mafia where I have a voice and a place." I smile. "Yes. Besides, I don't think I ever really left the mafia behind."

"That's good to hear." There's a quality to his tone that has me stepping back. I scan his features. "What did you do?"

"Elaine said you were sad about losing your grandmother's pasta press. You had to leave it behind when you ran from Detroit."

"Technically, I ran from the Revello family cabin, but yes."

"You never told me that story."

"You don't like me talking about being married before."

He grunts.

"What does my grandmother's pasta press have to do with that look on your face?" And then it hits me. "You contacted my family to get it for me, but how did you know it wasn't at my house when it got blown up?"

"I contacted your mother to ask for help getting one like it to replace the one that got blown up, only to learn that you'd never taken it from your childhood home."

"There was already a pasta press in the kitchen when I moved into the Revello home." And Agustino Sr. said I didn't need to use an old relic when I had a brand new pasta press at my disposal.

For as hidebound to tradition as he was, he placed very little value on items passed from one generation to the next.

"You talked to *mamma*." Dazed, I stare up at him. "Did you talk to my father too?" What about Rocco? Do they all hate me for letting them believe I'm dead?

"You said you didn't want to withhold our baby from your family."

Yes, I said that, one night while he held me after we made love.

"It should have been my choice about when to contact them." If ever.

"They're flying in tomorrow."

"What?"

He winces. "You don't need to screech."

"I'm not screeching, I'm exercising my need to punch you with my voice."

"I'd rather take the hit."

"I would rather you had let me contact my family in my own time."

"Our baby would be starting school by the time you worked up the nerve. You were scared to tell them you're alive. So, I told them for you."

"How did that go for you?" I demand, but I really want to know. "Is my mother furious with me?"

"No. Both your parents are happy and relieved you are alive and your brother is too, though he's not as expressive about his emotions."

Pieces start to fall into place in the puzzle that is this man. "If they hadn't been happy, if they had been angry with me, would they be flying in tomorrow?"

"No."

Suddenly him going behind my back to contact my family makes sense. "You were protecting me."

He's trying to say it was about getting my pasta press, but it's really about him making sure no one hurts me. In any way. Not even my family.

"Would you have ever told me about it if they were angry with me?" I ask.

"Eventually, after I got them to see their error in being angry with you for being the amazing person you are."

The tears from earlier come back and this time I cannot blink them away. This man.

"I love you, Atlas."

"I love you, *ilios mou*."

"I know." There's no way to doubt him when he keeps showing me over and over again how important I am to him and how much he cares about my happiness.

Epilogue

Dímios in Russia

ATLAS

Ivan pulls an obviously drunk, or high, young woman into his penthouse apartment with him. It's her lucky night. She won't end up the recipient of his vicious bedroom games.

Dead men can't strangle women at the point of climax.

He doesn't notice me in the shadows near the window. Why would he? His attention is on the woman he is mauling. She's trying to push him away with uncoordinated movements.

Probably roofied.

The alarm starts to beep more insistently and he shoves her down on the couch before turning to disarm it. The woman throws her hand over her mouth and makes retching noises.

Ivan curses in Russian. "If you vomit on my furniture, you'll clean up your mess with your mouth."

Looking around wildly, she lurches to her feet.

"Find the toilet or pay the consequence." Ivan's voice is filled with anticipation.

He's played this game before. The thought of Lucia on the receiving end of his sadism makes rage erupt inside me.

The woman runs down the hall, the sound of her heels clicking on the marble floor joined by the splatter of vomit. She had no nope of finding the toilet before being sick and Ivan knew it.

What he doesn't know is that he's about to die.

Slipping up behind him on silent feet, I maneuver the garrot around him with quick movements. His laughter cuts off and turns into a gurgle as I pull the razor-sharp wire tight with the leather tethers.

A hard kick to the back of his knees sends him crashing downward. He tries to get his fingers between the wire and his neck, but it cuts right through skin and cartilage at the joints. He rears back, but has no leverage and I make sure he doesn't get his feet under him again.

All the while pulling that wire through his neck.

Blood sprays when his carotid artery is cut and seconds later, he goes limp. A few seconds after that, the blood stops pumping out of him.

He's dead and can't ever hurt another woman again. Lucia is safe. From him.

And I will continue to keep her safe from anyone and anything.

A woman's moans reminds me I'm not alone with the dead man. Not that my lizard brain ever forgot.

Dropping the body to the floor, I leave my garrot where it is, the leather tethers dangling down the back of Ivan's suit jacket. I sign my work into his cheek with the tip of my knife. δ for Dimios.

His Golubev brothers will know their *palach* killed the *vtoroy*.

Jumping lightly to my feet, I go in search of the woman Ivan was tormenting. She's sitting against the wall, tears streaming down her face.

When she looks up and sees me, she doesn't even flinch. She's too wasted.

"You are not safe here," I tell her in Russian.

She wipes at her face with the back of her hand. "I know."

In the past, I would have gotten her out of the apartment and left her to figure out what came next. But Lucia's face keeps superimposing itself over the younger woman's. I cannot leave this innocent for the bratva to punish for the justice I doled out.

"You need to leave St. Petersberg."

"I have nowhere to go."

Not good. Killing the *vtoroy* is sanctioned but that doesn't mean the *pakhan* won't look for someone to make an example of.

"What about your family?"

"I have none."

"Friends."

"If they could protect me from him and his brothers I would not be here." Her words are slurred, but their meaning is sound.

Maybe throwing up got some of whatever Ivan gave her out of her system.

"How do you feel about America?"

"It's not here."

"Does that mean you want to go?" She can fly back on the jet with me.

Getting her papers and a new identity will be child's play for Orion. With the large Baltic community in Portland, it's a good place for her to disappear.

"Yes."

Lucia will say that I should wait for the young woman to sober up so she can make an informed decision. I don't have time.

I text my brother.

Atlas: *I have a job for you. Be waiting at the tarmac when the jet lands.*

Taking time to clean the apartment of trace DNA from the woman, I leave her where she is until the last. Then I clean up around her and we go.

"Do you have things you need from your home?" I ask.

"Aren't you afraid of the bratva coming for you if we stay in the city?"

"No."

Ivan's attempt to have me and my brothers killed was a violation of the truce between us. Because my uncle was also a party to that truce, it was considered an act of war against the entire *Ádis Adelfótita.*

Dimitri is now enjoying my uncle's hospitality. The *pakhan* wants his son back and he does not want full out conflict with my uncle.

He offered Ivan's head as a peace offering. My uncle told him I planned to take it anyway and if the *pakhan* didn't want me to keep killing after the *vtoroy's* death, he had better offer something else to guarantee peace.

Whatever he offered satisfied the *Nonós tis Nýchtas* and my uncle told me to leave Russia after killing Ivan.

In the past, I might have argued, but I need to get back to my fiancée.

Such a beautiful word, but I like wife even better.

Getting her in touch with her mother should have waited though. The older woman immediately contacted my own mother and they are insisting on a huge Italian-Greek wedding with traditions from both sides being honored.

Lucia told them they have two months to plan the wedding. She refuses to waddle down the aisle heavily pregnant. Her words, not mine.

Determined mothers, with the force of two powerful syndicates behind them, could probably plan Armageddon in sixty days. The ostentatious Christmas wedding they have dreamed up is a piece of cake for them.

The woman packs quickly and efficiently and we are flying back to the U.S. before Ivan's cooling body is even found.

LUCIA

I wake up from a restless sleep to see Atlas undressing in the dim light spilling from the open bathroom doorway.

With each piece of clothing he drops to the floor, more of the assassin melts away to be replaced by the man that only I see when we are alone. Even around his brothers, there is something of Dímios in him.

It's why they hadn't heard him whistle since childhood.

He's whistling softly now. That must be what woke me. Or my body is so attuned to his presence that it pulled me out of sleep.

I sit up and smile at him. "When are you going to expand your repertoire to something from this century?"

The soft notes of "My Girl" accompany him across the room until he sings the last line in his panty melting baritone. Since I'm not wearing panties, my thighs get slick with my juices.

He puts one knee onto the bed. "Tell me what song you want me to whistle, and I'll learn it for you."

"I have something better for you to do with your mouth." I pull him down to me.

Delight shimmers to the depth of my soul as he blankets me with his heavy, muscled body and shows me he knows exactly what I'm talking about.

THE END

Greek & Italian Glossary

G REEK

Ádis Adelfótita - Hades Brotherhood
anax - head (of the family)
dímios – executioner
(Atlas is called Dímios as a nickname by his mafia.)
eidikós - specialist (above foot soldier)
eromenis mou - my lover
gamó - fuck
ílios mou - my sun
kai - second in command
kalós sýntrofos - goodfellas (foot soldiers)
Nonós tis Nýchtas - Godfather of the Night
Hades Brotherhood Motto: *Dóste tous típota, allá párte tous ta pánta.* Give them nothing, but take from them everything.
Nemesis: Greek goddess of vengeance
ITALIAN
brava regazza – good girl
caspita – polite way to say holy shit
Che cosa? – What?
Dio mio- my god
Ho bisogno di te. – I need you.
Ho bisogno del tuo cazzo. – I need your cock.
per favore - please
porca miseria - damn it

Acknowledgements

I am grateful to the people who have helped this book become what it is. My husband, Tom, who not only supports me during the writing, but who reads the finished book and lets me see the story through a reader's eyes. Andie, my editor at Beyond the Proof. Her insights made Ruthless Enforcer more emotional and a stronger story. Two very special ARC readers who take the time to proofread after the copyedits are done before writing their reviews, Dee Dee & Haley. Any remaining typos or errors are my fault and mine alone. Thank you all! You are the very best!

Brutal Capo

Lucy Monroe

LUCY MONROE LLC

For all my angst loving girlies who appreciate a good grovel.
This one is for you.
With a special mention for Kathleen B.
who gave her name to Bianca's bestie,
a pole dancer known on stage as Candi.
(And who will eventually get her own
story with the SAF, super intense Angelo.)

Cosa Nostra Territories & Hierarchy:
New York: Five Families
Bonanno (Queens), Colombo (Bronx), Gambino (Staten Island), Genovese (Manhattan), and Lucchese (Brooklyn): each founding mafia is led by a don who could be from any of the families loyal to them.

New York Genovese family
Don/Boss: Severu De Luca
(Also known as The Genovese and King of New York)
Underboss: Miceli De Luca
(Severu's brother)
Consigliere: Big Sal De Luca
(Severu's uncle)
Capos: Domenico Bianchi, Salvatore De Luca (Severu's cousin), Tomasso Marino, Niccolo Costa, Lorenzo Ricci, Stefano Bianchi
Head Enforcer: Angelo Caruso
(Also known as Angel of Death)
Soldiers: Luigi, Carlo, Aldo (Severu's men)
Fausto, Marco (Big Sal's men)
Las Vegas
Don/Boss: Patrizio Mancini
Underboss: Raffaele Mancini
Detroit (Don: Pietro Russo)
New England
Boston (Don: Lombard)
Known as the Lombardi Family, despite
the Americanized name for the don's family.
Chicago aka The Outfit

* All names and positions are fictional or used in a fictional capacity, a product of the author's imagination, loosely based on La Cosa Nostra structure in America.

Prologue

SALVATORE

Age 20
New York, New York

Monica's eyes plead with me, her shiny blonde hair, the only genuine thing about her, hanging in messy clumps around her head.

Have mercy.

Don't kill me.

Don't kill my lover.

Her mouth is gagged so she can't beg for their lives out loud, but I hear the words echo in the silence around us.

Until this morning, I thought I was her lover and the only man she had in her life. I told her I loved her.

I fucking loved her.

I told her everything about my family, except that we are part of the New York Cosa Nostra.

I have to get my don's permission to do that and Uncle Enzo insisted on a background check on Monica before giving it.

Since my dad is my uncle's top capo, Big Sal got the job of investigating the woman I wanted to marry.

Criminals are excellent at finding the dirt on other criminals. But I was so sure Monica was clean, I gave every piece of information I had on her to my dad's guy. Only to find out that Monica is five years older than she told me, and she's not a botany student either.

She never even went to community college.

She's been living with the same man since they were teenagers. They move around the country scamming unwary schmucks.

I'm just her latest mark. A *scemo* like every other person they've bilked.

A $250,000 orchid plant is sitting in my apartment right now as irrefutable proof of what a *scemo* I am. Finding it was the hardest part, but I belong to the most powerful Family in New York. We have connections. I bought the rare orchid believing the plant would protect Monica from getting kicked out of school, or being prosecuted.

She spun a fucking good story.

Oh, Salvatore, I don't know what happened, but I killed it. If the professor finds out, he's going to press charges. I wasn't supposed to touch it, but it was so perfect. So beautiful. Blue eyes shimmer with unshed tears. *I don't know what to do.*

Not once did she ask for my help. When I offered, she adamantly refused it. This only made me more determined to save the woman I loved.

I'm a De Luca, at the top of the mafia food chain. My father might not have as much money as his brother, our don, but his net worth would put him on the Forbes Real Time Billionaires list if so many of his assets weren't hidden from the government.

"You thought you could steal from the Cosa Nostra?" I ask her, looking at Monica and her guy with disgust.

Her eyes widen with fear.

"Are you just now realizing I'm connected?" I shake my head. "What did you think? A regular student would drug you and your boyfriend and hang you up like a couple of punching bags from the ceiling?"

Like she thinks I'm going to start beating on her like the punching bag I compared her to, she starts screaming behind the gag and twisting her body. Her fear is a balm to my ego, but nothing can undo what a fool she made out of me.

"I'm not going to hit you." Her lover on the other hand?

Him I punch in the nuts. Fucker touched what was mine. That can't go unanswered.

He goes green and retches behind the gag.

"You'd better get a move on, Salvatore," one of my father's men says. "Or he's going to choke on his own vomit before you get a chance to kill him."

We aren't here alone because this isn't just between me and the couple that tried to scam me. It's Cosa Nostra business when an outsider comes for one of us. We can't let it stand.

Reputation is everything in the mafia.

My father hands me a gun. "You know what needs to happen."

I nod. My arm doesn't want to lift though. Bile rises in *my* throat at the thought of pointing the gun at Monica. Less than twenty-four hours ago, I was buried balls deep in her cunt believing I had found my home.

Like a woman could be that. Especially an outsider.

Swallowing back my urge to vomit, I ruthlessly cut my feelings off, just like papà taught me. There's no place for sentiment in a made man's life and tonight I get made. With this act of judgment.

As I lift my gun, the front of the guy's jeans turns dark from his piss. Monica is still screaming behind the gag, her legs kicking like she's going somewhere.

I pull the trigger and the boyfriend's head jerks back. His body goes limp in death.

"At least you'll be together in hell." I pull the trigger again and red blooms on the left side of Monica's chest.

Her faithless heart destroyed by my bullet.

My father claps his hand on my shoulder. "Well done, my son. You'll make a hell of a second for me."

I stare at him. Is he saying what I think he is?

"You still have to finish school, but from tonight, you're my second in command. I told Enzo you would do it." Papà sounds proud.

He should be. I'm exactly the man he raised me to be. Loyal to the mafia. Ruthless to our enemies. Willing and able to kill when necessary.

Everything his son has to be.

And all I had to do was shoot the woman I loved and kill her boyfriend.

Chapter 1

BIANCA

I swipe my sweaty palms down the sides of my skirt and wish I'd opted for the black one with the zipper instead of the pleather designer knock off.

It's three in the afternoon and the sidewalk outside Amuni is quiet, no long line waiting to get into one of the hottest nightclubs in New York.

After overhearing one of my roommates tell another that Amuni is hiring cocktail waitresses, I'm here to apply for a job. A job I need.

Even if my roommate hadn't gotten the part in the off Broadway show she auditioned for last week, I'd still be here. Trying to get this job instead of her. We share an apartment in Queens with another girl and the couple on the lease. They aren't my friends, but roommates by financial necessity.

The same necessity that has me here, looking for a job. I can't pay even the rent on half a sofa sleeper in the living room if I don't have a job. And I can't work at Pitiful Princess anymore.

Despite the generous curves I inherited from my nonna, I got hired to dance on the pole. I'm good at it and a favorite with the patrons because of the way my tits and ass bounce when I move.

I don't make what the girls who strip, and then come down off the stage to work the patrons, do. I'm okay with that. My boss is not.

Gino is trying to force me to work the floor too. I know what that means. Lap dances and *more* in the private rooms in the back of the club. I don't like being touched. And I sure as hell am not selling my mouth and ass so Gino can get his cut of the increased revenue.

Amuni is a nightclub, not a strip club and it has a strict policy against servers turning tricks on the side. A server can make bank on her tips without offering *extras* to patrons too.

I really, really want this job.

Now it's time to convince them that they want me.

"I'm Bianca Gemelli," I say to the security man at the door. "I'm here to interview for the server position."

He looks down at his clipboard and then waves me inside.

My name isn't Gemelli. It's Russo. Or at least it was when I was born. But when I turned eighteen, my mom offered me $5,000 to change it so there was less chance I would ever be connected back to her and my twin sister, Beatrice.

Having my own reasons for wanting to change it, I agreed. I picked Gemelli for my new last name because it means Gemini in Italian, the twins. A reminder that even if Bea never wants to see me again, she's still my twin. I am not alone in the universe. There are two of us. No matter what her and my mom want to pretend.

"I'm sorry for wasting your time, Bianca, but we aren't a strip club." Sierra, the waitstaff manager says mere minutes after my arrival, sounding anything but sorry.

More like bored.

I can't let that get to me. Getting this job is more important than clinging to pride that won't pay the bills.

"Believe me, I know."

Sierra continues as if I hadn't spoken. "We don't use dancers. If you're looking for a move up from the Pitiful Princess, try the club on 48th, Alladin's Cave."

I knew I shouldn't have listed my current employment. "If you look at the job I held before that, I was a server at a bar. I have an excellent memory and lots of experience handling a packed house."

"Yet you left to become a pole dancer at the Pitiful Princess." The older woman isn't quite sneering, but it is close.

"They offered more money and as I'm sure you are aware, living in the city is expensive."

"Tips here are decent, but I doubt you'll make more a night than you do stripping."

I don't strip. I dance the pole, wearing a sexy lace mask and practically naked. I don't take what clothes I do wear off for the patrons and I never remove my mask.

Not that Sierra is going to make the distinction between dancing and stripping.

"No one will expect me to work anything else here, though," I tell her with honesty born of desperation.

The waitstaff manager's eyes narrow. "Providing sexual services to patrons is grounds for immediate dismissal at Amuni."

"Did you miss the part that I don't *want* to provide anything more?" I ask, my temper getting the better of me.

This uptight bitch isn't going to hire me anyway, so I might as well stand up for myself.

"It's common practice at clubs like Pitiful Princess and I'm not judging that," Sierra says. "But it isn't allowed here. This club is entirely legitimate."

Someone else might not realize what she's alluding to, but I grew up mafia, even if no one knows that about me anymore. Amuni is owned by the Cosa Nostra as one of their legitimate business fronts.

Making it the ideal place to work. It's under syndicate protection, but dirty business doesn't get done here.

"Good!" I emphasize. "I'm looking for a legitimate job as a server without a boss that will pressure me to start offering my body to patrons."

Sierra sucks in a shocked breath. "Oh, I...that definitely would not happen here."

"Please, Sierra, call my references. I'm a good server. You won't regret hiring me." And I need this job.

Like yesterday.

Her phone buzzes and she picks it up to look at the screen. Not a great sign when she's willing to take a call in the middle of the interview.

She answers and steps away so I can't overhear the phone call. As she's talking, two bright color spots form on her cheeks. Then she looks up and around the club like she's trying to spot someone.

The call only lasts a couple of minutes and Sierra turns to come back to me and sets the phone face down on the small round table we are sitting at.

"Excuse the interruption," she says perfunctorily.

Kindness costs nothing. That's something my mom used to say. She's not so great at giving away that free commodity, but it is something I try to do. To prove to myself that I am not either of my parents.

"No problem," I say.

Sierra's phone buzzes again and she appears reluctant to answer. Picking it up gingerly she looks at the screen with furrowed brows. It must be a text this time.

Her shoulders stiff, she forces a smile that looks as plastic as one of my roommate's tits. It looks like someone is using a hook on either side of Sierra's mouth to draw her lips up.

She taps on her phone screen a few times and then looks up at me with that sick smile still in place. "Yes, well, I'll check your references. Is this number good to reach you at?"

She rattles off my pay-as-you-go number.

"Uh huh, I mean yes."

Sierra visibly swallows without meeting my eyes or looking around the club again. "Good. We...I'll be in touch later today."

That's a lot more positive than I expect. I jump to my feet and offer my hand to shake. "Great. I'll look forward to hearing from you."

If she really does call my references, she will only hear good things. Even Gino won't risk bad mouthing me, not after the last girl he did that to called the cops and dropped a tip about what goes on in the back rooms.

Sure, the cops are paid off, but they had to pretend to investigate and having them around made the clientele nervous. Several regulars disappeared and didn't come back to the club for nearly a week.

My temper is worse, and my boss knows it. That's the only reason he hasn't yanked me off the stage and onto some guy's lap for a dance.

Gino doesn't know what I'll do to retaliate.

SALVATORE

I'm not supposed to be at Amuni today, but Franco needs to take his pregnant wife to her appointment with the obstetrician. That leaves me here, accepting a delivery of flavored tequilas for this week's specialty drinks.

When the gorgeous redhead walks in looking nervous. I can't see what color her eyes are from across the club, but there's no missing the burnished copper of her hair pulled back in a ponytail. I bet it reaches the middle of her back when it is down.

Little tendrils stick to her temples with sweat and the fake leather skirt that should hit her mid-thigh is riding higher, teasing at what I will see if it rises just a couple more inches.

A pretty little panty clad pussy? Or is she going commando? Looking that nervous, I doubt it, but a man can fantasize.

It doesn't take superhuman vision to see that Sierra, the waitstaff manager, is giving the curvy job applicant a hard time. The beautiful woman's face shows every emotion she's feeling. Frustration. Hope. Anger.

I don't know what Sierra's problem with the woman is, but I'm lifting my phone to call her before I think about it.

"Hello. Mr. De Luca?"

"Yes. What is your problem with the woman you are interviewing?" She's young, attractive and doesn't have any of the physical tells that indicate regular hard drug use.

"Um..." Sierra looks around the club, but she won't see me.

My vantage point allows me to see her and the beauty she is talking to without revealing my own presence.

"Does she have experience?" I demand.

"Uh...yes."

"References?"

"I haven't checked them yet."

"Call them. If they recommend her for the job, hire her." I don't plan for her to keep the job long, but I want her accessible.

She makes my cock hard and she's not naked.

"Sir, that's not—"

"Did I ask for your opinion?" My employees don't talk back to me. Ever.

"No, of course not. I'll call her references."

"Tonight. I want her on the schedule by the weekend." Saturday night is the next time I plan to be in Amuni.

I'm a busy man. I don't have time to chase my prey, no matter how fun that might be. I have an itch and the beauty interviewing with my waitstaff manager is going to scratch it.

"I'll talk to Mr. Colombo about it."

"Sierra, do you like working at Amuni?"

"Yes, sir, very much."

"And you like being the waitstaff manager?"

"Oh, yes."

"Franco says good things about you."

"That's nice to know." She sounds a little more confident now.

I nod to myself. "I'll still fire your ass if you ever hesitate to follow my orders again."

She gasps.

"Are we clear?"

"Yes, Mr. De Luca. We're clear. I'm sorry, I didn't intend to—"

"Save the fucking apology. Don't do it again." I can be polite, but manners are a tool like everything else.

Right now they aren't the tool I want to use. Intimidation works.

"What's her name?" I ask.

"Bianca Gemelli."

"Send me her application." I want to know what there is to know about the woman I'm going to spend Saturday night balls deep in.

I hang up before Sierra can say anything else.

Gemelli? Huh. It's an Italian name, but not New York Cosa Nostra. If she was, I'd know. No way would I forget those mouthwatering curves and that beautiful face. Mamma would say she has the face of an angel.

I'm too much of a devil to be interested in angels. Though she's as beautiful as a painting of the Madonna, Bianca's tight skirt and the sensual way she moves says she's no innocent.

Good. Because I have zero interest in virgins.

I want to know more about the sexy beauty, but Sierra hasn't forwarded the application to me. I text her.

Salvatore: *Send the application. Now.*

Less than a minute later, my phone dings indicating a message. It's the link to Bianca's application.

Reading her previous work history, my already hard cock twitches in my suit pants. She's a pole dancer at the Pitiful Princess. I own that club too, but my second-in-command oversees the strip clubs, while I oversee our night clubs.

The rules for employee behavior at the Pitiful Princess are very different than at Amuni. No wonder Sierra is hesitant to hire Bianca.

The strippers and dancers there can offer extra curriculars to the customers and have a safe space to conduct their business. If they want extra income, and they all do, they offer hand jobs, blowjobs and fucking. We provide rooms at the back of the club for their use, and in exchange they give us half their take.

Considering they get access to clients without the risk of being picked up for solicitation, it's a fair trade.

We pay to keep vice out and they pay us to stay safe.

Bianca Gemelli was already a sure thing, but now I know I don't even have to seduce her. It doesn't bother me to pay for sex.

There are less complications that way.

Chapter 2

BIANCA

The strong techno beat thrums through me. It's my third night on the floor at Amuni.

I had to leave the Pitiful Princess without giving notice. Tough on Gino. Too bad. So sad. Not.

He's a greedy creep. Once he got promoted to assistant manager and put in charge of the dancers, he started pushing all of us to offer extra curriculars. Since only me and Candi *with an i* (real name Kathleen B) are holding out, he's upped the pressure on both of us.

I don't like leaving her to face him alone, but I have to get out of there to keep myself safe. No one else is going to do it.

My family taught me that lesson long before our capo tossed me on the street after executing my dad when I was sixteen.

Hoping I can protect my friend too, I'm keeping an ear out for any other job opportunities for Candi. She likes stripping, so moving to another club will be easier for her. I only danced the pole.

I don't care about being mostly naked and dancing with the pole like it's my only lover, but peeling my clothes off for an audience, bit by bit? That feels more vulnerable, and I can't do it.

Finding another club that has pole dancers who don't strip and that doesn't require lap dancing is like looking for a unicorn. And I stopped believing in fairytales when I was thirteen and had to kill a man to protect my sister.

"The big boss is coming in tonight. Look lively." Armando, the head server tonight, swats my ass.

I jump and glare at him. "Knock it off."

"I'm desensitizing you. You jump like a startled giraffe any time someone touches you. That doesn't make for good server-patron relations."

"The patrons aren't supposed to touch the waitstaff." Sierra was very clear on that.

"In theory, that's true. In practice, a harmless pat on the ass is not going to kill you."

"I'm not letting anyone smack my ass and that includes you, Armando. Next time you do it, I'll put ground glass in your shoes."

Armando's eyes widen almost comically. "What are you? Some kind of female assassin? Who even says stuff like that?"

"It wouldn't kill you, but it would hurt like hell and make you lose a few days of work for sure. Don't test me."

"How do you know I won't tell Sierra about your threat?" Armando asks, sounding more curious than threatening.

"Because then I would tell her about you touching me inappropriately." I stress the word inappropriately and give him my best look of vulnerable innocence.

I haven't been innocent in a long time, but I know how to project what I need to in order to protect myself.

"Wow. That's good. Okay, I'll leave your ass alone, but don't come crying to me when the boss finds a reason to fire you that isn't about the customer patting your ass."

Disgruntled, I glare. Armando is not wrong. If I piss the customers off, Sierra will find a way to let me go. Even if she gives lip service to the club's official policy of hands off.

"Whatever you do, be on your best behavior tonight. The big boss is coming in."

"Isn't he here every night?"

Franco manages the club and I've never actually spoken to him, only seen him from afar, but he's always here.

"Franco's the GM, but Salvatore De Luca owns the club. He comes in once a week to meet with Franco, but he does a walk through on the floor first. Whatever you do, don't threaten a customer with ground glass when he's around."

"I reserve threats like that for my coworkers," I deadpan, my mind spinning.

Salvatore De Luca. As in the don's cousin? His dad, Big Sal, is the new consigliere.

I may not be part of the life anymore, but I keep my ear to the ground for any news about the Cosa Nostra in New York.

Salvatore De Luca is a capo now. I shiver when I think of the only other capo I've met. It's not a good memory.

My dad on his knees, his expression resigned. Lorenzo Ricci, his capo, behind him, holding a gun with a silencer against his head. The muffled snick of the shot, my father's face exploding, blood and brain matter going everywhere.

Lorenzo turning the gun on me, the threat in his soulless eyes. "You a rat too?"

Me shaking my head vehemently, tears streaking down my cheeks.

"Get the hell out of here. Don't say anything to anyone. If I see you again..." He points the gun at me.

He doesn't have to say the words. I know.

I spin around to run out the door and he barks at one of his guys to stop me. Terrified he changed his mind about killing me, I try to rip out of the man's hold.

"You're covered in your dad's blood. Go. Shower it off. Pack a bag. What do you think I am? A monster?"

I don't answer because the truth might just get me killed.

"You have thirty minutes," he says, like he's being magnanimous.

I take the fastest shower of my life, everything inside me numb as I scrub my dad's blood off my skin.

And then I pack what I can just as fast and rush down the stairs.

I'm not giving Lorenzo a reason to change his mind and I never question that if I don't do what he says, Lorenzo will kill me, or order one of his men to do it.

Capos have a lot of power. They answer to the don, but that's it. Each capo has his own second-in-command and crew of soldiers.

Salvatore must run the clubs for the Genovese, like Lorenzo runs the drug trade.

I don't know what Salvatore looks like, but that doesn't stop me watching all the men in suits who enter the club. None of them have the level of arrogant entitlement in their stance that I remember Lorenzo Ricci having.

Before the owner arrives, Sierra sends me up to the VIP area to serve. I get a sulfuric glare from the server trading places with me on the main floor of the club. I shrug mentally. I don't know why Sierra wants me in the VIP area on my third night as a cocktail server, but I'm not about to tell her how to do her job either.

I'm sure that as soon as I learn what I need to serving in the VIP area, I'll be back on the main floor and the other server, or someone else, will be back working the VIP floor.

My ears, almost numb from the volume downstairs, adjust to the lower level of sound up here and I look around.

There are four different white leather sectionals with low tables to place drinks on up here. All are occupied.

One by a group of rich frat boys if I had to guess. Another has a mixture of businessmen and women dressed to impress in club clothes. They're drinking from two opened bottles of champagne.

Yeah. No one is getting up here without at least a seven-figure annual income. And they're probably considered the poor relations to most of the patrons drinking the top shelf whiskey and real French champagne.

My gaze snags on a man in the center of a group on one of the sectionals. And I can't look away.

He's lava level hot.

Even sitting, he's a few inches taller than the other three men at the table. And they aren't shrimps. Neither is the woman I can see out of my periphery sitting to his left.

My eyes are stuck on the gorgeous guy with raven dark hair and close-cropped beard framing his chiseled features.

I need to look away before I get caught staring, but my eye muscles forgot how to shift. Until the woman lays her light brown hand possessively on his arm, saying something into his ear.

Released from its imprisonment, my gaze flicks to a beautiful face framed by short black curls, trimmed close to her scalp. She's talking to the man, but her eyes are on me. And they aren't friendly.

Does she recognize me? Because I recognize her. Nerissa James, the woman Gino's boss calls boss at *Pitiful Princess*. She doesn't talk to the dancers, doesn't even acknowledge our existence. But I know who she is.

Is she pissed at me for leaving without notice?

Menaggia! I need this job.

I might as well say damn. No one can hear my thoughts and I can't get fired for what they can't hear. But I'm so used to cursing in Italian, I even do it inside my brain.

Bea and I learned to swear in Italian young. Mom doesn't speak it and she never wanted to learn, so we got away with saying stuff she would have washed our mouths out with soap for otherwise.

And this little walk down memory lane is an unproductive attempt at avoidance. The boss of my former boss isn't going to disappear with any amount of wishing.

Be real. Why would boss lady know who you are, much less that you quit her club without notice?

I wish I could be as confident of that as my inner voice. Forcing myself to look away, my gaze skims past the center of the VIP space where there are more low tables, each surrounded by four armchairs.

For smaller groups? Or just the ten percenters instead of the one percenters?

One of the bartenders waives me over and I go.

He tells me how the tables are numbered and expects me to remember. There are no convenient little maps tucked away where the customers can't see like in the last bar I worked at.

Okay. I can do this. My memory is excellent.

"Watch the level of champagne at booth two. When a bottle is empty, open a new one and replace it. Standing order."

"Will do."

"Booth three just got their round, so you don't need to check on them immediately, but both one and four need to be served."

Calling the small sectionals that wouldn't look out of place in a millionaire's living room booths is weird, but what do I know? Maybe to the extremely rich, that kind of seating is a booth?

I walk quickly, but not too quickly, over to the group of women in booth four. There are two unfinished drinks on the table, but the rest of the glasses are empty or close to it.

"What can I get you?" I ask them, memorizing their order as they give it to me.

After relaying the order to the bartender nearest booth four, I make my way to booth one.

His booth.

He watches me approach with unnerving interest, trapping my gaze with his.

Nerissa is sitting several inches away from him now and nothing about their body language screams intimacy. That doesn't mean she isn't hoping.

I don't blame her. I'm irreparably broken in that department, and I'm still drawn to him.

Encased in a Brioni suit, tailored to fit his muscular form, he relaxes on the leather sectional, one arm slung along its back.

Yet the aura of leashed power surrounding him makes me think he could spring into action at any moment. From the heated look in his eyes, he might be springing in my direction.

My heart beats a rapid staccato in my chest while I struggle to get enough air. Who is this guy?

Instead of scaring the crap out of me like he should, my ovaries wake up screaming from their lifelong nap. I don't feel sexual attraction. Not to men. Not to women. Not to anyone.

Tell that to my now weeping vagina. What the hell is going on?

Unable to break eye contact with him, I stop when I'm a foot away from the table. This close, I can tell that his eyes are the color of gray.

I force words past my tight throat. "What can I get you?" My voice is a husky timber I have never heard from my own throat before.

Caspita! Could I sound any more ready to go to bed with this man?

"Are you on the menu?" he asks.

It's a totally cheesy line, so where is the ache in my core coming from? Why are my thighs pressing together with the power of vise?

"No." Very cool, Bianca.

At least smile, or something to let him know you get the joke. Even if it is at your expense. No way does someone with VIP access *not* know the servers don't fraternize with the club patrons.

"You sure?" he asks, his voice whiskey smooth.

My thighs clench tighter, and I go through an entire litany of Italian curse words in my head.

"I'm sure. Would you like a drink?"

He orders top shelf Frangelico in a rock glass. Nerissa James orders a specialty coffee I know we don't offer.

When I explain that, she gives me a mocking glance and says, "I'll just have a black coffee then."

Something tells me she knows Amuni doesn't do specialty coffees. Ignoring her petty power games, I get the orders from the remaining people at the table. The two men sitting on either edge seat of the sectional want sodas, their hyper vigilant attitudes exposing them as bodyguards.

The man sitting across from Mr. Gorgeous orders a mixed drink with a smile that doesn't reach his assessing blue eyes. That look crawls over my body like ants at a picnic and I have to suppress a disgusted shudder.

Mr. Gorgeous is deep in conversation with the skeevy guy when I bring the drinks back and doesn't look up when I place his Frangelico on the table.

That is not disappointment I feel.

I refuse to let it be.

Leaving, I notice booth two needs more bubbly. I drop one off and snag the empty bottle to put in the recycle bin. Fingers snap around my wrist as I'm returning from the kitchen.

I yank at my arm and spin around to face my assailant, still trying to get loose.

"What the fu—" Realizing it's the man from booth one, I cut myself off before I curse out a customer.

Letting go of my wrist, he puts his hands up, palms out, and smiles at me, even white teeth flashing in his handsome face. "I didn't mean to startle you."

I am right. He *is* tall. Really tall. I'm five-foot-four and he's got to be almost a foot taller than me.

"Do you need something?" I ask, rubbing my wrist with my other hand.

It doesn't hurt. It tingles. Where he touched me. What is happening to me?

He leans his shoulder against the wall, blocking my exit and creating a pocket of privacy for us. "When is your next break?"

"Not for a couple of hours. Don't worry, I can get you whatever you need."

"Two hours is a long time to wait."

Uncomprehending, I stare up at him. "You don't have to wait. I'll get you another Frangelico now, if you want it."

"I meant wait to taste your lips."

Chapter 3

BIANCA

The penny drops and I groan. "Why are all your pickup lines so lame?" And still so freaking effective?

"You think I'm lame?"

I give him a once over, ignoring the way my body wants to lean toward his. "You're gorgeous, I'll give you that, but you don't have game."

"No one has ever complained before."

Arrogant much? "And were you paying these women for their time?"

I can't believe I'm teasing him. I'm going to get myself fired and I need this job.

His laughter is rich and dark. It goes straight to my cooch, and I stifle a gasp as unfamiliar feelings ricochet through me.

"Sometimes. I'll pay you for some of your time."

I shake my head. "No can do."

He pulls a money clip from his pocket and pulls five crisp hundred dollar bills off. "I'll pay you five hundred to let me kiss you."

"Do you even realize what a creeper you sound like right now?" I ask.

His dark eyes narrow and his jaw tenses. "I am a businessman. Money talks."

"And you want me to listen."

"Yes."

"No, thank you. My time is not for sale."

As if he doesn't even hear me, he pulls another five bills off. "A thousand. For one kiss on your break."

"Now, you sound desperate."

He jerks away from the wall, towering over me, his relaxed demeanor gone. "I am not desperate."

"And yet you're offering me a thousand bucks for a kiss." I won't pretend that money wouldn't come in handy, but at the cost of getting me fired?

So not worth it.

"I prefer the expediency of transactions."

"Makes sense." I don't blame him. If I wanted sex, I'd probably like paying for it too.

You can't be betrayed when there are no expectations other than the give and take of a business transaction.

"I'm glad you think so," he purrs. "Take half now and I'll give you the other half after the kiss."

I ignore his outstretched hand and shake my head. "My kisses aren't for sale. Neither is anything else, in case you were wondering."

Though I'm hella tempted and that? Is so far out of the norm, I'm seriously freaked out.

"I need to get back to work."

His fingertips brush down my neck and instead of jumping a mile and taking off like I would with anyone else, I shiver. Pleasure sparks from one nerve ending to the next until I'm ready to press myself to him and offer my lips for that kiss.

I cannot believe this. My body is on a whole other wavelength when it comes to this man.

"Do you need something?" My voice breaks on the word *need* and I want to sink into the floor. "Other than to harass the help, that is." At least I end strong.

"You know what I need." His eyes burn into me with hungry fire, leaving no doubt what that is. "I'll pay you five thousand to sleep with me tonight."

"Are you for real?" We're up to five thousand? I shake my head even though I'd rather say *yes*. And *please*. "I. Am. Not. For. Sale." I enunciate each word of my refusal, making it its own sentence. "No."

"Do you want me to seduce you? Would you rather that than money?" He sounds intrigued by the idea, like I just increased my attractiveness to him.

Who is this guy?

Clearly someone who isn't used to being told *no* and taking it as a personal challenge when it happens.

"You're not as irresistible as you think you are," I inform him. Lying.

Everything about this situation should reinforce my lack of desire for physical intimacy.

The opposite is happening. My nipples are peaked and achy. My breasts feel heavy in my bra. My lips keep parting like they're getting ready for the kiss he wants. And I'm not even going to think about how wet the gusset of my panties is.

"I will exhaust you with orgasms," he promises me.

I roll my eyes, but my core clenches. "Why don't you try your luck with that lady at your table? She seems interested."

Che palle. Why did I say that? I don't want him to start macking on Nerissa James while I'm serving them their drinks.

His face twists with genuine revulsion. "Nerissa is my sister, or as good as."

Totally inappropriate relief floods me. The beautiful and successful Nerissa James is his sister. *Or as good as.* Which means she isn't really. The relief sours in my belly.

For whatever reason, that finally breaks the stasis in my body. Unwilling to give the gorgeous stranger a chance to offer me any more money for a kiss, or more...I scoot around him.

Because I might take it. And not for the money I legit need, but for the pleasure he promises. Pleasure I have never once experienced or craved in my adult life.

The next time I come to booth one to get drink orders, Franco, the man I *thought* was the big boss, is sitting with them. Tension invades my limbs. Is the dark-haired Adonis part of the mafia too, or is this the club manager schmoozing a wealthy patron?

"Bring a chilled bottle of Belvedere, unopened. And shot glasses from the cooler," Franco says to me.

"Of course, sir. Anything else?"

"I'll have another coffee, and if you could bring it while it's still hot, that would be great," Nerissa says.

Franco frowns. "Your coffee was cold?"

"It was fine," Mr. Gorgeous answers before the woman can.

She smiles at Franco. "I'm sure your new waitress will get the hang of things."

The words sound like she's trying to be nice, but she's not. She's undermining me in front of my boss and she knows it. I'd like to pour the next cup of hot coffee over her head.

Forcing a smile, I say, "I'll do better."

Mr. Gorgeous is frowning, and the look isn't directed at me. "Knock it off, Nerissa."

"I only pointed out that my coffee was cold last time. If she served it like that to a regular patron, it would be a problem."

She's not a regular customer? How so?

I don't stick around to find out. If I do, I'm more likely to tell her where to shove her supposedly cold coffee.

The two years I danced on the pole, I forgot how much I hate customer interaction. It's one of the reasons I went for the dancing job in the first place. As long as I stayed up on the stage, I didn't have to deal with entitled or bitchy customers.

I return to the table with chilled vodka, shot glasses and a cup of coffee, still steaming.

Giving the hot drink to Nerissa first, I offer her the fakest smile in my repertoire along with it. Candi says that smile is as good as saying fuck off. I'm more likely to say *che palle*, but the meaning is pretty much the same.

Nerissa's eyes narrow. She's reading my facial expression fine.

I dismiss her with a subtle shift of my head and offer the vodka and glasses to Franco.

"You want to do the honors Salvatore?"

Salvatore. As in the *real* big boss, Salvatore De Luca?

Suddenly this whole situation takes on new meaning. He is testing the new girl, trying to tempt me into screwing up.

Che palle. What a jerk.

I know how serious the club is about the no turning tricks on the side, or dealing drugs. You'd have to be an idiot to try to deal drugs on mafia territory anyway. But Salvatore is trying to set me up to fail. To get fired.

Why? Does he do it to all the new servers? Or am I special?

It doesn't matter. I didn't fall for it. Even if I was close to doing so, he'll never know that.

Something inside me cracks. For the first time since puberty, I wanted to kiss someone.

No sloppy lips forcing mine apart, just hazelnut liquor flavored goodness that could set my body on fire.

But that someone isn't really into me. For all I know, Nerissa *is* his girlfriend and *as good as a* sister to him. After all, they *don't* share a last name.

I hold the drinks tray so tightly, my knuckles turn white.

"Would you like anything else?" I ask Franco, ignoring everyone else at the table.

My boss's gaze takes in the way I'm holding the tray and his eyes narrow. He thinks I'm annoyed with Miss Bitchy for complaining about my service. Or maybe he realizes I'm pissed at Salvatore.

Doesn't matter. I force my fingers to relax their grip and a smile that feels more like a grimace to curve my lips.

Franco gives a tiny nod of approval. "That's all for now."

I don't wait for someone else to stop me, but quickly turn away.

Was Franco in on the plan to test me tonight? Was Sierra? Is that why I got put on the VIP floor my third night on the job? Is this their way of weeding out servers who don't abide by the rules?

Hell, maybe there wasn't a plan at all. Maybe Salvatore De Luca gets his kicks out of trying to trip up unsuspecting servers when he's bored.

If that pile of rat pellets accosts me by the kitchen again, I'm suing this place for sexual harassment.

Letting myself fantasize about taking Amuni to the cleaners, I serve the other tables in the VIP lounge. By the time I circle back to Salvatore's table, rational thought is overriding my temper.

I'm not suing a mafia owned business. I like breathing too much.

Chapter 4

SALVATORE

Franco says my name and Bianca goes rigid. After exchanging a few words with Franco, she walks away from the table. Without looking my way once.

Call me arrogant, but this is not how women usually respond to learning who I am. They see a rich businessman, not the brutal capo. My wealth and power only make me more appealing to them.

Bianca's response is unique. And interesting.

Making no effort to hide the way I watch her, I track the sexy redhead's movements around the VIP lounge.

She doesn't return my obvious interest. Unlike before Franco revealed my identity as the club's owner, there are no furtive glances my way as Bianca walks between the tables and the bar.

She has a hurried, whispered discussion with the other server on the floor, but after an unsubtle look at my table, the waiter shakes his head. She's trying to trade with someone else to get out of serving us.

Why? Is she playing hard to get to increase my interest?

Women have been playing games to get my attention since my voice dropped. Only one woman's games caught me, but in the end it was her downfall, not mine.

Bianca is a novice compared to Monica. But this pretense that she's not interested in me is working. Damn it.

I only want her more.

"I don't think she's all that into you, Salvatore," Nerissa drawls.

I frown at my second. "Maybe she's avoiding your bitchiness."

"I wasn't being bitchy," Nerissa defends herself.

"You're always bitchy."

She shrugs. "It's part of my charm."

My bodyguard, Pietro, coughs in a poor attempt to hide his laughter.

"Your other *charms* make up for it," Juniper says, his eyes fixed on Nerissa's chest.

Nerissa picks up her coffee and looks over its rim at him. "One of them is how good my knife throwing skills are. Keep looking at me like that and I'll show you. I never miss the bullseye."

Instead of looking chastened like an intelligent person would, the man trying to offload a chain of decrepit bars smiles wider. "Youse only live once. Might as well do it dangerously."

Five-foot-eleven with her body toned with muscle and her shooting skills outstripping her accuracy with a knife, Nerissa killed to become made just like I did.

Juniper only sees my sister's beautiful exterior and is clueless about just how dangerous she really is.

Bianca arrives at the table and waits for Franco to acknowledge her before asking, "Can I get you anything else, sir?"

The urge to shoot Franco where he sits when she calls him sir is so strong, my hand goes to the gun in my shoulder holster.

"Sal!" a familiar voice booms from several feet away.

My jaw clenches. I do not go by Sal. That is my father. I am Salvatore and anyone with half a working brain acknowledges that fact.

The man approaching my table is proving himself to be lacking in that department on many fronts.

Pietro moves smoothly to his feet, making it possible for me to exit the booth if I want to. Nerissa groans. She doesn't like Lorenzo Ricci and now that she's my second-in-command, she can't avoid him like she did as one of my father's enforcers.

"Introduce us, Franco, I haven't met this one." Lorenzo is behind Bianca when he speaks.

He doesn't see the way she pales, a look of terror flitting through her gaze before she pulls concrete walls around her emotions, completely closing them off.

What the hell is going on?

Ignoring his demand to be introduced to my staff, I meet my fellow capo's gaze. "Lorenzo."

"Brought my friends to party. I knew you could fix us right up."

Considering that Lorenzo Ricci is in charge of drug importation, exportation and sales for *la famiglia*, he's not talking about getting them some Molly. Which he wouldn't get at Amuni anyway.

As one of our legit business fronts, drug dealing on premises is strictly forbidden. Just like my father before me, I have some inventive ways to discourage anyone thinking they can break that rule.

His gaze slides over Bianca's form as she hurries away without taking any orders or empties. "New meat?"

"My servers are not meat," I inform him. "If you are looking for companionship, take your friends to the Pitiful Princess or The Red Room."

That Bianca used to work at the former pisses me off for no accountable reason. What difference does it make if she's sold her ass to a hundred other men? I only want it for one night.

I've never fucked a virgin and I don't particularly want to. Pussy isn't like a bee's stinger. It's not a onetime use commodity.

Besides, sex is easier after a woman has learned how to find pleasure with her pussy.

His brows drawing together, Lorenzo fixes his gaze on Bianca's retreating back.

Only when she disappears down the hallway with access to the kitchen and bathrooms, does he look back at me. "I've got some business to discuss with you."

"I'm busy tonight." I indicate Juniper with an inclination of my head. "Call and we'll arrange a time to meet."

My role as capo is less than a year old, and some of the old guard are still struggling to adjust to my promotion. I could give two fucks.

If he wants to talk business, he'll make an appointment like anyone else.

Surprising me, Lorenzo nods almost affably. "I'll do that." He claps Franco on the shoulder. "Well, I gotta drain the dragon. Maybe we'll head to the Red Room after that. The music in here is better suited to teenagers."

Considering the drinking age in New York is twenty-one, teenagers are not Amuni's target demographic. But neither are men my father's age.

"More like drain the worm," Nerissa mutters under her breath as the older man walks the same direction Bianca went.

Suddenly I feel an urge to take a leak myself. I stand up and acknowledge Juniper. "Excuse me for a minute."

"Youse do what you need to," he says with a knowing look. "I'll keep your beautiful sist-ah company he-ah."

His New Jersey accent is thicker than when he started drinking. Not surprising considering the fact he drank at least a third of the Belvedere on his own.

BIANCA

My hands shake as I rush down the hall toward the restroom.

Che Palle. Why did Lorenzo Ricci pick tonight to come into the VIP area? Next shift I'll be back on the main floor, one server among many, and lost in the crowd of patrons.

Fuck my life.

I haven't seen that *stronzo* for six years and he hits on me the minute he lays eyes on me? I'm skeeved out and drowning in fear filled adrenalin at the same time. Because I still remember his threat when he threw me out of my family home.

Getting hit on by him is slightly better than having a gun shoved in my face, but only a little.

Back when I first started working at Pitiful Princess, I knew there was a risk that Lorenzo would come into the club and recognize me. But it wasn't a big one. I remembered hearing my dad say Pitiful Princess wasn't Lorenzo's style. The capo preferred The Red Room because it was more upscale.

One of the dancers there was his mistress at the time, which was probably the real reason. Regardless, the two years I danced the pole, Lorenzo never came into Pitiful Princess.

I wore a sexy lace Mardi Gras style mask as part of my costume, just in case though. The customers loved it, and I grew complacent. Even learning tonight that Amuni is owned by the mafia, I didn't worry about Lorenzo coming in.

He's old school. Amuni definitely is not.

From the first word he spoke, his voice went through me like an icepick. Instant recognition sent a jarring alarm clanging in my brain.

Get away. Get away. Get Away.

Shoving the door open to the ladies room, I hurry inside.

"Are you okay?" A woman reaches out like she's going to touch me.

I jump back and force a smile. "I'm fine."

It's a lie. I'm anything but. Doesn't matter. You don't let them see you sweat, even if they're trying to be nice.

"Are you're sure?"

I'm surprised at her continued concern. This is New York. Not some friendly small town. New Yorkers aren't heartless, but we do a good job of sticking to our own business.

Right now, this beautiful, rich lady is sticking her nose in mine.

It's weird.

"I'm sure." I figure there's a better chance she'll believe me if I say the words instead of nodding.

"Come on, Alisa, the guys are waiting." Her companion grabs the friendly woman's arm and drags her toward the door.

Getting my frozen limbs to work, I go into a stall. Not because I have to pee, but because I need a second of privacy and this is the only place I'll get it. I don't have time for a meltdown.

I don't indulge in them anyway. Crying never got me anything but a headache.

Lorenzo probably didn't even recognize me. Why would he?

The last time I saw him, he'd just executed my father and tossed me out on the street after threatening to shoot me if he ever saw me again.

That's pretty memorable.

Me? Not so much.

I was a teenager with bad hair and even worse dress sense. Don't forget the red, blotchy face from crying. He got to witness the last time I let myself cry in front of anyone else. How's he going to recognize me from that?

Okay. I'm alright. Stop panicking and get back to work.

When I come out of the stall, there are a couple of women at the mirror and sink. They don't notice me because they're too busy looking at the man standing near the doorway, glaring.

It's Lorenzo Ricci and the way his eyes narrow when they land on me, he's not in here because the men's room is suddenly out of order.

Oh, *merda*. Shit. He did recognize me.

Trying to brazen it out, I pretend ignorance and go to scoot by him. He won't do anything in front of witnesses, right?

Wrong. He grabs my arm and shoves me against a wall. "Where the fuck do you think you're going?"

When he looms over me, it's nothing like Salvatore, trying to get his freak on. This capo scares the hell out of me. He always has.

Fear makes me angry and I glare up at him, refusing to answer.

"What are you doing working for a family owned club?" he demands.

"I didn't know it was." Not until tonight.

Lorenzo glowers at me. "Does your boss know your dad was a rat?"

"Why would I tell anyone about my dad?"

"You keep it that way. You know what happens if you don't keep your mouth shut," he hisses.

My stomach rebels as every word sends a gust of Lorenzo's bad breath in my direction.

I don't react to his threat because I've been living under it since I was sixteen. And I don't react to him calling my dad a rat because it's true.

Not of the telling on the mafia to the FEDs kind, but the stealing money from his boss kind. That's what got Dad killed. The same weakness that left his daughters vulnerable to his debtors.

"Thirty days on a good probiotic will take care of that," I mutter, probably picking the least sensible thing *to* react to.

"The fuck are you talking about?" Lorenzo shakes me.

Pain shoots up my arm, but I don't react. Never let them see you sweat, especially when they are *stronzo* capos trying to intimidate you.

"Your bad breath. Mints help, but they don't treat the root of the problem. Sometimes a probiotic will." It worked for Candi when she got that godawful breath after trying one of her weird diets.

He makes a sound like a rusty door being yanked open. "Listen, you little bitch—"

"Get the fuck out of here, Lorenzo," Salvatore's voice cuts off the other man with the force of an axe being swung by Paul Bunyon. "I told you my servers are off limits."

"You don't belong here. You're not family anymore," Lorenzo hisses at me, squeezing my arm again for good measure.

His words don't hurt like he thinks they will.

I stopped being part of a family a long time ago. After the way my dad's buddies in the mafia made me pay his bad debts, I want nothing to do with the Cosa Nostra family either.

"We're just talking." Lorenzo's hold on my arm loosens so he can turn to face Salvatore. "Do you mind?"

"I fucking mind you ignoring me. Get the hell out of my club and don't come back."

"You can't ban me from this place," Lorenzo shouts, his face going florid with fury.

Taking advantage of his focus on the other capo and loosened hold, I yank myself loose and scoot under Lorenzo's arm. Salvatore blocks the doorway and my headlong rush out of the bathroom. Abruptly stopping in front of him, I wait for the younger capo to move.

He doesn't.

After several long seconds of silence, I school my features and look up at my boss's boss. The man who offered me a thousand dollars for a kiss and five thousand for sex, hoping to get me fired.

Though I've been thinking about it ever since, I still don't understand why.

"Did he do anything to you?" Salvatore studies me like he's memorizing every inch of my face.

He and Lorenzo are like two bulls snorting and pawing at the earth, ready to charge. I'm not playing the part of capeless matador caught between them.

No way am I going to tell him about my throbbing arm. "Can I get by?"

Salvatore's gaze doesn't break away from mine.

"I need to get back to work," I remind him.

With a jerk of his head, he moves aside just enough to let me by. Our arms touch, sending jolts of electric pleasure dancing along my nerve endings. I don't let that show on my face though.

Never let them see you sweat, especially not the boss.

Chapter 5

SALVATORE

When I reach the hallway, I don't see Bianca or Lorenzo. Is he hitting on her? Rage heats my blood as I slam the swinging door to the kitchen back. The dishwasher looks up, startled, from a tray of glasses he's preparing for washing and sanitizing. His mouth gapes, but no sound comes out of it. No one else is in the kitchen. I spin on my heel and head to the bathrooms. If Lorenzo is in the men's room, there's no issue.

So, I walk right past it and shove the outer door to the ladies' room open. While two women fix their makeup and another washes her hands like nothing is happening, the asshole I'm chasing down looms over Bianca.

He's got her backed against the wall with his hands on either side of her head, speaking to her in tones too low to hear.

"Get the fuck out of here, Lorenzo. I told you my servers are off limits."

The older capo jolts like I hit him with the cattle prod I am known to use to drive a point home. Fists are good, but sometimes 5,000 volts are better.

He says something to Bianca and then turns to face me. "We're just talking. Do you mind?"

Does this slimy bastard really think I'm going to turn around and leave him to harass my staff? Not fucking likely. "I fucking mind you ignoring me. Get the hell out of my club and don't come back."

"You can't ban me from this place," Lorenzo yells.

That is where he is wrong. I own this club and he's not getting back inside. My crew don't bow to any other capo. When I tell the bouncers to keep him out, they will obey me.

Because they know how far I'll go to maintain order and obedience.

Bianca ducks under Lorenzo's arm and rushes toward me, her face that same expressionless mask she donned a few minutes ago. She stops in front of me. I wait until she looks up and meets my eyes.

"Did he do anything to you?"

Her shoulders tense, but nothing shows on that beautiful, stoic face. "Can I get by? I need to get back to work."

The words are reminiscent of what she said when I cornered her near the kitchen earlier. This time they are said with no breathless inflection. Her beautiful blue eyes hold no reluctant interest.

They reflect nothing at all.

I step to the side a few inches and she scoots around me. Her arm brushes mine, the scent of cherries and vanilla I noticed earlier teasing at my senses.

When she is gone, I give Lorenzo a sardonic lift of one brow. "What are you doing in here? It's got to be hard when you're too old to stand up and piss, but there are stalls in the men's room too."

Lorenzo's face goes florid. "You little shi—"

"Uh, uh, uh. Ladies present."

The women titter and one sends me a sultry look in the mirror. Her body is on display in a skintight mini dress and she's got curves in all the right places. Normally, I would wink and might even take her up on the invitation in her eyes.

Right now, I'm disgusted, and I turn away from her blatant interest to glare at Lorenzo. She and her friend ignored the way the other capo was forcing his company on Bianca.

Besides, my cock only wants one woman. The skittish server who hightailed it out of here.

Putting my hand out toward the door, I indicate Lorenzo needs to leave. "Maybe you should start bringing your bodyguard with you so he can ensure you don't get the words on the doors confused again."

"Watch it, Little Sal. Making me an enemy isn't smart."

No one has called me Little Sal since I punched a made man in the nut sack at age eight when he did it. If Lorenzo doesn't watch it, I'll do more than punch his family jewels. I'll castrate them.

I let the imminent demise of his junk show in my eyes. "The ladies might be impressed with your posturing, *old man*. I am not."

"Severu is going to hear about this disrespect." Lorenzo takes a step backward.

My gaze flicks sideways to the women watching us and listening with blatant interest. Lorenzo left subtle behind a decade ago. He swaggers through life, throwing his weight around. Not only does he not care who knows about his connection to the mafia, but he revels in the fear it usually causes.

Stronzo. This guy really is an asshole.

And my patience is all used up. I grab Lorenzo by the back of the neck and shove him out of the women's restroom. He squawks the whole time.

"You better watch your back," he shouts as I strongarm him right into the men's room.

I toss him forward. "Piss and then get out of my club, Ricci."

He yells and windmills his arms, barely avoiding a fall against the black marble back wall of the urinals where a steady stream of water runs.

The man using the urinals cuts off his stream and shoves himself back into his jeans. "I'm outta here." He takes off without washing his hands.

Unsanitary.

Two men rush out of the stalls and wash their hands. *Grazie a Dio.* Casting a nervous glance our way, they hotfoot it out of the bathroom. A quick glance confirms the rest of the bathroom is empty.

Unless someone is standing on a toilet to eavesdrop on us. But this isn't a fucking afterschool special.

Lorenzo is puffed up like an angry chicken. I'm not calling him a rooster because he's a dickless piece of shit as far as I'm concerned.

"You cannot treat me this way. Severu should never have promoted you to capo," he sneers. "You are too fucking young and immature to respect the role."

I'm 31 not 14. "The fuck I care what you think. I'm a better capo than you. I take care of my people."

Lorenzo runs one of the most lucrative industries for the mafia, but he has men on his payroll that are forced to work a second job to cover rent. It's one of the reasons Severu is investigating the other capo.

Where is the money going, if not to his people?

"Who has been complaining?" Lorenzo demands.

Not once has he looked around to make sure we are alone. How pissed would Severu be if I killed the stupid son of a bitch?

"You think the rest of us don't have eyes?" I ask derisively. "We can see when your guys show up looking haggard from working two jobs."

"I don't coddle my soldiers like you and your dad. I expect them to pull their weight."

"Your men swear loyalty to *la famiglia* and in return, their don and capos take care of them. It's not coddling to pay a man what he is worth." I don't call him a stingy piece of shit.

He should thank me for the restraint.

I move until I'm looming over him like he was doing to Bianca when I found them. "You are banned from this club. Piss me off again, Lorenzo, and I will ban you from all of *my* clubs."

"You can't do that!"

"Watch me."

Without another word, I execute an efficient search of the bathroom stalls. No, it's not a movie, but I'm not a man to take chances either.

Something my father taught me.

When I'm done, having found the stalls empty of potential informants for the FEDs, I wash my hands because I've got no interest in becoming a walking petri dish. I leave the bathroom without saying another word to Lorenzo, who is still standing there glowering.

I guess he doesn't need to piss after all.

Returning to the main area, I signal the bartender that we want another round.

Bianca is at another table, talking to the patrons, but he'll let her know.

Impatience scores my brain like nails on a chalkboard. It's not good enough. I want her attention on me *now*. And I want her within touching distance if Lorenzo accosts her again.

I will get great pleasure out of knocking him into next week if he does.

She turns from the other table and I signal to her, indicating my booth with a tip of my head. She pretends not to see me and goes to another table to pick up empty glasses. Her back to me, she talks to the two men sitting there. Probably taking their order for the next round.

It pisses me off.

When she heads to the bar without looking back toward me, frustration is a louder beat than the club music in my head.

Reaching the table, my mood sours even further. "Where is Juniper?"

"He's dancing." Nerissa indicates the lower level with her thumb. "He asked me to join him. I declined."

Good. We want the man to sell us his string of bars, but if my second stabs him for being handsy, that's not going to happen.

Franco is gone too, but that's not a surprise. He is the club manager and it's a busy night.

Lorenzo comes storming out of the hallway and shouts at his companions. "Let's go!"

The two men and their arm candy jump up and scurry after the capo who is giving his bodyguard an earful. Typical. He probably told the man not to follow him because he wanted to try it on with Bianca.

When things didn't go his way, Lorenzo blames his bodyguard instead of his own obnoxious behavior.

"Something happen in the bathroom?" Nerissa asks. "Lorenzo doesn't look too happy and you look like you want to kill someone."

"I do. Him."

"Why?"

"Do I really need a reason with that *stronzo*?"

"Not in my opinion, but you're usually the cooler headed one between the two of us."

"He accosted Bianca in the bathroom."

"The curvy little waitress you've been making calf's eyes at all night?"

"Fuck you, Nerissa. I'm not a sap."

"First, eww, no thanks. Second, before tonight, I would have agreed, but you have it bad for the waitress and she's got no time for you." My sister smirks. "I never thought I'd live to see the day that my big brother got shot down by a working girl."

"She's not a working girl. She's a server." Bianca turned me down flat when I offered her five grand to fuck me.

Nerissa makes a dismissive gesture. "She worked at Pitiful Princess."

I'm not surprised she knows. As my second-in-command, it's Nerissa's job to oversee the strip clubs.

"Not all of the dancers sell extra curriculars," I say, wondering for the first time if Bianca is one of the extremely few that chose not to.

Nerissa scrutinizes me like she can tell what I'm thinking. "Right. And not all guys jack off after they discover what their dick is for besides pissing."

"Did she?" I ask, a powerful need to know pounding through me.

Nerissa shrugs. "Don't they all?"

My look tells her I don't appreciate her flip answer.

She sighs. "I don't know, okay? You know I don't deal with the dancers. I only recognized her because she was one of the only two plus size dancers we had there."

One of the only dancers with generous curves, and maybe the only one who didn't make money from offering extra-curriculars.

Chapter 6

BIANCA

My feet hurt and my brain is on a sluggish spin cycle when I finish my closing shift at Amuni.

Lorenzo never came back, and Salvatore finally left around two. It's just my luck that my night of training on the VIP floor brought me to the attention of two powerful capos. And not in a good way.

The tips might be twice what I earn on the main floor, but the extra money isn't worth it for this kind of stress.

In the employee locker room, I take off my uniform. It's a sleeveless mini dress, with a flared skirt and square neckline, cut low enough to show a couple of inches of cleavage. I am allowed to wear flats with it, but not tennis shoes.

My feet are thankful I splurged on a pair of black comfort-support ballet style flats before my first night as a cocktail waitress. They're doubly grateful tonight. Who knew that serving a smaller clientele would require so many more trips across the floor?

I'm not wearing either going home. Not when I have the walk to the subway station ahead of me and a ride on the F train alone at four-thirty in the morning.

"How was your night up on the VIP floor?" Armando asks, ignoring my partially undressed state.

I slip on a form fitting t-shirt that says, *I didn't mean to push all your buttons. I was looking for mute.* "Okay. I prefer the main floor."

"I hear that the VIPs can be demanding." He changes his shoes, pulling on trainers nearly as beat up as mine.

Despite looking so worn out, my tennies are comfortable. More importantly, they won't get me mugged for my shoes.

Pulling on jeans I got from the rag bin at a second-hand store, I ask, "You don't know? Didn't you train up there too?"

I thread my belt with a knife hidden in the buckle through the loops of my jeans. According to the psychology class I took, needing to have a weapon handy is a trauma response from what I experienced as a teenager.

It feels like a natural native New Yorker response to me.

"Nope. I've worked at Amuni for over a year and have yet to spend a single night serving VIPs. I hear the tips are great?" He makes it sound like a question.

I shrug as I shove my new shoes in the bottom of my backpack before careful folding my uniform and putting it inside too. I don't know the other server well enough to tell him I have twice as much cash on me right now than I went home with last night.

"Oh, yeah," he says, like I said something. "Your trainer probably took most of the tips. They wouldn't have let you serve tables on your own your first night up there."

He doesn't make this a question, so I don't feel the need to correct him, but I didn't have a trainer. I had assumed that was because I'd already done my first night with a trainer on the main floor. Only he makes it sound like I should have had one tonight.

"How was the main floor?" I ask. Not because I care, but because I don't want to answer any more questions.

"Busy. We could have used you. I didn't know the woman who took your place, but she's gotten soft serving the VIPs."

"You think? I ran off my feet getting to all the tables in my section as fast as they expected." Shoot. I should have kept that to myself.

"Yeah? Even with a trainer?" Armando asks me with unsurprising interest.

I need to think before I speak.

I hum, not wanting to lie, but not wanting to admit my lack of a trainer either. Because then he'll ask why I didn't have one and I don't know. I'll ask Sierra when I come in for my next shift though.

If she's in a better mood than tonight.

I zip up my threadbare, oversized hoodie that turns my curves from my neck to mid-thigh into a nondescript single shape.

I'm going for invisible because invisible means safe. When I flip the hood over my red hair, my armor is complete.

Almost.

Before sliding my arms through the straps on my backpack, I pull out my pepper spray. I never walk alone at night without it. Or the knife

"That backpack looks like it's ready for the garbage heap."

"I know," I say proudly.

It doesn't have any rips, but worn duct tape covers strategic spots making the bag look about ready to disintegrate. If you don't look like you have anything worth stealing, then no one tries to steal what you have.

More invisibility.

"The duct tape is a nice touch," he says admiringly.

I repay his admiration with my own. "Yours looks like you pulled it out of the trash heap." I wrinkle my nose. "It smells like it too."

"My mom's fish oil. Prick a couple of capsules and rub it into the zipper. Instant stink and my zipper doesn't stick."

"Smart."

Armando doesn't change all his clothes like I do, but he pulls on a worn flack jacket that covers the uniform.

The other waitstaff and kitchen staff who closed join me and Armando as we leave the locker room. We'll walk together to the subway station. None of the others ride the F train with me, but there's safety in the group for the walk.

I keep my pepper spray in my hand anyway.

We're almost to the door when I hear my name called. Turning, I see Sierra waving at me.

Wishing I had pretended not to hear, I trudge over. The others are going to leave without me and that will end up with me walking alone. Not for the first time, but I prefer going with the group.

I stop in front of Sierra. "Yes?"

"I wanted to know how it went up on the VIP floor."

Seriously? She called me back to chat about my night? I couldn't have told her when I came in for my next shift? Or better yet, she should ask the bartender for his opinion. She's going to anyway. It's not like she's going to trust me to critique my own success.

"Fine, but I'll be glad to get back to the main floor."

Sierra frowns. "Didn't I make it clear? You're assigned to the VIP floor now."

"But I'm new," I can't help saying.

"Are you saying you don't want the VIP floor?" she asks with disbelief. "You told me you need the money."

"Who doesn't?" Any of the main floor waitstaff would be thrilled to be assigned to the VIP level.

So, why am I, a new hire, getting the assignment?

Did Salvatore arrange this? But from what Sierra is saying, the decision to put me in the VIP lounge was made before I ever met the big boss.

"Just out of curiosity, is Mr. De Luca the usual honey trap you all use to weed out servers willing to take money on the side for sexual favors?" I ask, my annoyance at the capo surging all over again. "It seems like it would be beneath the general manager, though."

"I don't know what you are talking about. Are you claiming that Mr. De Luca offered you money for sex?" Sierra asks, doing a good imitation of shocked offense.

It's close, but I manage not to roll my eyes. Sure, she doesn't know what I'm talking about. "Did you need anything else?"

"I would like you to clarify your question," Sierra says.

"That will not be necessary. I'll take it from here, Sierra." That voice rolls through me like a swirl of hot fudge in my blood stream. "Bianca."

Sierra walks away without another word to me. This is why she held me back from leaving. Not because she cared how I found my first night on the floor, but because her boss told her to.

I turn slowly, knowing what I will see.

Salvatore De Luca stands way too close, looking as immaculately put together as he did at the beginning of the evening. Not a dark hair on his handsome head is out of place. His tie is gone, but he looks far from disheveled.

Black ink from a monochromatic tattoo is just visible on the strong column of his neck revealed by the open top two buttons on his shirt. His neatly trimmed beard frames his sensual lips.

I swallow in my suddenly dry throat. "Mr. De Luca."

"I wanted to make sure you are alright after earlier. It is not acceptable for one of our employees to be accosted in the bathroom."

"I'm fine." I'm not about to make a big deal about Lorenzo Ricci's actions.

He's the kind of man who holds a grudge and punishes those who cross him. My father's death is testament to that fact.

"Some might say your behavior earlier in the hallway was on par with Mr. Ricci's."

"Do you say that?" Salvatore asks.

I cock my head to one side. "Does it matter?"

"It does."

"Mr. Ricci scared me."

Tension fills the muscular man's frame. "Did he proposition you?"

"No."

"What did he want then?"

"I don't know." It's a lie, but a small one.

Lorenzo Ricci wanted to know if my new employers were aware of my father's past with the mafia. I'm not about to bring that up and I hope he doesn't either. He and Salvatore are clearly not friends.

"Thank you for making him leave me alone," I say, realizing I should have said it earlier.

"No thanks necessary. If he comes onto you again, you tell me."

So, Salvatore doesn't believe me that his fellow capo didn't proposition me. Not surprising, but it stings.

I wish it didn't. I should not care what this man thinks of me, other than as it pertains to my job.

Yeah. Right.

I care way too much.

"I'll tell Sierra," I promise. Not that I think the waitstaff manager will do anything about it.

"You tell me. Not Franco. Not Sierra. Not the head bartender."

"Um..." How am I supposed to tell Salvatore.

"Give me your phone."

"Why?"

Salvatore waits for me to comply without answering.

Sighing, I pull my phone out of my front jeans pocket with the hand not holding my pepper spray and offer it to him.

"Unlock it."

"Why?" I ask again, this time determined not to do what he says until he gives me an answer.

"I'm going to put my number in it."

"What? Why would you do that?" He can't mean his regular cell number.

He has to mean an extra he keeps around for calls from people outside his inner circle. He's a capo, for goodness' sake. He's not going to give me his main phone number.

"You can't tell me if Lorenzo bothers you again if you can't call me. I'm only in the club one or two nights a week."

"Wouldn't it be better if I told Franco? He could tell you if he thinks it's necessary?" Not that I plan to tell anyone because there won't be anything to tell.

Now that I know he's an Amuni patron, I will stay out of Lorenzo Ricci's way.

Chapter 7

SALVATORE

Why is Bianca arguing with me about this?

Getting my number is a privilege. How does she not know that? Her reaction to hearing my name tells me she's aware I am her boss's boss, even if she doesn't know I am a mafia capo. What other cocktail waitress gets offered my number?

Niente. Zilch. None.

"Unlock your phone," I tell her again.

The more she balks, the more determined I am to get my number into her contacts. Her number is already in mine. Ridiculous for what I planned to be a one night stand, but maybe the sex will last longer than one night.

It would be unethical to fire her just for having sex with me. Not that business ethics are a high priority for me.

Making no move to obey me, she stares up at me through narrowed eyes. "Is this another test?"

What the hell is she talking about? "Who tested you?"

Is that what Lorenzo was doing in the bathroom? Testing her about something? Why the fuck would another capo be testing an employee of one of *my* establishments? Lorenzo is one of the few arrogant enough to do it though.

"You tested me." She rolls her eyes. "Like you don't know it. Or maybe you think I'm so stupid, I don't."

"When did I test you?"

"Offering me money for sex." The look she gives me is all attitude.

"I can fire you as easily for insubordination," I warn her. "And that was not a test. I want to fuck you."

"Have you heard of sexual harassment? I mean I know you're practically a dinosaur, but it's been a thing for a long time."

The fuck I'm a dinosaur. I'm one of the youngest capos in the Cosa Nostra. "I'm only thirty-one."

"That's still almost a decade older than me."

She's right. Her application says she's twenty-two, old enough to drink and serve alcohol. And old enough to fuck.

"I have more stamina than the twenty-somethings you're banging." White hot rage burns at the thought of her letting another man touch her perfect curves.

"Nice to know," she drawls smartly. "But I think I'll keep my job, thanks. No dick, no matter how attractive the package it comes with, is worth getting fired."

Getting even backhanded confirmation she's attracted to me takes my semi to full in a few heartbeats. "I offered you five-k. That would tide you over while looking for another job."

"You aren't even going to deny that saying yes would have gotten me fired?" Her bright blue eyes flash with hurt, but she hides it as her too kissable lips purse in disapproval.

My erection pressing painfully against my trousers, my mouth salivates for a taste of her. I want to nuzzle into her neck and inhale her earthy scent from working all evening mixed with the cherries and vanilla.

"We don't let our staff moonlight in the sex trade." Even if they don't do it out of the club.

As a legit business front, we can't risk having Amuni employees that might bring the heat down on us for any reason. That includes sex work, or dealing in their off hours.

"And you say you weren't testing me. Right."

"It wasn't a test. I wanted you to say yes."

"And you didn't care if that got me fired. You are a piece of work, Mr. De Luca."

Unused to being looked at like a pile of dog shit she stepped in, I cross my arms and frown down at her.

"Salvatore," I correct, not wanting her to create distance between us with formality. "And you are still risking getting fired for insubordination."

"You think?" She couldn't look less impressed. "New York may be an at-will employment state, but you still can't fire someone for illegal reasons. And firing me for turning down your sexual advances is illegal in all fifty states."

"You're pretty damn knowledgeable for a twenty-two-year-old with no college education."

"Condescending much? I'm working on my degree."

I'm never surprised. I'm too cynical, but shock rolls through me. Is she lying? "You didn't say anything about going to college."

"When was I supposed to mention it? When I was taking your orders, or maybe when I was clearing the table of dirty glassware?"

It's not on her application, but I don't bring that up. Because it's not unheard of to hide an education. She might not have her degree yet, *if* she's telling the truth, but she would still be considered overqualified for a lot of jobs.

"What are you studying?" I ask.

"Business."

That shouldn't spark approval in me, but it does. We have that in common. And that shouldn't matter for a one-night stand either.

Will she be graduating in a few weeks?

That could explain her not putting her schooling on her job application. She needs a job while she's looking for one in her field, but she won't be staying at Amuni.

Disappointment twinges in my chest. Ridiculous. That is exactly what I want.

"You're twenty-two," I prompt.

"And you're not."

Smart ass. I almost smile. "When do you graduate?"

"Thinking of offering me a job behind the scenes?"

"No."

"That was fast." She shrugs. "Doesn't matter. I won't graduate for another year and a half."

"Why?"

Her look says *none of your business*.

Mine says *tell me anyway*.

Surprisingly, she does. "Most of the time I have to take the bare minimum number of classes to maintain my grants."

"I would think you'd want to get through school as soon as possible."

"Sure. I also want to live in an apartment with no roommates and work a job that doesn't leave me with sore feet at the end of my shift. But none of that is going to happen right now."

"Why?"

"You hire someone to do the books, don't you?" she asks condescendingly.

My eyes narrow and I cross my arms, taking a stance that makes made men nervous.

This little spitfire rolls her eyes at me. "Do the math, *Salvatore*. Working at night makes it easier to attend classes during the day, but there are still only so many hours in a day."

According to her, that means she has eighteen more months of juggling school and work. And she turned down five-k because she did the math and figured keeping this job is worth more to her than that.

She's pragmatic, smart and determined. Which is as much of a turn on as her luscious body.

"You're smart. You have scholarships." She has to.

A look passes over her pretty features I cannot read. "How I pay for school is none of your business, but I know what I know. You can't fire me for refusing to have sex with you. Not without risking financing my early retirement with a lawsuit payout."

Too bad one of the things she knows *isn't* that I'm a mafia capo. She wouldn't be spouting all this shit about reasons I can't fire her, that's for damn sure. She'd know that trying to sue me for sexual harassment would not go well for her.

My don would be pissed as hell if I drew attention with a lawsuit of that nature though.

"So, what's it going to be?" she asks borderline belligerent. "Are you going to fire me for turning you down or can I go home now and come back to work tomorrow?"

"I'm not going to fire you for refusing to have sex with me." I am not desperate, and I don't need to threaten women to get them hanging off my cock.

Even if I don't give a rat's ass about business ethics.

She's good at hiding her emotions when she wants to, but her shoulders relax a little and the tension around her eyes eases. She's relieved.

For all her bravado, Bianca does not want to lose this job, but she doesn't back down from me either. Her refusal to be cowed only makes me like her more.

This beautiful creature has the inner strength to be an asset to the mafia. Like my sister. Unlike my sister, I doubt Bianca could kill to become made though.

There's a reason, besides backward thinking and blatant chauvinism, that there are so few made women in the Cosa Nostra. They tend to seek resolutions that don't require bloodshed.

Nerissa would tell me believing that makes me a chauvinist too. My sister could be right, but like Bianca, I know what I know.

I also know those resolutions could well be better than the ones we employ so easily in mafia business.

Bianca turns and starts walking away.

I should let her go. We've established she's not going to relieve my aching cock tonight. She wants to go home. Alone. Walking the streets alone. Riding the train. Alone.

She does it every night. She's fine.

Cazzo.

I stride after her and grab her upper arm. "Come on. I'll take you home."

"Giving me a ride home isn't going to get your dick wet. I don't even have a bed." She tries to tug her arm away.

I tighten my hold. "Where do you sleep then?"

"I pay for one half of the pullout sofa." How much she does not like that arrangement is in every word.

"And the other half?"

"One of my roommates."

"You share your bed with a roommate? Is he the reason you don't want to fuck me?" I guide her past the door the other employees use to the exit for me and my people.

"Get over yourself. *She* doesn't swing that way and I already explained. I'm not having sex with you if it means losing my job. Besides..." Her voice trails off and I want to know besides what?

But I ask, "And if it didn't mean losing your job?"

I want to know the answer to that more.

Can I promise to keep her at Amuni after fucking her? My plan is to bed and forget her. Will I be able to forget Bianca if she's around to turn me on with every swish of her hips?

"Do you ever stop?" she demands, exasperated.

"Not when it comes to getting something I want." She might as well know that right now.

I want Bianca and I *will* have her.

"Does that mean I have more sexual harassment to look forward to in the future?" She doesn't sound worried by the possibility, or mad. More intrigued.

This woman.

"Probably." Honesty is probably a mistake, but I'm not going to pretend. I'm not hiding what I want.

The only thing I hide is my illegal business transactions as a Cosa Nostra capo from the FEDs.

I shove the door open to the alley behind the club.

My armored RS7 is waiting with my driver and bodyguard. The Audi is the fastest armored vehicle on the market and can make tactical turns in a very tight radius. Ideal for city driving synd evasion.

Things are calm right now and the security level is green. Tail cars and additional security are at my discretion.

I choose not to use them. Nerissa bitches, but I am the boss. What I say, goes.

"How have you not lost your club in a lawsuit yet?" She grinds to a halt before we reach my car, tugging at her arm and trying to get loose. "I don't need a ride home."

"Most women want my attention," I inform her, ignoring her comment.

"How about you give it to one of them then?" She yanks at my hold.

"Get in the car, Bianca."

"I'm fine. I have my pepper spray." She holds up the small canister. "I'm dressed to avoid attention. I know how to get myself home safely."

"Tomorrow night, you can do just that. Tonight, I'm driving you."

"Pretty sure you aren't the one driving," she snarks.

"I can be, but my bodyguard won't like being relegated to the backseat."

"Listen, I get that in your rarified rich world with bodyguards and shiny black cars, you think you're doing me a favor."

"I am doing you a favor. This time of night, we'll get you home before the train will and you won't have to walk to and from the station."

"It's not a favor if I don't want it."

"Get your ass in the car, Bianca. I have better things to do than argue with one of my cocktail waitresses in an alley."

"You are super arrogant. Like you could give classes in it."

I don't repeat my demand but tip my head toward the open door of the car.

With a gusty, rich-men-are-such-a-pain-the-ass sigh, she finally starts moving again.

I tell my driver where we are going before sliding into the backseat with Bianca.

She's frowning at me. "How did you know my address?"

"You work for me."

"You looked it up?"

As good as. I read her application for employment. "Yes."

"What else did you look up?"

"I read your application." My phone buzzes and I pull it out.

The text is from Nerissa, wanting to know where I am. I tell her and then tap to access my curated newsfeed.

It's silent in the car. Bianca fidgets, zipping and unzipping her backpack, but she doesn't take anything out.

"You can text a friend to tell them I'm giving you a ride if that will make you feel better."

"No thanks." She huffs and unzips the backpack again. "Did you really read my application?"

"Yes." I don't bother to look up from my phone and I don't tell her I read it right after instructing Sierra to hire Bianca.

"So, you know I worked at Pitiful Princess. Is that why you offered me money for sex? You thought I was a sex worker."

I turn my head so I can see Bianca's beautiful features. "Were you?"

"No."

Shrugging, I look back at my phone. "I must have got it wrong then. I thought that strip joint let the dancers use the back rooms for clients."

There's no way she knows about my connection to the Pitiful Princess. No one outside my inner circle does.

"They do, but it's voluntary. Or it's supposed to be anyway."

That gets my attention. When I look at her, she's staring out her window.

"What do you mean supposed to be? Does the owner pressure you to offer extra curriculars?" I know he doesn't because I'm the owner.

No way is Nerissa pressuring women to sell their bodies. Besides, my second called it earlier. She has nothing to do with the dancers.

"Not the owner. Not even the general manager."

"Then who?"

She finally turns her head back so I can see her troubled expression. "Gino. Ever since he took over as assistant manager and got put in charge of the talent, he's been pushing me and Candi to offer lap dances with a happy ending at least, but he made it clear he wants us to do more."

"More?"

"Turn tricks. I shouldn't have left Candi to fight him alone."

"What do you mean?"

"The other dancers work in the back already. They're not happy about the extra ten percent he takes from them, but me and Candi are the only ones who refuse to touch the customers sexually at all."

"I'm sure your friend is fine. She's been saying no to Gino to this point." And she's not going to have to worry about him if he is taking the extra ten percent Bianca thinks he is and pocketing it.

"Right. He's already put her on the slowest nights. What happens when he cuts her dance time even more? She can't live on what she's making now, and he knows it."

"Is that what happened to you?"

"He went the other direction with me. He knew I worked short shifts four nights a week by choice because of school, so he put me on longer shifts and scheduled me six nights a week."

The sudden need to see her dance is riding me as hard as the desire to bury my cock in her tight pussy.

"What's the difference between giving a lap dance and following through with a hand job?"

"Are you really asking me that? What's the difference between doing a no contact lap dance and participating in a sex act with a stranger? You tell me."

I let her attitude slide because she's right. That was a stupid question.

"Besides, I didn't do lap dances." The glare she gives me would shrivel a lesser man's dick. "I was hired as a pole dancer and that's all I did. I worked the pole four hours a night, Wednesday through Saturday."

"Until Gino changed your schedule."

She jerks her head in an angry nod. "He thought he could force me into doing what he wanted."

The revulsion in her tone says that even if she hadn't gotten the job at Amuni, that was never going to happen.

"And your friend Candi?"

"She'll do lap dances, but she doesn't touch the customers when she does them and she doesn't want to sell her body. That's her choice," Bianca says fiercely.

Like maybe I'll argue with her.

I won't. The Genovese Family does not force women into sex work. Men either. There are plenty of women eager to work our clubs for the safety we provide in exchange for half their take.

We protect our own. Working for us, they don't need a pimp. No one to steal more of their money than the agreed upon take, or beat them when they don't make enough in a given night. If Bianca is right, Gino is acting like a pimp in one way at least.

Taking more than he should of their money.

"Of course it's her choice. Did you try talking to the general manager before looking for another job? Gino is probably trying to impress him by increasing the nightly take."

This woman and her looks.

The one on her face right now questions my intelligence. It should piss me off, but it's having the opposite effect. I'm so hard for her, I could pound nails with my dick and not end up with a piercing.

"You think he doesn't know Gino is pushing the dancers to turn tricks?" she asks with an eyeroll. "Yeah. Not likely. The GM is there almost every night. Maybe he's the one pressuring Gino to bring in more revenue."

I bite down on the need to defend Ugo. He's loyal mafia. No way is he aware that Gino is trying to force reluctant dancers to turn tricks. Nerissa is going to blow a gasket.

I see punishment and maybe death in Gino's future. Nerissa is not one of the women who looks for nonviolent solutions.

"You don't believe me." Bianca shakes her head. "Typical. You assume that because Ugo is upper management, he can't be dirty when we both know that usually means he *is* dirty."

I assume it because Ugo would have to be a fool to take the risk of pissing me off. No way in hell does he want to take a trip to The Box.

Not on any of the building schematics filed with the city, The Box is on a subfloor of the Oscuro building along with holding cells. It's where we keep, interrogate and torture our enemies.

If Bianca is right, that is where Gino will spend his last hours. If she's wrong and it's a matter of an overenthusiastic guy in a new position breaking the rules to impress the boss, he still has to be dealt with.

Nobody breaks my rules. For any reason.

Chapter 8

BIANCA

Candi: *The GM asked me a bunch of questions about Gino tonight.*

Bianca: *???*

Candi: *Like am I being coerced to work in the back rooms? That's the word he used. Coerced. Felt like I was talking to a lawyer, or something.*

Wow. For once, my plan worked. When I realized who Salvatore was, I also realized that if Nerissa is his sister, she's mafia too. Which means mafia owns the Pitiful Princess and even though I've never seen him in there, it's under Salvatore's control.

Even if his sister is the face of ownership at the strip club, Salvatore calls the shots. His insistence on taking me home gave me a chance to try to help Candi and I took it.

Bianca: *And?*

Candi: *I told him the truth. Figured it can't get much worse than only two weeknights on the schedule.*

Gino, that greedy pig, cut her from five to four nights and now two? *Stronzo.* Candi can't make rent on that.

Bianca: *Do you need money for rent?*

The nest egg I've managed to save is hidden in an offshore account, but I can transfer funds to my digital bank within twenty-four hours. It would be instant, but I filter the money through other accounts to obscure my connection to the offshore bank.

Just like my dad taught me.

The last couple years of his life, dad grew increasingly paranoid and insisted I learn how to hide my money, showing me how he set up similar accounts for Lorenzo.

Candi: *Looking for another gig.*

Which is not an answer, but I don't push it. Candi doesn't like to depend on other people any more than I do. She knows I'm here if she needs me.

~ ~ ~

After two days off, this is my third night back in the VIP room. I rush through putting on my uniform and ballet flats even though I have time before I have to be upstairs.

I *should* want to avoid Salvatore. Only, I can't stop my eyes from sneaking a peek at the entrance to the VIP area every few minutes when I'm working. I should *not* be disappointed by Salvatore's continued absence, no matter how panty-meltingly hot he is.

I don't do sex. Not ever. His absence absolutely should be a relief. It's not.

I'm nothing but hella relieved that *stronzo*, Lorenzo, is nowhere to be seen though. My phone buzzes as I put my backpack in my locker. I'm not due upstairs for ten more minutes. I like to be early, but I have time to check the text.

Candi: :dancing girl emoji: :celebrate emoji: *!!!!!!!*

Bianca: *What?*

Candi: *Gino didn't come in last night. The GM told us tonight the creep won't be back.*

Bianca: *That's great!*

Relief swirls through the stew of emotions I keep a tight lid on. Candi is going to be alright. Salvatore came through for me and he doesn't know I'm aware he's the owner of Pitiful Princess.

He didn't do it to butter me up enough to slide my panties off.

A little curl of warmth unfurls inside me.

Candi: *The GM redid the schedule too.*

Bianca: *More nights for you?*

Candi: *Yes! And get this. I don't have to pay the house a cut of my tips for the entire weekend to make up for my inconvenience.*

Inconvenience. What a tool. Losing her home because she can't make rent would be more than inconvenient for my friend. It would devastate her. Her mom and sister too. They rely on Candi to support them.

Her mom does what she can, but her arthritis is so bad, she can't make it down the stairs to the outside, much less hold down a steady job. She hasn't left the apartment in all the time I've known them.

Bianca: *Because Gino tried to force you to turn tricks?*

Candi: *Because he cut my hours to do it. The GM says Gino asking is okay and it's on me to say no.* :screwdriver emoji:

Candi clearly agrees with my tool assessment of Ugo. He has probably never been asked to do something by the one person standing between him and being able to make rent.

Candi: *But trying to force me by cutting my income is on the club.* :shocked face emoji: $$

That's something at least. Not having to give a cut of her tips will help Candi make up for lost income. But I'm still surprised at Ugo's generosity. I might expect him to offer a single night, maybe Wednesday or Thursday, but the whole weekend?

While most nights of the week, there's a steady stream of johns for the dancers who use the backroom, tips for dancers are way higher on Friday and Saturday. And Candi earns more tips than anyone else. The other dancers don't mind because when Candi dances, they make more money in the back rooms too.

She's got banging curves and this innocence that drives the customers wild with lust.

The GM must not realize how much she earns in tips on a Friday or Saturday night.

He wouldn't give up the club's cut for both days if he did. His bottom line is the business and how much Pitiful Princess earns for mafia. Which is why no one thought talking to him about Gino's behavior would do any good.

We all figured he knew.

Bianca: :party horn emoji: $$

Bianca: *Gotta go. Due upstairs.*

Candi: *Slay, girl! Get your* :moneybag emoji: *tips.*

Tips are good on the VIP floor. My new job is perfect except when I'm not watching out hopefully for a glimpse of Salvatore, like some love-struck teenager, I'm looking over my shoulder for Lorenzo. If he comes in again, I'm going to fake throwing up and go home sick.

Even when he doesn't come in, I spend enough time worried he's going to tell Franco, or worse, Salvatore, about my dad. No one in the mafia wants to hire the daughter of a rat.

Guilt by association is the Cosa Nostra motto. Or close enough to it.

Neither man comes in tonight.

With a celebration for some corporate suit getting promoted and a bachelorette party for Daddy's Little Girl, I'm run off my feet. I don't know if Daddy is her actual dad, or the guy she's marrying, but her and her posse order expensive drinks all night.

A party like this goes two ways. One, they tip generously. Two, they barely tip at all. When the women stay past closing and resist every attempt to clear them out, a sour feeling in my gut tells me it's going to be the latter.

"Che palle," I grind out under my breath when they are finally gone, and I see the small stack of cash left on the table.

It's not even a five percent tip. Cursing in Italian, the whole time, I clear the table before dropping the bartender's cut of my tip on the bar.

"Big spenders, not big tippers," I warn him.

He looks at the few bills and shakes his head. "Keep it, Bianca, you earned it. I was worried you were going to suck and screw things up for the rest of us when the big boss insisted a brand-new waitress be put in the VIP lounge, but you work hard and know how to interact with the patrons."

"Uh, thank you." I grab the bills he refuses.

I can't afford to play the oh-no-you-take-it game. I'm saving every penny I can so I can move away from New York and start a new life somewhere else as soon as I graduate from QC.

"What do you mean, the big boss insisted I got put up here? I thought it was Sierra's decision."

I saw Salvatore for the first time five nights ago *after* I got put in the VIP lounge, but why would Franco want me in here?

Salvatore makes more sense. That guy is used to getting what he wants. But how could he know he wanted me if he hadn't seen me yet? Maybe he saw me on the main floor? And waited to come up to the lounge until I was settled in?

"Mr. De Luca," the bartender says, confirming my unlikely suspicion.

Wow. Salvatore's maneuvering should piss me off, or scare me at the very least. It doesn't. He did me a favor, even if his intentions were purely selfish. That first night wasn't a fluke. I take home twice in tips what I did on the main floor.

Even on a night like tonight with the bachelorette party from hell.

And unlike with Gino, when I say no to Salvatore, he doesn't pull out the big guns to try to force me to do what he wants.

He expects me to cave to his hotness.

Which is kind of sweet. And thinking that means I should probably start therapy.

No matter how hot he is, or how much I'm starting to like the bossy capo with the cheesiest pickup lines ever, my vagina is dusty and wearing an out of business sign so old it's starting to weather.

Even if she acts weird around Salvatore, going from dusty to soaking my panties.

Soaking. My. Panties.

That does not happen to me.

It's after five a.m. when I finally clock out and change in the now empty locker room. I'm practically falling asleep standing up.

Sleeping during the day on the sofa bed is never great, which is one of the reasons I started sleeping on the floor of the closet in one of the bedrooms. My roommates like having access to the couch and the television, so they're happy to let me sleep on the floor in there.

I feel safer in the closet too. It's also quieter and darker, so I get better sleep all around. Only the last two days the super has been doing some plumbing repairs that require access to the wall in the back of the closet.

It's no use trying to sleep in the other bedroom's closet. It's too small and the floor is covered with shoes.

One of my roommates offered her bed, but sleeping there makes me feel exposed. Deep sleep is impossible and my body is craving my bedroll on the floor of the closet. Even if it is stuffy and warm in there today.

The sun will rise soon and with it the temperature in our fourth-floor walkup. It's only May, but even seventy-degree days make for stuffy heat on every floor above the second one in our old building.

Summer will be way worse. When I graduate and leave New York, I won't miss the hot and muggy summers in the City.

Walking to the subway station alone isn't my favorite thing, but everyone else is gone already.

Throwing my shoulders back, and putting my head down, I walk with the confidence of a native New Yorker. A poor one with nothing to steal. My tips are inside a pouch tucked in my underwear and my phone is in the front pocket of my jeans.

If someone cuts the straps on my decrepit looking backpack, they're going to get my uniform dress and shoes. That's it.

Holding tight to my pepper spray in my left hand, my right hand empty so I can easily grab my phone or the knife from my buckle, I head toward the entrance to the subway station. My head might be down, but I'm fully aware of my surroundings.

So, when two dark shapes step away from the buildings on my right, I notice. Adrenalin floods my system, blowing away my exhaustion as they rush toward me. I quickly release the knife from my buckle with practiced movements as I pivot away from the hand reaching out to grab me.

I slash downward, slicing through fabric and skin with ease when another hand comes around my waist.

"Fucking bitch!" the man shouts. "She cut me."

Shifting to my right foot, I spin and I unload my pepper spray on my other assailant, hitting him with over five-million scoville heat units right in his face.

He screams, reaching up to rub his eyes, which is only going to make it worse, but I'm not about to tell him that.

A beefy, tattooed hand lands on my shoulder and I drop down, surge forward and slash upward, giving his right forearm a gash to match the one on his left.

I don't want to kill him. I want him to give up and go help his friend who is now sobbing and rubbing at his eyes with the hem of his t-shirt. This guy is tougher than his friend though. The cuts on his arms don't slow him down and he grabs me...or my hoodie.

Unzipping it, I peel right out of it and my backpack. The flight part of my fight-or-flight instincts finally kicks in and I start to run. Something heavy hits me in the back and knocks me forward onto my hands and knees. My pepper spray goes flying, but I manage to keep hold of my knife.

I roll and just miss the knife intended for my chest.

Che palle. These guys are playing for keeps.

And there are three of them, not two. Not good.

Rolling again, I use the momentum to shove myself to my feet, but the man with the knife is too close. I shuffle backward and a hand covered in blood crosses in front of my face before the attached forearm presses against my neck. He grasps my shoulder with his other hand in a bruising grip.

Reaching up I stab the forearm against my throat and slice sideways.

"Fucking vicious bitch." The arm loosens but doesn't leave my neck entirely.

I can breathe. That's what matters.

The guy with the knife waives it in front of my face. "Think you're so smart, bitch?"

"Smarter than you." Using the other man's hold on me as ballast, I swing my knee up and right into the knife wielding *stronzo's* nut sack.

His face blanches and he doubles over, wheezing.

I stab the guy holding me in the thigh this time and drag my knife upward, pulling it away when he bellows in my ear. He releases me finally and I jump sideways, spin and start to run, but the guy I kneed follows and manages to grab my upper arm.

Throwing myself forward, I try to dislodge his grip. He doesn't let go and my feet drag against the sidewalk as he pulls me back toward him. Then, suddenly, I am free and my body flies forward.

Pain explodes in my head as I collide with the ground. There is a gurgling sound followed by a thump behind me. With no time to worry about nearly knocking myself out, I shove myself back up to my feet and start to run again.

"Bianca, stop. You are safe," a voice that has played a starring role in my dreams the past five nights says harshly from behind me.

My legs stop moving of their own accord, my body reacting to the assurance of safety in Salvatore's tone even more than the command. That's what I tell myself anyway.

There is more scuffling behind me and wanting to see what's happening I start to turn.

"Don't," Salvatore barks. "You do not want to see this."

He's wrong. I do want to see my assailants laid out, but he's right too. Because if I look, then I'm a witness and that's not something I want to be. Not when a Cosa Nostra capo and his security team just took out three men.

"Not turning," I gasp out, winded.

The adrenaline giving me energy takes a nosedive and it's all I can do to stay standing, even more exhausted than before. I try to suck in air, but something in my chest hurts. Sweat drips into my eyes from my forehead. I swipe at it. Damn New York muggy weather.

Blood is smeared on my hands from my assailants. Assholes. It's so hard to get out from under your nails. That's a lesson you never unlearn.

I sway.

"Boss—"

Whatever Salvatore's man says is muffled and I can't make it out. My hazy vision goes black around the edges.

Chapter 9

SALVATORE

"**B**oss, there's blood on this asshole's knife. She might be wounded," Pietro says.

Bianca sways. I catch her as she crumples. She's bleeding like hell from a gash on her forehead and the back of her t-shirt is soaked with it.

Pietro reaches out like he's going to touch her and I jerk her backward, snarling.

He puts his hands up. "I won't touch her boss, but she needs a doctor. There's a rip in the back of her t-shirt and she's still bleeding."

Cazzo. We have to get the Lucchese soldiers off the street, but Bianca needs medical attention now.

I shove my handkerchief against the wound on her back and start jogging to the car. "Franco is still at the club. Call him and then wait here for backup."

Severu De Luca, the Genovese don, and my boss, will go nuclear over this.

"Already called him boss. The Audi is fast, but not ideal for disposing of bodies," my driver says.

A black metallic SUV slams to a halt right behind my SR7. Franco and two men jump out.

"Take the one still living to The Box," I bark. "Store the others on the sublevel until Severu decides how he wants this handled."

He'll want to make a statement with the bodies, but whether it is a pile of dismembered parts dumped on the don's front lawn, or something else is anyone's guess. Some people might think our don has grown soft since getting married, but the opposite is true.

Keeping Catalina safe makes my boss twice as deadly.

"Tell Severu I want to be there for the questioning," I yell toward Franco as I slide into the backseat with Bianca.

What are Lucchese soldiers doing mugging a woman on Genovese territory? Interrogating the *stronzo* my feisty server hit with her pepper spray will have to wait.

"Take us to the hospital and show me how fast this fucking car can go getting there."

We peel away from the curb as I press one of the black hand towels, we keep for situations like this, hard against Bianca's back over my handkerchief. I take another and press down on the oozing wound on her forehead.

She sucks in a breath and her eyes pop open. Her face contorts in pain, but she doesn't cry and she doesn't complain. Her silence bothers me.

"You will be alright. We're taking you to the hospital."

She names a hospital on the other side of the river. I tell my driver to take us to the Cosa Nostra hospital instead.

Her eyes narrow and I have no doubt that the woman in my arms would argue with me, except she loses consciousness again. Cursing out the Lucchese bastards who attacked her, I press harder on the towels.

Too bad there is only one still alive. He's going to pay in pain for attacking a woman in our territory.

For attacking this woman, he will pay double.

~ ~ ~

Bianca is not a good patient. She wakes up to argue with the doctor about treating her here, only to grudgingly give consent to treatment when the doctor explains that not doing so could result in a much longer convalescence.

She answers the questions about her health history grudgingly and asks her own about every damn test they want to run.

I make it clear to both her and the doctor that the tests *will* be done. Every last one of them.

"Bossy," she grumbles.

"Irreparable damage could be done to your spinal cord if we don't find out exactly where the knife went in," the doctor explains patiently.

"What knife?"

"The one you were stabbed with." I text Franco for an update and my driver to bring me a fresh suit.

Franco: *Street cleanup done. On our way to work.*

Good. New Yorkers aren't going to faint at the sight of a little blood on the sidewalk, but nobody needs to see the dead bodies. Witnesses are a mess to clean up. Even when you pay them off, you have to monitor them.

It's a headache.

They should be at the Oscuro building soon. I text Severu to give him a heads up.

Bianca is still arguing with the doctor. "He didn't stab me. One of them hit me in the back. It hurts, but I'll be fine."

I walk over to the bed and grab the hand not getting an IV and press it against my blood-soaked shirt.

The blood is starting to dry, but her hand comes away smeared with red. "You bled all over me and my car. You were stabbed."

Her eyes round and she blinks at her hands like she's trying to make sense of what she sees.

The nurse frowns at me. "Her hands will have to be cleaned again and what if some of that blood is from the other involved parties?"

Involved parties? Is this a nurse, or a lawyer?

I shrug. "She doesn't have any open wounds on that hand."

The nurse looks like she doesn't believe I checked. I don't care what she believes.

My phone rings. It's Severu. I go to the outer room to take the call and give my don a sit rep.

"She's in treatment. I need to get back in there before she tries to sign herself out of the hospital against doctor's orders."

"Why would she do that?"

"Why do women ever do the things they do?"

When I come back into the treatment room, Bianca is laying on her stomach and there is an imaging machine above her. I'm right and she's still bitching, but she's not moving so they can get their pictures. And she's not trying to deny treatment, so I don't intervene.

"There has been no damage to the spinal cord or major vascular structures."

"Then why the hell did she bleed so much?" I demand.

The doctor's explanation sounds like he's throwing out big words because he's getting paid by the syllable.

"In English," I demand. "Medical speak isn't one of the four languages I'm fluent in."

"Excuse me, but I'm the patient and I understood just fine." The defiant words seem to exhaust Bianca.

Refusing to tire her further, I don't argue. I will get my answers from the doctor later.

"Does she need a transfusion?" I ask.

"We can make do with plasma and fluids."

"What part of being a doctor at this facility has anything to do with *making do*?" I fist my hands to keep from grabbing him by his pristine white coat and shoving him against the wall until he apologizes to Bianca for merely wanting to *make do* with her treatment.

He can apologize after she's better.

"A transfusion would be best," he hurriedly adds.

"What's your blood type?" I ask Bianca.

"I have already ascertained that," the nurse informs me in a snippy tone.

What the hell is going on with this place? Have these people forgotten who their patients are and who pays their salaries?

Bianca doesn't seem to hear the nurse and says, "B negative."

Satisfaction I don't understand settles in me. "I'm B negative." I glare at the doctor. "You'll transfuse my blood to her. If she needs plasma after, you will take it from my stores."

I expect an argument from Bianca, but her eyes are shut and her breathing is even.

I walk swiftly toward the bed. "Is she sleeping, or passed out?"

I don't wait for the nurse or doctor to answer and jostle Bianca's arm.

She hunches her shoulder, winces when that hurts her and mumbles. "Leave me 'lone. Tired."

Her eyes don't open.

"Fix her." I let the doctor see his own broken body in my eyes if he doesn't repair the damage done to Bianca. "Give her what you need to not hurt her patching her up."

The nurse grumbles about treating a patient without consent, but the doctor instructs her to administer local anesthetic before irrigating the wound on Bianca's back, or doing anything else.

I insist on a plastic surgeon being brought in to do the stitches on both her back and forehead.

When Bianca wakes up, she immediately goes for the IV needle in her hand. I'm on the phone discussing the purchase of Juniper's bars with Severu, but I see the movement and grab her wrist before she can rip it out.

"No. You need the plasma." She's already had a pint of my blood.

"Is she awake?" Severu asks me.

"Yes."

"Find out why they targeted her."

"You could ask the Lucchese asshole I sent to The Box if he was still alive," I say in Italian.

Fury rolls through me in impotent waves. Since when does a made man bite off his own tongue and choke on his blood rather than face interrogation?

"Whoever sent them had them more afraid of our interrogation techniques than death," Severu says with disgust.

"Pretty sure you and Angelo are the reasons the other families fear being interrogated by us." Not that I can't inflict damage when necessary, but both the don and his head enforcer have torture down to a fine art.

And the New York underworld knows it.

Bianca gasps, drawing my attention back to her.

"Do you need something for the pain?" I ask her.

"You sound damn solicitous," Severu mocks me.

Bianca shakes her head. "I'm woozy as it is."

"Is it true that you insisted on giving her your blood for the transfusion?" my boss asks.

"We're the same blood type."

"And I'm sure they have pints of B or O negative on hand."

"No doubt." We keep a supply of O negative available at all times because it's the universal donor blood type. "I wasn't letting the doctor put some random guy's blood into her veins."

"That's how blood transfusions usually work," Severu says, sounding inexplicably amused. "You didn't have to use your private supply."

"I didn't." Not for the first bag anyway.

All capos and their inner circles in the Genovese Family keep plasma in cryo storage, refreshing the supply once a year, or after it gets used.

"You had the doctor take directly from your vein?" Severu asks, all humor leached from the tone that reveals nothing of his thoughts.

"She needed the blood." I'm glad Bianca doesn't speak Italian.

This whole conversation is not something she needs to hear.

"Is there something I need to know about her?" Severu asks.

I grimace at what he's implying.

I'm a capo. I don't get married without the don's approval. Not that Severu exercises his right of refusal. So far anyway and he's been don for over five years.

"Other than I want to fuck her until her throat is raw from screaming my name?"

Bianca squirms with discomfort again and I push the call button. She's getting pain meds, whether she likes it, or not.

Severu barks out a laugh. "It's like that?"

"It's like that."

"Sounds like she's got some healing to do before that can happen."

"Doctor said minimum two weeks before anything strenuous."

"You asked?" Severu's laughter lasts longer this time. "You have got it bad, Salvatore."

"You know how it is. You want what you can't have."

Cold water saturates my chest and down the front of my slacks. Shouting, I jump back and lose my grip on my phone.

"What the hell?" I demand.

Bianca looks up at me, her pallid face showing exhaustion and pain, but no remorse. "I knocked it over."

"And the lid slipped off too?"

"It was hard to get enough water, so I took the lid off."

Cazzo. I should have been paying attention. "I'll get you a new bottle of water."

This one had better be easier for her to sip from or the medical staff here will find out how unpleasant it can be to deal with untreated pain.

Chapter 10

BIANCA

The truth hiding reality rolls off my tongue like Mr. Ruhnke taught me. "Don't lie when the truth will protect you better," was one of his favorite sayings.

Since everyone who mattered in my life before him hurt me with their lies, I follow his advice whenever I can.

I did knock over my water bottle. Right down the front of Salvatore De Luca's expensive suit, which he must have changed because it looks pristine with no splotches of dried blood.

And I *couldn't* get as much as I wanted to use with the lid on.

Hopefully the ice water bath cooled off his libido.

The *stronzo* wants me because I refused him.

He's only taking care of me because he wants to use my body. I don't know what the deal is with his blood, but he probably wants me to feel more beholden to him.

Newsflash: I don't.

Who is going to pay for this swanky hospital he's got me in? The room I'm in is light years away from a cubicle in a public hospital ER. It's like the kind of hotel rooms my mom insisted we stay in for our family trips before she left my dad and me, taking my twin with her.

I told Salvatore to take me to the one covered by my insurance. I know I did, but did he listen?

No.

Well, I didn't sign anything agreeing to treatment and I'm not paying a dime for any of this.

My glare is wasted on him because he's too busy picking up his phone from where he dropped it on the floor.

"You still there?"

Pause.

"I'll talk to her."

Her has got to be me, but I don't know what he wants to talk to me about. Or who he's talking to. My guess is someone in the mafia because they're speaking Italian.

Whoever it is, Salvatore feels comfortable telling them he wants to have sex with me. Jerk.

If there was any water left in the bottle I found on the swing table by my bed, I'd trick him into leaning over and dump it on his head.

He doesn't know I speak Italian. Just like he assumed I didn't have a college education, he assumes I don't speak our mother tongue.

Okay, I have my mom's blue eyes and my grandfather's red hair. And maybe I do look more like my mom's side of the family than my dad's, but my name is Bianca Gemelli. You can't get much more Italian than that.

Salvatore should know that not all Italians have dark hair and eyes. My nonna's mother was blonde with blue eyes the same shade as mine. The same shade as nonna's.

My *bisnonna* came over from Italy to marry my great-grandfather. An arranged marriage. I shudder internally at the thought.

They still happen in the mafia, even now. One good thing came from getting kicked out of the Genovese Family by Lorenzo Ricci. No one is pushing me to marry some stranger for the sake of *la famiglia*.

Salvatore demands pain meds, which I tell the nurse I don't want, and another water bottle for me. "This one had better be easier for her to drink from."

"The bottles are designed to require minimum suction, Mr. De Luca," the nurse assures him.

"She had trouble drinking out of that one," he says like it's the nurse's fault.

Her face mottles under his tone. Is she scared, or angry at being spoken to like her life is on the line if I don't get a working water bottle?

"Do you need a towel?" she asks him politely enough.

Salvatore glowers down at his wet clothing. "Yes."

The nurse turns away, probably to get the towel, but she winks at me and gives me a subtle thumbs up. She knows the water bottle isn't defective. She assumes that I dumped the water on him on purpose. She's right.

I smile back.

"Don't smile at her, she's doing her job," Salvatore barks.

The nurse rolls her eyes and I have to stifle the urge to laugh. Not least because it will hurt if I do. Any kind of movement, including breathing, hurts right now. My whole body feels like one big ache and tomorrow is going to be worse.

The second day always is.

So, no laughing. Because pain, but also because I don't want to get the other woman in trouble.

"As a person who makes her living in the service industry, I will always show my appreciation for someone doing their job." My voice isn't strong, but I don't slur my words and Salvatore gets the message.

The nurse hands him a neatly folded towel.

"Thank you," Salvatore says shortly, still frowning.

Surprise flashes in the nurse's eyes, but her lips remain pressed together in a straight line. "As you said, it's my job."

It sounds like she's saying *you're welcome* but I have a lot of experience saying something that sounds like one thing, but I mean in a totally different way. The nurse isn't a pushover and she's not impressed by the capo's grudging appreciation.

Salvatore doesn't seem to care either way, which fascinates me.

My only experience with another capo is Lorenzo Ricci, as limited as it was. But my dad talked about Lorenzo. A lot. The older capo is not the type of man to let even the tiniest indication of disrespect slide. He would go ballistic if I spilled water on him too.

The nurse bustles from the room and Salvatore moves closer to the bed. "Why did those men come after you?"

"You'll have to ask them." He said something about a Lucchese soldier on the phone.

The Luccheses are another one of the Five Families in the New York Cosa Nostra and the family of the current godfather, Don Caruso. Why would their men mug someone in Genovese territory?

The Five Families are allies and sometimes rivals, but they usually stick to their own territories.

Salvatore is not impressed by my answer. "I'm asking you."

"I don't know."

Salvatore knows more about what happened than I do. I only know three men attacked me. He knows they are from a rival family.

"You must know something. Three Lucche—three men attacked you. What are you mixed up in that has made you a target?"

"Are you victim blaming?"

"I am asking you: Why were you targeted by three killers?"

They were a kill team?

"Maybe I wasn't the target." Talking is harder than it should be, dizziness making the words hard to string together.

Nausea makes my stomach roil too and I take shallow breaths, trying to control it.

Salvatore strides to the door, yanks it open and says something to someone outside. His voice is muffled and I can't tell what he says, but his tone is easy enough to decipher. He's angry and impatient.

I'm not surprised when a few seconds later, the nurse returns with a tray holding a fresh water bottle, a vial of clear liquid (probably the pain medication I said I didn't want) and a hypodermic.

"Give her something for the pain," Salvatore demands. "She can't talk without it hurting."

Of course, he's worried about my ability to communicate. Why else would a busy and powerful capo be hanging around my hospital room? He wants answers.

Too bad for him. No matter how easy it becomes for me to talk, I still won't have anything to say he wants to hear. I don't know why I'm the one lying here in a hospital bed. I don't live in Lucchese territory. I don't know any Lucchese made men.

The nurse prepares the hypodermic before approaching the bed. Her steady, compassionate gaze meets mine. "This is a mild opioid. It won't knock you out, but it will make you drowsy."

Even with my dad's history, I want that shot. I hurt.

But I shake my head. "No. I still have to get home."

Thinking of trying to deal with this pain in my current living situation would make me cry. If I let myself cry.

Bile rises in my throat and I take a hasty sip of water to settle my stomach. It doesn't work. The room is spinning around me.

Salvatore says something, but his words sound like they're coming through a wind tunnel.

"Are you feeling nauseated?" the nurse asks, her face too close to mine.

I don't like people close to me. Even medical professionals. Maybe that's why I'm feeling so sick. This whole hospital thing is triggering my need to get away from people big time.

I swallow, trying not to vomit.

"I'll take that as a yes. Is your heart racing?"

"Just anxiety." Something I have to live with.

She looks worried. "Are you feeling dizzy?"

"Room is spinning," I get out before clenching my teeth on the need to throw up.

"I think you're having a reaction to the local anesthetic."

"You were supposed to ask about allergies," Salvatore says in a deadly tone.

"I did, but a patient can be fine with a medication the first ten times they are exposed to it and have a reaction on the eleventh."

"Fix it!"

I don't know about the nurse, but my body wants to obey Salvatore's roar.

Chapter 11

SALVATORE

It's another harrowing forty minutes before the medical team have Bianca's reaction to the local anesthetic treated. It leaves her looking even more exhausted and fragile than before.

My response to her saying she still doesn't want the pain meds is not calm.

"The fuck are you talking about? You're not leaving the hospital." If she tries to get out of that bed, she will fall flat on her face. Before she can argue more, I tell the nurse, "Give her the codeine."

The nurse makes a point of looking at Bianca and pretending I am not standing right here. "Do you want this medication? I can give you the analgesic by itself, but it won't help as much with the pain."

"No strong meds." Bianca blinks, clearly trying to stay awake.

She needs rest. And to be comfortable. "You are in pain. You will allow the nurse to administer the drug."

The stubborn woman shakes her head at me. "I can't stay here."

What the hell does she think she is going to do? Go back to her shitty apartment and rest on her half of the sofa bed?

"You are staying," I tell her.

Despite the dark bruises under them, her blue eyes flash defiance at me. What the fuck is wrong with her? I'm her boss. I am *the* boss and she may not know I'm mafia, but she knows I own the club she works at.

She's still out of it from everything that has happened. That's why she's not thinking straight.

And it's the reason she needs to stay right where she is. In that hospital bed.

"Don't bother looking at me like that, Bianca. You are staying the night here and probably tomorrow too. And you are taking that damn shot. "

"That's not your choice." She's trying to sound tough, but her voice is so thready it makes my argument for me and if she wasn't so out of it, she'd realize it too.

Patience gone, I don't softshell this. "It is if I say it is." I zero in on the nurse. "Give her the pain medication, or look for another job, because you won't be working here any longer."

Getting her fired is the least I can do to her. And working at this hospital, taking care of the patients she does, she has to know that.

She squares her shoulders and looks me right in the fucking eye. "I am not one of your soldiers, Mr. De Luca. I have an ethical duty to treat my patient as *she* requires."

"Wow. I just got a lady boner," Bianca says, obviously impressed by the other woman's foolish bravery.

I'm done dealing with this woman. "Get the doctor in here now."

Alarm washes over Bianca's features.

"I'll take it if you're footing the bill for all this." She frowns at me and sweeps her arm to indicate the hospital room.

Wincing, she lets the arm fall back to the bed.

"Don't wave your arms around like that," I bite out. What the fuck is wrong with her? "You'll tear your stitches."

"Are you sure you want this?" The nurse holds the needle up for Bianca to see. "Yes."

The nurse nods to Bianca and then gives me a baleful stare, "I will instruct accounting that all charges related to Miss Gemelli's care are to be billed to you."

Like that is some kind of threat. "I already took care of it."

Bianca's tired eyes show shock and then something else. Maybe gratitude? But then her expression turns mutinous. "I'm not having sex with you because you pay my medical bills."

That's one thing we agree on. "You'll let me fuck you because your pussy weeps for me and for no other reason."

BIANCA

Heat climbs up my neck and into my cheeks at Salvatore's crude words. I cannot believe he said that and in front of the nurse.

My ovaries are *not* swooning. Not.

Oh, yes, they are, my inner voice sings.

Pretending not to hear it or his arrogant, and strangely arousing claim, I focus on the woman prepping the syringe.

When she's done, she administers the medication through my I.V. port. "The codeine phosphate will act more quickly this way, but you'll have to take the accompanying analgesic orally."

I nod.

"It will take about ten minutes for the full effect, but you should start feeling relief immediately."

I feel woozy. And it's easier to breathe. So yeah. Relief.

Feeling thirsty, I reach for my new bottle of water, but my hand misses. Okay, really woozy.

Before the nurse can help me, Salvatore is there, grabbing the bottle and holding it so the straw is right in front of my mouth.

I take a drink and almost regret pouring my other water over him immediately. The cold liquid sooths my throat so much.

"Don't drink too much at once," the nurse warns me. "Some people get nauseated when they take opioids."

"Get her something for the nausea."

Frowning, I push the water bottle away from my face. "Don't be so bossy. I'm not nauseated anymore."

"But you might get that way. She should be prepared."

"We are always prepared, Mr. De Luca," the nurse claims. "If you could step aside. I need to give my patient the acetaminophen."

Salvatore puts his hand out imperiously. "I'll do it."

The nurse looks to me for permission and I give a small nod. She may not realize how deadly the capo's anger can be, but I do. He killed three men only a couple of hours ago because they were mugging someone on his turf.

The nurse hands the tiny paper cup to Salvatore. Only, instead of handing it to me like I expect, he slides one arm behind my shoulders and helps me sit up.

Then, guiding the cup to my lips with his other hand, he says, "Open up."

The position feels intimate, but it's not uncomfortable. For some mysterious reason, having Salvatore inside my personal bubble doesn't bother me.

"I could do this myself," I mumble anyway.

He ignores me and waits for me to obey him. The man is not going anywhere until I do. So, I open my mouth and he tips the pills into my mouth, and offers me the water bottle straw immediately after.

I manage to swallow the pills and take a few extra draws of water because I can. When I'm finished, he puts the water bottle down and settles me back against the bed, but doesn't step away from me.

Right. More questions.

"Okay, get it over with," I say with what should be a wave of my hand but ends up being a wiggle of my fingers.

Huh. Not sure how mild the opioid is if I can't even control my limbs properly.

"Get what over with?" Salvatore asks.

"Your questions." The words come out a little slurred and my eyelids grow heavy.

"You're not going to question her now?" The nurse sounds scandalized.

Or annoyed.

Maybe both.

"Leave." What patience the capo has is used up and he's giving the poor nurse a death glare.

With him the death part isn't a euphemism, so I shoo her which turns out to be another series of finger wiggles. "Go. It's okay. Gonna fall asleep soon anyway."

And Salvatore can blame himself for that. He's the one that insisted on the pain medication.

"Did you give her too much? She shouldn't be this affected by codeine. It's not as strong as morphine."

"Ooh, you wanted to ask your question and now you're gonna have to wait." I giggle.

"I gave her exactly what the doctor prescribed." Offense vibrates in every word of the nurse's defense of herself. "Your girlfriend lost a lot of blood, that can impact how strongly she will react to medications until her blood supply has renewed itself."

"She's on her second transfusion bag."

Alarmed, I manage to get my eyes open to stare blearily up at Salvatore. "Can't donate that much at once."

"You're not donating any blood," he tells me condescendingly.

"Not me. You."

"Mr. De Luca donated one pint of fresh blood and another of his stored plasma, Miss Gemelli."

"Not his girlfriend," I slur as my eyes close again and my body drags me toward sleep.

SALVATORE

Bianca sleeps through the nurse taking her vitals and a woman coming in to ask if either of us wants breakfast.

I'm reluctant to leave and order breakfast. Bianca needs looking after. The woman clearly doesn't take her own health seriously. She has a stab wound and gash on her forehead. Not to mention her rejection of the local anesthetic used on her. Her body needs rest.

If I leave, she'll probably try to check out the minute she wakes up again.

While I wait for my food and coffee, I check messages on my phone. Severu wants the three bodies delivered to the godfather, Don Caruso. Miceli is going to do it, but asks if I want to come along.

Hell, yes, I do.

Those Lucchese *stronzos* attacked one of my employees, outside of one of my clubs. Whoever sent them needs to know I'm coming for him.

Bianca moans and my head snaps up. Her eyes are closed, but she's frowning and moving restlessly on the bed.

I stand and go to her, saying her name softly. "Bianca."

She doesn't respond, locked in her nightmare. No dream would make her face contort in that rictus of agony. She's dreaming about the attack, I bet. Her head whips violently back and forth on the pillow and that can't be good for her concussion.

Mild, or not.

I lay my hand against her cheek, holding her head immobile. The zing of connection surprises me under the circumstances.

"Bianca, it is alright, little one," I tell her in Italian, leaning down so I am practically whispering in her ear.

She stops moving, her face losing some of the stress lines. I rub her arm and talk to her in Italian until she's breathing deeply, and her body shows only the relaxation of sleep.

"Boss, your breakfast is here," Pietro says from outside the door.

My men have strict instructions not to come into Bianca's room. She is only wearing a thin gown and no bra or underwear.

I found a stack of cash in a pouch tucked into her underwear when I undressed her. That was the first time the nurse gave me attitude. I told her Bianca is my girlfriend to get her off my back.

No way was I letting someone else undress her. Not even the nurse.

The cash is probably her tips from last night. I put it with the rest of her things in the closet.

"Let her through." Pulling my hand away from Bianca's soft skin, I turn to face the woman returning with my breakfast and point to a desk-sized table on the other side of the private room. "Put it over there."

But before I can sit down, Bianca gets restless again. I return to her, laying my hand against her neck, brushing my thumb along the underside of her jaw and speaking to her in low Italian. She settles almost immediately.

"Put my food here." I indicate the swing table by Bianca's bed.

After the woman leaves, I drag the chair closer and maneuver myself so I have one hand on Bianca's arm and the other available to feed myself. I speak to her between bites of food and sips of coffee, telling her about my plans to buy a string of bars and turn them into nightclubs.

To make my own mark on *la famiglia* and prove I didn't get named capo because of who my cousin is. Being my father's son will always influence my role within the family, but I'm *not* Little Sal. I am Salvatore De Luca and I can make those bars into something that will make millions for the Genovese Family.

I speak in Italian, too low for anyone outside her room to hear me. Not that I'm worried. I have men in the outer room that will make sure no one comes near the door without me knowing.

I'm taking my last sip of coffee when my phone buzzes. It's Franco.

Chapter 12

SALVATORE

I move away from the bed to answer. "What do you know?"

"I sent their pictures to the don's security team. They came back with names and their affiliation."

Most likely the request for information was forwarded to Catalina, the don's wife. No one outside my cousin's inner circle knows that his wife has more intel than the FEDs when it comes to organized crime families.

"Who do they work for?" I ask Franco.

We know they are Lucchese soldiers because of the tattoos on their left wrists, but we don't know what capo they are under.

The Genovese mark our people too, but we hide the symbol with other tattoos in ink only visible under black light. Every one of us from soldier to don is required to have the black light app on our phones, so we can confirm affiliation when necessary.

The invisible tattoos make us harder to spot by law enforcement and Severu has been pushing for all the Five Families to adopt the practice. Most have, but some capos still require a visible mark of loyalty.

Which narrows down who the capo is that the dead men worked for.

Before Franco can answer me, a moan comes from Bianca's bed. Shit. She kicks her blanket off and flails. She's going to rip out her IV. Rushing over, I grab her hand and settle her down before going back to my phone call.

"Who?" I ask again.

"Caruso's nephew."

Cazzo. There is no such thing as coincidence in the life. Bianca has nothing to do with those soldiers being in our territory. She was just in the wrong place at the wrong time.

Henrico (call me Henry because I'm a douche) Caruso thinks he should be the next godfather because he is his uncle's heir and will become Don of the Lucchese after the godfather's death.

But Don Caruso has already told the other Five Families that Severu should be made godfather upon his death. Even if Severu is younger than any Cosa Nostra godfather in the last hundred years.

The other dons will listen and cast their votes for Severu as long as nothing happens between now and Don Caruso's death that makes our family look weak.

Like not being able to protect our territory.

This morning, we killed the *bastardos.* A win. But if Bianca hadn't fought like a fucking warrior, she would be dead and we would still be looking for who did it. She kept her attackers busy long enough for us to drive by on the way back to my place.

It was good luck, but not coincidence, we got there in time. I instructed my driver to take a small detour by the club after Franco texted me to tell me that the VIP lounge closed late. A bachelorette party that didn't want to leave. I knew Bianca would be heading to the train and wanted to make sure she got there alright.

Nothing soft in that.

Once we have sex (repeatedly), this obsession with the cocktail waitress will abate. Amazing lay, or bad one, I'm not looking for a relationship. Especially with a woman nine years younger than me.

Offering her a ride home was just another opportunity to persuade her into my bed.

"You're going to have to get someone to cover Bianca's shifts for the next few weeks."

As long as her stitches hold and her concussion doesn't get worse, she could return to Amuni in only a few days. However, no way am I letting her go back to work where other men can ogle her gorgeous curves until we've had our fill of each other.

This jealousy is new. I'm a possessive guy. I don't share, but I also don't do relationships where that possessiveness lasts beyond a night, or two.

Once I bury my cock in her hot pussy, this need to keep her out of circulation will abate.

Franco's long silent pause makes me itch.

"You want me to keep her job open for her?" he finally asks.

"What the hell? Are we fucking heartless? She got mugged on her way home from working at Amuni. Even if those assholes hadn't targeted her for her connection to us, we wouldn't fire her for taking sick leave, would we?"

"Is this a trick question?" Franco asks, sounding amused. "That's exactly what we would normally do."

"Well, we're not doing it this time. And we need to take a fucking look at how we treat our employees."

"Says the man who intended to pay a waitress to sleep with him and then fire her for it."

I regret telling Franco my plans. "When you say it like that, I sound like a heartless jerk."

"Uh..."

"Okay, enough with the comedy routine." I was going to pay her 5K.

It would have been enough for her to live on while looking for another job. Probably.

"I wasn't joking, boss."

No, he is just telling it like it is. I am no soft touch. Not even close. Pops raised me to be hard and life did the rest. Whether the 5K would have been enough, or not, should not be a blip on my conscience.

But it's the clang of a five-alarm fire. "Keep her position open for her, or create one when she's ready to come back. I don't give a damn which. She's got enough to worry about without stressing over losing her job."

"Did you get religion, or something?"

Or something. "I'm Catholic like all good capos."

"Right, boss." Franco laughs. "The last time you were in a church was for the don's wedding."

There's no point in denying the truth, so I don't.

My cock is ruling my head right now, and worse, I'm letting it.

What the hell?

After I end the call with Franco, I take off my suit jacket and tie. Hanging them in the closet I can't help noticing Bianca's beat up bag and threadbare clothes. She's got multiple roommates and makes good tips, as the thick bundle of cash sitting on the shelf attests.

Why does she dress like she's barely getting by?

Does she have a drug habit?

Considering how opposed she is to taking pain meds, that's unlikely. But then what?

I ponder the conundrum that is the sexy cocktail waitress I will now have to wait two weeks to fuck vigorously while I kick off my shoes and remove my belt.

After tucking both in the closet I cross the room to her bed, reaching her just in time.

She's already having another bad dream. Damn it.

Is it the codeine? I know from experience morphine can cause some pretty lousy dreams. I don't like how distressed she gets.

Bianca isn't going to sleep quietly without me. After putting my gun in easy reach, I don't feel a drop of guilt climbing onto the bed beside her. I put my arm over her waist and she turns her face toward me, inhaling like she's seeking my scent.

My dick grows predictably hard, but I ignore it, closing my eyes and willing myself to sleep.

BIANCA

A deep rumbly voice infiltrates my consciousness. "Leave her the fuck alone. She's sleeping."

"We need to take her vitals, Mr. De Luca," another male voice responds, this one softer and almost chipper.

The body underneath me tenses. "Get a female nurse in here then. You aren't coming near her."

Someone is with me? In the hospital bed? And I slept? How?

My head is nestled in his neck, and I'm laying half on top of him. A familiar scent of expensive aftershave mixed with a unique fragrance I have only smelled once. When Salvatore De Luca had me cornered outside the kitchen at Amuni.

Shocked, my eyelids fly open and I try to shove myself away.

His arm over my hip stops me going anywhere. "Relax, *dolcezza*. No one is going to hurt you."

Before my brain processes Salvatore's words, my body obeys him, going boneless and relaxing into him. What the hell?

How did he do that?

I tilt my head to look up at him and our eyes lock. Whatever he's thinking is hidden behind expressionless steel gray orbs. While I'm sure he can see the battle between nerves and confusion going on inside me.

Opening my mouth to tell him to let me go, a jaw cracking yawn comes out instead. I slap my hand over my mouth, wincing when the movement pulls something in my back.

"Do you need more pain meds?" He studies me, like he's making his own determination. "You only went into deep sleep after draping yourself over me."

Cheeks hot with mortification, I try to move again.

"Settle." He holds me against him while brushing my hair back from my face. "Are you in pain?"

"Not enough to need more codeine." I can't believe I slept next to someone else. Not even next to. On top of.

A male someone too. One who makes no bones about wanting to sex me up.

I don't feel hypnotized, but this is weird. Even how relaxed I feel right now is freaking me out, but my body is not sliding into a panic attack. No, my heartrate and breathing are totally chill.

"Are you a vampire?" Aren't they the ones that are supposed to be able to hypnotize?

His gaze narrows. "Are you feeling alright? You have only had two doses of codeine and they were four hours apart."

It's the codeine. It must be. That's why I'm so chill like this with him. More than chill, I do not actually want to move.

My brows draw together in confusion. "I don't remember a second dose."

"You were asleep when it was administered."

"I thought they were supposed to wake me up."

"I woke up." He says it like him making medical decisions for me is a given.

It isn't.

"You aren't the patient," I remind him.

"I took responsibility for you."

"That's not how it works." Like at all. It doesn't matter who is paying the bills for my stay at this luxurious medical facility.

I am the patient and an adult. He isn't even related to me. He can't legally make decisions for me.

"It is here." He's complacent.

Me? Not so much. "I bet the nurse was pissed at you."

"She refused to administer the second dose without waking you. I called the doctor in to do it."

"You're a bully. You know that right?"

"I am the boss."

"But that doesn't make you a god." Not even if he is a capo.

"God would be less wrathful."

Caspita. What did he threaten the doctor with? "You didn't get the nurse fired, did you? I like her."

"No. She was watching out for you."

And he likes that? "You're a very confusing man."

"Not at all. I am who I am and everyone around me knows who that is."

Lie. Lots of people don't know he's a capo, or what that means if they do know. I doubt all his employees know he's a made man who has killed before.

"So, they all know you sleep in hospital beds with wounded waitresses?" I push.

"This is a one off. You would not settle. The codeine gave you bad dreams."

I remember some of those dreams and they have nothing to do with the codeine. "And you insisted they give me a second dose? Thanks a lot."

"You're welcome. As long as I stayed near, you slept fine, despite your dreams."

But why? I don't sleep well with anyone near. Not even my savior, Mr. Ruhnke. For sure not my roommates. And a man who wants to screw me? I shouldn't have slept a wink with him in the bed.

"How long since the last dose?" I ask.

"Two hours."

"I slept six hours?" With him in the bed? Repeating it isn't making it any easier to believe.

"You did."

"I'm sorry."

"For what?" His eyes try to see into my brain. "Did you bring those men into my territory?"

"You consider the area around your club your territory? That's pretty arrogant." I'm teasing him and I'm not sure why.

But he doesn't know that I know he's mafia. So, his claim *is* arrogant.

"Answer my question," he demands without responding to mine.

Typical.

"No, they didn't come to Manhattan looking for me. I don't know why they were near the club or why they attacked me. I told you." That I remember.

"What are you sorry for then?"

"Keeping you here with me. I'm sure you had better things to be doing."

"Sleeping here, or at my apartment." He shrugs, lifting my body with the movement. "It's the same."

"I'm sure your bed is much more comfortable than this one." And I doubt very much he's the kind of man to let women sleep cuddled on top of his chest.

"You'll find out soon enough," he assures me, his arrogance very much in evidence.

"Yeah, that's not happening."

"You don't think so?"

"No." But for the first time in my life, I might be lying when I say I'm not interested in sex. "You need to go."

"Are you trying to kick me out of your hospital room?"

"If I say yes, will you leave?"

"Doubtful."

I sigh and let my head drop back to that super comfy, and ridiculously *comforting* position nestled into the strong column of his neck. "Bully."

"I am looking out for you."

"Until I give you sex, which is not happening."

"Until I am not," he corrects me, sounding as surprised by his own words as I am.

Huh. "That doesn't sound like a one-night stand that ends in me losing my job."

"No, it doesn't, does it?"

Chapter 13

SALVATORE

Why did I say that?

I don't do relationships. And if I did do a relationship, it wouldn't be with a barely making it cocktail waitress nearly ten years younger than me.

Yet, I practically promised not to fire her after we have sex.

"Will I be able to leave soon?" she asks, her breath puffing against my neck enticingly.

Now is not the time to get an erection.

Before I can answer, one of my men knocks on the door and then opens it a crack. "The nurse is here to take Miss Gemelli's vitals."

"A woman?"

"Yes, boss."

"You shouldn't have a let a man in here."

"I'm sorry, boss. He was a nurse."

I give a shit. "Orders are orders."

"Yes, boss." His voice is infused with a healthy dose of fear.

As it should be. I see to discipline personally when the refraction occurs under my orders. Unlike some of the older capos, I don't leave it to my second-in-command. My sister would enjoy it too much.

She is feared among my men, but my punishments are worse and I am feared more.

A woman dressed in nurse's scrubs comes into the room. She's younger than the nurse from early this morning, with bright blonde hair pulled up in a bouncy ponytail.

She smiles at me, paying no attention to Bianca. "Good morning, Mr. De Luca. Is it alright if I take the patient's vitals?"

Affront rolls off of Bianca and from one breath to the next she goes from lax and pliant to sitting up and glaring. "That question would be better directed toward me. I am the patient."

"I could take your vitals, Mr. De Luca," the nurse says in a flirty tone. "If you'd rather."

"Are you kidding me?" Bianca mutters under her breath.

She casts a glare up at me over her shoulder as if it's my fault the nurse is behaving like we're in a kink club and offering to play *doctor*.

"What part of me being in this bed with your fucking patient makes you think I'm open to your flirting?" I ask the nurse in clipped tones.

"You're not with her though. She told Amanda that she's not your girlfriend. We all understand why you said she was."

"Yes?" I ask in a tone that should clue her into how precarious her position is right now.

"Oh, yes. You thought you needed to say that so you would be allowed into the exam room with her."

I *had* said it to give my insistence on overseeing Bianca's care some legitimacy. That doesn't mean I enjoy having this woman bring attention to that fact, or knowing that she and her colleagues have been gossiping about me.

"You and your coworkers would be smart to keep your nose out of my business."

Instead of being frightened like an intelligent human being, the nurse looks like she just soaked her panties.

"Everybody knows you brought her in because you feel sorry for her. She was attacked outside your club, but that doesn't make it your responsibility," she says earnestly.

"There is no world in which I need your advice." I am done with this woman. "Take Bianca's vitals and get the hell out of here."

Finally, her smile drops and she blinks like she's going to cry. For fuck's sake.

"Do you even know how to take her vitals?" I demand.

"Y-yes. Of course. I'm trained."

"Trained as what?" I ask suspiciously.

"I'm a fully qualified medical assistant." Her eyes shine with suspicious moisture and I don't feel a spark of compassion.

"Get a fucking nurse in here and don't come back."

She turns and runs from the room.

"That wasn't very nice." Bianca presses the controller so the head of the bed raises.

Without her sharing my space, there's not really enough room on the bed for both of us. My reluctance to leave her is ridiculous.

"I need to go." Ignoring the weird twinge of conscience the words give me, I climb out of the bed.

With a look toward the bathroom door, Bianca shifts her legs over the side of the bed, doing her best to hide the pain the movement gives her.

"I am trained to read micro expressions," I tell her conversationally.

She shrugs, pretending that doesn't hurt either.

"Stop moving like that, or I'll instruct them to give you something to knock you out with your next dose of pain medication."

Fear flashes through her eyes. "No. Don't. I can't be unconscious here. Please, Salvatore."

It costs her to say please like that. Enough that she can't hide that either.

"You slept through the night," I remind her.

"Sleeping and unconscious are not the same thing."

No, they are not, but I don't expect her to make the distinction so adamantly. "Then, stop moving and hurting yourself."

"I won't heal if I don't move. Besides, I have to pee."

This woman. Even terrified of being drugged she can't help talking back.

"You argue with me more than anyone else." I put my arm out for her.

Sliding off the bed to her unsteady feet, she takes my arm without a word. At first, I'm uncertain about leaving her in the bathroom alone, but she is adamant.

So, I stand outside, with the door open, in case she falls.

She refuses to hold my arm walking back to the bed. But it's beyond her to get back onto the bed without help. Her solution is to stay up.

Mine is to lift her onto the bed.

She settles with the blanket over her.

"You're damn stubborn."

"Pot meet kettle." She rolls her eyes.

Rolls. Her. Eyes.

At *me*.

"You should do what I say," I inform her.

"Yeah, no. I am not one of your soldiers, capo."

Everything inside me stills. "Capo?"

Her expression does not shift from irritated. "Please. If you throw a rock in Manhattan, you can't help hitting someone that knows you're Cosa Nostra leadership."

"I do not know what you think you know." But I'm going to find out.

"I know that the medical facility caters to the Cosa Nostra, mostly the Genovese Family. I know that a De Luca is the don and your last name is De Luca. Even if I hadn't heard from someone that you are a capo, I would know you're connected."

"Not all De Lucas are connected to the mafia."

"No, but you are."

"Who told you I am a capo?"

"A friend."

I grab my gun and holster and put them on. "What friend?"

Were the Lucchese men there for her? Is she part of that mafia family? But if she is and spying for them, they would not have tried to kill her.

The knife wound wasn't fatal though, was it?

She sighs and closes her eyes, like she's tired and in pain. Which I'm sure she is. But giving into it like this? Feels timed.

"Does it matter who?"

"Yes."

Her eyes open and she bites her lip. "I don't want to get anyone into trouble."

"They are only in trouble if they spoke out of turn." Bianca is not wrong.

Probably half of Manhattan knows about the Genovese Mafia. Not that anyone outside our family has proof of syndicate ties. No one should have proof.

Do they?

"One of my roommates dated a guy named Marco. He knew a lot about the mafia in New York."

Fucking Francesco Jilani, Severu's former consigliere, had a made man running his security named Marco. My dad, the new consigliere, demoted Marco to foot soldier for being sloppy.

"Did you ever meet this Marco?" I ask, watching for any evidence of a lie falling from her beautiful lips.

"A couple of times. They broke up when he lost his job. Only I didn't know you could get fired in the mafia without...you know, *dying*."

"What did Marco look like?" I ignore her comment.

Unlike Marco, I don't have loose lips.

"Shorter than you. Thick like Franco, but with less muscle." She shrugs and winces. "Dark hair. Brown eyes. A couple of years ago, when I knew him, he wore a hipster goatee and his hair always looked like it needed a wash. He dressed the part though, complete with gold chains and silk suits."

Fucking Marco.

"You took a job at Amuni believing it was owned by a capo in the mafia?"

"I didn't know you were the owner when I took the job. I thought Franco owned it."

"He doesn't." Not even on paper.

Amuni is squeaky clean and one of my official business interests in New York. Like the chain of bars I'm buying from Juniper.

"When Armando told me the big boss was coming in I knew Franco didn't own the club."

"Armando is one of the servers?" I guess.

"Don't you know?"

"I own five clubs." Two nightclubs and three strip clubs in our territory. "I don't track every employee."

"He's a server on the main floor."

How did the waiter know I was coming in? Had Sierra announced it? Probably.

No doubt she believed my visit was me checking up on the running of my property and wanted everyone on their toes. When in fact, I showed up that night to see Bianca and to get the beautiful redhead into my bed.

My fascination with her is because she said no. Of course, it is. There's no other reason for the amount of brain space Bianca has taken up since that night.

"You didn't quit after learning I own the club," I observe. "And you think I'm part of a syndicate."

"Are you saying you aren't?" she asks.

This time, she's the one watching for any sign of dishonesty from me.

"No." I'm not saying I *am* either, but I'm not denying it to her.

I don't know why that feels important, but it does.

She nods. Her hand lifts to press gingerly at the bandage on her forehead. "Man, those jerks did a number on me. Speaking of, Mr. Not Going to Confirm or Deny Being Mafia, why do you keep asking me about them when they were probably there because of your organization."

"Only a fool would attack on territory claimed by the Genovese Family." It's still not a confirmation, but it's taking me further away from denial too.

"I heard you say something about Lucchese on the phone. Isn't that another mafia family in New York?"

"What else did you hear?"

She gives me a measured look I don't understand. "A lot of Italian."

Good. She might have picked a name out of my conversation with Severu, but she wouldn't have gotten anything else. And we talked about plenty in her hearing if she was awake longer than I realized.

"You still haven't told me why you continued working for a club you believe is owned by the mafia."

"You still haven't confirmed that you're a capo. I guess Marco was wrong about that, huh? I mean a capo wouldn't have brought an employee to the hospital, much less stayed the night watching over my dreams."

The hell is she talking about? The fuck I'm not a capo. I'm one of Severu's strongest captains.

"Marco was not wrong," I grind out.

A little flicker of triumph shines in her eyes and I know she played me.

"Reverse psychology? Really?" I demand.

She grins. "It worked, didn't it?"

"You played to my pride."

"Well, yeah." She's smug.

And gleeful. I'm charmed when I should be pissed.

"And now that you've admitted it, I can tell you that the idea of working in a mafia protected business felt safe."

Felt not feels. Because she was nearly killed on her way home from that *protected* business.

Chapter 14

BIANCA

The nurse who comes in to take my vitals is a huge improvement over the flirtatious medical assistant who acted like I wasn't even in the room.

When she's done I ask how soon I can get discharged. But Salvatore comes out of the bathroom looking like a GQ model before she can answer.

His suit and shirt are fresh and wrinkle free. I bet one of his guys brought him new clothes *again* while I was sleeping. The capo can't look anything less than put together. Salvatore's hair is smoothed into place with product that manages not to look greasy.

My dad always had the stereotypical Italian mafioso look. He could have been an extra on the Sopranos, with his slicked back hair, dark suit, shiny shoes and thick New York accent.

"All good?" Salvatore asks.

"Yes."

Salvatore does the clasp on his watch and looks at the nurse. "Make sure she gets some lunch."

He turns to leave without saying anything else. My eyes follow him while I bite back the need to say something. Anything. Like goodbye. Not as bad as the urge to ask him not to leave pushing against my vocal cords.

The nurse smiles at me. "The doctor should be in to talk to you soon. If she approves your release, we can have you on your way after you eat lunch."

Salvatore stops and turns around, his handsome face set in grim lines. "You will spend the night at least."

"Would you?" I demand, knowing he wouldn't.

The knife wound in my back hurts, but it didn't hit any organs or vital tissue. It's the equivalent of a flesh wound, only a little deeper. The doctor said it wouldn't take more than a couple of weeks to heal on the surface.

There's no reason I should have to stay the night in the hospital and I say so.

"You are staying."

"I am not."

"And if you get discharged after lunch, where exactly are you planning to go?" he asks mockingly.

"Home?" Why did I make it sound like a question? I clear my throat. "My apartment," I say more firmly.

"The apartment you share with five other people? The one where you sleep on a sofa bed in the communal living room?"

"I only have one apartment, Salvatore. We aren't all as rich as God with more than one place to live." I assume he owns multiple properties.

Even if he doesn't, his father does and the family home is still an option for the man glowering at me.

"You will stay right here." His expression dares me to argue.

Too bad for him, I'm not one of his soldiers. He can't tell me what to do. "I'm going home."

"Will the doctor release her if she has no one to care for her at home?" Salvatore's tone implies the nurse's answer had better be no.

Hugging the tablet where she recorded my vitals to her chest like a shield, the nurse takes a step backward. "I don't know, Mr. De Luca."

"And she can't find out while you've got her trapped in the room. Let her leave, Salvatore."

The look he turns on me is sulfuric. "You do not tell me what to do."

Save me from the egos of men.

I put my hands up in surrender only to wince and let the right one fall immediately. I'm not due for more pain meds for at least an hour and no way am I taking codeine again.

I need to stay alert to ride the train home.

Maybe I'll splurge on a rideshare. I assume my tips are with my clothes. I wonder what the nurse thought of my money pouch in my underwear when she undressed me.

"I'm not trying to boss you around." Like he does me. And everyone else, I'm sure. The man is a dictator. "I only wanted to point out that she can't leave the room with you standing there."

Salvatore steps aside without acknowledging my words verbally. "Tell the doctor we need her in here now. I have things to do today."

He's a capo. Of course, he has things to do. Him staying this long is surreal.

The nurse nods and scoots out the door, letting it close behind her.

"There's no reason for you to wait for the doctor's consultation. I'm not falling asleep sitting up like earlier."

"There is every reason because apparently you have no concern for your own wellbeing."

"I'm not about to check out against medical advice." Now that I know Salvatore has taken responsibility for the charges for my care here.

I have no intention of taking advantage, but neither am I going to leave if the doctor believes there's a genuine medical reason for me to stay. And Salvatore's general bossiness is not that.

"You are not checking out at all. Not until the wound on your back no longer requires care."

"That's ridiculous. That could take days."

"Two weeks at the very least," he corrects. "You could stay at my apartment. My housekeeper will keep an eye on you."

The look he gives me tells me that I wouldn't just be a house guest.

The look I give him tells him that's so not going to happen. "I already told you. I'm not paying for medical care on my back."

"And I told you that the only reason you're going to spread your legs for me is because your pussy is craving my big dick."

"Arrogant much?" I mutter while said ladybits react in a totally unpredictable way to him.

Again.

He shrugs. "It's not arrogance if it's true."

"I'm sure all men like to think their dicks are the size of the audience at a Taylor Swift concert, but reality says not."

"I'll have to stretch you to take me, but don't worry. I like playing with a woman's pussy to get her ready."

"What is wrong with you?" And what is wrong with me? Because those words should scare the crap out of me.

Instead, my vagina is all, *bring it on, bitch.*

"Nothing a few hours buried in your tight flesh won't fix."

Before I can blast him, there's a knock on the door. I *would* blast him, right?

A little voice in my brain says she has her doubts.

Salvatore's guy tells him that the doctor is here. The level of security Salvatore has in his life is unbelievable. Talk about stifling.

I don't remember Lorenzo's guys being so careful. I might have only met him that one awful memorable time before the other night, but I saw the capo out at restaurants and even attending his nephew's basketball games at the high school.

His men weren't nearly as conscientious about not allowing anyone near him without approval.

Salvatore is the don's cousin. Maybe that's why his security is so tight. They must be trained to blend in because I didn't notice it at Amuni.

After checking the wound on my back and forehead and applying new bandages, the doctor asks, "Have you gone to the bathroom on your own yet?"

"No," Salvatore says.

As I say, "Yes."

I roll my eyes at him. "You insisted on helping. That doesn't mean I couldn't go alone."

For a minute I thought he wasn't going to leave me to pee in peace. He refused to let me shut the door, but at least he stepped away from the bathroom and out of my line of sight.

"Were you woozy?" the doctor asks me.

"A little," I admit grudgingly. "But that was the codeine. Once that's out of my system, I'll be fine."

"Why would it be out of your system? You are due another dose in an hour."

"I'll be staggering acetaminophen with ibuprofen," I inform him. Not that it's any of his business.

"Will that manage her pain sufficiently?" Salvatore asks the doctor.

The doctor flicks her gaze to me. "Only Miss Gemelli can answer that question. It is what she wants."

"Didn't you say you have things to do?" I unsubtly try to get Salvatore to leave.

He doesn't react to my words by so much as a twitch of an eyelash. "Will the ibuprofen prevent her from receiving the codeine if the pain becomes too much?"

"No."

He nods.

Why do I want to throw something at him? I'm not a violent person, but this man's arrogance is getting on my last nerve.

"So, once I've proven I can get to the bathroom alone, you'll discharge me?" I ask.

"Yes."

"Doesn't she need to have a bowel movement first?" Salvatore asks, like that's a perfectly normal thing to inquire about another person.

A person he barely knows.

"That is only true for patients who are put under general anesthesia." The doctor turns her gaze on me. "If you have someone to help you change bandages and you can take your pain medication orally, there is no reason for you not to go home."

"I've been taking the acetaminophen orally since I got here this morning. Taking the ibuprofen won't be a problem."

"Pietro will be in the outer room to take you home when you are discharged." Salvatore turns to go and this time, he doesn't stop.

His easy capitulation surprises me, but I'm sure not going to ask him why he's suddenly decided to let me make my own medical decisions. I'm just glad he is.

Again, he doesn't bother to say goodbye.

And I'm not disappointed.

It's doubtful I'll ever see him again. No way are they going to hold my job for me at Amuni. Not for the time it will take before I can go back to work.

At least with Gino gone, I can probably get my old job back at Pitiful Princess when I'm healed enough to dance.

My stomach rebels at the thought of dancing the pole in front of lascivious strangers, but I'll get over it. The attack this morning brought up some old feelings, that's all.

The doctor gives me an encouraging smile. "Once the codeine has worn off and you've eaten something, you'll feel more like yourself."

"You think so?" I ask hopefully.

"Yes."

Relief pours through me. Maybe I won't lose my job after all if I only miss a few shifts.

The doctor frowns, like she's reading my mind and she doesn't like what she sees there. "Remember, you lost enough blood this morning to need a transfusion. You'll be able to go to the bathroom on your own, but you still need a lot of rest while you're healing."

"Okay, sure."

My quick agreement doesn't appease her.

If anything, the doctor's expression turns to one of deeper concern. "You shouldn't work for at least two weeks. Three would be better. Things might look healed from the outside, but your body still needs extra energy to fully recover."

"We'll see." Though I'll have to get through Salvatore to go back to work at Amuni and I don't see that going well.

He's weirdly worried about my health.

I'm not going to be doing any semi-naked dancing right away either, not with stitches still showing on my face and back. "When will the stitches disappear?"

"They won't, but the surgeon will remove them in five to six days depending on how you are healing."

Right. Because I'm going to come back to the bougie hospital that probably charges more for a meal than I make in a day to have the "surgeon" remove my stitches. Millionaires like Salvatore may be able to afford this kind of medical care, but cocktail waitresses aren't so lucky.

The doctor must read something on my face because she says, "Check in with your primary care doctor in a couple of days and if you have issues, you can of course consult them instead."

"I will."

Chapter 15

SALVATORE

I stop in front of Pietro on my way out of the hospital suite. "When Miss Gemelli is discharged, you are to take her home."

"Yes, boss."

"My home."

Pietro rears back like I smacked him. "You want me to take the waitress to your apartment?"

"Yes. She needs help with her wound and her living situation is untenable for recovery. Your mom is good with stuff like that." Rosa has been bandaging my scrapes since I was three.

When I moved out on my own, she came with me as my housekeeper. Her husband maintains the fleet of cars for our crew and my father's, now they are not one in the same.

Pietro is their oldest and he's been on my crew since the beginning.

Their youngest is on my father's payroll, but their sister married a professor ignorant of the life. They moved to California when he got an endowed chair at one of the state universities. Her children will grow up to live normal lives without any knowledge of the mafia their mother was born into.

One day, when I have children, they will never know anything but *la famiglia*. Just like I don't.

Pietro grimaces. "Mamma will make sure Miss Gemelli rests, that's for sure. She'll stuff her with *healing* soup too."

"That's what I'm counting on." I don't need to be worried about Bianca when I should be focused on business.

Worried is too strong a word. I don't *worry* about potential bedmates. But she won't heal if she doesn't rest. If she doesn't heal, I can't slake this incessant lust I feel around her.

That's why I need Rosa watching over her.

"You're going to a lot of trouble for a piece of ass." Pietro looks at me like he's trying to figure out my angle.

My head of security who also leads my security detail is nowhere near ready to settle down. He knows I'm not either. When I marry it will be an alliance that is best for *la famiglia*. Emotion will have no place in my decision about a bride, no matter what my mother thinks.

"Bianca is more than a one-night stand. I think it will take at least a few nights to get her out of my system," I admit.

Pietro nods knowingly. "I figured. You spent six hours sleeping with her in that hospital bed, and you weren't banging. That's got to be a first."

It is. I haven't slept the night in the same bed as a lover for more than a decade, much less during the day.

Damn it. "Shut it. She had nightmares unless I was nearby." I'm not analyzing why I slept so soundly beside her. "Since she was attacked by our enemies because she works at one of the Genovese clubs, I wasn't going to abandon her to her nightmares."

"Uh, sure. Whatever you say, boss." Pietro doesn't look or sound convinced.

Giving him a pissed off glare, I double down. "It was a matter of expediency."

If a part of me is hoping that expediency is necessary again tonight when I can share her bed in much more comfortable circumstances, I'm not acknowledging it.

But until I get this woman out of my system, normal rules of sex and non-dating do not apply.

"Yeah. Okay. So, I bring this totally normal piece of ass to your apart—"

"Stop calling her a piece of ass," I bark over him. "Her name is Bianca." Thinking of him using it with her, I growl. "Call her Miss Gemelli."

Pietro salutes with a sardonic twist of his lips. "You got it. Miss Gemelli who is not just a piece of ass that you are moving into your place before you have even known the heat of her pussy."

"Do not mention her pussy." I grab Pietro by the neck. "Or any other fucking body part on her."

Although he is only two inches shy of my own six-foot-three, I lift until only his toes touch the floor and his face is beet red.

He nods the best he can in the situation.

"Do not look at her. Do not talk about her. If you so much as mention her gorgeous rack I will cut out your tongue." I drop him.

Coughing, he tries to suck in air. "I apologize, Salvatore," he gasps out. "It won't happen again."

"Good." I meet the eyes of the other men in the room, one by one.

I don't have to say anything. They bow their heads in obedience.

I told the hospital that Bianca is my girlfriend so there would be no argument about me staying in the room for treatment. Not that I would have let them keep me out, but the claim was the easiest path to my goal.

Now, I tell my men. "Get the word out. Bianca Gemelli is off limits."

"Yes, boss," they say in unison.

"Should I send one of the guys to get some of her things from her place?" Pietro has his phone open ready to send a text.

Thinking of her crowded living situation, I nod. "Tell him to pack up everything and give her notice."

"You think that's a good idea? Where's she going to live after?" Pietro asks, his voice still raw.

"Where I put her." When our passion fizzles out like it always does, I'll find Bianca someplace safer where she can have her own room.

First, she has to heal. Two weeks. At minimum. Before I can wreck her. Before she can wreck me.

Ignoring the speculation in Pietro's gaze, I leave.

~ ~ ~

Severu, Miceli and Angelo are waiting in the don's office at the Oscuro building when I get there.

Severu De Luca is my don. Miceli is his brother and underboss, and Angelo is Severu's top enforcer. Interrogator. Killer. Whatever the title, Angelo has as much power in *la famiglia* as any capo.

"What did you find out?" Severu asks me as soon as I enter the room.

I sit down in a chair across from his desk. "She doesn't know anything. They attacked her because she was in the wrong place at the wrong time."

"Is this Henrico Caruso making his move, or feeling out our reactions?" Severu asks to the room at large.

"He thinks he should be godfather when his uncle dies," Miceli says. "Hell, I don't envy the Lucchese family with him as their don. He'd be a goddamn fucking disaster as godfather to the Cosa Nostra."

"He will be godfather over my dead and decomposing body." The words are no surprise. Everyone in this office feels that way.

However, who says them is. Angelo is not a big talker.

"I have to meet with Don Caruso before I can sanction a hit," Severu says.

The only man our don answers to is the godfather and it doesn't sit well with my cousin. But he kissed the ring like every other don in the Cosa Nostra and he's loyal. Like we all are.

"You think Caruso would sanction a hit against his own nephew?" I ask, doubtful.

"No, but he'll have to offer restitution."

"Do we have video footage of the attack?" If we don't, Henry might claim the deaths of his soldiers were unprovoked.

Miceli does something on his phone. "Sent it to you. They come into the frame when they are already chasing the waitress."

In other words, there is no proof that she didn't do something to instigate the attack. "They fucking tried to kill her. No matter what they think happened out of frame, that was not sanctioned on our territory."

Severu nods. "Which is exactly what you and Miceli will say to Henrico when you return his men to him."

"I cut off their hands before I sanitized the bodies." Angelo steps away from the wall.

"Good." They dared to touch what is mine.

They will be buried with mutilated bodies for their mistake.

Angelo stops at the door. "The bodies are ready for transport in the Beemer."

Even with the large cargo capacity, three bodies will be a tight fit in the BMW's spacious trunk.

I stand. "Let's get this done."

Miceli nods, but Severu inclines his head. "A word, Salvatore."

The other two men leave the office and I wait to hear what my don has to say.

"With this incident, it is imperative that we get those bars."

In full agreement, I nod.

He's talking about the bars that Juniper is selling. My plan to buy them and turn four of them into nightclubs, providing income and a place to launder money, is now secondary to securing the properties for the sake of protecting our territory.

"Whatever the cost," Severu emphasizes. "I don't care if we have to buy all five to get the three we want."

Juniper owns properties in three of the five boroughs of New York, including Manhattan. Genovese territory. The others are in Brooklyn, Lucchese territory, and Staten Island, Gambino territory.

Severu plans to use the property in Staten Island to solidify his alliance with the Gambino don. He had the same plan for the one in Brooklyn, but that could change with Henry's recent aggression.

That bar might become leverage rather than a source of goodwill. So far, no one in either of the other families knows about the deal I'm making with Juniper, or his desire to sell the properties he inherited from his dead uncle.

The other two properties are outside the state, but I still want them. My cousin isn't convinced.

I'm determined to prove to him my plan is solid and good for *la famiglia*. "They'll all be good earners eventually. Having more businesses outside the city to launder money spreads out our risk too."

Severu nods. "Get it done."

Taking that for the dismissal it is, I go to leave.

My cousin's voice stops me at the door. "Catalina is having your parents over for dinner next week."

"Okay." His wife is something of an introvert, so having a dinner party is notable, I suppose.

"She wants you to come too."

I turn and look at Sev. "Why?"

"Does she need a reason?"

"I guess not." But my cousin isn't telling me something.

"Her sister is going to be there as well."

Cold chills run down my spine. "Your wife cannot be matchmaking. Her sister is too young for me."

Neither of us mentions that I'm five years younger than Sev and he was engaged to Carlotta a year ago when she was only nineteen. The ten-year age gap between him and his wife, Catalina, is big enough. Not that I'll say anything about that either.

I'm fond of life.

"Come to dinner. You can ignore Carlotta, but not my wife."

"I would never ignore Catalina." I like my cousin's wife and I respect her.

She's strong and loyal. Her sister is neither.

Severu says I can ignore Carlotta, but if his wife is matchmaking, I don't like my chances. My parents are going to be there as well, which means my mother is onboard with this scheme.

"Bring a date if you want a buffer," Severu says, reading my mind.

An image of Bianca flashes through my brain, not that I'm bringing the woman I want to get into my bed and out of my head.

But a date is an excellent idea, especially if she's someone who will have no expectations after. Maybe Bianca *is* a good idea. My mother won't see a pole dancer turned cocktail waitress as wife material. So, I won't have to worry about her hounding me later about how things are going with Bianca.

And Bianca knows I'm not looking for commitment, or even anything longer than a few nights.

It started with me wanting one night, sure. But that won't be enough. For either of us. She thinks I didn't notice how she pressed her thighs together trying to contain her arousal, or how her pupils expanded with desire when I talked about fucking her.

I'd make a lousy capo if I was that oblivious. "Let your wife know I'll be bringing a date."

Chapter 16

BIANCA

The doctor is right. After I eat and the codeine has more time to wear off, I'm a lot more lucid.

Clear headed enough to feel the pain in my forehead and back every time I move wrong. The pain is manageable though, so I don't say anything to the nurse when she comes to check on me and offer me street clothes to change into.

I manage to get into the brand-new underwear and leggings, but no way am I going to manage the bra. It's the stretchy kind that fits more than one cup size, but the clasp is in the back. Not happening.

There's a thin cami to wear underneath the oversized off-the-shoulder t-shirt. Both are made of ultra soft fabric and don't irritate my bare skin. I don't know where the clothes came from, but I'm not upset to be going home in something other than my blood-soaked shirt with a knife slash in the back.

I don't see it, or my jeans, anywhere. My tennies are in my backpack, but I opt for the ballet flat style slippers the nurse brought with the new clothes. They don't require socks or bending to get on.

The leggings are the kind with slip pockets on the side of the legs. I take my phone (with cracked screen courtesy of the *stronzos* who came after me) and put it in one pocket. My ID goes in the other one.

My pepper spray is gone along with my clothes, all of which are replaceable, but I want my belt and buckle knife. After I tuck the pouch with my tip money into my underwear, I call the nurse and ask about my belt and buckle knife.

She doesn't know where they are. Apparently, neither does anyone else. I don't like being defenseless.

It will definitely have to be a rideshare home and not the train. No way am I riding the train without a weapon to defend myself.

After I go to the bathroom by myself, the doctor discharges me, as promised. The nurse goes through a sheaf of instructions for my wound care and follow up before I can leave.

Honestly, I don't know how I'm going to check the wound in my back for infection. Maybe one of my roommates will help. They're not bad people. Most of us just live very different lives from each other.

Some of my roommates are aspiring actors or musicians. The only person with a normal job is the primary renter's girlfriend. She teaches third grade and they share the largest bedroom.

She will probably check my wound and help me change my bandages if I ask.

"Are you ready to go, Miss Gemelli?" a deep voice asks when I come out of the hospital room.

Thinking I'm alone, now that the nurse is gone, I jump.

But I don't look toward the speaker. I'm too awed by the room I'm in.

Ma va'.

I thought Salvatore's men were hanging out in the hall outside my room. But no. My hospital room is part of a freakin' suite.

This outer room has more space than the living room of the apartment I share with five others. There's a big screen TV mounted on the wall in front of a brown leather couch and chair. The four-person table for dining looks like real wood. There's even a full-size desk with a charging station on top and an executive desk chair.

Dark wood and rich colors make the room feel like a luxury hotel.

It's light years away from the rundown hospital room Mr. Ruhnke breathed his last breaths in. If I could have given him this for those last days, I would have.

He deserved it. I'm only here because the man who wants in my pants is a capo from one of the wealthiest crime families in the world, much less New York.

I let my gaze settle on the man near the outer door. A little shorter than Salvatore, he still exudes strength and power. There's no expression in his dark eyes. No smile meant to make the invalid feel better.

That might be a red flag for some people, but I trust no emotion over fake emotion any day. Besides, he's one of Salvatore's guys.

"I remember you." He was seated at Salvatore's table when I served them. "You were at the club with Salvatore."

"I was in the car this morning, too, but you were mostly passed out. The name's Pietro."

Even though I know passing out like that was the culmination of lack of sleep, adrenaline fatigue and the knock I took to my head, I'm still embarrassed.

When I get embarrassed, I get cranky.

"Hope you got the blood off the leather seats," I say with sickly sweet insincerity.

Getting blood out of leather is almost impossible.

"Not my job," he says with a shrug.

"Okay, well, whatever your job is, you probably want to get back to it." I wiggle my fingers toward the door, dismissing him.

His dark brows rise mockingly. "My job right now is to take you home."

"Not necessary. I already booked a rideshare and if I don't get downstairs, he's going to drive off without me." Technically the car shouldn't be here yet.

Because I don't risk stuff like that, I booked him to arrive fifteen minutes from now. Better to wait on him than not be there when he pulls up and chance losing my ride.

"Cancel it." Pietro grabs my backpack, which I'd been holding rather than wearing because *stab wound in my back.*

I try to snatch it back, but he's already out of the room and I'm hustling to keep up. Not so easy right now. "Hey, slow down. That's my backpack you're stealing."

There's not much in it, just my Amuni uniform and shoes, but it's *mine* and I want it back.

Pietro doesn't slow down, but when he reaches the elevator, he stops and waits for me at least.

When I reach him, I put my hand out. "Give it back."

"You don't need to be carrying anything right now."

"Listen up, bub. That's my backpack and you are not my boss. Give it here."

Ignoring my outstretched hand, he steps into the elevator when the doors open. Aargh!

There's no one else in the elevator and I'm not getting in there alone with him.

I turn and shout down the empty hall, assuming in a place like this someone is around to hear me. "Nurse! Doctor! He's stealing my backpack."

His eyes grow comically wide and he steps back out of the elevator, clearly intent on shushing me. Not going to happen. I start backing up fast, shouting for help the whole time.

"Stop that, Miss Gemelli. I'm not stealing anything."

Not having my pepper spray or knife has me on edge and his looming presence isn't helping.

"I'll take the stairs and meet you." It's a practical plan. "Just give me my stuff."

"You're being irrational. You aren't walking down six flights of stairs."

Six flights? Okay, yeah, that feels like a little much. "So, you take the stairs."

Pietro doesn't answer, but lunges for me.

Fight or flight adrenaline floods my system for the second time in less than twenty-four hours and I pivot, grabbing Pietro's arm and yanking so his forward momentum takes him into the wall opposite.

Not waiting to see how effective the move is, I turn and run, going left as soon as there's an opening. I get winded fast and have to slow down. Looking over my shoulder all I see is an empty corridor. No *stronzo* chasing me, but no one to help me either.

Giving up on the yelling, and moving a lot slower, I try to find my way back to the elevator. He's not going to be there waiting for me. Why should he?

He has your backpack. You know he's not stealing it. Salvatore told him to drive you home. He's just following orders.

I still don't want to get on the elevator with him and I'm willing to give up my backpack to avoid it.

Didn't I pass that doorway before?

I'm not lost. I will find the elevator. Or the stairs. I can make it down six flights. On my butt, scooting step to step maybe.

"Miss Gemelli." It's him. And he still has my backpack dangling from his meaty fist.

I glare. "Go away."

"No."

"Nice. My rideshare is probably gone and it's all your fault."

"Let me drive you home."

I shake my head and regret the movement immediately as the low-level headache I've had since waking up turns it up a few thousand notches to intolerable. My sprint down the hospital corridors didn't help either.

I need to sleep, but that's not going to happen and there's nothing I can do about it. Even if the closet is empty and available, sleeping is hard on a good day. Today is not one of those.

"I just want my backpack."

He shakes his head, looking at something over my shoulder.

I'm not falling for that trick. Only what if someone is behind me? I feel a sting in my arm that shoots pain deep into my muscle. A bee? A mosquito? How does a bug get into a place like this to fly around?

Trying to rub the sting away, I look over my shoulder. There are no flying insects, but I discover an orderly right behind me. I sidestep, putting distance between us without getting closer to Pietro.

The orderly is holding an uncapped hypodermic in his hand. Maybe he's a nurse? I don't think orderlies administer shots.

"You're not getting near me with that."

He puts his hands up in surrender. "Not coming near you."

Only then do I see the plunger is already depressed.

"*Bastardo.* You drugged me!"

"It's just something to calm you down."

"I don't need to be calm." Okay, maybe I did overreact to Pietro wanting me to get on the elevator with him. A little. "I want to go home. Point me to the elevator."

Pietro can keep my backpack. I don't care anymore.

Is that the sedative talking? How fast acting is it?

"I'll show you the way to the elevator," Pietro offers.

I shake my head and point at the guy who stabbed me with a needle. "You do it."

The man shrugs and walks past me. I scuttle back so there is always at least two feet between us, but I follow him. Pietro's heavy tread sounds behind me.

My shoulders tense, but I do my best to ignore his nearness. I've embarrassed myself enough for one day. As we get closer to the elevator, my legs feel wobbly but I don't stop walking.

The orderly-slash-nurse, whatever he is, pushes the button for the elevator.

"There you go. You got it from here?" The question is clearly not for me, but for the hulking mafia thug behind me.

"Yes."

The man in scrubs walks off without asking if I'm alright.

"Let's go." Pietro grabs my arm and tugs.

I yank away from his hold. Or I try to. It's more like a slow sidestep. "You go first. I'll take the next one."

"There's only one elevator on this side of the building."

I don't ask why. Probably something to do with mafia security. Why the orderly...I've decided he's an orderly because a nurse would be more concerned about my wellbeing.

What was I thinking?

Oh, yeah. Why the *orderly* guided me to the elevator reserved for the mafia is a mystery, but right now I'm too woozy to care. I just want to get to ground level.

There are taxis and maybe even my rideshare at ground level.

"I'll wait for it to come back." Go me for remembering what we were talking about.

"Salvatore's instructions are for me to take you home." When did Pietro get so close?

"Get away," I slur and close my eyes against the way the wall starts expanding and contracting.

SALVATORE

My phone rings on our way to Brooklyn. I check the screen and see it is Pietro.

I swipe the phone to answer and press it to my ear. I don't need Miceli and the other two men in the car to hear this conversation.

"Talk." I'm not big on greetings and my men know that.

"She's resting in your guestroom bed. Mamma will wait for her to wake up and feed her. She's saying she's going to stay until you get home."

Manaja. That means Rosa wants to talk to me, or she's worried about Bianca.

"Is something wrong with Bianca?"

"No." The word is a negative, but he doesn't sound convinced.

Why the hell should I be? "Tell me."

"We had to drug her to get her out of the hospital, boss." Pietro's tone is worried.

It should be. Images of killing my head of security six different ways flash through my mind.

"You drugged her?"

Miceli goes on alert beside me, settling his full attention on me.

Cazzo.

"Yes, boss. We had to."

"Why?"

"Miss Gemelli was hysterical. Yelling all sorts of shit about needing help, that I was stealing her stuff. I don't think she should have been discharged. The drugs are still playing with her mind."

"And you thought giving her more drugs was the answer?" How much would I regret killing one of my best friends?

"She wasn't going quietly, boss."

"You scared her."

"Not on purpose. One minute she's all sarcastic, pissed off woman, the next she's running and screaming for someone to help her."

"You made her run?"

"I didn't make her do shit. She went bananas the second I stepped onto the elevator with her backpack. I wasn't trying to leave without her."

"But she ran from you?"

"Yes."

"She was afraid of you?"

"Yes."

"So, you drugged her."

"Yes." Pietro says the last affirmative through gritted teeth.

He's pissed he had to drug Bianca to gain her compliance. He's used to women falling all over themselves to do what he wants. That's no excuse for drugging her.

"With what?"

"I had one of our guys give her a shot of K."

"Ketamine? What if it reacted with the codeine still in her system?" My insides turn to ice.

Bianca could have stopped breathing. Her heart could have stopped. Mine skips in my chest. *Cazzo.*

"She's breathing okay?"

"Of course. Better than when she was practically hyperventilating with hysteria."

"Get a doctor in to check her out," I bark. "If the K causes her any problems, I will give you twice the dose and leave you in an alley in Colombo territory to sleep it off."

It's not an automatic death sentence, but he won't make it home unscathed.

"*Manaja.*" He sighs. "I'm sorry, Salvatore. I didn't know how to get her to calm down."

"Words."

"I tried words. She just kept screaming."

"You didn't try hard enough."

"Did you want me to carry her out of the hospital kicking and screaming?"

I hang up without bothering to answer. We both know he had to touch her to carry her at all and I'll make him pay for that. As for the kicking and screaming, Pietro had to have done something to set her off.

Bianca never screamed once with me. Not even when she woke up with me in her bed.

Chapter 17

BIANCA

The first thing I notice is the silence. There are no street noises. No shuffling feet.

Only silence.

Am I still in the hospital?

Opening my eyes cautiously, I blink and then blink again, trying to make sense of what I see. I scramble to sit up and the wound in my back pulls, piercing me with a shard of pain.

I grunt and stop moving to breathe in shallowly through my nose until the fiery pain in my back settles to less than scream inducing levels.

Okay. Note to self: *no fast movement.*

With a lot more care than I used sitting up, I scoot off the big bed and stand up. My body lists from one side to the other and I grab the top of the headboard to steady myself.

This bed is ridiculous. If it was in either of the two bedrooms in the apartment where I live, there would be no room to walk or even open the closet door. But in this room? It fits fine.

Because this bedroom that I have never seen before is freakin' huge. And wow. Seriously elegant.

It's even more bougie than the Cosa Nostra hospital.

The heavy drapes on the floor to ceiling windows that cover one wall are a slightly darker shade of tan than the duvet cover. There are wood nightstands on either side of the bed with smooth lines, no decorative detailing.

Everything about the room is sleek and modern. Even the bench at the end of the bed. Covered in off-white leather, it has no tufting or ornamentation.

But it's what's sitting on top of the bench that has my heart beating faster.

With the sight of my backpack, everything floods back. Pietro's insistence I go with him. My ignominious flight. The unwelcome sedative.

Che palle. The *stronzo* had that bastard orderly drug me and then when I got woozy, Pietro freakin' kidnapped me.

Gingerly making my way to the windows, I cuss Pietro out under my breath and push one of the curtains aside. I catch my breath.

Looking down, not up, at the familiar New York skyline tells me that I'm in one of the taller skyscrapers and this apartment is way up. Maybe even penthouse level.

Clouds have moved in, bringing spring rain, but it's still light out, which means I was either out for only a few hours, or overnight and into the next morning.

A flash of memory from earlier plays in my brain. I reach down for my phone in the side pocket of the leggings I'm wearing. Relief gusts out of me in a big breath as my hands touch the hard lump of my phone.

I fish it out and the cracked screen lights up to reveal that it is 5:17 p.m. on the same day. So, I was only out a little over an hour.

Long enough to kidnap me from the hospital and bring me to this rich man's dream of an apartment.

And I know what rich man. Salvatore De Luca.

The controlling jerk.

He knew I wanted to go home. I still want to go home.

A red tide of anger rises, making my muscles tense and my heart beat fast and hard. I jab at the screen until I get into my contacts. Without waiting a single beat, I call Salvatore.

The phone rings twice before going to voicemail. I call again. Same thing, only it goes to voicemail immediately this time.

Yeah, no. I'm not giving up and the capo is going to learn he isn't the only stubborn person around here.

I dial again. And again.

He probably put his phone on do not disturb, but I don't care. I keep calling.

Finally, instead of the call going to voicemail, Salvatore answers. "What?" he barks.

Nice way to answer the phone, douchebag. "You had Lurch drug me!" I shout without preamble.

"His name is Pietro, not Lurch."

"I care." My voice drips with sarcasm.

"He did not have my permission to drug you."

I scoff, "I'm supposed to just take your word for that?"

"Yes." The call drops.

He hung up on me. Rude.

I immediately dial again.

"I'm busy," he barks instead of a greeting and hangs up again.

I cannot believe this guy. Who does he think he is? The president?

Reality bites me in the ass with the truth. He's a Cosa Nostra capo. Practically a god in his own mind, and lots of other people's. Of course, he thinks his time is more valuable than my mere human problems.

Too bad. I dial again.

SALVATORE

Miceli gives me a look when my phone rings *again*. He wants to know why I haven't put it on DND, or at least silenced the ringer.

Our situation is precarious.

Three dead bodies, wrapped in plastic, lay at our feet on the driveway behind the godfather's house.

He is also the don of this territory and taking them anywhere else would have been disrespectful.

A dozen of Caruso's men surround us with their guns pointed in our direction.

Our two soldiers' hands hang loose so they can draw their guns quickly, but Miceli gave the signal not to. The Genovese underboss looks bored, but I know better.

He's on high alert. Just like I am.

Neither of us is worried though. Killing us would trigger an all out war among the Five Families. Henrico Caruso might be stupid enough to risk it. His uncle is not.

That doesn't mean the situation lacks any danger. Twelve fucking guns are pointed at us.

That's why I answer the phone. I'm telling the godfather how unworried I am. We're in the right and we know it.

"Excuse me, I need to take this," I say to the godfather.

Respect flashes briefly in his eyes and he nods, giving permission. I step through his perimeter of guards and create enough distance none of them will overhear me.

Miceli can handle the explanation. I'm here because the aggression happened near my club and that makes it personal to me. He's still the don's underboss and spokesperson for the Genovese right now.

I slide my finger across the screen to answer. "Stop calling. I'm busy," I repeat, in case she didn't get it the first time.

"You had your thug drug and kidnap me, Salvatore. Excuse me if I don't care if you have business to attend to."

Flicking my gaze to the tense tableau less than twenty feet away, I frown. "Pietro is not a thug. He's the head of my security."

"Oh, I'm impressed. *Not*."

"He was not supposed to drug you."

"But kidnapping me is okay?" she shouts. Then groans.

"Hurt your head yelling?" Which is exactly why she needs to be in my apartment and not her own.

She has too many roommates. With all that noise her headache will be constant.

"You cannot just kidnap me to your lair, Salvatore."

"I'm not a super villain. It's a penthouse apartment, not a lair."

"You're a Cosa Nostra capo. It's a lair."

In her mind that makes me a villain? She is not wrong. And still she works for me? She said it made her feel safe. In the past tense. Maybe my villainy now overshadows the security of working for the most powerful mafia family in New York.

"It's my home and you are safe there. Rosa will help with your wound care and make sure you eat."

"Who is Rosa? Your wife?" Bianca asks, clearly horrified.

"My housekeeper."

"You really had me brought to your *home*?"

"As opposed to?" I ask with more curiosity than I have time for.

"Your fuck pad."

"I don't bring women to my apartment to fuck them."

"Good to know."

"That doesn't mean I won't be fucking you there." A picture of her spread naked across my bed sends blood surging into my cock.

I don't have time for this.

"You won't be screwing me at all." Her ire is sexy as hell and her words do nothing to dampen my libido.

"I have to go." Right now is not the time to spring wood. "Stop calling me."

"Fine. I won't be calling you again," she says like it's a threat. "But don't expect me to be here when you finally deign to show up."

It's her turn to hang up but I smile. She's not going anywhere. My apartment door does not open without security clearance and the penthouse elevator does not move without it either.

Bianca won't be able to access either.

BIANCA

Walking like an old woman who needs a hip replacement, I cross the room and pick up my backpack. The pull of the weight in my hand turns the throb of pain in my back to a more acute sensation.

I was planning on getting some ibuprofen and acetaminophen on the way home. That didn't happen.

Because Pietro, the thug, kidnapped me.

Leaving is even more imperative. I need pain meds and I need them now.

The handle on the guestroom door turns easily, surprising me a little. I half expected to be locked in here.

Since I'm not, I pull the door open and step into the hall. I turn left, assuming that's the way out because about twenty feet down on my right, the hall ends in a large window with no covering. I bet it's bullet proof.

All the windows in this penthouse apartment are probably bullet proof. Or *impact resistant*. Whatever, no way does a mafia capo live here without taking precautions. Especially one with security as heavy as Salvatore's.

The hallway ends at a door, which I open, finding myself on a landing before a set of stairs. To my right is a reading nook that overlooks the large living room below. The back wall is lined with bookcases that reach the ceiling, their shelves filled with books and no nicknacks.

The temptation to check out the titles is huge, but I don't succumb. Even when I imagine Salvatore sitting in one of the comfy looking armchairs wearing a pair of black rimmed reading glasses and an open book in his hands.

Swoon.

I'm halfway down the stairs when a woman bustles into my line of sight. She looks so much like my nonna, only younger, that I freeze, trying to decide if she's real or the result of the knock to my head and the drugs I've been given.

Chapter 18

BIANCA

"**M**amma mia. What are you doing child? You should not be out of bed." She rushes up the steps, muttering in Italian about the foolishness of youth the whole way.

Closer to my mom in age, this sweetly rounded, motherly Italian woman even sounds like Nonna. She stops in front of me, her hands out like she's going to catch me if I fall.

Or grab me to her in a hug.

I take a hasty step back but stop before she gets the wrong idea that I'm going back upstairs. "I need to go home."

"You need to rest," she counters, trying to shoo me back the way I came.

Gripping the rail tightly, I shake my head. "I'm leaving."

"What are you talking about? You are staying here where I can take care of you." She's bossy like my nonna too.

"You might as well give up. Mamma never loses an argument when she's got her mind set on something," a familiar voice comes from the bottom of the steps.

Tensing, I look down. Pietro.

Anger shoots up my spine and right out of my mouth. "You jerk. You drugged me! You can get arrested for that. Kidnapping is a federal offense too."

Not that I'm going to the cops about any of this.

Not even my attack in the wee hours of the morning. I'm sure those men are long gone and not in the leave-the-area-of-their-own-volition way.

Not Pietro drugging and kidnapping me. Though I'm freakin' tempted. It would be just my luck to file my report with a cop on the Genovese payroll.

So not happening, but the thug frowning up at me doesn't need to know that.

He rolls his eyes. "I didn't kidnap you. I told you I was bringing you home."

"To *my* home, not here. And you drugged me to do it. I'm not here of my own volition. That makes this kidnapping."

"Come, let's get you back to the bedroom. Pietro will apologize for drugging you and promise never, ever to do anything like that again to a defenseless woman." The look she shoots Pietro could incinerate concrete.

And I could swear she got it from the same storehouse of looks as my nonna.

If I revel a little in her son's wince and obvious discomfort at his mother's disapproval, who could blame me?

Knowing Rosa is on my side doesn't make me want to stay though. "I'm tired and in pain. Please let me pass so I can leave."

It's the wrong thing to say and I realize it almost immediately.

"Of course, you are tired. You need your rest as I have said. Pietro, bring up the pain relievers and a carafe of water," she orders her drug-happy son and then turns back to me. "Let's get you back upstairs."

It's clear she's not moving and I'm not about to push her out of my way. She might fall and then getting drugged again would be the least of my worries.

Pietro would probably kill me.

Still, I try. "I'm not going to be alone. I have five roommates."

"With that kind of chaos around you, how do you expect to get better?" she asks with clear disapproval.

I feel a little of Pietro's pain, and she's not even my mother.

"Mrs.—"

"It's Rosa," she says firmly, herding me up a step before I realize it.

I stop. "Rosa, please. You cannot hold me here against my will."

"I am not holding you anywhere," she says with clear affront. "Salvatore will return in a few hours. Take a nap and then you can talk to him about leaving when he arrives."

In other words, no matter what she says about not keeping me here, that is exactly what she's doing. I'm going nowhere without the capo's approval.

My stance on calling the cops might be shifting. Only what do I tell them?

A really nice lady is holding me in this totally swank apartment against my will? Sure, with the human trafficking problems in New York, I might get listened to. But then Rosa would get in trouble.

Maybe even arrested. While I don't care if her son, Pietro the thug, spends a night or two in jail, I don't want that for the woman who reminds me of my nonna.

It's not a rational response, because Rosa isn't my grandmother or any sort of relation. But I can't help feeling the way I do. She is so much like the woman that stars in the best memories of my childhood there is no way I'm going to do anything to hurt her.

Nonna died when Bea and I were twelve. If she'd still been alive, the stuff that happened when we were thirteen wouldn't have. And neither would any of what happened later, but her death was the first blow in the destruction of my family.

"*Per favore, dolce ragazza*, let me take care of you."

Tears spring to my eyes. *Sweet girl.* Just like my nonna used to call me. She called my twin, Bea, *bella regazza*. Pretty girl. Nonna always said we were both pretty and sweet, but that I was sweeter and Bea worked harder to be pretty.

It was true. Back then. Before.

I'm not sweet now. Not even a little. But Bea is still beautiful.

Unable to deal with memories that usually never see the light of day, I give in. "I'll go back to the room and take my pain meds."

Anything to get this sweet Italian mamma to stop using endearments with me. And taking the medication will make escaping easier too. I'll be able to move faster than I am right now. That's for sure.

Rosa and Pietro left me alone once. It's just bad timing they caught me coming down the stairs. They'll leave me alone again. Especially if I pretend to take a nap like Rosa suggests.

My plan would be foolproof except Rosa insists on helping me undress and put on a borrowed nightgown, so new she has to remove the tags. My phone and ID wallet end up on the bedside table before Rosa helps me into the bed.

Fluffing the pillows behind me so I can sit up in the ginormous bed, she gives me a motherly look that makes my heart ache. "I will bring you some food. You should not take pills on an empty stomach."

"That's not necessary. Really. I had lunch." I look longingly at my phone and then my backpack, once again resting innocently on the bench at the end of the bed.

"That was hours ago. And hospital food. Pfft."

Her disdain for the chef prepared cuisine I had for lunch makes me smile.

"Ah, that is good. You smile. You are feeling better already now that you are off your feet."

I don't argue. Just like nonna, Rosa isn't about to let facts get in the way of her perception of life. Nonna believed pastina soup could cure all ills and no doubt Rosa thinks the same.

She bustles out of the room to get me something to eat, but she comes back a couple of seconds later carrying the carafe of water she'd told Pietro to bring up. "We'll just put this here on the bedside table for you, but you need to eat some soup before you take the pain pills."

Half tempted to take the ibuprofen as soon as her back is turned, I nevertheless nod.

As much as I want to take the meds now - because hello, stab wound in my back and stitched up gash in my forehead complete with accompanying painful goose egg - I don't want to see the disappointment on Rosa's face when she realizes I didn't listen to her.

Which is ridiculous, because resemblance to my nonna, or not, Rosa is a practical stranger to me.

Nevertheless, I know I won't be giving into the temptation when she leaves. Which she does almost immediately.

Sighing, I pull out my phone and check my texts.

There's one from Candi. And another from Mr. Ruhnke's daughter-in-law. I read the message from her first.

Lynn: *Call me when you get a chance.*

That will have to wait. Contacting Lynn will never be at the top of my priority list, but right now I'm a little busy being held hostage.

Tapping into Candi's message stream, I smile. There's a gif of an ATM spitting out money sent early this morning, before the attack.

Candi: *Making Ugo regret letting me keep all of my tips for the weekend.* :smiling devil emoji:

Me: *Dance tonight like only rich guys are watching. $$*

I put my phone down when Rosa comes back into the room. She is quicker than I expect. She must have had the broth on simmer.

I smile at her. Pietro walks behind her, carrying a wood bed tray. The kind with legs that can sit over your lap so you can eat in bed.

Him, I frown at.

He rolls his eyes, like I'm oh so annoying. Which makes me smile inside, satisfied I've irritated him.

She takes the tray from her son and places it carefully over my legs. "This will help you heal faster than any drugs."

Casting a glare at her son to let him know she hasn't forgiven him for drugging me, she tsks.

Hiding my grin, I inhale the delicious aroma of the soup. I was right. Rosa's answer to all ailments is pastina soup. Just like Nonna.

The scent of chicken stock and garlic makes my nose tingle and my mouth water. "This looks yummy."

The large ceramic bowl is filled with tiny star shaped pasta and the light yellow of egg swirled in the broth to cook. A little convinced that both she and Nonna are right and the soup can heal anything, I scoop up a spoonful and blow on it so I won't burn my mouth.

Warm memories from my childhood play around the edges of my brain as I eat the soup with near reverence.

"Mamma's cooking will have you feeling 100% in no time," Pietro says, like he has anything to do with the delicious soup I'm eating.

I frown at him. "Do you need something?"

He spins on his heel and heads out of the room, muttering, "I don't know what the boss sees in her," in Italian as he goes.

"Pietro!" his mother admonishes.

"Don't worry, mamma. She doesn't speak Italian," he calls from the hallway.

Pretending ignorance of their exchange, I eat my soup. Apparently, I'm still not telling Salvatore I speak Italian. Which means not revealing it to his people either.

Even if it didn't give me a tiny sense of power in my suddenly out-of-control life, it is probably better for my health for Salvatore not to know I understood the parts of his conversation with the don I overheard.

He might want me to spend a night in his bed, which is so not happening right now, but he's still a Cosa Nostra capo with a brutal reputation. He wouldn't hesitate to finish the job my attackers started if he thought I was any kind of threat to the security of *la famiglia*.

After Rosa bullies me into eating nearly the whole bowl of soup and I take my pain meds, I'm yawning like I haven't slept in a week.

"I shouldn't be so tired," I complain.

Rosa helps me lay down and tucks the blankets around me. "Nonsense. Your body is healing. Rest is the best thing for you."

I would argue, but I can't work up the energy to lift my eyelids much less open my mouth.

Chapter 19

SALVATORE

"Are you finished talking to your girlfriend?" Miceli asks with a heavy dose of sarcasm when I return to the circle.

The godfather's men have lowered their guns, but not put them away. Progress.

"Maybe you want to explain to me how this is not an act of war on behalf of your don?" Don Caruso asks me. "Your cousin hasn't been very forthcoming."

We all know that Severu called the godfather and Caruso knows exactly why there are three dead bodies on his drive. He's posturing.

Why? Has he decided to withdraw his support of Severu as the next godfather and back his incompetent, hot headed nephew instead?

Henry Caruso looks like he just got a hand job he didn't have to pay for the first time in his life.

Cazzo.

"Three of your capo's men came into Genovese territory and attacked one of our own." I let Henry see his death in my eyes.

If not today, then later. Because his uncle isn't going to last much longer, no matter what the godfather wants us to believe by coming out of his house and away from his medical team.

I make no effort to hide how pissed off I am when I meet the old man's eyes. Yes, he is our godfather, and we swore an oath of loyalty to him. However, we are Cosa Nostra, not dogs to be led around by a leash.

He gives me a gimlet stare. "A cocktail waitress who shakes her ass for tips and doesn't even make your club extra money is hardly one of your own."

A red mist of fury drops like a curtain in front of my eyes at his dismissive attitude toward Bianca. Those *bastardos* nearly killed her.

Miceli, who has been relaxed since we arrived at the compound suddenly tenses, like he knows how close I am to saying something I shouldn't to the godfather.

"Amuni is one of our legit businesses," I remind the old man from between gritted teeth.

"Which makes this *puttana* even less one of your own." That's Henry sticking his broken-down oar into the water.

"Call my girlfriend a whore again and I will end you." I stare him down until he looks away.

"It is true then?" the godfather asks. "The woman is your girlfriend. I had heard that is what you told the hospital, but I dismissed it as provocative gossip."

Provocative because she's not in the life? Probably. I doubt Don Carusa has so much as flirted with a woman outside the Cosa Nostra in his entire long life.

His words aren't meant to chastise my choice in bedmates though. He's telling us that he still has his finger to the pulse of the Five Families in New York.

"I thought Captain Playboy didn't do committed relationships," Henry sneers.

I dislike the moniker Captain Playboy almost as much as being called Little Sal. But if I let the *stronzo* see how much I hate it, he'll use it. And I give my enemies nothing to use against me.

"She is mine," I say to the godfather, ignoring his grandstanding shit-stain of a nephew.

"What was she doing walking alone that time of the morning?" he asks, sounding genuinely perplexed. "I know things have changed since my younger days, but my mistresses never went without protection."

This admission of his age is more worrying than his nephew's play for power. Don Caruso just admitted he doesn't keep a mistress any longer.

Fuck and double fuck.

Severu's timeline for building the support he needs for his bid for godfather just got jacked.

"She's my girlfriend, not my mistress." And too damn stubborn and independent for her own good.

Not something I'm going to tell the godfather and his nephew though. Especially when Bianca herself has no clue she's now my girlfriend. I don't need to increase their interest in her.

But she's not a secret and I'm not married. So, not my mistress.

"Only a fool doesn't protect what is important to him." This time there's no question the godfather is censuring me.

Rather than worry about disappointing him, I will capitalize on his words. "I'm glad you see it that way, Godfather, since I killed the three men who tried to harm her."

Henry sucks in a breath. He knows his uncle just played into my hands and by proxy, Severu's. It's not a mistake Don Caruso would have made even a year ago.

If it is a mistake. Maybe he *wants* to sanction the hits.

"Regardless of their target, your capo's men were in our territory and they tried to kill someone without Severu's approval." Miceli's voice is pure ice.

Both of my cousins were raised not just to hide weakness, but to have none. As I was.

"Was it a hit?" I ask Henry, sure the answer will be no, but wanting to shake the other capo up a little.

He blanches and shakes his head vehemently. "No."

In his urgency to set me straight, he has just confirmed that his men were in Manhattan on *his* behalf to screw with us.

Does he realize that?

The dawning look of chagrin on his face says he does.

"Does your don seek reparations?" the godfather asks.

"Uncle—"

"Shut it," Don Caruso cuts his nephew off. "You need to control your men."

So, Henry has convinced his uncle that the men weren't there on his orders. Or at least that is what Don Caruso wants us to believe.

The godfather turns that gimlet glare on Miceli. "And your brother needs to prove his strength if he wants my support to take my place."

I ignore Henry's pathetic objections, as does everyone else.

Miceli shrugs. "Severu's inclination is to wipe out your nephew and all his men in retaliation for this act of aggression. I thought you would be against it, but if you're sanctioning retribution..."

Don Caruso goes nearly purple with fury, realizing once again he's left himself open. Oh, hell.

How the mighty have fallen.

He was once the scariest man in New York. Now he's barely keeping it together. If his nephew was any kind of a second, this entire conversation would have gone differently.

"My uncle said *reparations* not retribution," Henry is quick to correct Miceli.

Again, Severu's much better second ignores him, waiting for the godfather to speak.

"My nephew will pay a tithe to Severu for three months." He glares balefully at the wrapped bodies. "One for each man on his crew he could not control."

Henry glowers in impotent fury. "Did you have to cut off their hands? It's going to upset their families."

"You're damn lucky we didn't chop them up into bite size pieces and dump them in the river." Not that we dump bodies in the river.

We use a chemical bath under the floor of The Box for disposal. Enough time in that morbid soup and there is no body, much less DNA evidence left to trace.

"For the three months of the reparation tithe, we expect Lucchese soldiers to stay out of Manhattan." Miceli meets the godfather's gaze without a single glance in his nephew's direction. "Any found in our territory will not be returning for a proper burial, or otherwise, regardless of their reason for being there."

"We have always had good relations between our families," Don Caruso lies.

None of the Five Families can claim a history without bloodshed between them.

"And that will continue if there is no further aggression." Miceli's tone makes it clear that this is the only concession the Luccheses will get from us.

Next time Henry decides to rattle Severu's cage, he'll face the teeth of the lion.

~ ~ ~

Rosa reads me the riot act about letting that poor, sweet girl get hurt when I return to my penthouse.

"She should never have been walking to the subway alone." My housekeeper slams the cupboard closed after putting away a freshly washed pot. "I thought the men in this family had more sense."

"We can't provide an armed escort for the employees, Rosa."

Rosa crosses her arms and taps her foot, frowning up at me. "And why not? Are you saying you don't have enough soldiers to keep a couple available to walk your employees to the train after closing?"

"They usually walk together." Which admittedly I only know because Bianca told me.

"Then why wasn't she walking with them? Did you keep her late at the club and then send her on her way without a second thought?" Rosa is as good as any Italian mother I know at dishing out guilt.

Even my own.

"I wasn't there at closing. She had a table of customers that were slow to leave."

"What?" Rosa is incensed. "You allow your customers to keep your employees after closing hours? Are you a man, or a doormat?"

I don't bother reminding her that Franco is the Amuni's general manager. As far as Rosa is concerned, I am responsible for anything related to any of my businesses because I am capo.

She is right.

"I will make sure the female employees are escorted to the subway station after closing."

"What you think men can't get mugged? And what about employees whose shifts end before closing?" she demands, not giving an inch. "The streets of Manhattan aren't any safer at midnight than at four in the morning."

"All employees, whatever time their shift ends, will either walk in a group or be escorted. Happy?"

She smiles and pats my cheek. Like I'm ten fucking years old again. "You're a good boy, Salvatore. Now, go check on your guest. She keeps trying to leave."

I find Pietro standing like a sentry at the bottom of the stairs. When he sees me, his shoulders drop with relief. Which is not the emotion he should be feeling, knowing how badly he screwed up drugging Bianca earlier.

"Boss." He nods.

Without telegraphing my intention, I hit him with a left jab to his stomach, followed by a right cross to the head and a left uppercut to his chin. He falls like a damn tree.

I whip out my gun and have it pointing at the center of his forehead by the time he sits up. "You ever going to drug Bianca again?"

"No, boss." He shakes his head like he's trying to clear it.

I didn't pull my punches.

"Don't know how you're going to keep her here without drugs, unless you plan to chain her to the bed in the guestroom?" he asks hopefully.

An outraged gasp comes from behind me. "No one is chaining me anywhere."

Looking over my shoulder, I find Bianca standing on the top of the stairs. The light behind her turns her thin nightgown into a sexy peep show, revealing every luscious curve.

"Get the fuck back into your bedroom," I bark.

Then I whip my head around to see if Pietro is looking. He's got his gaze fixed firmly in the other direction. Smart man.

"You don't tell me what to do, Salvatore De Luca," the termagant shouts from where she is still standing at the top of the stairs. "I want to go home. Now."

She thinks she is going to give orders to me? Her capo?

Fucking hell no.

"Shit." Pietro jumps to his feet. "She's not in the life, boss. She doesn't know."

Now he's defending her?

"I don't need you defending me, Mr. Kidnapper!"

"You need to be quiet," my top bodyguard shouts right back. "I'm trying to help you."

"Why the hell are you trying to help her?" I press my gun against his forehead.

"Rosa," Bianca screams and then she's yelling at me. "Salvatore, what is the matter with you? What if it goes off?"

All of this shouting cannot be good for the headache she admitted to earlier. The woman clearly doesn't know how to take care of herself after being hurt.

Most people outside the mafia don't have my experience with it. That's why she needs to stay here, with people who do.

Rosa comes rushing into the living room. She's still wearing her apron. Is she not planning on going home tonight? What the hell is happening in my home?

"Salvatore?" Rosa asks, sounding a lot less worried than Bianca and it's *her* son I'm pointing my gun at.

Unlike the woman stomping down the stairs behind me, Rosa knows I won't kill him though. Not for pissing me off. If he's trying to get with Bianca, that's another story. I'll cut off his dick and then kill him.

"Are you and Bianca *friends* now, Pietro?"

His eyes widen and he swallows. "No, boss. It's not like that."

"What's it like then?"

"Am I not allowed to have friends?" Bianca's small hand lands on my arm.

"My men are not your friends." I think for a beat. "Rosa can be your friend."

"Tell me I'm still sleeping and this is some bizarre nightmare."

"I don't star in your nightmares," I inform her.

"You can't dictate my dreams."

"Bet me."

"Yeah, no." The eyeroll is in her voice.

I don't have to see it.

"Do you honestly think I'm going to be friends with the thug who drugged and kidnapped me and then stole my clothes?"

"Explain." I shift my body so Bianca in her unexpectedly revealing nightgown is standing behind me.

I ordered nightgowns intended to be modest so they would not make my already volcanic lust erupt and cause me to do something I would regret. Like seduce her and undo the painstaking efforts of the plastic surgeon to repair the wounds on her forehead and back.

The modest cut is deceptive however, because of the thinness of the cotton. And the buttons down the front make me want to undo them, kissing every silky inch of skin revealed as I do.

"She wants to go home and she's..." Pietro pauses, clearly struggling with what he wants to say.

"Resourceful?" Bianca asks with a heavy dose of sarcasm. "Smart? Unwilling to be trapped in my rich boss's penthouse?"

"She tried to go down in the food service elevator."

"How?" It has a shelf cutting it in half, making it impossible for anyone to fit inside.

"The shelf is not welded in."

It's not? That's a huge potential breach of security. And Bianca found it.

Wired to the security system, the food service elevator does not move without someone on my team knowing about it. The motion detectors in the shaft will draw attention to anyone who gets past the guard and locked steel door at the bottom and is foolish enough to try to climb the forty stories to my penthouse.

As irritated as I am with Bianca, I can't help feeling some admiration too. Nerissa couldn't have done any better herself.

"Get it fixed." I shift my gun away from Pietro and put it back in its holster.

Watching over the escape artist is its own form of punishment, I guess. Doesn't mean I feel bad about the bruises he'll have tomorrow from my punches.

He doesn't step back but his shoulders relax infinitesimally. "Already done."

Bianca tries to step around me. "But not before he took my clothes away."

I step to the side so she's still behind me. That nightgown might as well be made of plastic wrap. It shows everything.

"You are wearing a nightgown," I observe, wondering if I put my gun away too soon.

Pietro hastily explains, "Mamma helped her change again."

"You can't go around firing people just because I don't want to stay here," Bianca admonishes me. "Making your sweet housekeeper an accessory to kidnapping is just wrong."

That explains how Rosa convinced Bianca to change into the nightgown after her failed escape attempt. My *sweet* housekeeper lied.

Chapter 20

BIANCA

Any hope I had of Salvatore's return being the catalyst for getting me out of this ridiculous situation lay in ashes at my feet. The man is even more irrational and bossy than Pietro.

No wonder Rosa has been so stressed about me trying to get out of the apartment. Our boss is an ogre. I'm not sure why she doesn't want to get fired though. Working as domestic staff for Salvatore can't be a picnic.

But she'd practically been in tears when she begged me to put my nightgown back on and get back into bed. I'd decided then that I would wait for Salvatore to return and confront him without putting an innocent woman who reminds me of my nonna in harm's way.

Maybe getting fired entails more than just losing her job. Salvatore is a mafia capo after all.

A mafia capo who put his gun back into a holster on his belt. Not a shoulder holster, which would make what I'm about to do impossible.

My hand snakes out and I grab for the gun.

Salvatore is faster and his fingers clamp around my wrist like steel bands.

Che palle!

Keeping hold of my wrist, he turns and suddenly his entire attention is on me.

Fear thrills through me, but that's not the only reaction my body has to his fierce regard. My vajayjay gives a single, powerful pulse of want as wetness soaks my panties.

He inhales like he can smell it. He can't, can he?

That's not a real thing. Is it?

The predatory look that comes over his features says maybe it is.

Merda. Am I in trouble.

Because that look on his face is only making the situation between my thighs more acute.

"You tried to run away?" he asks, like he's my father and I've broken a house rule.

Too bad I have no respect left for father figures and his rules wouldn't apply to me even if I did. I'm not a member of Salvatore's household.

"It's not running away when I don't live here," I inform him.

At the same time, Pietro narks, "Twice. First, she tried to short the door lock mechanism."

"How?" Salvatore asks, looking like he wants to laugh.

If he does, I will knee him in the nut sac.

"I'm not sure what the plan was," Pietro says. "But I found an empty glass, a wet wall and a metal object wedged into the trim around the security panel."

Salvatore regards me with curiosity. "Metal object? Water? What was your intention? To electrocute yourself?"

"My intention was to open the door."

"The security panel is tamper proof. I could shoot it and it wouldn't crack."

Which explains why the metal cocktail stirring stick I pilfered from the drink's cabinet bent rather than breaking through the panel. I tried wedging it behind too, but it got stuck in the wood casing around the panel.

In a hurry because I could feel my time while Rosa and her son were otherwise occupied dwindling, I left it there and snuck into the kitchen to get a knife.

Which I now know would not have worked either, but when I found the dumbwaiter, I focused on using it. Pietro and Salvatore wouldn't fit inside, even folded up like a contortionist. I might not be model thin, but I'm a lot more compact than they are.

"Not sure how she thought she was going to call the elevator without access if she'd been able to get the door open." Pietro's patronizing tone makes me want to hide thumbtacks in his bed.

"I assumed the elevator has a button like normal buildings," I gripe. Not that I got anywhere near it.

"When that didn't work," Pietro, the snitch, continues. "She tried the food service elevator."

"Tattletale." I lean to the left so I can glare at him only to be reminded in vivid detail why moving like that is not a good idea.

"How the hell did she have enough time to do all that?" Salvatore spins to face his housekeeper and head of security, his body rigid with anger.

"I am your housekeeper, not jailer for your unwilling guests," Rosa says with wounded dignity. "I was relaxing in my room off the kitchen."

"Watching her soaps, she means," Pietro says sotto voce.

He's right. I could hear the sound of Rosa's program through the door. It was the only reason I risked taking the shelf out of the dumbwaiter with her so nearby.

"What were you doing?" Salvatore asks Pietro in a voice that gives me chills.

I have no idea what it's doing to Pietro.

"Working in the office with the door open. I *thought* Miss Gemelli was sleeping." He makes it sound like me faking sleep is worse than him kidnapping me.

I don't think so. "Yeah, I heard you on the computer when I tiptoed by."

The clickety-clack of a keyboard warned me to drop to a crawl going by the doorway. Too bad for him, stealth movement is one of my skills, honed by necessity in my teens.

"She heard you, but you didn't hear her?" Salvatore sounds less than impressed by his guard's observational skills.

I think Pietro got complacent, believing there was no way I could get out of the apartment without help from him or Rosa. Considering the fact, he brought the dumbwaiter back up to the penthouse before I could reach ground level and get out, odds are in his favor.

That doesn't mean I'm going to give up and remain a good little prisoner for them. "Salvatore, you have to let me go home."

"When was the last time she had pain meds?" Salvatore demands of Rosa like I didn't even speak.

I mean, I assume he's not talking to Pietro. Considering how special Salvatore is being about his guard seeing me in this nightgown. Which is perfectly decent, covering way more than my cocktail waitress uniform. It's a little thin, but it's hardly see through.

Not that I want to run around Manhattan wearing it, but still.

"Bianca has refused the acetaminophen she was supposed to take two hours ago." Rosa's voice rings with disapproval.

Apparently, Pietro got his tattling ways from his mother.

"Why did you refuse your pain meds?" Finally, Salvatore is looking at me again.

I'm only the person in question.

"The ibuprofen made me sleepy. The acetaminophen would too." Probably. It's not worth the risk.

"It did not occur to you that you are tired because your body is recovering from the trauma of this morning."

"Oh, so when you get into a fight, you nap the day away after?" I ask with sarcasm.

I don't think so.

"You did not get into a fight. You were chased down by three large men intent on doing you harm."

"And I fought back."

"Yes." Admiration reflects in the depths of his gray gaze. "Very well too."

"Not well enough." I would be dead if he hadn't shown up with his men. As much as it pains me to utter the words, I say, "Thank you for stopping them."

"Show your appreciation for me saving your life by allowing me to take care of you."

Right. He's not taking care of squat. My so called care is all on Rosa.

"Your housekeeper doesn't need extra work. I can take care of myself."

"Like when you tried to electrocute yourself opening my door?"

"Give me a break. I used my phone's silicone case to hold one end of the stick. I was never at risk of getting a shock, much less being electrocuted."

"For a pain in the ass, you're pretty smart," Pietro says from behind Salvatore.

His boss doesn't seem as pleased by the praise as I am. It's honest admiration after all and that is in short supply in my life.

My banging body gets plenty of approval, but that's different. This is my brain we're talking about.

"You do not care that he called you a pain in the ass, just that he said you are smart," Salvatore says with narrowed eyes.

I shrug and wince, questioning those smarts. How many times am I going to move the wrong way and add to the pain radiating out from the stitched up wound in my back?

"That's it. You are going back upstairs and taking your pain medication. All of it. Argue with me and I'll carry you."

I roll my eyes. Men. Logic isn't always their friend.

"How are you going to do that without hurting me?" If he wants me to take pain meds, it follows he doesn't want to add to my discomfort.

Salvatore doesn't bother to answer verbally but moves with the speed of the predator he is. Trapping my own arms in the process, he wraps one arm around my waist and the other around my hips right under my butt. Then he lifts, like I weigh no more than a child.

"This is ridiculous." I squirm, but I can't even move enough to pull at my stitches. "Put me down!"

He heads up the stairs with a smooth gait that doesn't jar me. Okay, maybe he's got the no hurting thing down. It stands to reason that a capo knows how to cause pain, which probably makes him expert at knowing how not to cause it too.

"I didn't do anything wrong, why am I being kept a prisoner?" I complain all the way to the bedroom.

I might have called him a few names in English that I usually reserve for my Italian muttering. He ignores all of it. The name calling. The demands. The appeal to his better nature, of which I'm increasingly convinced he does not have one.

"Is that your dick?" I screech as a hard bulge presses against my thighs. "This is turning you on?"

"Everything about you makes my cock hard, Bianca. Holding you so close to my body is only a bonus."

"I could have walked."

"But would you have?"

I turn my head away, refusing to answer because of course I wouldn't have come back up here under my own steam.

He releases his hold on my thighs and controls my slide down his body with his other arm.

"This is sexual harassment." And it is not turning me on to be so close to this man.

Even in pain and cranky about being held prisoner *for my own good*.

Not.

"I'm not your boss right now."

"That's not how it works, Salvatore. Besides, you're always the boss, aren't you, Mr. Capo?"

"Then perhaps you should learn to obey me?"

"You aren't bossing me into your bed."

"While that could be another kind of turn on, no I am not. When it happens, you'll come of your own free will."

When, not if. I shake my head. "Over confidence was Napolean's downfall, you know."

"It's a good thing I'm not a French dictator then, isn't it?"

I realize he is no longer holding me against him and step back, refusing to acknowledge the sense of loss I feel when we are no longer touching.

Yes, I want this man, but I'm not screwing him until I have full freedom of movement. And maybe not even then.

Though, probably? I am.

Because as annoyed as I am right now, the fact that his touch doesn't make my skin crawl is huge. That I can stand with my body trapped against his without having even a mini panic attack? Unprecedented.

I don't spend time along with men. At all. Not ever. There are two male roommates in our apartment, and when they are the only ones home, I leave. No matter what time it is, no matter what the weather is like, I'm out of there.

Right now? I want to leave on principle, not because being alone with this man makes me anxious.

He's a capo. A made man. He's a killer. A criminal. Dangerous.

He should scare the crap out of me, but he doesn't.

"You have a weird look on your face." He steps toward the bed.

I don't move. "Do I? It's probably my irritation at being kept a prisoner."

"You are not a prisoner."

"The locked door and inaccessible elevator says otherwise, not to mention my jailer, Pietro the thug."

"Again, not a thug."

"Maybe you need to rethink his position as your head of security. I got past him pretty easily." Because he underestimated me.

What if Pietro underestimates one of Salvatore's enemies? A sick feeling in the pit of my stomach says I never want to find out.

"He won't make the same mistake again."

I wouldn't like to have that anger directed at me, but then again, I'm making zero effort to avoid pissing off the mafia capo.

Huh. Maybe the knock to my head had more impact than the doctors thought.

Then again, it's hard to be afraid of a man who is currently straightening the sheets and duvet on the bed for me. He even fluffs the pillows.

"Uh, shouldn't Rosa be doing that?"

"You think I should leave everything to my housekeeper?"

"You don't?"

"No." He pulls the bedding back into a perfect triangle, so I can slide in easily.

"I don't want to lay down."

"You need to rest and trying to escape down food service elevators isn't helping."

"Maybe if I didn't need to escape, I could be sleeping right now." I yawn, highlighting how tired I am. "In my own bed."

Or on the floor of the closet. Which admittedly does not seem nearly as appealing as the bed Salvatore just made up for me.

Chapter 21

SALVATORE

Why is she still arguing with me? There are purple bruises under her eyes. That yawn is no sympathetic reaction either.

Her beautiful body needs rest.

And I need those curves safely tucked out of sight. "Do you need the toilet?"

"I'm not a toddler. If I need to go to the bathroom, I'll go."

"Do you need to go now?"

"No."

I nod. Good. "Then get in the bed." I'd much rather be saying those words under different circumstances.

"I want my clothes and I want to go home."

"Do you remember the doctor saying the dressing had to be changed with new antibiotic ointment applied daily? That even if you do everything right, the wound on your back could become infected?"

"Yes," she says grudgingly.

"Who is going to help you with that?"

"My roommates."

"Even you don't sound convinced. Why the hell would I be?"

"It doesn't matter if you are. It's my life."

"Which I saved. I have a vested interest in you not losing it to an infection that could be avoided."

"Are you kidding me? This isn't some tale in King Arthur's court. I don't owe you my life for saving it. Or my ass for that matter."

"I killed three men for you." Two to be accurate. One killed himself, but that's extraneous detail she doesn't need. "Even in the twenty-first century mafia that means I have a claim on your life."

And her ass as she so eloquently put it, but that argument can wait. She will come to my bed because she is no more immune to this pull between us than I am.

She bunches her fists and puts them on her hips, her eyes sparking fire I have to ignore.

For now.

"You might be right about my roommates, but I have a friend I can stay with."

"Does this friend work?"

"Of course, she does. Who doesn't work?" she snarks.

"Then she can't be with you all the time," I point out more reasonably than I would with someone else. I am used to being obeyed, but this woman challenges me. And it turns me on. "Here, you will always have someone with you."

"That's not the benefit you seem to think it is," she grumbles.

If I can't get her into the bed with logic, there are other ways. "Did you know that with the light behind you I can see the outline of your luscious tits and hips. I can't accept the invitation your hard nipples are making, but I promise when you are healed. I will."

She squawks and rushes to the bed, practically diving under the covers despite the pain it causes her, evidenced by her wincing. She pulls the duvet up to her chin and glares at me.

"You're damn shy for a woman who used to dance at a strip club."

"Sue me." She huffs.

I smile. "Not necessary. I find it intriguing."

"Don't."

"What?"

"Be intrigued by me."

"Too late for that." Much too late.

She caught my attention the first time I saw her fiery red hair across the club and hasn't let go of it a single day since.

"I'll stay the night, but tomorrow I want my clothes back and escort out of this apartment."

"If you won't stay here, then I will pay for your stay at the hospital." I'm not a monster. Well, not all of the time. "You cannot tend to that wound on your own."

"Candi can help me."

"The friend who works?"

"Everybody works, Salvatore. Even Rosa. She won't be with me twenty-four-seven and I don't need anyone to be. That would stress me out."

"Why?"

"I don't like being around people."

"And yet you share your apartment with five roommates."

"Six if you count my couch-mate's boyfriend."

BIANCA

Salvatore's eyes narrow, the space around him going still in some weird way.

A shiver goes down my spine.

Because his mask of urbanity is gone and he is pure predator. "He shares a bed with you?"

"Not with me. With her." Like I'm going to participate in a three-way when I'm not even interested in a one-on-one.

At least I wasn't. Before Salvatore.

Not sharing that little tidbit.

He stalks toward the bed, a prowling panther, ready to spring. "But you sleep on that same sofa bed."

"I pay for half of the sofa." Keeping a firm grip on the duvet covering me, I scoot to sit against the headboard. "I don't sleep there."

"Where do you sleep?" He lowers his powerful body to sit beside me on the bed.

Strange. There's just enough room. As if I somehow unconsciously made space for him when I scrambled into the bed to get covered. Like I want him near me, or something.

Salvatore's big hand drops onto my duvet covered thigh and stays there.

My nipples grow achingly hard and I have to fist my hands so I don't try to soothe them. There are tingles in my core, his nearness sparking a strange electric current through me.

There is none of the usual panic that having a man in my sleeping space would cause. Just like at the hospital.

It's all I can do not to embarrass myself completely and lean forward to inhale his scent.

The hand on my thigh squeezes. "Where?"

"Where what?"

His smile is pure masculine arrogance. I lose my train of thought and he assumes he's the cause.

He is, but I'm not stroking his ego and admitting it.

"Where do you sleep in your overcrowded apartment if not in the sofa bed you pay for?" he asks.

Oh. Right. "The couple that sleeps in the main bedroom lets me use the floor of their closet."

"You pay for half of the sofa bed, but you sleep on the floor." He speaks slowly, like maybe he's got it wrong and he's giving me a chance to interrupt and set him straight.

I can't. "It's not as bad as you're making it sound. I don't sleep well with other people nearby." Or not at all.

"You slept with me."

I have no explanation. "The pain meds," I say, but don't believe it.

Neither does he by the look on his handsome face.

"You are telling me that you have a bed in the closet?" he asks with narrowed eyes.

"More like a yoga mat, blankets and a pillow." I mean, it has been my bed for a couple of years, but it's not really *a* bed.

"Even better." Sarcasm saturates his tone and the air around him is redolent with that panther-about-to-pounce energy.

And instead of having a panic attack, my ovaries are sending out all sorts of *get me some of that* signals.

When other women claim they can't resist their lovers, I judge them inside my head. Every single time. Of course, they can resist. It's their body.

Only my body is awash with chemicals sending messages to my brain I thought were on the blocked list.

Desire. Want. *Need.*

No, I'm not going to give in to these feelings, but for the first time, I want to. And if I didn't have stitches in my back and forehead, it might be a different story about the giving in.

More like enthusiastic participation.

Both terrified and exhilarated by that truth, I stare in silence at Salvatore. Can he tell what I'm thinking?

The banked anger in his steely gaze says he's not thinking about sex right now. For once.

And I can't get my ladybits to shut up about it.

How the tables have turned.

"You were going to go back to that apartment to heal? On an old yoga mat on the closet floor?"

"Some of us make do with what we have, Salvatore." If Mr. Rhunke were still alive, I would be able to stay with him.

But two years ago, the man who saved me from homelessness at sixteen had a stroke that left him first paralyzed and then dead. His family evicted me so his younger son could move into the rent-controlled apartment.

After Mr. Ruhnke's death, and having no other option, I moved into an apartment with five strangers, including one man who officially lives there and one who does not.

Life. It's full of twists you don't see coming.

Like me being here.

"You making do would have ended up with you in the ER, or worse." Salvatore looks at me like he's trying to figure out my brain.

Good luck with that. I still don't understand what drives me sometimes. "What's worse than the ER?"

"Your roommates not noticing you in delirium from infection and you dying of dehydration."

"Man, you have a talent for coming up with the worst-case scenario, don't you?" Maybe it goes along with being a capo in the mafia.

Death feels like the natural go-to.

"It's a gift."

"Was that a joke?"

"Capos don't joke."

"Uh huh. Pretty sure that was another one." What the heck is going on?

Who is the humorous version of the man determined to get me under him? Or maybe he wants me on top? X-rated images of different positions with Salvatore play like an unruly porno in my head.

"Candi isn't going to ignore an infection." But neither am I willing to put that stress on her.

Not when she's home she has her little sister and arthritic mom to take care of. Going to stay with Candi would not be fair to her.

Accidenti.

I'm not about to share that revelation with Salvatore. Once he lets me leave, I can just go home. To my many roommates, one of whom will hopefully be willing to help me with the daily dressing.

"Does Candi have a guest bedroom?" Salvatore asks, like he can see right into my brain.

"Not exactly."

"What exactly?"

"A twin bed." In a room she shares with her little sister.

"You would rather put your friend out of her bed than stay here?" Salvatore asks, the look on his face judging me.

"No." I chew on my lip, thinking.

This is too much for just a one-night stand. His concern makes no sense. Even his bossiness. Why does he care so much? He could sit back and wait for me to heal and then pounce.

I'm pretty sure we both know I want him.

"You're not used to allowing others to help you."

"Are you saying you are?" Not likely.

"We are not talking about me."

"We kind of are and your need to take care of a perfect stranger."

"One. You are not perfect."

"Another joke?" Seriously?

"Two," he says smoothly as if I did not interrupt him. "You are not a stranger. You work for me."

"For Franco, technically," I have to interrupt.

Though we both know that as the club owner Salvatore has the power to fire me just like Franco.

One dark brow raises. "We both know that technically, everyone who works at a Cosa Nostra club in this territory works for me."

"That makes your attempt to coerce me into bed even more skeevy."

The long suffering look he gives me is everything. "I don't coerce women into bed. I offered to pay you. You turned me down."

"Go me. I bet you're not used to women saying no."

"It doesn't happen. Maybe that's why I want more than a single night now."

Oh no. No. No. No. I did not supercharge his desire to screw me by turning him down.

Only, I think I really did.

And my vagina is not unhappy about that. Which, considering my past, is some kind of sexual miracle. But wanting and being able to do something about it are two very different things.

Chapter 22

BIANCA

"What do you mean you want more than a single night?" Is he talking about dating?

"We will discuss that when you are feeling better," he says blithely. "Have you considered that once Rosa knows about your living situation, she'll worry herself sick about you?"

"And I suppose you're going to tell her the minute you get the chance."

"I would prefer my housekeeper not believe I kidnapped you with no reason."

"I thought you didn't approve of kidnapping."

"I disapproved of Pietro's use of a drug to gain your compliance."

"But it was okay to kidnap me?"

"Considering the situation you were returning to in order to convalesce, forced compliance should not have been necessary."

And was therefore okay? Judgy much? "Convalesce. Who talks like that?"

"Educated men?"

"Here I thought all you learned in the mafia was how to intimidate and kill people, not to mention kidnapping." My sarcasm is as thick as his judgment.

"As my father's second, that was definitely part of education. However, I got my degree in business and then my MBA because I knew that his second-in-command wasn't all I would be."

Right. He's probably known since he was a toddler that one day he'd take over as capo from his father.

"Please tell me Pietro isn't your second."

"Nerissa has that privilege."

Privilege, right. Of course, he thinks it's some kind of honor to intimidate, kidnap and even kill on his behalf.

"Your sister is your second-in-command?" That's not the mafia I remember.

He shrugs. "Miceli is underboss to our don and his brother. It's a solid system. Keep it in the family."

"What does Nerissa's husband think about being married to a capo's second?"

"My sister's not married."

"But her last name is different than yours."

"She joined our family when she was fifteen."

Apparently, that's all the explanation I'm going to get, but it's more than I expect.

"Aren't you worried about telling me this stuff?" It's a real turn around from the man who didn't even want to confirm he is a Cosa Nostra capo.

Now, he's telling me mafia stuff, not to mention a pretty personal piece of information about his family dynamic.

"You witnessed me kill a man."

"According to you, three men." And he's decided that somehow makes me trustworthy?

Or maybe that's the real reason he had me kidnapped. To stop me going to the cops. "It happened behind me."

"You'd still make a credible witness."

"Are you going to kill me to keep me quiet?" Has all this talk about getting me into bed been a smokescreen?

Only if he wanted to kill me, wouldn't I already be dead? Why go to the trouble of having Rosa help tend to my wound? "Is that what this keeping me in your apartment is really about?"

"No."

"You need time to get rid of the evidence."

"The *evidence* was gone by the time you woke up the first time in the hospital."

"Except me. I'm not gone."

"You're not evidence either."

"You said it yourself. I'd make a credible witness."

"To a crime there is no evidence was ever committed."

"Oh."

"It is safe to say your brain doesn't travel the same tracks as mine."

"Duh. Not part of the mafia." Not anymore anyway. "Let me get this straight. Since I witnessed a crime there is no evidence for, you have decided it's okay to tell me who the Genovese underboss is."

"Are you trying to imply Marco didn't already? If he mentioned me, he definitely spilled the beans about Severu and Miceli."

"You are not wrong."

"So, I'm not telling you anything you don't already know."

"And you're so arrogant you think you know everything without even asking me to confirm it?" That tracks.

He shrugs, not bothered by being called arrogant.

It figures. "Did you really threaten to fire Rosa if I didn't cooperate?"

"Does it matter?" His eyes bore into mine.

I'm not trying to hide anything. Right now. So, I look back. "Yes."

"Why?"

"If you'd fire her for something like that, I'd know I can't trust you."

"You *can't* trust me."

"You know what I mean."

"Not sure I do. I don't trust anyone outside *la famiglia* and few within."

Which is a pretty clear way of saying he doesn't trust me. "You don't need to trust a woman to have sex with her."

"No."

"But I do. Need to trust a partner, I mean. I couldn't let a man into my body that I didn't trust." I'm not sure I can ever let a man into my body that way at all.

"What if I lie and say no, but the real answer is yes?"

"What if you don't lie to me?"

"No," he says with conviction. "Rosa is like a second mother to me. My own would disown me if I fired her."

His words ring true. But then so did Rosa's. "She lied to me?"

"Did it work?"

"You know it did." It had to have been the tears.

They convinced me. Not to mention her too believable manner. Huh.

Salvatore shrugs. "Rosa is a smart woman and she didn't want to cause you further stress, but you weren't being reasonable."

"Wanting to leave my prison isn't unreasonable."

"My apartment is not a prison."

"Right. You've got other places to keep prisoners."

"Do you really want me to confirm that?"

"No. Your thug drugged and kidnapped me, so you know...even a penthouse can feel like a prison under the right, or wrong, circumstances."

"Pietro deeply regrets drugging you."

"But not kidnapping me." It's not a question.

Salvatore doesn't regret it. Why would his guard?

"You were heading back to a yoga mat on the floor and planned to take a rideshare to do it. You might as well put a sign out welcoming infection."

"You are such a drama llama."

His eyes widen fractionally, and the edges of his mouth start to curve before he stops the smile forming. "No one has ever called me that before."

"No one has insisted on taking care of me since Mr. Ruhnke had his stroke." And maybe Salvatore is a tiny bit right.

I might be reacting to him wanting to do it slightly irrationally. I'm feeling more emotional than usual. I blame the drugged kidnapping. So, basically, it's Pietro's fault.

"Who is Mr. Ruhnke?"

"Someone I used to know." I should call his daughter-in-law to find out why she texted. "I need my phone."

Salvatore looks around like he expects the device to materialize. "Where is it?"

"Pietro took it." When I made my empty threat to call the cops after my failed escape attempt in the dumbwaiter.

"I will see you get it back."

"Thank you."

"Will you stay and allow your body to heal in an environment conducive to it doing so?"

"You sound so formal."

His expression is not amused.

"You're actually asking me now?"

"Yes."

"And if I say no?"

"I will arrange for you to return to the hospital or a rehabilitation facility until you are healed."

He is really determined to take care of me.

Doing my best to pretend I don't notice that warm sensation in the center of my chest, I nod. "I'll stay."

SALVATORE

A tormented scream yanks me from my uneasy doze and I'm jumping from my bed with my gun in my hand before a second one shatters the nighttime silence.

Bianca.

Adrenalin spikes and I rush to her room, slamming open the door without knocking. Jerking my head from side to side I look for the threat, but no one else is here.

Two of my men guard the penthouse at night from inside and two more in the hall. Another team patrols the parking garage and the lobby.

None of them would come up here, but that scream.

Cazzo.

I am ready to kill and there's no one to shoot.

"No!" Bianca flings herself to the side.

The covers are twisted around her and she's fighting them, trying to kick her feet. Tears track a silver streak down her cheeks in the near dark.

She's having nightmares again.

Yesterday's attack is still affecting her.

Reparation isn't enough. I want retaliation. If that *stronzo*, Henry, or any of his people make the mistake of coming to Manhattan, I will get it too.

I won't disobey the godfather and hunt them in their own territory, but if they come to ours, it will be the last mistake any of them make.

It only takes a few seconds to tug the duvet and sheets away from Bianca. She doesn't wake, even when I say her name.

There's only one way to calm her down. The same as at the hospital. But no way in hell am I sleeping in a guestroom bed in my own house.

Picking her up, I hold her against my chest, but she's still trying to thrash. Then she turns her face into my neck and inhales. Her body goes limp.

How? There's no white knight in my gene pool. We're mafia back five generations.

And this sweet woman finds solace in my nearness. There's something wrong with her olfactory senses. My scent is that of a predator. It should frighten her, not calm her down.

My presence brings terror and submission, not this...this peace.

Carrying her into my bedroom, I dismiss how right she feels in my arms. My cock is aching and hungry for her. It doesn't want any other pussy. That's all this is.

Until I fuck Bianca a few times and get her out of my system, my lizard brain is going to approve of her in my arms. And I can't bang her if I can't touch her.

That's all this is.

Settling Bianca into my bed on her side, I make sure she's not irritating her wound. She rubs her face against my pillow and a soft little sigh puffs from between her parted lips.

I climb into the bed and pull the covers up over both of us before putting my hand on her hip. She squirms until her arms are pressed up against my front and her head is tucked under my chin.

My cock is hard, like it has been all night, from knowing she's in the room next to me. In a bed. In my home. Where she belongs.

For now.

For now, I repeat to myself.

Despite the arousal pulsing through my veins, my body relaxes and the pull of sleep finally takes hold.

~ ~ ~

I wake a couple of hours later to a quiet moan.

"Bianca?"

"What are you doing in my bed?" she whispers.

She's in my bed, but she'll figure that out soon enough. And probably start yelling at me about it. I'd like both of us to get a few more hours of sleep before that happens.

I ask the smart speaker what time it is and realize Bianca is past due for her acetaminophen.

"Stay there. I'll get your meds and be right back."

When I return with the pills and a glass of water, she swallows them without argument. I tell the smart speaker to set an alarm for when she needs her staggered dose of ibuprofen and climb back into the bed.

"I suppose you're going to tell me that I was having a nightmare until you got into bed with me." She's still whispering.

"If you already know, there's no need for me to tell you."

"I'm too tired to argue." She turns so her back is to me.

My muscles bunch with the need to pull her against me, but because of the still raw wound on her back, I won't. I settle onto my own back, but somehow my right hand makes it onto her thigh.

Her breath catches, but then the tension drains out of her body. "I don't sleep with men."

"With a bed in the bottom of a closet, I'm not surprised," I say drily.

"It's not that." She sighs. "Never mind. But..." She pauses and then says, "Thank you, Salvatore. I don't know why you're being so nice to me. Why you are willing to be my woobie blanket, or why my subconscious feels safe with you, but I appreciate you helping me sleep."

I don't know how to respond to her gratitude.

Women thank me for screaming climaxes and expensive gifts. They don't thank me for being *nice*. I am not a nice man.

And what the fuck is a woobie blanket?

Chapter 23

BIANCA

My fifth day at the penthouse, I decide enough with the nightgowns.

Today I am getting dressed.

The only problem is: I still don't know where my clothes are. So, I ask Rosa when she brings up my breakfast.

To Salvatore's room.

I go to sleep alone in the guestroom bed every night, but wake up in Salvatore's massive bed every morning. Again, alone. But memories of him taking care of me linger along with his scent on the pillow.

My super-hot, violently dangerous nurse makes sure I take my pain pills in the middle of the night.

And he touches me. Not intimately. But his hand is always connected to me somewhere on my body. My hip. My shoulder. The back of my neck. Whenever I wake it's there and I sleep better and more deeply than I have since my nonna died.

I don't know why he carries me into his bedroom and shares his bed with me when he is not getting the one thing men seem to want. Sex.

It feels like connection and that's even scarier than Salvatore, Cosa Nostra capo.

Every morning, he's gone when I wake up though and doesn't return until after I fall asleep. Which isn't that hard since I fall asleep so easily right now, it feels like I have narcolepsy.

It's weird. I usually doze at best. Sometimes I can't sleep at all at the apartment, but although I'm sleeping more than ever, I'm exhausted.

I can only be grateful I took my last final the day before the attack. There's no way I have the focus or energy to attend classes. Even if I could do it without Salvatore having a meltdown.

Who probably thinks that QC is as rife with germs waiting to attack my healing wounds as the closet I sleep in at the apartment.

Wearing street clothes will be a signal to my body to stay awake.

"I put them with the rest of your clothing." Rosa lays the tray on a table by the windows.

"The rest of my clothes?" Salvatore must have sent one of his men after some things for me to wear.

I wish he'd said something. I've been living in these thin cotton nightgowns. Even though I am not allowed to shower, Rosa gives me a clean one to put on after I get my wounds checked by the doctor every day.

Washing myself with a fluffy wash cloth isn't cutting it and today, I'm taking a shower. The doctor said on Sunday it would probably be okay, but she would prefer I waited one more day.

That day is done.

I'm getting clean. Today.

"They are in the guestroom dresser and closet." She presses a button that draws the drapes back to reveal the stunning view of New York from Salvatore's corner bedroom.

"Oh, okay. Thank you." I never even thought to look in what I assumed was an empty dresser and closet.

Why would I? I don't live here.

Which makes what I find in the guestroom after breakfast so astonishing.

The dresser is full. My entire, though yeah sparse, collection of t-shirts, yoga pants, and jeans are mixed in with clothes of the same size with the tags still on them. "Did you buy me clothes, Rosa?"

"That's all Salvatore." The older woman straightens the fresh bedding on the bed. "He had everything delivered."

Salvatore bought me clothes? Rosa must be mistaken. But then where did the soft t-shirts with smartass sayings on them come from? Or the designer jeans mixed in with the ones I got from Goodwill?

Maybe he told one of his guys to do it. I grin at the thought of Pietro being forced to shop for my clothing. That would explain the t-shirts. Though, they fit my personality to a *t*.

Is it a pun if you only say it in your head?

When I open the drawer with bras and panties, my cheeks heat and I fervently hope Pietro *did not* buy these for me. I've never owned a pair of La Perla panties in my life. Now I have seven. With matching bras.

They're all ridiculously feminine and sexier than anything I own.

I could live for months off of what was spent on this drawer alone. Also, I haven't had underwear to wear since Rosa took the pair from the hospital away with the first nightgown to wash. Only, apparently, I did.

Lots of them.

Pride makes me reach for a pair of my cotton panties that came in a pack of five, but my fingers slip along the soft satin of a pair the same blue as my eyes and I cannot resist them.

I grab the panties and matching bra before I can stop myself. Slamming the drawer closed, as if that will negate my choice in underwear, I inhale a deep breath.

The t-shirt I grab is silk and the same shade of blue with pink lettering that says, *I'm not responsible for what my face does when you talk*. The yoga pants I pick are mine and one of my most comfortable pairs.

Opening another drawer, I stop in stunned amazement. The man even bought me socks. My five pairs of well washed black ankle socks reside in a single small stack next to a plethora of ankle and no-show socks in every color. The drawer is practically stuffed.

Feeling like I'm selling my soul, I pull out a pair of pink fuzzy slipper socks. But I'm already going to be wearing over $500 worth of underwear, what's a pair of cozy socks compared to that?

"I'm a little afraid to look in the closet," I admit to Rosa.

The look on her face says I have reason to be worried. Which only makes it impossible to ignore my curiosity.

But it's not the dresses hanging in the walk-in closet that have me sucking in a breath and forgetting how to let it out. It's the neat rows of shoes and other items. This is not picking up a few things from my place so I have something to wear, which considering all the shopping Salvatore did, is a complete waste of energy.

And yes, now I accept Salvatore did the shopping. No way would he let one of his men buy me underwear when he wouldn't even let a male nurse near me at the hospital.

All of my things are here. Not just my clothes. Everything. My box of keepsakes sits on the top shelf next to my pillow. My yoga mat is rolled up and leaning against the wall. My bedding is folded and stacked neatly in one of the closet cubbies.

My school bag empty except for my laptop and charger sits lonely on another shelf. I already sold my physical textbooks back for the semester. Ebooks are more convenient, but since they can't be sold back, the more cumbersome but economic physical books are usually what I end up getting.

I don't own a lot, but what I have is here. If I go into the attached bathroom and start opening drawers, I bet I'll find my makeup, my toothbrush (even though I've been using a new one straight out of the package since I arrived), and everything else I kept stored in my bathroom basket in the apartment.

"Did they bring my food from the fridge too?" I ask Rosa sarcastically.

She looks at me reprovingly. "I told them not to bother, but I purchased items similar to what you had."

Similar, but not identical. Rosa isn't going to buy store brand pasta. *Accidenti*. She's not going to buy dried pasta at all.

Even the tiny star shaped pastina in her soup tastes fresh. "No wonder my coffee tastes perfect. You got my cinnamon dolce creamer."

"Bite your tongue." Rosa is scandalized by the suggestion. "I put real cream and cinnamon with a dash of vanilla in your morning latte."

There's only one thing missing. The African violet Mr. Ruhnke got me that first year he helped me. He showed up with the plant and a used grow light, saying it was good to have something to take care of.

He'd been right. That plant is like family to me.

I'll need to call one of my roommates. It's due watering tomorrow. But what if they water from the top, or give it too much? Maybe Salvatore will give me a ride back to my apartment now that I'm doing better.

"Why?" I walk out into the bedroom and wave my arm, encompassing the dresser, the made bed with the covers turned back invitingly. "Why all this?"

"You need to heal, *dolce ragazza*."

"It doesn't take all my worldly goods to help me get better." But if they're all going to be here, I really wish my violet was among them.

"Salvatore does not like your living situation."

She cannot be saying what I think she is. Salvatore would not move me out of my apartment without even asking me.

Who am I kidding? He's a capo.

He thinks he's at least a minor deity. Of course, he would.

"How and where I live is none of his business." I say it as much a reminder for myself as for Rosa.

Being looked after, even if it is by an arrogant mafioso is dangerously appealing. Independence is woven into the fabric of my being, but being alone is not the same as being independent.

And I've been alone a long time. No safety net. No one to rely on when even my independent nature bows under the weight of life.

"Are you sure about that?" Salvatore's smooth tones have me spinning around to see him.

He's leaning against the doorjamb, his big body encased in a tailored suit and a cool expression on his features.

My heart surges with an erratic beat. Heat and want coalesce between my legs. My nipples tighten and poke against the thin cotton of my nightgown.

Why this man and no other? Why does my body go nuclear for him? Why does he make me feel safe?

My response to Salvatore is primal and rooted so deep in my atavistic instincts, logic has no hope of influencing it.

"What are you doing here?" I hold the pile of clothes in front of me like a shield.

His eyes say he notices and that he knows what I'm hiding behind that shield too. Hard nipples, aching for a touch they have never experienced.

Gah! The scream inside my head does not make it past my lips.

A tiny tilt of his too handsome mouth says he's amused. He knows. All of it. That I'm wet for him and can barely breathe past my desire for him.

"I live here," he drawls.

"But you're never home during the day." Okay, maybe I'm not qualified to make that statement.

I've only been staying here a few days.

"I'm not?"

"But..." My voice trails off because I don't know what I want to say.

My brain is too busy cataloguing every inch of the gorgeous capo determined to keep me locked in his penthouse like some kind of princess in a tower.

Until I heal.

But the fact all my worldly possessions are here indicates his plans might last beyond that and not just for a night of hot and steamy sex.

It's ridiculous. Salvatore doesn't want me living with him. He can't. We barely know each other.

But you're here now.

I shush that little voice inside my head. *Remember,* I tell it, *he's a mafia prince and I'm no princess.* Not anymore.

If I could be tossed away as easily as Lorenzo threw me out of my home and the mafia, abandoned by both my parents, I never was one to begin with. No matter what my parents claimed.

"The doctor is here to examine you."

Looking past his shoulder, I don't see anyone. "She is?"

"She's waiting in my bedroom."

"Why your bedroom?"

Not bothering to answer, Salvatore leaves.

The sound that comes out of me is not pretty. That man. Could he be any more irritating?

Chapter 24

BIANCA

"Give me these," Rosa says with a smile. "I'll put them in the bathroom for you."

I let the bundle of clothes go but shake my head. "I'm not going in there like this."

I'm not even wearing panties for crying out loud.

That didn't bother you last night when you were cuddled up against Salvatore in his bed.

Shut up, inner voice. No one asked you.

Rosa disappears into the bathroom and returns a second later with a blue silk robe. I'm starting to sense a theme here.

It's thin, but something is better than nothing. Pulling it on, I'm not surprised by how soft it is against my skin, but I am startled by how opaque it is. Tying the belt in a bow, I immediately relax a little.

I head to Salvatore's room, where the doctor is waiting for me. Again. Why here?

The previous visits with her to check on my wounds have been in the guestroom.

When I reach the penthouse's primary suite, I step inside and ignore the sense of being in my own space that it gives me. Sleeping so well has made my brain associate this room with comfort and home.

But I don't have a home and haven't had one in so long, it's not worth thinking about.

This is *not* my space. *Not* my room. *Not* my home.

But you want it to be.

Ignoring the thought with more bananas than an ice cream sundae, I smile at the doctor. "Thank you for taking the time to come here and check on me."

"It is her job," Salvatore says dismissively.

"Yeah, no. Doctors don't make house calls anymore, Salvatore." I don't look at him because if I do, my body is going to go haywire again.

"They do for me."

"It is no trouble, Bianca. You're one of my best patients. If only they were all as cooperative." Her smile invites me to share the joke.

The sound of disbelief Salvatore makes adds another layer onto the annoyance I feel toward him. "You find Bianca to be cooperative?"

Why do I desire a man who irritates me as much as he turns me on? Hormones and primal libido have a lot to answer for.

"Your houseguest has complied with every instruction I have given her."

"Too bad you didn't *instruct* her not to recuperate on the floor of a closet."

The doctor gives me a concerned look. "You've been sleeping on the floor of the closet?"

I look at Salvatore only long enough to singe him with my glare. "No. That's where I sleep usually."

"But not anymore," Salvatore says bossily.

Like he gets to decide.

"Well, it's a good thing you're sleeping in a bed with clean sheets. Your wounds are healing very nicely with no sign of infection."

"Your pronouncement is premature." Salvatore's voice is so cold it makes the doctor shiver.

Or is that fear?

He moves closer so I can't help seeing him in my periphery. "You haven't even checked her over yet."

"Let's get to it then, shall we?" The doctor indicates one of the chairs by the window. "Why don't you sit down, Bianca?"

Her things are already on the table where I ate my breakfast earlier.

Eager to get away from the too-sexy-for-my-own-good capo's proximity, I quickly walk to the chair and sit down. The doctor starts her exam with the healing gash on my forehead.

"Your skin is knitting together nicely. The plastic surgeon did an excellent job. I doubt you'll have much of a scar, if any at all."

"Plastic surgeon? You didn't put the stitches in?" I ask, confused.

I don't remember talking to a plastic surgeon.

"Mr. De Luca insisted your wounds be seen to by a plastic surgeon after my colleague cleaned them and determined the depth of the damage in your back."

Her colleague? She's not the doctor who saw me initially? Now that I think about it, I remember a male doctor talking to me when I woke up the first time in the hospital.

Considering how over the top Salvatore was about the male nurse who tried to take my vitals, having this doctor assigned to my care is his doing for sure.

"Why a plastic surgeon?" I let my gaze settle on Salvatore finally because I need to see his expression.

Not that it does me any good. He might as well be wearing a mask for all the emotion he's showing. Until I look into his eyes.

Molten metal stares back at me, heating my body with their intensity.

But when his voice comes out, it is cool and emotionless, just like his too gorgeous face. "I assumed you would prefer no scars."

"I do," I whisper.

There are enough scars inside, my outside doesn't need to match.

"There is your answer."

Because I want it? That's his answer. My ovaries swoon.

"Your forehead is healing nicely and you can leave the bandage off now. The plastic surgeon will be here Wednesday to remove the stitches."

"That's not a full week for healing. Is that wise?" Salvatore asks.

"Plastic surgeons don't like to leave stitches in longer than five, six days max because it significantly increases the chance of scarring."

When Salvatore doesn't say anything further, the doctor looks at me questioningly. "Do you want him to remain for the examination of your back?"

The question startles me. Does the doctor think the capo will leave his own bedroom if I say no?

Do I?

I narrow my eyes at Salvatore. "Will you leave if I ask you to?"

Tension immediately fills the air between us, but Salvatore grudgingly nods. "Yes," he says from between gritted teeth, like it pains him.

I'm tempted to roll my eyes at his reaction, but part of me, the vulnerability that hides behind stubborn snark, likes how invested he is in my wellbeing. This isn't only about sex between us.

If it was, I wouldn't be here, in his home, to heal.

Fear wars with comfort inside my chest, making it ache.

"You can stay." It's not like he's going to see anything but my back.

I don't like being naked in front of others. Even when I'm dancing, I always wear something. I'm known for my creative outfits that reveal what I want them to. On the stage, I feel removed and in control.

Here, not so much. The doctor hasn't complained yet that I don't take off my nightgown for the exam.

Like the previous exams, I unbutton the front of my nightgown. Then I untie the silky robe and allow both to slide down my shoulders and upper arms. I keep the fabric over my chest, but my back is on display for the doctor.

And Salvatore.

His heated stare sends frissons of responding desire through me. Unfamiliar excitement I can't act on, even if I want to.

At least not until I'm healed.

The doctor carefully peels the gauze and paper medical tape away from my back. "There's no sign of infection."

Of course there isn't. Rosa checks it six times a day. She insists it's necessary because of the risk of infection to a knife wound. I comply because she reminds me of my nonna and her concern brings back good memories.

Rosa applies the prescribed salve and changes the bandage for fresh, sterile gauze every time too. It feels like overkill to me, but she says Salvatore will be furious if it gets infected.

Considering how weirdly concerned he is for my health, I believe her.

"This cut is healing just as quickly as the one your forehead." The doctor sounds happy.

So, I smile.

"Good," Salvatore says.

Could he make the affirmation sound grumpier?

"You no longer need to bandage this wound either, but continue the use of the salve once a day."

"It only needs to be applied once a day?" I ask.

The doctor's lips twist wryly, like she knows about Rosa's zealousness. "Technically, yes, but it certainly doesn't hurt to apply it more frequently."

Yeah, no. Rosa is going to have to dial it back a few notches. I have the doctor's recommendation on my side.

"Can I take a shower?"

I don't ask for my sake, because I already know it's okay and that I *will* be bathing.

I ask for Salvatore's. I don't like his chances of coming out unscathed if he tries to tell me I need to settle for another session with a soapy washcloth.

Every inch of my skin itches with the need to get clean.

"Yes, but no direct spray on either wound. You do not want to soak them until they are closed fully, so no baths or swimming."

"I haven't had access to a pool since high school," I say with a laugh. "And it's been longer since I had a bathtub where I live."

Specifically, since I got booted from my childhood home at sixteen.

"You have access to both here but using them will have to wait until you are healed." Salvatore talks like I'm going to be here long enough for that to happen.

"I'm sure the plastic surgeon will have further instructions when he removes the stitches." The doctor starts packing up her things.

I'm surprised he allowed the plastic surgeon to operate on me and say so.

"The time it would have taken to wait for a qualified female surgeon to arrive would have taken too long."

"Too long for what?" I wonder out loud.

"Healing without a scar," the doctor offers.

I'm still not sure why that's so important to Salvatore. "Are you that turned off by imperfection?"

"No. It is simply a matter of making sure you get the best care."

Do I believe him? I think I do.

Does that make me intuitive, or foolish?

"If that's all, I'll be going." The doctor smiles at me.

I nod.

Rosa appears in the doorway. "I'll see you out, doctor."

When the other two women are gone, I shake my head. "I swear Rosa's psychic. She always knows just when to come into the room to tidy it, or when to show up to escort a guest back downstairs."

"Have you had other guests?" he asks, sounding suspicious.

"You're kidding, right? You think there's even a remote possibility that a visitor came to your apartment you weren't told about?"

"There'd better not be."

"Don't worry. I'm sure Pietro would rat me out in a nanosecond."

"It's not being a rat to tell me what is happening in my home."

"About that."

"*Che cosa?*" He grimaces. "What?"

I roll my eyes. "I know what *che cosa* means."

"I suppose you have been around enough Italians to pick up a phrase or two."

It's all I can do not to roll my eyes. "You could say that," I say wryly.

Only my entire childhood. I could tell him I speak Italian fluently, but I'm having fun seeing the perfect capo get it wrong. Besides, I don't want the questions that would come after revealing my fluency. Like, how did I learn Italian? Who are my parents? Where is my family?

People can be nosy, and Salvatore is more intrusive than anyone I've ever met. Comes with being a capo, I guess.

"About what?" Salvatore prompts, his tone bordering on impatient.

"Do you have somewhere to be?"

"In fact, I do."

"Oh. Well, then you better go."

"Ask your question."

"Bossy."

"Bianca," he says warningly.

"It's just, you keep talking like I'm going to be here longer than a few days to recuperate. You bought me enough clothes to triple my current wardrobe—"

"Which is not saying much."

"Every piece of clothing I owned, I paid for, so get over yourself about how many pairs of jeans I have."

"Had. And it was one."

"It *was* two, but you had my clothing thrown away at the hospital." It's a guess, but none of the clothes I was wearing during the attack are in the guestroom.

"They were covered in blood and your shirt was torn."

"Blood can be washed out and tears can be mended." I puff out a breath of frustrated air. "Never mind, that's not what I'm asking about."

He gives me a look that says, *get to the point already.*

"Not only did you buy me a ridiculous amount of clothing, but you had your guy pack up all my stuff from the apartment."

"And it did not even fill the trunk."

"The fact he only had to take one trip is not the point. It's that you moved me out of my apartment. Without talking to me about it, which we will get to. But you moved me in here, like we're..." My voice trails off.

I don't know what we are.

"Right now we are friends."

"Are we really?"

"What else would you call it?"

"I don't know what to call it," I admit with exasperation.

His warm hand cups my neck and reaction tingles along my nerve endings. "I'm not ready to let go of this thing between us."

"Thing between us?" I ask incredulously. "What thing? You mean the *you want to get me into bed* thing? Or the *you had me kidnapped and then forced me to stay at your apartment to recuperate* thing?"

"Do not pretend you don't want to open your sweet pussy for me as badly as I want to be inside it. Your pulse is erratic from this simple touch."

"Again, not the point. I can't suddenly be living with you." And that's not something I should have to mention. "Who does this? You're a capo! You can't move a perfect stranger into your home."

"My *secure* home," he points out, rubbing in the fact I couldn't leave without help, despite my best efforts. "And we have addressed the perfect stranger concept. You are neither."

"You are not cute. We aren't dating. We don't have a relationship. We haven't even kissed."

His eyes darken. "Do you want to change that?"

"No." Then more honestly, I admit, "Maybe, but I—"

I don't get to finish my thought because his mouth takes possession of mine.

My brain shorts out. He's kissing me. And I like it.

Why did I think his lips would be hard like him? They're not. They are soft.

His scent surrounds me, the heat from his body drawing me to him like a moth to a flame. Though I feel more like a butterfly, coming out of my chrysalis to bright sunlight and a new life where touch is possible.

Where having a man touch me without throwing me into a tailspin is possible.

Where warm lips mold to my own so perfectly moisture burns at the back of my eyes.

Salvatore does not grab at me, or squeeze my boob until it hurts. There is no sweaty stench. No cruel demands.

Just touches that makes my soul sing.

He traces the seam of my lips with the tip of his tongue, sending shivers of delight through me. I always thought if I were to be kissed like this, with tongue, it would sicken me.

It doesn't. The opposite happens and I revel in how good every tiny touch between our mouths feels.

Salvatore nips my bottom lip and I gasp.

Chapter 25

SALVATORE

Bianca's lips part like I want them to and I take advantage of the opening to push my tongue inside the warm heat of her mouth.

Vanilla and cinnamon slide across my tastebuds along with a sweetness that is uniquely Bianca. My dislike for dessert forgotten, her sugary essence becomes my new favorite flavor.

She doesn't respond, her own tongue unmoving, but she's not trying to push me away either. Her body is almost preternaturally still as she seems to be relishing our connection as much as I am.

But I want more.

Lifting my head, I order, "Kiss me back."

Her lids snap open but her pretty, blue eyes are unfocused, nothing in them to indicate she registers cognition of my words. Knowing the barest touch of my lips affects her this way feeds my already healthy ego.

Only I will see her like this. No one else.

Right now, my brain taunts me, *until she gives herself to the next man.*

It won't be enough for her to leave Amuni. I need her out of New York after this thing runs its course. My primal nature will never allow another to touch what I have claimed as my own.

But I can't keep her. I am capo. I marry to further the interests of *la famiglia*. That is my duty.

In the future.

Right now, she is my pleasure.

"Bianca." I rub my thumb along her bottom lip. "Kiss me back."

Confusion flares in her gaze. "How?"

She wants to know how I like it? *Cazzo.* Why does that turn me on so much?

"Like this." I kiss her again, harder this time, forcefully thrusting my tongue into her mouth.

Hers slides against my own, making no effort to eject the marauder. Because we both want this. For however long it lasts.

My cock strains against my slacks, the pantleg not tailored to make room for my oversized erection. Because I'm not a teenager who gets hard when a sexy woman walks by.

Bianca sets my control over my hormones back fifteen years.

Groaning, I deepen the kiss as I pull her body close, pressing her stomach against my aching dick, teasing myself with what I cannot have. Yet.

Her soft little moan is almost my undoing. I want to rip the silky robe off her and her nightgown with it.

If I don't end this kiss, I'm going to do exactly that and she's not healed enough for the kind of sex that will lead to. But even as the thought forms her lips finally start to move under mine and I am lost.

Her mouth moves perfectly against mine with just the right amount of pressure, just the right amount of softness. She's the best fucking kisser I have ever laid my lips on.

Her body presses even more tightly against me. Hands that have remained at her side bury themselves in my hair, grabbing two clumps to yank my head closer.

She's too short. Sliding a hand under her ass, I lift her up so nothing can break our kiss. Her legs dangle. But then they come around my torso, locking like a vice, her years dancing the pole evident in the strength of their grip.

The only barrier between her hot, drenched pussy and my skin is my rapidly soaking shirt.

Cazzo.

She's not wearing panties. How often has she been naked under the nightgowns?

Without permission from my brain, my free hand slides under the thin cotton and over the silky skin of her ass. My middle finger dips between her swollen, wet pussy lips. No thought to hesitate, I spread her honey to her clit and rub there, my thumb pressing inside her hot tunnel.

She goes rigid against me. Does she want me to stop?

Fuck that. She wants this as much as I do. She's not trying to break the kiss. She's just not moving. Not her body. Not her tongue. Not her lips.

Then a switch flips inside her and she starts riding my hand like a rodeo queen. Her lips are suddenly eating at mine like she's ravenous and her tongue meets mine, thrust for thrust.

This woman is going to be a tsunami between the sheets. Or against the wall. In the bath. Wherever the hell we decide to bang, which my libido demands will be *everywhere*.

Her pussy soaks my hand as her vaginal walls clamp around my thumb, her nearly instant climax making her muscles spasm so tightly I feel like a boa constrictor is around my torso.

I don't stop moving my finger on her clit, forcing another orgasm to follow the first and she screams into my mouth, nearly biting my tongue.

Turned on to the point of madness, I reach down to undo my slacks so I can shove my cock into her right where stand.

"Salvatore!" That is not Rosa's voice.

It's my mother.

Managgia la miseria!

Bianca is still too out of it to realize we've been interrupted by the one person who could stop my rampaging libido right now. Even my father's presence wouldn't. But I'm not burying my cock in Bianca's heat in front of my mother.

"What are you doing to that poor girl? She's supposed to be resting." Of course, my mother knows all about my houseguest.

She and Rosa are thick as thieves.

Breaking our kiss, I surreptitiously slide my hand out from under Bianca's nightgown and robe.

Her eyes still closed, she mewls, trying to capture my lips again with her own.

I want to destroy something.

She's so hot for me, she doesn't even realize my mother is here.

"Shh...*bellissima*. We must stop. We have a guest." I look back over my shoulder. "Give us a minute, mamma. We'll meet you downstairs."

Skepticism twists my mother's perfectly painted lips. "For shame, *mi figlio*. If I leave you now, that young woman is going to end up flat on her back on your bed. And considering her recent troubles, that is the last place she should be."

The only saving grace to that little speech is that my mother spoke in Italian.

Bianca makes a sound of distress and it's not sexual need this time. She realizes we are no longer alone. Her legs unlock from around me and she tries to throw herself from my arms.

With no intention of allowing her to hurt herself further, I keep my arm tight around her hips. "Calm down, you're going to hurt yourself."

"I'm going to *murder* you if you don't let me down this very second." The anger and embarrassment blazing in her eyes is a potent combination.

She might actually try to do it. Maybe strangle me with those amazingly strong thighs of hers? The thought does nothing to deflate the log in my pants.

Which is why, after I carefully lower Bianca and make sure she is steady on her feet, I don't turn to face my mother.

Besides, there is a wet spot on my shirt my mother does not need to see.

All she could have seen was us kissing passionately. From her angle she can only speculate that my hand was buried between Bianca's thighs.

Chapter 26

BIANCA

Mortified does not begin to express the scope of my humiliation at being caught by Salvatore's mother while getting fingered by him. I have never been so embarrassed in my entire life.

Worse, I resent the intrusion with every fiber of my being. For the first time in my life, I enjoyed a man's touch. Salvatore made me come. Twice.

And I want more.

Which is terrifying enough to have me backing away from him as fast as legs still shaky from my climaxes will carry me.

"Uh...you need to..." I waive my hand toward his mother, who smiles kindly at me.

I want to sink through the floor. But I also want to find a place to revel in my newfound sexuality.

Sex can feel good. I know that on an intellectual level, but after my experience at sixteen, my body has always equated sex with humiliation, pain and fear.

Of course, we weren't actually bumping uglies, but his thumb was inside me and I liked it. A lot.

I just want to be alone to revel in that a little.

Why isn't he leaving? He has to realize his mother won't go anywhere until he does.

My gaze skitters down his body, yanked to a stop with a force stronger than even my will when I reach the noticeable wet patch on his shirt just above the waistband of his pants. I did that. My arousal soaked his shirt.

I should be even more embarrassed. But the awe I feel at the evidence of my own sexual desire pushes everything else out.

Salvatore pulls his jacket together, buttoning it and only then do I notice the pipe straining against his pants. If the monsters in my past had been that big, they would have split me in two and killed me.

For the first time, not even a tiny part of me wishes they had.

"If you keep looking at me like that, I'll never be able to turn to face my mother," Salvatore says without a trace of embarrassment.

He may not want his mother to actually see the erection that looks painfully constricted in his tight-fitting trousers, but he's not ashamed of it. Not even a little.

"Eyes up here, *cara.*"

My gaze snaps to his and I do enough blushing for both of us.

His gorgeous mouth is twisted in a smirk. "Are you going to be alright?"

I nod, no words at the ready.

He nods too and then turns, severing the tether between us. My heart burns. Like he literally took a knife and cut our connection.

Dio mio. I have to get out of here.

"Come, mamma, you can explain why you dropped in without calling first downstairs."

"I can't drop in on my favorite son? Never say so," she scolds him.

Salvatore offers his arm to his mother. "I am your only son."

Isn't he going to wash his hands? His fingers must smell like me. Like my juices.

The thought sends another burst of arousal pulsing through my ladybits. *Che palle.* I am in so much trouble.

Mrs. De Luca looks back at me before they exit the room. "Come downstairs after you have taken a moment to freshen up, my dear."

Without waiting for a reply, she turns her head to face forward again and lets Salvatore lead her from the room. She just expects me to obey her.

Like mother, like son.

And like her son, Mrs. De Luca will learn that I'm not great at being told what to do.

I scurry to the open door and peek around it to see mother and son disappear down the hall. Once their voices fade entirely, I make a beeline for the guestroom. It is blissfully empty when I get inside. Slamming the door shut, I press the lock and then lean back against it.

Closing my eyes, I replay the kiss that turned nuclear.

My first ever orgasm.

I've never even masturbated. The attempted assault on Bea happened when we were thirteen and just starting to have hormone driven urges. What happened to

Bea and the aftermath that followed turned off any instinct I had to explore my budding sexuality.

That might have changed later. Maybe. I don't know.

But then that horrifying, painful night happened when I was sixteen, two weeks before I watched Lorenzo execute my father. It's all wrapped up in my subconscious as one trauma because I spent those two weeks in a fog of pain and disillusionment, abandoned by everyone I trusted.

Equating sex with agony, abandonment and betrayal, nothing about it or my own sexuality interested me. At least until I met Salvatore.

He sparked a reaction in me that I didn't believe I was capable of feeling. And now, he's given me my first climax and my body is still humming from it.

Tugging my nightgown and robe up my thighs, I slide my own hand down over my stomach, reveling in the sensation of skin-on-skin contact. Even if it is my own.

Maybe especially because it is my hand on my body causing this pleasure. My fingers brush over the hair at the top of my mons and I shudder. It's as if every individual hair follicle is sensitized. Do other women feel this when they touch themselves?

I could ask Candi, but I might combust from embarrassment if I do. Even if I'm pretty sure she would answer without hesitation.

My hand drops lower and I slip two fingers between my folds. The wetness coating my most intimate flesh is copious and silky. This is what Salvatore felt when he touched me, this slippery liquid covering plump labia.

If I slide my finger inside my vagina, will it feel as good as his? Unable to resist finding out, I press my middle finger inside. It's not nearly as thick as his thumb but I still feel it in my tight channel.

Sliding my forefinger in beside my middle finger, I shudder. That's closer, but it still isn't the same.

That unfamiliar feeling of euphoria is starting to wash over me again though. I want it. The loss of self for the brief time my body drowns in ecstasy. Pushing my heel into my clitoris, I slowly fuck myself with my fingers.

The climax hits me by surprise and my knees try to buckle. I press back against the door, not ready to give up this feeling of bliss. I don't stop touching myself until I have wrung every last drop of pleasure from my body.

I've never done drugs. Not even weed. But friends have described a really good high like the floaty feeling I'm experiencing right now.

The monsters stole this from me along with my innocence, but Salvatore De Luca, dangerous mafioso, gave it back.

I have never had any desire to touch the part of myself I consider soiled, or let anyone else near enough to do it either.

Self-help books and Mr. Ruhnke's wisdom did a lot to help me realize what happened to me didn't make *me* dirty. It made the men who did it monsters.

But I have yet to find the inner sex goddess Candi says we all have. Well, until now.

Until a capo burst into my life with his brutal good looks and refusal to believe I don't want him as much as he wants me.

I guess today proved without a doubt that he is right.

SALVATORE

"So, you have a house guest." My mother pauses and studies my face, seeing inside me as much as anyone can do. "That you kiss in your bedroom."

Never let it be said that Ilaria De Luca is not as adept as any made man at interrogation. Her techniques don't include torture, but they are damn effective.

"He was kissing her?" Rosa asks, her tone scandalized.

"You knew I had someone staying, or you would not be here now." I speak to my mother, but give Rosa a look meant to quell.

Her complacent expression shows a woman of stronger mettle than most of my men. "You did not tell me to keep your involuntary guest a secret from your family."

"She is not here under duress," I grind out.

"She is free to leave?" Rosa sounds surprised. "That is not the impression I got when you instructed me not to use my access to open the apartment door for her."

"Is this true, *mi figlio?*"

How does my mother manage to imbue five words with so much disapproval?

"Bianca does not know what is good for her. She was going to return to a tiny apartment she shares with five other people, six if you count the roommate's boyfriend. She doesn't even sleep on the pullout couch she pays for. Bianca sleeps on the floor. She would have been back in the hospital in a matter of days. If her roommates even noticed she was ill. She could have died," I say with exasperation.

The whole time I am talking, my mother's eyes grow rounder and rounder. "Have my prayers been answered? Is this you showing concern for the welfare of one of your girlfriends?"

"I don't have girlfriends," I remind my mother. And if I did, she wouldn't be a pole dancer, turned cocktail waitress.

"More's the pity," Rosa mutters.

Mamma pours me a cup of coffee before serving herself and Rosa tea from the other urn on the tray. "What do you call a woman living with you if not your girlfriend?"

My obsession.

Rosa takes a sip of her tea and says, "His kidnap victim who he forces to sleep in his bed."

Managgia la miseria. These women.

"Is this true?" my mother asks with brows raised.

I am not about to explain Bianca's nightmares. She deserves her privacy even if Rosa does not believe I deserve mine.

"I did not kidnap her. That was your son," I remind my housekeeper-slash-second mother.

Bianca's suggestion of taking her to a fuck pad is sounding better by the minute. Not that I have one, but a penthouse suite at the Ritz-Carlton will do.

"On your orders," Mamma chides. "We did not raise you to shirk responsibility, Salvatore Enzo De Luca."

Shit. My full name. Mamma is going to mount a rescue mission any minute if I don't calm her down.

"She agreed to stay."

Mamma looks questioningly at Rosa who shrugs. "If she has, I didn't hear it."

If? Fucking if?

That is it. I have had enough. "When have I ever lied to you?" I demand of my mother. And then I glare at Rosa. "*If* you find it so onerous to work for someone you clearly don't trust, perhaps you should cease doing so."

"Are you threatening to fire your housekeeper again, Salvatore?" Bianca asks lightly with a teasing smile from the archway of the living room.

Mamma's head snaps up and she turns to watch Bianca's unhurried progress across the room.

Her long red hair pulled back in a wet ponytail, my soon-to-be lover's luscious curves are encased in one of the snarky t-shirts I bought her to replace the one destroyed in the attack. The snug fitting yoga pants she's wearing with it send my heartrate spiking.

She's not wearing shoes, though she has several pairs in her closet. Both new and old. Instead, she's got on one of the pairs of fuzzy slipper socks that looked too comfortable to pass up.

I don't need a lot of sleep, so I woke well before Bianca that first night she was here. Unwilling to leave her to her nightmares, I worked on my phone and ended up ordering Bianca clothes after checking my email.

Ensuring she would have adequate clothes to wear was surprisingly gratifying.

The smile playing at the edges of her mouth is even more so. If I had known giving her an orgasm would put her in this good of a mood, I would have found a way to eat her out at the hospital.

"Hello, Bianca. It is a pleasure to meet you." My mother stands and offers her hand to Bianca. "Since my son did not see fit to introduce me upstairs, I am Ilaria De Luca. You will call me Ilaria."

Shock reverberates through me. My mother is a stickler for propriety. Very few outside of our family are given permission to use her first name. Rosa being one of them, but even Pietro calls her Mrs. De Luca.

"Thank you, Ilaria." Bianca smiles and shakes my mother's hand before sitting beside me on the sofa.

Right beside me. Her thigh presses against mine.

What the fuck is going on?

"Would you like coffee, or tea, Bianca?" Mamma asks.

"Coffee please."

Mamma pours Bianca her coffee and hands it to her before giving me a gimlet stare. "You threatened to fire Rosa?"

My housekeeper is offering the cream and sugar to Bianca and apologizes for not putting the doctored creamer she made specially for my houseguest on the tray.

I shake my head. She's more solicitous of Bianca than she is of Nerissa. Not that my sister tolerates being coddled, but this is ridiculous.

My mother taps the side of her teacup once with her fingernail, her signal to pay attention.

Meeting her eyes, I let my irritation reflect in my own and don't try to keep it out of my voice either. "No, I did not threaten to fire Rosa. She lied and told Bianca I had to get her to cooperate."

Rosa shrugs. "It worked. The child needed her rest."

So, it is okay for my housekeeper to decide what is best for Bianca, but not me? Fuck that noise.

I am capo.

Chapter 27

BIANCA

Salvatore is so angry; steam should be coming out of his ears.

Neither his mom, nor Rosa appear worried.

But it's the hurt lurking behind the furious capo façade neither of them seems to see that concerns me. I arrived in time to hear both Rosa and Ilaria question his truthfulness. He doesn't like it.

At all.

Which tells me three things. One, he expects to be believed. Two, he isn't used to having his honesty questioned by either woman. And three, he doesn't lie to his family.

That last one is a leap, but it fits what I know of him so far.

"I've only known Salvatore a short time." I smile toward him before meeting his mother's eyes. "But he doesn't strike me as a man who lies."

"I'm a Cosa Nostra capo, of course I lie." Tension vibrates from his big body.

Glancing toward him, I bite my bottom lip. The look he's giving his mother and Rosa dares them to deny his claim.

Something about that defensiveness tugs at my heart. It's as if he wants them to admit he lies when he has to. Which is not the same as lying for convenience, or to the people that should matter most.

I know. I've been the recipient of those lies. Salvatore is nothing like my father.

Che palle.

Give a girl an orgasm and suddenly she's looking at you like you're some kind of superhero and your feelings matter.

To be fair to myself, that orgasm was pretty spectacular and it wasn't isolated, not to mention my first ever. It's bound to impact me more strongly than it would someone who is used to having them.

"I'm sure you do," I pat his thigh. "To your enemies. Not to family."

Salvatore goes still, that predator about to strike aura surrounding him again. Then he turns his whole body to face me without dislodging my hand.

He studies my face like it's a map he has to memorize. "How is it that you realize that truth, but my own mother and the woman who is as close as family do not?"

Ilaria makes a sound of hurt disagreement and Rosa mutters something about never being too old to be questioned by the women who love him in Italian.

Salvatore ignores them both and waits for me to answer.

"Even when you knew it would piss me off, you told me the truth." I don't mention what that truth was.

I get the feeling neither of the older women would approve of his offer to give me five thousand dollars to have sex with him. Especially if they knew that me taking the money would automatically mean losing my job.

Now that I know how good sex can feel, I'm rethinking my position. Not the getting paid part. The actually having sex part.

He knows exactly what I'm talking about though. I can see it in his eyes and the way they travel from my lips to my chest. The La Perla bra fits my DD boobs perfectly and makes them look amazing. Which he is definitely noticing.

It's also surprisingly comfortable. I wouldn't expect him to get the cup size wrong, but the band size is another matter. Most men are clueless and think 36 is the norm. There are a lot of bralette tops at Pitiful Princess that are too big around the band for most of the dancers and too small for both me and Candi.

Either he checked my other bras, or he has excellent size guessing skills, because Salvatore got it right.

Ilaria taps on her teacup and Salvatore's gaze snaps to her, his mouth tipped down in a scowl. "Yes?"

"I did not accuse you of lying."

"The De Lucas take responsibility for their actions, mother. You looked to Rosa for confirmation of my words, implying you believed I could be lying." There is no give in Salvatore's tone.

Whatever hurt he's feeling is buried down deep now and the only face he's showing is that of arrogant capo.

And still, I just want to climb in his lap and rub myself all over him. How long is Ilaria planning to stay? Will Salvatore be returning upstairs with me when she does?

"You had the girl kidnapped," his mother defends herself in Italian.

"English, mother. It is impolite to speak in Italian when not everyone present understands the language."

As much as I enjoy knowing something Salvatore doesn't, this is getting ridiculous.

"There is no need to worry about only speaking in English around me," I say in Italian.

"You speak Italian?" Salvatore demands, his deep tones filled with shock.

I shrug, the pull on my stitches negligible at this point. "My father's family was from Italy."

"Where are they now?" Ilaria asks.

"They're all gone." The Russos in Detroit are just names to me, not family.

I've never met any of them. While I might have distant relatives among the Genovese *famiglia* if I do, I don't know who they are either.

Ilaria gives me a look filled with compassion. "I am sorry to hear that. Family is important."

"Why didn't you tell me before now?" Salvatore's voice drips with suspicion.

He's not talking about my family being gone. He's still harping on *me* not telling *him* I understand Italian.

Really? I frown at him. "You just assumed I didn't speak the language. Considering how many Italian speaking people there are in New York, I wouldn't think you'd be so quick to dismiss the possibility."

"You aren't part of *la famiglia*."

"There are plenty of Italian American's who aren't." And he's right.

I'm not part of the mafia, not since Lorenzo kicked me out of my home, cutting my ties with the Genovese Family when he killed my father for being a traitor.

"You should have told me. I discussed sensitive information in front of you."

"It's not Bianca's fault if you didn't show enough sense to mind what you said around her." Rosa's staunch support warms me.

But it's having the opposite effect on Salvatore.

His gray eyes are icier than a glacier. He opens his mouth, and my gut tells me the words that will come out aren't going to be pleasant for Rosa to hear.

I like Rosa. I don't want Salvatore to hurt her feelings.

I also don't want Salvatore hurt by more criticism from his mother, or housekeeper. He's clearly not used to it.

It still surprises me that I believe the arrogant capo can be hurt, but I do. I know what I saw when I got in here, even if he's got his top dog face on now.

I jump in to say, "You said it yourself, I witnessed you killing my attackers." Not that I actually watched, but for the sake of this discussion we'll go with it. "Not much you could talk about that would be more sensitive than that." I do air quotes as I say *sensitive*.

His eyes narrow and I just know this conversation isn't over. How disturbed am I that I'm looking forward to arguing with him later?

"You will tell my mother you are here of your own volition," he demands, apparently ready to shift back to the original volatile topic.

"Bossy much?"

"Bianca," he warns.

I roll my eyes, but then I meet Ilaria's eyes. "Pietro kidnapped me and I wasn't happy to be here at first."

Salvatore lets out a frustrated breath.

"I'm being honest here, Salvatore. Your mom knows Pietro drugged me and carted me back here like an abandoned puppy."

"Pietro drugged you?" Ilaria demands.

I nod an affirmative.

Then she shows she's got a temper every bit as volatile as my nonna's ever was and starts yelling. When she's done, Salvatore's face looks like granite and Rosa is dabbing at her eyes in shame for her son's behavior.

Are these women for real? They are married to made men. Their sons are made men. Even Ilaria's daughter is made. *Dio mio.* Nerissa is Salvatore's second.

What do they think happens in mafia business?

"I have dealt with Pietro's overzealousness in carrying out my orders."

"He did," I agree.

With panty melting efficiency. Not that I will ever admit seeing him dole out punishment to his top bodyguard turned me on.

Definitely disturbed.

Before another argument can erupt, I say, "I have agreed to stay here while I heal."

"Not under duress?" Ilaria probes.

That granite line of Salvatore's jaw goes diamond hard. *Accidenti.* His mother does not know when to quit, but I also like that she's watching out for me like Rosa. I am not alone here and ultimately, if I want to go, they will help me, I realize.

Even if Salvatore forbids it.

I let my gratitude for her concern shine in my eyes. "He actually used logic. I guess the risk of infection to knife wounds is high, even those that have been treated at the hospital."

At least that's what I take the doctor's warnings to mean. And sleeping on the floor of a closet, no matter how clean I keep my little spot, isn't the best way to avoid it.

And even if I had wanted to leave before, now that I've experienced sexual pleasure with Salvatore, I definitely don't. I want to explore what else my body can feel with someone who doesn't trigger a panic attack when he gets intimately close.

"I have to admit that you didn't look like you were here against your will upstairs." Ilaria winks at me.

She winks.

Like we're friends and are sharing a joke. Heat blooms in my cheeks while embarrassment crawls like a spider up my spine. I'm more grateful than a dancer taking off her heels at the end of the night that Salvatore's big body blocked his mother's view of mine.

I would die if she'd had a front row seat to his fingers inside me.

Which doesn't look good for me going back to pole dancing if I have to once my wounds heal. I haven't had the nerve to ask Salvatore if I'm fired, or not. But the chances of Franco holding the job open for a brand new cocktail waitress are worse than the odds of the guy obsessed with watching you dance turning out to be your soulmate.

This self-consciousness about my body has to stop.

But then getting caught by my lover's mother while his thumb is buried in my wet vagina and his fingers play with my clit isn't the same thing as dancing on a stage where no one can touch me. Where I choose what to show and when.

Lover? Did I just think of Salvatore as my lover?

Because of one, probably super tame for him, sexual experience in his bedroom? I need to slow my roll.

Or stop it all together.

He's not my lover. Not my boyfriend. Not even my friend with benefits. We barely know each other and me temporarily living in his house doesn't change that.

You go on telling yourself that, girl. The man brings you to his bed every night. He touches you like he has the right to. And you let him.

My groan is spontaneous and loud. And it has the two older women and Salvatore all staring at me.

"Uh, sorry about that." Hiding in my coffee cup, I take a slow sip, but eventually I have to set it back down.

No one's attention has moved from me by a single iota. I stifle my sigh, like I should have the groan.

"Do not be embarrassed. I should not have come upstairs unannounced," Ilaria says soothingly. "Not when I knew Salvatore had a guest staying here."

"Bianca merits courtesy and I do not?" Salvatore does not sound impressed.

Ilaria takes a sip of her own tea, pointedly not replying to her son's question.

Oh, man. There are some complicated relationships going on here. Do they even realize how much push-pull is happening between them? Ilaria is Salvatore's mother, but he is *her* capo.

Having grown up in a mafia family, I know that means that family, or not, she is supposed to treat him with deference and respect. Is it because he's only been a capo for about a year?

Or maybe it is because she is his mother, and that role gives her special license to treat him like a human being.

She's also the wife of the consigliere. I'm not sure where that puts Ilaria in the mafia pecking order. Despite my dad's pride in being (distantly) related to the Detroit don, our family didn't interact with anyone in the Cosa Nostra higher ranks.

The first day I actually spoke to Lorenzo was the one when he kicked me out of my home.

He was rude to Salvatore at the club too. Not that the younger capo allowed it. If Salvatore gave me the look and warning he did Lorenzo, I would probably piss myself.

I guess taking over as capo isn't all that easy, even if the role is inherited.

Chapter 28

SALVATORE

Not for the first time, I question the wisdom of keeping Rosa as my house-keeper now that I am capo.

It doesn't surprise me that she called my mom and told her that Bianca is staying here. They are like sisters.

But it is not acceptable either.

Neither is either woman questioning my word when I told them that Bianca is not here under duress. If I needed to keep her here against her will for the good of *la famiglia*, I would. I am capo.

And I would not hesitate to tell either woman that is the case, like I did not hesitate to tell Rosa to keep Bianca here that first day. For Bianca's health and safety.

The welfare of the people under my authority rests on my shoulders.

My mother and Rosa can get as pissed as they want at me. Ultimately, my word is law. The only voice with authority to override mine is Severu's. As his underboss, Miceli can override me only when speaking directly on behalf of the don.

My father is consigliere, which is a position of great influence, but he does not have the authority to override my will either. So, why the hell do my mother and Rosa think I would stoop to lying to them?

I don't need to.

But it is obvious neither woman sees things that way. Rosa will never give me the unquestioning loyalty I need from a member of my household staff. She loves me, which she believes gives her leeway to question my actions and motives and share her concerns with my mother.

It does not.

I'm going to have to fire her. I don't like it, but I trained my entire life to be what I am and there's no room for sentimentality in a capo's decision making.

She does not see her actions as disloyal, but they are.

And I cannot let that stand.

Which means I need a new housekeeper.

But not today because you also need someone here to watch over Bianca. What is more important? Her wellbeing or demanding the respect due you as capo?

There is no contest. I'm not like that loser Lorenzo. I don't need to throw my weight around to feel the heft of my position. Rosa will have to go, but not until after Bianca has healed.

Her brand of disloyalty is not dangerous for *la famiglia*. Or even me. It is simply unacceptable.

"If you two are finished convincing yourselves that I have not suddenly started participating in the flesh trade," I stand. "I have work and Bianca needs her rest."

"You're leaving?" Bianca asks, surprising me.

I expected the feisty beauty to argue with me about her need to rest, not question whether, or not, I am sticking around.

"No." I have phone calls to make in my office.

Juniper is dragging his feet about finalizing the sale of the bars and I want to know why. Money should be enough to convince him to sign his properties over to me, but if it isn't, I'll persuade him in other ways.

Taking possession of those locations as soon as possible is key to Severu's bid for becoming the next godfather. The sale needs to happen. Now.

"You are so dramatic, Salvatore." My mother shakes her head. "No one accused you of human trafficking."

Bianca gasps, like she's just registered what I said. "You would never."

"No, I would not." That is not something we allow in our territory, but how is she so certain of that?

"I'm sure your mom and Rosa never meant to imply that either." She gives them a reproving look, her tone admonishing.

The urge to smile startles me. But her defense pleases me and for once Bianca's ire is directed at someone else.

"Of course, not. My son is too honorable a man to participate in business so heinous." Mamma's righteous indignation is overdone for a woman who as good as accused her capo of lying.

Rosa manages to look wounded despite being the one to tell my mother I force Bianca to sleep in my bed. And mamma soaked it up like a sponge, only too eager to believe the worst of me.

"Salvatore is a good man," Rosa says with a pointed look at me. "We all know this."

Most of the time, both women see me through the rose-tinted lens of love and willful obliviousness. They spend their lives ignoring the seamier side of their husbands and children's lives.

Par for the course in the mafia.

However, I am *not* a good man. I do heinous things. What I do not do is: buy, sell, or keep sex slaves.

I put my hand out to Bianca. "Come."

"I am not a dog, Salvatore. You could ask." Crossing her arms over her chest, her beautiful eyes narrow at me. "We just established I'm your guest, not your prisoner."

I am a capo. I do not ask. And no matter how much I want to fuck this woman, it isn't going to make me into some tame lapdog.

"Do whatever the fuck you want," I say and turn to leave.

"Salvatore." My mother's tone is admonishing. "You did not kiss me goodbye."

In no mood to show familial affection, but also unwilling to disrespect her, I return to give her a perfunctory kiss on the cheek.

"Goodbye, mother," I say in Italian with a glare for Bianca.

She should have told me she speaks the language.

Bianca rolls her eyes like she knows exactly what I'm thinking, and she's not impressed.

This woman.

If my cock didn't see her as true north, I would not say another word to her while she's healing. Better yet, I would send her to stay with the Gallos and Rosa could watch over Bianca in her home. Then I could I hire a new housekeeper immediately, killing two birds with one stone.

Not going to happen. *Manaja.*

I don't make this kind of effort for bedmates. Not fucking ever.

"We will see you at the don's for dinner on Thursday," my mother says smoothly.

Like she can't feel the black cloud of temper hovering over me right now.

"We'll be there."

"We?" my mother asks pointedly.

"I'm bringing Bianca." As long as she has the doctor and surgeon's approval to leave the penthouse.

But since the doctor was going to let Bianca check out of the hospital only to go to that tiny apartment with more roommates than square feet, I doubt she'll have any objections.

"What? Bringing me where?" Bianca demands.

"My cousin's wife invited us for dinner."

"The don's wife knows I'm staying here?" she asks, her beautiful face creased in confusion.

"I told Severu I'd be bringing you," I explain. When I never explain.

My mother makes a sound of surprise and Rosa tuts. Ignoring both of them, I turn to leave. Again.

"Aren't you even going to ask if I *want* to go to dinner at a mafia don's house?" Bianca asks, her tone critical.

"No."

BIANCA

Salvatore walks out of the living room without looking back.

"He doesn't date a lot, does he?" I ask Rosa wryly.

The man has no clue.

"My son doesn't date at all," Ilaria answers for the housekeeper. "And yet he wants to bring you to a family dinner. Just how long have you known Salvatore?"

"Less than two weeks," I answer honestly, as bewildered by Salvatore's pronouncement as she clearly is.

Ilaria looks at Rosa like she expects the other woman to have the answers.

But the housekeeper shrugs. "I don't know what is going on with him. Since that she-devil, Monica, he keeps his heart closed off. He doesn't bring women here, but he won't let this one go."

Not comfortable being talked about like I'm not in the room, I insert, "Maybe he feels bad about the attack." And who is Monica, besides being a *she-devil*?

Also, I'm pretty sure that it's not Salvatore's heart involved. It's the impressive lead pipe in his pants, but I'm not about to say that to his mother and adopted aunt. I've done enough blushing for today.

"Why should he?" Ilaria asks. "He didn't attack you."

It occurs to me that Ilaria does not know the attack was from another Cosa Nostra family.

The Five Families are all part of the same syndicate. That doesn't mean they all get along. Cousins fight. So do the different families. But they always stand as one against an outside enemy.

At least that's what my dad used to say to explain the rivalry between the different families.

Rosa hmms. "Pietro said the attack happened when Bianca was late leaving Amuni."

She and Ilaria give me identical looks of censure.

Going from having no mom to two. It's a lot. Not that either are my mom, or ever likely to be by marriage, no matter what kind of stories they are telling themselves.

But the mom vibe is strong.

"I didn't have a choice," I defend myself. "The patrons wouldn't leave." And they'd been lousy tippers.

The knock on the head didn't make me forget that.

"Franco should have made them leave," Rosa says, disgruntled.

Ilaria nods. "Salvatore needs to talk to him. Employees shouldn't be put in such dangerous situations."

"I had a word with him already," Rosa says. "He promised to tell Franco not to allow the employees to walk alone to the subway station without an escort."

Wow, that is quite a concession. Is there a heart under that gruff capo exterior after all?

Content to listen to the older women chat, I sip my coffee and revel in being downstairs.

But the third time I smother a yawn, Rosa tsks. "It is time for you to rest."

Ilaria agrees and with both of them adamant, I take myself back upstairs.

The open door to Salvatore's office draws me like a beacon.

Chapter 29

BIANCA

His jacket and tie gone, his shirtsleeves rolled up, Salvatore sits back in a burgundy leather wingback office chair talking on the phone.

The sight of the black ink covering his muscular forearms locks me in place. I have seen tattoos peeking out of the neck of his dress shirts, but his forearms are covered. And it is seriously hot.

Do they cover his whole body, or just his arms?

He sleeps in boxer shorts, but he's always gone before I wake in the morning and there is no light to see him by when he wakes me up to take pain meds.

"Tell your boss I expect a call back today," he says into the phone and then swipes to end the call.

Steel gray eyes trap mine. "Finally decided to let your body rest?"

"I can't sleep the days away."

"That's exactly what you should be doing while your body heals. Getting as much sleep as possible."

"I've been sleeping too much," I argue. And when he's not here, that sleep isn't exactly restful anyway.

"Take a nap before lunch and I will take you up to the rooftop garden to eat."

"You have a rooftop garden?" Awe colors my tone.

Sue me. I know some buildings in New York have them. I've seen pictures but never been anyplace that had one, much less been allowed to visit it.

"Yes. Worth taking a nap to get to see?"

"If I take a nap now, can I go to my apartment later?"

"No." He looks ready to lecture me on the germs inherent in an apartment shared by so many people again.

I put my hand up. "Stop, Salvatore. I'm not moving back until I'm fully healed but there's something I need to get."

"My men got all of your things."

"They missed something."

"What?"

I don't want to tell him. He'll think it's ridiculous to be so worried about a plant, but I am. "My African violet."

"Where is it?" he asks.

It's that simple? No question about whether I really need it? Or why a plant is important enough to me to go get it?

Not willing to look a gift horse in the mouth, I tell him.

He pulls out his phone and sends a text. "Pietro will pick it up this afternoon."

"Tell him to be careful with it," I say, panicked. "If he hurts it, I'll—"

"He knows how to transport delicate plants. Don't worry," Salvatore interrupts before I can think of a threat dire enough toward Pietro.

"He does?" Does Rosa keep houseplants?

"Yes. You'll find out why after your nap."

In the rooftop garden? Curiosity and interest piqued, I nevertheless don't let this opportunity to bargain go by. "If I nap like a good girl, I want to go for a walk in the park tomorrow."

"I already acceded to the retrieval of your plant."

"If your guys had done their job the first time, it would already be here. They grabbed everything else. I want to go for a walk in the park."

He frowns, the muscles in his forearms flexing and distracting me. "You can walk in the garden."

"Even if it spans the whole building, that's still not the same as walking in the park."

"You don't need to tire yourself out getting fresh air."

"I'm used to working, Salvatore. My body needs to move."

"I have a gym. Once you're approved for mild exercise, you can use it."

"I'm already approved for mild exercise. The fact you and Rosa want to keep me wallowing in bed is beside the point."

"You will find that what I want is never beside the point, Bianca. I am capo."

"And I am an adult woman, capable of making my own decisions. I chose to stay here. I am not a prisoner. Remember?"

"As much as I might enjoy tying you to my bed, I don't want to keep you prisoner."

The image sends heat flooding through me. And not of the embarrassment variety.

"Don't think that you can start bossing me around since you gave me an orgasm."

Salvatore's gaze heats and he stands up. "Maybe you need another climax to help you sleep."

"What? No." My ladybits disagree and let me know with a thrum deep in my core.

He comes around his desk, moving with the grace and determination of a tiger stalking its next meal.

I should not have let Mr. Ruhnke talk me into watching so many nature documentaries. My imagination is slotting Salvatore into too many scenes I watched with the old man.

Of their own volition, my feet start moving backward, but instead of going out the door into the hall, I bump into the wall beside it.

Oof.

His grin is as predacious as his sensual glide toward me. "Your mouth says no, but those diamond hard nipples crowning your gorgeous tits are telling me that's exactly what you need."

Each word hits me right in the vagina, sending wetness gushing into my La Perla underwear. Everything down there pulses with anticipation for the pleasure he's offering.

My nipples are as hard as he says. And tight. They tingle with the need to be touched.

What is happening to my body? "I don't react like this when I dance the pole."

"That's because you were never dancing for me."

His words send my imagination spinning in another direction as an image of me dancing the pole in an empty club, except one patron. Him. In my mind's eye, the spotlight isn't on me. It's on him.

Suppressing a shudder of want, I say, "You're so arrogant."

"Is it arrogant if it is true?" He stops scant inches from my body. "Put your hands on me, *bella mia.* Show me you want this."

My hands clench. Can I touch him? Can I do what he wants and show him *I* want more pleasure?

His fingers curl gently around my wrist and he lifts my fist to place it against the hard muscle of his chest. Needing to explore in a way I never have, my fingers unfurl from the fist and splay across his pec.

Heat emanates through his shirt. The heel of my hand is over a small nub. His nipple. Hard like mine. Rubbing my hand in a circle, my heel and palm pass over it.

Strong fingers clasp my nape. "Yes. Like that, Bianca. Touch me."

I want to. So much.

So, I do, mapping his chest with my fingertips as I inhale his masculine scent. When my hand travels lower, it's like the appendage belongs to someone else.

To a curious and sexually open woman.

My fingers curl around the hard bulge I find angled toward his belt. Angled because this monster penis would be sticking out of his waistband if his belt wasn't in the way.

My core clenches and I shiver with atavistic recognition of what his hardon represents. The urge to merge two bodies in the most fundamental way. My mind might not be ready for him to be inside me, but my body is going nuclear at the thought.

Tracing his length from root to tip, I squeeze when I reach it, the column of flesh stretching my hand.

He groans, thrusting his hips forward. "*Cazzo, bella mia.* I want you."

"I..." I'm not sure what I want.

Him? Yes. But am I ready for penetrative sex? Pretty sure I'm not.

"I know." He groans again. "We have to wait. If I fucked you the way I want to right now, every one of your stitches would tear."

Why does that turn me on instead of frightening me? Memories from my past should have me trying to get away from him. They flicker dimly, like an overexposed reel under the hot sun of his passion.

My body is on meltdown and all I can think of is ways we could do the deed without ripping stitches.

No, Bianca. Bad idea. You don't even know if you could go through with it. You might freeze up at the last second and what if he doesn't stop?

That thought finally chills the raging inferno inside me and my hands still.

Salvatore inhales deeply. "Yes, you are right. We must stop." He steps back and looks into my eyes, his nearly black with lust.

A sound of need that I have never made before comes from my mouth.

Jaw looking hewn from granite, his gaze traps mine. "That doesn't mean I can't help you relax enough to sleep. Let me make you climax."

And all the air whooshes from the room.

The muscles in my neck jerk my head up and down in a nod without any input from my brain.

Salvatore doesn't hesitate. Careful not to jostle my back, he lifts me into his arms, and carries me into the hallway. I think he's going to go right past the guestroom, but he stops and sort of step pivots before pushing the unlatched door open and carrying me inside.

Was he going to take me to his bedroom? Did he change his mind? Why? He touched me in there earlier. What is different about now? Is it because I'm going to sleep after? Only he carries me to his bed nightly for me to sleep beside him.

My thoughts go static when he lays me on the bed and begins to undress me. Like this is normal. Like having a man take off my socks is nothing out of the ordinary for me.

It so is.

He pulls my leggings down my thighs slow inch by slow inch while he stares at what he reveals. I know what he sees.

I'm a dancer, so my body is strong, but that hourglass shape so popular in the middle of the last century? I've got it. I'm curvy.

The emcee called me the big girl with the juicy thighs whenever I got introduced on stage at the Pitiful Princess. Men appreciated my jiggle but I didn't care. I didn't dance for them.

I danced for myself because I love it. And I danced for the money I needed to support myself. For tips that went into savings toward my dream of leaving New York. It didn't matter how lasciviously the customers looked at me, it didn't touch me.

Salvatore's gaze burns through me though, setting my insides alight with desire. His eyes caress my body and leave shivery pleasure in their wake. He leaves my panties on and helps me into a sitting position so he can remove my shirt.

I don't know why I don't offer to help, but I don't. Letting him undress me feels nice. Like he's pampering me. Surprisingly, I enjoy that feeling. It is turning me on in ways I don't expect it to, as well.

His hands skim up my sides and cup my bra covered breasts. My nipples poke against the soft lace, begging for attention.

Caspita! What this man does to me.

"This looks better on you than I expected and I knew your gorgeous tits were going to look amazing in it." He fingers the bra strap. "La Perla should pay you to model their lingerie, but if they did, I would have to kill the photographers who looked at you to take the pictures."

I laugh breathlessly. "And all the men that saw me dance the pole at Pitiful Princess?" I tease.

Salvatore's face goes dark and his eyes are filled with death. "Give me names and I will take care of them."

Pretty sure *take care of* is mafia speak for kill. "You should be joking, but I don't think you are."

He shrugs. *"Sei mio."*

Chapter 30

BIANCA

My world shrinks down to his molten gray gaze as my breath stills in my chest.

You are mine.

Sex talk. That's all it is. All it could possibly be.

For a second though, my entire being thrums with the idea of belonging. Not being alone. Having someone who claims me as theirs, that I can tell the world belongs to me too.

It's ridiculous of course. We've known each other eleven days. He wants to have sex with me.

He does not want to keep me.

Only a fool would take his words to heart and I am no fool. I learned my lessons the hard way and they stuck because of it.

Doesn't stop my body from vibrating in anticipation of the pleasure it knows is coming though. Whatever the future holds, Salvatore is determined to send my ovaries into the stratosphere in the present.

He squeezes my breasts and I suck in air as sensation that borders on pain turns into pure ecstasy as his thumbs brush over my turgid nipples. My hands land on his hard, muscular shoulders.

"I want you to take your shirt off." I don't ask him to take his slacks off.

Because one, I don't know if I'm ready to see his naked body. Touching him through his trousers is sexy but safe. And two, even a novice like me can see that he's on the edge of his control. I'm not giving him a reason to tip over.

Especially when I don't know if him trying to penetrate my body will send me into a freakout, or not.

He lightly pinches my nipples. "I cannot nap with you."

Jolts of sensation travel straight from my nipples to my pulsing vagina.

"I know, but I want to see you." At least his chest and arms.

"You do it." He rolls my nipples between his thumbs and forefingers. "My hands are busy."

My body electrified with pleasure, I don't wait for a second invitation. I start unbuttoning his shirt, taking in his hairy chest as it's revealed to my greedy eyes.

His pecs ripple as he reaches around and undoes the clasp of my bra and peels it away from my heavy breasts.

"Perfect," he says under his breath.

Warmth unfurls in me, but I don't look up from my task. His chest is covered in dark hair that vees down his abs until it disappears enticingly into the waistband of his trousers.

Sliding my fingers through his chest hair, I am startled by how soft it is. There's black ink under it on his right pectoral, but the image is hard to make out at first because of the hair he allows to grow over it.

After a couple of seconds of intent appraisal, I realize it's a viper. A dead one. I ruffle his hair to get a better look. The shading is done so perfectly, that it takes a second to realize what I thought were scales at first are parts of letters.

His hand traps mine against his chest. "Forget the tattoo. Touch me *bella mia*."

Mouth dry, I nod. But I saw what the letters spelled out. A woman's name. Monica.

The name of the woman Rosa mentioned downstairs.

What does she mean to Salvatore? Hot jealousy spikes inside my chest knowing he has her name inked permanently into his body. Even if it is mostly covered by his silky black chest hair.

Is she dead? Is that why the snake is dead? Why a snake? Why her? Who *is* she?

"Stop thinking about it. She doesn't matter. She'll never matter."

That's pretty definitive. "So, no girlfriend?" I ask just to be sure.

If I'm going to keep letting this man touch me intimately, I need to know there aren't any other women. I know it's not forever, but this physical closeness means too much to me for it to be any other way.

"I don't date. How would I have a girlfriend?" His hands slide down my back and he caresses my butt.

First outside the underwear, and then beneath it.

Losing my ability to focus, I demand. "Say it."

"No girlfriend. There is only you."

The words zing along my nerve endings like an electric current, leaving pleasure and anticipation in their wake.

"Now you say it."

"What?" I ask, barely tracking as his middle finger slides between my butt cheeks.

The tip of that finger taps my pucker. "You are mine."

I jerk as new sensations pour over me.

"Say it," he demands with another tap.

Dio mio.

"*Io sono tua,*" I gasp out. *I am yours.*

He growls in primal approval. Then he's laying me back on the bed sans bra and seconds later I'm without my panties too. My thighs clench in response.

Not sure what about that thigh clench triggers him but he growls again, lifting and bending my knees so my thighs spread wide.

His finger runs down my slickened slit as he inhales the crotch of my panties. "Your pussy smells like heaven." His gaze settles between my spread legs. "And looks like it too. *Dolcezza.*" He shakes his head and adjusts the giant bulge in his slacks. "So fucking sweet."

There is no warning before his face is buried between my legs. Nothing about this reminds me of the past. It is Salvatore pleasuring me, not taking his own from my unwilling body. He inhales deeply and a guttural sound comes from deep in his chest.

Dio mio. I am going to die, and he isn't even touching me yet.

His tongue stabs into the heart of me and I gasp in shock, a moan following right after. It feels good. Better than good. This is bliss.

That marauding tongue pistons in and out of my overjoyed vagina like a mini dick and it's all pure pleasure. Every glide brings more noise tumbling from my lips until a deep thrust makes me shriek.

Salvatore lifts his head and smirks, his lips glistening. "Good thing I locked the door this time, or we'd have Rosa in here wanting to know what I'm doing to you."

His words only half-register. I'm still pulsing from the bliss of his tongue in my most intimate place.

"Do that again," I order.

"It would seem I am not the only bossy one in this relationship."

I don't dwell on his use of the word *relationship*, but I notice. How can I not? Even with my brain and body fully occupied by sensation.

"Salvatore..." His name is another demand while my hips tilt upward in a silent plea.

"Your wish, *bella mia*..." His head drops, but his tongue does not thrust back inside me.

Instead, he slides it up between my labia, sending shivers of delight along every nerve ending until he reaches my clit.

He circles it. Over and over again. Teasing me with hint after hint of what I *could* be feeling.

"Do it," I demand, my voice hoarse with need.

But he ignores me, sliding his finger inside me and dragging more of my wet arousal out only to spread it down to my bottom. This time when his fingertip presses there, it slides in a little.

In automatic reaction, my thighs try to slam together but his head is in my way. "Salvatore?"

He pushes his fingertip inside me.

Dio mio. It doesn't hurt. Not even a little. It feels good. Amazing. I should definitely not be enjoying this. Should I?

Why not? If it feels good. That's Candi's voice in my head and I like it better than the shrieking surprise of my own panicked inner voice.

Then Salvatore's tongue finally centers on the throbbing and neglected bundle of nerves at the apex of my labia. And both voices splinter into shards of nothingness as my brain goes static from an overload of pleasure.

Bucking up, I try to get closer to Salvatore's mouth. He nips and sucks at my clit, one of his hands traveling up my body to squeeze my breast and pluck at my nipple. Ecstasy sparks along the direct neural pathway between my nipple and my clitoris, creating a feedback loop that makes it all bigger.

So much bigger.

Suddenly, every muscle in my body contracts and I scream as pleasure so intense it borders on pain rushes over me. My body bows and Salvatore's hands grab my hips, supporting me as he continues to feast on my most intimate flesh.

The agony of intense pleasure goes on and on until it's too much. I try to drop my hips, but his hold stops my body from moving away from his mouth.

"It's too much," I gasp out.

Salvatore's tongue softens, but he doesn't move his mouth. He continues to stimulate over sensitized flesh until only moments later, I feel a second cataclysm building inside my core. He nips my swollen bundle of nerves and ecstasy detonates through me like an erupting volcano, leaving devastation in its wake.

My muscles lock, my uterus cramps, adding to the pleasure he's forcing into my body with his mouth.

My juices are running down my crack and he uses my arousal to lubricate my sphincter so his finger can slide inside that dark, secret place. Another orgasm crashes over me, sending me into blissful oblivion.

Chapter 31

SALVATORE

Bianca goes boneless. The kind of boneless that comes with unconsciousness.

Something I am well acquainted with. Although, usually when I knock someone out, it is not with pleasure.

Sitting back on my heels, I enjoy the view before me without a shred of guilt. She is mine.

That pretty pussy, lips plump and flushed from her climax, is mine.

Her thighs are spread wide, revealing how those delicious nether lips shine with her cream. She squirted the last time she came, and her juice is so damn delicious, I'm salivating for more.

But the whole point of this exercise was to relax Bianca enough to sleep. Her somnolence and the relaxed state of her body is proof I did my job.

I swipe the back of my hand across my mouth and then lick the pussy juice off of it. *Merda.*

She tastes like honey with a little bit of spice.

Miceli claims to have read some kind of study that said when two people are sexually chemically compatible, their arousal excretions taste good to the other.

Miceli is always reading weird shit like that. It's why he and Catalina get along so well. He's the brother she never had and he's the only one in the family who wants to know as much random shit as she does.

I thought he was talking out of his ass, but there is no hint of the underlying sourness I usually taste when going down on a woman. I don't find it unpleasant, but this?

It's fucking ambrosia.

Bianca's eyes flutter open, her blue gaze unfocused. "You can touch me whenever you want, if it will end in pleasure like that," she slurs.

Then her eyelids drift down again.

What is she dreaming about to prompt her to say that? It sure as hell is not the nightmares that keep waking her since those *bastardo's* attacked her.

My primal instincts growl in satisfaction at her words while lust prowls like a beast inside me, insisting I take her up on the offer and get myself off with her body. But I am no boy to allow my sexual need to dictate my actions.

My self-control is legendary.

Except around her.

I force that inner voice into silence. I can control myself. To prove it, I undo my slacks and shove them and my boxers down my hips so I can jack myself off. I will not go near the bed. I will not shove my aching dick in her tight, sweet pussy.

But fuck if I will wait one more minute to come.

Spying her panties on the floor, I grab them and shove them in my face, letting her fragrance drive my arousal higher. Then I wrap that soft silk around my cock, rubbing up and down with the pressure and speed I know will take me over quickly.

I'm leaking so much precum that I soak the panties with only a couple of swipes up and down my shaft and over my sensitive head. Shuddering, I hold back from coming, reveling in pleasure more intense than anything I have felt with a sex partner in a long time.

If ever.

I am not even inside her beautiful body, but watching her sleep? Her heavy round tits tipped with nipples still erect from her climax, and her pink pussy lips beckoning me, desire explodes in my blood like a roman candle.

My balls ache with the need to come. Squeezing harder, I increase the speed of my hand on my cock.

Ecstasy roars up my shaft exploding in streams of cum that land in pearly pools on her soft, smooth skin. A few drops shoot as far as the tops of her breasts, one small streak landing on the base of her throat, marking her as mine.

Using her panties, I swipe one warm puddle up so our scents are mixed on the silk and stuff them in my pocket. Then, using my fingers, I rub the rest of my cum into her skin so she will smell my primitive claim while she sleeps and it will imprint on her subconscious.

While my fingers are still wet with my release I gently rub them over her lips. Her nose wrinkles, but then my knees nearly buckle when the tip of her tongue comes out to swipe over where my fingertips have just been. Her lips smack and a soft smile plays at the edges of her mouth.

This woman is going to be the death of me.

My cock is still ready for action, but I shove it back into my boxers and then zip up my slacks where a dark wet spot from earlier shows just how turned on this woman makes me.

Using all my vaunted self-control I move Bianca under the covers, turning her onto her side to take pressure off her wound. Not that she seemed to notice it while my mouth was feasting on her.

I hide her too tempting body from the predator in me that wants to strip out of my clothes and join her. No matter how much I want to, I cannot bury my cock so deep in her body, she will feel me for the next week.

After I tuck the blankets around her, I lean down and kiss her forehead, lingering to inhale her sweet fragrance underlying the heavy scent of sex. It makes me want to do things I do not do with women.

Touch? Yes. Fuck? Definitely.

Hold in my arms while she sleeps? Never before. Not even Monica.

The need to protect Bianca, to keep her near, to know she is safe is constantly in the background. It is why I was there the morning she was attacked. Knowing she left work late and had no one to walk to the train with drove me to instruct my men to take me on an alternate route home. The one that made sure I would see her walking between Amuni and the subway station.

I am not like this.

I do not worry about my playmates. I do not think about women when I should be working.

She is an outsider. Off limits for the long term. Understandable that my libido does not care, but my primal need to protect and possess isn't hampered by that truth either.

Managgia la miseria!

No matter what Bianca wants to claim, she is just as affected. My scent calms her nightmares. *Mine.*

She shies away from other men, even when she is working, she keeps a barrier up between herself and everyone else. Except me.

Does she realize that?

It has to be some kind of pheromone compatibility. I bet Miceli's article talks about that too, but no way in hell am I asking my cousin about this shit.

He'll start thinking I'm getting serious about Bianca.

I'm not.

I can't.

After Monica, I vowed I would never again consider commitment to someone outside *la famiglia*. It's too risky. If I had told Monica the truths I planned to, she could have destroyed me and maybe even my pops. Instead, I had no choice but to destroy her and the man she partnered with.

They say your first kill is your hardest. I did a damn good job of hiding how true that was for me from my father and my uncle, the don. Executing the woman I had sex with and told I loved only hours before? Had been hell.

But that hellfire had forged me into the strong capo I am today. I no longer feel remorse when I have to kill for my family.

I will not let Bianca, another outsider, be my undoing. Or put *la famiglia* at risk for her.

That doesn't stop me wanting her, or needing to possess her. She is mine until the lust that burns like a thousand suns between us goes out.

If it ever does.

Deliberately stepping away from the bed where Bianca sleeps so peacefully, I ignore the taunting inner voice.

Then, in defiance of the desires I cannot seem to control with her, I go into the adjoining bathroom where I wash my face and hands, before patting myself dry with a hand towel. I do *not* sniff the towel before tossing it in the hamper.

Refusing to acknowledge how I immediately miss her taste on my lips and scent under my nose, I grab my shirt and pull it on, only to be inundated with the perfume of her pussy dried into the fabric from earlier.

I rip it off on my way to my bedroom. Seeing my empty bed only darkens my mood.

Bianca should be sleeping there, not in the guestroom.

Fucking inner voice is as much of a meddler as Rosa.

I stomp into the walk-in closet and drop my shirt with Bianca's juices in the hamper only to grab it back out again. I shove it against my face and inhale, my still hard cock pulsing with renewed need.

I fold it up so the spot that has her essence is protected from the air and tuck it into a drawer. After I pull on a fresh pair of slacks, I put the panties with our mingled scents into the pocket.

I count it a win when I don't hesitate to drop my dirty slacks into the pile for the dry cleaner.

Why not? They only have your cum on them. Not her delicious juices.

Fucking inner voice. My phone rings as I finish buttoning my new shirt.

Juniper. Finally.

I swipe to answer.

"De Luca," I say by way of greeting when I want to ask why the hell it has taken him two days to return my call.

We're supposed to meet later today. Why do I think he's not calling to confirm the appointment?

"Hey, Salvatore."

"Juniper."

"Uh..."

My sixth sense for trouble sends the hairs on the back of my neck to standing attention. And I walk-jog to my office, where I grab one of my Bluetooth earbuds and put it in my ear. I never wear both.

I need to be aware of my surroundings at all times. When I see people jogging on the streets, oblivious to the noise around them, I cringe. The least of the dangers around them is getting knocked down by someone they don't hear coming.

If Bianca had been wearing earbuds on her walk to the subway, she never would have reacted quickly enough to fight off her attackers until I got there. She would be dead.

The thought sends rage spiking through me.

"When are we signing papers?" I ask Juniper bluntly as I text Nerissa.

Salvatore: *Get a fix on Juniper's location. Now.*

Nerissa: *Do you know if he is with his phone?*

"About that," Juniper pauses.

I remain silent, letting him hang.

Salvatore: *He's talking to me on it now.*

"I got a better offer," Juniper finally admits, like my silence forced the words out of him. Weak. "No hard feelings. It's just business. Right?"

His death is going to be my business if he doesn't sell me those bars. "Who gave you the better offer?"

I don't ask what the offer is because it doesn't matter. Juniper is selling those bars to me at our agreed upon price, whether he signs the papers or we forge them after dumping the body.

"It's a property development group out of Boston. They offered me nearly twice what you did. How could I turn them down?" His hopeful tone tells me two things.

One, he hasn't signed papers with the developers. Two, he's hoping to drive the price up even further.

Nerissa: *Got a lock on his location.*

Salvatore: *Pick him up.*

Nerissa: *Ninety minutes out by car.*

Fuck. It would be too easy for him to be in the City to meet me like he promised.

Salvatore: *He's in Trenton?*

Nerissa: *At home.*

Not his store? Until his windfall inheritance, Juniper's only property was a rundown corner shop in East Trenton. He probably doesn't think he needs to worry about the shop, with the money from the property sale coming in.

Especially if he expects to drive the price up with rival bidders.

Black fury rolls through my body, but I control it, like I control all my emotions when necessary.

Chapter 32

SALVATORE

"Are you trying to jerk me around to get more money?" I demand over the phone to Juniper.

"No, man." He pauses. "I mean, if you want to outbid the developer, I'll listen to any reasonable offer."

Fucking Juniper.

My phone dings.

Nerissa: *Helicopter?*

Reaching the area by helicopter would take thirty minutes instead of ninety. I do a quick calculation in my head, accounting for Nerissa and her crew getting to the helicopter, the flight and then driving to Juniper's home. Assuming we can source a vehicle and have it ready at the landing site.

Best case it saves her team thirty minutes in real time to reach him. Worst case, it takes as long, or longer than the drive.

The Irish control Trenton. Calling on our connections in the area to source a vehicle prevents this from being a clandestine snatch and grab with the local mob none the wiser.

Getting approval from Trenton's mob boss to land the helicopter and do business in his territory alone could take longer than the drive south.

Cazo.

Salvatore: *No helicopter.*

Nerissa: *Roger that.*

Salvatore: *Keep the tracker on his phone live.*

Nerissa put the tracking app on his phone when he came to the club. She is going to enjoy *encouraging* him to keep our bargain. I'd do it myself, but he pissed her off with one too many innuendos uttered while leering at her tits.

Bad choice, Juniper, not checking your phone for spyware.

He is babbling about land values and development potential the whole time I'm texting with my second.

"Youse can't expect me to take the first offer that comes along. That's bad business, man."

"You want me to believe some developer from Massachusetts contacted you out of the blue to offer you twice what I did?" I let disbelief I do not feel infuse my tone.

This offer is legit. I can feel it in my gut. But who are the *stronzos* willing to outbid me?

"I'm not lying. It's Stellar Holdings. They're big in Boston."

More dark fury brews with the rage already bubbling like lava in my gut.

Stellar Holdings are big all over the East Coast.

Except New York.

Owned by the Lombard family, who are still known in our circles as the Lombardis, Stellar Holdings is one of the front corporations for the Boston Cosa Nostra.

What are the Lombardis doing messing with New York real estate? The whole fucking state is off limits to them without the godfather's approval. Buying in the City could be construed as an act of aggression against the Five Families.

No way is the Lombardi don that foolish.

Which means he is working under the auspices of the godfather, or with one of the other Families.

"Who contacted you?" I ask Juniper as I text an update to Severu and request an information dive by his wife.

"Does it matter?"

"Answer the damn question," I bark.

"Okay. Shit, cool your jets, *amigo*."

Juniper is not Latino. Neither am I. Does he think amigo is Italian?

"You are not my *amico*," I stress the proper Italian word for friend. "We are business associates."

"Nothing to stop us from being friends is the-ah? Me and your sist-ah got a thing, if youse know what I mean." His New Jersey accent is thickening.

Either he's drinking, or he's nervous.

"My sister certainly has a thing for men who keep their word in business," I inform him.

"Hey, hey, hey...I'm not breaking my word. We ain't signed nothing yet."

"We shook on our deal." In the mafia a handshake is as good as a signed contract and in some cases, more binding.

The consequences of reneging are more severe than anything the courts could impose. Those outside the life learn quickly that when they make a promise on a handshake, *we* expect them to keep it. Regardless of whether they know we are connected, or not.

"Look, I gotta go. Youse take some time and think about if youse wants to up your offer."

"Do not fuck—" The call disconnects before I can finish telling him not to fucking hang up on me.

Stronzo.

Maybe I won't allow Nerissa to teach Juniper the error of his ways.

I'll reserve that pleasure for myself.

Twenty minutes later, I get a text from my second.

Nerissa: *We lost the trace on his phone.*

Salvatore: *WTF? How?*

Nerissa: *He could be in a dead zone.*

Our spyware utilizes GPS data, which is accessible even when a phone is out of cell tower range. There are few places it would not continue to send out signal. But they do exist.

Salvatore: *Where was he when you lost him?*

Nerissa: *The NJ Turnpike. He exited and five minutes later, we lost signal.*

The New Jersey Turnpike could take him to Manhattan, or Boston, depending on what he does when he reaches the I-278 interchange. If he stays on the interstate headed north.

Nerissa: *There are two helipads near the exit.*

Someone is flying Juniper north, and it's not us. Whoever it is has technology on their helicopter to block GPS transmissions like we do.

He's on his way to meet with Stellar Holdings.

Fuck.

I send a quick text to Juniper.

Salvatore: *I want those bars. I am willing to pay.*

The greedy bastard better not make a deal with the Lombardis without letting me make a counteroffer. Assuming they give him the chance. If I had my hands on him, I wouldn't.

I text my don.

Salvatore: *We need to track a helicopter heading from New Jersey to Boston.*

Salvatore: *Scratch that. Probably New York.*

The paperwork has to be filed in each county where the bars reside before the transfer of ownership is complete. If Stellar Holdings know about my offer, they'll want to file with the county clerk's offices immediately.

It's not something that can be done online.

I text Nerissa instructing her to send teams to each of the courthouses involved to be on standby to stop the filing of the paperwork.

Nerissa: *On it. Where will you be?*

Salvatore: *Here.*

Where the hell does she expect me to be? Until we know where they are headed first, there's no point in me leaving the penthouse.

Nerissa: *You keeping watch over your unwanted houseguest?*

Pissed off by the out of bounds question, I make no effort to explain my actions, or lack thereof.

I'm waiting for the intel from Catalina and a conference with Severu before deciding on next steps.

The Lombardis would not risk a Cosa Nostra civil war.

It would be guaranteed destruction for them to go up against New York's Five Families. Which means they are working with one of us and believe the decision to buy property in our territory will not blow back on them.

One of the bars is in the Gambino territory, the other is in the Lucchese territory. Either family could have learned about the property sale. Or any of the other families, for that matter.

The don's wife has scary mad skills for gathering information. Her being the best does not mean she is the only one with the intel though.

If the Lucchese family is involved in the deal, my path forward is limited. Especially if the godfather is behind Stellar Holdings' offer. Why would Don Caruso hide his interest behind an outside company brokering the deal though?

Maybe, like me and Severu, he does not want the other Five Families to know about the bars changing ownership before it's a done deal. He's the only member of the Five Families that could broker a backdoor deal like this through another mafia without incurring the wrath of the other families.

That doesn't mean he is the only one who *would* do it, however. I can think of a couple of dons and three times as many capos who are arrogant enough to believe they won't be found out until the leverage is in their hands.

The godfather could have plans to use ownership of the properties as leverage himself. It's something he would have done back in the day.

Not so much lately, but maybe he's more on top of things than our last meeting would imply.

Nerissa: *Getting this deal signed and sealed should be your priority.*

Stuffing down my rage at her insolence, I call her. This is not happening over text.

"Who the fuck do you think you are to question my priorities?" I ask as soon as the call connects.

I don't yell. I keep my voice even, but there's no question I am pissed.

"Getting these properties under our control is more important than you getting your rocks off," Nerissa says, disapproval dripping from her tone.

What the actual fuck?

"Who is in the SUV with you?" I demand.

Her punishment will be commensurate with how many of her team overheard her disrespect.

Her pause says she realizes her mistake. "I'm alone in the back with the privacy panel up."

Do I believe her? "Put me on video call. Now."

Her angry face pops up on the screen. "Are you really checking to see if I'm telling the truth?"

"Show me."

Eyes narrow, her mouth set in a firm line, she turns the phone so I can see that no one else is in the backseat with her and that the privacy panel is in place. "Satisfied?"

"You do not chastise me." My words are clipped, my temper too close to the surface.

This is the third woman in my family to challenge my authority and integrity as their capo today. I'm not sure what I'm going to do to fix this problem, but none of us are going to enjoy it.

"Mamma said she caught you kissing the little stripper in your bedroom." Nerissa's words prove she is either obtuse to my growing fury, or unimpressed by it.

Neither is acceptable from my second-in-command.

"Bianca is not a stripper." Why I need to address that point before the issue of respect, I don't know, but I fucking do.

"You don't deny kissing her."

"I have no need to. Mamma did not *catch* me doing anything. She walked into my bedroom unannounced and *found* me kissing Bianca."

And doing other things my mother has no idea about because the angle of my body blocked her view of my fingers buried between Bianca's leg.

"Who I kiss, fuck or put in my bed is not your business, or hers." I can't be any clearer without breaking out the hand puppets.

"I thought you were smarter than that." Nerissa's condescending tone is the last straw.

First, she questions my priorities. Now, she's disparaging my decisions and my intelligence? Not happening.

"And I thought you were smart enough not to disrespect your capo," I bite out.

My word is law. My actions not up for her scrutiny.

"You're also my brother."

From boss to brother. Fuck. All the women in my family do think they are immune to my status.

"Ask Miceli how often he disrespects Severu. I'll give you a hint, it starts with zero and ends with never."

"I mean no disrespect."

"Then shut your mouth because it's leaking out around your tongue."

"Salva—"

Too pissed to continue this conversation, I tap to disconnect the call. When my phone rings seconds later, I send Nerissa to voicemail.

She texts next.

Nerissa: *I am sorry, capo. It won't happen again.*

Salvatore: *It won't if you want to remain my second.*

Something is going on with the women in my family and it's crystalizing around my very much wanted houseguest.

Chapter 33

SALVATORE

Thirty minutes after I hang up on Nerissa, Severu calls with information on the helicopter. It is headed for Boston, not New York, which gives us time we didn't think we had.

He also updates me on what Catalina has uncovered. "Henry Caruso's mother is a Lombard. Her brother is the current CEO of Stellar Holdings and their cousin is the don of the Boston Cosa Nostra."

"If Don Caruso is behind the offer from Boston, I cannot kill Juniper and forge his signature on the sale documents." A frustrated sigh gusts out of me. "Even intimidating him into taking my offer could cause a rift between you and the godfather."

"His behavior at the meeting with you and Miceli has already made that rift." Severu's tone matches my cold and even one.

Miceli might be the only other person who would realize it, but our don is as furious as I am.

"Do you think Don Caruso decided to back his nephew to replace him as godfather?" He knows what is best for the Five Families, and Henry Caruso is not it.

But a man changes when he is staring death in the face. Sometimes for the worse.

"Our godfather's interest in his legacy could be stronger than his concern for the longevity and prosperity of the New York Cosa Nostra," Severu says, mirroring my thoughts.

"He has to know that shifting support from you to Henry won't get him voted in by the Five Families council."

"Our godfather isn't thinking as strategically as he once did," Severu says heavily.

"I can't argue with that." A shift in his support will complicate the battle for the position of godfather and could lead to a bloody civil war.

A war Severu will win, but not without cost to *la famiglia*.

Out of respect for Don Caruso and fear of Severu's power, the other dons of the Five Families will back Severu as things stand. My cousin Giulia is married to the underboss in Las Vegas. Severu will get their vote as well. Chicago, Boston, Detroit and New England remain noncommittal. But with the Five Families behind Severu, it doesn't matter.

He has the majority. Remove Don Caruso's support, and the same two dons arrogant enough to try a backdoor deal with Juniper through a third party would put themselves forward for the position. Chicago and New England's dons probably will too.

There's a chance they will anyway.

None of those dons are happy about a man as young as Severu stepping into the role of godfather. The other dons are all at least twenty years my cousin's senior. Even Henry is ten years older than him.

And not a damn one of them would lead the Cosa Nostra into the future as well as my cousin.

"We need to know who is behind the attempt to outbid you with Juniper."

I agree before hanging up.

Catalina and Domenico Bianchi's tech wizards dig deep to figure out which of the Carusos is involved in the property deal with Stellar Holdings.

Juniper's phone records show he is in contact with a phone registered to Stellar Holdings, but there is no record of who that phone is assigned to. This does not surprise me. We don't keep records like that for the FEDs to find either.

There is no obvious link between Stellar Holdings and a particular Caruso either, Henry's family ties notwithstanding. Which in itself could be an answer. If Don Caruso were in contact with Boston's Cosa Nostra, there would be phone records to show it.

Maybe.

But we do know that with his family connections, Henry could be in contact through his mother or another unofficial channel, making him the more likely suspect.

My phone beeps and I see I have multiple texts. Two from my second and the other from Juniper.

Nerissa: *Juniper's phone tracker is working again.*

Nerissa: *He is in a moving vehicle headed away from Stellar Holdings head-quarters.*

Juniper: *Don't worry, amigo. I'm busy tonight but tomorrow you can make me another offer.*

While I'm still typing a response, another text comes in.

Juniper: *You're going to have to up your game though. Tell that sister of yours to be a little nicer, yeah? Stellar Holdings really know how to treat a guy.*

I will get the deeds for the bar properties, but Juniper may not going to live to enjoy the money.

I text Nerissa.

Salvatore: *Keep me informed of his whereabouts.*

Then I text Juniper, picturing myself putting a bullet hole in the center of his forehead the whole time.

Salvatore: *Great. Looking forward to it. Don't worry. We know how to take care of our friends.*

And our enemies.

The alarm I set to remind me to wake up Bianca for lunch goes off. My fury banks as satisfaction settles in my chest.

Bianca did not wake up screaming in the past two hours.

When I walk into the guest bedroom, my beauty is on her side, the covers shoved down to her hips. One arm is tucked under the pillow and her other rests over her belly, leaving her gorgeous tits on display.

My cock wakes up, ready to party.

Shaking my head, I approach the bed and the curvy Siren lying there. There's no time to have sex right now. Taking time out for lunch is pushing it, but I have to eat and I'll have my phone with me. I can monitor information as it comes in.

Right. No sex. You might as well eat at the desk in your office after you wake up Sleeping Beauty.

Okay. Sexual gratification is not totally off the table. I don't have to be sitting at a desk or a table to monitor my phone. I set my phone, screen up, on the nightstand.

There. Problem solved.

Focusing on the buffet of temptation laid out before me my cock strains against my slacks. I reach out and cup one of Bianca's lush breasts, brushing my thumb over her nipple. It stiffens as quickly as my cock, turning the color of a raspberry almost instantly.

So fucking pretty.

My mouth waters for a taste of those sweet peaks, but there is something I want to taste even more.

Not wanting her to wake just yet, I carefully tug the blankets down until her entire body is exposed to my gaze. The scent of her arousal and the cum I rubbed into her skin earlier clings to her, sending hot desire pounding through my veins.

Cazzo. This woman turns me on like no other.

And you thought one night would be enough?

I shake off the thought but can't dismiss the one that comes right after. *A month of nights will not slake this lust.*

That should put a lid on my libido. Allow me to wake Bianca without touching her.

It doesn't.

I prefer to keep sex transactional. Bianca will not allow it. I still want her.

It has been more than a decade since I spent more than a couple of nights with the same woman. Yet Bianca has been in my bed for the last four nights. I have never allowed another woman to sleep in my penthouse, much less my bed. And I fucking moved her in.

Bianca is the exception to too many rules.

And knowing that does nothing to dampen the raging inferno of need inside me.

Fuck.

Rules be damned. I want to taste her sweet honey and that's what I'm going to fucking do.

My mind flips through scenarios that don't put her on her back. I should have gone for a different position earlier. I won't make the same mistake now.

The stitches come out tomorrow, but that does not mean she is healed.

With a detour to lock the door, I make my way around the bed.

My movements are stealthy as I climb onto the firm mattress, barely causing any disturbance. Who knew my training to be a made man would come into use in a situation like this?

But the idea of waking Bianca up with my tongue buried between her legs is too much temptation to resist. She gave me permission to touch her whenever I want, as long as I give her an orgasm, which I fully intend to do.

At least one of us will be satisfied this afternoon.

Salivating for another taste of that sweet, juicy pussy, I lie down on my side and gently lift her leg so I can rest my head between her thighs, my mouth pressed against her pussy lips. She mumbles but does not wake and I grin before licking her from her perineum up to her clit.

Her faintly tart, but mostly sweet, earthy flavor bursts across my tongue. Delicious.

Caressing her gently with my tongue, I stimulate her so she grows wetter and wetter. Little mmming sounds drop from her mouth and her hips cant against my face, but her limbs are still loose from sleep.

I could spend all afternoon feasting on her, but there's too much happening right now with the Juniper deal. Wanting her to wake on her orgasm, I simultaneously slide two fingers inside her slick, hot channel and suck her swollen clit.

Her tight vaginal walls clamp around my fingers and she wakes with a cry, her cum soaking my hand.

Bianca tries to close her legs in reflex, but my head is in the way.

Gripping her thigh with my free hand, I pull my mouth away from her still pulsing pussy. "Do not move. If you move, I stop."

She's good for at least one more orgasm and her body knows it, even if her mind has not caught up yet.

Chapter 34

BIANCA

My body reacts to Salvatore's words on a primal level before I even parse what he's saying in my conscious brain.

I go completely still, the only movement in my body my lungs sucking in and expelling gusts of air.

I woke from a dream about Salvatore to an orgasm courtesy of his mouth and fingers. Ecstasy is still sparking along my nerve endings. His tongue against my clitoris is too much, but do I move to stop him?

No, I do not.

Before I fell asleep, I told him he could touch me whenever he wants. As long as it ended in this carnal bliss.

I can barely believe I said that. Wasn't sure I'd even managed to utter the words I never expected to say, I was that out of it. But I did and I cannot regret it.

This kind of pleasure drowns out everything. Physical pain. Memories. Worries. All of it.

My second climax hits me like a freight train and I scream. Salvatore's name.

With a final kiss to my nether lips, he shifts his head from between my thighs and scoots backward off the bed.

"What was that?" I ask, still panting.

His grin is predatory. "You needed to wake up to eat your lunch and take your pain meds."

"So, you thought, hey, I'll wake Bianca up with my mouth on her?" Is this guy for real?

He wipes his fingers over his lips and then licks my juices off of them. "Can you think of a better way?"

The earthy gesture sends another pulse of remembered ecstasy through my lower half.

"You could have nudged me, or jostled my shoulder, or I don't know...said my name loud enough to wake me." I'm a light sleeper.

At least I usually am, but I slept through him taking the covers off of me and getting situated with his face up close and personal with my ladybits.

"This was more fun."

"For me maybe." He hadn't climaxed before, and another impressive erection is tenting his slacks now.

"I enjoyed it, trust me, Bianca. But if you are offering to return the favor, I will not turn you down."

Am I? Do I want to taste him? I think I do.

Oral isn't something the monsters that ripped my virginity away forced on me that night.

This is something of myself I can give that no one has taken from me. Salvatore never has to know he's my first blowjob. Unless I really suck at it. Then he might figure it out.

But I want to try.

I sit up and scoot around so I'm sitting on the edge of the bed, my feet dangling over the side. "I'm offering."

I don't try to sound sultry. Pretty sure I couldn't pull that off. But I don't hide how much I want this either.

He comes around the bed with flattering speed and stops in front of me.

Putting the side of his hand under my chin, he lifts my head so our eyes meet. "Are you up to this?"

The ice around my heart that has protected me for so long melts a little more. This man.

"I want to taste you too."

"I can get myself off." He makes the offer but shifts a little closer.

I smile. "Not necessary."

"*Brava ragazza.*"

Something unexpected shivers through me when he calls me *good girl*. I want to be good. For him. And only him. The rest of the world can take me as I come.

All gentleness vanishes from his gaze and his hand snakes around my nape to grab my hair in a tight grip. "Take me out."

Desire gushes from my core at his demand and the hold he has on my hair. Because it makes me feel safe. Like everything else, he has this under control.

After undoing his belt and then his slacks, I slide the zipper down carefully so I don't catch the tented silk of his boxers on the teeth. I push the slacks down his hips first, paying no attention when they fall to the floor around his feet.

I'm too focused on the monster dick barely covered by the silk boxers in front of me. Pulling the waistband away from his body, I gasp as his erection surges up, the leaking tip an angry purple.

Eating me out did this to him. Making me come turned him on so much that there's a dark, wet spot on the front of his boxers. Inhaling his scent, I push his boxers down. Because of the elastic, they get caught on his hips.

I don't care.

His erection is bobbing in front of my face, tempting me to taste. To touch. To smell. I lean forward and inhale, taking in the unique scent of his precum only to jerk my head up and stare at him.

I've been smelling this since I woke up. "Did you come on me after I fell asleep?"

"Yes." There's no apology in his eyes.

I don't want there to be.

"Good."

"*Cazzo*. You are perfect for me *carina*."

A smile is flirting at my lips as I press them against his rigid column of flesh. I kiss him. *Hello, Salavatore's sex.*

Eager for a taste, I flick my tongue out and lick him from root to tip, swiping my tongue over the pearly essence beaded on his slitted opening. Tang slides over my tastebuds with a hint of salt.

More. I want more.

Licking and swirling my tongue all over his bulbous head, I lap up every bit of it I can get.

He's swearing in Italian and I think that's Russian? Is that Arabic? Not even sort of willing to stop what I'm doing to ask, I let the litany of incomprehensible words pour over my head.

Then I open my mouth as wide as I can and take him inside. My lips stretch as he immediately hits the roof of my mouth. Flattening my tongue against the underside of his hardness, I caress the warm, velvety skin.

"*Cazzo!*" His grip on my hair tightens and he pulls my faced forward, pushing more of his dick into my mouth.

He hits the back of my throat and I gag a little.

"That's right, my beauty, gag on my cock like the good girl I know you are." He says it all in Italian.

Which makes it hotter somehow.

"Open your throat for me. Let me in."

For a panicked second, I don't know if I can trust him enough to do it, to give him control of my airway like that. But then I just...do.

He pushes forward as I swallow and relax my throat. He roars as loud as any lion and then groans pushing more of his sex down my throat.

Power surges through me. I am a sexual being capable of giving and receiving pleasure. My past has not neutered my sensuality. It may have been in hiding, but it is still there.

Salvatore pushes deep, stretching my throat and the last bit of air exhales through my nose. My airway completely blocked, I put my hand on my throat to feel him inside me. A shudder works its way up my body.

He is inside me. I didn't think that I would ever allow this to happen. And I'm not just allowing it. I want it.

So much.

Laying his hand over mine, he slowly pulls his hips back until his hardness is in my mouth, not my throat. I inhale precious air through my nose and suck on his large sex, hollowing my cheeks around him.

"*Cazzo,*" he groans. "That's good, *brava ragazza.*"

The mix of English and Italian is endearing. And hot.

I swirl my tongue around his erection before I suck on him again, repeating this over and over, getting more and more of his precum to savor.

"Your mouth is so fucking good, I am not going to last," he says gutturally.

The words of praise add another layer of pleasure to what I am doing. Unbelievably, my clit is pulsing with the need to climax. *Again.*

Salvatore surges forward. "Take my cum, Bianca."

Air expels through my nose as he pushes into my throat again and then no air can move in or out. Only hot, viscous fluid jetting down the back of my throat.

"Swallow," he demands.

But I'm already doing it, taking his essence into my body. He's still coming as he withdraws so his semen pulses onto my tongue and spills out the corners of my mouth.

The way he is looking at me, he did it on purpose. He likes seeing his cum on me. No wonder he released on me when he masturbated earlier.

Will he do it again? When I can watch?

Does it make me a freak if I ask him to?

Not wanting to release him yet, I breathe through my nose and savor his taste. He swipes at the corner of my mouth with his thumb before pushing it between my lips as he withdraws his sex.

I suck his flavor off his thumb, my hand sliding between my legs and rubbing my clitoris with my middle finger. His big hand covers mine, his rougher finger sliding over my slick nub, sending shards of ecstasy through me.

"Come for me *brava regazza*." Pushing his heel against my finger, he thrusts two fingers inside me and hooks them. "Now."

I see stars. Entire super novas. As my body explodes for the third time since waking from my nap.

My head falls forward against him, my heart racing from the pleasure, my lungs sucking air like a spasming vacuum. His hand lands on the back of my head and he holds me like that as my breathing begins to slow and my heart no longer feels like it will beat out of my chest.

His phone rings, the sound a shrill interruption to the private cocoon we have created between us, his world intruding.

He swears, his fingers tightening their grip on the back of my head, but then he lets his hand fall away.

"Take a shower while I answer that." He caresses my cheek before stepping away.

I don't watch him as he picks up the phone. I jump up and hightail it into the bathroom, needing a minute of solitude to process what just happened.

What I did. What I let him do. What I *wanted* him to do. I crave that hardness inside me and not just in my throat. Vaginal walls contracting at the thought of him claiming the most intimate part of me, I force myself to step into the shower and turn on the water.

It is only a few seconds before the water is hot enough to step under. Steam begins to fill the space around me as I run my hands over my tingling body.

My mind playing both this morning and just now on repeat, I let the hot water soak my hair before washing it for the second time today. I use extra conditioner and leave it in while I wash the rest of my body, taking inventory of how things feel different and yet the same.

My skin is sensitized but it is also still *my* skin. Washing my vulva with the hot water, my fingers slide through the silky slickness at my core. I shudder.

That feels so good.

I'm tempted to pleasure myself again, but Salvatore said something about needing to eat lunch. I am ridiculously reluctant to lose the chance to spend time with him, so I quickly finish washing and turn off the shower.

Salvatore leans against the wall, his eyes locked on me like lust filled missiles. "If only we had time to do all the things I want to you."

"I thought we needed to wait to do them until I am more healed," I tease breathlessly, grabbing a towel to dry off.

"Until I fuck you through the mattress? Yes." He pushes away from the wall, coming to stand in front of me. "But there is so much pleasure to be had without putting your healing wounds at risk."

Things like putting his head between my legs while I am on my side? That's a pretty amazing way to wake up. Heat pools in my core as the memory of waking to an orgasm plays in my head.

Salvatore's body tenses and the air between us thickens with want. "Stop thinking about it."

"What if I don't want to?" I drop the towel and look up at him through my lashes.

Who *is* this woman?

His hands clenched in fists at his sides, he shakes his head. "No." But then belying his denial, he yanks the towel from my hand. "You are a lot of temptation for such a tiny thing."

"I'm hardly tiny." Okay, five feet, four inches isn't exactly tall, but it's not a shrimp either.

And if one of the strippers from Pitiful Princess was on the other end of a teeter-totter, I'd send her flying.

I like my body, but it's not tiny.

He makes a sound like I'm oh-so-annoying and turns me around so he can dry my back. "Compared to me, you are."

Well, I guess that's true. Still. Not tiny.

"Your presence takes up all the space in the room and my thoughts," he mutters the last bit. "Does that make you feel better?"

"Yes."

He finishes his gentle pats on my back with the fluffy towel. "It's a little red from earlier, but the stitches look fine."

"It's probably just red and has nothing to do with earlier." Plastic surgeon, or not, skin takes time to heal.

"Probably? You don't know?"

"As you pointed out so adamantly, I can't see that spot on my back and can barely reach it with my fingers." Not that I'm about to touch it. I don't want to accidentally pull on the stitches.

Removing the gauze bandage before my shower was easy. I just pulled on one corner of the medical tape. If being on my back earlier had caused any damage, the gauze would have been stuck to my back with blood.

It wasn't.

He carefully dabs the towel around the cut. "Does it still hurt?"

"A little."

"I shouldn't have had you on your back earlier."

"It doesn't hurt any more than it did when I woke up this morning," I tell him honestly.

"Rosa told me you refuse to take pain meds during the day." He brushes the towel over my butt cheeks, one at a time.

It feels like a caress, and I have to stifle the moan that wants to come out. "It's not unbearable and I don't like taking meds I don't have to."

The air shifts from movement behind me and then he's drying my legs, pushing them apart to gently wick moisture from between my legs. I'm not sure all of it is water from the shower.

A soft whisper of lips at the base of my spine and then Salvatore stands and taps my bottom. "Get a move on, or I'm going to be eating a lunch wrap in the car on the way to Oscuro and you are going to miss out on your time in the rooftop garden."

"Why can't I go up with Rosa?" He says I'm not a prisoner, but he sure wants to control my comings and goings.

Not that there's actually any *goings*.

"You don't want my company?"

A week ago, sheer self-preservation would have forced me to say *no*. Now? I can't deny the truth to a man who not only saved my life, but has taken very good care of me since, and keeps my nightmares at bay.

Impossible not to crave his company.

The best I can do is hold back saying how much.

Chapter 35

BIANCA

Access to the rooftop garden is via a set of stairs at one end of the terrace off the living room.

The view from the terrace is impressive enough, and Salvatore has to tug me by the hand to keep me going.

But from the roof? *Accidenti*. The 360º view steals my breath right out of my chest. This is my city and seeing it like this does something weird inside my chest.

Our family home had been in East Rutherford because my dad couldn't afford the cost of living in Manhattan on what he made working for Lorenzo. However, everything important in our lives took place 30 minutes away by train. In Manhattan. Genovese territory.

I'd gone to school here. Even after mom left and dad put me in public school, he fixed it so I attended one in Manhattan. Every dance lesson and recital happened here. Every job I'd held. The three years I lived in Queens with Mr. Ruhnke were the same. It was a place to sleep, just like the apartment I lived in with my roommates.

This is my home.

For the first time, I acknowledge moving away is going to be hard.

Leaving Salvatore's home might even be harder and it's not because of the luxury. Though breathing in the fresh air on the rooftop and basking in the warmth of the sun's rays isn't a hardship.

The sky, not even visible from the street in parts of the city, is blue with puffy white clouds.

The rooftop garden itself is as incredible as the view. Statuary are placed among the plants and shrubbery laid in a way that reminds me of the pictures I've seen of the formal gardens at the home where my *bisnonna* grew up in Italy.

Salvatore leads me to a large rectangular wrought iron table set for two in the shade of a freaking conservatory.

I can't call this elegant building with carved white wood dividers between beveled glass windows a greenhouse. It looks like it belongs attached to that same Italian villa.

Again, I feel that punch to my gut from how rich Salvatore and his family must be to own something like this in the middle of New York.

He pulls a chair out for me, and I sit down. His spot is at the head of the table to my right. Despite the size of the table and grandeur of the garden, it feels intimate.

My ovaries swoon a little and I grit my teeth against renewed arousal.

What is this man, this mafia capo, doing to me?

Salvatore presses something on the wall of the conservatory. When the wall slides back to reveal a familiar opening, I realize the dumbwaiter comes all the way up to the roof. The only thing I'd been interested in, when I was trying to find a way out of the penthouse, was going down.

He withdraws two covered plates and places them on the table as well as two glasses and a pitcher of Rosa's freshly squeezed lemonade. I've watched her make it. The housekeeper crushes mint leaves before pouring the hot lemonade over them and then chills it after.

It's delicious and my mouth waters for a taste.

I pour some in each glass before taking the lid off my lunch and smiling. "Rosa must believe I'm getting better. This is my first lunch here that does not include pastina soup."

Asparagus spears lay over a bed of pasta farfalle aglio e olio. I used to beg my nonna to make the bowtie shaped noodles because they are my favorite. And I like them best served this way, tossed in olive oil, garlic and grated parmesan. A fat link of grilled sausage is arranged in a neat line of slices to one side.

If we were eating inside, the meat would not be on the same plate as the pasta, but I guess some rules get bent for outdoor dining.

"It is my favorite. This is her way of apologizing for calling my integrity into question."

Even as I store the bit of information that we share the same favorite pasta, I wince at the anger lacing Salvatore's tone. "I'm sure that's not how she meant it."

"Never mind Rosa, or my mother, if she's the next topic on your conversation list. I want to enjoy my lunch." He gives me a pointed stare.

I shrug. "If you say so. Only I think you love both women and you're mad at them right now, but you'll realize eventually they're doing their best to look out for you."

A harsh bark of laughter erupts from his mouth. "You are lousy at following directions. I would punish one of my soldiers for disobeying a direct order like that."

"It's a good thing I'm not one of your soldiers then because I don't like orders," I sass.

His hot gaze sweeps over my body. "It is indeed."

Three guesses what he's thinking about and the first two don't count, girl. My pesky inner voice holds more snark than any words I say out loud.

From any other man, the insinuation would get a big eyeroll from me. But Salvatore's eyes on me sparks a very different reaction, one I don't attempt to hide from him.

There's no reason to. I'm going to enjoy the physical intimacy while it lasts and hope that the sensations he wakes in me do not go dormant when our relationship, such as it is, inevitably ends.

We talk about my business courses over lunch and what I hope to do with my degree when I get it.

"I've been saving up and I'm going to move away from New York."

"Why?"

The better question is why I have stayed at all. At first, I had a place to live, which made going to college more doable. Then after Mr. Ruhnke died and I got thrown out, I was already set up with financial aid at QC.

To establish residency for instate tuition somewhere else could take up to two years. With no guarantee the grants I receive would transfer, or that I would be able to get others.

And maybe a tiny part of me has always hoped my mom or sister would reach out, that I would be invited to move to Boston to be with them.

"I want a home with a yard," I say, answering the why of leaving. "A life that doesn't require working two jobs just to make ends meet without a roommate."

"You don't have to leave New York to get that, just move outside the city."

"It's not always that easy." Now that Lorenzo knows I'm still in the City, my need to move far, far away is growing by the minute.

I'm pretty sure I can't go back to Amuni and risk running into him again. My only excuse for sticking around after that first confrontation is desperation. I need the job, but I need to be safe more.

Weird how getting attacked and stabbed reworks your priorities.

Are you sure it's not having a gorgeous, rich capo moving you into his penthouse and promising to help you get settled when you move out?

"There you are!" A woman's voice cuts across my mocking inner voice. "I brought you this dead plant Pietro was carrying around like it's a freakin' Faberge Egg."

Dread bubbles upward until it's choking me at the words *dead plant*. Salvatore told me he would send Pietro for my African violet.

"He should have just thrown it into the trash." Nerissa plops a bedraggled African violet in a large margarin container on the table with zero care. "It's not an orchid. What do you even want with it? "

I grab Vee. Yes, I named my plant. Vee for violet. Not inspired, but it works. I talk to Vee too. When I'm alone.

Looking for some sign it can be saved, I brush the end of a stem where it's obvious a flower has been violently torn off. My roommates haven't killed her, but the violet is knocking on death's door for sure.

"What did they do to you?" I ask Vee, drawing my own conclusions from its condition.

The loss of its beautiful ceramic pot hits me like a blow in the center of my chest. Mr. Ruhnke gave me the pot made by a local artist when I graduated from high school. It means...meant...almost as much to me as the violet.

Someone must have broken it, and they rehomed my violet in this plastic container. How much damage to the roots did they do?

A quick look at the bottom has me groaning. No holes for water drainage also mean any watering done was from above. And the soil is moist. Too moist. The leaves that aren't curled and brown at the edges are too pale a green for a healthy violet.

"How could they do this much damage in a week?" I wonder out loud.

Salvatore looks from me to the plant with a frown. "Who?"

"My roommates. Who else? If I had to take a guess, they broke the pot, over-watered when they replanted it in the butter tub and put it in the windowsill to *help it recover*." Queens has fewer skyscrapers than Manhattan and being on the fourth floor means our apartment gets several hours a day of direct sunlight on our south facing wall, the only one with windows in it.

Usually, I keep my plant on a table far enough away from the window for sufficient indirect light. I give it two hours a day in the windowsill, but any more and the leaves lose their dark green color and the beautiful deep purple flowers fall off their stems.

Any less, and pretty much the same thing happens.

"They broke the pot?" Salvatore frowns. "On purpose?"

"No. Of course not, but when they have parties, it can get pretty wild." I always make sure to put Vee someplace safe before the party goers start showing up.

After the near disaster when I put it on top of the fridge for safekeeping, I started putting Vee on the top shelf of the closet during their parties.

Looking at the butter tub, my heart squeezes with grief. Mr. Ruhnke picked out the ceramic pot especially for me. It was glazed the same blue as my eyes with gold specks that he said reminded him of light that shines from inside me.

I don't feel very shiny right now. I feel like the connection I had to the last person to really care about me is both suffocating and drowning in that awful little plastic container.

Nerissa puts her hand out. "Give it to me. I'll throw it away. When you leave, you can get another plant. It's not as if that one is some rare genus of violet, or something."

I shrink back in my chair, hugging the near dead plant to my chest. "It's the only one of its kind because my friend, Mr. Ruhnke, gave it to me."

I have managed to keep it alive for six years. I'm not about to throw Vee in the trash now.

Also, why is a mafia soldier talking about the plant genus?

Maybe I'm being a little judgy here, but botany isn't something I would expect Nerissa to have studied. I'm only familiar with the term because of all the research I did on how to care for an African violet in a city apartment.

"Sentimentality." Nerissa sneers the word.

I've been living with her brother, the capo, for nearly a week. She does not intimidate me.

"Not all things have to be worth tons of money to have value," I sneer right back.

Nerissa's dark eyes flare with surprise before she masks it. She's not used to people standing up to her.

The look on Salvatore's handsome face can only be described as pride and he's directing it at me. "Who is Mr. Ruhnke?"

He's asked this before, and I never gave him a full answer. Sexual pleasure seems to have loosened my tongue though, because now I want to.

"My father died when I was sixteen. I didn't have anywhere to go." Not anywhere I was wanted.

An old ache echoes through my heart. I once asked Mr. Ruhnke if it would ever stop hurting. He said some wounds never heal completely, but they get easier to live with.

After today, I finally believe him. Because the slashes carved into my soul when I was sixteen are finally not the deciding factor in my life experience. It is amazing. And a little scary.

Maybe the way my parents abandoned me when I needed them most will get more bearable too. Right now, though, every time I think of that period of my life, anxiety and pain rip my heart to shreds all over again.

My solution? Don't think about it.

Yet, here I am, ready and willing to revisit it to explain the importance of the African violet to Salvatore.

"No family?" Nerissa's stance softens slightly, and her expression turns almost sympathetic as she sits down across from me at the table.

"No." None that wanted me. "I tried a shelter, but I couldn't sleep with everyone around me."

The reasons for that I am *not* willing to revisit mentally, much less go in to verbally.

"What did you do?" Salvatore asks, his own expression back to the stoic mask of capo.

I recognize it for what it is now. A protection, similar to the façade of uncaring I wear most of the time myself. I'm not sure why he needs that protection right now though. This story is my pain to bear.

Neither of them asks why I didn't go to social services. It's the mafia way. We don't trust outsiders and we especially don't trust government authority.

The realization I still think like I'm in the life hits me hard. Maybe I didn't leave my mafia roots as far behind as I thought I did.

Chapter 36

BIANCA

"I started sleeping between the dumpsters behind my high school."

"Bet you didn't sleep much," Nerissa says, like she knows.

I shake my head. "It was Manhattan, not the Bronx, but that didn't mean it was safe."

Sometimes, I marvel that I survived those first weeks without a home without suffering more physical trauma. Maybe my dad made a better guardian angel in death than he had a protector in life.

"So, you grew up in Manhattan?" Nerissa asks.

She's not as clever as she thinks she is. I recognize fishing when I hear it.

"I went to school in Manhattan."

"Where did you live?" Nerissa asks bluntly, clearly aware that I hadn't actually answered her question.

Changing my last name at eighteen makes this question a safe one to answer. "Before my dad died, we lived in East Rutherford."

Thirty minutes by train and forty-five minutes by car from Manhattan, it's in New Jersey, a territory that does not officially belong to any of the Five Families. Lower ranking soldiers can afford to live there without fear of stepping on another don's toes.

So can a lot of other people.

"How does Mr. Ruhnke come in?" Salvatore asks.

"He was the head janitor. He found me sleeping between the dumpsters one morning." I had finally gotten exhausted enough to sleep past the sunrise that usually had me packing up and getting out of there before the cleaning crew arrived.

"What did he do?" Salvatore asks when I stop talking, lost in my memories.

I shake myself, physically dislodging the tendrils of fear those memories still evoke. "He gave me a safe place to sleep and made sure I had what I needed to survive."

"He took you home to his wife?" Nerissa asks. "And she wasn't furious? I mean..." She gestures to me. "You're sex on a stick. You would have been a real temptation to a man even back then."

No doubt Nerissa considers her words a compliment, but they only bring back more devastating memories that have nothing to do with my savior. I don't let a flicker of that show.

Knowledge is power. And I don't want this hard woman having any power over me.

"Mr. Ruhnke wasn't like that." Not like the monsters that still invade my dreams. "Anyway, his wife was dead already and he didn't take me home with him."

More feral than a stray cat born in the streets, there was no way I would have gone to his house with him then. That came later, when I moved in with him so he didn't have to move in with his oldest son after Mr. Ruhnke broke his hip.

Officially? I was Mr. Ruhnke's ward and caregiver. Unofficially, I was the daughter he'd never had that he liked way more than his daughter-in-law.

Who I have yet to text back. Oh well. It's not like we're friends.

"He called social services on you?" Salvatore demands, his tone implying he finds my gratitude for that fact incomprehensible.

"The system isn't all bad. There are some amazing foster families out there." Candi's mom, who was actually her foster mom, is one of them.

"There are also nightmares," Nerissa says, like she has personal experience with that.

I nod. "True. But Mr. Ruhnke didn't put me in the system."

"What did he do?" Salvatore asks, like he's getting impatient for the answer.

I smile. "You're way too used to being catered to, you know that, right?"

"I am capo. The world moves at my direction."

Nerissa gasps. "Why would you trust her with that, Salvatore?"

"She already knew," Salvatore tells his sister. "Marco dated one of her roommates and had loose lips."

"Did you tell papà?" Nerissa's frown is downright scary.

I'm glad I'm not Marco.

Salvatore jerks his head in affirmative. "Yes."

There's a wealth of meaning in that one word. Marco is definitely in trouble with the consigliere. His punishment for being so candid about *la famiglia* isn't something I even want to contemplate.

I would feel bad for him and my part in getting him in trouble if he hadn't been such a jerk when he was dating my roommate.

"Marco likes to throw his weight around." In more ways than one.

The boyfriend that takes my spot on the sofa sleeper is a huge improvement over the violent mafioso.

"Enough about that *stronzo*. What did this Ruhnke guy do, if not put you in the system or offer you a home himself?"

"He did offer me a home." The only one I was able to accept at the time. "Mr. Ruhnke fixed up a supply closet in the basement of the school for me."

Then he put a new lock on the door in front of me and gave me the only keys to it so I could sleep at night without being afraid someone would come in.

"You lived in a janitor's closet?" Salvatore asks, his voice dark with disapproval.

"There are worse places," Nerissa says before I can.

I nod in agreement again. "Between the dumpsters on the cold ground was one of them. I had a bed. A desk. Heat. A place to shower. Food."

"What did the janitor expect in return?" Salvatore asks suspiciously.

"For me to bring my grades back up." My straight As has turned into Ds and Fs that year.

I'd stopped trying to keep my grades up when I realized my best attempt at being the perfect daughter wasn't going to convince my mother to make a place for me in her life.

"Was that all?" Salvatore's tone is skeptical.

Looking away from him, I push the remaining pieces of farfalle around on my plate. "His only other rule was for me to stay safe."

Mr. Ruhnke was adamant I couldn't sell drugs or my body to earn money. Which was never going to happen after my experience living with my dad.

Only I'm not sure what he would think of me becoming a pole dancer after he died. As long as I was safe, I think he would have approved. And I did stay safe, even when it meant finding another job.

I could not have foreseen the job at Amuni would put me back on Lorenzo's radar.

"He insisted on paying me an allowance, just like I was really his kid," I add.

Even after Mr. Ruhnke finally convinced me to contact my mom and she gave me a ten-thousand-dollar payoff to leave her and my sister alone.

Ten thousand dollars felt like a fortune to a sixteen-year-old. Five thousand dollars two years later wasn't nearly as impressive.

After Mr. Ruhnke sat me down and went over what it would cost to rent my own place, buy food and pay utilities, I realized that initial ten K wouldn't last more than a few months.

With roommates it could last longer, but at that time, roommates were not an option for me. For lots of reasons.

SALVATORE

For her to stay safe.

Why do those words hit so hard? And why do I have this inexplicable urge to find Mr. Ruhnke and thank him?

Standing from the table, I put my hand out.

Bianca hugs the bedraggled violet more tightly to her ample chest.

"Bring it with you."

Her beautiful blue eyes narrow in distrust. "Where?"

"To the conservatory."

"I knew it was too bougie to be a greenhouse."

Her words make me smile.

"That's the De Lucas," Nerissa says snarkily. "Full of pretentious airs."

"Since you are a De Luca, I guess that means you are too." Bianca sasses my sister as she skirts around the table to join me.

She shows no fear of my intimidating second-in-command. Her courage impresses me.

I like the way Bianca calls Nerissa a De Luca too. Even though my sister never changed her last name from James, Bianca doesn't question that my second is also my family. I told Bianca that Nerissa is my sister and she believed me.

Because my beautiful lover trusts me on a gut level whether she's willing to admit it, or not.

Pulling her by the hand, I lead her into the warm humidity of the conservatory. The light, temperature and moisture in the air are kept precise for the very rare, very expensive orchids residing in pots throughout the space.

Bianca pulls her hand from mine and I have to force myself not to grab it back. She walks to the nearest orchid and fern grouping. Her fingertips hover above the petals of my Koki'o Orchid, as if she knows how rare and fragile it is.

After the barest brush over one of the perfect green leaves, her hand drops.

"It's beautiful." Bianca's head turns first to the right and then to the left. "They're *all* beautiful and every pot is unique."

Her brow furrows as she slides her fingers across the uneven glaze on the orange and gold somewhat misshapen pot holding my Shenzhen Nongke Orchid. It is the most expensive specimen in my collection but isn't much more impressive than the pot it is in.

Only blooming once every four to five years, the rest of the time, it looks like any other orchid plant with light green foliage. The last time it bloomed, I sold each flower for more than I paid for the plant.

I am, after all, a businessman.

"That is my mother's first attempt at throwing and glazing ceramic," I inform Bianca.

"And you have it in here."

"Housing my most expensive specimen."

"That's sweet."

"I am not a sweet man." My mouth twists with distaste on the word *sweet*.

I'm glad Nerissa didn't follow us into the conservatory to hear that.

"If you say so." Bianca's tone implies she doesn't agree.

I suppose it is alright if *bella mia* thinks I am sweet. "Don't call me that in front of others," I order.

"I can think it, but I can't say it?" she teases as no one is allowed to do to me.

"Yes."

"Fine." She points to my Shenzhen Nongke Orchid. "Is that what Nerissa meant by a rare genus?"

"It's one of them. Every orchid in here is difficult to obtain, but none as unique and scarce as that one." I bought many of them on the black market.

Not this one though. The first in my collection, I purchased that one directly from the Shenzhen Nongke Group for nearly a quarter of a million dollars. More than I would have paid if I had been willing to be put on the waiting list.

I was not.

I bought it to save a woman from being expelled from a university she did not actually attend. The woman, I killed, but the orchid I kept.

"And you put it in your mother's pot."

"At my father's request. He rescued the pot from the garbage after finding my mother in tears."

"Because it didn't turn out the way she expected?" Bianca asks.

"She considered it ugly, a complete failure and told my father she was never going to work with ceramics again."

"But her fingerprints are hidden in the clay, her DNA mixed with it under the glaze. He didn't want to let the pot be destroyed," Bianca says dreamily.

"I'm not sure my father thought of it that way, but he has never liked seeing my mother upset."

"So, he asked you to plant one of your orchids in her pot?"

"Yes. And ugly, or not, it works for what it was intended to. Putting that orchid in it was fitting." There are many ugly things in my world.

Torture. Death. Greed. Human weakness.

What I did that resulted in me being the final owner of the orchid, was one of ugliest of them all.

Necessary in my world. But ugly. I'm capable of heinous acts others could not stomach to see, much less perpetrate. It makes me a hell of a capo, but not a good man.

"After I planted the Shenzhen Nongke Orchid in it, papà arranged for mamma to visit my conservatory."

"Did it make her happy?"

I shrug. "She went back to learning to cast pots, paint and glaze them."

"So, it worked."

"Yes."

"That's really romantic."

"If you say so." My lips twist wryly. "No question, my father is soft for my mother."

Their marriage was arranged, like so many in our world, but they fell in love and my father has never taken a mistress. My mother treats him like a king and she is his queen.

There was a time I thought I would have that. Now I would rather slit my own throat than be that gone on a woman.

Bianca frowns. "You say that like it's a bad thing."

"Weaknesses can be exploited."

"Is love and devotion a weakness?" she asks like she really doesn't know the answer.

"It's fucking inconvenient. His need to make her feel better ended up with me having to repot every plant in my conservatory." Orchids and ferns alike.

"Because your mom kept giving you pots?"

I nod. "My dad said if I threw one away, he'd set fire to my conservatory to hide my cruelty from my mother."

Pretty blue eyes wide with surprise, Bianca throws her head back and laughs, her red hair rippling over her shoulders.

I wait for her to finish.

She's still smiling when she says, "It sounds like you're pretty soft for your orchids."

"I made more than a million dollars on the flowers from the last blooming cycle. The plants might not cost what a Faberge Egg would, but your Mr. Ruhnke could retire on what I would get for selling them."

She sobers. "Not soft, just practical."

"You'd make a mistake to believe anything else."

The look she gives me is unreadable as she reaches out to touch my Shenzhen Nongke Orchid's pot. "There can be beauty in ugliness."

"You think?"

"Don't you?"

"I don't think about things like that." Especially not whether this woman could find any in my scorched soul.

Bianca walks from one orchid pot to the next. "Mr. Ruhnke never got a chance to retire, but I think even if he had, he would have been more impressed by the ceramic pots made with love than the rare plants living in them."

Mr. Ruhnke is dead? Fuck. No wonder the plant means so much to her.

Opening a cabinet under the bench I use to prune and replant when necessary, I pull out two pots. "These are mamma and Rosa's latest gifts to my conservatory. Which do you want for your violet?"

Bianca stops running her hand over the smooth sides of a pot glazed in tans and creams.

Her eyes take in the two I am holding with longing. "You are giving one of those to me? But your family made them."

"It would make either woman happy to provide a new home for your plant."

She looks down at the bedraggled African violet.

"I don't think Vee is going to survive my roommates not so tender care." Bianca's voice is light, like it's a joke, but her eyes darken with grief.

The violet can be saved, but it will take effort.

"You named it?"

She shrugs. "It's the only living thing reliant on me."

And that means she gives a plant a name? As expensive as my orchids are, I have never considered naming any of them. If I did, I would call the Shenzhen Nongke Orchid, *Betrayal*.

"Which pot?" I lift both for her inspection, putting us back on track.

"But..."

"Choose, or I will choose for you Bianca."

"You're so bossy."

"We've discussed this. It's in my job description."

"You are not my capo though."

I am your everything. The words are on the tip of my tongue, but I don't let them past my lips. I am her *temporary* lover, nothing more.

My brain rebels against that reality and I frown. "You work for me. You live in my territory. *I am your capo.*"

"Uh, I'm pretty sure that's not how it works. Besides, I don't live in Manhattan. I live in Queens."

"Not anymore."

"That's right. You had your soldiers move me out of my place without my say. And just where am I supposed to go when this thing that isn't a thing between us ends?"

"I told you, I'll make sure you have someplace to live where you don't have to sleep on a closet floor."

She looks down at the violet held closely to her chest. "I would prefer not to return to an apartment filled with plant assassins, but I doubt I can afford anything you would find acceptable."

"Leave that to me."

"You want me to trust you?" Disbelief replaces the grief on her face.

"Why so shocked?" Doesn't she realize how many people rely on me? Trust me? How much *she* already trusts me? "My word is good."

"I'm sure when you make promises to your mafia brethren, you keep them."

"I keep every promise I make."

"If you say so."

I'm starting to dislike that phrase, but especially the way she says it. "I shouldn't have to."

"Only in your world is that true. The rest of us have to earn trust and only give it when it's proven we can."

She cannot be that naïve. "That is not true. Too many people trust without proof of worthiness."

"I'm not one of them."

Neither am I. It doesn't matter though. "You will trust me."

"The pot with the lemons and blue swirls," she says, avoiding a reply to my statement. "It reminds me of my nonna's dishes."

I set Rosa's pot on the bench and return mamma's to the cabinet. "I'm not surprised. It's a popular pattern in Southern Italy and Sicily. Rosa made this as practice before making pieces to replace those lost over the years in the dish set passed down through her family."

"It must be amazing to be able to do something like that." Bianca sounds wistful.

"If you would like to try it yourself, I am sure my mother or Rosa will teach you." Probably both, considering how much the women like my temporary roommate. "Give me your violet."

Bianca approaches me reluctantly. "You really think Vee can be saved?"

"Yes. Haven't you ever had to nurse a plant back to health?" I have had orchids show up worse for wear, despite paying more money for them than some people spend on a car.

"This is the only plant I have ever owned."

"I, on the other hand, have all the experience necessary." I waive my hand around to indicate the healthy orchids and their shade ferns. "Trust me with your plant, Bianca."

She hands me the little butter tub. Our fingertips brush as I take it from her. Electric current travels up my arm from the contact.

This woman and what she does to me.

I put the plant down on the bench beside Rosa's pot and turn back to Bianca. She's looking up at me like I'm something amazing, her blue eyes glowing with approval.

I pull her against me and claim the mouth I find irresistible, kissing her until we are both panting and I'm wishing I'd turned the windows opaque when we came in. I've come with her twice already and my body is still clamoring for more.

When we fuck, it is going to measure on the Richter scale.

That is just sex though.

This? I picture the bedraggled plant on the bench behind me. This is something else.

Why in the hell am I insisting on nursing her unimpressive, garden variety African violet back to health?

Nerissa is right. We could replace it with another just like it easily.

But it wouldn't be the plant a dead man gave her.

Manaja. "Go finish your lunch while I re-pot Vee."

She's got me calling the plant by a name now.

"Uh...okay. I'll just go spend time trading barbs with your sister. Sounds like fun."

"You'll survive." My voice is brusque as I shove down the need to warn my underboss to be nice to my lover.

Merda.

I am not soft for this woman.

That is a weakness I will never indulge in again.

Chapter 37

BIANCA

Nerissa has her own plate of nearly finished food in front of her when I come out of the conservatory. Putting her phone away, she watches me with cold eyes as I walk toward the table.

Finishing what is left of my lunch loses its appeal at the look on Nerissa's face. Instead of sitting down, I decide to explore the rest of the rooftop garden.

I'm trailing my fingers in the water of a small fountain when I hear the sound of steps on the white gravel behind me.

I turn with a smile, expecting to see Salvatore.

It's his sister. *Che palle.*

My smile slips from my face. "Hello, Nerissa."

"Miz James."

"Really?" I ask, rolling my eyes and shaking my head at the same time.

Her perfectly shaped brows draw together in a frown, her dark brown eyes as cold as Central Park in the dead of winter. "My brother may be mesmerized by your pussy, but I am not."

"Uh. Good?" I don't want this barracuda anywhere near my ladybits.

"I'm not letting any *puttana egoista* take advantage of my brother."

Selfish bitch? "I'm really getting the feeling you don't like me."

Nerissa's...excuse me, Miz James. No. Fuck that. She's going to call me a bitch?

Nerissa's eyes narrow. "You think you've hit the jackpot with my brother, worming your way into his home and playing on his sympathy."

I match the other woman's judgmental gaze with a dismissive glare. "First, I didn't worm my way anywhere. Pietro kidnapped me on your brother's orders and Salvatore refused to let me go home."

"Because he felt sorry for you," she inserts.

"Anyone else, and I'd say sure, but you know your brother better than me. Do you think the capo does anything he doesn't want to do? That he could be influenced by pity? Because I gotta tell you, I have my doubts."

"He wants to fuck you."

"Yeah, I got the memo."

"Playing hard to get isn't going to get you an engagement ring.

"Wow, that went from blinding him with my magical vagina to trapping him into marriage by withholding it. Pick a lane, why don't you?"

"When my brother marries, it will be to a mafia princess who can carry De Luca heirs and make the Genovese family stronger." Nerissa looks at me with something close to sympathy.

Wow. Okay, maybe not a raging bitch then.

Not an ex-pole dancer. I get it. "Listen, Miz James, I get the protective sister thing." I've played that role and with a lot more reason to. "But I'm not looking for any man to be my *jackpot*. I can take care of myself."

"My brother—" she starts to say.

I roll my eyes. Hard. And interrupt her, "Read the room, Miz James. Salvatore is a rich and powerful capo. I am a cocktail waitress. My vagina isn't capable of casting the spell you think it is."

And also, how many times is Miss Possessive Pants going to call Salvatore *my brother*? It's starting to feel a little pathological.

"My brother..." There she goes again. "Is not going to get taken in by a hot body and pretty face. I won't let him."

And she thinks he needs her protection? Does she know her brother?

"Your compliments leave a lot to be desired."

"It's not a compliment. You're used to trading on your sex appeal, but unlike Daryl Ruhnke's family, I won't let you take advantage of Salvatore."

Okay, definitely a raging bitch with a side of stooping low enough to scrape the ground.

"Shut your nasty mouth about Mr. Ruhnke. I never took advantage of him." I never did anything to get Mr. Ruhnke to help me, especially not what Nerissa is implying.

I'll never know why I was the one kid he chose to help. I sure wasn't the only teenager at that high school who was struggling, but Mr. Ruhnke picked me, and I'll always be grateful.

That doesn't make me a leach. It makes me lucky.

Then it hits me. "I didn't tell you Mr. Ruhnke's first name."

I never used it. At first it was a sign of respect and a way to keep emotional distance. Later, it meant something else. He told me when I said Mr. Ruhnke it sounded the same as when his sons called him *dad*.

I never called him anything else after that.

"How do you know his name was Daryl?"

"The same way I know his family are still furious about how you took advantage of an old man."

She looked him up? How? We were only in the conservatory for a little while. "Seriously, how did you find all that out so fast?"

The look she gives me. "You were in there with Salvatore for thirty minutes."

I was? It sure didn't feel that long to me. That kiss though. It could have lasted hours and I wouldn't have noticed.

"The name of your high school is on your employment file," Nerissa says dismissively. "Finding the janitor named Ruhnke that worked for them wasn't hard. A quick search on social media did it. One of the posts that tagged him was by his son after Ruhnke's death."

Then she found the son's phone number, or more likely work number considering what time it is, and called him. If she wasn't such a nasty minded troll, I would have a lady boner for her efficiency and tech savvy.

"If you try to play my brother, you'll get burned," Nerissa warns me darkly. "Just ask the last woman who tried to milk him for money. Oh, wait..."

My lips zipped, I refuse to take the bait.

The second gives an exaggerated look of having just remembered something. "You can't." She pauses dramatically. "Because she's dead."

Okay. There's a lot to process here.

First, Nerissa is a bona fide drama queen.

Second, a woman tried to make Salvatore De Luca her mark? Was she living under a rock? Anyone in New York knows you don't mess with the De Lucas, even if you don't know they're Cosa Nostra.

Third, that woman is dead.

And Nerissa is just itching to tell me about it. So, of course, I don't give into the curiosity burning like a hot coal in my chest.

"Who do you think killed her?" Nerissa demands when I remain silent.

"I don't know." But my brain is spinning with the possibility of what she's implying. "Your bitchy tongue, maybe?"

"You little..." Nerissa takes a threatening step toward me.

I instinctively fall back into a defensive stance, ready for her attack.

"What the fuck is going on?" Salvatore barks as he powerwalks over the gravel path toward us like an avenging demon.

"Your sister was just about to tell me about the woman you killed. I mean, I guess I'm making an assumption it's just the one." Two assumptions really because I'm also assuming Nerissa is implying Salvatore killed the dead woman.

I mean his second as good as said it, but it's still an assumption.

The look Salvatore gives his sister is lethal.

I expect her to drop from a heart attack any second.

Showing she's got more fortitude than I give her credit for, Nerissa glowers right back at her brother. "You already told her about you being a capo and she witnessed how you handled the men who attacked someone in our territory."

Not attacked *me*. But *someone in their territory*. A distinction I'm sure is important to the second.

"So, you decided it was okay to trust an outsider with my secrets?" Salvatore asks with glacial disgust.

Nerissa's face changes, and she looks sick at the realization of what she'd been about to do to make a point.

I'm not doing so great myself. The reminder that Salvatore considers me an outsider hurts in a way that it shouldn't.

Not if this thing between us is just sex.

Then Nerissa's whole demeanor changes and she smiles at me.

The smile of a hyena just before going in for the kill. "Do you know why my brother keeps rare orchids?"

Clearly, it's not for the money he earns on the blooms. A million dollars might be life changing for someone like me, but for him? It's basically pocket change.

"You ask a lot of questions you can't wait to give the answers to." I make a gimme motion. "Go ahead. Tell me."

Salvatore looks like he's going to say something to stop her, but he doesn't.

He wants me to know too.

"Every day he tends to them is a reminder that we cannot trust outsiders. That *he* should never trust a woman just because he's fucking her."

I don't know how the orchids connect to the dead woman who tried to pull something over on Salvatore, but somehow, they are his constant reminder not to trust another woman like her.

Another outsider. Another woman like me.

My gaze shifts to him, as my heart seeks assurances my brain insists I don't need for *just sex*.

But the avenging demon is gone. In its place is a man so aloof, there might as well be ten-feet-high steel wall between him and any possible emotion he could ever feel for me.

My heart proves my brain wrong. Because that hurts. A lot.

SALVATORE

I harden my heart to the flash of pain in Bianca's blue eyes. She needs to remember this thing between us is physical and transitory.

We both do.

My preoccupation with her has to end. Forcing myself to look away from my beautiful redhead, I let my sister see the fury and disappointment fighting for supremacy inside me.

She winces and her mouth opens. Probably to apologize to me. I do not fucking care.

I put my hand up. "Shut it."

Today is not the day for my second to go rogue. It looks like Nerissa did not get that memo though.

There is one sorry she needs to say that I want to hear. "Apologize to Bianca."

"For what? Telling her the truth?" my sister asks incredulously.

"I heard your whole conversation." Or at least most of it.

I started listening in the second I realized that my sister was no longer at the table. I have listening spyware installed on all my crew's phones and devices, but she and Pietro are the only ones who know.

Choosing to confront Bianca when she knew I could listen had to be deliberate on Nerissa's part. Did she think I would be swayed by the garbage she spewed?

"I didn't say anything wrong."

"I disagree. Ignoring for a moment what I stopped you from telling her, you disrespected a guest in my home. You made unfounded accusations against Bianca and you *will* apologize to her for them."

"They weren't unfounded."

"Did it sound like I was making a suggestion?"

Nerissa's lips twist like she's sucking on sour candy. "I am sorry if I disrespected you, Bianca."

Before Bianca can reply, I shake my head.

"Do better," I bark.

This is no longer only about Nerissa's words to my lover, it is about Nerissa's respect for me as her capo.

Showing more smarts than she has so far today, Nerissa's head snaps to the side so she's looking at Bianca. "I am sorry for accusing you of being a leach."

"I wouldn't mind if you included calling me a selfish bitch in that," Bianca goads.

My lips twitch but I don't let myself smile.

"I should not have called you that," Nerissa forces out from between clenched teeth.

She does not like apologizing. We have that in common.

Bianca nods. She's not offering forgiveness for an apology given under duress, but she's not turning her back on it either. Admiration for her dampens some of my rage toward my sister.

"Go to my office and wait for me," I say to Nerissa.

It's time to remind her that being family does not make her immune from the expectations of mafia hierarchy or discipline.

Without another word, my second turns smartly and heads toward the stairs down to the terrace.

"Don't be too hard on her. It's her job as your sister to watch out for you, even when you don't want her to."

Bianca's words hit me on the raw. How the hell is she standing up for Nerissa after my sister did her best to warn Bianca off?

The idea that Nerissa could have succeeded fills me with rage. Bianca isn't from this life. Learning I killed my ex would terrify her. Not that Nerissa left much doubt about what happened.

Bianca is too smart to miss the implication of my second in comand's disloyal words. Why isn't she bothered? She's angrier about the implication that she took advantage of Ruhnke than worried I killed my ex.

She's not afraid of how I handled Monica's betrayal because Bianca has no intention of betraying me, *or* sticking around.

Inexplicably, that knowledge fills me with more fury than my second's insubordination.

Bianca doesn't care if Nerissa doesn't like her. She sure as fuck doesn't make any effort to get along with Pietro. She's made it clear she doesn't want to be here and only stayed because she finally accepted that she couldn't care for the wound on her back by herself.

Despite me promising to help her get settled, she'll probably start looking for a new place to live as soon as the surgeon gives her a clean bill of health.

My hands fist at my sides, every muscle in my body rigid with tension. If she tries to leave me, Bianca will find out the difference between being a prisoner in my home and a guest.

How does that make you any different than the human traffickers you despise? The voice in my head sounds uncomfortably like my mother's.

But I know I'm different. I'm not keeping Bianca as a sex slave. I will never force myself on her, but she isn't leaving until she's fully healed and has a decent living situation to go to.

Until I'm *ready* for her to go.

And if that never happens?

Slamming the door on that question, I barely control my rage at my sister for creating this situation and Bianca for not caring about it.

"How the hell would you know?" I demand of Bianca harshly. "You don't have any family and how I deal with mine is none of your business."

Bianca blinks, that stoic façade cracking to show hurt at my words before her face is once again wearing the emotionless mask I'm coming to hate. "My family circumstances don't matter."

"They do if you think you know more about a sibling relationship than I do." I have a sister.

Bianca has no one. She said so herself.

"Transitioning to capo at your age can't be easy," she says, ignoring my jibe. "Navigating relationships that are both family and professional makes it even more complicated."

Why is she trying to reason with me?

She wants to leave. My success as capo doesn't matter to her. Neither do I.

"How I treat my soldiers has even less to do with you," I grit out, ignoring the truth of her words.

"You're right, it's none of my business, but that doesn't make my observations any less valid. Maybe you should talk to Severu. It seems like he's faced a lot of the same challenges."

She's still trying to be reasonable. Nice. While my temper is overheating like a nuclear reactor with a broken cooling system.

I am not running to my cousin like a whiney child. "You know too fucking much about the Genovese Family. I'm going to tell my father to cut Marco's tongue out."

Or I'll do it for him. I smile at the prospect.

"*Che palle.*" Bianca shakes her head. "I've never seen a smile that scary."

She looks impressed, not scared. Fuck. This woman!

"Come on. I've got more important things to do." At least that's what I'm telling myself.

Why does it feel like nothing is as important as this woman?

That is fucking madness and I am not going there. *La famiglia* comes first, last and always. It is the mafia way.

"I'll stay up here for a while." The way she says it, like it's her decision to make slices through the last tether on my temper.

Striding forward, I reach for her. She tries to evade me, but she's not fast enough and I swing her up into my arms.

"My orders are not suggestions." No matter what the women in my family seem to think.

Shock of all shocks, Bianca does not squirm, or try to get down.

She pats my fucking chest. "Okay, caveman. But you're going to spoil me into thinking I don't have to walk anywhere with this kind of service."

She's laughing at me. It's in her tone. Her eyes have lost that dead look and sparkle with mirth. At my expense.

I like it so much better than the fucking mask, I don't tell her off for it.

Chapter 38

SALVATORE

I don't hesitate to tear a strip off my second after leaving Bianca in her room with an order to rest though.

"The fuck are you thinking? Talking to me like that?" I pound my fist on the desk.

My second is fucking lucky she is my sister because I will not deal with her the way I did Pietro. But I have no doubt when she finds out what her punishment is, she'll wish she'd gotten off with a couple of punches.

"I meant no disrespect, Salvatore. I apologized. I shouldn't have said things the way I did."

"You shouldn't have said those things at all."

She looks ready to say something else and I slice my hand in the air. "No, you do not fucking speak again. Your earlier disrespect is the least of my worries."

I wait to see if she's going to try to interrupt again, but this time Nerissa's lips remain sealed in a flat line.

Good. "You were about to tell an outsider something you shouldn't even tell one of our own without my permission. That's the closest anyone on my crew has *ever* come to betrayal."

Nerissa winces, guilt and affront both glinting in her dark eyes. "I would never betray you," she says forcefully.

"What would you call it?"

Her shoulders slump, the anger draining out of her. "A mistake. I shouldn't have brought Monica up to her, but Salvatore, I don't want to see you hurt."

"You think she can hurt me?" My disbelief makes my tone even sharper.

"Anyone can be hurt when they fall for somebody. Even you. If Dad's people hadn't investigated Monica at Uncle Enzo's request, who knows how much money she would have taken you for before she disappeared with her partner."

Reminding me of my idiocy in the past isn't improving my mood. "I'm thirty-one, not twenty anymore. And Bianca isn't asking me for money."

"Not yet, she isn't." Nerissa holds up her phone, like it's proof of something. "I checked into Bianca's past. Did she tell you that Daryl Ruhnke is dead?"

"Yes."

I want to shut my sister down, but I am capo. I cannot allow emotions to rule me. So, I wait for her to continue. I will hear everything she discovered.

"I called his son at work. He told me how Bianca took advantage of his elderly father. Ruhnke paid her an allowance. It's not hard to guess what she did to earn that money."

"Ho detto basta." I bark. That is enough. "Bianca told us about that."

She'd said it made her feel like one of his children, something she'd clearly treasured.

"Why did she tell us? Was it to soften you to the idea of taking care of her financially?"

"You are so far off base, you're not even on the playing field. Bianca categorically turned down my offer of five thousand dollars for a single night of fucking." No way would she have doled out sexual favors for a measly few bucks every week. "She did not have a sexual relationship with a geriatric for money."

"Salvatore...listen to me," Nerissa insists. "Bianca convinced that geriatric to leave her fifty-thousand dollars in his will. She refused to sign it over to the family even though she has no real right to it."

"Cazzate!" What kind of bullshit is this? "If he left the money to her, it's hers."

Fifty thousand is nothing. To me. Fuck.

What portion of a school janitor's estate would fifty-thousand dollars be?

But if she has a fifty-thousand-dollar nest egg, why was she so worried about losing her job over taking money for sex? Was turning me down part of a long game to soak me for cash?

My gut rejects that idea. It doesn't fit who she is.

Or who you believe her to be.

"Did Ruhnke's son say anything else?" I force myself to ask.

I am not weak. I don't hide from the tough shit.

"He wanted me to convince her to meet with him and his brother and sister-in-law."

"What did you tell him?"

"To fuck off. I'm your second-in-command, not his damn messenger."

That sounds like my sister. Short tempered and unwilling to give an outsider the time of day.

"You didn't think it was strange that he was willing to tell a complete stranger about his family business?"

"Outsiders tell grocery story clerks their life story."

"He obviously had an agenda. He wanted you to convince her to meet with the family."

"That doesn't mean he was lying about the will."

"It doesn't mean he was telling the truth either." I shake my head.

My sister is usually much more cautious about believing unconfirmed intel.

"Give me some credit, capo. I planned to order a copy of the probated will."

"I am only going to tell you this one more time: I am your capo. I am not a twenty-year-old with dreams of true love and a house full of blonde babies. I have not been that man since the night I killed Monica."

"I know, Salvatore, but—"

"Zitto." Shut up. "Investigating Bianca's past was smart."

Nerissa's lips don't tilt into a full smile, but her expression turns pleased, and she relaxes.

I tap on the desk once. "Telling me about your intention to do so would have been smarter."

I tap again, this time more forcefully. "Almost telling her about Monica was not smart at all."

I tap a third time. "Assuming the intel you gathered was the only side of the story and confronting Bianca about it was short sighted, something my second cannot be."

Giving my second the benefit of the doubt, I ask, "Did you ask Bianca about the inheritance or for further information on the allowance?"

Maybe I missed enough at the beginning to misinterpret the conversation I overheard.

Nerissa swallows audibly and shakes her head.

"You thought scaring her with a story from my past about how I handle thieves was a better approach." It's not a question.

"She pissed me off."

I can imagine. Bianca has snark down to a science and my sister is used to being deferred to. Even before I made her second-in-command, she was a top soldier on my father's crew, not to mention his daughter.

"And that excuses you revealing mafia secrets?"

Nerissa's jaw sets stubbornly. "I was trying to watch out for you."

She still thinks she is in the right. When she is so fucking clearly not. Why?

"Did papà tell you to run a background check?" I know the order didn't come from Severu.

My cousin would have had his own people do it. The same team I'm working with right now to figure out who is trying to outbid me for the bar properties. And he would not hide doing it either.

He would tell me.

Nerissa's expression says it all.

"You are no longer on the consigliere's crew. You are on mine," I inform my second.

As if she could forget. Except, she did exactly that. Launching an investigation into Bianca without consulting me first.

"I know that, Salvatore. You have my loyalty. That's why I did what I did."

"No, you did it because you think I am weak. And stupid."

"No." Nerissa's tone is adamant, her expression horrified. "He's our father, Salvatore. Of course, I did what he asked."

"We are the damn mafia, Nerissa, not a fucking family company. I am your capo and my word is law. He is counselor to our don, that does not make his orders supersede mine."

"I know that."

"Then you know what has to happen. If I let you get away with this shit, I *am* weak." And we both know I am not.

Contrary to what her actions imply.

She clasps her hands behind her back. "Do what you have to do."

"For the next two months, your pay will be split between the top tier soldiers as a bonus for their loyalty."

Nerissa sucks in a shocked breath.

The punishment is a blow to her pride. She can easily live without that income, but for the next sixty days, she will be reminded of her disloyalty to me.

So will the rest of our soldiers.

Nerissa will lose respect from our crew and will have to work to regain it. She will have to fight to keep her position as my second-in-command.

Like I fight with every action, every decision, and every reaction to maintain the fear and respect my crew and the rest of the Cosa Nostra have for me.

She fucked up and now she will have to fix it. With them. With me.

That knowledge is dawning in her eyes.

"And Nerissa? If you ever call Bianca a bitch again, I will take it as a personal slight against me."

"She's not your wife, or even your girlfriend!" Nerissa argues.

"She is my girlfriend. She is living in my home. She is mine."

My sister's eyes go wide and then she scowls. "Have you told mamma and papà?"

"They are both aware she's living here." No way would my mother have kept that information from my father.

"Salvatore."

"Basta!" I raise my hand. "Do you understand?"

"Yes," my sister grits out.

We both know what happens to soldiers shortsighted enough to blatantly disrespect their capo like that. And it's not something my sister wants to experience.

"And Nerissa," I say before dismissing her. "I will have her background investigated, but not by you. If I find out you disobeyed me on this, being demoted and returned to our father's crew will be the least of your worries."

BIANCA

The temptation to eavesdrop on the conversation between Salvatore and his sister is strong, but I resist.

Mostly because I need to process. Not nap. Process.

I don't like the pain I felt when Salvatore referred to me as an outsider. Later, when I could tell he was trying to, if not hurt me, at least shut me down, I felt more compassion for him than anger on my own behalf.

Whether or not he wants to admit it, the war he's fighting inside himself over how to respond to his family as brother vs. capo is plain. Yes, he got short with me, but how obvious was it that he was compensating for his frustration over Nerissa's behavior?

I can hardly blame him for dismissing my advice on handling a sibling when he doesn't know I have one.

The way he rubbed my nose in my lack of family sucks though. Almost as bad as his sister's implication that I somehow took advantage of Mr. Ruhnke. Nerissa's words were cruelly similar to what Mr. Ruhnke's adult children said when I moved in with him.

It wasn't about me. No matter how they want to paint it.

He'd fallen and broken his hip at work. He needed help while he recovered. His daughter-in-law wanted him to move in with her and his son and their kids while he recovered. Mr. Ruhnke loved his grandchildren, but he didn't want to live with them.

His younger son offered to move into the family home in Queens to watch over it. Only, Mr. Ruhnke confided he was worried that while he was convalescing, his kids would pack the house up and put it on the market.

His children had been pressuring him for years to sell the house, divide the proceeds between them and move in with his oldest son's family. They insisted Mr. Ruhnke didn't need all that space and with the proceeds from the sale, his oldest son could afford to buy a larger house to accommodate them all in a nicer neighborhood.

It was win-win. Except Mr. Runke hadn't wanted to move from the home he'd shared with his beloved wife and raised his children.

So, with a mix of fear and determination, I pushed myself to get over my aversion to sharing my space with another person. I was determined to stop his sons from forcing Mr. Ruhnke to leave his home of forty-two years.

It worked and he got to stay in his home until his death.

If his daughter-in-law thinks I'm answering her text after her husband trash-talked me to Nerissa, she's delulu.

It's bad enough they kicked me out of his house the day after he died, but they didn't let me attend the funeral either. I owe his family nothing.

For the sake of his memory, I've been polite to them and respected their wishes about the funeral, but I'm done being nice.

Whatever they want they can suck it.

Maybe it shouldn't matter to me if Salvatore thinks I'm a greedy scammer, but it does. Whatever lies they told Nerissa about me, she's going to repeat to Salvatore.

Che palle. I should have listened in on their talk in the office. Then I could be ready to defend myself.

Because I want him, even if he is an ass sometimes and over-the-top protective pretty much all the time. His touch does not spark panic, but desire.

Until I met him, I assumed having a partner, much less a family was totally out of reach. My mom and sister may never be my family again, but if I can have sex with a partner, I can build my own family.

Yes, I can go the single parent route. I've thought about it and in every realistic scenario, I'm in my forties by the time I build up enough savings to be financially secure enough to adopt. That's not too young to become a parent, but it means living alone, without a family, for at least two more decades.

But if I can let a man into my personal space, I can hope for something other than being alone. I could be a part of a family again, even if it's just the two of us.

Continuing sexual exploration with Salvatore is the key I never thought I'd find for the lock on the door holding all those possibilities on the other side.

Keep telling yourself it's all about the future and not about having Salvatore in the now.

Can you muzzle your own inner voice?

Okay, so I want Salvatore. So, I have feelings for him that make no sense. It's too soon. He's too arrogant. He's tactless, bossy, grumpy and part of the mafia I got kicked out of like garbage.

And so damn sexy, my ovaries have learned a whole new set of dance moves for him.

I feel safe with him. He makes me feel like nothing and no one can hurt me when he's around.

Even Nerissa's words only pierced so deep because he was there and part of me knew he would show up any minute and shut her down. Which he did.

I can fight my own battles. I've been doing it a long time. I don't need some billionaire mafia prince to take care of me.

But having someone stick up for me? Since coming to stay in Salvatore's place, I've discovered that feels amazing. And when he does it, little chinks of the wall around my heart fall away.

That scene on the rooftop ripped out more than a chink of my protective armor though. It left a big chunk of my heart unprotected.

I'll just have to rebuild the wall. Because Salvatore wants my body for a limited amount of time.

And I can't let myself get emotionally invested to the point that walking away from him will leave me as uninterested in other men as my past trauma.

It starts by taking back some of my control.

First, I'm going back up on the roof and soaking in more spring sunshine. Second, Salvatore isn't carrying my sleeping body into his bedroom tonight.

Because I'm going to be there already.

If he wants me to sleep in his bed, he doesn't get to say when that happens. It's either when I want it to happen too, or not at all.

You'll give up sleeping deeply for a point of pride? I don't think so.

For once, my inner voice is talking garbage. Because, yeah, I so will give up sleeping with Salvatore if he thinks it's only going to happen on his say so.

He might be capo, but he's *not* dictating all the terms of our physical relationship.

It is *not* transactional.

It *is* temporary.

It is *not* limited to the times he wants to touch me.

It *is* going to happen when I want to touch him too.

And I *am* sleeping in his bed.

Chapter 39

SALVATORE

I'm exhausted and still angry when I return to my penthouse that night.

After my meeting with Nerissa, I went to Oscuro to meet with Severu, Miceli, Angelo and my dad about the Juniper situation. The don, his underboss, his head enforcer and his consigliere all had something to say about it.

My receptivity was not high.

Resentful of my dad's interference in my life through Nerissa, I put his advice under the harshest scrutiny. When he tried to corner me after the meeting and scold me for disciplining my second, I told him to fuck off.

The argument that followed drew blood on both sides. He brought up my past.

My reply still rings in my head and I hope it is ringing in his.

"If you don't think I am fucking fit for my job, then advise our don to replace me, consigliere. Otherwise stay the fuck out of my business. As long as I am capo you will show me the respect I am due. If you ever undermine the loyalty of one of my people again, I will kill them, no matter who they are, and then I will fucking shoot you."

I didn't threaten to kill my father. We both know even I'm not capable of that. I won't kill my sister either, but I wasn't willing to admit that to him. So, I let the threat stand as I spoke it.

The look on my father's face told me he believed my words. All of them. Because I am the man he raised me to be.

He was a good father. However, he was always capo first, father second. I am a good son and brother, but I am capo first, like he taught me.

I don't even stop at my room before heading to the guestroom. I want to see Bianca. Feel her skin against mine. Breathe in her scent.

If I don't, I'm going to kill someone.

Rosa told me that Bianca went back up to the roof and stayed there for two-and-a-half hours. She ate dinner with Rosa in the kitchen and then retreated upstairs. Rosa thought to rest, but my check on the guestroom smart television shows Bianca watching it until a little after ten o'clock.

Rosa left after dinner, leaving only security to watch over Bianca, so of course I checked in on her. That I could only do so by checking her phone's activity and the smart TV, irked me.

Pietro needs to up his game. He's the head of my security and clearly, he should have installed cameras in the interior of the penthouse by now.

Everywhere but my bedroom.

I'll tell him tomorrow.

My eyes adjust quickly to the dark in the room, the light from the hallway enough to illuminate the empty bed.

There is no light coming from the attached bathroom and I don't hear anyone peeing, or breathing for that matter. I check the small room anyway.

It is empty. The closet is empty. Where the fuck is she? Did she decide to sleep on the roof? There are chaise lounges she could use, but it's not fucking safe up there.

What if someone got past the motion detectors around the perimeter? What if a sniper got a bead on her and thinking she's important to me, took her out?

My thoughts are spiraling as I sprint back down the stairs and through the door to the terrace.

"Is she up there?" I demand of the guard on duty out here.

"Who? Oh, you mean Miss Gemelli? She's upstairs, boss."

"She is not fucking upstairs. Her room is empty."

"Did you check the other rooms?" my soldier asks.

My racing heart thumps louder in my chest. I locked my office, didn't I? She wouldn't go snooping anyway. Why would she?

But memory of leaving my office includes watching my sister walk away with stiff shoulders. It does not include shutting and locking the office door.

Fuck.

I run back up the stairs and to my office, but Bianca isn't in there.

Is something wrong with her bed? Did she change to a different guestroom for a reason?

I check the other guestrooms on this floor. They are all empty. If my security let her leave the apartment, I am beating the shit out of every single one of them.

I'm heading back down the hall toward the stairs when a sleepy voice from my doorway halts me in my tracks. "What's going on Salvatore?"

Spinning to face her, I stare, my mouth hanging open like a new recruit on the first day of training.

She's wearing my t-shirt instead of the nightgown I know Rosa left out on Bianca's bed.

"I didn't mean to wake you up." Those are not the words I should say.

I should be asking her what the hell she's doing sleeping in my room. But fuck if I don't want her there.

"You galloped up and down the hall like a herd of rampaging elephants and expected me to sleep through it?" She yawns, covering her mouth.

I want to tug her hand away so I can see her pretty pink tongue.

"I didn't gallop." I ran. My movements might have lacked my usual stealth.

"Whatever you say." She turns back into the room. "Are you coming to bed, or do you have some more late night exercise you need to do?"

I can think of some exercise that will keep us both awake, but then she yawns again.

"Did you skip your nap this afternoon?"

"I'm not a downy haired baby, Salvatore. I don't have scheduled afternoon naps."

"You are definitely all woman," I say with appreciation for how my t-shirt stops midthigh, revealing her sexy as hell thighs.

"Put a pin in that thought for tomorrow," she says with a cute wink and another yawn before climbing back into her side of the bed.

Her fucking side.

Of *my* bed.

You started this by carrying her in here every night. Don't pretend you weren't going to do the same damn thing tonight.

"Why didn't you tell me you were going to sleep in here?"

"You mean none of your minions told you?"

"Security is not allowed upstairs while you are here."

"Okay. Well, now you know."

"I thought you ran away," I admit.

"I am too tired to explain everything wrong with that statement. Come to bed."

"I'm not the only bossy one in this relationship."

She groans and waves her hand. "Noted. Goodnight."

This is the first time I've seen her voluntarily give into her need for sleep. The first time she's even admitted she is tired.

That's another layer of trust right there.

I'm smiling as I walk into the bathroom to take a shower.

BIANCA

The sun shining through the big windows wakes me and the smell of coffee brings my eyelids fluttering open.

The spot beside me on Salvatore's bed is empty.

"What time is it?" I ask Rosa as she puts my coffee down on the table where she usually puts the breakfast tray.

Did I sleep so late there's no time for breakfast?

"Nine o'clock."

"Wow, I slept in." Even with all the sleeping I've been doing since arriving here, I usually wake around seven.

Salvatore is never here, even that early, so his absence is no surprise. It's disappointing though. I was too tired last night for more sexual adventures, but if he were here, I'd be totally down for them now.

"The surgeon will be here in an hour to remove your stitches." Rosa smiles at me. "You've got time for a shower. Do you want to eat here or on the terrace?"

I get a choice? "Terrace, if that's not too much trouble."

"No trouble at all. It saves me a set of stairs."

I'm on my second cup of coffee and eating my breakfast when I hear the sliding door open.

Expecting Rosa, my warm smile turns to something else, something more, when I see Salvatore striding toward me. That explains the second coffee cup on the breakfast tray.

"Good morning, *bella mia*. How are you feeling today?" His gray gaze roams over me, like he's looking for any sign I am not 100% while he takes the chair closest to me at the round table.

The table here is smaller than the one up on the roof, meant for more intimate meals. Not that he kept his distance during lunch the day before.

"Great. I slept in until nine." Duh. He knows that.

Rosa would have told him.

"I know. The temptation to wake you as I did yesterday from your nap was strong."

Tingling between my legs from his words, I pour him a cup of coffee and doctor it the way he likes before placing it on the table in front of him.

"If you're going to wake me up like that, I'm happy to take another nap." Even if, for the first time since the attack, I am full of energy and not at all sleepy.

"If I'm here to wake you, count on it."

My body responds predictably to his promise. I'm going to have to change my panties soon. "It's a deal."

However, the reminder that he has a job and spends very little time at his penthouse during the day deflates me. What are the chances he'll be here when I wake up from a nap?

He takes a sip of his coffee and gives me a look of approval. "You remembered how I like it."

"That's what I'm trained to do." Remembering the preferences for a regular customer is a necessary server skill if you want to make good tips.

"You're saying you remember how Nerissa takes her coffee from that night in the club?"

I frown at the mention of his underboss. "She wants it extra hot."

Salvatore must see something on my face because he asks, "What did you do?"

"I put that second cup of coffee in the microwave for a minute before serving it." Fresh coffee isn't supposed to be microwaved, but I wasn't giving her another excuse to complain.

He shakes his head. "She could have burnt her tongue."

I shrug. "She wanted it hot. I gave it to her hot."

"You weren't worried about her leaving you a tip."

"Give me a break. Nerissa wasn't going to tip me regardless." If the drinks had been on her tab, I would have been stiffed.

But they were on Salvatore's and he tips generously.

"She thinks I'm too into you."

"Does she vet all your sex partners?" I can't help asking.

"You're the first one, but to give her credit, you are also the first woman I have brought to my penthouse. I don't do overnights."

Which means he does not move women in on a whim. "Why me?" I put my hand up. "Don't give me the spiel about me needing someone to take care of me."

Yes, he offered to send me to a rehab facility or pay for me to stay in the hospital, both of which were ridiculous options in my opinion. But he wants me *here* in his home and he's made no bones about it.

"The plastic surgeon will be here soon," he says completely ignoring my question.

Maybe he doesn't know the answer. Any more than I know why this man makes me feel safe and triggers my libido, when no one else does.

"I still can't believe you've got a surgeon doing house calls."

"There's no reason to take you into the hospital for something as minor as removing stitches."

Which is pretty much the opposite of how normal people interact with medical professionals. If Salvatore wasn't involved, my stitches would have been put in by a doctor I would never see again. If they weren't the dissolving kind, I would see a nurse to remove them.

I suppose plastic surgeons do things differently and those that serve clients as wealthy and powerful as men like Salvatore, making house calls isn't out of the norm.

But it still feels weird.

Chapter 40

BIANCA

The surgeon, who identifies himself as Dr. Anders-Powell, examines me in the guestroom next to Salvatore's private gym downstairs.

The reason for the change of location for my exam becomes apparent pretty fast.

The surgeon leans over me to take a look at my stitches and brushes my hair back from my forehead. Fervently wishing I'd put my hair away from my face in a ponytail or braid, it's all I can do not to jerk away from his nearness.

In only a few days, I've become too used to not fighting my own reactions. Spoiled to no one but Salvatore invading my personal space and having more alone time than I have since living in the storage closet in my high school's basement.

I'm not mentally prepared for the surgeon's nearness and him touching me.

Salvatore growls and the look he gives the surgeon is borderline violent. "If you need Bianca's hair moved out of the way, tell me and I'll do it."

"Or he could, I don't know, tell *me*," I point out drily.

"I will need her hair pulled back to complete the exam and remove these stitches," Dr. Anders-Powell says to Salvatore, paying no attention to my suggestion.

"If you can wait a minute, I'll run upstairs and grab a hair tie." And put my hair up into a ponytail while I'm at it. "It will make it easier to remove the other stitches too."

My hair is long enough that it will interfere with the examination of the wound on my back otherwise.

"Stay put." Salvatore pulls his phone out of the inner pocket of his suit jacket and taps something on the screen before putting it away again. "Rosa will bring you a hair tie."

No one says anything while we wait for the housekeeper. She arrives a minute later carrying a brush and some hair ties.

I put my hand out. "Thank you."

"I should have thought of this before the surgeon arrived." She moves around to stand behind me, both items still in her hands.

Knowing it's useless to insist, I let my hand drop. The capo isn't the only bossy person around here.

"That would have been preferable, yes," the surgeon agrees, clearly unhappy with the delay.

What a tool.

He's all polite fawning to Salvatore, but the rest of us don't rate courtesy.

"If you were aware it was necessary, you should have provided preparation instructions ahead of time." Salvatore's critical tone makes Dr. Anders-Powell flinch.

Because I'm annoyed by how the surgeon is treating Rosa, I don't point out that it's only necessary because the capo doesn't want the other man touching me more than absolutely necessary.

And that is when the penny drops.

Salvatore's soldiers aren't allowed upstairs while I am here. That is what my lover said. Now I get that he meant absolutely no men are allowed up there, not even a medical professional.

Over protective, much? Or is that possessive?

Both seem excessive for a temporary sex partner. The whole one-night-stand thing is already blown out of the water, but it's not like I'm living here. Well, okay I *am* living here, but only because of my healing wounds.

Right? If that hadn't happened, Salvatore would have been happy with a single night of screwing. At least that's what his offer of five-thousand-dollars implied.

And because of my hangups, it never would have happened, no matter how attracted to him I am.

Our forced cohabitation worked a miracle in my reactions to him that I'm still not sure I understand.

Rosa finishes pulling my long red hair into a smooth, high ponytail and pats my shoulder. "There you go."

I smile up at her. "Thank you."

"My pleasure *dolce ragazza*." She leaves without another word to the two men.

The surgeon steps forward, leans close, and presses his fingertip to first one side of the gash and then the other. "Good. No blood seepage. It's healing nicely."

I force myself not to wince from the sting. It's not that bad. Dr. Anders-Powell removes the first stitch. It pulls a little, but that's all.

Doing a good impression of a brooding romance hero, or a cranky capo, Salvatore leans against the wall nearest me. "Does that hurt?"

"Not really."

"And when he pressed around it?" Salvatore asks, his tone definitely on the cranky side.

"Nothing much." If not for the wound in my back, I wouldn't still be taking pain meds. "I barely know it's there most of the time."

"Then we did our job," the surgeon congratulates himself. "I am going to put Steri-Strips on to make sure it doesn't open again and undo my work."

"Can I shower with them on?" I do not want to go back to cleaning myself with a washcloth.

"Yes, but keep your wound out of the direct stream of water."

That's better than the first few days after coming here from the hospital. "Okay, thank you."

"How long will she need to wear them?" Salvatore asks.

"The Steri-Strips can take up to ten days to fall off. If they don't by the four-teen-day mark, contact my office and I will send a nurse out to remove them. If the scab has not fallen off the wound in her back, new Steri-Strips will need to be applied."

"When can I take a bath?" The beautiful jetted tub in Salvatore's bathroom taunts me every day with how much I want to luxuriate in it.

Just once.

I would settle for the tub in the guestroom bath too.

"Not until the final Steri-Strip comes off."

I sigh. Too bad. I'll probably have Steri-Strips on my back for three to four more weeks. I'll be long gone from here before I can indulge in a soak in one of Salvatore's big tubs.

I never assume the best-case scenario. Less disappointment that way.

"I need you to remove her top and bra for me to examine her back," Dr. Anders-Powell tells Salvatore.

Crossing my arms, I glare at the surgeon. "I'm perfectly capable of taking off my own clothes."

"No," Salvatore barks.

I roll my eyes at Mr. Cranky. "I've been dressing and undressing myself for years."

An animalistic sound comes from deep in Salvatore's chest. "You are not taking your top and bra off in front of him."

Che palle.

I should be pissed at Salvatore's over-the-top possessiveness, but that growl sends my vagina into spasms.

Having a very different reaction to Salvatore's threatening behavior, the surgeon jumps away from me.

"I will do it in the bathroom where I can grab a towel to cover my front," I tell Salvatore.

I'm no more excited about being nude from the waist up in front of the self-important doctor than Salvatore is about me doing it. I'm not about to flash Dr. Anders-Powell my boobs if I don't have to.

Yeah, I know. I am sure a therapist would have a field day with my career choice as a pole dancer considering how much I don't like being undressed in front of other people. Salvatore being the confusing exception.

Or maybe a therapist would tell you that dancing the pole was as much about taking back your power as making money.

Since when did that little voice in my brain get so smart? About the time I read my tenth book on recovering from trauma maybe.

For the first time it occurs to me that the two years I spent dancing on stage, not ignoring my sensuality but not being vulnerable to it either helped me to heal.

So, when I met Salvatore and my ovaries started their impression of a Mariachi band, there was space in that healed spot inside me to explore those feelings.

Regardless of my subconscious reasons for taking the job at Pitiful Princess, I'm pretty sure I don't want to go back to dancing at a strip club. Even if I could get the same terms of employment I had before that *stronzo* Gino took over the dancers.

The attack brought back memories I don't want to keep reliving. I'm afraid the leering customers will trigger them now too.

"Need I remind you both that I am a medical professional? I am not about to look lasciviously upon Miss Gemelli's bare breasts." The surgeon's voice is loaded with affront.

Salvatore shifts away from the wall, the air around him filled with predatory menace. "Do I need to remind *you* that what I want, I get? And I don't want you looking at any more bare skin on my lover's body than absolutely necessary."

His lover.

My ovaries swoon like a teenager at a K-Pop concert.

"Perhaps you should get a different sur—geon..." Dr. Anders-Powell's voice breaks and goes high as Salvatore takes a step toward him. "T—to consult on this case."

"Maybe you should do your fucking job before I decide your services are no longer required." The threat in Salvatore's tone is unmistakable.

If Salvatore decides to fire the surgeon, the results will be longer term than losing income from one patient.

Finding Salvatore's threatening attitude hot is wrong. I know it is, but that doesn't stop my vagina getting wetter and wetter. My clitoris is throbbing for his touch too.

How quickly has my body adjusted to sexual pleasure?

"If you want to help me take off my shirt and bra..." I let my voice trail off in husky invitation.

The surgeon gives me a judgy glare but I don't care what the self-important douche-canoe thinks of me. I'm pretty sure this whole situation makes me a freak. I still want Salvatore to follow me into the bathroom.

And I'm not ashamed of that.

His eyes devouring me, Salvatore orders the surgeon, "Go to the living room and ask Rosa for some coffee."

"I have other appointments today." The other man's bravado is back now that Salvatore's attention is fixed on me.

My capo does not look away from me when he says, "You leave when I say you leave."

The surgeon makes a sound of disbelief.

"Take it from me, Salvatore is not talking out of his ass." The penthouse is a fortress. No one comes in or goes out without the capo's approval.

What initially pissed me off is just cause for another level of arousal now.

I don't wait to see if the plastic surgeon obeys Salvatore. He's smart enough to have gotten a medical degree and savvy enough to have landed himself a job at one of the most exclusive hospitals in the country. He's got to have enough sense not to goad a deadly predator like Salvatore any further.

Big hands land heavily on my shoulders when I cross the threshold to the bathroom, moving with me as I step over the tile in another pair of fuzzy slipper socks.

Stopping when I'm in front of the sink vanity, I am mesmerized by the image in the mirror.

My own blue eyes stare luminously back at me as I take in the tall, gorgeous capo with dark hair and olive toned skin decorated with sexy as sin tattoos standing behind me. My own skin is only a shade lighter than his, our Italian heritage obvious, if only to me.

We look like a pair that belongs together.

I shift my gaze to meet his and gasp at the desire turning his gray irises molten.

Whatever this thing is between us, it affects us both. Strongly.

"You are too damn tempting." His hands slide down my arms, making pleasure spark in every nerve ending along the way.

"Your fault."

"No, *brava ragazza mia*. It is all you."

His good girl.

Ovaries swooning yet again, I shake my head. "Agree to disagree."

Salvatore slowly tugs the loose oversized shirt I'd intended to simply lift for the exam up my overheated body. First, he reveals a wide slice of skin above the waistband of my leggings, then the underside of my breasts covered in red lace.

Stopping his movement, he scowls. "You were going to let him see you in this?"

Then the shirt rises so my entire chest is exposed along with the sexy style of the La Perla demibra. It barely covers my engorged nipples, but the cups support my ample breasts surprisingly well.

"I didn't plan for my shirt to go any higher than an inch or two above the knife wound." I'm still not convinced it needs to.

"Next time he comes to examine you, you wear a sports bra," Salvatore growls.

My thighs clench with need but I give him a look in the mirror that lets him know just how ridiculous I find his suggestion. "Yeah, no."

His eyes narrow and I can't help poking the bear. I'm not afraid of being eaten by the apex predator. In fact, I'm looking forward to it.

"If I wore something like this when I was dancing, I would have gotten double my tips," I gasp out between panting breaths, my body on fire for his touch.

The sound he makes as he rips my top off over my head sends thrills through me. My panties definitely need changing now.

"You are never dancing for other men again."

I know he doesn't mean it like it sounds. He's not laying claim to me or my future. He can't, but we can enjoy each other while I'm here.

"Does that mean you want me to dance for you?" I ask in an honest to God purr.

I didn't even know my voice could do that.

His hands dive into my demibra and he grabs my fleshy mounds. For all his ferocity, he does not squeeze so tight they hurt, but kneads them and plucks at my nipples until I moan with needy lust.

Leaning down, he growls into my ear, "Yes, *brava ragazza mia*, I want you to dance for me."

Shivering from the sensation of his hot breath in my ear, I lift my arms and clasp them behind his head while I press my butt back against him.

I crave the pleasure he gives me. I want him inside me, and I'm so turned on, that doesn't even scare me a little.

He pulls one hand from my breast and slides it down my torso until he reaches the stretchy waistband of my leggings. Running his finger along the waistband, he teases me.

"Touch me, Salvatore. Touch me now," I demand.

"Be a good girl and ask me nicely."

I shudder. "Please, *il mio lui*, touch me." *My him. My man. My guy.*

"Say that again," he demands in a hoarse voice.

He likes me laying claim to him, maybe even as much as I like when he gets possessive over me.

"*Il mio lui,*" I repeat. "*Sei mio.*" You are mine.

Salvatore goes nuts, ripping my leggings and underwear down and off along with my socks. He lifts me up onto the vanity, so my butt is on the edge of the sink and my feet planted wide apart on the countertop.

Chapter 41

BIANCA

My knees frame my raspberry tipped breasts and my thighs are open wide, revealing my most intimate flesh.

My capo's eyes burn back at me from the mirror, his gaze fixed on my flushed slit wet with invitation. Around it, my swollen nether lips glisten with my juices, a tiny nub peeking from the top of my labia.

"Look at that beautiful pussy, so wet and ready for me and that engorged little clit, just begging to be touched." He moves one big hand down my thigh and over my mons while his other arm holds me tight so I do not fall.

His forefinger and middle finger split to slide down on either side of my clitoris. His big, masculine hand goes lower until both fingers dip into my slit before drawing my arousal back up, coating my labia and clitoris with his now slick fingers. He does it again and again, driving the sensations coiling inside me tighter and tighter.

Squeezing his fingers together, he pinches my pleasure button as he rubs up and down along my now slippery flesh. Ecstasy explodes outward from the bundle of nerves and I cant my hips upward.

I need more.

That final cataclysmic eruption I know is coming.

"Touch your tits, *brava ragazza mia*."

Letting go of my hold on his neck I cup my breasts and moan at how good it feels. I brush my thumbs back and forth over my sensitive nipples, sending frissons of ecstasy directly to my core.

My climax hits with unexpected power, and I scream Salvatore's name as my hands convulsively close over my sensitive breasts. It feels like every muscle in my body contracts and pleasure washes over my body in wave after wave.

He touches me through it until I go limp. The only thing holding me upright is his arm around my middle.

I'm floating in post-orgasmic bliss when I feel his hand moving behind my back. Then I hear the sound of his zipper lowering and his hot erection slaps against my spine.

His hand comes between me and the velvet covered steel and he starts jerking off. I want to help him, but in this position, there is nothing I can do but watch us in the mirror, my legs still splayed lewdly.

"Look at that soaked pussy." His hand moves faster. "And those perfect tits. My pussy. My tits. *Tu sei mia!*"

Aftershocks of pleasure roll through me at the intensely possessive claim.

"Say it," he demands.

"Io sono tua." I am yours.

I am afraid that my plan to get over my sexual hangups has backfired. Because even when I leave, I am still going to belong to this man.

"Capo mio." I barely whisper the words, but he hears them.

And they send him over the edge.

Warm fluid bathes my skin and he keeps jacking until I feel it all across my back.

He rubs it in with leisurely strokes. "You will smell like me and that fucking doctor won't be able to miss that you are mine."

"Okay, caveman," I tease, but secretly I like knowing that just as much as Salvatore's ferocious expression says he does.

He's careful only to rub the viscous fluid into my skin and stays away from the gauze, which he removes before finishing undressing me by taking off my demi bra.

"I'm not going out there naked," I tell him.

The ferociousness in his expression takes on a more demonic cast. "You think I would let you?"

"Considering how this got started in the first place because you didn't want Dr. Anders-Powell to see my naked upper half, I'm going with a no."

Salvatore pulls out his phone, tapping on the screen for several seconds. Other than his cock hanging out of the opening in his slacks, he's still fully dressed.

Unreal.

"Next time you are getting completely naked," I tell him. "I like seeing your tattoos."

"Done," he immediately agrees.

We both wash our hands, but neither of us mentions him washing the cum off that he rubbed into my back. I'm drying my hands and contemplating putting my messy underwear back on or going commando under my leggings when there is a knock at the bathroom door.

Salvatore opens it without letting whoever is on the other side see past his big body blocking their view to the bathroom. "Good. Thank you, Rosa."

He shuts the door, his hands filled with one of his button up shirts, and a new pair of underwear and a freaking sports bra for me.

Laughter bursts out of me.

"He does not need you to be without a bra to examine the stitches that are at least two inches below the band."

"I can just wear the red bra," I challenge.

"If you want the underwear, you put on the sports bra."

"That is blackmail."

"Is there anything in who I have shown myself to be that makes you think I would hesitate to use blackmail to get what I want?"

Still smiling, I shake my head. "Nope. But don't think that because you won this round, you'll win the next one."

His sardonic look says he thinks just that.

Too bad for him, I'm not easily led. The next time I'm examined by the doctor, I'll have on a damn thong and the demibra that *doesn't* cover my nipples.

"I don't like that look on your face."

I grin. "Probably because you know it means I'm plotting against you."

"Plot away, but remember, I play to win."

"I never doubted it, but so do I." Which is pure bravado on my part, because I have never once played games with a lover.

I've never had a lover, so it tracks.

Pulling up my leggings after I put on the new underwear, I scrutinize his shirt. "I don't think you got anything on you. Why do you need to change shirts?"

"This isn't for me." He holds the shirt toward me.

Ten minutes later, I'm on the chair, straddling Salvatore's lap and facing him, wearing both the sports bra and Salvatore's shirt backward so my arms and front are completely covered but the shirt is open in the back.

Salvatore is holding the edges of the shirt so it is open just enough for the surgeon to see my healing wound.

Dr. Anders-Powell tsks when he sees us, but wisely says nothing critical. You'd think after what happened in the bathroom Salvatore would be less possessive, but it's the opposite.

My nickname for him fits to a T as he plays the role of grunting caveman with a side of menace to perfection.

"It is healing very well. You should barely see the scar after six months, but it may take longer for it to heal completely." His fingertips run over the skin on either side of my wound.

Salvatore's arms shifts and I hear flesh slapping against flesh. "Watch it!"

I look over my shoulder to see my capo holding the surgeon's wrist in what looks like a painful grip.

Smacking my lover on the chest, I remind him, "He has to touch me to take out the stitches, Salvatore."

"I can take them out," Salvatore claims. "I've done it for myself before."

But he releases the other man's wrist.

"You demanded a plastic surgeon because you wanted your girlfriend to scar as little as possible," the surgeon says with afront. "But by all means, remove them yourself."

I wince internally. Taking that attitude with a Cosa Nostra capo isn't going to end up well for the surgeon.

"You tell me exactly how to do it and if Bianca still has scars six months from now, I will carve the same marks in your fucking face. Are we clear?"

The next ten minutes are fraught with tension. Not Salvatore's. He's confident he can do this. Not mine. I don't really care if there's a scar even a year from now.

But the surgeon's voice shakes as he gives my bossy lover instructions on how to remove the stitches and apply the Steri-Strips after.

"You need to thoroughly cleanse the area with an alcohol swab," he instructs Salvatore.

Salvatore tenses. "You only wiped over the area on her forehead once. Do we need to redo it?"

"Her forehead does not reek of efforts at copulation."

It's all I can do not to laugh at the man's prissy attitude. I smell like Salvatore's cum and I like it. Sue me.

"What kind of fool do you take me for? I didn't spread my cum over the scab." Something in Salvatore's tone tells me that once the scab is gone and the only thing left behind is a scar, it won't just be the anti-scarring cream he'll insist on rubbing on the pink ridges though.

I'm a freak, but the idea of him marking me that way sends a shiver of desire through my sated body.

The plastic surgeon winces at the word *cum*. "Be that as it may, cleanse the area thoroughly, but do not rub and do not disturb the scab."

Salvatore starts muttering about officious pricks in Italian and I press my face into his neck to hide my smile.

Chapter 42

SALVATORE

Two texts come through back-to-back as the surgeon is leaving.

One is a regular text from my don. The other is on the secure group chat with Catalina and the tech guys on Domenico's crew that have been working with us to figure out who is trying to steal the bar properties from under our noses.

Severu: *Call me.*

Group Text (QC): *Confirmed Henrico Caruso behind the Stellar Holdings bid.*

Group Text (DTC1): *Sending details via secure link.*

QC stands for Queen Catalina, because she is both my cousin's queen and the queen of gathering and analyzing information. The FEDs only wish they had someone as good as Catalina on their payroll.

DTC stands for Domenico's Tech Crew. 1 is his top guy, but they are all good.

We don't use names on our proprietary chat app. It's an extra layer of security, allowing us to talk mafia business. We still use coded communication if the information we're exchanging is too volatile.

My phone dings with another notification for a new email message.

Turning to face Bianca, I cup her nape and tug her forward. "I have to make a call."

"Okay. I'm going to go change my shirt."

"Leave it on." I like the idea of her wearing my shirt.

She rolls her eyes, but doesn't answer.

Leaning down, I kiss her soft mouth and inhale our combined scent. *Cazzo*. I have to go, but for the first time in memory, I don't want to jump to my don's bidding.

Kissing her one last time, I force myself to step away.

This woman is a fucking disaster for my self-control.

I wait to call Severu until I am in my office and the secure link is pulled up on my computer.

There are statements for a bank account we didn't uncover in our initial search. It is a joint account for Henry Caruso with his cousin Matthew Lombard. I know the Lombardis Americanize their names because of their political connections, but Henry is just a tool.

He acts like he's ashamed of his Italian heritage, or maybe it's his connection to the Cosa Nostra he is trying to hide. Unlike his family in Boston, pretending not to be connected is more likely to put him under scrutiny in New York, than if he stuck with his given name.

And this brain trust is our godfather's choice of successor to run the Lucchese Family?

"Why didn't we find this on our first pass?" It would have saved us the time looking into the other Families.

"We needed a thread to tug on to unravel the layers of obfuscation," Severu replies. "We got that in the copy of the earnest money agreement from Stellar Holding's offer."

Nerissa's team broke into Juniper's office at the convenience store while he was busy with the woman Stellar Holdings sent home with him. An effective watch dog for a man like him with the side benefit of gaining his favor.

It's not a job I would give one of my crew. That's not how we operate. A willing sex worker could keep him occupied without having to know why though.

I wonder which one the woman with Juniper is.

If she's made, she'll be more cautious around our people. And more dangerous if she figures out our plan.

"Nerissa is planning to dose Juniper when they prefunction at his place." Waiting to drug the man until they reach the strip club has too many variables that can go wrong. "She'll give his babysitter a knockout dose to keep her out of the way for the rest of the night and Juniper enough to make him malleable."

Neither will remember the night before. One of the benefits of Rohypnol.

I scroll down to the seven-fucking-figure earnest money check accompanying the offer for the bar properties. It doesn't list any individual names, only the company, Stellar Holdings.

It reveals two things immediately though:

1. Stellar Holdings is willing to pay well above market value for the prop-

erties.

2. Juniper's greed is the only reason he didn't sign that offer.

He thinks he can get more money out of me.

"Once Domenico's people had access to the account and routing numbers," Severu says. "It was just a matter of time before they found the actual names associated with the account."

"Why not use one of the company's usual accounts. It would have given them another layer of security?" I ask.

Our guys are exceptional hackers. They would have unraveled all the threads no matter how layered, but it's something we would do if we were trying to hide our involvement in a deal. Few hackers have the skills of Domenico's crew.

"My first thought is that they don't want The Lombardi to know they are partnering on this deal," Severu replies.

"You think Matthew Lombard is acting without the approval of his don?"

"Yes, I do. Now that we know it's Henrico and not our godfather involved in the attempt to purchase the properties, it's highly unlikely that the Boston don would sanction the action."

"The potential for blowback is too big."

"Buying land in our territory is an act of aggression that would not be ignored."

"You aren't going to ignore the attempt, are you?"

"No. Matthew will be punished in a manner commensurate with the crime, or his uncle will have to deal with me."

That is why Severu will make a good godfather. He doesn't hesitate to act. His show of force isn't always as blatant as torturing a man to death, but he never leaves his opponents in doubt of how badly they fucked up.

I scroll down with my mouse, marveling at Henry's cursory effort to hide his actions. "This leaves no doubt about who is working with Stellar Holdings."

There's a clear trail between Henry Caruso liquidating and shifting assets into the account. Technically, his actions are not against mafia protocol. As long as he takes full possession of the New York properties.

If his cousin maintains even a small stake in them, Henry is guilty of treason to the Five Families.

"Since Don Caruso is not involved, you have full freedom to proceed as planned," Severu tells me.

While Henry can buy property in New York by any means necessary, so can I.

Unfortunately for Juniper, I have no intention of outbidding the other capo. I have other ways to make him abide by our original agreement.

And if he squawks after, I can silence him for good. Once the properties have gone through transfer of ownership. With two other Cosa Nostra families involved, keeping a low profile with this is imperative.

We operate so effectively because we operate under the radar.

~ ~ ~

Bianca is dozing in the sun when I find her on the rooftop. She's wearing my shirt, the right way around, and the sleeves rolled up. Possessive pleasure rolls through me at the sight.

I'm making no effort to hide my approach, so I'm not surprised when her eyes pop open.

The smile that comes after sends 150 joules of reviving electric current through my heart. Enough to start the organ all over again, this time with feelings I've walled off for over a decade.

My step falters for a second, but I force my feet forward, dismissing the fanciful thought.

I cannot have feelings for this woman, but I can enjoy her while she is here. And make sure she enjoys being here too.

"Hi." She pulls her knees up and wraps her arms around her legs. "All done with your phone call?"

"Yes." I finished with Severu a few hours ago, but had a lot of work to catch up on.

Figuring out the Juniper angle has taken up time I don't have in my busy schedule.

"I have a business meeting tonight at Pitiful Princess."

Her eyes light up, but then dim. "Oh. So, you'll be gone. You didn't have to tell me."

"I am aware." I answer to no one for how I spend my time. "Do you want to come?"

"To a business meeting? Is that wise?"

Probably not. But I'm no neophyte soldier. She won't see or hear anything I don't want her to. "Your friend Candi is on the schedule. I thought you might want to see her."

"That's really nice of you?"

"You don't sound so sure."

"I'm just trying to figure out your angle."

"I have to have an angle?"

"Is this like a date with work stuff thrown in? Are those the only kind of dates a busy capo can go on."

"You can think of it as a date if you want."

"But you don't?"

"It's an opportunity to spend time together and for you to see your friend."

"That would be great. Really," she says like she's not sure I believe she thinks that. "I haven't seen her since I quit working there."

"You text every day though."

"You went through my phone?"

I shrug. "I'm a nosy guy."

More like security conscious, but she doesn't need to know that after tasking Pietro with doing a background check on her, I decided to do my own investigating.

Yes, Nerissa got in my head.

So, I did my due diligence, pressing Bianca's finger to her phone to unlock it while she was sleeping. Domenico may be the capo in charge of online money laundering and tech security, but I know my way around a phone.

Not that I found much.

There are no apps, hidden or otherwise on her phone. No social media. No internet history with a login page for her college. The phone is old and pay as you go. She probably deals with any apps or websites that require higher bandwidth on her laptop.

But it requires a password to access. If necessary, I'll have it hacked, or just demand she unlock it for me.

I did a quick Google search of her name on my own phone. No social media accounts popped up, which makes sense, considering her former occupation. She probably felt safer having no online presence.

There are phone numbers for Pitiful Princess, Gino and Ugo. I delete Gino's contact information after blocking his number. That *stronzo* is never talking to her again.

Her former roommates are listed in her contacts along with names that are clearly other dancer's stage names, including her friend Candi. There are no numbers associated with family though, supporting her claim that she is alone in the world.

Her call log is short. Apparently, she doesn't like to talk on the phone. And the only person she texts regularly is her friend Candi. Those texts were illuminating, but not condemning.

I saw a text from Ruhnke's daughter-in-law too. I had to unblock the number to read the text stream. It isn't long. And there is not a single mention of money or Bianca's inheritance. I blocked the number again and put Bianca's phone back where I found it on the charger.

"That is an invasion of my privacy, Salvatore."

"You are living with a mafia capo. There is no such thing as privacy when it comes to me staying on top of what is happening in my home."

Her eyes narrow. "Do you have surveillance cameras in the penthouse?"

"Only outside the access points." For now. "I value my privacy."

She snorts. "But no one else's?"

I consider it and then shake my head.

"You are something else. I can't believe you just admitted that."

"Would you rather I lie to you?"

She sobers completely. "No."

"Do you want to go tonight?"

"Yes. What time?"

"We need to be there by nine, but I thought we could get dinner first."

Bianca jumps up from the lounger. "It *is* a date."

"We both have to eat, *bella mia*."

"Stop trying to be such a grouch and just admit it is a date."

"I already said you are free to see it that way if you want to."

She shakes her head like I'm the most annoying person ever. No one treats me like that.

It should piss me off, but I feel my mouth curving into a smile instead.

Her eyes widen, like my smile surprises her. Then she grins. "I am calling it a date and since it's a date, I need to go get ready."

"You're fine in what you are wearing." More than fine. She's delectable.

"Yeah, no. I am not wearing a man's shirt and leggings on a date." She grabs her phone and looks down at it. "How long do I have?"

"An hour." Which I had planned to spend naked with her.

"*Caspita!* Are you kidding me? An hour? I won't be able to wash my hair, but I am definitely taking a shower."

"You want to wash off my cum?" I demand.

"I've enjoyed getting little sniffs of your sex scent all afternoon, but no, I don't particularly want to go to a strip club smelling like a guy's cum."

"Not a guy, mine."

"You know that. I know that, but any random customer at Pitiful Princess won't. They'll probably assume it means I'm available to take clients in the back."

"I will kill anyone who touches."

Her laugh cascades over me and she pats my chest, which is becoming a habit of hers. "No need for such drastic action, caveman. No one's coming near me with you by my side."

"Then why wash my scent away?" The primitive core of all made men craves marking her as mine.

"Better safe than sorry."

"You stay by my side."

"If that starts now, you're going to have to follow me to the bathroom for my shower."

It will be an exercise in temptation, if not downright sexual torture, to watch her naked body under the falling water without touching.

I am right behind her.

Chapter 43

BIANCA

After the most sensual shower of my life, where I am not ashamed to admit, I put on a show Salvatore will not forget soon, I rush through putting on my makeup, so I have time to style my hair.

I use the straightener to make big curls in the waves that cascade down my back. The whole time, Salvatore watches. He doesn't talk, and he checks his phone every time it dings with a notification, but the way his attention stays on me regardless is unnerving.

Going into the walk-in closet, I riffle through the hangers, trying to decide which dress is perfect for a not-date of dinner and going to a strip club after. I've never owned sexy designer dresses like the ones hanging in the guestroom closet. I've never owned so many dresses at all.

Not even when my mom and dad were still married and she made sure Bea and I had the latest styles "appropriate to our age" to wear every season. At thirteen, the need to go clothes shopping every few months was annoying.

I'm pretty sure I would find it no more exciting now. My mom and Bea have way more in common than I have with either of them, despite Bea being my identical twin.

The LBD is always a good choice, right? I grab a short black number to wear and carry it out of the closet.

Salvatore looks up from his phone. "Wear the blue one."

"I like this one." Black is easy to accessorize.

"I've been imagining you in the blue one since I bought it." He looks at me like he's imagining me naked, not wearing the blue dress.

"What is up with that anyway? You bought me a whole freaking wardrobe."

"I didn't know what you would need."

"So, you got me everything?"

He shrugs, which I interpret as *pretty much*.

"What do I get if I wear the blue one?" I ask.

His gorgeous face goes blank. "What do you want?"

That's easy. "No getting lap dances or tucking tips in the dancer's panties."

He can tip through management. A lot of the customers that appreciated my dancing designated tips for me on their bar tab. It wasn't my favorite because I had to wait to get the tips on my paycheck, but it works.

Salvatore's face clears and he smirks. "Feeling possessive?"

"Feeling like I have no desire to be one of the many women I've seen in the club watching their dates have eyes all over other women."

"I wasn't planning on doing either." His heated look sends tingles through my nether regions. "Only a fool would spend the evening watching someone else with you sitting beside him."

Warmth fills my chest that I do my best to ignore. "Those are pretty words for a man who insists this is not a date."

He shrugs. "The truth is the truth."

If only. There are so many shades of truth and honesty. There is so much about me that he doesn't know and so much about him that I have no clue about.

"You're going to tip though, right?" I ask after replaying his answer in my mind. "That's how dancers make their money. Or does the boss not tip on principle?"

"No one at Pitiful Princess outside of Ugo knows I own the club and I want to keep it that way."

"Okay." It's not like I'm going to announce the club's connection to the mafia, much less that he's a capo who owns several clubs in Manhattan for his Family.

I have a fully developed sense of self-preservation.

"You can tip the dancers on my behalf."

"I get to decide how much each dancer gets?" I ask suspiciously. I'm not looking at some kind of threesome energy.

"Yes, *bella ragazza mia*. You decide how much to tip."

Any dancer who makes a play for Salvatore while I am there isn't getting a dime. I'll have Candi spread the word.

"You look very pleased all of the sudden."

"Worried?"

"No. Intrigued though."

I just grin and go back into the closet to grab the blue dress.

Salvatore takes me to one of the hot restaurants in Manhattan I never thought I'd see the inside of as a server much less a patron. He silences his phone and tucks it into his inside suit pocket.

He'll feel the vibration of a notification, but I still appreciate the effort.

We talk about my life with Mr. Ruhnke over dinner.

"You moved in to stop his children from forcing him out of his home?"

"Yes." Still leery about living with another person, I installed my own lock on my bedroom door with a deadbolt and kept the only keys.

It wasn't safe if there was a fire, but I would never have slept otherwise. The past two years dozing in a closet and only sleeping when I knew all my roommates would be gone proves it was a good move.

"No wonder he left you money in his will."

"What? No. Mr. Ruhnke didn't leave me anything." If I hadn't had my savings, I would have been in real trouble when his children evicted me from Mr. Ruhnke's home after he died.

Salvatore's eyes narrow. "That is not what his son told Nerissa."

"The lying little weasel. I'm glad I blocked all their numbers now."

"You are saying he didn't leave you fifty-thousand dollars?"

"If he had, do you think I would be living in an apartment with five other roommates and my roomie's boyfriend that didn't pay rent?" The idea of having that money blows my mind.

I could have finished college faster and be planning to move away from New York already. Chances are, I would never have taken the job at the Pitiful Princess either. And I wouldn't have moved on to Amuni...or met Salvatore.

Suddenly the idea of a $50,000 windfall two years ago doesn't look so shiny.

"You no longer live there."

"Thanks to you, I don't live with plant assassins," I snark. "Is that what you want to hear?"

"Appreciation from a beautiful woman is always appreciated."

"Watch it, Salvatore. You're slipping into cheesy line territory again." This time though? I'm totally down with the idea of showing that appreciation in a fun and physical way.

He doesn't take the bait and our conversation moves on to how badly mobster movies get it wrong.

But I'm still thinking about what Mr. Ruhnke's son told Nerissa. Unless Salvatore called him and talked to him too?

Doesn't matter. What does is that he claimed Mr. Ruhnke left me $50,000 in his will.

What if he did? What if they have spent two years trying to hide that fact? What if that's why his daughter-in-law wanted to get ahold of me?

I only stop thinking about it when we reach Pitiful Princess. Walking in, the familiar scent of sex and alcohol mixed with perfume and perspiration hits me. I remember the first time I came into the club, when I auditioned for the job of pole dancer.

The smell of vagina clung around the stage and the pole, even though it was wiped down with disinfectant between each dancer's sample set.

That same earthy odor is under all the other scents in the club now. Wednesdays are not our...*their* busiest night, so there are only five dancers on the T-shaped stage in the center of the room and two on the four small circular stages mixed in with the tables.

There are three poles down the center of the stage that the dancers share. All three are being used by the strippers. The two poles on the ends of the cross part of the T are reserved for dedicated pole dancers. Like I used to be.

Both are occupied by dancers I don't recognize who are also dancing stripper style. Friday and Saturday nights there will be a dancer doing exotic flow in heels like I used to do on one of the dedicated poles. The other will have a dancer doing exotic hard in heels.

I never got into the faster paced and more physically demanding style of exotic hard dance.

Wearing a hot pink corselette that barely confines her boobs and matching six-inch stripper heels, Candi is performing on one of the circular platforms when we walk in. Her long brown hair is up in a high ponytail so she can whip it while she dances.

One of the patrons watches every move she makes, with the clear hope her breasts will pop out of the corselette. It's not happening. I know the brand of body tape she uses and there will be no accidental exposure.

She has routines that include stripping down to a g-string, but she reserves them for the weekend, when tips are highest.

There is an empty table with a *reserved* sign on it near her stage.

Waitresses, whose only uniform is a g-string and pasties, weave between the tables. One of them approaches, walking with a roll of her hips that makes her boobs jiggle. She's good with makeup because the contouring she's done makes her C cups look like my DDs.

I would be impressed if she wasn't eyeing Salvatore like a hungry cat. "Let me show you to your table, sir," she purrs.

I am the only woman allowed to purr for *my capo*. At least as long as I'm living in his penthouse.

I texted Candi to tell her we were coming and to spread my warning.

Did this server not get the memo? Or does she think she can convince Salvatore to leave her a big tip anyway? The dancers come from a lot of different backgrounds, but they learn fast how to spot wealthy patrons.

We've all been schooled in rich people's shoes, suits and watches. Not that I needed the schooling after being raised until I was thirteen by my socialite mom, not to mention a dad who always tried to dress like he was a capo and not a soldier.

Salvatore looks like the billionaire that he is in his bespoke suit (no tie), black silk hand-tailored dress shirt, Gucci oxfords and Patek Phillipe watch.

This chick is going to miss out on the brass ring if she makes a play for the golden goose.

"Lead the way." Salvatore slides his hand around my waist, keeping me close as we follow the naked and contoured ass of the other woman.

Ignoring the view, his gaze flicks side to side to make sure I don't come into contact with any of the other customers. A man leers at me and Salvatore, hooks his chair leg with his foot dumping him on his back as we pass.

Servers rush to help the man cursing loudly and throwing threats in Salvatore's direction. Somebody whispers in his ear and the angry man goes silent.

"Stop rubbernecking, *bella mia*. He's not that interesting."

"No but your caveman tendencies are kind of hot." I slide my arm under his suit jacket and around his torso.

My happy feelings evaporate when I see who is approaching the table from the back of the club.

Nerissa.

Looking elegant in a silver jumpsuit and heels that makes me feel gauche in the blue dress that made me feel beautiful and sexy only five minutes before, she walks confidently toward us.

Ugh.

The general manager, Ugo, is with her. So, Salvatore's business is club related? Still not sure why they're taking their meeting here and not someplace else. Especially with Salvatore so insistent on keeping his connection to the strip club under wraps.

"You weren't kidding when you said it wasn't a date," I gripe. "You could have told me your sister was going to be here."

He pulls a chair out for me. "Is that a problem?"

Candi's back is to us as she slides into a slow split looking to the side over her shoulder toward the other side of the club. I'll have to wait to say, "Hi," until she is done with her set.

So, I sit down.

"Why would spending the evening with the woman who called me a selfish bitch and accused me of trying to scam you be a problem?" I might understand Nerissa's protectiveness toward her brother, but I don't have to like it.

"She will not call you that again."

"You sound very certain."

"Because I am."

I don't get a chance to ask how because Nerissa and Ugo arrive at the table.

Chapter 44

BIANCA

Salvatore might be convinced Nerissa is done name calling, but the look she's giving me isn't filled with warm fuzzies.

She turns a no friendlier look on the waitress that led us to our table. "A round of tonight's rum special for the table."

The server looks hopefully toward Salvatore. "Would you like anything else?"

"No."

"You've been given our order. Bring enough drinks for the entire table," Ugo instructs her, indicating the empty chairs. "There will be others joining us."

The cocktail waitress finally leaves.

"What is she doing here?" Nerissa demands of her brother with a head tilt toward me.

"Watch your tone," Salvatore barks. "She is here as my cover."

Nerissa leans between us toward her brother. "Your cover?"

"A man like me doesn't come to strip clubs alone," he says in a low tone only the two of us can hear. "It was her, or a group of our men pretending to be my friends. This was easier and more believable."

"I guess the fact that your supposed girlfriend used to work here makes your patronage of a club like Pitiful Princess more credible too," Nerissa muses quietly.

The little bubble of joy that has been floating inside me all evening begins to deflate. I am his expedient cover. This really isn't a date.

"But the only people who think she's your girlfriend are our family and the hospital staff," Nerissa points out.

I really wish I wasn't privy to this conversation. I was having fun, but now the evening is tainted with the knowledge I'm being used. I thought Salvatore wanted to spend time with me, even if he did have to work.

"Which means everyone in the Family knows," Salvatore says wryly. "But I took her to dinner at Per Se to be seen."

So, we could be seen as a couple.

Even dinner was part of the cover. I thought that at least was the date part of the evening. I knew Salvatore had business, but dinner was just us.

"The car with Juniper will be here shortly. His date from Boston is currently sleeping off the effects of her pre-function drink," Nerissa says quietly in Italian, apparently mollified by her brother's explanation for my presence.

"Hello, Bianca, it's good to see you again." Ugo slides into the chair beside me. "If you ever want to come back to work, you'll be welcome. The customers miss you."

Yeah. That is not happening. No matter what the future holds with me and Salvatore, I've gotten what I needed to from exotic dancing.

His smile seems genuine, but he doesn't offer his hand. My own smile is noncommittal and hiding the turmoil roiling through me. I don't offer to shake hands either.

"Nerissa, you sit there. Ugo, move over a chair." Salvatore's tone demands instant obedience.

Because Ugo and Nerissa work for him, he gets it. After the shuffling, there are two empty chairs left at the table.

I lean toward Salvatore and ask quietly, "More scheming for whatever you all are doing here tonight?"

"I don't want another man sitting next to you."

This show of possessiveness would have turned me on five minutes ago. Now, it's just annoying.

I lean back in my chair and speak loudly enough to be heard over the music by the others at the table. "Get over yourself, Salvatore. I'm not going to trip and fall on some other man's dick just because I'm sitting beside him."

Ugo turns his head, pretending interest in what one of the servers is doing at a table nearby. Nerissa snorts a laugh she tries to cover, but there's no missing the amusement in her dark eyes.

Salvatore's not laughing though. "I didn't say you would."

"Didn't you?" I stand up. "Excuse me."

Salvatore grabs my wrist. "Where are you going?"

"To see Candi."

Done with her set, my friend has exited her stage via the climb down on the other side that looks like part of the club's décor. Our table is close to the stage, but the route she has to take through the other tables means she's still making her way toward us.

Suddenly, I have no desire to talk to her in front of Salvatore and his people.

"You can catch up here at the table."

"No."

"Why not?"

"I don't want to." I tug on my arm. "Don't worry. Her break only lasts fifteen minutes. I'll be back to play my part in your little farce then."

"It is not a farce. You *are* my girlfriend." He makes that last claim loudly enough to be heard at the surrounding tables.

Candi hears it because her eyes go wide and she gives me a thumbs up sign.

"Who is not on a date with you." I yank at my arm. "Yeah, that tracks." My voice is heavy with sarcasm.

"We'll go on a date tomorrow."

"To dinner at your don's? That's some date, Salvatore." I roll my eyes.

"I'm starting to like her," Nerissa says, but her tone is sarcastic.

I give her a look, one brow lifted. "Yeah? Is it because your brother is so willing to use me?"

I speak in Italian like she did earlier. I'm not willing to mess up Salvatore's *business*, whatever that is, but I'm not pretending everything is fine either.

"I am not using you," Salvatore snaps, tugging me into his lap.

"Che palle. Let me go," I demand, squirming to get up. "I'm your cover to be here. How is that *not* using me?"

A hard bulge under my hip tells me my movements are turning him on.

"No lap dances, remember?" I ask scathingly.

"You are the only one I would want one from," he says in a sexy growl.

I shove against his chest and shock of shocks, he lets me stand up. Only he pushes me to the side and a little behind him, which is not where I want to go because Candi is approaching from the other direction.

I know why a second later when I hear an unfamiliar voice talking, or should I say *slurring* in a New Jersey accent. "Salvatore, buddy. They-ah you ah."

The man who was at his table at Amuni the first night I met Salvatore comes up and lists forward, offering an unsteady hand to Salvatore to shake.

Apparently, those pre-function drinks were strong.

The capo indicates one of the empty spots at the table. "Sit down, Juniper. Your chair has a great view of the stage."

"My date's not he-ah," Juniper slurs. "She fell asleep." He looks like a child deprived of his favorite toy and not understanding how it happened.

"Don't worry. We've got you covered," Nerissa says, like she's trying to sound accommodating, but there's an underlying current of disgust in her voice.

An actor she is not.

"Bianca!" Candi calls my name and tries to step around Juniper to get to me.

I point to my right, indicating I'll meet her the next table over.

But before either of us can move, Juniper turns fast and leers at Candi. "Are you my date for tonight?"

Ugo leaps from his chair like it caught on fire and inserts himself between Candi and Juniper. "No, sir. If you'll have a seat, one of our dancers will be over to give you a lap dance in a moment."

"I want that one." He points toward Candi.

Ugo blanches and shoots a worried glance toward the other side of the club where a few of the tables are deliberately situated in the shadows. They're reserved for Pitiful Princess's version of VIPs.

"No," Ugo says. "She's on break. Let me just help you to your chair."

Ugo grabs Juniper and guides him with a white knuckled grip on his arm toward the other side of the table.

Salvatore obviously has plans for Juniper tonight and doesn't want him latching on to the wrong dancer. Not that Candi would give Juniper the kind of companionship he's looking for. Her lap dances are strictly noncontact.

Knowing I'm here for a purpose, and determined to play my part in a way that will make Salvatore squirm, I lean down and place a lingering kiss on Salvatore's cheek.

"Back in a bit, daddy," I purr loudly enough for the tables around us to hear.

Not to mention the server who has returned with our drinks. Giving me a sour look, she places the drinks around the table. But when she tries to pass Nerissa's chair to hand Salvatore his, the second snatches the glass from the tray and sets in front of her capo herself.

So, I'm not the only one Nerissa doesn't want near her brother. Pretending not to notice the byplay, I scoot around Juniper and grab Candi's hand.

I immediately start tugging her toward the back.

"Candi's taking a little extra breaktime, Ugo. You don't mind, do you?" I call toward the GM. "I'm sure daddy would be appropriately grateful for making me so happy," I sing song.

Ugo stares at me like I've grown a second head, and Nerissa looks like she's going to hurl.

Oooh, added bonus. Grossing out the overprotective sister.

Chapter 45

BIANCA

Candi leans forward as we head toward the back. "You call him *daddy*?"

I turn my head so I can speak close to her ear, though the two inches she has on me in height and the additional six inches of her heels means my mouth is closer to her chest. Oops.

Standing on my tiptoes, I cup my free hand near her ear. "Not my kink, but he wants to play my sugar daddy tonight so I'm letting him. It's a one night only pass though."

"That sounds more like you," she says with a laughs and then she sobers. "Not that actually having a boyfriend sounds like you."

The worry is clear in her tone.

"Who knew? I was just waiting for the right bossy billionaire to come along," I tease.

Candi yanks me to a stop, not laughing. "Did you hit your head during the attack?"

"You know I did," I try humor again. "I told you everything about that morning.

Well not everything. I didn't tell Candi that Salvatore killed three men to protect me, or that he slept with me in my hospital bed to keep the nightmares away.

She shakes her head but nudges me to start walking again. We pass through the velvet curtain into the hallway leading to the rooms for private lap dances (and other things) and the dressing room, which is where I'm headed.

But Candi stops again as soon as we're behind the curtain and pulls me around to face her. "Are you alright? I can't believe I haven't seen you since you got attacked."

Her eyes scan over me like she's taking inventory.

"I'm fine. I texted you pictures."

"That weren't as reassuring as you think they were. You were stabbed!"

"He didn't hit anything vital."

Candi glares. "Don't joke."

"I'm not."

"Your whole body is vital, Bianca." Her voice wobbles. "You could have been killed."

"I'm okay. More than okay. I'm living the high life in a billionaire's penthouse."

"Like you care if he's rich," she scoffs. "The only thing that matters to you with people is how they treat others."

"He's taking very good care of me."

"I just bet he is."

"Not like that." Though the sexual satisfaction is very welcome from my side. "I mean, like making sure I eat and rest."

"That's good." She doesn't sound convinced though.

"My roommates tried to kill Vee and he's trying to nurse it back to health." Because he knows the plant is important to me.

"That's something real, I suppose. And he's making sure you rest, like actual sleep?" Candi knows how hard it is for me to sleep, if not why.

"He's big into me taking naps." His new way of getting me to sleep isn't something I'm going to share, even with my best friend, though.

She nods grudgingly. "He got you out of that awful apartment where you slept on the dang floor, so he can't be all bad. Even if he is rich."

"Most people would not see that as the detriment you do."

"Is he trying to force you to do anything?" she asks as she tugs me toward an unoccupied private room. "If you need to get away, I can smuggle you out the backdoor and you can go to my apartment. Mom knows you might come, so she'll let you up."

"You already talked to her?" Unexpected tears prickle at my eyes.

What is with me and this surfeit of emotion lately?

"Of course, I did. You can live with us as long as you need to. And I'll check your wounds every day," she says wryly, clearly remembering the excuse Salvatore made for me staying at his place.

I told her in one of my texts with laughing emojis. Apparently, my friend didn't take my agreement to stay at face value.

"I want to be there," I tell her. "When he touches me, I don't freak out."

Candi is the only person I've ever told that I don't like being touched by men. I didn't give her the details, or tell her about my past, but she didn't need me to. She accepts my limitations for what they are and doesn't judge me for them.

She's the only dancer who never gave me crap for not working the floor at least.

"You sure you don't want to run?" she asks. "I know rich guys think they can have whatever they want."

"Positive. He's not like that." My defense is vehement.

When the truth is? Salvatore does think he can have whatever he wants. Not because he's rich, but because he's a capo. Only, he would *never* force me to have sex with him.

Keep me trapped in his apartment until I saw reason? Yes.

Hurt me physically? No.

With a final measuring look, Candi flips the sign to occupied and goes into the room. The smell of sex mixes with citrus and mint based disinfectant is strong, reminding me what these rooms are used for.

"Are you sure we should be using one of these rooms?"

"It's not that busy tonight and we won't be here very long." Candi shrugs. "We've got thirty minutes max before Ugo comes knocking. He's figured out how much I make in tips and he wants the house's split."

There are two seating options: a sofa, upholstered in easy to clean microfiber and two armchairs. They look like expensive armchairs with tufted backs like the sofa, but the vinyl upholstery means that there are no lingering body fluids caught in the fibers after being wiped down with disinfectant.

"Are you two doing the dirty?" With no concern for what the microfiber might be hiding, Candi kicks off her heels and plops down sideways on the sofa, putting her feet up.

I gingerly lower myself into one of the chairs, keeping my arms close to my sides. "That's on a need to know, and you, my friend do not need to know."

"Well, everyone out there sure thinks you are. Sitting on his lap like that sold it." Candi jerks her thumb in the direction of the club.

"Sitting on his lap was Salvatore's idea."

"You didn't scream bloody murder or throat punch him, so we all figured you wanted to be there." Now that I've allayed her worries, Candi is in full on nosy friend mode.

"You all?" I ask.

"Girl, if you don't think your warning caused a buzz of gossip then you don't remember this place very well."

Fair point. "Our server didn't get the memo."

"Oh, she got it alright, but she's new and thinks she's irresistible because of all the new girl attention she's getting."

"I was ready to punch her in the vagina," I admit.

Candi laughs. "Yeah, well if she moves on one of Piper's regulars like she tried to move on Salvatore, she's going to get a six-inch stiletto up her ass."

Piper is one of the dancers who has been at Pitiful Princess the longest. "Yeah, well you don't mess with a fellow dancer's income."

"Not if you don't want that stiletto heel in your back."

We smile at each other in understanding.

"So, Salvatore..." Candi says leadingly.

"He's mine." I shrug. "For now."

"We all definitely got the *he's mine* impression."

And Candi still checked in to make sure I wasn't putting on an act. I love her for that.

"No one in the club has seen you so much as touch a guy. Then you walk in on the billionaire's arm and sit on his lap?" She fans herself. "Girl, he would give a lot of women daddy fantasies. Now that I know he's not a typical rich douche, I don't blame you for playing."

They'd better keep their kinks to themselves around Salvatore.

Dio mio.

You are getting very possessive for a temporary bedmate, aren't you, Bianca?

Temporary is right. I can't forget that. But I can't deny that my snarky inner voice is right either. Again.

"Like I said, it's just for tonight." After what my dad put me through, daddy play is a big fat *no*.

"The possessive way he looks at you doesn't seem like it's only for the night. He didn't glance at the stage once."

"You were watching?"

"Weren't you?"

I shrug again. "He promised no lap dances."

"That's not the same as looking and he didn't."

We both know how rare that is. Men come to the Pitiful Princess to look.

Even when they're here with business associates. This time my inner voice sounds thoughtful, not sarcastic and that's dangerous. That means my subconscious is considering things we've got no business thinking about.

"Do you have a daddy kink I don't know about?" I tease Candi, not wanting to dwell on my thoughts, or the inner voice that is right more than she's wrong.

Someone else might call it my intuition manifesting in self-talk. I read that in a self-help book. I call it annoying.

Candi bursts out laughing. "I think you have to have experience with sex to have a kink."

My friend, the virgin stripper.

"How are things now?" I ask seriously. "You okay?"

"Ugo has taken over management of the dancers personally and he's making sure no one is being pressured to offer extra curriculars they don't want to."

"Good. He's still a tool."

"Pretty much." Candi grabs some paper towels from the handy access dispenser on the wall behind the couch and starts dabbing at the sweat on her face, careful not to ruin her makeup. "Piper told me she'd fix the problem if he didn't. I'm glad he came through though."

More like Salvatore did, but I can't say that and give away his connection to the Pitiful Princess.

Candi tosses her paper towels into a discreet trashcan. "Now, tell me everything."

"You already know it all." Well not the details about the sex stuff, but no way am I sharing that.

"Texts are not the same as talking. I've missed you." Sadness washes over Candi's face. "It's not the same here without you. No one else even remembers my real name."

"It's Kathleen."

"I prefer Kath."

I know that. And I never use it because calling her by her stage name is how I keep my friend at a distance.

Since Mr. Ruhnke died, I haven't let anybody in. But living in Salvatore's penthouse has made me remember what being part of a family feels like. What having people around me who care feels like.

I stand and take my chances with the couch to sit down beside Candi's stretched out legs.

Pulling my friend in for a hug, I say, "I miss you too, Kath."

Candi grills me some more and reiterates that I'll always have a place to live with her at least three times before Ugo sends someone looking for her.

SALVATORE

Nerissa shifts over to sit beside me and Ugo rises to leave. Then the two women we hired to keep Juniper company arrive at the table, one sitting on either side of him.

Neither woman is aware of my plans for Juniper, but they don't need to be. They only need to be willing to keep him occupied while his lower dose of Special K takes full effect, making him malleable enough to sign the paperwork.

Ugo has one of our lawyers and notaries waiting in his office to oversee the proceedings.

How long is a little extra break time?

"Staring at the curtain to the backrooms isn't going to make her magically appear, Salvatore," my second informs me wryly.

"How long is a little extra? Five or ten minutes? More?" It had better not be more.

Candi's break is supposed to last fifteen to begin with.

"Chill out, Salvatore. She's only been gone a few minutes."

It feels longer. I don't like her being out of my sight. "This is not a safe place for her to be hanging around the back room."

"We make sure it is a safe place for all our girls."

I whip my head around so my sister can see my pissed off expression. "She's not one of the working girls."

"Never said she was."

It's too close to the conversation I had with Bianca before she left. I don't think she's going to fuck another man, but that doesn't mean I want any other men close enough to touch her.

"I should go check on her."

"Would you relax, capo? Pietro followed them. Per your orders, he's always got his eyes on your *baby girl*." Nerissa snickers.

I know he's with her. I don't know why I'm so antsy.

"What the fuck was that daddy shit?" I ask to change the subject.

"You're asking *me*? If I had to guess, I'd say Bianca's not thrilled about being your cover and decided to get a little of her own back."

"Probably. She's no pushover." And why that should make me proud, I have no idea.

She's my temporary girlfriend.

Right?

"You seem different." Nerissa cocks her head and studies me. "Not so broody. Are you happy Salvatore?"

"You ask that like it would be a miracle if I was."

"Ever since you became made I would have said it was."

"What the hell are you talking about? I'm happy." I'm fucking glad the music and angle of the tables around us mean no one else can hear our conversation.

Not even the security teams taking up the tables on either side of us.

"No, really. This is different." She waves at me. "I was too busy worrying she was another Monica yesterday to notice, but when she's around, you're relaxed. At peace."

"Are you getting soft on me, second?"

"No, capo, but if she makes you feel good like this, keep her around a while."

"Even if she's an outsider?"

"I'm not saying marry the woman, but..." Nerissa shrugs. "She makes you happy."

"That wasn't your attitude yesterday."

"I was in protective sister mode then."

"What are you in now because you are not sounding like my second-in-command. We don't talk feelings and shit."

"Because you don't have them."

"Are you saying you do?"

She shrugs. "None that I'm willing to share."

"What the hell does that mean? Are you dating?"

Nerissa's laugh is too spontaneous not to be genuine. "Salvatore, I've been dating the same guy for a year. He's met mamma and papà and been vetted by dad."

"That guy you brought to Thanksgiving?"

"Yes."

"You didn't bring him to Christmas. I figured you broke up."

"And you didn't ask."

Unlike the rest of my family, I don't feel the need to force my way into personal business. If her relationship impacted her job as my second-in-command, that would be different. But Ernesto is part of Domenico's crew. The only other crew I trust as much as my own.

Besides Severu's crew, but that is to be expected. They work directly for our don. If they aren't trustworthy, they are dead. No demotion from any of his personal teams.

"You weren't sad," I explain. "I didn't have to kill him."

"No killing my boyfriends."

"He is your boyfriend now?"

"He wants to be more."

"What do you want?" Is my sister going to get married?

She shrugs. "I'm not sure. Ernesto understands the life because he's in it. He doesn't treat me like I'm too fragile to be your second."

"Smart man." The whole time we're talking, I'm watching that damn curtain leading to the back rooms.

It doesn't move. No one goes in. No one comes out.

"You sure Pietro went with her?" I ask over whatever Nerissa is saying now.

"Yes, capo, I'm sure." My second sounds exasperated. "I also think it's time to take Juniper into Ugo's office."

She indicates the man now leaning sideways, the woman beside him the only thing stopping him from face planting on the floor.

Chapter 46

SALVATORE

"Watch for Bianca. Make sure she stays at the table while I'm gone." I don't want her roaming around the strip club on her own.

Some *stronzo* would try to touch her and I would have to cut off his hands.

"You do remember she used to work here, don't you?"

"She doesn't anymore. And never will again."

"Ugo already said he'd have her back any time," Nerissa taunts.

"If Ugo wants to keep breathing, he'll rescind that offer." I grab Juniper by the shoulders and yank him up. "Let's go."

"Huh? Whe-ah ah we going? Ah the ladies coming?"

I jerk my head toward the one he was leaning on and she jumps up, sliding her arm around Juniper from the other side.

Once we reach the office, I dismiss her with gesture of my hand.

"What ah we doing he-ah?" Juniper looks around the office hazily. "Whe-ah's my date?"

"You just need to sign some paperwork and you can get back to her."

"Paperwork?"

"I've got the deed transfer on the properties ready for you to sign."

"You're going to pay me a lot, right?"

"Yes." My original offer was more than fair.

I wanted to finish the deal quickly, so I initially offered the high end of fair market. Juniper was salivating for that deal before Stellar Holdings stepped in.

Too bad for them and Henry fucking Caruso, I fight dirty, and I fight to win.

After reminding Juniper that his dates are waiting, he signs every single document, including the permission to transfer the funds directly into his bank account.

Proof of that transfer and the signed sales agreement is all my people need to expedite the sale of three out of five of the bar properties. We have people on our payroll in the Manhattan County Clerk's Office already and the transfer of ownership will be finalized first thing tomorrow morning.

We were able to bribe clerks in two of the other offices to bypass what could be as much as a ninety-day wait and record the deed changes within twenty-four hours.

The other two aren't in the City. In counties with smaller Clerk's Offices, it's not worth the risk of trying to bribe someone when taking ownership of them is not critical.

"Any sign of Gino?" I ask Ugo while one of my guys leads Juniper out to the club to a different table, where he can party as long as he wants with his dates on my dime.

Don't say I'm not generous in victory.

"About that." Ugo tugs at his collar. "I think he's in the soup."

The way he says *soup* lets me know he's not using a euphemism for in trouble. He's talking about the chemical bath we use to dispose of bodies in the subbasement of the Oscuro building.

"Che cosa?"

Ugo swallows. "One of the dancers mentioned to Angelo that Gino had been pressuring Candi to work the backrooms."

"When?"

"Before I got a chance to talk to him."

"Because you weren't doing your job, she told our don's top enforcer so he'd do something about fucking Gino stealing her money."

Ugo nods, misery in his expression. I was already pissed at him, but this makes our crew look bad and me look like I don't have control of my people.

I point at the GM and then to the chair Juniper vacated. "Sit."

Ugo sits.

Going to the door, I instruct one of my men to get Bianca and Nerissa. He doesn't have to tell Pietro to come. My top bodyguard goes where Bianca goes.

A couple of minutes later Nerissa brings Bianca into the office.

She walks across the room, her hips swaying with exaggerated motion, her pretty lips pursed. "Daddy! I missed you."

She's mocking me and about as sincere as the guy selling "Rolex" watches on the sidewalk. Those fucking words still hit me center mass.

"Knock that shit off," I tell her even though what I really want is for her to say it again. This time without the sarcasm

Refusing to examine why, I pull her into my body and hold her tight to me. My cock wakes up and my hands itch to caress every luscious curve her dress clings so sensually to. I knew I'd love this on her.

Bianca looks up at me through her lashes, her eyes glimmering with disdain. "But I thought you wanted me to play your girlfriend."

I don't like that disdain, or the implication that she's only playing the role of my girlfriend.

"You *are* mine." I lean down and speak softly directly into her ear. "You are my good girl. If you want to be my baby girl, I can be persuaded."

She shivers against me and sighs. "I'll pass."

"You sure?"

"The whole daddy thing does not carry good memories for me," she says with more candor and less rancor than I expect.

I want to ask her why but not in front of everyone else. So, I let her move to the side of me.

"Make Ugo's demotion to Gino's position permanent," I say to Nerissa, informing Ugo of his change in status at the same time.

The former GM doesn't look happy but he's smart enough not to protest.

Bianca goes stiff beside me. What is that about?

Finding out will have to wait. Her being here for this meeting is not the norm, but I don't want her out of my sight for one more minute in a club full of horny customers.

"Put someone in the GM position who will pay better attention to what is happening under their watch."

Giving Ugo a look of frustration, my second tells me, "I've got some candidates. The assistant manager at the Red Room is ready for more responsibility."

"I want to interview her before you offer her the position." I'm not risking this happening again.

"Is that really necessary? Having you participate in the interview will further undermine the confidence our crew has in me as second-in-command."

She's right. Under other circumstances, it wouldn't cause much comment. But coming on the heels of her punishment for disloyalty, it will be another blow to her reputation among our people.

Maybe they should question her fitness to lead. Maybe I should.

Nerissa should have noticed how much leeway Ugo was giving Gino. I may not know every employee at Amuni and Festa, but I sure as hell know the bar, kitchen and staff managers at both clubs. And how they perform.

My second should know the same for the strip clubs. "Yes. It is necessary. And I want you spending more time here and at the other clubs under your purview."

She can oversee our business

"This was a one-time thing, Salvatore," she says in protest. "Ugo delegated to the wrong guy."

"Ugo delegated too much and so did you. If you don't think the strip clubs are worth your time, I'll give them to someone who sees differently," I tell her.

The strip clubs are the second's responsibility. If I give them to someone else, I'm giving them her job too.

Nerissa's jaw clenches, but she nods without saying a word.

"Well?" I say, wanting the acknowledgment made out loud.

"I know I fucked up, okay? It won't happen again. The strip clubs are worth my time," she grits out, showing she knows exactly what I want from her. She flicks a glance to Bianca and sighs. "I will apologize to the dancers personally for letting them down."

Bianca's tension eases a little. "I think that's a good idea. They need to know they can come to you, or the GM, if there's a problem."

"I am sorry, Bianca," Nerissa says sincerely. "It is my job to oversee the strip clubs and I let you all down. I'll be checking in with the dancers at the other clubs too."

"Thank you," Bianca says.

I'm not sure if she's thanking my sister for the apology or the promise to check the other clubs.

"We aren't going to have any more problems with management, are we Ugo?" I ask the other man in a tone that lets him know there is only one right answer.

"No, no, of course not."

I turn to Bianca. "Happy now?"

"Not particularly, no."

She's still pissed about me using her as cover tonight. I need to take her on a real date and show her that temporary, or not, she *is* my girlfriend. And yes, I fucking want everyone to know it.

"Are you ready to leave?" I ask her, done with this place.

But she might have more friends she wants to catch up with. And for some reason, I'm channeling a guy who cares.

She steps away from me and turns toward the door. "Yes."

Bianca moves fast when she wants to and if Pietro wasn't blocking her way in the hall she would be outside before I caught up with her.

I grab her hand and incline my head toward my lead bodyguard. "Let's go."

When we get to the car, instead of sitting beside me like she has been all night, Bianca sits as far away from me as she can on the bench seat.

"I told you it wasn't a date," I remind her.

"You didn't tell me you were using me." Her look could incinerate a high-rise to a pile of ash. "You didn't tell me dinner was just so we were seen together to support the girlfriend pretense."

"For the fucking last time, it is not a fucking pretense. You are my girlfriend. And yes, I wanted you fucking seen with me. I want everyone to fucking know you are mine and to stay the fuck away."

"That's a lot of *fucks*."

"Not as many or the kind I really want," I tell her with frustrated honesty.

"You're not funny."

"Good, because I'm not joking."

Pointedly looking away from me, she stares out the window. "Why was I there for that?"

"I already told you." And she wasn't happy to hear it, so am I going to repeat it? Fuck, no.

"I meant for your meeting with Nerissa and Ugo."

"Did you want to hang out in the main area watching the dancers?"

"It's always fun to see what new moves or techniques other dancers are trying."

"But you don't work the pole any longer."

"It's still great exercise. Whether, I dance to make a living, or not, I'm not giving it up."

My cock likes the sound of that way too much. My inner caveman? Not so much.

"Where would you dance?"

"At a studio." She shrugs. "Does it matter?"

"I could have a pole installed in my gym."

She gives me a look that's a lot less angry, but a lot more questioning my intelligence. "I won't be able to use it until the cut on my back is completely healed. It would put too much strain on the recently repaired tissues."

"You sound like a doctor."

"I can Google like everybody else."

"I apologize that using you as cover tonight hurt your feelings." If my second can express regret, so can I.

No matter how little experience I have doing it.

"I wish you'd told me instead of just saying it wasn't a date."

If I told her, she wouldn't have acted naturally, making people wonder why we were together. Okay, so I used her and knew I was doing it.

I sigh. "I am sorry for that too."

"Don't do it again."

"I won't."

She turns her head and our gazes meet. "Promise."

"I give you my word as a capo." Does she know how serious that is?

Something flares in her bright blue gaze that says she does. "Okay."

She opens her mouth and then closes it again, looking uncertain.

"Che cosa?"

"Nerissa sounds like she really wants to do better overseeing the strip clubs."

"Yes." She'd better if she wants to remain my second-in-command.

"But Ugo..." Bianca's voice trails off.

"What about him?"

"I get that demoting him to assistant manager works to punish him, but is that what's best for the dancers?"

"He wouldn't dare pull the shit Gino did." Especially knowing that Gino died for his misdeeds.

And that if Angelo hadn't killed him, I would have. Nobody steals from the mafia and lives.

"That doesn't mean he'll be a good manager over the talent. If he doesn't respect them..." Her voice trails off.

"Why would you say he doesn't respect them?"

"Because he never once checked to see how Gino was managing us. He checked in with the bar manager every night to see if there was enough liquor stocked, but when it came to managing people who earn as much, or maybe more, for the mafia as the fricken liquor license, he left it entirely to Gino."

"That doesn't mean he won't do his job."

"Really? Is it worth the risk? Most of the dancers are sex workers, all of them are in the sex industry. That puts them at risk in a way other employees are not. Half of their job is illegal and there are no OSHA guidelines for how many johns a dancer takes into the backrooms in a single shift."

"We provide healthcare and they're routinely screened for STDs."

"To protect the customers. What protections do they have?"

"The mafia protects them from overzealous customers and getting picked up by the cops. And the women get to choose whether to take on a customer," I remind her.

"Really? Once a dancer starts offering extra services, she has to pay a base rate per night for protection."

"That's normal and it's less than our average 50% take." They don't pay protection on top of their 50%, but Bianca is right.

There is a minimum amount every dancer is expected to pay for the use of the back rooms and the security we provide. Some nights their 50% doesn't cover it, but most nights it does.

"Do you know why their 50% take covers that base rate so many nights?"

"Because it's not hard to make enough to cover it." I'm sure about that. It's a policy I instituted when I was in charge of the strip clubs before my father moved me to the nightclubs.

He wanted me working the legit businesses in public to distance me from the illegal aspects of our business on paper in preparation for me taking over as capo one day. We thought that was a lot farther into the future than it turned out being.

"You make money offering hand jobs, your mouth and your ass for one night and tell me how easy it is."

"The sex workers never complained to me when I was in charge."

"And no one complained to Ugo or Nerissa when Gino started his shit either."

"Are you saying I wasn't paying attention? Because I was. I checked in with Ugo when he was assistant manager."

"Yeah? Did you talk to the dancers?"

"I didn't have time to talk to every employee then any more than I do now."

"Your employees at the nightclubs aren't facing the same kind of risks the dancers and cocktail waitresses who turn tricks are. When a dancer is too sick to dance, she still has to cover her backroom fee for every night she's on the schedule, whether she works or not."

"That's business."

"That's shitty."

"Look, I pay taxes, rent and utilities whether we are open or not."

"You mean your shell company."

"The shell company is me." Effectively.

"More like the mafia," she mutters, but then her jaw sets at a stubborn angle. "Whoever. That shell company makes tens of millions of dollars in profit."

"At least," I say proudly.

"So if you have to eat overhead costs the impact on your bottom line is minimal. If one of your hourly workers has to, the difference could be between making rent that month and not. Or between groceries and paying the heating bill."

"It's too hot to run heat right now."

"Don't. This isn't funny."

"You never did back room work. Why do you care so much?"

"You've never been don, but that doesn't stop you from caring about Severu De Luca's wellbeing."

"I owe him my allegiance."

"If you expect loyalty from your employees, whether they manage the bar or make the mafia extra money with their bodies, and I know you do..." She pauses, daring me to contradict her.

I don't. I do expect loyalty.

"Then you have to give it to them too."

"Write up your concerns and send it to Nerissa. I'll give you her email address."

"What stops her from dropping it straight into the trash folder?"

"Do you think she would do that?" I'm genuinely curious what Bianca's take on my sister is.

I know Nerissa will consider Bianca's concerns and if she finds them valid, look for a way to mitigate them. Despite overstepping out of concern for me, she's a good second and there's a reason our soldiers are loyal to her which has nothing to do with being my sister.

Bianca takes a minute to consider my question. "No, I don't think she would. Especially if you tell her to expect my email."

No one pushes me like this woman. "Done."

Chapter 47

SALVATORE

Bianca stares up in awe at the Art Deco building through the car window. "Your don owns this building and the top two floors are his home?"

I don't like how impressed she sounds. "I own the building my penthouse is in too."

Her head turns so our eyes meet. I have no interest in the view out the window. I have seen it many times before, but I will never tire of looking at Bianca.

"How?" she asks, her brows furrowed. "No wonder the only access to the rooftop garden is from your penthouse."

"My father signed it over to me when I became capo." I'd been managing the building as part of my duties as his second-in-command for nearly a decade at that point.

I still manage it and assign other responsibilities to Nerissa.

"You know that's ridiculous right? To be given an entire Manhattan high-rise as a gift for a job promotion."

I shrug. "My grandfather gave it to my father when he was named capo. My father gave it to me when I was."

"How does that work? One son became don, and the other was a capo."

"When the capo in my father's position had to be removed from his position. My grandfather needed someone to take over he could trust. Since his underboss, Uncle Enzu would become don after him, he chose his younger son."

"Your father."

"Yes."

"How did your grandfather become don?"

"He was a behind the scenes money guy without an arrest record. After RICO, the leadership had to be squeaky clean to keep us off law enforcement's radar."

"Makes sense, I guess." She bites her bottom lip and gives me a worried look. "Have you been to prison?"

"No." All my illegal deeds are buried along with any evidence they ever happened. "We're a lot more careful not to get caught for even petty crimes now."

Once they get you in the system for anything you fall under more scrutiny and are more vulnerable to search warrants and being held for questioning.

Not that either would do law enforcement any good. We are too fucking careful. And a modern Genovese doesn't talk. They know it's a death sentence with a side of grisly.

"I'm glad."

"You don't think I should pay for my crimes?"

"No. There's too much corruption and greed that's legal for me to think you deserve jailtime for protecting your family." She smiles softly. "You might have been bossy about it, but you watched out for me. You're even trying to save my poor Vee."

I still find it hard to believe she named her African violet. I should set Bianca straight and tell her that I am more monster than man. But I won't.

I like the look of admiration in her beautiful blue eyes too much.

My driver pulls into the parking space set aside for me in the underground parking garage.

Bianca doesn't unbuckle her seatbelt right away. "Why am I here?"

"Because you are my guest and I was invited."

"But *why* am I your guest?" she persists.

I realize where this is coming from. "It's not like last night. There are no ulterior motives."

Not now anyway.

"This is dinner with your *family*, Salvatore. You had a reason for asking me to come."

She sounds completely convinced of that fact. And she's right, damn it. "I thought bringing you would stop my cousin's wife matchmaking without getting my mom's hopes up about marriage and grandchildren."

"Because I'm not a mafia princess." The way she says it bothers me.

Like she's somehow less than.

It bothers me even more that she's not wrong. "My mother is usually a stickler for people knowing and staying in their place. She doesn't even let Pietro call her Ilaria and she's known him since birth."

"But she was really nice to me when I met her and she was pretty adamant I call her Ilaria."

"I am aware."

"That doesn't mean she'll start imaging wedding bells in our future. If she didn't know before, I'm sure Nerissa has informed your mom by now that I am a pole dancer turned cocktail waitress."

"She knew that you were a server at Amuni."

"Did you tell her?"

"No, but I'm sure Rosa did." What Rosa knows, my mother knows, which is why I need to find a new housekeeper.

"But I'm still an outsider." She sighs. "Your mom was just being nice."

My mother is unfailingly polite. She can be kind. She is loyal. She loves her family fiercely, but she is not *nice*. I don't burst Bianca's bubble about that either.

I tell her the one thing that should not be true. "You don't feel like an outsider."

Maybe my sister is right to be concerned about my judgment when it comes to Bianca. I've been patting myself on the back because the skittish woman so obviously trusts me, all the while being blind to how much I am growing to trust her.

A temporary lover and an outsider, like she just reminded me.

But she doesn't feel like an outsider. She feels like mine. Like my crew is mine. Like my family is mine.

Fuck.

Bianca opens her mouth and closes it without saying anything.

"Are you angry?" I ask after several long seconds.

"No."

"But I was going to use you again."

"Yeah, you're kind of mercenary like that." She doesn't *sound* angry. Only thoughtful.

"Your presence will still stop Catalina from throwing her sister at me all night long."

"Good."

Good? What the hell does that mean.

A tap on the window reminds us it's time to go.

Bianca jumps like it was a gunshot and the click of her undoing her seatbelt is loud in the back of the car.

We're in the elevator with Pietro, the rest of my men in the freight elevator per protocol, when she speaks again. "Tell me about the don's wife trying to play matchmaker."

Pietro covers a bark of laughter with a cough.

I scowl at him. He won't think it's so funny if I put him forward for the position of Madonna Carlotta Jilani's husband. Lottie has grown up a lot in the last year and done her best to be a good sister to our don's wife. She's still a self-involved princess, used to getting her own way though.

"Catalina invited her younger sister to dinner too."

"She'd be a good match though for you, right?"

I shake my head in firm negation. "Lottie is too young, impetuous and selfish."

"A dangerous combination for the sister of the don's wife."

Surprised she gets it so easily, I nod. "I'm lucky Severu doesn't consider me the answer to his sister-in-law headache."

"She wouldn't be any less problematic as a capo's wife," Bianca says.

"Got that right," Pietro mutters.

They're both right. And Severu is savvy enough to know it.

"If I wasn't here, your mom might get in on the matchmaking too," Bianca guesses. "That woman wants grandchildren. "But she's too polite to trip another woman and watch you land on top of her when you have a date."

Neither Pietro, nor I stifle our laughter at this assessment. That is my mother in a nutshell.

"You got to know mamma very well in a single afternoon."

"She's pretty open about what she wants, and that's you married."

My mother is in fact *not* open around people outside the family. That she was so open with Bianca surprises me.

That Bianca figured mamma out from whatever she did share doesn't. "You're good at reading people."

"Sometimes," Bianca says, like she has memories of bad judgment calls about people in the past.

"Who hurt you?" I ask.

"Too many people."

"Do not fall for me," I warn her, though the words taste like ash on my tongue. "I don't want to be one of them."

"You're driving into conceited territory there, capo."

"I like it better when you call me your capo."

"Both you and your sister have a hard time sticking to a lane. Is it a family trait, or something? You don't want me to fall for you, but you want me to claim you. That's fine for sex talk, but bordering on delulu outside the bedroom."

She's absolutely right. It still pisses me off.

"While you are living in my home, you are mine and I am your capo."

"Dream on, caveman."

Pietro cough-laughs again, reminding me he's there. How the fuck did I forget, for even a second, that her bodyguard was in the elevator with us?

There's no time to answer her sass before the elevator dings and the doors slide open to Severu and Catalina's foyer. Stepping in front of Bianca so she can't exit, I shove my friend out of the elevator and push the button to close the doors.

Pietro's guffaws of laughter echo off the doors as they close.

I pull the button that stops the elevator from moving and then press my thumb against the print scanner beside it, effectively creating a locked room for privacy.

Spinning to face Bianca, I am determined to get her to admit she is mine.

She's got a point, genius. You are crossing lanes like a racecar driver making for the outside track.

And like that driver, I am fucking determined to cross the finish line as the winner.

Bianca's arms are crossed, lifting her beautiful tits framed by a sweetheart neckline in mouthwatering display. She's wearing the black dress tonight. More modest than the blue one I convinced her to wear last night with its lowcut neckline and spaghetti straps, this one is still sexy as hell.

Too sexy. A trash bag would be too sexy on this woman.

"Staying on the elevator defeats the purpose of us actually going to dinner at your don's home," she drolly points out.

"You are not stepping off this elevator while you are pretending to believe you are not mine."

"Uh...this thing..." She waives her hand between the two of us. "It's temporary, dude. You said so yourself."

"As long as it lasts, no other man touches you."

"That's not the problem you seem to think it is." Her eyeroll questions my intelligence. "I don't like being touched."

"You like my hands on you." But I notice how she avoids close proximity with others.

"You're the exception." She gives a disgruntled sigh. "I don't know why, but you are."

"Don't sound so happy about it."

"You're a freaking capo in the Cosa Nostra. Of course, I'm not happy about it. There's no future for us, no place our lives meet and stay connected."

"What if there was?" What the fuck am I saying?

She doesn't latch onto my words like a lot of women would though.

Sadness flashes briefly in her pretty eyes before she dispels it. "There isn't. We both know it. In eighteen months, I finally get my degree and I'm leaving New York. In two months, or sooner, you forget about me altogether."

"Are you saying you are going to forget me?"

"I'm not saying anything."

"Which means you won't." It had better mean that.

"Don't get a big head. It's not every day a woman ends up in the bed of a mobster. It's pretty unforgettable."

"Fuck that. I'm not just any made man. I am *your fucking capo*."

"We've only known each other thirteen days." She's still arguing.

And I won't fucking have it.

I step forward until I am a hair's breadth from her banging body. "Say it. Or I will fuck you against the wall of this elevator until you're screaming it."

"Can't do that yet. The plastic surgeon would yell at you for messing up his work."

"That supercilious fucker has too much instinct for self-preservation to yell at me about anything." But she's right. I'm not fucking her against a wall. Yet. "And you are too damn smart not to know that I'll have you yelling *capo mio* loud enough for them to hear in the penthouse if you don't say it."

"Stop it! *Ho detto basta*." She pounds the side of her fist against my sternum. "Are you trying to break my heart?"

I have no answer for that. Not two minutes ago, I told this woman not to fall for me, so I don't hurt her. But there is nothing I want more than for her to go head over heels for me.

No woman has touched my heart since Monica and now I want to own Bianca's. No matter what is best for her. Or my mafia.

Cazzo.

Grabbing her curled up hand, I gently unfurl her fingers and press her now flattened hand over my heart. "What if we don't put an expiration date on it? What if we just see where this goes?"

"Can a capo do that? See where it goes? I thought you had to marry for the good of the family. For heirs and other medieval crap like that." She's glaring at me like I'm the one who made the rules.

But I'm not that man. I'm the man, who for the second time in my life, is considering breaking them. For her.

"I'm not talking about marriage." Yet.

But I'm not letting her go. Not today. Not a week from now. Not two months from now when she's fully healed and can go back to work.

And you can fuck her into the wall.

Maybe not ever.

"Marriage should be the furthest thing from my mind." Bianca's nose squishes in disgust. "We were complete strangers two weeks ago. This is ridiculous."

"Pretending there's nothing real between us, no matter how quickly it developed, is more ridiculous." I know what I feel, and I know that I'm not alone.

"I'm not."

"You are. I have too, but that ends now." I'm not falling alone.

"Salvatore," she sighs my name like a prayer.

I cup her nape and squeeze. "Admit that I am yours."

She keeps her lips together, silently refusing.

Leaning down, I kiss her. At first her lips are immobile, but as I flirt at the seam of her mouth with my tongue, she makes a soft little sound and lets me in.

I devour her mouth until we are both panting and then I lift my head just enough to speak against her lips. "Say it, *brava ragazza mia*."

Her breath hitches.

"*Io sono tua*. You know it."

"You're *my capo*," she says with a gusty sigh, trying to sound fed up with me, but the words hold weight and she knows it.

"And you are mine. "

"Yes." She kisses me like she can't stop herself and then ruins it with her next words. "For now."

"For as long as we want it to last," I promise her.

She shakes her head, but she doesn't argue with me again.

"Are you two coming out?" Severu's voice comes over the elevator speakers. "Or are you staying in there all night? We have guestrooms if that's what you need."

Stronzo.

Bianca groans and her forehead lands against my sternum. "I can't believe this."

"Be careful," I admonish her. "You've got a healing wound there."

"I know." She looks up at the ceiling where the speaker is. Does she see the camera as well? "Can he hear us? Has he been listening this whole time?"

"I can hear you now, Miss Gemelli," Severu says. "But no one has been listening in on your *conversation*."

"He thinks we've been in here having sex," Bianca whispers to me, horrified.

"We haven't been fucking," I inform my cousin, trying to make her feel better.

Severu makes a sound that might be amusement. "Noted."

He jokes more since he married Catalina. By more, I mean at all.

My statement and Severu's agreement should make Bianca happy but now she's scowling at me while she tries to push away from me, her cheeks bright red.

I'm not going anywhere just yet.

I squeeze the back of her neck again. "Remember who your man is when you meet Miceli."

Women fall all over themselves to be with him. God knows why. His charm is a thin veneer over a stone-cold killer every bit as ruthless as any other man in our family.

Bianca's gaze softens and she whispers, "*Il mio lui,*" before pushing my suit jacket aside to press a kiss over my heart.

The word *sempre* is heavy on the tip of my tongue but I hold it back. Barely. I cannot claim her forever.

Yet.

Chapter 48

BIANCA

My thoughts are spinning while I am introduced to the rest of the De Luca family.

Salvatore wants to be *my capo* which is not the same thing as merely being a Cosa Nostra capo. He wants, no *insists* on me laying claim to him.

He wants to see where this thing goes.

He said he wasn't talking about marriage. He didn't say *yet*, but I heard it whispered between us, a silent word that we both refused to voice.

This is so messed up.

"Pleased to meet you," I say by rote to Don De Luca when we are introduced.

Incredibly handsome, he gives off an aura of menace that would terrify me if it weren't for the way he looks at his wife, Catalina. Like she is the sun, the moon and the stars all in one beautiful package.

He does not invite me to call him Severu and studies me like a bug under the microscope. I would probably fidget under his intense scrutiny if my mind wasn't so occupied with my conversation with Salvatore in the elevator.

Still, I'm relieved when he, his brother, Miceli, Salvatore, and his dad leave to talk in private. Big Sal De Luca seems about as impressed with me as his daughter.

Speaking of, where is Nerissa? Isn't she joining this family dinner?

The don's mother, Aria De Luca is good friends with Ilaria and those two are chatting on the far side of the luxurious Art Deco living room.

Pietro stands aloof near the entrance to the room, his eyes scanning back and forth like there could be a credible threat in the don's home. He's not alone in his diligence though. No less than two other mafia soldiers have similar stances around the room.

The don is just a little over-protective of his wife.

She and her sister seem happy to include me in their conversation. Though it's pretty much the Lottie show, with her talking about her adventures at culinary school while Catalina (who did insist I call her by her first name) and I listen.

I don't mind because I'm still playing that elevator conversation over in my head. Word by confusing and heart wrenching word.

Salvatore went from telling me not to fall for him to demanding I admit that he is *my* capo. And the most messed up thing about it is how much I wanted to say the words, how good it felt to tell him I am his.

Che palle.

"Excuse me," I interrupt Lottie's lecture about a new cooking technique she learned this week . "Where is the bathroom?"

"I'll show you," Catalina says before her sister can answer.

Even though Catalina is only a smidge shorter than my five-feet-four-inches, she's wearing ballet flats. I'm in three-inch heels, so I'm half a head taller, but her curves are a little more pronounced. Not that I'm slender by any stretch, but dancing keeps my muscles more toned than an average woman of my size.

She also has one of the kindest dispositions I have ever encountered, which shows itself in her words on the way to the guest bathroom.

"I'm sorry," she says for the second time after I told her not to worry in response to the first. "I didn't know Salvatore was in a relationship. If I had, I wouldn't have invited Car— I mean Lottie. She doesn't like being called Carlotta anymore."

"He said you were hoping to get them together."

Catalina winces. "I just worry about her. My sister is not exactly my husband's favorite person."

"Why?" I ask. "She seems nice."

"She can be, but she's also the woman who left him standing at the altar."

I feel my eyes grow wide, my own spinning thoughts forgotten for a second. "He was supposed to marry her? But she's younger than me."

I slap my hand over my mouth. I should not have said that.

Catalina's laugh is like tinkling bells and it makes me want to laugh too. "He's the Genovese don. She's the most beautiful mafia princess of our generation. Our father was his consigliere. It all made sense at the time."

"Nope. Still not getting it. Your sister is no more beautiful than you are. And I mean it's pretty obvious he's so into you, other women don't exist for him."

Catalina blushes, but smiles. "The feeling is mutual."

I can't help the little squiggle of envy that slithers through my brain. If my father had been a different man, a loyal mafioso, Salvatore and I could have something like Catalina and the don.

Maybe. Probably. Oh, I don't know.

She leaves me to it outside the surprisingly small bathroom for such a spacious home. I suppose with all the bathrooms attached to bedrooms; the guest toilet doesn't need to be that big.

I close the door before plopping down to sit on the closed toilet lid. I need a minute. Maybe ten.

I look up and realize this is one of those bathrooms where you can see your face and shoulders in the vanity mirror while sitting on the commode.

Like yesterday morning, I find myself looking intently at my reflection, but there is no Salvatore behind me now. No sexy view of us together.

It's just me.

Bianca Gemelli. *Bianca Russo.*

My red hair may be the exact same shade as my sister's, our features identical and our bodies so similar, it would be hard for our mom to tell us apart at first glance, but my life is nothing like Bea's.

She's the acknowledged daughter of a wealthy socialite married to a minor politician. I am the hidden daughter, left behind when our mom decided I was too much like her mafia husband to take me with her.

Bea might be my twin, but as far as the rest of the world knows, she's an only child.

The only other people, besides my mom and sister, who knew she was a twin are dead.

If Salvatore and I stay together, I have to tell him though. About Bea. About what I did to protect her. About what happened to me later?

Is this the real source of my refusal to even consider a future with the capo?

My stomach twists. What happens when he finds out my secrets?

There's so much about me he does not know.

How angry will he be when he learns that I've been lying to him about being part of the mafia? If he can get past that, will he be able to stomach it when he finds out that my father was a rat?

Even if he can get past all that, will he reject me like my mother did when he learns I killed a man when I was thirteen?

Unlike my society mom, Salvatore has killed plenty of men and at least one woman. Maybe he can deal with that part of my past. I can't apologize for it because nine years later, I still feel no remorse for killing the man trying to assault my sister.

Telling him about what happened when I was sixteen is worse though. The shame is not mine. Didn't Mr. Ruhnke say that over and over again? And all the books I read trying to get a handle on the dark shadow inside me said the same. To reject the shame. To refuse to own it.

And still, this ball of humiliation and pain is always there, deep down inside me.

No matter how much I don't want to, I have to tell him about it. Isn't that what you do when you love someone? Tell them everything.

I look into my own troubled gaze.

Girl, you can't fall in love in a couple of weeks. That's not the way it works. No matter what you think you're feeling, it's not love.

For once my inner voice is talking sense and I don't want to listen. It *feels* like love. All consuming. Terrifying. Impossible to ignore.

If he loves me, he'll accept my past like I accept his present. Right?

Only, wanting to possess me is not the same thing as love, is it? Hard enough to believe I have feelings this deep after such a short time, how can I even begin to think the brutal capo shares them?

A brisk knock sounds at the door.

SALVATORE

Severu's office has subtle changes since he married Catalina a year ago.

A stack of Catalina's composition notebooks sits on a small table kitty-corner to Severu's desk. To Domencico's crew's dismay, she still insists on keeping her records analog. She has her own office, but these two are sickeningly inseparable.

There is even an armchair behind the desk beside where my don sits. It's for his wife whenever she is in the room and *not* in his lap. Which when it is just family, is pretty damn rare.

For the first time, I get it.

"Everything still going smoothly with the bar properties?" Severu asks leaning on his giant desk facing the rest of us.

The rest of us make up a semicircle around him.

Since I'm the one giving a report, I'm in the center facing my cousin. "The transfer of ownership for the three New York city properties have gone through. The other two have been filed with their respective county clerks and are awaiting approval."

"No interference from Stellar Holdings?"

"Juniper didn't wake up until after all the papers had been filed. He did so with three women in his bed and hasn't tried to use his phone yet or leave the house."

We've had his cell phone jammed since my people picked him up yesterday. The jammer drains the phone's battery, so it looks like it's dead because he forgot to charge it. A side effect of his pre-function cocktail is Juniper's memory will be too fuzzy to know the truth.

"What about the escort Lombard sent with him?"

"Nerissa dumped her phone in a full margarita pitcher once she passed out last night." That phone is toast.

"Good thinking," my father praises my sister.

I agree with a nod. Nerissa is hella smart.

"And the jammer on Juniper's phone?"

"Now that the paperwork is filed it is set to self-delete once he sets his device to charge."

"I'm surprised Matthew Lombard hasn't sent people to check on him."

"No reason to. The GPS on the woman's phone still registers at the house and the false GPS signal Domenico's people set up for Juniper's phone does too."

Miceli frowns. "It's still sloppy."

I agree.

"Lorenzo called me." Severu looks at me expectantly.

The little bitch went running to the don and tattled on me like the rat he is.

I cross my arms, meet my cousin's gaze and say nothing. If he's looking for an apology for my actions, it's not happening.

"He says you were very disrespectful when he came to Amuni," my father drops into the silence between me and Severu.

I flick a glance toward my father. "I'm sure Nerissa already told you, but he followed one of my people into the ladies' room and accosted her."

Papà doesn't even flinch when he nods his acquiescence to my accusation. "Still, your reaction was not respectful."

"I should respect that pile of shit?" Everyone in this room is aware that Severu has Lorenzo under investigation for skimming the drug profits. "He's lucky I did not kill him. If he tries to touch her again, I will slit his throat."

Miceli barks a laugh. "It's Severu all over again. No woman is going to turn me into a Neanderthal like you two."

Severu frowns at his brother. "Good luck with that. You share my DNA."

"But not your obsession for your wife."

"If you did, I would have to kill you."

Another joke from my serious cousin? Something has put him into a good mood tonight.

"You know what I mean, brother. I will never obsess over a woman like you do Catalina."

"Never is a dangerous word you could end up eating," Severu warns.

Miceli just shakes his head.

But my father is looking at me with both anger and concern. It has been more than a decade, but I remember that look.

I put my hand up. "Do not tell me you would do any differently if he tried to maul mamma."

"Oh how the mighty have fallen," Miceli says pityingly.

My father stares at me in blatant disbelief. "Are you saying this nobody, this outsider you have known less than two weeks, is your woman? Monica worked you for six months before you were serious enough about her to ask Enzu's permission to tell her the truth about your role in *la famiglia*."

The way my father says *worked you* would have made me check myself in the past. Not now. Yes, I was a fool when I was twenty. I'm not one now.

Bianca is not Monica.

Severu doesn't speak, there's a question in his silence though.

I have a choice to make. I can back down, or I go with my gut. Backing down has never been my strong suit. It's not even in my deck of cards.

My gut it is. "She is mine."

"Are you saying you are not open to being the husband in the alliance deal with Shaughnessy?" Severu studies me intently.

Miceli is supposed to marry the Irishman's niece. I do not know what Severu wants me to say right now. But for the first time in my life as a made man, what my don wants is not my top priority.

I am not giving Bianca up.

Miceli glares at his brother. "I'm the sacrificial lamb in that scenario. The deal is done."

"You two fight like cats and dogs," Severu tells his brother. "Maybe Salvatore won't piss her off so easily."

"She is my fiancée," Miceli grinds out between clenched teeth, his hands fisted at his sides with white knuckle intensity.

"I am not marrying her," I insert before the argument between the don and underboss comes to blows.

Both men stare at me in surprise. My father's mouth gapes like a fish.

I just refused my don. Point blank.

Instead of jumping down my throat, Severu nods and then turns a glare on his brother. "Figure your shit out with Róise then. This marriage is supposed to cement an alliance, not start a war."

Chapter 49

BIANCA

"Bianca? Let me in." Salvatore's deep tones are muffled by the thick wooden door, but I have no trouble understanding him.

"I am using the bathroom, Salvatore. Go away."

"You have been in there a long time."

"What are you? The bathroom police? I'll be out in a minute."

Now that I need to rush, I have to pee. Of course I do. It only takes a minute and then I wash my hands.

When I open the door, I'm not even a little bit surprised to find Salvatore leaning against the wall opposite, waiting for me.

I roll my eyes. "Seriously? You're going from cheesy pickup lines to stalking? You have zero game, Salvatore De Luca."

"I have all the game you need, *bella mia*." His expression intent, he pushes away from the wall.

I shake my head and sidestep, knowing if I back up into the bathroom it is game over. "No way. You are not getting me all wound up before we have to sit down to dinner with your family."

"I'll make sure you are sated when we join them."

My ladybits are shouting *hell, yeah* while my brain is yelling *don't you do it*.

"There you two are. Everyone else has gone up to dinner," Ilaria says. "Your father was wondering where you were, Salvatore."

"Was he?" My lover sounds less than impressed.

A minute later, I find out what Ilaria meant by *gone up*. Two rooftop gardens in one week? How freaking wealthy is the De Luca family?

"Where is Nerissa?" I ask Salvatore as he pulls a chair out for me at the table between his mother and Miceli.

"She's working tonight," Ilaria answers while Salvatore taps his cousin's shoulder.

With his fist. "Move, Miceli, this is my seat."

"Catalina didn't assign seats tonight," the other man says, reaching for his glass of wine.

Salvatore snatches it up first, walks around the table and trades it with an empty glass at the only other unoccupied spot. "I'm assigning them. Move your ass."

"Salvatore, you cannot speak to the don's underboss that way," Ilaria admonishes her son.

"That's rich coming from you," Salvatore retorts with some bite while glaring at his cousin.

"Miceli, come and sit by me." The unoccupied spot is beside Catalina. "I want you here when me and Severu make our announcement."

Announcement? The don's wife glows with happiness and I'm pretty sure the whole table knows what's coming next.

Miceli jumps from his chair though and circles the table to sit down beside Catalina. "Have you got a bun in the oven, *cara?*"

"Don't call my wife endearments," Severu orders. Then he smiles at Catalina before turning to look at the rest of his family at the table. "We're expecting the next little De Luca around Christmas."

I do some quick calculations in my head. That would make the don's wife about two months pregnant.

What would it be like to have so much confidence in the future, you were willing to announce your pregnancy before passing the three-month mark when the chances for miscarriage drop significantly?

I'd probably wait until I was showing and couldn't hide it anymore.

Everyone congratulates the couple, including me. We drink sparking grape juice because Severu won't have everyone drinking champagne while his wife abstains. A surprisingly sweet move from the scary don.

It's surreal to be here for this important family moment. The De Lucas are all welcoming though. Well, except Iliaria's husband, Big Sal. He watches me like he's expecting me to start taking notes for the FEDs.

Salvatore keeps one hand on my thigh while he eats with the other and whether I belong with his family, or not, I feel like I belong with him.

Dessert has just been served when one of the don's security people comes up and says something in his ear.

A mask drops over Don De Luca's face, taking away every speck of humanity from his expression. "Don Caruso had another stroke." He fixes me with a deadly stare. "That information will not go beyond those at this table."

I nod in instant agreement, unable to speak under the weight of his look.

Ilaria and Aria gasp, giving Severu identical looks of concern. Is he close to the other don. Wait, isn't Don Caruso the godfather?

If he dies, it's not just the New York Five Families that lose their godfather. It's the entire freaking United States Cosa Nostra.

Che palle. The city of New York, the whole fucking country, has no idea how fragile peace between the Families will be in the days ahead. Does Salvatore know who is likely to take Don Caruso's place?

I don't ask.

He's too busy to talk to me, constantly on his phone. But he insists on taking me back to the penthouse. He doubles the security team both around the building and in the apartment.

Once we are in the penthouse, he grasps my shoulder, meeting my eyes. "Do not leave the penthouse for any reason."

A snarky reply about how that's no different than the past two weeks is on the tip of my tongue, but I swallow it back. Now is not the time for snark.

"I won't," I promise.

"Brava regazza mia." He kisses me. "Go upstairs and stay there for the rest of the night."

I nod.

"You do not go outside."

He is seriously concerned about my safety.

"No going outside," I promise.

He kisses me again and then he's gone.

I'm surprised when Pietro doesn't leave with him.

"I thought you were head of his security," I say to Pietro, who is busy texting on his phone.

He looks up. "I am."

"Shouldn't you be with him then?"

"He wants me here."

Protecting me?

"Yes." Pietro smiles at my surprised look. "You asked it out loud. In Italian by the way."

I nod, too flummoxed by how important Salvatore is making me feel with his choices.

The feelings of love I've been fighting shatter the last defenses around my heart.

It doesn't make sense, but I love him.

SALVATORE

Two days after the dinner at Severu's, Pietro texts me to say he'll be waiting in my office when I get back to the penthouse. So, instead of going directly to my bed and Bianca like I want to, I head to my office first.

Pietro is sitting in one of the chairs facing my desk, doing something on his phone.

Veering to the drink's cabinet, I ask, "What do you have for me?"

He didn't tell me why he wanted to meet, but I assume it is because he finished Bianca's background check.

"Everything has been quiet. No problems at the clubs and no attempts to gain access to your penthouse."

"And Bianca?" I pour myself two fingers of my favorite whiskey and take a sip. It slides down my throat with a smooth burn.

"She doesn't have any social media accounts. Her high school records only list Daryl Ruhnke as her guardian and his contact information. No parents are listed."

It's a little odd, but not completely unexpected, since both are dead. Ruhnke must have gotten himself assigned as her guardian. "What else?"

"Her work history includes a bar, Pitiful Princess and Amuni. No one had anything bad to say about her at the bar or strip club."

"You didn't talk to Nerissa then." My lips twist wryly.

Pietro shakes his head. "Yeah, no. I did talk to Ugo and some dancer named, Piper. He said she's worked there the longest and knows the other dancers the best."

"What about Bianca's friend Candi?"

"She told me to go fuck myself and then went straight to Ugo to tell him that some creep, as in me, was asking personal questions about the dancers and wanted me thrown out."

Amusement alleviates some of my exhaustion. "She's a firecracker, just like Bianca."

"That's one way to put it." He blows out a breath. "Before she went ballistic on me, she confirmed Bianca doesn't use social media."

Pietro's dry tone suggests that the words Candi used to tell him that weren't friendly. "She wasn't impressed with your charm?"

"She told me that Bianca doesn't do social media to keep creeps like me at bay, but I think it's your charms she's the least impressed with. Candi didn't tell me to fuck off until I explained I'm in charge of your security and doing a background check on your girlfriend is part of my job."

"She's offended on Bianca's behalf. They're tight." I bet there are some less than flattering texts about me on Bianca's phone right now.

"Queens college is out for the summer," Pietro continues. "I can have men track down students and professors from the business school, but it will take time."

"It's not a priority." His crew is stretched thin between guarding me and keeping the penthouse secure right now.

While the godfather lingers on the edge of death, I'll be doing a lot of traveling to meet with other capos to solidify Severu's support for godfather with other Cosa Nostra syndicates.

Being both capo and my don's cousin gives me a unique position we are taking advantage of.

"Did you follow up with Ruhnke's family?"

"Both sons and the daughter-in-law refused to talk to me."

That gives me pause. "One of his sons was happy to air their grievances with Nerissa."

"He stonewalled me completely."

"Check into the will through the probate office. That was Nerissa's next step."

"Okay, but why does it matter if the old man left Bianca money?" Pietro asks.

"Any red flags?" I ask.

"None. But I'll feel better when I can identify her parents. That information will be in the registrar's office at QC."

"Now is not the time to break into a university." The city is on edge with the godfather's imminent demise and we need to keep a low profile.

"Do you want me to ask Domenico's guys to use their facial recognition software to dig deeper?"

"No. We'll keep this inhouse. She's my girlfriend, not my fiancée." As soon as we bring in Severu's people, he and my father get access to their discoveries.

I've had enough of papà's interference in my personal life to last me a lifetime.

Chapter 50

BIANCA

My heart leaps into my throat when I read Candi's text.

Candi: *Your asshole rich boyfriend sent his security guy around to ask questions about you. Are you sure you like this guy?*

My stomach twists. This is not what I wanted to wake up to this morning. It doesn't help that Salvatore isn't beside me in bed.

Did he find out who I really am? Is he going to kick me out of his apartment and life because my father was a rat?

"I assume by the expression on your face, your friend texted to tell you Pietro is running a background check on you," Salvatore's voice cuts through my spiraling panic.

Jerking my head up, our eyes meet. His are not filled with loathing or anything like that. They gleam with heated desire sending a spear of want directly to my core.

He stands there completely naked, his hair still wet from the shower, his penis already semi-erect. He does not look like a man who just found out secrets about his lover that disturb him.

"Why? Is it because of what your sister told you?"

"It's because you are living in my home."

"So why not run the background check before you had Pietro kidnap me and bring me here?"

"The kidnapping was all Pietro's idea."

That's not an answer, but then maybe Salvatore doesn't have one he wants to share. He *should* have had me investigated before bringing me to his home. The fact he didn't is more proof that whatever this thing is between us, it's more than sex.

And his judgment is just as affected as mine.

"So you say," I tease.

"You can tell Candi that Pietro didn't find any skeletons in your closet."

"You assume there are some to find?"

"We all have secrets."

I nod. Because, truth. "If things get serious between us, I'll share mine. Will you share yours?"

"Yes."

"Okay then." That's crisis averted. For now.

But why should I tell him about my parents or the most painful moments in my past if we aren't serious? As long as this thing between us is temporary, my lips are sealed.

So are his, apparently, because Salvatore is done talking. He wants to do something else instead.

If our relationship doesn't last, I am going to miss the pleasure he gives me.

Almost as much as I will miss him.

~ ~ ~

A few days later, I acknowledge it's not just Salvatore I will miss when I leave here. But Rosa and Ilaria as well. Maybe even Nerissa.

"Stop daydreaming, *dolce ragazza*, or that plate is going to end up as thin as paper on one side and swollen like it has the mumps on the other," Rosa's voice scolds me, bringing me back to the present.

I grimace at the misshapen mess of clay on my wheel.

"Do not look like that," Ilaria admonishes me. "No one throws the perfect plate their first time."

Remembering her pot in Salvatore's conservatory, it's hard to believe the same hands that created it make the beautiful pieces she does now.

So, she must be right.

"Okay, no giving up. But I do think I have to restart," I say ruefully.

We are working in Ilaria's ceramics studio. She and Big Sal have a large apartment one floor down in Salvatore's building, coincidentally on the same floor as Nerissa's place.

While they only use the apartment when they are staying in the city for something, Nerissa lives in hers full time. Ilaria and Big Sal have a mansion on Long Island, where they raised their children and still live.

Since the night of the dinner at the don's, Ilaria and her husband have been staying in their city apartment for safety reasons.

Rosa is thrilled because she gets to spend more time with her friend. They're both trying to teach me how to cast ceramics.

"Are you sure I can't just learn how to paint the pieces?" I ask for the umpteenth time.

But this is really not my skill set.

"You will learn by doing," Rosa encourages me.

The sound of Big Sal's voice booming from the other room makes me flinch.

Ilaria pats my arm. "Do not be afraid of my husband."

"That's easy for you to say. Every time I see him, he looks like he wants to squash me like a bug." And he shares enough features with Salvatore that the older man's disapproving looks are really unnerving.

"Sal has always struggled with the balance between duty and love for family," Ilaria says with a sigh. "He wants our son to marry..."

She doesn't finish her thought, but she doesn't have to.

I blow out a breath and start pounding my clay back into a ball. "Someone who doesn't have pole dancer on her resume."

Ilaria shrugs.

That's one of the things I like about her. She's diplomatic, but honest. With family almost brutally so. That she feels comfortable being this honest with me is a compliment.

I think it's time I returned the favor.

I've been trying to think how to approach this since the first time we met, but it never seems to be the right moment. The reminder that Salvatore and I don't have a future, *can't* have a future, allows me to say what needs saying.

And maybe piss off two of the nicest women I have ever known, but who sport a severe blind spot where Salvatore is concerned.

"You're not as proud of your son being capo as Mr. De Luca is?" I ask Ilaria. "There's someone you think would be better? Or maybe you think he's too young?" This I direct at Rosa.

"Why would you ask such a thing?" Rosa demands, her tone severe, her expression filled with shock.

"No one could fill his father's shoes better than Salvatore," Ilaria says, throwing her hands out in a gesture of vehemence and sending drops of clay colored water flying.

I wipe the water from my cheek, smearing more clay on and roll my eyes at myself.

"Oh, that's it then." I start spinning my plate again, guiding the clay to spread slowly. "You expect him to continue to be a mouthpiece for Big Sal?"

"Of course not. I am proud of my son. He is his own man."

I shrug one shoulder. "If you say so."

"I do say so. Why would you imply otherwise?"

"You undermine him. That first day, you doubted him when he told you I wasn't in the penthouse under duress."

"My son can be brutal."

"So can your husband," I say, certain Salvatore learned how to be a mafia capo from the father who raised him.

"Yes, but..." Ilaria shakes her head. "Never mind."

"Is this about the lover he killed?" I ask.

"*Dio mio,*" Rosa breathes.

"Salvatore told you about Monica?" Ilaria asks, sounding shaken.

Shoot, I shouldn't have brought that up. I'm pretty sure Ilaria would be furious with Nerissa, just like Salvatore was if she finds out her daughter almost spilled the beans.

"I didn't know her name," I say, to put the older women on the defensive. "You know there are rumors about the most brutal capo in the city."

I'm taking a shot in the dark, but the expression on both women's faces confirms my guess.

"If you have heard the rumors and that awful title," Ilaria says sadly. "Then you know that my son's sense of morality is skewed."

"Huh." I stop my wheel, giving up on the lumpy clay. "Who exactly ordered Salvatore to kill her?"

Ilaria looks uncomfortable. "You know I cannot answer that."

"Let me take a guess. His don. Or maybe it was his father. But you think *Salvatore* is the one with a skewed moral compass?"

"I..." Ilaria's voice fades.

Rosa stops her wheel and studies me. "Why are you bringing this up?"

"Because I care about Salvatore, and it hurts him the way two of the most important women in his life doubt him. You are forcing him to either distance himself from you or..." This time it is my voice that trails off.

"Be seen as weak," Nerissa says from the doorway.

I acknowledge her words with a nod.

"Maybe that's what you want." I decide to drive the point home. "You're still training your son to be the emotionless, ruthless man you believe he should be."

Ilaria's protests are drowned out by Big Sal's voice. "You don't know what you're talking about."

I meet his furious gaze. "Yes, I do. My nonna used to tell me I couldn't blame my father for his weakness. That in trying to train it out of him, my grandfather destroyed the good parts of my dad that would have been strong enough to compensate for the pride and the greed."

They don't know my father was mafia, but it's a concept that plays out in other families outside the life too.

"Do you want to destroy your son's ability to love? I get you don't want him to fall in love with me, a nobody in your world, but would you condemn him to a life without the love you and your wife share?" I can't believe I'm asking this.

That I'm challenging the Genovese consigliere.

"You have to stop judging him for killing her, mamma," Nerissa says. "That doesn't make Salvatore a monster. It makes him loyal. To the man you love."

Big Sal makes a sound of grief.

Does he regret pushing his son to do what he did?

I don't know the details, but I guessed that killing the woman he was in a relationship with wasn't Salvatore's idea. He *can* be brutal, I have no doubt. But that was something he learned. He wasn't born with it.

There's too much caring in him for that to be the case.

"I think you might be very good for my son." The words are startling, but who says them makes me breathless with shock.

It's Big Sal. Ilaria is nodding in agreement, her eyes shiny with tears.

If only I could believe they might feel the same later, when emotions aren't running high.

"That's enough drama. You've given us something to think about, Bianca. But now it is time to get back to making that plate. You aren't leaving this studio until you've cast at least two of the same size."

I stare at her in horror and everyone else laughs, breaking the tension.

Chapter 51

SALVATORE

*T*hree Weeks Later

It has been a busy and rough few weeks, but when Don Caruso breathes his last, Severu will have the support he needs to step into the old man's role. Part of that certainty is the result of gifting the bar property in Gamino territory to their don.

Henry Caruso hasn't made a peep about throwing his hat into the ring. If he did, it wouldn't do him any good. Not after we informed the other Families he was working with another Cosa Nostra syndicate outside of New York to buy property in our territories.

Breaking longstanding treaties comes with heavy consequences. The Lucchese capos will not allow him to become don upon his uncle's death either. Jockeying for the position is already beginning among them.

The Cosa Nostras outside New York have all agreed to count Don Caruso's endorsement of Severu as that family's vote for the next godfather.

The Boston don has already offered reparations for Matthew Lombard's attempt to buy property in another syndicate's territory. Severu demanded a guarantee from the family that Matthew will never be made capo, much less don to maintain peace between our two syndicates.

The don and his capos all swore on their oaths as made men.

Matthew Lombard's power and reputation within his own syndicate is gone because of his failed attempt to help his cousin become the next godfather.

Try to fuck with a De Luca and you get fucked. Right up the ass without lube.

Which Lorenzo Ricci is going to find out soon enough. Severu's investigation into the capo is done and Lorenzo's death is a matter of when, not if.

When the corrupt capo's name comes up on my phone's display, I narrow my eyes at the timing.

I swipe to answer. "Lorenzo, to what do I owe this interruption?"

"Always the smart ass, aren't you Little Sal?"

"The next time you call me that, I will cut out your tongue," I tell him conversationally.

He gasps and then coughs. "I didn't call to trade insults," he says finally.

It wasn't an insult. It wasn't even a threat. It was a promise and if he knew me at all, he would be aware of that.

"Why did you call?" I ask, what little patience I have for the man already used up.

"Is it true you moved that little whore into your penthouse?"

I clamp my jaw so tight, my teeth grind. The only woman living in my home is Bianca. "Call her that again and I will let you choke on your own blood after I cut out your tongue."

"It's true then? You moved her in? When my mistress told me last night that you took up with a stripper from Pitiful Princess, I didn't believe her. What are you thinking?" he practically whines. "You don't date strippers. You don't even go to your own clubs."

I did with Bianca. Not that I was interested in what was happening on the stage. Why would I be when I had her in my bed?

"I am thinking that who I have in my home is none of your fucking business." And if it took him this long to figure out Bianca is staying here, he's dangerously out of touch with what is happening in *la famiglia*.

"I'm sorry to have to be the one to tell you this." He sounds nervous, but not even remotely sorry. "But when I found out you had her living with you, I didn't have any choice."

I'm not listening to some bullshit story he's concocted to try to get me to kick her out so he can make his play for her. "Give it up, Lorenzo. Bianca is out of your league."

Pathetic loser. He thinks he's going to convince me to throw Bianca out so he can pursue her? Not happening.

"It's not like that," Lorenzo squawks. "I don't want to fuck her, but she's not who you think she is."

"I might believe you if I hadn't caught you trying to corner her in the women's bathroom at my own club."

"Her father was one of my most trusted soldiers," Lorenzo rushes on like I didn't say anything. "Until I found out he was a rat."

That's rich coming from the greedy piece of shit who has been embezzling mafia money for years.

Severu is beyond pissed it took us this long to figure it out. But between paying his soldiers way too little and moving more product than he reported, Lorenzo flew under the radar until last year.

"Her father is dead."

"I know. I killed him."

"I have no doubt you have executed your own soldiers." Probably to cover his tracks when they started asking questions. "But that's got nothing to do with Bianca's dad."

She would have told me if he had been murdered.

"I'm not lying." When someone has to tell you they aren't lying, they probably are. "Alberto Russo was part of my crew."

"Her name is Gemelli."

"She was born a Russo."

"Bullshit."

"I'm sending you proof."

How desperate is this guy to get his hands on my woman? For that alone, I will kill him. My cousin will have to deal with me being the one to mete out Lorenzo's punishment and death.

My phone dings. There are three texts from Lorenzo. All images.

The first is a screenshot of an employment record for Alberto Russo. According to the record, he was Lorenzo's bookkeeper until six years ago. His single dependent listed is Bianca Russo, daughter.

His ex-wife's name is not given, which would not happen in my files. Even though we don't keep centralized files on our people...that would be a FEDs wet dream come true...my records include all important family members. Including ex wives and husbands.

The only files we keep are legitimate employment records linking a capo's crew to his businesses. All of my people work for me, or one of my clubs, in an official capacity. Except Pietro and his team. Pietro owns a security company, and I am his only client. His team are on his payroll.

The next picture is of an urn holding cremated ashes on a dais at a funeral. The framed photo next to the urn is of a dark-haired man in a suit who looks vaguely familiar. A placard in front says, Alberto Russo with the year of his birth and death.

It's not uncommon to give a funeral for a rat, either as a way to spare the family grief, or to keep his death from looking suspicious. But more likely, the funeral was Lorenzo's way of not drawing attention to his supposed rat.

So, why draw that attention now?

Is he trying to set the dead bookkeeper up to be the fall guy in his organization? Does he realize Severu is on to him? There's no question that as his bookkeeper, Alberto Russo would have had to be complicit in the embezzlement or dead because he refused to be.

Six years in his job makes the former more likely.

But how does Lorenzo plan to explain the missing money and product from the past six years? Another conveniently dead patsy the capo will try to convince Severu was Russo's accomplice?

The last image is of a short memorial obituary that says Alberto Russo is survived by his daughter Bianca. The memorial obituary could be faked because it's not from a newspaper and I can't confirm its origin.

For that matter, all of this so-called proof could be faked. Although checking the death record for Alberto Russo wouldn't be difficult. Which means that the man really did die because even Lorenzo Ricci isn't stupid enough to lie to me about something I can check that easily.

Even if Roberto Russo had a daughter named Bianca, that doesn't mean it's my Bianca.

The dates fit and she speaks Italian fluently. You know she's way too accepting of our world for an outsider.

She said she wasn't part of the mafia.

No, you said that, and she didn't disagree.

Cazzo.

"All any of this proves is that you had a bookkeeper who died six years ago." His funeral doesn't prove he was a rat, or that Lorenzo killed him.

"It's Bianca. I'm telling you. When I saw her in Amuni that night, I recognized her right away."

"And then you accosted her?" I ask, letting the skepticism I feel coat my voice. He called her *new meat*. I'm definitely cutting out his tongue.

"You got that all wrong. I was warning her off. I kicked her out of the family when I passed judgment on her father."

"How old was she?"

"A teenager. Couldn't make myself kill a kid even if that's what she deserved."

"Like fuck."

"I'm old school, Salvatore. We don't kill kids."

"You'd kill your own mother to get what you want."

He gasps, sounding genuinely shocked. "I would never, God rest her soul!"

So, his mother is a trigger for him. Good to know considering my plans for him later.

"Just ask her, Salvatore," Lorenzo stresses my full name. "Ask her what her father's name was."

"Get me a copy of her birth certificate and I might believe you." If he really was her father's capo, that shouldn't be any problem for him.

"You know Domenico's crew is busy with Severu's attempt at godfather right now."

It's not an attempt. Severu will be the next godfather. "It doesn't take a tech genius to order a birth certificate."

"I'm not your secretary. You get it yourself." Lorenzo disconnects the call.

Another thing to punish him for.

Dismissing him and his accusations about Bianca, I get back to work, but the conversation itches at the back of my brain. Has my lover been lying to me from the beginning? Hiding who she really is?

Why would she?

Maybe she thinks I would be *old school* like Lorenzo and blame her for her father's sins. But I judge people on their own merits. She should know that.

She should know me like I know her.

Do you really know her though?

I know she has secrets. Which she says she will tell me if our relationship becomes permanent. Reasonable. There are things I don't tell her now, that I would tell her if she was my wife.

My wife. I shake my head.

Am I ready to take that leap? Yes, everyone expects me to marry a woman who will bring benefit to the mafia, including me. But I am capo and no one, not even my don can force me to let Bianca go if I don't want to.

Every time we have sex, I give her a piece of my soul, something I thought had been destroyed long ago by Monica's betrayal. I would swear on my oath as a made man Bianca gives me a piece of hers too.

My feelings for her are so fucking powerful, they push everything else out. I haven't told her I love her, but I can't think of another label for the way I feel.

However, the last time I told a woman I loved her, I had to kill her hours later. That cured me of any desire to *fall in love* again. Love's a game for suckers.

What if I'm the biggest sucker of them all?

Because damn if I'm not in love with the enigmatic redhead. I need to know if Bianca is who I believe she is, or someone else. A liar.

My gut churning, I text Pietro.

"Get me a copy of Bianca's birth certificate," I say without any preamble when he answers.

Chapter 52

BIANCA

The feelings I grudgingly acknowledged the night the godfather had his stroke are stronger than ever. I'm pretty sure Salvatore is feeling them too. Even if neither of us has said the words.

I'm planning to. Tonight. Salvatore said he'd be home for dinner and I have plans for after.

Dr. Anders-Powell says my back is healed enough for the strenuous movements of participatory penetrative sex. That's how he put it, *participatory penetrative sex*. Apparently, there is a nonparticipatory kind where one partner does all the work and the other one lays there and counts the dust motes on the ceiling.

In the penthouse cleaned by maids overseen by the exacting Rosa, that number would be zero. But I have no intention of playing possum in bed. I love what Salvatore and I do together and I'm ready for more.

Salvatore is out of town more often than he's here lately, but we talk on the phone every day. And when he does manage to sleep in our bed, we pleasure each other with hands and mouths. And it is glorious.

I've taken his sex into my mouth and down my throat many times. He's eaten me out and pistoned his fingers in and out of me until I'm screaming his name. I'm confident I'm ready for the one act we haven't performed.

Because every fiber of my being craves his body's connection to mine.

I know Salvatore is waiting for the all-clear from the doctor to fuck me through the bed. Those are *his* words.

I want the final act those monsters stole from me. Consensual sex. Those are *my* words for it.

Tonight is the night.

SALVATORE

I am bone tired. If Bianca were not waiting for me at the penthouse, I would skip dinner and crash in one of Severu's guestrooms.

Ever since Lorenzo's call earlier, I've had a sense of dread, like time is running down on the clock of me and Bianca being together.

Even if I sleep like the dead tonight, I want her in my arms while I do it. Bianca's wounds have healed to the point I can spoon her at night, my front pressed right up against her back.

She sleeps more deeply when we're like that. So do I.

My beautiful houseguest still has nightmares sometimes, but it's not like it was at the hospital. Should I suggest she go to therapy? Find a therapist for her that I trust?

If it's what she needs, I don't care that it's not the mafia way.

When I get home, Bianca is waiting in the living room for me. Her eyes light up, like they do every time she sees me. She presses the button that turns off the TV and recesses it back into the ceiling before dropping the remote and jumping up from the couch.

"Salvatore!" She rushes toward me, eager and sweet.

Exhaustion forgotten, my cock fills with blood.

She's fucking sexy, wearing one of the dresses I bought her. I picked it out because the off the shoulder plunging neckline and short skirt looked like it would make for easy access to her luscious curves. What I didn't anticipate was how much of the curve of her inner breast would be on display.

The deep purple stretchy velvet barely covers her areolas and does nothing to disguise the way her nipples pop at the sight of me.

"You are never wearing that dress outside our home," I say, my voice guttural from the desire coursing through me.

She hooks her forefinger on the bottom of the V and tugs just a little. "Why not? Don't you like it?"

The sound that comes out of my throat is more animal than man and I do not fucking care.

Reaching out, I yank her to me and slam my lips down on hers. She opens for me immediately, allowing my tongue to spear inside like my cock is straining to do to her pussy.

We kiss until we're both breathing heavily.

I lift my head just enough to speak, our eyes locked. "You look beautiful and too damn tempting for anyone else to see you like this."

"You're the only one I want to tempt."

Alberto Russo's daughter, or not, this is my woman. I kiss her again until she squirms, trying to put space between us. While I allow it, I keep my arms around her.

"I helped Rosa make dinner," she says, her lips rosy and swollen from our kisses.

"Did you?"

Bianca nods. "It's one of my nonna's recipes. Rosa's is almost identical."

"Did you have fun comparing?" I ask, loathe to let her out of my arms, even to walk into the dining room.

So, I don't. Leaning down, I slide one arm under her legs and pick her up bridal style.

Her hands come up to cling around my neck and more lust surges through me at her immediate trust and acquiescence.

"Yes. She reminds me a lot of my nonna, though she's a lot younger."

"You miss her, don't you?"

Bianca never talks about anyone else in her family, but whenever she brings up her grandmother, it is with a smile.

"I do. When she died, I lost the only adult I could rely on."

"Were your parents already gone?"

"No." Bianca kisses the underside of my jaw. "I don't want to talk about people who aren't in my life anymore."

It's not the first time she's avoided discussing her parents, but it is the first time I wonder why. Not enough to push it right now. Instinct even deeper than what drives my inner thoughts tells me that if I do, I will regret finding out what I do not know.

Shoving aside thoughts triggered by a corrupt capo's words, I ask, "What do you want to do?"

Bianca has the formal dining room set up as an intimate oasis for us. Candlelight illuminates the single place setting at one end of the table.

"You've already eaten?" I tease, though I'm pretty sure I know her plan here.

"Nope."

She wants to eat off the same plate while sitting on my lap. We've done it a couple of times before, but always at my insistence. Because I crave her closeness. Now, that she's instigating the intimacy, I'm so turned on I will probably come from her squirming in my lap while we eat together from the same plate.

"You know, I'm not really hungry," I tell her. "For food."

Bianca's expression turns serious, all flirting gone. "I want you, Salvatore."

I spin on my heel to head out of the dining room.

She laughs and tugs the short hair at my nape. "Stop, caveman. Eat first, then sex. Nerissa told me you skipped lunch."

My sister and Bianca are slowly thawing toward each other. They aren't friends, but they aren't enemies either. Nerissa has admitted to me that Bianca's ideas for managing the dancers and sex workers are smart and well thought out.

They've been discussing the best way to implement changes since the first email.

"We can eat after." Do I carry Bianca upstairs or is tonight the night we christen the couch?

Bianca's breath speeds up, the scent of her arousal reaching my olfactory senses and increasing my own lust tenfold.

"No. Please, Salvatore. Let me take care of you."

"You are going to take care of me, *brava ragazza mia.*"

"You promise to eat after?" she demands a hitch in her breathing.

"Prometto."

Leaning forward she buries her face in my neck and sucks on a spot with a direct connection to my dick.

The couch it is.

Chapter 53

BIANCA

Salvatore sits down and maneuvers me around to straddle his lap.

Panting with desire, I lean forward to kiss him, my lips already slightly parted. His mouth is open when our lips meet and our tongues clash, sliding against each other and sending zings of desire straight to my core.

Dio mio. I want this so bad.

He tugs me forward, spreading my legs wider. The hem of my dress slides up my thighs, bunching at my hips. My clitoris presses against the hard column of flesh trying to bust through his slacks.

I moan and rock my hips.

His hand slides over the curve of my ass and into the crease, encountering my naked flesh.

I'm not wearing my pretty La Perla underwear. I'm not wearing any panties at all.

Salvatore's groan mixes with mine as his finger slides unimpeded into the slick folds of my sex. I've had his fingers inside me. Many times.

Tonight, I want more.

Yanking me against him even harder, he thrusts his hips up, abraiding my clit. It's too much. And not enough.

My knees jam into something and I freeze.

The back of the sofa.

Memories flicker behind my eyelids, warring with the need storming my body with gale force.

Going still, my eyes fly open and I take in the scene around me. Salvatore's penthouse. His living room. His sofa. Not the couch in my family home. Not the site of my most painful memories.

Pulling his mouth from mine, he immediately asks, "What is it?"

I stare into stormy gray eyes filled with concern. Yes, there is lust there too, but it's banked. He knows something is wrong because he cares.

Because he is tuned into my tiniest reaction and that's more important to him than the desire making his dick feel like a steel shaft against my ladybits.

I shake my head. "Nothing."

He doesn't go back to kissing me, but searches my expression.

And I know...I know this is exactly what I need to vanquish the ghosts of the past. Us together on a couch. Him still dressed. But I want to be naked and I want to be the one to take off my clothes, not have them torn from me while I am helpless to protect myself.

I am replacing the awful memory with the glorious present.

"I want to take off my dress," I tell him in a husky voice I barely recognize as mine.

He nods and reaches down to help me. This is right. This is better. Together we pull the stretchy purple fabric up over my unfettered breasts and over my head. I throw it over my shoulder.

His hands are already cupping my heavy breasts and playing with my nipples.

I unbutton his shirt and spread it open, so his tattooed chest is on display.

When he goes to shrug the shirt off, I stop him. "No. Like this."

"If that's what you want *carissima*."

"Mmm..." I hum agreement. It's what I want.

Reaching down between us, I manage to get his belt undone. I pull it through the loops on his slacks and toss it in the direction of my dress.

Then I squeeze his hard shaft, marveling at the size, like I do every time we are intimate. He's big and I can't wait to feel stretched by him. Good memories replacing the old.

Unwilling to wait any longer, I open his slacks and push the waistband of his boxers down so his sex springs free. Unable to resist, I swipe my finger through the viscous fluid beaded at the tip and then suck it into my mouth.

His taste bursts on my tongue, turning me on even more.

Lifting up so I can position his head at my entrance, my heart is beating a mile a minute.

Thump. Thump. Thump

His hands drop from my breasts to grab my hips so I cannot move. "Wait," he orders. "What about your back?"

"It's good."

He doesn't release his hold on me.

"I called the surgeon's office."

"And?"

"And he said I'm cleared for participatory penetrative sex."

Salvatore barks out a laugh, then he sobers. "How can he tell? He wasn't here to examine you."

"Rosa sent him a picture of the scar and then he guided her through a physical exam and asked very pointed questions. We're good."

Something wild and dangerous flares to life in Salvatore's eyes.

"Take me into your pussy," he demands in a guttural tone that sends shivers of delight through me.

I press down with my hips, the head of his large erection stretching my sensitive, intimate flesh more than his fingers ever have.

"*Dio mio*. You are huge."

"Do not make me laugh right now, *carissima*. I'm trying not to shove my cock into your wet pussy."

That's the second time he's called me his *very* dear one and it does something to my insides.

"I'm not joking," I breathe, my voice rising at the end as his bulbous head pops into my vaginal channel.

He groans, his hold on my hips tightening. "You are so fucking tight. You feel like a virgin."

I do feel like a virgin. Like he is my first. My one. My only. I am not prepared for the emotion that washes over me and have to blink back tears.

Pushing down, I take more of him inside and release my grip on his dick. Moving my hands to his shoulders, I squirm, trying to get more of him in me.

My breasts swing side to side with my movement, rubbing my nipples against the silky hair on his chest. It feels so good, I do it again on purpose.

"You're killing me."

"Not trying to."

He laughs, the sound filled with unexpected joy. "No, you are trying to bring my heart back to life and it's fucking working."

I have no words to respond, my own heart too full. And then something shifts and my body allows his shaft to surge up inside me.

I cry out.

He yells my name.

And then we are moving together, his hips thrusting, my body meeting his in delicious union.

If he's hitting the infamous G-spot, I don't know, there's so much sensation inside me. Every drag of his thick erection against my tight walls feels like a thousand electric sparks are igniting.

He grabs one of my wrists and guides my hand back to where we join. "Touch yourself, *bella mia.*"

My middle finger slips down over my clitoris and the sparks of sensation turn into fireworks of ecstasy.

My juices are dripping around his hardon, making my passage slick and our movements more and more pleasurable. The sound of our bodies slapping together mixes with our labored breathing.

My forefinger slides alongside my middle finger and I try pressing them together like he does when he's touching me.

Everything inside me contracts as bliss washes over me in a cataclysm of endorphins and pleasure.

"*Capo mio,*" I scream as I come so hard, my vaginal walls clamp around his sex so tight it almost hurts.

He grabs the back of my neck and tilts my head back before slamming his mouth down on mine. His tongue demands entrance and I open for him, letting him conquer both my mouth and my most intimate flesh at the same time.

Moments later, he breaks the kiss and shouts. *"Amore mio."*

The words land on the unprotected expanse of my heart and carve his name into it with indelible marks.

~ ~ ~

For the first time in over a week, Salvatore is beside me in bed when I wake up. He's sleeping so deeply, he does not stir when I turn over to face him.

There is no innocence in his face in repose. He still looks like the hardened mafia capo he is. He also looks like mine.

Amore mio. He called me his love last night.

I didn't ask him if he meant it because I'm not ready to know if it was just sex talk.

We ate dinner together like I'd planned.

Unlike I planned, we were both naked and he licked the rich caramel sauce I made to pour over the homemade gelato off my breasts. Then he laid me back on the table and ate his gelato off my ladybits.

I screamed myself hoarse with my orgasm.

He didn't want me to return the favor, but wanted back inside me.

"I am already addicted to the feel of your tight pussy around my cock."

"Don't exaggerate," I teased before getting lost in the sensation of our joined bodies, coming again before he filled me with his seed.

After he woke me to make love twice more in the night, I no longer think he was exaggerating.

If I hadn't asked the doctor to get me birth control pills, I have no doubt I'd be pregnant after last night. The thought of carrying Salvatore's baby is unexpectedly sweet.

What isn't sweet are the naughty thoughts I'm having about waking up Salvatore the same way he has woken me so many times. With my mouth on his sex.

He becomes alert way faster than I usually do. I barely get my mouth on him before he's groaning and making demands for how he likes it.

Afterward, we cuddle in the center of his bed while I work up the nerve to tell him about my past.

"What we have isn't transactional," is what comes out of my mouth.

He lays me on my back and looms over me, a slashing smile on his handsome face. "The only currency between us is orgasms."

I can think of a currency I would like more. But I'm no more ready to bring up love when I'm not sure of his feelings, than I am my messed up history. Without love on both sides, I'm not sure I'll ever feel comfortable revealing my past to Salvatore.

So, I settle for another orgasm. Or three.

Chapter 54

SALVATORE

A few days later, Pietro texts me while I'm working in my office at the penthouse that there is no birth record for Bianca Gemelli in New York on the date of her birth.

In addition to telling him to search vital records in the surrounding states, I tell him to search for Bianca Russo.

My gut clenches at the thought of him finding something under the Bianca Russo name and what that could mean.

I've been in Manhattan for four out of the last six nights, even when I'm out of the state during the day. Because I cannot get enough of Bianca's pussy. Not her taste and not the way it feels strangling my cock when she comes.

The way she fusses at me to eat and drink my water does weird things in my chest too.

I crave everything about her when I am away from her and if things weren't on such a razor's edge with the godfather's impending death, I wouldn't be in my office right now. I would be with her.

My head of security texts again an hour later.

Pietro: *Bianca Russo born on that date in Manhattan.*

Salvatore: *Anything else?*

Pietro: *Father is A. Russo from East Rutherford, NJ.*

I recognize the name of the town immediately. That's where Bianca said she lived with her dad before he died.

Or his capo killed him.

Fuck.

Salvatore: *What did you find out about the will?*
Pietro: *Bianca Gemelli is listed as a beneficiary.*
Salvatore: *How much?*
Pietro: *Fifty K but there's something off.*

There sure as hell is. Bianca lied to me about inheriting money from the old man she lived with. She lied about everything.

She's not an outsider, alone in the world. She has family from here to Detroit.

Dread twists my stomach into a gordian knot while my brain plays back every conversation between us. Every fucking lie that fell from her beautiful lips.

Eleven years ago, Monica lied about everything and I killed her.

An image of Bianca with a gunshot wound in the center of her forehead and her eyes drained of life flashes in my brain. I retch uncontrollably, sprinting to the bathroom attached to my office.

I barely make it to the toilet where I throw up the contents of my stomach and then dry heave.

"Salvatore!" My sister's voice sounds from my office.

Cazzo.

I force my heaving stomach to settle. She cannot see me like this. Splashing my face with cold water from the sink, I refuse to look at myself in the mirror.

I don't want to see the face of a man who has managed to fall in love twice in his fucking life to women who turned out to be con artists.

My hand trembles as I open the door after I dry off. I force it into stillness by sheer will alone and my face into an emotionless mask before I step into my office to face my sister.

Nerissa looks almost as bad as I feel. She sits in one of the chairs facing my desk, but instead of looking at me she stares at the floor.

"What the hell is going on, Nerissa?" What more can this day bring?

She lifts her head, her eyes filled with both rage and pity.

Ice forms in my twisted gut. Nerissa knows.

I sit down and keep my features schooled. "Talk."

"I didn't want it to be true. You were happy, like I haven't seen you in years. I was even starting to like her. But they're genuine. Ernesto analyzed the photos in secret. They're not fakes," Nerissa rambles.

My sister never rambles.

"What photos?" I ask in a voice devoid of emotion.

If I let the smallest crack form in my façade, the tsunami of rage and grief swirling through me will crash through and lay waste to everything and everyone in its wake.

She sets a large manilla envelope on the desk. "There's a copy of the will in there too. She lied about it. Ruhnke left her fifty-thousand dollars just like his son claimed he did."

It's not as bad as it could be. Nerissa makes no mention of Bianca being Alberto Russo's daughter. And the will is no longer a surprise, so it's not hard to maintain control of my features.

But she says there are pictures too. Of what?

Bianca in a risqué position with the old man, Ruhnke?

Foreboding making my hands clammy, I pick up the envelop and upend it to spread it's contents on my desk. At first, I can't make sense of what I am seeing.

It's Bianca dressed like a socialite in a long designer gown and wearing diamonds worth at least a million. I would have adorned her in jewelry worth ten times that.

But she's with another man.

That man is Matthew Lombard.

Son of a fucking bitch.

Cold fear washes over me. It should be fury, but there's no room for that when I see the proof of her betrayal in front of me.

It is one thing for her to lie to me about her past. It is another to sell out the mafia.

Severu will order me to kill her.

I won't. And I won't let him kill her either. Even if it means burning down the city and the mafia I've spent my life serving.

"No one is killing her," Nerissa says, her dark gaze filled with sisterly worry.

I stare at her, nothing in my brain but white noise and the constant refrain. *I will not kill her.*

Not this time. Not this woman.

Somehow, Nerissa is standing beside me, her hand on my shoulder. "Calm down, brother."

I don't know how many times she has said those three words, but they finally penetrate. I don't have time to lose my shit.

I force my brain to look at this situation through the strategic eyes of a capo. "Where did you get the pictures?"

How many people know about Bianca's betrayal?

"They came in as texts from an anonymous number."

Relief sends more synapses firing in my brain.

That's one person. My guess is Lorenzo. Since I don't see him following Bianca around like the paparazzi to get her picture with Matthew Lombard, he probably sent one of his guys to do it.

That's two men I have to neutralize.

"We burn the printouts and delete the files."

If Severu sees those pictures, Bianca is dead.

There's a slim chance he will let her live if he continues to believe she's an outsider. None if he discovers she's a Genovese.

Nerissa nods without hesitation. "But Salvatore, someone took those pictures."

"Probably fucking Lorenzo."

Nerissa's brows draw together in confusion. "Why? What does he get out of this?"

The reality of why Lorenzo called me and told me about Bianca's past suddenly hits. I would have seen it sooner, but I wasn't thinking straight.

She fucking does this to me.

"Turmoil," I say. "If it gets out, it will undermine the confidence of the other capos and their dons. I'm not just Severu's capo. I'm family and his top campaigner."

I've spent the past three weeks talking to other capos and dons all over the country, encouraging them to support Severu as the next godfather.

If I'm shown up for a chump, everything I've said to them comes into question. Image is everything in the mafia.

For some fucking unfathomable reason, Lorenzo doesn't want Severu to be the next godfather.

"Lorenzo has to die," my sister and I say at the same time.

"And we have to get Bianca out of New York." Even if I wanted to keep the manipulative liar, I couldn't.

I can't kill her, but I'll never trust her again.

Nerissa nods.

"Why are you going along with this?" I question my second's easy acquiescence.

"You love her, Salvatore. Killing Monica changed something in you. You lost part of your humanity. If Bianca is killed, you'll lose what's left of it."

"Some would say that's what a good capo needs to be."

"No." Nerissa shakes her head firmly. "Even if he is harsh and even brutal at times, a good capo has to care about his people. If you lose that last link to your heart, you stop caring about everyone."

I don't know if my sister's perception is right, but I do believe she believes what she's saying. I either trust her, or I kill her.

"Bianca's father was a Genovese soldier," I tell my sister, choosing trust. "Lorenzo claims he executed him for being a rat."

Nerissa's face contorts in shock and fear.

She knows what this means.

"Bianca is not an outsider," she breathes.

"No one else can know about any of this, not our family, not anyone."

I'll have to swear Pietro to secrecy about the research he's done on Bianca's birth. He's not stupid. He'll have guessed that she was born Bianca Russo. But without the pieces that I have, his puzzle won't show a Genovese mafia princess in the picture.

I won't tell him she was a Lombardi plant.

Nerissa nods. "I know. I made Ernesto give me his word he wouldn't tell anyone about the pictures. Right now, he has no idea who is in them. You've kept Bianca out of sight the whole time she's been here except that one night you took her out to Per Se and Pitiful Princess."

There are no pictures of us at either place. Standard security protocols I am grateful for now. It's all word of mouth about my gorgeous redhead girlfriend.

No one will be surprised when they see me next week with a blonde on my arm. I don't do girlfriends.

Pain spears through my chest. I ignore it. "Do you trust him?"

More importantly, do I trust him? Can I afford to let him live? Can I risk killing another capo's soldier?

Fuck.

"As much as I trust anyone besides you." She frowns. "I deleted the files from his computer and cloud storage myself."

"He knows what she looks like."

"So do a lot of people. But can he link her to the bar deal? Would he even think to? The reports on the Lombards list his girlfriend as a Boston socialite, with no connection to the mafia. Bianca must be his side piece."

One they didn't come across when they researched the Lombards for connections with the Five Families. Once we uncovered the familial connection between the Lombards and Henry Caruso, that's where we put our focus. Not on Matthew Lombard's girlfriend.

Rage overrides my fear for Bianca's life and I roar out my frustration.

She is *not* his girlfriend.

She is my woman.

That I have to let go. That I should want to let go.

Chapter 55

BIANCA

The sound of Salvatore yelling has me jumping up from the couch where I've been pretending to read.

Nerissa came in about twenty minutes ago and rushed past me without even saying, "Hi." She glared at me though.

I've been trying to figure out why the renewed hostility. Ever since she walked in on me talking to her mother and Rosa about how they treat Salvatore, she's thawed toward me. I consider her a friend.

She listens to my ideas for the women working in the strip clubs. We talk about other stuff too.

She even confided in me about her brother's harsh punishment for what he considers her disloyalty. Nerissa thinks she deserves having to earn the respect of their men again. I disagree, but I don't get a vote.

The sound of Salvatore's harsh shout tapers off. Did the godfather die? That shout sounded filled with pain. Even if he's not close to the godfather, the loyalty he feels toward the man has to be deep.

Or maybe something has gone wrong in his cousin's bid to be the next godfather. I know that's important to my lover. Salvatore hasn't told me about it, but he doesn't make me leave the room when he takes phone calls and I've heard plenty.

Because he trusts me.

It's time to prove I trust him with more than my body. I'm not sure how much of my past I want to reveal to him, but at the very least, I need to tell him that I used to be part of the Cosa Nostra.

Unsure how he's going to react to learning who and what my dad was, I'm so nervous I'm sweating. Salvatore despises disloyalty. He even told me he is planning to replace Rosa with a housekeeper who has more loyalty to him than to his mother.

Rosa's cooking and pottery lessons are the only reason I'm not climbing up the walls with boredom. Salvatore won't even consider me going back to work while things are so volatile in his world. When he played *the you could be kidnapped or hurt to get to me card*, I gave in.

Since I'm not paying rent and don't even have to buy my own groceries right now, it's not a hardship.

If this godfather thing isn't resolved yet, things are going to get dicey when classes resume at QC though. There's one I can take online, but most required for my degree are in person this semester.

Climbing the stairs to the second floor, I smile tentatively when I see Nerissa walking toward me. "Hey!"

I wait for her to notice today's t-shirt. She says if she wasn't second-in-command, she'd wear the shit out of shirts like mine. I don't tell her that Salvatore bought them for me, but I do plan to get her the perfect one for her birthday.

The black t-shirt I'm wearing with jeans today says: *My dark little heart skips a beat when I see KARMA catch up to somebody who deserves it.*

Nerissa's eyes widen when she sees me. Her gaze drops to my t-shirt but instead of smiling, she looks like somebody kicked her in the stomach.

Her tone grim, she says, "The capo wants to talk to you."

The capo? She never refers to him like that to me anymore. It's always Salvatore, or when he's not around, *my lovesick brother*.

If only.

"I need to talk to Salvatore too." Saying it out loud makes it real.

It's a promise to Nerissa to come clean to her brother, even if she doesn't know it.

"But will you say the things he needs to hear?" Her words should be a joke, but Nerissa's dark eyes reflect disappointment.

I put my hand on her arm. "Are you okay?"

Is Salvatore okay? I don't ask because that's not a question for Nerissa to answer. I'm careful never to ask her things that Salvatore should tell me himself.

He'll never consider her disloyal on my behalf again.

She jerks her head up and down. "Don't keep him waiting."

Okay, whatever this is, it's serious.

But not an excuse to put off telling him about your dad.

My inner voice can be such a judgy bitch sometimes.

I knock on the partially open door when I reach it.

"Enter." It's Salvatore's capo voice.

Is he on a call? I'm quiet as I go inside just in case, closing the door behind me. What I have to tell Salvatore is for his ears only. We'll decide together if we need to tell the rest of his family about who my dad was.

His phone is silent and he's sitting rigid behind his desk, staring down at some papers on his desk.

"Nerissa said you wanted to talk to me about something?"

He looks up, no expression on his handsome face. "Want to talk to you? No. However, it is necessary."

"That doesn't sound good." I grip my hands together in front of me.

Is the A/C turned down in here? It feels as cold as a walk-in cooler.

He stands and comes around his desk, his movements deliberate, an aura of menace settled around him like a dark cloud. "It's not."

Not good? "What's not good?"

"Tell me about your father, Bianca."

He hasn't called me by name in weeks. It's always *my beauty*, or *my good girl*, or *dearest darling* and always in Italian. My favorite is *my love*. But he only says that during sex.

Why am I zoning out on endearments when he just asked me about my dad?

"Funny you should ask that. Timing wise, I mean." I cut the babble short before it can get out of control and swallow. "His name was Alberto Russo. He worked for Lorenzo Ricci as a bookkeeper."

Not a flicker of surprise shows in Salvatore's expression. No emotion leaks into his gray eyes at all. Why do I feel like I'm not telling Salvatore anything he doesn't already know?

"You fucking lied to me."

I glance at the papers behind him on the desk. What are they? My birth certificate, or something?

"I withheld the truth from you."

"Don't play fucking semantics with me. You lied. You are part of the Genovese mafia."

"No, I'm not. When Lorenzo executed my dad, he kicked me out." Out of my home. Out of the mafia.

The murderous capo ripped every mooring from my life.

"Is that why you did it? To get back at him?"

Did what? "I don't know what you are talking about."

"You were raised in the life." He says it like an accusation.

"Yes." I am not ashamed of that, or of the life I have built for myself since. Both are me.

"My father cut Marco's tongue out on *your* word. Did you get off knowing your lies cost a good man so much?"

"Good man? Are we talking about the same Marco? Because not only is he a big-mouthed Soprano wannabe, he beat my roommate so bad she was in the hospital for three days."

"You didn't get your inside knowledge into the Genovese mafia from him."

Like hell I didn't.

"Everything I told you I know because of him is true. When I got kicked out six years ago Enzo De Luca was still alive and he was still the don. You weren't a capo. How would a sixteen-year-old girl know that stuff anyway?" I'm talking fast, but it's like my words are sliding right past him.

When he says nothing, I add, "I only figured out that the Genovese control Pitiful Princess after going to work there. I didn't know about your connection to it until *you* told me."

"Fuck that!" He looms over me, for once his nearness not making me feel safe. "I stood up for you with my father. I vouched for you to Severu. I told my sister to fuck off. *For you*. And you've been lying to me about everything since the beginning."

"What beginning?" I ask snidely, getting angry too. "The one where you propositioned me for five thousand dollars to have sex, knowing it would cost me my job?

"No wonder you didn't take the money. You already had a sugar daddy for your whoring ass."

I shake my head, my ears ringing. "Did you just call me a whore?"

"If the title fits. Or is he your *boyfriend?* Newsflash: fucking me to get information for him still makes you a whore."

"Is who my boyfriend? Do you think I'm dating Lorenzo?" I ask, confusion interrupting my anger. "First, eww. Second, did you miss the part where he threw me out on the street?"

"Stop with the innocent act. I know the truth."

"That my dad was a rat who stole from the mafia? So what? Newsflash," I throw back at Salvatore, my anger back in full force. *"I'm not him."*

My father's sins cost me more than anyone but him. And for a long time I wondered if dying wouldn't have been better than what happened to me.

Salvatore grabs some papers from the desk behind him and shoves them at me. "Go ahead. Lie some more and tell me that's not you."

I take a small stack of photos and flip through them. Stifling a gasp of shock, pain pierces my heart.

They're pictures taken without the knowledge of the people in them. If Bea knew her picture was being taken, she would have changed her expression. I don't do social media. Neither did Bea before she and mom left. But they both set up on the different platforms after.

I created a catfish account for a glamourous model living in the UK to stalk them. It's not tied to anything related to me and I only sign in the web at Internet cafes. My dad's insistence we keep a low profile is drilled into the depths of my consciousness. Besides, I didn't want to come to Lorenzo's attention.

Bea's social media shows my sister is very good at curating her image.

In these pictures, she's dressed like the socialite she is, her hair pulled up in an elegant French twist. The guy she's with looks just like her type.

White. Preppy. Rich.

I like the candidness of the photos though. Until I notice a detail that sends shards of more pain slicing through my heart.

Bea is wearing an engagement ring. A classic, tasteful diamond solitaire. Not too showy, but I bet the clarity and cut are perfection.

She's engaged.

And I didn't know. Our dreams of being each other's maids of honor are ashes. I'll never even meet her fiancé. And if she has children? I won't be allowed to meet them either.

Because I'm tainted with my father's blood.

Which somehow Salvatore seems to realize even though he doesn't know about the most shameful moments in my past.

The ones that draw the dividing line between me and Bea with permanent marker.

So, why is he so convinced I'm the one in the pictures?

Even though the style hides the fact her hair is about eight inches shorter than mine, the differences between the two of us are obvious. Bea might be my identical twin, but she is at least two sizes smaller than me. Diet, exercise or surgery?

Or maybe just really good shapewear.

It doesn't matter. Her cleavage is still impressive and that's probably all Salvatore notices.

"This is not me."

"Stop with the fucking lies."

"You know who my father is, so you have to know that could be my sister." Why is he acting like this? "Why swould you even assume it was me?"

"You are a good actress, I'll give you that." He sounds disgusted, not impressed. "You don't have a sister."

The words hurt in a way nothing has in a long time.

Because in their own way, they are true.

"No matter what she and my mom like to pretend, I do. Bea is my twin." But he has to know that.

Derisive laughter flays my already lacerated heart. "Alberto's employment file lists one daughter. *One,*" he emphasizes.

"Well, our birth records prove he has two!"

He grabs more papers from his desk and waves them in front of me. "Did you fucking sleep with that old man to get him to leave you the money, Bianca? How low will you go?"

Sickened by his question, I snatch the papers from him and skip to the highlighted parts. Mr. Ruhnke really did leave me $50,000? And his greedy sons hid it from me? Doing a quick scan of the unhighlighted first paragraphs, I see that Mr. Ruhnke made his oldest son executor of the will.

Well, that explains how they got away with not informing me of my inheritance.

Is that why his wife texted me? Maybe slipping my existence by the probate court isn't as easy as they thought it would be.

My eyes prickle with tears. This is too much.

The reminder that my sister is no longer my family. Apparently, she and my mom weren't even listed in my dad's employment file.

The knowledge that Mr. Ruhnke left me something in his will. The reminder that he considered me family, the daughter of his heart, hurts too. Because he's dead. And his children withheld his final act of love from me.

I am alone.

The man I've fallen in love with thinks I'm a whore. If he loved me, this conversation would have been questions, not accusations. He would be glad to hear I'm not the one in the picture, not flat out refusing to believe it.

No wonder he never calls me his love outside of sex.

He does not fucking love me.

Chapter 56

BIANCA

Turning, I stumble toward the door.

"Where the fuck do you think you are going?"

"Away from you." I need time to process all of this.

I reach for the doorknob but a heavy hand on my shoulder spins me around. The cold mask is gone. Hot rage is in its place. It radiates from Salvatore, filling the air between us.

"You are not leaving without telling me the truth." He grabs my throat with his big hand, shoving me up against the door.

My heart races. Panic flares for the first time from his touch. I thrash, trying to pull away.

"Please," I gasp out. "I can't breathe."

"You're talking. You're breathing," he says pitilessly, his eyes chips of granite under the lights.

For a second, there's more than fury in his expression. There's pain too. Then it's gone. Was it ever really there? More likely my wishful thinking, wanting him to be affected by this like I am.

"You're fucking lucky your plan didn't work," he grits out. "You whored yourself out for nothing, didn't you?"

"Not a whore."

"Call it what you want." His face set in a rictus of disgust, he lets me go and shoves me away from him. "You're lucky I don't kill you, but you're not worth it."

Scored by a thousand tiny cuts from his disbelief, I don't feel lucky.

"Get out!" he shouts, the muscles in his neck cording with strain.

Without turning my back to the angry predator, I feel for the door handle. When my hand latches onto it, I twist my wrist and pull the door open before sidling around it and slipping through the opening.

Something heavy lands against the door as I yank it closed. The words he shouts are muffled, but the rage in them bleeds through even the heavy wooden door.

Intent on getting my birth certificate and the small photo album I brought with me when I left my family home, I turn away from Salvatore's office and rush down the hall. If he can take pictures as proof of my guilt, he can accept the ones of me and my sister together as children as proof of my innocence.

I don't know if we can come back from this, but I'm not leaving here with him believing I'm a liar.

The whore part I can't change.

I have no proof I never had sex with Mr. Ruhnke. That I had no clue about the $50,000 he left me in his will. The wording of it should be proof enough though. Only a sicko would call a woman he's used sexually *the daughter of his heart*.

Bile rises in my throat at the thought of someone thinking Mr. Ruhnke was that kind of man when he had been all that was decent and good.

I force it down and shove open the guestroom door.

Nerissa is near the dresser, putting clothes into a Louis Vuitton duffel bag I've never seen before.

"You're packing my things?" I ask, my voice accusing.

She doesn't bother to look at me when she says, "Yes."

"Why?"

"He wants you out."

My newly vulnerable heart cracks in my chest.

Salvatore is throwing me out. Just like Lorenzo. Just like Daryl Ruhnke's family. Once again, I am losing my home through no fault of my own.

And Nerissa is helping?

"I thought you were my friend." Why am I so stupid?

She spins, a pile of underwear in her hand, her beautiful face twisted with contempt. "Friends? Well, you know the old saying, keep your friends close and your enemies closer. Who do you think gave the capo those pictures? I ordered that copy of the will from the courthouse."

Who doctored my father's information to list only one daughter? It could have been Nerissa, or their father. As consigliere, Big Sal has access to all the capo records.

Neither one of them wants me in Salvatore's life, but I stupidly believed that both had changed their minds.

Nerissa drops the underwear in the duffel. "Now that you are here, you can pack your own shit. You have fifteen minutes."

She leaves. Numbness starts in my feet and moves up my body until the pain inside me smothers under it too.

Even though Salvatore and I have shared a bed every night since the first one I spent here, all my stuff is still here in the guest room. What does that say about what has really been going on?

I told Salvatore I wouldn't sleep with him for money, so he figured out my currency. Orgasms. Affection. Feeling like I belonged.

Now that he's done with me, he's ripping it all away.

The last two months have been a lie. Every touch, every moment of protectiveness was a pretense. His demands I call him *capo mio* part of the Off-Broadway production he was directing to keep me in his bed.

My need to prove my innocence to him disappears in the face of this painful truth.

Knowing my time is limited, I quickly repack the duffle with practical clothes. The first thing I will do when I get a chance, is hock the pretentious designer luggage and get something that will make me less of a target for predators.

After taking a quick picture of my birth certificate, I transfer my important papers and money stash into a pouch meant for travel I got at the secondhand store. It attaches to my belt and flips over my waistband to tuck inside my jeans.

Shoving a smaller stash of money into my backpack, I also put a change of clothes and my essentials in there along with the photo album I refuse to leave behind.

I don't know what I'll do about Vee. I don't even know if Salvatore managed to bring my African violet back from death's door. I've been too afraid to ask, not wanting the grief that would come from a negative answer.

Alive, or not, I can't take the plant with me when I don't know where I'm going.

The beat up looking backpack looks wrong with the designer duffle. Just like I look wrong in a billionaire's penthouse.

I'm still packing the rest of my things into the set of matching luggage I find in the closet when Nerissa comes stomping into the room. "Time's up."

Ignoring her, I finish packing.

When I'm done, I stack the luggage and boxes against the wall of the walk-in closet.

"What are you doing?" she demands.

"I can't take it all with me now." I don't even know where I'm going. "I will text you an address to ship my things later."

"Fine," she agrees, surprising me.

No threat to burn them or throw the stuff away like Salvatore is doing to me.

After slipping my arms through the straps of the backpack, I pull the handle up from the back of the rolling duffle. "Let's go."

Without a word, Nerissa spins and stomps back out of the room.

I follow. Hating myself for it, I turn to look back over my shoulder to see if Salvatore has come out of his office to watch me leave.

The hall is empty.

SALVATORE

My chest tight, some kind of weird burning at the back of my eyes, I slam back a double shot of eighty-year-old whiskey.

This is not fucking happening again.

Compared to Bianca, Monica was an amateur.

With a rich boyfriend in Boston, no way Bianca is a student at Queens College like she claims. I keep calling Matthew Lombard her boyfriend, but that damn ring on her left hand says he's more.

How did we miss it?

Or is the piece of jewelry a shut-up-ring for a *goomah?*

Just like Monica, Bianca Russo has been playing me for a fool while committed to another man. And I let her do it.

A master manipulator, she wove a complete backstory that made her look like the plucky heroine who never gives up. And she played the part so damn well.

Right up until I saw the pictures of her with Matthew Lombard, I was looking for excuses for the lies about the will and who she is.

I never would have gone with the twin farce though.

How did Bianca think she was going to convince me of that bullshit?

I pour myself another shot, but I don't pick it up.

I am not weak.

You're so strong, you arranged to get Bianca out of New York before anyone else finds out about her lies and you can be ordered to kill her.

I slam my fist down on the desk. I fucking despise her, but I am not killing her.

BIANCA

Nerissa drives and I don't ask where we are going.

Right now, I can't make myself care. My heart hurts and my brain insists on playing over every minute in Salvatore's office. My throat constricts as if his hand is still around it, squeezing.

"Why did you stay after the attempt to buy the bars out from under us failed?" Nerissa asks in the heavy silence of the car.

Her words burn through the fog of memories playing like a loop in my brain.

Why is she still pretending to think I'm some kind of spy? She knows about Bea. She has to. She's the one that gave the pictures to Salvatore.

Does she want to be able to tell Salvatore she grilled me and I refused to answer? Why not just tell him that anyway? What is one more lie on top of all of the others?

Or is she rubbing in her success at getting rid of me? Pushing home how easily and quickly Salvatore believed the ugly pretense she created.

"Answer me, damn it!" Nerissa pounds on the steering wheel. "Do you even realize how much Salvatore is risking by letting you leave?"

I press my lips together, refusing to answer the crazy.

"My brother put his position as capo and his own fucking life at risk for you," she says passionately.

I almost believe her.

"If my dad or Severu figure out you ratted on Salvatore to Matthew Lombard about the bar properties, they'll want you dead. And maybe him too."

The only two things I take from that are the name of my sister's fiancée and the threat against Salvatore's life.

"Why would they kill him?" I ask.

"You don't rat out the mafia and live. If Severu orders Salvatore to kill you like his dad ordered him to kill Monica, he will not only refuse, but he will protect you to his last dying breath." She sounds disgusted and angered by that fact.

Can I believe her? Is it possible she doesn't know about Bea? Does Nerissa believe the story the pictures tell too?

"Where did you get the pictures?" I ask.

At first, I think she's not going to answer.

But finally, she says, "They were sent to me via an anonymous email address."

"You didn't trace it?"

"We don't have tech guys on our crew that can do that. Once Ernesto confirmed they are genuine, I didn't want him tracing them back to their source either."

"Why?"

"To protect Salvatore."

Cold dread slithers through the numbness enveloping me. Because I believe her. I hate him, but I don't want Salvatore to die.

"Tell them the truth then."

"You *want* him to die?" she demands with disbelief.

"Those pictures aren't of me. They are my twin," I tell her.

"Right," she scoffs. "Even if that were true, and trust me, I don't believe a single word out of your lying mouth, then it just means you fed her information and not directly to Matthew Lombard. You're still a rat and Severu will still want you killed."

I know I can prove the lack of connection between me and Bea no matter how much it hurts, but I don't mention that. I want answers to other questions because if she's telling me the truth, things aren't adding up.

"Why not just let them kill me then?"

"Salvatore won't and I'm not letting him die because he insists on protecting you."

He killed Monica, but he won't kill me? That doesn't make any sense. Not if I'm right and he doesn't love me.

I can't even think about that right now. Letting hope blossom in my heart after everything would be beyond stupid. It would be suicidal.

"What happens to you if someone finds out you hid this too?" I ask. "Your loyalty to the don will be put in question just like his."

"You think I care? My first loyalty is to my brother. My first priority is protecting Salvatore."

"So, you're not going to tell your dad or your don?" I press, to make sure.

"No. But you have to stay out of New York. If this comes out, I'll make sure you die slowly. A day of torture for every hour they put Salvatore through."

Severu De Luca would torture and kill his own cousin? Big Sal De Luca would stand by and let him do it? What am I asking? Of course, they would. It's the mafia way. Loyalty above all else.

My father forgot that and that's why he's dead.

I won't let the same thing happen to Salvatore. Or Bea. She might not recognize me as her sister anymore, but no way am I going to risk her being tortured and killed because of mistaken identity and a misunderstanding I can put right.

The sound of a jet overhead answers the question I did not ask. We are headed to the airport.

"I texted you the details of your flight while you were packing."

I haven't checked my messages since Salvatore blew my world up with his cruel words and accusations. I check now and see the text Nerissa is talking about.

The flight isn't for three hours. Way more time than I need to get through security screening, but not enough time to leave and come back.

I'm not doing either.

The only way to protect both Bea and Salvatore is with the truth. The whole sordid story that started when I was thirteen. I have to spin it though. It doesn't protect Salvatore if his don thinks he hid things from him.

Unfortunately, the only way to sell it, I have to make Nerissa the heroic messenger.

Instead of the deceptive manipulator she really is.

Keep your enemies closer.

Stop pretending like you could live with yourself if she was killed as punishment for hiding information.

Once again, my inner voice is right. Nerissa might not be my friend, like I believed, but my feelings toward her are genuine.

I was *her* friend.

As soon as I get inside the airport, I call Catalina De Luca and ask if we can meet.

"Will you come here? I'm not allowed out of the building right now without a security team bigger than the president's."

I would rather meet at a restaurant where I have at least a slim chance of getting away if things go wrong, but I agree to come to her home. I don't have a choice if I want to make her my ally.

Without that happening, we're all screwed.

I spend an hour and a half drinking overpriced coffee on the main level of The Atrium Business & Conference Center at LaGuardia while I compile the evidence I need to prove the truth of my story to Severu De Luca. After putting together the digital file, I make a print copy too.

My ready cash in my backpack seriously depleted, I head toward the rideshare pickup location.

Remembering the rideshare Pietro made me miss by kidnapping me from the hospital makes me ridiculously nostalgic. What do he and Rosa think of my abrupt departure?

Or have they been expecting it all along?

Their boss, *Captain Playboy*, has a different beautiful woman on his arm every time he attends a notable event. He isn't known for having serious relationships either.

Yeah, I found that nickname while compiling the things I need. Searching my name connected to Salvatore De Luca didn't bring up anything about us. However, it brought up a ton of articles about *Captain Playboy* and his many women.

There aren't even any pictures of us together at Per Se. Other than the selfie I took, which I'm not deleting.

It's a reminder that he was using me all along.

Just like his orchids remind him not to trust women. I should have taken that for the stadium sized red flag it is.

I didn't and here I am. About to step into a rideshare to take me to Don De Luca's building and maybe my own death.

Chapter 57

SALVATORE

I hang up my phone after arranging with Lorenzo Ricci to meet at Amuni. Tonight, that miserable cretin's time is up.

A perfunctory knock sounds on my office door before Nerissa steps inside. Her expression is grim.

"What?"

"She hasn't checked in for her flight yet."

She's not leaving New York. Why not? Lombard is in Boston. Is he sending his plane for her, or maybe a car?

I pull up the tracker app I put on her phone. The little dot is moving back toward the city.

Managgia la miseria. Where the fuck is she going? To Henry Lucchese? But why would she go to him?

What is there for her here in New York?

A tiny kernel of hope sparks in my battered soul.

Not you, genius. You threw her away like trash.

A first-class ticket to Boston is not the garbage heap.

A ticket she's not using.

"Lorenzo is meeting me at Amuni in two hours," I inform my second. "I want you and your team to take him."

"Done."

"Put him on ice until I decide how I want to spin killing another capo without my don's approval," I spell out for her.

Nerissa is putting her life on the line for me, for my need to keep Bianca alive. She has to go into this with her eyes wide open.

"We're in this together, brother. Lorenzo is a rat. He betrayed *la famiglia*. We're just taking out the trash for Severu."

It's too close to what I thought about throwing Bianca out. *Cazzo.*

I pound my chest to dislodge the weight that settles there.

A loud knock sounds.

I nod to Nerissa. She opens the door and Pietro steps inside, his mom hot on his heels.

Sweat is beaded on my top bodyguard's forehead. "Boss, did you give Bianca permission to leave the penthouse without an escort?"

"She's gone, Salvatore. I looked everywhere, even the roof." Rosa rings her hands. "How did she get out? I thought she wanted to be here."

"We broke up." The words cause a cavern to open up inside my chest.

"But why? She's so good for you." Rosa's eyes fill with tears. "I thought you were finally over what happened when you were young."

Do you ever get over killing a woman you believe you love? It changed me permanently. But not so much I am capable of killing Bianca.

"It is what it is."

Pietro is looking at his phone. "Is she going to stay with the don while you work things out?"

"She'll be safe there, I suppose, but you two need to make up quickly. This is where she belongs," Rosa says. "I don't understand why she didn't go to your parents' apartment though. That is just an elevator ride away."

"What are you talking about?" Nerissa demands. "Bianca is not going to Severu's place."

Pietro shows his phone screen to my second. Of course, he's tracking her. He's the one I asked to install the app on her phone, and her safety has become his number one assignment.

I should have relieved him of those duties before I kicked her out. I wasn't thinking.

When am I ever not thinking?

Right now, apparently. Because it is only registering now what the tracking information means. Bianca is headed to talk to Severu.

She's going to get herself killed.

Without another word to anyone else, I sprint out of my office. Pietro's big feet pound behind me.

I don't close the door behind me when I hurtle out of the penthouse. Jabbing the button over and over, I will the elevator doors to open.

I have to get to Bianca before she gets herself killed.

BIANCA

My hands are clammy as Severu's security checks my identification and then scans my bags and tests them for who knows what all. Explosives? Drugs?

It's definitely more thorough than anything I would have gone through at the airport if I'd taken that flight to Boston. Finally, I'm back in the elevator headed to the top floor of the building.

I try to block out the memory of my last ride up to the De Luca's home, but little bits keep flashing in my brain like one of those best of your life highlights videos.

Che palle. My time with Salvatore was not the best of my life.

Wasn't it?

I want to throat punch my inner voice, but then I wouldn't be able to talk to Catalina and tell her the things I need to. Because that inner voice is me calling me on my own bullshit.

The don's wife is waiting for me when the elevator doors slide open.

Her hazel eyes widen when she sees the duffle beside me.

"Um..." She gives me a questioning look.

I step out of the elevator, pulling the Louis Vuitton bag behind me. "Salvatore and I broke up."

"I'm sorry to hear that. I thought you two were good together."

Did she? Then he fooled her too.

"It was never going to last. A capo doesn't marry a pole dancer turned cocktail waitress." I hate the sound of self-derision in my voice.

I am not ashamed of who and what I am. Salvatore has killed how many people? He's not too good for me. If anything, it's the other way around.

"He's not exactly royalty." Catalina leads the way into the living room.

"Pretty sure his dad would disagree with you."

"Big Sal? Is he the reason you two broke up? Maybe Severu can talk to him."

I shake my head. "No point."

She sits down on the end of one of the sofas without replying. Putting my duffle out of the way behind it, I take the closest chair to her. This is not a conversation I want overheard. Not even by her ever present security.

One bodyguard stands near the entrance and the other is closer, probably so he can leap on top of her in case of an invasion.

Like anyone is getting up that elevator without approval.

I keep my backpack in my lap.

"Do you need a place to stay for a few days?"

I'm tempted to say yes because Salvatore would blow a gasket over me staying here.

"No but thank you for the offer." Her kindness makes my throat tight with emotion.

"I have some things to tell you that I'm hoping you will be willing to share with your husband." On the way here, I decided that Catalina telling him would give the truth a better chance of being heard.

"Things about Salvatore?" she asks warily.

"No. Things about me. Things Salvatore doesn't know." I tell my first lie. "Things that Nerissa has shown me could be misconstrued without the whole story."

"Why aren't you telling these things to Salvatore?"

"Our breakup wasn't pretty. We're not speaking to each other." Not a lie. "But I have to tell someone in your um...family." I don't know how much Salvatore has told the don that I know about the mafia. "Or my sister could be in danger."

"What do you mean?"

"My sister is engaged to Matthew Lombard. I guess he's one of Salvatore's enemies, or something." My lack of knowledge is not feigned.

I still have no idea what the property developer has to do with the New York Cosa Nostra.

"A rival maybe," Catalina muses. "Do you mind if I take notes?"

I shake my head.

I'm surprised when the don's wife jumps to her feet and leaves the room, one of the security team hot on her heels. Is her phone not with her? I keep mine with me all the time, even at home.

And I barely have anyone contacting me on it.

That number decreased by all but one as of a few hours ago. Of course, my phone rings right then, making a liar out of me. I jump in shock.

I can't talk to Candi right now. I look down to ignore the call and see it is Salvatore. Did he check to see if I took my flight and find out I didn't? Is he wondering what I'm doing?

Well, he can keep wondering. I decline the call.

A text dings second later.

Salvatore: *Do not speak to Severu. Get out of there.*

I don't know how he knows I'm here and I don't care. I power down my phone. The bossy capo abdicated all rights to try to tell me what to do when he dumped me.

Catalina returns carrying a composition notebook and a pen.

"Wow. Old school."

She laughs. "I prefer pen and paper. It helps me keep my thoughts in order."

To each their own. I take notes on my phone. I don't remember the last time I carried a pen, much less a pad to write on.

I'm glad I printed out the documents I compiled though. I get the feeling, Catalina will find them more compelling than an image on a screen.

She opens her notebook and looks at me expectantly. "Okay, start at the beginning."

I do. Sort of. I tell her about meeting Salvatore for the first time.

"You told him he has no game?" Catalina asks with a grin.

"Yep. Honestly, I find it difficult to believe he's called Captain Playboy. Not that he hasn't had a bazillion lovers, but being a playboy implies a certain level of smoothness. And smooth, he is not."

Catalina laughs, her whole face lighting up with her amusement. "I hope you two can patch things up. The De Luca men tend toward bossy arrogance. Salvatore needs you in his life."

I wish I could agree.

Once I tell her the rest of the story, she'll change her mind too.

"My dad was Alberto Russo. My mom is, was, Elizabeth Butler. For a while she was a Russo and now she's a Harrington."

"Your father died?"

"He was executed by his capo for stealing from *la famiglia*."

"The mafia has no mercy for traitors." Catalina's eyes reflect deep grief.

I don't know why, or how, but she gets it.

"My dad was my mom's big rebellion against her society parents. Their marriage wasn't a happy one."

Catalina scribbles away as I talk, but her pen stills when I tell her about that night when I was thirteen.

"She left you there?" Catalina asks, horrified. "Alone?"

"I had my dad."

"Who was stealing from the Family." Catalina grabs her phone and sends a text. "Severu is in his home office. He'll be here as soon as he can break away."

"Why?" I ask, terrified.

I don't want to talk to the don.

"Because my husband will insist on hearing your story directly from you to judge your honesty."

"Doesn't he trust you?"

"The question is, do you? You must have at least a little to come here to talk to me. Trust me when I tell you, talking directly to Severu is the best thing you can do right now. This situation is complicated in ways I'm not sure you know about."

"Honestly, I don't. All I know is that Nerissa said the don might think I'm a rat like my father." Not a lie, but not the strict truth either.

"The best way to convince him otherwise is for you to be completely honest with him."

I'm scared and it must show on my face because Catalina pats my hand. "Don't worry. My husband has a soft spot for courageous women who try to protect their sisters."

Catalina offers to play the piano for me while we wait. Not wanting to engage in meaningless chatter, I accept.

Surprisingly the beautiful, sometimes haunting music she plays helps my nerves to settle.

Until the elevator dings and the sound of footsteps approaching from different directions jerks me back to my terrifying present.

Chapter 58

BIANCA

Forcing myself to turn and face the don, shock holds me immobile. It is not Don De Luca heading toward us, but Salvatore.

And he is running across the marble floor like the hounds of hell are nipping at his heels, not Pietro.

"Do not say a word, *bella mia*," he orders.

That breaks my paralysis alright. Glaring at my ex-lover, I jump to my feet. "You are not the boss of me, Salvatore De Luca. This isn't about you."

Another lie. It is about protecting him as much as it is about protecting Bea.

He skids to a stop in front of me, his eyes narrowed, his jaw set in that stubborn way he gets. "You are not talking to my don."

"I most definitely am." There is so much I want to say right now, but if I say it, my implication that he doesn't know about my sister and Matthew Lombard goes out the window.

From the top of a high-rise like this one, that's a pretty big fall.

"What is this about?" Severu De Luca looms behind Salvatore, his expression forbidding, proving his are one of the sets of footsteps I heard.

"Bianca is trying to protect her sister from mafia reprisal. Does that sound familiar?" Catalina smiles at her husband like she can't help doing so.

The don's stern face softens when he looks at his wife. "Yes."

"For fuck's sake, Bianca, stop this." Salvatore yanks me to his side, like that's where I belong.

When we both know it isn't. Not anymore.

"Something you want to tell me, cousin?" Don De Luca asks as the room fills with his men.

Okay, there are only four, but with Catalina's bodyguards, that's six. They block the only avenues of escape, to the foyer and the hallways on either side of the living room. Two of them come to stand near the don and his wife, the menace in their postures making goosebumps of terror break out on my skin.

Salvatore meets his cousin's gaze unflinchingly, like there are no men with guns glaring at us. "Bianca is mine. She's not talking to you."

There is so much wrong with that statement. I start with the most important bit. "I am *not* yours. You threw me out."

"I don't want you talking to her. Whatever she may have done was done in ignorance," Salvatore says to his cousin, ignoring me. "She is not part of our world."

What is he trying to do? If Salvatore doesn't knock it off, there's no way I convince his don that the capo didn't know about the Bea situation.

All the softness that came into Don De Luca's face when he looks at his wife is gone. He is tense, like he's ready to strike and it's scaring the crap out of me.

Salvatore's insistence on opening his big mouth is not helping.

"That's not strictly true, is it?" Catalina asks before I can tell Salvatore to shut up. "She was born into the Genovese family."

"You were?" The don looks at me, both question and demand for an answer in his expression. "And you have done something my capo believes I will punish you for."

"Like hell you will," Salvatore grits out.

The two guards nearest him draw their weapons, but for now, they don't point them at anybody.

"Stay where you are!" Don De Luca barks. "If you pull that gun from its holster, my men will kill you."

I look where his glaring gaze is pointed, because it's not directed at me and Salvatore right now, and my terror ratchets up several notches. Pietro is standing in the foyer, his hand on his weapon.

"He is Bianca's bodyguard. Her safety is his top priority."

"I am his don." Don De Luca's glacial tone freezes my insides.

"Stop it," I cry. "Pietro, don't you dare touch your gun, or I'll shoot you myself."

When he doesn't move, I spin to face the don. "Will you please tell your men to put their guns away?"

"No."

Catalina makes a sound of disapproval, but this time the don does not spare his wife a glance.

Dio mio.

Neither Pietro, nor Salvatore are getting out of this alive, much less me.

I will not wet myself.

Two weeks after I was assaulted to pay his debts, I watched my father's execution. I killed a man to protect my sister when I was thirteen. I might be afraid, but I am not weak. I can handle this. Even if it feels like there's enough tension in the room to squeeze the life out of me like a hungry boa constrictor.

There is only one way to get through this situation. With the truth. And that's not a guarantee for amnesty.

I can only hope it will be enough.

There has been no betrayal here, no matter what Salvatore believes.

"My father was Alberto Russo," I say. "He was Lorenzo Ricci's bookkeeper until his capo killed him."

Don De Luca looks at Salvatore, his expression grim. "Did you know?"

"Not until today."

Che palle. Does the man have no sense of self-preservation? He couldn't tell one tiny lie?

Severu opens his mouth to speak, and I'm pretty sure it's to tell his men to take us into custody.

Catalina stands up quickly from the piano bench. "Let's move this discussion somewhere more comfortable. I don't know about Bianca, but this pregnant lady doesn't need a bunch of trigger happy made men looming over her."

The change in Don De Luca is instantaneous.

His attention goes from Salvatore to his wife, his gaze showing deep concern he does nothing to hide. "Are you alright *mi dolce bellezza*?"

She nods. "Yes, but I would prefer not to risk my piano if you and Salvatore start trading blows."

By blows she means gunfire. I shiver.

Don De Luca sweeps his wife into his arms. "As you wish."

"You don't have to do this anymore." She loops her arms around his neck, showing her protest is an empty one.

"I enjoy it, as you know." He leads the way down to the sunken living room, carrying his wife.

The bodyguards follow them, moving their bodies between us and the married couple. Catalina's attempt at diffusing the situation is clearly a temporary stay of execution.

I swallow on a dry throat, terror for Salvatore and now Pietro mixing with the storm of emotions inside me.

Taking a breath for courage, I try to follow King and Queen of New York, but Salvatore's hold keeps me from moving.

He spins me to face him and leans down so our faces are almost touching. "What the hell are you trying to do? Get yourself killed?"

"I am trying to clear up a misunderstanding that could get more than one person offed," I hiss back angrily.

"Stop this. I will protect you. Trust me."

My laugh is harsh. "If you had trusted me, none of this would be necessary." I glare up at him. "You didn't and it is. But maybe stop trying so hard to get yourself in trouble with your don."

"I'm going to admit to knowing all along and wanting you anyway. I'll remind him that Lorenzo kicked you out of *la famiglia* and offer to take whatever punishment Severu wants to mete out in your place. You just need to stay quiet."

For a second, I am completely speechless. Believing what he does about my supposed betrayal, Salvatore knows if he does that, Don De Luca will order his death.

"Why would you do that?" I demand.

"Because I will not let you die, *amore mio*."

It is the first time he has called me his love outside of the bedroom.

What should be a profound moment of joy is soured by the circumstances in which he uses the endearment. In one breath accusing me of whoring myself out for the business interests of another man and the next saying he will as good as die in my place.

"You're a very confusing man, capo."

"Your capo."

"Now is not the time," I say harshly. "Focus, Salvatore."

"I am focused." And all of it is on me.

No, that's not true. His body is held taut, like he's aware of where everyone else is in the room. Particularly in relation to me as he shifts us around so he's between me and the others.

Like *he's* my bodyguard, not Pietro. "And could you please tell Pietro to stand down?"

"No."

I'm going to be sick. "You and your cousin have a lot in common and that's not a compliment for either of you."

Salvatore doesn't bother to reply.

I sigh. "I have done nothing wrong, Salvatore. But according to Nerissa, you trying to smuggle me out of town could get you killed."

"Stop this. *Per favore*. I know you think your story is a good one, but the fantasy of a twin sister isn't going to convince my cousin of your innocence. And even if he believes you have a sister, he'll assume you were feeding her information for her fiancé."

"You really don't trust me." What am I supposed to do with that?

He is begging me to let him handle this. The man is willing to take any punishment for me, up to and including death, but he doesn't believe a word I say in my own defense.

I don't understand what's driving him, but it can't be love. If he loved me, he'd trust me. He wouldn't have thrown me out like yesterday's garbage.

"I am not going to shut up and if you don't, you could get us both killed." I shove away from him and this time he lets me go, his gorgeous face filled with uncertainty for once. "Don't think I've forgotten that you accused me of having sex with the only decent father I ever knew either."

With that, I turn my back on him and head to the don and his wife, my anger overriding my fear.

The don is standing near the sofa, his wife still in his arms. They are kissing. I'm pretty sure that's Catalina's attempt to give me and Salvatore time to talk with a hint of privacy.

As if he senses the moment we come close, Don De Luca lifts his head and kisses Catalina's forehead before settling her in the center of the sofa and taking the seat beside her closest to the chair I was in earlier.

Two bodyguards are now stationed at either end of the couch though, preventing me or Salvatore from getting too close.

I grab my backpack and sit down before pulling the papers out and laying them face down on the coffee table.

Salvatore is hovering beside me.

I look up at him. "I need you to send me an email with the don copied on it."

I don't explain why. This is his chance to show he trusts me at least a little.

After jerking his head in acknowledgment Salvatore pulls out his phone and taps on the screen. A few seconds later, I get a notification for a new email.

Clicking into it, I see that Salvatore hasn't sent a blank email, but written something.

No matter what happens, I will protect you.

Same here, caveman, same here.

Instead of copying his cousin, he has included Don De Luca's email address in the body of this message.

After copying and pasting the don's email address after Salvatore's in the *To* field, I send the email I prepared with the attachments. Then I flip over the papers I printed off at the airport business center and push them toward Catalina.

The page on top is a screenshot from my sister's social media. It is dated the first night I started work at Amuni. It's a selfie of her and Matthew, along with a picture of both their dinners. They are eating out at one of Boston's most exclusive restaurants.

They're both smiling and looking happy.

More screenshots follow. Some are like the first one, my sister chronicling her dates with her fiancé. Others are pictures of them at social events from sites like TMZ.

All are with dates and times that Salvatore and the don can easily verify as ones I was either working, or living with Salvatore at his penthouse.

Today is the first time I have left the penthouse without Pietro as my bodyguard and Salvatore knows it.

Chapter 59

SALVATORE

Seeing more proof of an ongoing relationship between Matthew Lombard and my woman fills me with jealous rage. I want to bellow my anger and break things, but most of all I want to kill that fucker after at least a week of torture.

"Look at the dates," Severu says.

All I can see are that *bastardo's* hands on her, their faces next to each other selfies I want to fucking obliterate from existence. I growl, my fingers tightening on my phone until I can feel the case crack.

My cousin barks, "Calm the fuck down and look at the damn dates."

Instead of doing what my don orders, I lift my gaze to Bianca. She is watching me, no sign of guilt on her beautiful face. Her brows lift in challenge. *Are you going to look at the dates?*

I finally look and pain rips through me as one thing becomes inescapably clear. There is no way that these pictures are of Bianca. One was taken last night for fuck's sake, while she was wrapped tightly in my arms. In *my* fucking bed.

Then other details start to register. The woman in the pictures wears her make-up differently than Bianca. She prefers more muted colors of clothing. Instead of blue the color of their eyes, she chooses sky blue and sage green instead of bright emerald.

Lavender instead of violet. The only color they wear in common is black.

"She looks just like you, Bianca," Catalina remarks.

But I disagree.

"Her hair is shorter than yours," I say hoarsely. "And she's too fucking skinny."

"She's a socialite like our mom. Keep looking." The expression of vulnerability on Bianca's face tells me I'm not going to like what comes next.

She's right.

The next attachment is a picture of two birth certificates side by side. Dated the same, one is for Bianca Butler Russo and the other is for Beatrice Butler Russo.

What I thought impossible is the truth. Why was I so quick to dismiss her claim to have a twin? Maybe because she said she had no family.

Any way I look at it, Bianca still lied to me. But now I'm wondering if the reason is because of something other than betrayal.

The next attachment is another screenshot. This one is from Elizabeth Butler's social media made on Bianca's fourteenth birthday. She wishes her beloved daughter *Bea* a happy birthday with gushing affection.

There are pictures of a baby, a toddler, a little girl and then a young teenager. With red hair the exact same shade as hers and heart shaped face so like what I imagine my lover looked like as a child, they could all be Bianca. They aren't though.

They are her sister, with nothing to indicate that Bea has a sibling, much less a twin. Their mother makes no mention of Bianca at all.

I go hot and then cold. I thought her mom was dead too, but Bianca never said that. My vulnerable lover said her mom was *gone*. And from these pictures, it's clear Bianca has no place in the socialite's life.

"What happened?" I ask, a leaden feeling in my gut.

Severu asks, "Why does your mother only mention one daughter?"

Did Bianca's parents each take one of the girls in the divorce? That would explain Alberto's employment record, for a sloppy capo like Lorenzo anyway. Why didn't Bianca go to her mother after her father died?

Bianca takes a deep breath and then starts talking, her voice like it is coming from someone else's body.

"Things were rocky between my parents for as long as I can remember. Mom came from Boston high society. Marrying my father was her act of rebellion, but it didn't turn out the way she expected."

"In what way?" Severu asks.

"She didn't like not having money. I guess my dad flashed a lot of cash around when they were dating, saying what a big man he was in the family. He was only 19 and not the son of anyone important, just another soldier. He didn't get promoted to bookkeeper until a couple of years later when he finished his associate degree."

It's no surprise Lorenzo made such a young, inexperienced man with only a two-year degree his bookkeeper. The corrupt and soon-to-be-dead capo was hiding his own thieving and would have wanted someone malleable in the position.

"My dad played up being related to the Detroit don, but that connection is a distant one. I don't think Don Russo ever even knew my dad's name. But my mom didn't know any better. She expected the same pampered life with people to cook and clean for her that she'd had back in Boston."

"As the bookkeeper for Lorenzo's crew he made more money than some of them, but that cheap *stronzo* doesn't have *any* rich soldiers," I say with disgust.

"How did you learn all this?" Severu asks.

"My parents fought constantly. I knew every lie Alberto had told and every way he fell short of her expectation by the time I was five."

Catalina scrunches her nose. "Your mother sounds like a piece of work."

Bianca smiles wryly. "If she hadn't gotten pregnant, the marriage probably wouldn't have lasted past the first year, but she did and they stayed acrimoniously married for almost 14 years."

"What happened then?" I am compelled to ask.

I need to know everything about this woman.

"When we were 13, my mom was at a luncheon with some of the other wives." Bianca shudders and stops for several long seconds. "A man came to the house. When we didn't answer the door, he forced his way inside."

Unable to stay away when she sounds so vulnerable, I drop to my knees beside Bianca's chair and put my arm around her shoulder. "You don't have to say any more."

"I do though, don't I?" She looks at me with unfocused blue eyes. "If you and Don De Luca are going to believe me when I tell you that there's no way I'm feeding information to my sister and her fiancée."

"I believe you, *amore mio*."

She sighs. "Good." Then she looks at Severu, clearly determined to finish her story. "We didn't call the cops because we were more scared of what the capo would do to us if we did than the man."

Catalina makes a wounded sound.

Bianca nods. "We should have called 911."

How did I ever think this woman was an outsider? She thinks like mafia.

"He said my dad owed him money. We told him our dad wasn't there, but he searched the house anyway. He couldn't find any money though. He said..." Bianca swallows. "He said..."

"I can tell them what you told me if that's easier," Catalina offers.

But Bianca shakes her head and squares her shoulders and keeps talking. "He said that he was going to take payment on account and leave a message for my dad."

Fury erupts inside me with volcanic force and somehow I keep it from exploding outward. Whoever this man is, I will find him and I will kill him. Slowly.

I press a kiss to Bianca's temple. "We get the idea. You don't have to say anything more."

"We didn't know what he meant, but then he grabbed Bea and he threw her onto the couch," Bianca continues, her voice devoid of emotion. "At first I didn't understand what was happening, but Bea screamed, and I saw he was tearing at her underwear."

Chapter 60

BIANCA

9 Years Before

I try to pull him off of Bea, but he's too big. He shoves me back and I land hard against the coffee table. His jacket rides up and I see a gun in a holster at his waist. I grab it.

He doesn't notice. Bea is kicking and screaming.

I point the gun at his head and pull the trigger. It just clicks.

He looks up and laughs. "Put that down before you hurt yourself."

I pull again and again, but the gun just clicks and clicks.

"I can see you're a feisty one," he says with a disgusting leer. "You'll get your turn soon enough."

I can't make the gun work and he's not afraid I'll figure it out. The gun must be empty. What *stronzo* wears an empty gun?

He thinks I'm funny. That what he's doing is funny.

My sister screams again. I grab one of my mom's crystal lamps we aren't allowed to touch. She can punish me as much as she wants, but I have to get this man off of Bea.

I swing for his head, but he shifts at the last second and it hits him on the shoulder.

"Fuck. You little bitch!" He yanks it from me fast and throws it against the wall, where it shatters into tiny sharp bits.

Except one big piece still attached to the base. It looks like a knife and it gives me an idea. I run into the kitchen and grab the knife my nonna used to use to filet fish from the market.

A memory of my dad talking to one of his friends, his voice thick with admiration, plays through my mind. "That's how you use a knife. You don't stab the fucker. You cut his throat so he can't scream."

I approach the man again, being as quiet as I can, trying to tune out my sister's screams. If I mess up, there's no one else to save Bea.

He's unbuckling his belt and I know it's now or never. I jump on his back and slash the knife across his throat with all my strength. Blood sprays everywhere, covering Bea, the sofa and the carpet around them.

He throws himself back, landing on top of me, knocking all the air out of me. He rolls off me and tries to crawl to where I'd dropped his gun.

If he wants it, then the gun must work. I didn't do it right. My lungs burning, I crawl faster and shove the gun out of his reach. The man tries to crawl toward me, but he's getting slower. Eventually he stops.

Bea is still screaming and trying to wipe the blood off of her. I want to help, but she won't let me touch her.

Suddenly, mom is there and she's yelling while she checks Bea for injuries.

"It's not her blood," I say, hoping to calm my mom down. "It's his."

Mom looks from me to the dead man on the floor, horror etched in every line of her face. "What happened to him? Where is your father?"

"I killed him." I drop the knife.

SALVATORE

Present

"That night, she and my sister left," Bianca's voice is hollow as she finishes her account of what must have been the worst day of her life.

"She didn't take you?" I ask in the hushed silence that falls after Bianca stops speaking.

My precious love shakes her head. "Mom said I had my dad's bad blood, that I was a violent criminal just like him."

Severu looks as furious as I feel. "That bitch."

"I sickened her, and Beatrice couldn't even look at me," Bianca says like anything could explain her mother's actions. "Maybe my mom was right. I still don't feel any remorse for killing that creep. They split custody in the divorce. Bea went with mom, and I stayed with our dad."

Catalina's brows furrow. "There's no divorce in the mafia."

That's the rule, but there are exceptions. Divorces happen. More often made men abandon their wives and children to live with their lovers, without the formality of divorce. As long as they provide financially for their family the don and his capos don't get involved.

"There are annulments," Bianca says on a sigh.

"How can you get an annulment when there are children involved?" Catalina asks.

"The state grounds for annulment and in the Catholic church are broader than you'd think, love," Severu says. "But don't go getting any ideas."

Catalina rolls her eyes and then looks at Bianca expectantly.

"My dad felt guilty about what almost happened." Bianca's head tips infinitesimally toward mine, seeking comfort.

Or at least that is what I tell myself.

"He didn't dispute what mom claimed when she filed for the annulment in New York and with the Church."

"That would have made you and your sister illegitimate." Catalina sounds shocked.

As well she should. No made man with any honor would deny the parentage of his children. To allow his daughters to become legally born out of wedlock goes against centuries of tradition and belief, stretching back to our Sicilian roots.

"I'm pretty sure my mom's parents preferred their daughter and granddaughter to carry their name rather than Russo. They're kind of waspy, if you didn't figure that out from the types of events my sister attends."

"When your father died, Lorenzo didn't send you to live with your mother?"

She laughs, the sound harsh. "He threw me out into the street and told me I was lucky he didn't kill me too."

Lorenzo is a cruel man. He'd known that a sixteen-year-old girl had no chance of surviving on the street on her own. He would have expected her to end up dead or turning tricks.

After I kill Lorenzo, his son will be ten times the capo that old bastard is.

"How did you survive?" Catalina asks.

Bianca told me and Nerissa the gist of this that day on the roof, and says pretty much the same thing now, adding that she had been terrified Lorenzo would change his mind about killing her.

"What about Elizabeth?" I ask, planning the woman's slow demise in my head.

"She gave me ten thousand dollars and told me to stay away. There was no place in her life for my father's daughter."

"You and Bea share the same fucking DNA," I say, incensed on her behalf. Identical DNA.

Bianca shrugs. "Mom was right. If I suddenly showed up, it would have hurt her reputation and Bea's too. That's important in the world they live in."

"You should have been important," I growl.

She shrugs me away. "People find it easy to throw me away."

I have no excuse. I fucked up and the look she's giving me says fixing it isn't going to be easy.

But it starts with the words I owe her. "I'm sorry I didn't believe you when you told me the pictures were of your sister."

"I told you my family was gone." She shrugs again and I'm learning to dislike that particular action from her. "We were never going to last anyway. You're destined for a mafia princess and I've got a whole world outside of the New York *famiglia* to explore."

She is not leaving New York, but I'm smart enough not to say that out loud right now. I've got ground to recover with her.

"You're going to reconnect with your mother?" Catalina asks, sounding worried about that possibility.

Bianca shakes her head. "As far as she and Bea are concerned, I don't exist. I'm okay with that as long as my sister doesn't have to pay a price for looking like me."

She looks expectantly at Severu.

He's looking at me though and his expression isn't friendly. "You didn't just know about Bianca's connection to the Genovese mafia, you knew about her connection to Matthew Lombard."

"She doesn't have a connection with that *stronzo*," I say forcefully.

"But you thought she did, and you were going to hide it from me." Severu silently signals to his men.

I use a quick hand gesture to tell Pietro to stand down. Bianca is no longer at risk from our don, and I will not allow Pietro to stand against our don on my behalf.

The four guards not standing beside the couch all draw their guns. I release a silent breath of relief when Pietro makes no move to follow suit.

"I wasn't going to let anyone hurt her," I tell my cousin.

"Even if she was a rat?"

"Even if she fucking sent Matthew Lombard the information on a silver platter," I affirm.

Now that I know Bianca is safe from my cousin's wrath, I will not stoop to hiding anything from him.

Severu gives another silent signal and the four men close in on me. My cousin's reaction is no surprise. I betrayed him and Severu isn't going to settle for monetary reprisal to punish my disloyalty.

Unaware of what the movement of my don's men means, Bianca stares at me in disbelief. "What is wrong with you? Do you think I came here and laid my soul bare to your don for shits and giggles? I'm trying to save your stupid life."

"I don't lie to my don."

"Unless it's to protect the woman you love," Severu says with an edge.

I shrug. I'm sure as hell not going to admit to my cousin that I love Bianca before I tell her. Would it make any difference if I did?

Catalina worriedly chews her bottom lip. She's worried. Unlike Bianca, she notices the movement of her husband's men and knows what it means.

She, more than anyone else, knows that Severu will not spare family for the sake of sentiment. I don't regret my actions though. I would do it again with the same information.

The only thing I regret is not believing *mi amore* when she told me the truth about her sister and being stupid enough to throw her away.

Chapter 61

BIANCA

I cannot believe the big dope kneeling on the hard marble floor beside my chair. He's been there since I started talking.

His knees have to be killing him.

"Get up. Sit on a chair like a normal person," I tell him.

"Stay there," Severu barks, once again scaring the crap out of me.

The look he's giving Salvatore is 100% merciless don without a trace of caring cousin in there.

Salvatore doesn't move, but there's no fear emanating off of him either.

Stupidity or courage?

The don stands and draws his gun before pointing it right at Salvatore's forehead. "You broke your vow to me."

"He didn't," I disagree, trying to stand up so I can put myself between the gun and Salvatore.

These two predators needed a cool down moment.

But Salvatore's arm over my shoulder turns into concrete. I'm not going anywhere.

"Do not move, Bianca," Salvatore bosses, his gaze never leaving Don De Luca's face. "If I survive the discussion to come, Severu, you and I will have words about you pointing a gun so close to her."

"What is wrong with you?" I demand, pretty sure it's not the first time I've asked today.

If he survives? Like that's in doubt and he's okay with it. He probably is. Severu isn't the only one who considers Salvatore's actions disloyal.

Both men have an overdeveloped sense of what constitutes loyalty and apparently Salvatore is willing to judge himself as harshly as he would anyone else.

"Let me go!" I struggle to get out from under that heavy arm.

"I don't like you so close to a gun," Salvatore explains. "But if I let you go, you're going to try to get between me and Severu."

I can't deny the truth. So, I say nothing.

"You are safer where you are." He squeezes my shoulders like he's comforting me.

I want to scream, but I'm not risking tipping the scales of this dangerous situation with my very understandable frustration with the capo and his don.

I'm not going to stay entirely silent though. "He only found out today," I tell Don De Luca. "Telling you he knew all along was a lie." The one lie he was willing to utter, the *scemo*.

"Severu knows that because there was no betrayal on your part," Catalina says pointedly.

The fear in her eyes is not giving me any comfort. She's worried her husband is going to kill my capo.

Che palle.

"But there was on his," Don De Luca says, his gun unwavering.

"He didn't want you to kill me."

"If he had trusted you, the issue would be moot."

"I know," I grumble, but I don't mention my other grievances against Salvatore. The don has enough of his own.

"Correct me if I am wrong, but I assume the breakup today happened *because* my cousin believed you to be a rat."

Not sure I would correct him even if he was wrong, not with a gun pointed at Salvatore's head. But in this case, he's not wrong, so I just nod.

"After taking advantage of you sexually, he threw you away."

Pain spears through my fear. "I am aware."

"I did not take sexual advantage of her," Salvatore says, emotion bleeding through this voice for the first time.

And I remember that day with his mom and Rosa.

"Of course not. Severu didn't mean it that way," I say, with a frown for the don.

Doesn't he realize his opinion matters to Salvatore?

"But you did throw me away," I can't help adding to Salvatore.

His chest rumbles, but he doesn't agree verbally. What the heck is that supposed to mean?

"Salvatore, you have two choices. Both require you to give up your life."

"No," I shout. "What kind of man are you that you could kill your own flesh and blood?"

How do I get out of this nightmare? Equally important, how do I get Salvatore out of it?

"I am not a man. I am a don," Severu De Luca says with a shrug.

"Hate to break it to you, but a don is still a man."

He does not deign to answer me but stares at Salvatore, like he's waiting for something.

"I willingly offer my life," Salvatore says solemnly.

Don De Luca intones, "I accept your sacrifice."

Tears burn the back of my eyes and I blink rapidly, but they don't go away. Hot moisture spills down my cheeks. I shouldn't have come here.

My attempt to save Salvatore is what is going to get him killed.

The don re-holsters his gun and then makes a hand motion and the sound of other guns sliding back into their holsters penetrates the pounding in my ears. The soft glide of shoe leather on marble tells me the men I didn't realize were so close are moving away.

The don is so confident in Salvatore's promise, he doesn't feel the need to keep his men on alert. Even the bodyguards at either end of the sofa melt into the background.

Salvatore releases my shoulder and stands. I look up at him, but there is no grief on his handsome face to match the feeling in my heart. Why would there be?

He's a made man and death is part of his life.

But not his death, my heart cries.

I wait for him to move away so I can breathe.

But instead of moving back to his seat, he picks me up and a second later, he's sitting where I was and I'm on his lap. "That's better."

Catalina's laugh startles me, especially under the present circumstances. "That's definitely a De Luca trait."

"Well, I'm not a De Luca wife," I mutter.

Salvatore takes my left hand into his right, and laces our fingers so our arms create a band across my body. "Yet."

My confusion and grief morph into horror as his exchange with his cousin plays back through my head.

I willingly offer my life.

I accept your sacrifice.

It cannot mean what I think it does. I shake my head in denial, but a rock settles in my stomach.

I accept your sacrifice.

That rock starts to play with some friends, making me queasy.

"If your father or even your capo had done right by you, they would have arranged a marriage for you." Severu looks intently at me, like he's expecting me to agree.

"Maybe in a medieval mafia fairytale." But we're living in the real world. "I am the daughter of a thief. I don't belong in *la famiglia* anymore."

"The New York Cosa Nostra does not make the child pay for the sins of the father."

Personal experience tells me this is not true. However, I know what he is trying to say. Don De Luca does not believe that I am responsible for my father's betrayal. He doesn't see me as dirt because of what my dad did.

I would appreciate that more if Salvatore's life had not just been offered and accepted as payment for his disloyalty to the don.

"Your capo betrayed you." The look on the don's face would send those rocks in my stomach knocking against each other if it was aimed at me, but it's not. His next words prove it. "It was his job to make sure you were taken care of in the absence of your father."

Like that was ever going to happen. According to him, I was lucky Lorenzo Ricci didn't sell me to make back the money my father stole.

"What is done is done," I say now. "My past cannot be changed. I am no longer part of *la famiglia*."

"That is not true. You were lost but now you have been found and we will do right by you." Why does that resonate with as much threat as promise?

"That sounds almost biblical." I say it like a joke but no one else laughs.

"One of my capos put you on the street when you were still a child. Another took you as his mistress." The look he gives Salvatore sends a chill of dread through me. "You should have been protected."

"Everything that happened between me and Salvatore was consensual." Other than Pietro kidnapping me. "And I am nobody's mistress. Again, not the Middle Ages here."

"And that is why I will not kill him," Don De Luca says.

Relief pours through me. He is not going to kill the man holding onto me like he will never let me go.

"If we can make this right," the don adds, sending that relief on a long trip without a return ticket.

He cannot be saying what I think he's saying. Salvatore is destined for a mafia princess, someone who brings benefit to the mafia. A woman with the upbringing and pedigree to match his.

Offer my life. Accept your sacrifice.

The word *sacrifice* resounds through my brain over and over.

I look at Catalina and say, "Please tell me your husband is not talking about what I think he is."

"If you think he's talking about marriage then I cannot do that." She gives me a sympathetic, almost hopeful smile.

"No, no, no." Panic courses through me. This is not happening. "My life is not getting derailed by mafia don guilt."

What else could this be? He believes two of his capos screwed up in their treatment of me, so now, he's determined to make it right. With Salvatore's sacrifice.

And mine.

Wait, what if he's not talking about making his valuable capo marry me, but someone else? What if the sacrifice is letting me go before Salvatore is ready to?

Does that even make any sense?

My brain is spinning and I'm pretty sure that if I try to stand up right now, my knees will not hold me. Panic courses through me, sending the rocks in my stomach tumbling and every nerve synapse firing with stress.

"I'm pretty sure mafia don guilt is not a thing," Severu De Luca says, sounding amused.

Gone is the grim reaper.

The man I met at dinner that night we were all here is back, but now I know who lurks under the calm façade. An emotionless killer who would sacrifice his cousin for the sake of mafia loyalty.

Catalina gives him a look. "It so is a thing."

Oh, God. What am I going to do? I can't let Don De Luca choose a husband for me.

"If my father had done right by me, I wouldn't get nauseated when a man touches me." I speak the only truth that might change the don's mind.

Salvatore makes a pleased sound. The jerk. "You don't mind when I touch you."

"You're the only exception I've found so far. Go figure," I say with no attempt to blunt my sarcasm. "But that doesn't mean I can get married and have a normal sex life with some stranger."

Despite my lofty hopes when this thing between us started, the thought of another man touching me sends horror crawling along my skin.

"I know I am not your favorite person right now, Bianca, but I am no stranger," Salvatore whispers in my ear.

My first conclusion was the right one. Why doesn't that make me feel better?

"This is ridiculous," I nearly shout. "I have been living on my own since I was 16. No one can tell me who I have to marry."

Instead of getting angry at my outburst, the don gives me an appraising look. "Are you willing to allow Salvatore to die? He promised his life in exchange for his insult against his don."

I look to Catalina, hoping for a sign that her husband doesn't mean what he says. He cannot kill Salvatore. But the grief in her hazel gaze says her husband is capable of doing just that if I don't marry the capo.

"There has to be another way," I say desperately. "Salvatore, tell the don you are sorry and promise never to do it again."

"I am not sorry and I would do it again in a heartbeat to protect you," he says instead.

Whatever happens, I will always protect you.

Chapter 62

SALVATORE

Poor Bianca is on the verge of hyperventilating.

It's not an ego boosting response to hearing that Severu wants her to marry me, but after my fuckup earlier, it is an understandable one.

I let go of her hand to dig in my pocket for the item I've been carrying around for the last week. My grandmother's engagement ring. There is nothing understated about the ten-carat emerald cut diamond my grandfather got her after being made don.

Five years later, he had a three-carat yellow diamond added on either side of the main stone. I replaced them with dark purple amethysts two weeks ago.

I place the ring in her hand and curl her fingers over it. "I'm going to ask you the way you deserve, but I want you to hold onto that until then and remember that I've been carrying it with me since I got it back from the jeweler."

"Is that nonna's ring?" Severu asks.

I nod. Most of our nonna's jewelry was passed down to Aunt Aria, but she left this ring to my mother. Mamma had her own engagement ring and wedding set, so she never wore it.

She was over the moon when I asked her for it.

"It's your grandmother's ring?" Bianca asks. "You've been carrying it around in your pocket?"

"Yes. And yes. Now, please save my cousin from having to execute one of his favorite capos and tell him you will marry me. You can wait and give *me* your yes until I've asked you properly."

"You're so sure I want to save you?" she asks.

After the risk she took coming here to save me from my cousin's wrath? "Yes."

I'm under no illusions Bianca loves me after today. That feeling is on another continent when it comes to her heart. How can I expect anything else after how badly I fucked up?

But I can be a patient man when I need to, and my cousin's decree is giving me a lifetime to woo my beloved's heart.

"I killed a man and I'm not sorry," she reminds me.

"He deserved death. Do I?"

She huffs out a breath and makes me wait almost a full minute until she shakes her head. But she doesn't look happy about it.

"Is that a yes?" Severu asks.

Bianca glares at him. "It is a you-twisted-my-arm-and-I'm-not-going-to-forget-it yes."

"Welcome to the club," Catalina says with more humor than I think Bianca is ready for.

"The De Luca wives club?" The wry twist to Bianca's mouth indicates she remembers what she said earlier.

Does she remember my response?

"The forced to marry an arrogant De Luca who turns out to be a pretty great husband club." Catalina grins up cheekily at Severu.

"Less of the *pretty great* and more of the *supremely awesome* wife."

"I'll think about it."

"I see that you have luggage with you. You'll be staying here until the wedding then?" Severu asks Bianca.

She goes rigid, like she's remembering why she has the duffle with her.

My arms tighten around her reflexively. "Please don't. Come home with me." I am not ashamed to plead with this woman.

"It's not my home though, is it?" She pushes for me to let her off my lap.

I don't want to, but I do anyway.

She stands and takes a step away from me and I hate it.

I fucked up when I let my past superimpose itself over my present. I should have trusted her. At the very least, I should have heard her out. Asked questions and not made accusations. We both know it.

My only hope is that Bianca is even more furious with Severu for forcing her into the marriage than she is with me.

"Rosa is really worried about you." Yes, it's a blatant attempt at playing on her emotions.

No, I don't regret it.

"She noticed I was gone?" Bianca asks, flicking a glance to Pietro.

My head of security is now standing sentinel at the entrance to the living room. He backed off on my signal, but not so far away he couldn't intervene if she got in trouble. He's protective over her.

Since he looks at her like she's a sister, or something, I don't have to kill him.

"Mamma went gonzo when we couldn't find you in the apartment," Pietro says with a critical look for me, his capo. "I was not told you would be going anywhere."

Bianca opens her mouth, probably to say something about Nerissa taking her to the airport, glances at Severu and snaps her lips together.

How did I ever believe this woman was anything like Monica? She's protecting my second, even now.

"Rosa can come here and assure herself of Bianca's wellbeing." Severu indicates the hall that leads to his office. "Salvatore, we have business to discuss. Catalina can help Bianca plan the wedding."

"I can?" Catalina asks, her tone unimpressed.

"You did an excellent job planning ours."

"With your mother and sister's help."

"Now you will have both my mother and my aunt's help."

"I don't want a big wedding," Bianca inserts.

"You are marrying a capo, Bianca. That's not going to happen at the courthouse with two witnesses." My cousin smiles, like he's trying to be conciliatory. He looks like a shark going in for the kill. "With only thirty days to plan, it will be less of a spectacle than it would be otherwise."

"Thirty days?" Bianca shouts. "I'm not getting married in thirty days."

Severu looks at her stoicly. "That is your choice, of course."

Bianca doesn't look even a little relieved. Because she's learning how my cousin operates.

"If you are not married to my cousin in thirty days, I will order his execution. My patience only extends so far. Salvatore believed he was risking undermining my bid to replace Don Caruso as godfather. The only reason I am giving him an out is because up to this point, he has been one of my strongest and most loyal capos."

"Not to mention your cousin," Bianca says snidely.

"Who put the woman in his bed above family." My don's voice is arctic and uncompromising.

Severu is doing me a solid, demanding the marriage as a way to redeem my disloyalty.

If Bianca had been the rat I believed her to be, there would be no chance to redeem myself though. And he will follow through on his threat to kill me if the wedding doesn't take place.

That's why he'll make a good godfather. My cousin is utterly ruthless when it comes to protecting *la famiglia*.

"I'm not staying here with you," Bianca seethes. "Or are you going to threaten to kill *me* if I don't?"

"Where you live prior to the wedding is entirely your choice. As you said, this is not the Middle Ages."

Catalina's snort of derisive laughter causes the first crack in my don's expressionless demeanor. A flicker of worry enters his familiar gaze before he scowls at me as if his wife's unhappiness is my fault.

Which ultimately, it is, I suppose. Just like Bianca's anger and mistrust.

I have a lot to make up for.

"Since you *understandably* won't be staying," Catalina says to Bianca with a challenging side-eye to her husband. "Will you keep me company for lunch while the don and his capo conduct their business? We can eat on the rooftop."

Every word is a barb directed at Severu. Unless she has other commitments, Catalina would usually join us and put off eating until she could share the meal with her husband. I doubt he's thrilled she's decided to eat in their rooftop garden either.

Severu has the entire rooftop surrounded by a clear shield with a Level 8 bullet resistance rating and the latest anti-drone technology in place. He still doesn't like Catalina going up there when security is on high alert like it has been since Don Caruso's stroke.

"You can eat in the dining room," he says.

"Oh, I don't think so," Catalina replies. "After all, we have all sorts of modern technology, this *not* being the Middle Ages and all."

When we reach his office, Severu rounds on me. "You are welcome."

"Don't start calling yourself the mafia matchmaker just yet, but I owe you."

"Indeed, you do." Severu crosses his arms and gives me the stare that has made grown men piss themselves. "Lorenzo."

"He's on ice at Amuni."

"You had him picked up."

"I did."

"I didn't give the order," Severu observes.

"He was a risk to Bianca and he's a rat."

"Nevertheless, I was going to wait until things calmed down to take him out."

"Every day you let him live is a risk someone else finds out he's stealing from the Family," I say with force. "That will make you look weak."

Severu rubs his chin in thought. "That's what Micelli said and I agreed. Which is why I gave my brother the order to pick him up. But strangely enough Miceli and his team can't find Lorenzo."

I pound Severu's desk with my fist. "No one is killing that *stronzo* before I get a chance to ask him some questions."

"Do you want Miceli or Angelo there for the interrogation?" Severu asks without hesitation.

It's an easier concession than I expected. "Miceli."

I'm still pissed at Angelo for killing Gino before I got a chance to mete out his punishment.

My don nods. "Tell Bianca to call me Severu. We're family now."

Chapter 63

SALVATORE

Pietro is driving my Audi RS7 and the privacy screen is up between us, but Bianca gives me the silent treatment.

She keeps her lips pressed tightly together when I tell her what Severu said about using his first name, and when I bring up the wedding. She does not reply when I ask about her lunch with Catalina.

"We need to tell my parents you are a Russo."

"I am *not* a Russo," she claims.

"Whatever your last name is now, you are still part of the Genovese Family."

"Not according to Lorenzo."

"Lorenzo's opinion doesn't count for shit," I tell the side of her face.

She refuses to look at me, her gaze toward the view out the tinted car windows.

When she doesn't answer, I add. "Your don and *your* capo claim you. That is all that matters."

She flinches when I say *your capo*, but remains silent.

"Your mother is a selfish bitch and your father was a fool, but you are Genovese Family." And soon to be my wife. "Your new last name does not change that, but when you are a De Luca, no one will question your place."

"I prefer Gemelli."

"Did you take that name because it means Gemini?" The constellation that represents the twins, Castor and Pollox.

Greek heroes, not Italian, but the symbolism would matter to her more than their origin.

She shrugs, which I take for a yes.

"Have you tried to talk to Beatrice since you became adults?" Do I need to punish the sister as well as the mother?

"There is no place for me in her life." Sadness laces Bianca's voice.

I will bring her sister back into Bianca's life, kicking and screaming if I have to.

"She didn't run as far from the mafia as you think. Her fiancé is part of the Lombardi Cosa Nostra in Boston." Not that Matthew Lombard has any power in his syndicate any longer.

He has risen as high in the ranks as he ever will because of the peace agreement Miceli brokered on Severu's behalf.

Bianca's head turns quickly and she finally looks at me. "I thought he was a property developer."

"He is. Stellar Holdings is a front for the Lombardi Family. The Lombards are heavily involved in regional politics too."

"That must be how he and Bea met. The Butlers have been part of local politics for generations. The guest list for their wedding probably includes a senator or two." Pain dulls her blue eyes.

"If you want senators at our wedding, we'll have them."

"It's not politicians I want at my wedding." She looks away again, her shoulders slumped.

She wants her sister there. Her twin.

"If Matthew Lombard is Cosa Nostra, why would me talking to him be a betrayal?" Bianca asks without turning back to me.

The thought of Bianca being with the other man even though I know the pictures are of her sister, sends killing rage through me. "You *didn't* talk to him."

She doesn't reply.

I grind my teeth. "He tried to outbid me for some strategic properties."

"That's what you thought I told him about?"

"I didn't think you told him anything before this morning." And this morning, I was too consumed with fury and hurt to consider what exactly she had told me.

"But you did think I told him about the properties?" she presses.

"If you want an answer, look at me."

She shrugs without changing the angle of her gaze, her answer as clear as if she'd spoken out loud.

Fuck off, capo.

I take another tack to get her to talk to me. "I think you should get therapy for the nightmares. A professional can help you work through what happened when you were thirteen."

It works.

She sucks in a breath and then says, "That's not the mafia way. Besides, my nightmares aren't about that day."

"What are they about then?"

I expect renewed silence.

But I'm wrong.

"What happened when I was sixteen." Her voice is hollow, like earlier.

I should have guessed that. Watching her father's execution had to have been horrifying for her. "Lorenzo killing your father."

"No."

What does she mean, *no*? What else happened to her that year? "Did something happen during your time on the streets?"

"No."

You're batting a thousand, genius.

"What then?"

She just shakes her head.

I lay my hand on her arm. "Please tell me, Bianca."

"I don't have nightmares about being there to protect my sister," she says. "My nightmares are about the day no one was there to protect me."

Regardless of what I say or ask, she remains silent for the rest of the ride.

Fuck.

No one was there to protect her. From what Bianca saved her sister from? From being kicked out onto the street not once, but twice?

All of the above?

I ask, but she just shakes her head.

Something scarred her psyche more than killing a man at thirteen, or watching her father get executed three years later. She'll tell me when she's ready. Maybe after I tell her my secrets.

We are in the elevator headed up to the penthouse when Bianca finally speaks again. "Will Don De Luca punish Pietro?"

My head of security frowns. "You don't need to worry about me, Bianca."

"You don't," I agree. "I convinced Severu to let me handle it."

My cousin understands loyalty. If Don Caruso had threatened Catalina back when he still had the strength to carry through on that threat, Severu would have killed our godfather before he let him touch her.

"What are you going to do?" Bianca demands as the elevator doors slide open.

We all step out and then I nod to Pietro. "Thank you."

His lips tilt at the corners. "My pleasure."

"That's it?" Bianca asks suspiciously.

"That's it."

She turns and heads to the door, waiting for me to open it.

But I guide her through putting her biometrics in the system so she can open it at will. "That gives you access to the elevator as well."

Her shoulders relax a little. Is that because she thinks she can run now? No matter where she goes, I will follow her.

This woman is mine.

When we get inside, she hugs Rosa and then goes straight upstairs. I follow her and watch as she makes a beeline for the guestroom.

I don't miss the snick of the lock after she closes it either.

BIANCA

A sharp rap sounds against the door, too firm to be Rosa.

Besides, she already came in an hour ago. Fussing over me, she insisted on unpacking my things. All of them. As if having my clothes back in the dresser and closet would make everything okay.

Like it never happened.

Salvatore must have told her about the upcoming wedding as soon as we walked in the door, because she was full of ideas for that too.

So many ideas.

"Go away!" I yell now.

"It's me, Bianca. Please let me in," Nerissa's voice calls through the doorway.

Accidenti!

"Fuck off!" Not wanting her to be killed does not equal wanting to be her friend anymore.

"I'm sorry. I should have talked to you before I took the pictures and will to Salvatore," she says through the door.

Pretty sure that was *never* going to happen.

"I'm not listening," I yell back.

Oh, that was mature.

Shut up. But I can't silence my own conscience.

"I have already resigned as Salvatore's second-in-command, but I don't want to lose you as a friend. Please talk to me, Bianca."

She did what?

I go to the door, but don't open it. "Why did you do it?"

"The pictures were delivered to me. I thought they were you with a mafia rival."

I have questions about Matthew Lombard I didn't want to ask Salvatore, the man who offered to *sacrifice* himself by marrying me to make up for his sin against his don.

I throw the door open. "Tell me everything you know about my sister's fiancé."

Nerissa drops her hand, clearly intending to knock again.

Her perfect brows draw together. "Didn't Salvatore tell you?"

Crossing my arms, I move aside so she can come into the room.

She does before I shut the door, relocking it. Then I wait in expectant silence for her to answer.

Finally, she says, "Matthew Lombard is part of the Boston Cosa Nostra. Your mom being from Boston, you probably know as much about them as I do."

"Are you serious? I didn't even know Boston had a Cosa Nostra syndicate before today."

Contrary to what Salvatore seems to think, my knowledge of the mafia is limited to the Genovese Family. And I didn't know the De Lucas owned so much real estate in New York either.

They're the kind of mafia family my mom thought she was marrying into.

"They do."

"I got that," I say dryly. "So, Matthew Lombard?"

"He's the nephew of the don."

"How close are his ties to the criminal enterprises of the Lombardi Family?"

Nerissa opens her mouth but I put my hand up. "Don't try telling me you don't know either."

"I wasn't going to." She hops up on the top of the dresser, planning to stay a while. "Up until he tried to outbid Salvatore for the bar properties, Matthew Lombard wasn't involved in mafia business. He's an aspiring politician. I guess he thought he would try his hand at mafia politics too."

"Explain."

When Nerissa is done telling me about his attempt to buy the bar properties and how it all plays into Severu De Luca's bid to be the next godfather, I'm sitting cross-legged on the bed, my back against the headboard.

Two things are clear. One, Nerissa's not the one who doctored my dad's file. Two, she acted as she did in the hope of protecting both me and her brother. She could have taken the pictures to her father, but she brought them to Salvatore, believing he would try to protect me.

"You're the one who told me he killed a woman he was fucking before. Why would you think he was going to protect me?" I ask skeptically.

"Because I know my brother. I saw how he was with Monica eleven years ago and I see how he is with you now. If my brother still has a heart in there somewhere, you own it."

I scoff at that.

But Nerissa's expression says she's dead serious.

"Why let me go if you thought I could take Matthew information. Why not just kill me?" I push.

"I couldn't. We'd become friends. I don't have friends. Mafia colleagues? Yes. Family? Yes. Friends?" She shakes her head.

That shouldn't matter. The mafia comes first.

"That's not what you said on the way to the airport," I remind her.

She sighs. "I was being a bitch because I thought you broke my brother's heart."

"He doesn't have a heart."

"Before you came along, I would have agreed with you. Now, not so much."

He was willing to *die* for me, to protect me even when it meant betraying his own family. Why else would he do that if he didn't feel something for me? But then why not *ask* me about the pictures instead of accusing me?

Those are questions only Salvatore can answer and I'm not ready to talk to him right now.

"He was willing to die for you," she says echoing my thoughts. "I think he's in love with you, Bianca."

I wave my hand, dismissing her words. I'm not accepting proxy declarations of love from my capo's sister.

"Why did you resign?" I ask.

Her face twists in grief. "Salvatore deserves a better second."

"Pretty sure there isn't one." Nerissa is fiercely loyal, smart and strong.

And yes, a Grade A bitch when she needs to be.

"How can you say that?" she demands.

"Everything you've done to hurt me has been in an attempt to protect your brother and capo. I killed a man to protect my sister."

"What?"

"Ask your brother." I'm not reliving that day again. "Tell him I said he could tell you. Or Pietro. He was listening in too."

"Pietro isn't speaking to me."

That's got to hurt. From what I have seen those two are as close as brother and sister.

"I can't believe Salvatore still is." She looks at me intently. "But he doesn't blame anyone else for his fuckups."

"You didn't look for an alternate explanation because I told you that all my family is gone," I give her the out because it's true.

"I didn't think you had *any* siblings, so the whole twin thing wasn't even on my radar. I'm sorry she's not part of your life anymore. I know how much it hurts to lose family."

She told me about her parents dying and ending up in such a bad foster care situation that the streets were a better alternative. That's when Big Sal De Luca found her and instead of walking on by, he took her home to Ilaria and suddenly they had a daughter.

A teenage daughter with a big mouth and even bigger attitude, according to Nerissa.

"I should have told you about my family when you told me about your past."
If I had, she would have known the pictures weren't me.

But the will still made it look like I'd lied about Mr. Ruhnke.

"You got used to pushing people away," Nerissa excuses me. "I lived with the De
Lucas for three years before I told them what happened to me in foster care."

"What did Big Sal do?"

"He told Salvatore. It was a couple of months after my brother was made. He
went after the man who hurt me and made sure he never got the chance to hurt
anyone else."

"Do you sleep better knowing he's dead?"

Would you sleep better if you knew the men who hurt you were dead?

I don't know.

"If I'd told the De Lucas right away, he would have been stopped sooner."

That's not an answer. Or maybe it is. Maybe she stopped dreaming about what
happened to her and started having nightmares about what happened after she
left.

"It's not your guilt to carry, Nerissa."

She shrugs. Then she sighs. "I know you won't forgive me right away, but I hope
someday we can be friends again."

"Tell Salvatore you want your job back and you keep working on improving
conditions for the dancers and sex workers in your club and we'll talk."

"Whoever he puts in my place can do that."

"Maybe they will. Maybe they won't. But you'll listen to me and that means
something." She's made changes based on my suggestions already, and it's not only
because I was Salvatore's girlfriend.

It was because underneath her gruff exterior, Nerissa cares about the people
that rely on her. Now that she sees the employees in the club in that light, they
are the recipients of her fierce loyalty and protection.

"I'll ask Salvatore if I can still manage the clubs, but I don't think he trusts me
right now."

I grab my phone and unblock Salvatore's number so I can dial it.

He answers on the first ring.

"Make Nerissa your second-in-command again."

"Okay."

A small thrill runs through me at his easy agreement, but I hang up and block
his number again. "You're still his second. Use your powers for good."

"You do realize what a second-in-command to a capo does, don't you?" But
there's a light in her eyes that has been missing since she walked into the guestroom.

"If you didn't mess with my dad's file, who did?" I ask her.

"If anyone messed with it, it would be Lorenzo."

"What do you mean if. He only had one child listed."

"Lorenzo doesn't keep records as meticulously as my brother. He doesn't care about the families of his men either."

"But my dad became his bookkeeper before my parents got their marriage annulled and my sister went with my mom to Boston."

Nerissa frowns. "Then he probably *did* doctor the file. We'll ask him."

The way she says it makes me think by ask she means interrogate. "Where is Salvatore right now?"

"Having a talk with Lorenzo."

And he answered his phone on the first ring. Huh. "What kind of talk?"

"The kind that doesn't have Lorenzo walking out of the room alive."

"Please tell me he got the don's approval for this talk. I didn't agree to marry him to save him just to have him throw his life away a few hours later."

"He has Severu's approval now."

"But he didn't before?"

Nerissa shrugs.

"That silence right there. That doesn't work for me."

"Salvatore had me pick up Lorenzo and put him on ice while he went running after you. And I do mean running. He sprinted out of the office faster than I've ever seen him move."

Another huh.

"Why have you got Lorenzo if you believed the pictures were real."

"Lorenzo was a risk to you."

"And you picked him up on Salvatore's orders without the don's approval?" Salvatore made those orders.

Just how far had he been willing to go to keep me alive?

You know the answer to that. He was willing to die.

He was willing to die.

Chapter 64

SALVATORE

Lorenzo's eyes are wild, darting between me and Miceli. Sweat runs down his forehead into his eyes and drool runs down his chin from the corners of his mouth stretched around a ball gag.

Too bad for him, he can't wipe it away. The traitor's hands are cuffed above his head, hanging from a chain attached to the ceiling.

The temperature in The Box is chilly and despite his sweat, goosebumps cover his bare flesh.

"While I appreciate not having to listen to the traitor lie and beg, we can't get the answers with that in his mouth." Miceli leans against the wall by the door, his arms crossed over his chest.

"After that Lucchese asshole bit through his own tongue to avoid interrogation, my crew don't take any more chances."

"You'd think we had a reputation for brutality, or something." Miceli's mouth twists sardonically. "We're not that bad, are we?"

Lorenzo tries to shout something, clearly disagreeing with the underboss's assessment.

I swing the specially designed cattle prod I'm known for using up from my side and slap it into my other palm to gain his attention. When his gaze finds me, his eyes widen in alarm.

I smile the smile I give before meting out punishment. There's nothing friendly about it.

Tears mix with the sweat on Lorenzo's face.

"I haven't touched you yet. You might want to save your tears for when it really hurts." I flick the on switch on the prod.

It buzzes and crackles just like it is designed to do.

Psychological triggers are as useful as pain in getting information, but no way is this asshole getting away without the pain.

Taking one slow step at a time toward him, I smack the non-electrified length of the cattle prod against my palm over and over. "You know how this goes, Lorenzo. Answer my questions and you spend less time with me and my toy."

I say nothing about the time he will spend with Miceli after. Or the denouncement in front of the other capos and their seconds he will have to endure before death.

Stopping two feet away, I press the prod against his inner thigh. Even the ball gag can't silence his screams completely.

"Miceli is going to undo your gag and you are going to answer my questions." I don't ask. This is not a negotiation.

The pain in his thigh and cramping muscles will last as long as twenty minutes. A continuous reminder of how much he doesn't want me shifting the prod a couple of inches to the left and pressing against his junk.

Miceli pushes away from the wall and removes the ball gag in silence and tosses it toward the wall of implements and metal bench under them.

He pats Lorenzo's cheek forcefully. "Start singing cuckoo before I feel the need to get involved because I'll cut your balls out of your nut sac and feed them to you."

"Her dad was my bookkeeper. He stole from me. I didn't want her around *la famiglia*."

"Wrong answer." This time, I press the prod against his other thigh so the pain radiates around but doesn't quite reach his cock and balls.

He screams and begs me to stop.

I do when his screams devolve to whimpers and his face is covered in tears and snot.

"Try again." I press him with the prod, but don't press the button to release the electric current.

He jolts anyway, trying to get away from it. "I thought he had told her stuff about me."

"Stuff like you've been stealing from the Cosa Nostra?" Miceli asks, his voice colder than the room.

"Drugs are *my* business," Lorenzo sniffles.

"Run with money from the mafia. You get to keep half of the profit and you're supposed to pay your soldiers 40% of that."

"No way is that happening," I add. "Not with how poor most them are. Hell, your bookkeeper couldn't even afford to live in our territory. You had him fucking living in New Jersey."

"He was stealing from me," Lorenzo squawks, like that's supposed to justify his stinginess.

Miceli makes a sound of disgust. "You stole from *la famiglia*. From your don and the men in your crew."

"It was my money," Lorenzo wheezes.

And then grunts in pain when Miceli kidney punches him.

"What were Lucchese hit men doing in Manhattan and why did they attack Bianca?" I've had time to reassess our meeting with Henry and the godfather.

Now that I know how desperate Lorenzo was to get rid of Bianca, I no longer believe the Lucchese capo that the attack was random.

When he doesn't answer immediately, I bring the cattle prod up and slide it along his thigh toward his low hanging balls.

"It was a hit," he sputters trying to kick his body backward.

Dark rage tightens my grip on the prod and I send a jolt of painful electric current into the crease between his thigh and scrotum. He shouts hoarsely and then starts to sob.

I wait until he's got his blubbering under control and then ask, "Did you tell Caruso you had our don's approval for the hit?"

"Yes. He wouldn't send his men otherwise."

"He would have checked," Miceli says.

He's right. Even Henry Caruso wasn't stupid enough to take the word of a *stronzo* like Lorenzo without confirming with Severu the hit on another Family's territory was sanctioned.

"He wanted to be godfather. I gave him a way."

"You knew about the bars." And he tried to frame Bianca as the rat.

I went to zap him again, but Miceli grabbed my wrist. "Information first then retribution."

"How did you know about the property purchase?" the underboss asks.

"I have my sources."

If he's trying to sound important, the effect is getting lost in his sniveling.

"What sources?" I demand.

It takes a prod directly to his nut sac before the cuckoo is singing like a canary. Two of my father's men are feeding him information.

One now. Marco isn't telling anyone anything with his tongue gone and working as a grunt without access to anything important. But one of the men my father transferred to his crew from Francesco Gilani's is Lorenzo's half-brother.

Cazzo. That explains a lot.

No one would expect the pompous capo to be friends with a lowly soldier, but blood tells.

"I actually liked that asshole," Miceli gripes. "Now I have to torture and kill him."

"You did not like that blabbermouth."

Miceli shrugs. "Okay, like is too strong a word, but I didn't object when Uncle Sal brought him onto his crew when he became consigliere."

"None of us did." There were no red flags, not like with Marco.

And even though my dad didn't take Marco onto his crew, the man still caused problems blabbing his mouth.

There's a theme here.

"You sold out your don and tried to have an innocent woman killed for what, you traitorous prick?" Miceli snarls. "Our don had you under investigation already."

"No." Lorenzo's denial is like a little kid thinking he can lie about eating the chocolate cake with brown frosting all around his mouth.

"His guy found your duplicate books and your hidden accounts," I say.

"All of them," Miceli adds with relish.

Lorenzo moans, the words hurting him as much as my cattle prod to his balls.

"You'll be happy to hear that money is already being disbursed to Genovese Family accounts."

Once we have the names of the soldiers who knew about what Lorenzo was doing, Severu will give the ones who weren't complicit a lump sum to make up for what their capo withheld from them during their years of service.

It takes another ninety minutes of interrogation and *persuasion* before we are sure we have all the names in the right column.

Lorenzo's son is one of the innocent. He spent his teen years living with his mother in Detroit when she left Lorenzo's cheating ass and returned to her family there. When it came time for college, she asked Severu to arrange for Dario Ricci to train with the don in Vegas.

He's an asshole, but his commitment to the Cosa Nostra is unfailing. By the time Dario came back to New York, he was everything his father wasn't. Lorenzo never promoted him to second-in-command and that's what is going to keep Dario alive during the coming culling.

Once we have all the information we need, I leave Lorenzo to Miceli. If I don't, I will kill him. But I have been ordered not to do that. Severu wants Lorenzo to die in front of his fellow capos and their seconds.

Like the last traitor who betrayed his don and the vows he spoke as a made man.

I'll return for the execution.

Right now though, I have things I have to take care of. Beginning in my conservatory.

Chapter 65

BIANCA

The marble floor is hard under my knees and cold seeps up my legs.

Salvatore and I kneel in front of Severu, the don's eyes cast judgment on us both. Catalina hands her husband a gun. A huge pistol, the end of the muzzle a gaping dark maw.

He walks around us and points the gun at the back of Salvatore's head, the muzzle pressing into my lover's dark hair.

My heart races and my stomach roils.

"Will you marry him?" Severu's voice reverberates around the room, hitting me from every direction.

Terror makes my throat tight. I try to open my mouth to say yes, but my jaw is locked. I desperately try to nod, but my shoulders and neck are frozen.

"It is your choice," Severu says. "This isn't the Middle Ages."

Catalina looks pityingly at Salvatore and accusingly at me. "It looks like your sacrifice was for nothing."

Then the don pulls the trigger.

Blood and brain matter spray, landing on my face and body.

Finally, my mouth opens and I scream.

And scream. And scream.

I try to wipe the gruesome bits of my lover off of me, but they cling.

Severu throws a chair and it bangs against the floor. He grabs my arms, and I thrash, yelling for him to let me go.

"Bianca, *brava ragazza mia*, you must wake up." Salvatore's voice infiltrates my mind, pulling me from the scene in the De Luca living room.

Gasping for air, my eyes snap open. The room is dark, but light filters in from the hall through the open door. A door I locked before going to bed earlier.

It's hanging at a weird angle.

"Did you kick the door in?" My throat is raw and the words hurt.

Salvatore lifts me into a sitting position and rubs my arms. "Shh... You are alright."

Only as his words penetrate do I realize I'm whimpering.

He jostles me and I hear the sound of water splashing into the glass from the carafe on the bedside table. Even though I don't need pain pills anymore at night, Rosa always leaves a fresh carafe of water on the table beside Salvatore's bed just in case.

Tonight, she left it in here.

Salvatore holds me like he has so many times after waking me to take my analgesics and tips the water to my lips. "Drink, *amore*."

I obey, first sipping and then gulping the water until the glass is empty. My throat is still a little raw, but it feels better.

"More?" he asks.

I shake my head.

There's a small click of glass against wood as he puts it down and then both of his arms are around me, holding me close. The dream is too fresh for me to push him away.

"Do you want to tell me about it?" he asks as my breaths become less labored.

"It was us in the living room at your cousin's house. Only I was kneeling beside you. Catalina handed him the gun. It was huge." I let out a halting breath.

"Your nightmare was about earlier?"

"Mostly. But Severu walked behind you and put the gun against the back of your head, like Lorenzo did to my dad. I couldn't get the words out to tell him I would marry you." I shudder. "He shot you and your blood and brain matter sprayed on me."

It doesn't take a genius to figure out that what happened at the don's triggered memories of my father's execution. My brain mixed them up with recent events to destroy my sleep.

I'm still tired, but have zero desire to go back to sleep and relive that nightmare.

"Sleep, Bianca." Salvatore, settles me so I'm resting more comfortably against his chest. "I'll keep your nightmares at bay."

"You won't sleep sitting up like this," I say softly.

"I won't sleep regardless. The door's lock is no longer operational."

"But your people are here, protecting the penthouse." Like they always are.

The number of guards on duty has doubled since the godfather's stroke.

Salvatore muscular chest rises and falls under my cheek as he shrugs. "And I am here, protecting you."

"You don't have to hold me in my sleep. I'll be fine." A lie, but not one meant to hurt.

"You think I am here for your sake?" he asks. "I have discovered I do not sleep well without my *woobie blanket* either."

Laughter bubbles up dispelling the lingering horror from the dream. "Are you trying to say that I am your protection from bad dreams?"

"You are my protection from loneliness."

Dio mio. This man.

"I already agreed to go through with the wedding. You don't have to convince me." Severu's threat to kill his cousin did that just fine.

"I have thirty days to court you and I am going to use every one of them, but that is not what this is. This is my truth. I sleep better with you in my arms."

And I sleep better surrounded by his warmth and scent.

"But you're not going to sleep at all like this."

There are no words accompanying the shrug this time. Just silence that says everything his mouth doesn't.

He's not going anywhere and he's not going to sleep in a room with the door hanging off its hinges. Because he thinks it's his job to protect not only my dreams, but my body too.

"When I was twenty, I fell in love," he says into the silence that has stretched between us. "Her name was Monica and she was everything I wanted in a woman."

My heart twinges at hearing him confess his love for another woman. But it doesn't bleed.

No, he hasn't said those words to me, but he has called me *amore* twice today. His beloved.

"Is she the woman you..." I let my voice trail off, not wanting to say the words.

"You know our world. It is brutal and I was raised to embrace that brutality."

"Yes."

"She took me in completely. Everything about Monica was an act put on to reel in the big fish."

"You."

"Me."

"She wanted to marry you?"

"No. I thought she did and I wanted to marry her. I wanted to tell her everything, that I was part of the mafia and would one day be capo like my father. I wanted to share everything in my life with her."

"My father always said made men didn't share business with their wives."

"No, but most wives know what business we are in."

"I'm not okay with being kept in the dark." He needs to know that.

I'm not my mother, willing to pretend my life is something other than what it is. I'm not Salvatore's mother either. I won't pretend not to see the brutality in his life, but I won't judge him for it either.

"There are things I won't tell you to protect you, but what I can share, I will."

It's more than I expect without an argument. "Okay. What happened to Monica?"

"Uncle Enzo ordered a deep dive background check on her when my father told him I wanted to bring an outsider into the family. And he instructed my father to do it."

"That makes sense. She could have been a FED planted undercover with you." It's why I didn't go ballistic when Salvatore searched through my phone.

Vetting anyone who gets close enough to learn their secrets is standard protocol for the mafia. A future wife would definitely fit that criteria.

"Was she a FED?" I ask when Salvatore doesn't continue.

"No. It was worse. At least to me. I was her mark. She and her real boyfriend were scam artists and they'd set me up for a quarter of a million dollar payout."

"How?"

"She pretended to be a botany student at NYU. She played me for six months, softening me up. All so that when she came to me sobbing and desperate because she'd accidentally killed a rare orchid she'd been studying but wasn't supposed to touch, I would insist on saving her."

"I don't understand." How had he saved her?

"I bought a replacement orchid. One so rare it cost a quarter of a million dollars and she would have been able to sell it on the black market for even more."

"You didn't buy it on the black market?"

"No. It was so rare, and took so many years to grow and flower, there weren't any available anywhere but through the company that had developed and nurtured the plant. I *convinced* them to sell me a plant intended for someone else."

He might not have bought it on the black market, but he'd used mafia tactics to persuade the growers to sell him the plant. All for a woman who was scamming him. That would have been a blow to his pride and his heart.

I scoot up Salvatore's chest until my head rests against his shoulder and I hug him.

His arm tightens around me too.

"Nerissa said your conservatory is a reminder not to trust women, especially outsiders."

"It used to be."

"It's not anymore?" What does he feel when he looks at his orchids now?

"No." He pulls me so my body is fully on top of his.

I think he wants to me try to sleep like this, which is seriously not going to happen.

But then he starts talking again. "I told Monica I loved her and less than twenty-four hours later, I was ordered to kill her and her boyfriend for trying to steal from the mafia."

"You didn't use mafia funds to buy the orchid." Salvatore would never have done that.

"No, but that didn't matter to my uncle. It was my test of loyalty and strength."

"That's awful." I'm not sure Severu would be any less merciless, but it sounds like his father was completely void of compassion. "Your father didn't stick up for you?"

"My father gave me the order. He and my uncle witnessed the kill together." Salvatore's tone is flat, like what he's saying didn't devastate him.

But he's not the unfeeling guy so many people seem to think he is.

"I don't think I like your dad. That was a cruel thing to do to you."

"It changed me. Molded me to be the man who could and would take over as capo one day."

Nerissa said something like that on the drive to the airport. "You refused to kill me though."

A thirty-one year old man might not be willing to do what a twenty-year-old would. Or is it something else? Something more personal.

Amore.

"Yes." His tone resonates with absolute conviction.

"Instead, it ended up being your life on the chopping block."

His laugh surprises me. "An unexpected outcome, but then that's how things seem to go with you."

I push against his chest and sit up, trying to read his expression through the gloom. "You offered to sacrifice your life for mine."

"Yes."

"And your cousin accepted your *sacrifice*." I still don't like thinking of us getting married as Salvatore's lifetime sacrifice.

"Marriage to you is not a sacrifice. Losing you would have been that."

"Are you reading my mind?" I ask, only half teasing.

How does he know me so well after such a short time?

"You didn't look happy when Severu accepted my vow."

"I'm pretty sure I didn't look happy during any of that."

"No, but when he said those words, you looked hurt."

It's my turn to shrug.

"It is my life to promise. My sacrifice to make. My loyalty to pledge."

"Uh...I'm not sure what that is supposed to mean. If those are your wedding vows, they need work."

"Those are the vows I spoke when becoming a Genovese made man."

Chills wash over me. "You were renewing your promise to your don."

"Reminding him of my promise."

"And it worked. He gave you the option of marrying me instead of dying."

"Yes."

"That was your plan all along. Well at least once you realized the only one who had betrayed anybody was you with your don."

He doesn't wince, or look even a little repentant. "I am coming to realize there are different layers of loyalty. Some commitments supersede even my vows to the mafia."

"Your mom, sister and Rosa will be happy to hear that."

A smile ghosts over his lips. "I am sure you are right."

A jaw cracking yawn takes me by surprise.

"You need to sleep, *amore mio*. You must take better care of yourself."

There it is again. *Amore mio*. My beloved.

"You're going to have to say the words at some point," I warn him. "Pretty sure that's part of courting."

Did he really mean it when he said he has thirty days to court me? Of course he did. Salvatore doesn't say things he doesn't mean. Which is why I want those three little words.

"When the time is right," he promises. "Now lie down."

I shake my head. "We *both* need our sleep."

"Are you trying to kick me out again?"

"Nope. I can compromise."

"Really?" He sounds skeptical.

Which...fair.

"If it means both of us getting the rest we need, I'm willing to sleep in your bed." It's not like I was getting quality sleep in here. "I can't believe you broke down my door because I was having a nightmare."

Salvatore stands and lifts me before I have a chance to change my mind. "I did not break down *your* door." He carries me into the hall. "I broke down the guestroom's door."

Stopping at the threshold to his bedroom, he says, "This is our door." He steps inside, shuts and locks the door behind us. "This is our room." He carries me into the walk-in closet that now stands completely empty on one side. "This is our closet."

"I get it. You know how to share."

"Only with you."

Warmth unfurls in my chest. I believe him.

He carries me to the bed and lays me onto the mattress before climbing over me to spoon against my back.

"You could have gotten into bed on the other side," I grouse without heat.

"Not as much fun."

We're snug in our cocoon of blankets, when I say, "When I was sixteen, my dad got in debt to some bad guys again."

Chapter 66

SALVATORE

My entire body goes rigid at Bianca's words.

She presses more tightly into my arms. "He was home when they showed up to collect, but he didn't have the money they wanted."

Rage burns through me, but I keep my arms gentle around her. She doesn't need my fury right now. She needs me to listen.

And I will, no matter how hard her words are to hear.

"They told him they would take something on payment."

The tension in her body. The way she shies away from touch. The little clues that while she was up for trying anything, she hadn't done very much before me. It's all there.

And it adds up to one word. An ugly, selfish act.

"They took you," I say.

She nods. "My virginity. It hurt so much Salvatore. I didn't know being touched there could feel so good until you."

"And your dad just watched?" I ask, unable to stop some of my fury from leaking into my voice.

"That was his punishment. To watch. They said if he didn't get them the money, they would come back and this time, they wouldn't settle for a fuck."

"They threatened to sell you?" I killed a made man who made a similar threat to someone who owed him money.

My crew knows that family doesn't pay the debts of others. Torture and kill the fucker who stole from you, but leave his, or her, fucking family out of it.

"Yes. But Lorenzo showed up first. Part of me was relieved when he killed my dad and kicked me out."

"You had to be afraid they would come after you though."

"I was, but they didn't know where I went to school and for the first year, I never left the building. Not once."

Fuck. What she went through. "I am sorry, *amore mio*."

She turns and presses her face into my neck. I'm starting to get that is her go-to when she needs comfort.

I pull her tight. "I will never let another man touch you."

"No one ever has, not since then. Until you."

My heart beats a staccato in my chest. "I was your first."

"No...they..."

"What those sick bastards did wasn't sex. It was rape. I was your first."

She nods, but her tears wet my neck. Bianca doesn't cry. But she trusts me. Even when I proved my own trust is shaky.

"Do you know their names?"

"Only one of them. He was on Lorenzo's crew with my dad. I never saw the other two before."

"Tell me."

She whispers the name, like it's a secret.

It won't be a secret when I cut off his cock and balls and shove them down his throat. But that will only come after I get the names of the two other men I have to kill out of him.

My wedding present for Bianca will be a world without her abusers in it.

~ ~ ~

"Uh, I don't think that's going to be the great gift you think it is, capo." Nerissa frowns at me after I tell her my plans.

I am going to find the men who assaulted my beloved. Then I am going to torture and kill them.

"She'll be glad they are dead," I argue.

"Probably, but the whole give her a picture of their faces twisted in pain just before death? No woman wants that as a wedding gift."

"You would."

"If that had happened to me, I would kill the men myself."

"You think Bianca wants that?" She killed the man who tried to rape her sister and doesn't regret it.

"Maybe. Ask her."

The more I think about it though, the more I think Nerissa is right. And if Bianca doesn't want to mete out the justice they deserve, she can at least see them reduced to nothing.

"I mean it, Salvatore. *Ask her.* Maybe she doesn't want to add images of mutilated rapists to the slide show in her head."

I think those are just the images she needs to counterbalance the memories of when she was helpless against their violence and cruelty.

"I'll ask." After I show her the changes I've made in the conservatory.

BIANCA

Warm sunlight across my face wakes me up and I smile at the sensation, snuggling against my pillow and inhaling Salvatore's scent. The lack of a warm body against my back tells me he's already gone from his...no, *our* bed.

Relief that I have time to process our middle of the night confessions before I see him again overrides my disappointment at his absence.

Last night was the first time since Ilaria caught us kissing in here that we slept in the same bed without touching sexually. After the rollercoaster of a day and our middle of the night revelations, I was emotionally and physically exhausted.

Somehow, Salvatore knew I craved the safety of his arms and gave me exactly what I needed, holding me tightly throughout what was left of the night.

A sound near the window catches my attention and my eyes flash open.

Rosa puts a tray with breakfast on the table by the window, the open drapes the reason for the sunlight that woke me.

When she sees that I'm awake, she smiles. "Good morning, *dolce ragazza.*"

"Morning." I yawn and stretch before sliding out of the warm cocoon of covers.

The air conditioning keeps the penthouse apartment at a moderate temperature, but the air feels cool against my skin and I grab the silk robe someone thoughtfully left at the end of the bed. Probably Rosa.

She thinks of everything.

Tying the belt, the sudden urge to pee has me hurrying toward the bathroom.

I'm surprised to find Rosa still in the room when I come out a few minutes later. She's staring out the window, her hands clasped in front of her.

When I sit down, she joins me at the table and pours steaming coffee into two mugs. She came up prepared to have a chat.

"Thank you." I take my coffee from her, inhaling the rich aroma and faint scent of cinnamon.

"It is my pleasure."

We both sip our coffee, but then Rosa puts her mug down and clasps her hands again. "Pietro told me what he discovered about your birth yesterday."

I thought Lorenzo told Salvatore about my father and I say so. She explains Pietro's search for my birth records and what he found when he searched under Bianca Russo.

"Last night, he told me that your father was Alberto Russo."

"Yes."

"My aunt married a Russo from Detroit."

Chills run down my arms. "What are you saying?"

"Your grandfather moved from Detroit to marry my aunt, but my uncle and my father never got along. After nonno died they had a big fight and never spoke again." Rosa dabs at the moisture pooling in her eyes. "I was only six at the time. From that point on, the name Russo was never allowed to be spoken in our home. I knew that I had a cousin, but I never met him."

She can't be saying what I think she is saying. "I don't understand."

"Alberto Russo was my cousin."

"But I never met you." I'd never met any of my nonna's family.

"My papa tried to reconcile with your grandmother after your grandfather died, but she rebuffed him."

I am not surprised. "My dad told my nonna that if she tried to reconcile with the family that had treated his father so badly, he would cut nonna out of our lives."

Nonna chose me and Bea over her own brother. It couldn't have been easy for her, but she never showed any resentment toward us. Not even to my dad.

"He sounds like he took after your grandfather."

I can only nod. Both nonno and my dad only adhered to mafia traditions that suited them.

"So many things make sense now. From the very first, you reminded me of my grandmother."

"Your grandmother's recipes are so similar to those I got from my nonna because she got them from the same woman."

"Her mom." My *bisnonna* was Rosa's grandmother.

"Even the pattern on our family dishes are the same." Because they came from the same place.

Although my nonna's dishes were lost along with my home.

Rosa laughs. "No wonder you and Pietro get along like siblings."

That's one way to describe our relationship.

"He's very good at playing the annoying older brother." And protective.

I will never forget his willingness to stand by Salvatore in protecting me, even in the face of the don's wrath.

"It's a new role for him, but he's taken to it very well." Rosa smiles, but the expression seems forced.

"What's wrong? If you don't want to acknowledge our family connection, I won't tell anyone." But saying the words hurts.

I want this woman to be my family.

"Do not even think that, *dolce ragazza*!" Rosa throws her hands into the air for emphasis. "You are my family."

"Okay, but you don't seem happy about it."

"If you do not want to marry the capo, we will get you out of New York," she says in a rush.

Che palle.

I throw my hand up in a stopping gesture. "Don't say another word. If Salvatore hears you, he'll be livid. I'm already engaged to one man to save him from the don. There's no one I can marry to save you from the capo."

"Our family let you down in the worst way possible. You should never have been thrown into the street." Rosa's nurturing nature is appalled by my past. "We won't let you down now."

"Pietro told you everything," I say with dawning understanding.

No wonder Rosa is ready to launch a mafia rebellion to save me.

Rosa shrugs. "I may have listened in on a conversation between him and Salvatore and then pressed my son for more details."

"None of what happened to me is your fault," I assure her.

Rosa's mouth sets stubbornly. "You will not marry anyone you do not wish to."

"Even your bossy tone is like my nonna's," I grumble. "This marriage thing is a done deal."

Even if I didn't love Salvatore, I wouldn't allow him to die for trying to save my life. But marrying him is not the big sacrifice Rosa is making it out to be either.

"It does not have to be," Rosa stubbornly insists.

"Your don would disagree. Pietro dodged a bullet yesterday. Let's not create another one with his name on it."

Rosa's face blanches. "What do you mean?"

After I'm done telling the older woman the stuff her son left out about yesterday, she's ready to give him an earful. "He went against his don? Has my son lost his sense?"

"Uh...what do you think hiding me from Salvatore and his cousin is doing?"

"That is different. A woman should not be forced to marry a man she does not want to."

"It happens in the mafia all the time."

"Arranged marriages. Not forced ones," she argues.

When the bride and groom have no choice in the matter, how are the two things different? I don't ask because that's not what is important right now.

"I am doing this willingly."

"I saw the guestroom door this morning."

Oh, no. No. No. We are not back to that. "You didn't tell Ilaria?"

Rosa's mouth sets in a mulish line. "And why should I not tell his mother about her son's deplorable behavior?"

"Maybe because it wasn't deplorable. I was having a nightmare and Salvatore wanted to comfort me. The locked door was in the way."

Rosa's mouth opens and then closes three times but no words emerge.

"You and Ilaria *have* to stop thinking the worst of him. I know you both love him, but you don't trust him and that's not okay."

"You do trust him," Rosa says wonderingly.

"I do."

"Even after yesterday?"

"Especially after yesterday. His lack of trust in me hurt a lot. I won't deny it, but Rosa, he was willing to *die* to protect me. In the mafia, every made man is willing to kill to protect *la famiglia*, but to die for someone else?" I shake my head. "That's rare."

Rosa's eyes fill with tears. "I owe Salvatore an apology."

"You do, but how about you keep it to your previous distrust of him and not mention today's misunderstanding?" That would hurt him.

Rosa nods. "I need to talk to Ilaria before she chastises her son for breaking a door."

As funny as that sight might be, it also has the potential to hurt Salvatore if Ilaria lets him see her concern for my wellbeing because of the broken door.

"What you said that day in the ceramics studio is true. It is time we stopped thinking the worst of him because he obeyed the orders of his capo and his don."

"I would take it as a personal favor if you did that. I would hate to lose the family I just found and have nothing but a chilly, distant relationship with my mother-in-law after my marriage."

I let the words and their meaning hang in the air between us. Salvatore might forgive them for the way they judge him, but I will not.

I killed a man for my sister. I will cut two women I have grown to love from my life for the man who owns my heart.

Rosa jumps up, as if galvanized by the underlying threat in my words. "My father will want to meet you."

"I would love that."

With a hug and an extracted promise from me to meet her for a cooking lesson later, Rosa leaves.

Chapter 67

BIANCA

I grab my phone to check messages while I finish my breakfast. There's a text from Candi. And before I read it, I change her name in my contacts to KathB.

My friend. She has never called me by my stage name, not even once. I'm lucky she's been so patient with my standoffishness and still worked at being my friend.

KathB: *Hey, girlfriend. What's up.*

Bianca: *I'm getting married. Want to be my maid-of-honor?*

KathB: *WTF?!!*

My phone rings the second the text comes through. I answer and somehow explain my whirlwind wedding without telling my best friend about the mafia or the don's threats.

"I knew you had it bad for him, but this is next level. Are you sure you want to marry him? I mean he's giving you the milk. Why buy the cow before you're sure you want to keep it?"

"I am sure."

"Okay, but you do realize the other dancers are going to want to come to your bachelorette party. I know you don't think anyone else is your friend, but you're wrong."

"Okay. As long as they don't mind partying with the boss lady."

"You want me to invite Nerissa James? That woman is scary."

"She's going to be my sister-in-law *and* she's the one implementing the changes to protect the dancers and backroom workers at the clubs."

"She listens to you so she can't be all bad, but you do remember that until a few weeks ago, she'd never spoken to a single dancer?"

"Attitude adjustment." And Nerissa had taken it without bitching.

"Okay. Gotta go. I've got a bachelorette party to plan and a bunch of dancers to tell about the wedding of the century. Oh..." Her voice trails off.

"What?"

"Um, I assumed you'd want to invite them to the wedding, but maybe not. Mr. Billionaire's friends probably don't mix with strippers in public."

"He's marrying a pole dancer, I think he can deal."

"Ex pole dancer."

"If our friends can't mix at our wedding, how are we going to mesh our lives after?"

It's a question I'm still thinking about when I meet Salvatore up on the roof later.

He's standing at the conservatory's doors, his gray gaze devouring me as I walk toward him. "You look beautiful."

"Um...thanks." I'm wearing my usual snarky t-shirt, capri yoga pants and tennis shoes.

He reaches for my hand. "You are always beautiful."

"You don't have to butter me up with compliments to tell me you couldn't save Vee."

"Who said I couldn't?"

Excitement surges through me. "You did? It's okay?"

"More than okay." He leads me into the humid warmth of the climate-controlled conservatory.

I blink and then blink again, trying to take in what I'm seeing. "Where are all the orchids?"

The super expensive, ridiculously rare orchids?

"Gone."

"I can see that."

"They reminded me of my past. These remind me of my future."

All the shelves are filled with African violets amidst the shade ferns. Purple ones, pink ones, white ones and variegated petals, but by far the highest number are the plants with blue flowers. All of them are planted in pots made by his mother and aunt.

In pride of place, where his Shenzhen Nongke Orchid is Vee in the pot I picked out. Thrown and painted by my own newly discovered second-cousin.

It's vibrant with life again, the leaves dark green and a plethora of furled buds in the center that will flower soon.

"How did you do this so fast?" I ask. "What did you do with the orchids?"

"I donated them to an arboretum."

"Even the Shenzhen Nongke Orchid?"

"Yes."

"But it was worth so much money."

"Not as much as the violets are to me."

"Um, I don't know much about rare African violets," I admit. "My botanical knowledge is pretty limited to how to take care of Vee."

"I don't either. These aren't rare, they are hardy. And the blue ones remind me of your eyes."

"You found all these this morning?" Yes, I know the man is rich, but I'm still impressed.

"Not this morning. I only wanted blue that exact shade and didn't want any others the same purple as Vee. Your friend should stand out."

Okay, that's really sappy. And so incredibly sweet. "What do you mean *not this morning*?" I ask. "Did you order all these last night?"

"I've been working on the transition from orchids to violets for the past few weeks."

"But why?"

"I already told you."

"But you didn't know I was your future."

"Didn't I?" His hand drops from mine.

Unable to believe the message in his words, I turn around to face him. He's kneeling on one knee, the expression on his face making my heart beat too fast.

"I should never have doubted you about your sister. My only excuse is that I was terrified."

"You aren't afraid of anything." My voice comes out just above a whisper.

"Before I met you, that was true. I did not fear death. I did not fear pain. Or killing. But once I met you I had something to fear."

"What?" But I think I know. The same thing I learned to fear.

"Losing you."

"Is that why you kept me locked in your lair like Beauty and the Beast?"

"It's not a lair. It's a home. Our home."

I notice he doesn't deny keeping me locked up, because even though he said I could go once I was better, I think we both know that's not true. This man is obsessed with me.

Another woman might hate that, but for me, who has been discarded too many times in my life, knowing this man will *never* let me go heals old wounds I never thought would stop hurting.

"You were going to let me go." I frown. "You sent me away."

"If you had gotten on that plane, I would have been right behind you."

"How?"

"Private jet." He shrugs. "It was waiting on standby at the airfield."

"Then why send me in the first place?"

"I was in panic mode. There was no way I would ever kill you, but I didn't want to have to kill my cousin either."

The true depths of the quandary he'd put himself in fills me with terror. He would have killed his don to protect me. And died, horribly, as a result.

"You threw me away. You hurt me."

"I will regret that for the rest of my life." He grabs my hand and presses it to the side of his face. "You are the very air that I breathe *anima gemelli mia*."

My soul mate. Literally the twin to his essence.

I will never stop missing Bea, but Salvatore's soul is twined with mine now, filling in the lonely hollows of my heart. And unlike my sister, he will never be horrified by who I really am.

"*Anima gemelli mia,*" I repeat. Because I accept and love the very essence of this man too.

His gaze traps mine. *"Ti amo."*

"I love you too," I breathe.

"Will you save me from a life of empty loneliness, *amore mio* and marry me? Become my wife for this life with our souls joined for eternity?"

"Yes."

A grin splits his face as he surges to his feet and picks me up to kiss me senseless. Only when my butt lands on the empty potting bench do I realize we were moving.

We tear each other's clothes off, our hands greedy for bare skin. My hands press on his chest and I feel plastic against my hand.

Breaking the kiss, I look down, panting.

Where there once had been a monochromatic black tattoo of a coiled viper over his heart, there is one so new, it is still red around the edges and covered with a transparent bandage.

A cluster of vibrantly colored blue violets, it has the words *anima gemella mia* in a stylized curve under it.

That is what he was busy doing this morning, putting my claim to his heart on his skin and erasing any trace of Monica. Just like he did in here.

"It's beautiful." I trace around the clear bandage. "You put me on your skin."

"You are carved into my soul."

"And you are twined with mine."

"For eternity."

"Now and forever," I agree.

This time when he kisses me, his lips are reverent, sealing our vows with more power than any clerical blessing.

The frenzied passion of seconds before turns into something profound. We touch and kiss, making promises with our mouths and hands until he slides his big hardon into my swollen and ready vagina.

Leaning back on the bench, my legs splayed wide and my knees hooked over his arms, I eagerly accept him inside me. He stretches me like he always does and it is perfect.

Salvatore fills my empty places. And I am his sanctuary.

Ecstasy dances along every nerve ending in my body until I come with a crescendo of pleasure as I scream Salvatore's name.

"Bianca, *amore mio*!" He shoves himself forward and hot jets pulse inside me. "You are mine, now and forever."

Chapter 68

BIANCA

For the next month, Salvatore courts me just like he promised.

He wakes me with orgasms. When he learns of my family connection to Rosa, he invites my great-uncle to dinner for us to meet and hovers protectively until he's sure the man who insists I call him nonno isn't going to say anything to hurt my feelings.

One day Daryl Ruhnke's sons arrive with a check for fifty-thousand dollars and obsequious, if not sincere, apologies for how they treated me. When they go to leave, the oldest begs me to call off the dogs and I know giving me what Mr. Ruhnke left me in the will isn't enough for Salvatore.

He's probably bankrupting the Ruhnke sons. That night I tell him to stop. That it is enough. Mr. Ruhnke would not want his sons to suffer complete annihilation. Salvatore isn't thrilled but he agrees to back off.

"I should have waited to have them come until they were both jobless and on the verge of losing their homes."

"Yeah, no. What they did was petty and cruel." But it doesn't rank with the other trauma in my past.

And we leave it at that.

Salvatore and I tend the violets together in the conservatory, adding a new plant for the first pot I make that doesn't crack in the firing. We have dinner with his parents and Big Sal is positively friendly, making jokes about grandbabies and beautiful daughters-in-law.

It's weird, but I'll take it.

When Salvatore's mother is concerned about me inviting several exotic dancers to our wedding, both my fiancé and Rosa set her straight. Catalina casts the deciding vote, decreeing my friends *will* be invited.

As the don's wife, she has seniority, even over her mother-in-law, and the not-so-subtle attempts to expunge them from the guest list end.

Rosa, Ilaria and Aria are forces to be reckoned with when it comes to planning a wedding though. It is Catalina who makes sure everything is what *I* want it to be on my wedding day. Having her as an ally is every bit as powerful as I suspected it would be.

The night before Kath and I are supposed to go for our dress fitting, we are having dinner at Catalina and Severu's again.

I haven't seen the don since the day he threatened to kill my soulmate.

But it's not his voice that jerks me to a grinding halt as soon as I step off the elevator. It is a voice almost identical to my own. Only now that voice speaks with a distinctly Bostonian accent.

Bea is here?

Salvatore's hand rubs my back. "She can't wait to see you."

"Why didn't you warn me?" I ask.

"I wanted to surprise you." He comes around to face me, his craggy face drawn in lines of concern. "Was that bad?"

"I..." I shake my head. "I don't know. You said she wants to see me?"

He nods. "Very much."

"Bia." My sister's voice is low and uncertain.

I haven't heard that nickname in almost ten years. My father always called me Bianca or Bibi. Beatrice is the only one who called me Bia.

Salvatore looks down at me in question and I nod.

He steps to the side, but maneuvers us so he has his arm around my back when my sister steps forward.

She is dressed like the socialite she is, but her eyes are filled with tears. "Is that really you?"

Suddenly, I can't stand the distance between us and I lurch forward to hug her. She does the same, and we collide in a bone-crushing hug.

"I'm so glad you were willing to see me," she says into my ear. "I've missed you so much, Bia, like a piece of my soul was gone and I couldn't get it back."

I pull back and stare, unable to comprehend what she's saying. "Mom said you didn't want to see me, that you were ashamed of me."

"Mom told me you didn't want to ever see me again after you had to..." She doesn't go on, unsure if I've told my fiancé and his family about my past.

I can still read my sister like she is myself.

"But that night, you wouldn't talk to me."

"I was in shock. I've never been as strong as you, Bia. I don't think I could have done what you did to protect you and I knew it. I felt so guilty."

"But it wasn't your fault."

"That's not how it felt."

Catalina steps forward. "Come on you two, you can use my office to catch up without an audience. I can have dinner brought to you."

Bea looks horrified. "We couldn't possibly miss dinner. That would be rude."

"Not at all," Catalina says smoothly.

But Bea is shaking her head. "We'll talk in your office if that's alright, but we'll join the rest of you for dinner."

The difference in our lifestyles in the last near decade couldn't be more apparent. I don't care about societal expectations, but Bea is bound by them.

"Could you send someone to tell us when everyone is sitting down for dinner?" I ask Catalina.

"Of course." She leads the way down the hall to the right of the living room.

Salvatore sticks right by my side the whole way, but once we reach Catalina's office, I put my hand on his chest to stop him. "That's as far as you go. I'll see you in a little bit for dinner."

"I don't want to leave you alone with her."

"You wouldn't have invited her if you didn't think I was safe in her company," I tell him.

"She might say something that hurts you."

"Probably. And I'll probably say something that hurts her, but we'll get through it. Please, Salvatore, I need to do this alone."

He glares at Bea, but nods. "I will be—"

"In the living room with the others," I instruct, with zero give in my voice.

Catalina tugs his sleeve. "Come on, Salvatore. Give them some privacy."

Once we are alone, Bea looks at me with wide eyes. "He's pretty intense."

I nod. No point in denying the truth. "I like it."

"Better you than me."

That makes me laugh. "Are you saying Matthew Lombard is a pussycat?"

"He's nothing like your Salvatore, that's for sure."

I wonder if she knows if he's in the mafia, but as we catch up on the past decade it becomes pretty obvious that Bea has no clue that Matthew Lombard is part of the Lombardi Family.

Salvatore told me that Matthew Lombard won't ever advance within his Cosa Nostra, so she'll probably never find out either. Ten years ago, hiding a big part of my life from my sister would have been unthinkable.

Now, sharing anything important with her is harder to imagine.

"I tried to see you, after I graduated high school. I wanted us to go to the same college, but I couldn't find you. I didn't even know dad was dead until then and Mr. Ricci said you had left New York."

"Mom paid me five-thousand dollars to change my name. Since I thought you never wanted to see me again, I agreed."

"I don't understand why she did that. You're her daughter too."

"Not since that night."

"But you saved me."

"That's not how mom sees it. She thinks I lost my soul." I know she's wrong. I have a soul and it is connected permanently to Salvatore De Luca's.

"I want you to be a bridesmaid in my wedding," Bea blurts out. "It will make mom mad, but I don't care. You're my sister and I'm done pretending like you don't exist."

"Are you sure? We don't have to go public with our family connection to have a friendship."

Bea chews on her lip. "Even if I was willing to do that, I don't think your fiance would stand for it."

"What do you mean?"

"He won't allow me in your life unless I'm willing to publicly acknowledge you." She shakes her head when I open my mouth to protest. "The warning wasn't necessary, Bia. You are my twin and I want you in my life. Mom is going to have a conniption though."

"Conniption? Who says that?"

"What would you call it?" Bea teases back.

"Temper tantrum. Heart attack. Aneurism."

Bea laughs. "All of those too." Then she sobers. "She's going to be humiliated when everyone finds out she has another daughter she's never mentioned."

"Knowing her, she'll play it off as if she was too heartbroken by dad keeping me away from her to talk about me." Not that I'll play along, but even I am not going to make a big scene at my sister's wedding.

Which is the only time I plan to see my mother in the near future. I'm sure as hell not inviting her to mine.

I learn that Bea is here now because Salvatore thought I might want her in my wedding and we're dress shopping tomorrow.

Chapter 69

SALVATORE

Bianca is very happy I brought Beatrice back into her life. Making her happy is my priority.

Not because I'm courting her but because seeing her happy is so damn satisfying.

I don't tell my beloved that I investigated Beatrice before I would consider approaching her. When I decided she could be a positive addition to Bianca's life had a necessary conversation with Matthew Lombard. I made it clear that if his fiancée hurt my beloved in any way, I would relieve the earth of both their presence.

"Bea thinks mom is going to play the poor, brokenhearted mother, when news gets out in Boston society of my existence." Bianca cuddles against my side, her body lax from lovemaking.

"Not going to happen." I have plans in place.

Not only will the fact that Elizabeth abandoned Bianca come to light, but everyone is going to know that when Alberto died, the socialite left her daughter to fend for herself at the age of sixteen.

My fiancée pushes me onto my back and drapes herself over me, in what has become both our favorite position after sex. Propping her chin on her fists, she's careful to rest her biceps against me and not her elbows. As if I might be bothered by the small pain.

"I feel like you have plans for my mom." Her beautiful blue eyes sparkle at me.

"Because you know me well."

"Care to share?" Beautiful blue eyes reflect a soul the perfect match to mine.

"She will be humiliated."

"I figured with you being adamant that Bea and me not keep our family connection under wraps."

"There will be no opportunity for her to play injured anything," I say with pleasure. "Everyone in Boston society will know what a horrible mother she has been to you."

The Boston Cosa Nostra has an effective disinformation machine developed over decades playing in the political arena.

"If Beatrice and Matthew don't distance themselves from her, his political chances will die the same death as his future in the Cosa Nostra."

"You are ruthless."

I shrug. My soulmate already knows that and she loves me anyway.

"She deserves to pay for what she's done to you, but if you want me to dial it back, I will." Only for this woman would I dampen my natural inclination to go for the jugular.

Bianca's grin is the sun coming out after weeks of gray skies. "She kept me and my sister apart for almost ten years. She deserves what she gets."

"You are so perfect for me *amore mio*."

"We're kind of perfect for each other." She frowns. "I'm worried that Bea will want to stand by mom and Matthew will dump her though."

"He's an opportunist. It's possible."

"I think he loves her." Bianca's lips twist in uncertainty.

"Maybe, but not as much as he loves her political connections. If she becomes a liability..." I don't finish my thought.

My sweet fiancée knows.

"If he's that shallow, Bea is better off knowing now than later," Bianca says with certainty.

"True."

She sighs. "We're so different now."

"You and Bea?"

"Yes. She thinks I'm stronger than she is, and she might be right, but I think I'm harder too."

"You were born twins, but your lives diverged that night nine years ago. She was a victim. You were a savior. She went to live among the Boston elite and you stayed in the mafia world."

"And then I was a victim."

"You survived and learned to thrive. You made the last years of Daryl Ruhnke's life better and fought hard for the life you wanted. The fact you danced at Pitiful Princess for two years after what happened to you awes me." Beatrice is right.

My woman is stronger than her twin. She's stronger than most of the people I know.

"It was my way of reclaiming my power. If I hadn't done it, I don't know if I would have been able to let you touch me, no matter how over the top our attraction is."

"You would." It is my turn to be certain. Because anything else is unthinkable. This woman was meant to be mine. "You have more courage and tenacity than anyone I know."

"I'm not perfect."

Running my hand up her back, I revel in the feel of her body so relaxed against mine. "You are perfect for me. You accept me as even my own mother struggles to do. You do not shy away from the darkness in me."

"It is part of who you are, but it is also part of who I am."

"No." I brush her face.

She turns and kisses my palm. "Yes. If I were Bea, that might hurt me to accept, but I'm not. I'm not even Bia anymore. I'm your soulmate."

"My heart."

"Your darling."

"My good girl."

"Maybe not so good."

"Very, very good, *amore mio.*" Then I once again show her just how good she can be.

BIANCA

The news of my mother's abandonment breaks a week later.

She calls, crying and trying to spin the story she wants to feed to the press.

"You're forgetting that I was there when you called me a monster and left me with dad," I say dispassionately. "I was there when you gave me a measly $10,000 to go away when I was sixteen and five more to change my name two years later."

"You can't tell anyone about that. Think of what it will do to your sister. Her reputation will be ruined right along mine."

She can't see my eyeroll at her attempt to manipulate me. "Not if she publicly denounces your actions."

"Bea would never do that. She's not like you."

"I think you'll be surprised at what my twin is capable of when it comes to protecting herself." We're all capable of things we don't expect when we're backed into a corner.

I've stared my darkness in the face and come out stronger for it. Bea has to decide how she wants to live her life. I can't do it for her, but I won't try to protect her by protecting my narcissistic mother either.

"I'll fight fire with fire," my mother threatens. "Get your fiancée to back off or I will go to the authorities with what I know about the mafia."

"I'm going to do you a favor and not pass that on to Salvatore because the result would devastate Bea."

"Are you threatening me?" My mom demands shrilly.

"No." It's not a threat and I'm not implicating myself.

My mother was married to a made man for over a decade. She knows what happens to snitches.

"I'm your mother!"

"You'll have to get better at defending yourself than that," I warn her. "Even Boston society isn't going to forgive a mother who abandons her child to the streets."

"I left you with your father."

"But then he died." And she'd refused to help me.

"I couldn't do anything then. Ronald would have been appalled to find out I had another child."

She's talking about Ronald William Harrington III, the man she married three months after my parents' marriage was annulled.

"I'm sure he would have been," I agree. I doubt he's thrilled about it now.

"My parents would have sent me and you girls away someplace without any real society to mitigate the scandal."

And that would have been hell for my mother.

"So, you sacrificed me for your own comfort."

"You wouldn't have done well here. You're too much like your father."

"You think so? I think I'm more like nonna and *bisnonna*. I do what I need to in order to survive and protect the people I love."

"You aren't doing anything to protect me," she accuses in a voice bordering on hysterical.

Elizabeth Harrington is seconds away from a full-on temper tantrum.

Not something I'm willing to listen to. "You aren't one of the people I love."

"How can you say that? I gave birth to you."

The words reverberate in my head long after I disconnect the call with my mom.

"What is wrong?" Rosa asks as I pound my clay back into a single lump for the third time.

"I don't love my mom."

Rosa's gentle face takes on a look of distaste. "I don't love her either."

"She didn't give birth to you."

"Giving birth to someone does not make you a mother." Rosa looks to Ilaria for confirmation and my soon-to-be mother-in-law nods her agreement. "Caring for your child. Protecting them. Raising them. That is what makes you a mother."

"She raised me until I was thirteen." Why doesn't that carry more weight with me?

Shouldn't I feel something for her?

"And then cruelly abandoned you."

"But shouldn't I feel something for her? I mean I hate that she manipulated me and Bea to keep us apart for so long, but I don't even despise Elizabeth." Calling her by her first name feels more natural that calling her mom.

Huh. Good to know.

"How did you survive her rejection?" Ilaria asks, eyeing her own beautifully thrown plate for imperfections. "You had to cut your heart off from her or wallow in never ending grief."

"How poetic you are today, Ilaria," Rosa teases. Then she looks at me with understanding eyes. "But my friend is right. You had no choice but to put away feelings of affection that only caused you grief. If your mother had returned sooner, or at all, you might have been able to resurrect those feelings."

She's right. Even now Elizabeth isn't returning to me with apologies and words of love. She only called me because she was desperate.

"It is not healthy to love someone whose every action toward you is selfish and harmful." Ilaria sprinkles water on her clay and smooths away an imperfection I cannot see.

"You don't think something inside me is broken because I don't love her?" I ask both women.

Bea still loves our mom.

"No, *dolce ragazza*, there is nothing lacking in you. Your love runs deep and strong, but you don't love indiscriminately."

"You love Salvatore and have forgiven him for hurting you," Ilaria adds. "That is not the action of a woman with a heart of stone."

Rosa nods firmly. "That you even worry about not loving that viper shows how tender your heart truly is."

"Salvatore told me that if I wanted him to leave her alone, he would," I admit to them. I leave unsaid the obvious truth. That I didn't.

"He might." Rosa shrugs. "But Pietro would not."

"Sal wouldn't either. Though my husband wants to kill her and be done with it," Ilaria says as she places the wet clay plate on the rack to dry.

"Big Sal wants to kill my mom?" I squeak. "I mean he's been nicer lately, but I thought that was because you and Salvatore read him the riot act."

"Nerissa did too, but that's not why."

My almost sister-by-marriage hired me as the talent manager for all three De Luca owned strip clubs.

My position is the same level as a general manager and my decisions supersedes all the other managers when it comes to the dancers and women who offer services in the back rooms.

The job is challenging, but I love it.

Determined to keep them as safe as possible and to provide good work conditions, I have met with each of the dancers and club sex workers one-on-one.

Those meetings have been enlightening and I have at least two more issues I plan to bring up with Nerissa at our next meeting.

Ilaria smiles at me. "Once Sal learned how you ran to Severu to try to protect our son at great risk to yourself, he became your fan for life."

"He asked me to call him papà," I admit.

"And?"

I shrug. I never called my dad papà per my mother's insistence, and Mr. Ruhnke became the name that meant dad to me with him.

But Big Sal De Luca is something else. "I have a feeling if I call him papà, he'll become as insufferable as his son about my wellbeing."

The consigliere supports his daughter in her position as a soldier in the Cosa Nostra, but he gives Nerissa a lot more grief than Salvatore about putting herself at risk.

"He won't be offended if you choose to call him Sal," Ilaria says. "But I'm hoping you will call me mamma."

Tears prickle at my eyes and I turn away from my wheel. That lump of clay is not turning into anything worth firing today.

"You deserved better than you got growing up, but you have a family that loves you now, Bianca," Ilaria adds.

Rosa smiles. "Two families."

Two families that don't think I'm a monster. Two families that don't judge me for not loving the woman who left me to suffer a fate I'll never tell her about. Two families who don't look down on me for being an exotic dancer when my mother did nothing but judge that choice earlier in our conversation.

Two families that I love deeply.

I am not broken.

I am a survivor.

Chapter 70

BIANCA

Salvatore and I are married in the same cathedral where Catalina married Severu De Luca, but our wedding has to take place in the middle of the day on a Wednesday because of the short notice.

I don't even try to guess what Salvatore is paying to have the sanctuary decorated and undecorated within the space of three hours.

My dress and veil are the same one worn by my *bisnonna* on her wedding day to the man she had never met. Rosa brought it to me after dress shopping netted gowns for Kath and Bea but nothing I liked.

"Your nonna would be so proud," my 78-year-old great-uncle says as he offers his arm to walk me down the aisle.

Pietro wanted to give me away. So did Big Sal.

But Umberto Abati told me he wanted to do it for my nonna and I couldn't say no. He lost his sister to my grandfather's intransigence.

I know what it's like to lose a sister and how grateful I am to have Bea standing at the front of the church, waiting for me along with Kath.

"Thank you," I tell him.

"Thank you for giving me back a part of my sister. I do not regret I never got to know my nephew, may God rest his soul." Uncle Umberto crosses himself. "He took too much after his father, but you are the greatest gift an old man could receive in his final years."

"Enough with the final years. You'll outlive us all. And Bea is happy to have gotten to know you too," I remind him.

Bea hasn't taken to our Italian family in New York like me, but she's cordial with them all.

He shrugs. "She is sweet, but you are so much like my sister, it is as if she is here again."

The compliment wraps around me like the perfect woobie blanket and I walk down the aisle in a cloud of bliss, my nonna's presence all around me.

Salvatore is waiting for me with Pietro and a man named Angelo, who is as beautiful as his namesake, but also scary. He's not the best man, but he walked Kath down the aisle. When I asked Pietro about it after the last minute substitution at the rehearsal, he said he liked his hands attached to his arms.

Salvatore's gaze locks on mine and the message in his molten eyes is one of absolute adoration. The most brutal capo in New York loves me to the depths of his stained soul. And I love him to mine.

I was born a twin, but now my twin soul resides in a man who will kill for me and willingly die to keep me safe too.

When he says he will follow me into the afterlife I believe him. That man will never let me go.

And I will hold on to him just as hard.

Epilogue: Punishment

SALVATORE

Henry Caruso thinks he is safe when my cousin does not take out a hit on him.
The fool does not realize that if Severu wants him dead, no contract is needed.

Miceli and I fucking rock, paper, scissors for the right to kill him. Miceli wins
with scissors to my paper.

I'm still pissed about it, but as long as Henry dies painfully, I can accept it.

BIANCA

Two weeks after our wedding, Salvatore brings me to the Oscuro Building, but
we don't go in the main entrance. We take an elevator from the parking garage
down to a sub-basement and he leads me to a room called The Box.

The sound of low voices and bodies shuffling reaches me before I see the men
filling one side of a large room. An impression midway down the wall on both
sides looks like it houses another wall that can be used to divide the space in two.

All the capos and their seconds are here. Salvatore leads me through the group
of mostly men so we stand in the front. Nerissa takes a position on my other side.
Pietro stands behind me.

He's not a capo or a second-in-command, but he's here like me to witness
justice being served.

"You are here today to witness the punishment of a traitor," Severu intones.
"Lorenzo Ricci has stolen money from *la famiglia* both in tithe and what he owes
his own men from the profits of their enterprises."

"It looks like he's already been punished," someone behind me says.

Severu shrugs. "One session of torture is not enough for such an offense."

"Damn right," a handsome man to my right says. His second is sending surreptitious looks to Nerissa.

Oh, this must be her boyfriend and his capo, Domenico.

"Because his offense was against the entire family, you are all here not only as witnesses but to participate in his punishment as well."

What follows is a brutal display of violence. After each of the capos and their seconds have taken a turn, Lorenzo hangs limply in his bindings. The capo that terrorized me and murdered my father is reduced to a whimpering mess.

"Put him on his knees," Severu says.

Miceli and Angelo step forward to do as the don ordered. When Lorenzo is kneeling on the floor like my father on that long ago day, Severu steps behind him, but he doesn't have a gun.

He grabs Lorenzo's head, lifts and twists. A sickening crack sounds and Lorenzo topples to his side. Dead.

"Lorenzo Ricci will have no funeral and no gravestone to mark his burial. He will return to the nothing he chose to become by breaking his oath to the Cosa Nostra." The floor opens silently and Severu kicks the dead capo over the edge.

A small splash sounds and the floor closes again.

Severu warns his people about disloyalty and each capo and second renews their vows to their don.

I am stricken to the depths of my soul how much Salvatore was willing to sacrifice for me. He squeezes my hand as if he knows what I'm thinking and he's telling me silently it was worth it.

I squeeze back telling him risking my life for him was worth it too.

The others file out, but Salvatore keeps me back.

After everyone is gone, Pietro and Nerissa drag three men into The Box, one by one.

All three men are naked and all their genitals are black and shrunken. The telltale string dangling down one of their thighs tells me why. They have something tied around them cutting off blood flow. For them to be in this condition, it must have been there quite a while.

The pain would be ferocious.

When Salvatore notices where I am looking, he says grimly, "I wanted to castrate them and make them choke on their own cock and balls, but that's not how they need to die."

"Oh." It's all I can think to say.

Then my gaze slides to one of the men's faces. Recognition hits instantly. I look quickly at the faces of the other two men and despite the bruises on one of them, I know exactly who they are. The men who raped me when I was sixteen.

"You found all three of them."

"He helped me find the other two." Salvatore indicates the man from Lorenzo's crew with his chin. "I am going to kill them, but you do not have to watch. Or..." He looks at his sister and then back at me. "If you want to kill them, that is your prerogative."

"I don't want to kill them." I'm sure of that.

I can kill to protect someone I love, but not in retribution. That doesn't mean I want them to live though.

As if he knows exactly what I'm thinking Salvatore nods. "I will kill them, then. Do you want to stay?"

"You know me as well as my own inner voice. You tell me."

For a second, Salvatore's lips twitch. "Now that I am with you, my inner voice doesn't get nearly as loud."

"Mine either."

Because we have become that to each other.

"Alright you two love birds. Rhapsodize over how your inner voices are as perfectly matched as you are later. We have things to do here," Pietro grouses.

"I want to stay," I say, in case Salvatore has any doubts.

Nodding, Salvatore picks up a knife that looks like the one my nonna used to filet fish and I suddenly know what he is going to do.

I am not wrong. He goes behind the first man, grabs him by the hair and lifts his head. Then he slices across his throat. As blood sprays onto the metal floor, it begins to wash the pain and terror of a sixteen-year-old from my soul.

When all three men are dead, Pietro pushes a button on the wall and the floor opens again. Pietro, Nerissa and Salvatore dump the now dead men over the edge of the floor.

There are splashes for each body.

I don't know what is under the floor. Maybe an underground river. I don't care.

My tormentors are gone. They can never hurt me again.

Salvatore turns me gently and holds me tightly to him. "I was not there to protect you six years ago, but I will never leave you unprotected now. I will always stop the monsters from hurting you."

I believe him.

THE END

Afterword

If you enjoyed BRUTAL CAPO, please consider leaving a review, or rating. Thank you!

Want to read bonus content for this book and the others in the Syndicate Rules series and to be kept up to date on her books? Sign up for Lucy Monroe's newsletter: https://www.lucymonroe.com/newsletter

Acknowledgements

A huge hug and heartfelt thank you to everyone who has helped me make this book what it is:

My husband, Tom, who listens to endless ideas, scene snippets and character revelations as I write and *still* reads the complete book from start to finish when it is done.

Andie, my amazing editor at Beyond the Proof who excels at catching dangling threads and inconsistencies. Her insights make my books better. Full stop.

Two very special ARC readers who take the time to proofread after the copy-edits are done before writing their reviews, Dee Dee & Haley.

And with special thanks to fellow authors Josephine Caporetto for her invaluable help on Italian phrases and Monica Burns who always wanted to be a villain and leant her name to Salvatore's scheming ex.

Any remaining typos, mistakes, or translation errors are my fault and mine alone.

Italian Glossary

Note: certain words are not italicized in the book because of their common use in American English. Also, these translations are not literal. They are the more common vernacular. Italian as it is used in Northern or Southern Italy (and Sicily) as the case may be.

accidenti – (positive) wow, gosh, my goodness (negative) darn, drat
amore mio – my love
anima gemella – soul mate (no masculine form/same for either)
basta – stop, that's enough
bastardo – bastard
bella mia – you are my beautiful one, or listen to me i.e. in an argument to get the person's attention (alternate uses from Southern Italy)
bella ragazza – beautiful girl
bellissima - gorgeous
bisnonna – great grandmother
bisnonno – great grandfather
brava ragazza – good girl
cara/o – darling
carissimo/a – very dear
cazzate – bullshit
cazzo – dick/fuck equivalent
caspita – yikes/wow
che palle – oh balls/fuck it equivalent
Dio mio – my god
dolce ragazza – sweet girl
dolcezza – sweetheart, honey (literally sweetness)
mamma – mom or mother
fottuto stronzo – fucking asshole (see also *stronzo del cazzo*)
goomah – mistress or side piece
il mia lei – my her (possessive endearment for a woman)
il mio lui – my him (possessive endearment for a man)

managgia – damn
managgia la miseria – damn it (literally misery or poverty)
manaja – damn (variant from Southern Italy)
meno male – thank goodness
nonna – grandma/grandmother
nonno – grandpa/grandfather
oh merda – oh crap/shit
per favore – please
porca miseria – damn it (not literal)
puttana – bitch
stronzo/a – asshole (also another way to say bitch)
stronzo del cazzo – fucking asshole (see also *fottuto stronzo*)
tesoro mio – my treasure
vaffanculo - fuck
Phrases:
A accidenti. – (teasing or serious) darn him/her/you
Ho detto basta - that's enough, I said enough
Io sono tua. – I am yours.
Prometto. – I promise.
Tu sei mia! –You are mine. (jealous: another man or woman involved)
Sei la mia anima gemelli. – You are my soul mate. (no masculine form – same
for either)
Sei mio. – You are mine.
Zitto. - Shut up.

Syndicate Sins

Check out Lucy's new spicy mafia romance series!

From USA Today Bestselling author Lucy Monroe comes a brand-new mafia romance series: Syndicate Sins

Welcome to the dark and dangerous world of the Irish mob... where the men are ruthless, the stakes are high, and the heat is off the charts. These morally gray antiheroes are possessive, obsessive, and panty-meltingly intense—with brogues that could make a good girl sin.

⇒Spicy, high-stakes romance
⇒Intense mafia intrigue
⇒Second chances, forgotten love, and forbidden desire
⇒Fierce, clever heroines who give as good as they get

Syndicate Sins has it all.

If you love the raw edge of Cora Reilly, the emotion of Neva Altaj, and the grit of Michelle Heard, Syndicate Sins will steal your heart.

Each story stands alone with a guaranteed HEA, but together they weave an unforgettable saga of power, passion, and Irish pride.

About the Author

With more than 10 million copies of her books in print worldwide, award winning and internationally bestselling author, Lucy Monroe, has published over 85 books and had her stories translated for sale all over the world. While her latest series is mafia romance, written as an indie author, all of Lucy's books are passionate, deeply emotional and adhere to the concept that love wins. Even if that victory isn't an easy one.

Want to talk about the characters, read snippets of Lucy's WIPs before anyone else, and chat with other readers who love Lucy's books? Join her FB Group Lucy's Book Nook.
https://www.facebook.com/groups/lucysbooknook

FOLLOW LUCY ON SOCIAL MEDIA
BookBub: Lucy Monroe
goodreads: Lucy Monroe
Facebook: LucyMonroe.Romance
TikTok: lucymonroeauthor
Instagram: lucymonroeromance
Pinterest: lucymonroebooks
YouTube: @LucyMonroeBooks
Threads: lucymonroeromance
Lucy's website: https://lucymonroe.com